The Modern Novelette

Prentice-Hall English Literature Series
MAYNARD MACK, *Editor*

PRENTICE-HALL INTERNATIONAL, INC., *London*
PRENTICE-HALL OF AUSTRALIA, PTY., LTD., *Sydney*
PRENTICE-HALL OF CANADA, LTD., *Toronto*
PRENTICE-HALL OF INDIA (PRIVATE), LTD., *New Delhi*
PRENTICE-HALL OF JAPAN, INC., *Tokyo*

The
Modern Novelette

Edited by **Ronald Paulson**   *Rice University, Houston, Texas*

PRENTICE-HALL, INC.,   **Englewood Cliffs, New Jersey**

Table of Contents

Introduction   vii

A Woman's Kingdom (1894)   1
    ANTON CHEKHOV

Youth (1898)   30
    JOSEPH CONRAD

Tonio Kröger (1903)   53
    THOMAS MANN

The Seven That Were Hanged (1908)   90
    LEONID ANDREYEV

The Bench of Desolation (1910)   137
    HENRY JAMES

The Dead (1914)   171
    JAMES JOYCE

The Burrow (1924, 1931)   201
    FRANZ KAFKA

The Virgin and the Gipsy (1926, 1930)   225
    D. H. LAWRENCE

Old Mortality (1939)   285

KATHERINE ANNE PORTER

Julie de Carneilhan (1941)   320

COLETTE

Introduction

The artistry of the novelette, its economical ordering of every detail toward a single, limited effect made it easily distinguishable from the diffuse novel of Dickens and Hardy, Balzac and Zola. But the novelists of the twentieth century who derive from Gustave Flaubert (from *Madame Bovary* and *Un coeur simple*) have drawn away from those genres with which the novel was originally associated—history and biography, the essay and the letter—and have strengthened its connections with poetry. The poetically dense novel is also the shorter, more compact, and tightly unified novel. Henry James, the great transitional figure between Flaubert and the twentieth-century English novelists, maintained this distinction between his novels and "the loved *nouvelle* form." But a novel like *The Ambassadors* can be distinguished from a novelette like *The Beast in the Jungle* or *The Bench of Desolation* only by its length and scope, no longer by its primary concern with raw, unordered reality (what E. M. Forster calls "life"). The Jamesian novel even shares the novelette's traditional concern with a carefully placed and regulated point of view.

"The short novel" as a term is now often used interchangeably with "the novelette." In *The Great Gatsby, Thérèse Desqueyroux,* and *L'Immoraliste,* to name only three, the distinctions among novelette, short novel, and novel can be based on little more than degree of compression and word count. Beyond these criteria we can only say that the novelette more rigorously maintains a single center of interest and so allows less autonomy, less full realization to the secondary elements of the fiction than do the novel and the short novel. Everything in *The Great Gatsby* elucidates the situation of Jay Gatsby, as everything in *Old Mortality* elucidates Miranda's knowledge of Aunt Amy and Uncle Gabriel. But Fitzgerald's minor characters are allowed more development, more appearances on stage, more freedom of action, and in some cases they exist as much for their own sake as for Gatsby's. For example, the story of Gatsby and the story of Nick Carraway, the narrator, are to some extent independent, whereas Katherine Anne Porter allows the memories of Aunt Amy and Uncle Gabriel to exist only in relation to Miranda's growing sense of discovery. A secondary character, old Aunt Eva or Uncle Gabriel's second wife, is permitted to appear only long enough to give *her* view of Aunt Amy, and then she vanishes.

The novelette still remains fairly distinct from the short story, although there is a shadowy area where the latter passes beyond the Chekhovian presentation of a fragmentary experience used as a metonymy and seeks the same rounded-off, fully developed effect of the novelette. Hemingway's *Snows of Kilimanjaro* and Ivan Bunin's *Gentleman from San Francisco* are in this area, although by word count both are classifiable as short stories.

If blurred distinctions among novelette and short novel and short story make the novelette a less clearly discernible genre in our time, they also point to its hegemony as the ideal expressive unit of post-Flaubertian fiction. The longer as well as the shorter forms gravitate toward the characteristics, conventions, even the length of the novelette.

Take the indisputable novel with its great length and its multiplicity of plots and situations. If the eighteenth- and nineteenth-century novel was also a loose collection of plots, rather like the Elizabethan play with its double and triple plots, the twentieth-century novel stresses not only the unity of these diverse parts but also the relative unity of each separate part. The novelist likes to include whole novelettes that could be lifted out without radically altering either the part or the whole. Nearly every eighteenth-century novel contained one or more novels-within-a-novel ("The Old Man of the Hill" in *Tom Jones* or "The Memoirs of a Lady of Quality" in *Peregrine Pickle*), but this old picaresque custom appeared only intermittently in the nineteenth century, as in "The Grand Inquisitor" in *The Brothers Karamazov*. The modern novelist uses the device with a vengeance, emphasizing the separation by the artistry of the inserted story. The stories of Willie Proudfit in Robert Penn Warren's *At Heaven's Gate* and of Cass Mastern in *All the King's Men* are among the best things in those novels. Faulkner's most brilliant writing tends to assume the form of the novelette: *The Sound and the Fury* is constructed of four self-contained and carefully wrought but interdependent novelettes; in *The Wild Palms* two novelettes run side-by-side in alternating sections; and in *The Unvanquished, Go Down, Moses,* and *The Hamlet* Faulkner's form is the suite of loosely related short stories and novelettes. In Hemingway's *For Whom the Bell Tolls* a few independent novelettes emerge as completely realized units in a generally unrealized novel. These novelists seem to think and imagine in the unit of the novelette, and it is no surprise that they have also written striking novelettes: Faulkner's *The Bear*, Hemingway's *The Old Man and the Sea,* and Warren's *Circus in the Attic.*

The old novel-novelette distinctions remain more firm in the writers who are outside the Flaubert tradition. Thomas Mann is well aware of the generic distinctions and of the tradition of the German *novelle* when he writes in it, and no one will confuse *Tristram* with *The Magic Mountain* or even with parts of it; they share only some common themes and techniques. If the Mann *novelle* illustrates the genre's close links with poetry (through its repetition of leitmotifs and the like), those links come with the form he inherited. He still constructs around the central, often symbolic event, though often, as in *Tonio Kröger,* he uses a basic contrast between art and society or romance and business as his symbol rather than an object. In Kafka the German tradition of the *novelle,* with its associations of the grotesque and supernatural as well as its central symbol, has reasonably enough drawn in Freud and carried the genre to its logical end in fantasy. His *novellen* present a single fantastic situation—the turning of a man into a beetle or the trial of a man for a crime he is never informed of—which projects a symbol of the contemporary world. But Kafka also demonstrates the tendency to blur novel and novelette: only length and elaboration separate *The Trial* or *The Castle* from *The Metamorphosis* or *The Burrow.*

If Mann and Kafka carry on the tradition of the *novelle,* D. H. Lawrence's novelettes (or "tales"), which are certainly the most completely successful of his individual works, bear little resemblance to his sprawling novels; they retain characteristics of both the German *novelle* and the French *conte moral.*

We have in Lawrence's novelettes, as in Andreyev's *The Seven That Were Hanged,* a combination of symbolism and didacticism. Each of Lawrence's long tales is built around a central symbol or an analogy between a character and an animal or object (a fox, a ladybird, a horse, a doll), but the symbol is used as a device for exposing a basic contrast of values, which is different in degree but not in kind from the educational novels like *Sanford and Merton* that contrast a good and a bad way of life. This contrast is almost invariably between the forces of vigor and the forces of stagnation and sterility, with little doubt left as to whether Lawrence is on the side of the gipsy or the vicar.

As Lawrence's example shows, the novelette offers a better medium than the novel for the stark contrast desired by the reformer or the moralist. The writer of fiction can either make a situation exemplary of some idea he already has in mind or he can search into the situation in an attempt to understand its real meaning. The inductive method is most appropriately the novelist's, though it sometimes leads to reportage, autobiography, and an attempt to relive or re-experience rather than to understand. The deductive method leads to fable and didacticism, reality rearranged to make a preordained point. This method, although often used by the novelist, especially by the American novelist, is most appropriately conveyed in a novelette. The novelette has increasingly tended toward fable and moral-satiric writing. The only stories in the present collection that go very far in the opposite direction are *Youth, The Dead, Old Mortality,* and *Julie de Carneilhan;* and most of these, though not didactic, illustrate rather than penetrate. In general the novelette has no room for searching about; it must find a striking and economic correlative and present it.

It is therefore not surprising that satire has been a prolific offshoot of the novelette form. From the fable of Orwell's *Animal Farm* or Waugh's *Love Among the Ruins* to the striking central symbol of Nathanael West's *Miss Lonelyhearts* or Muriel Spark's *Memento Mori,* the novelette has offered the economical form needed by the satirist. Although Kafka himself is more interested in psychological than moral reality, he has shown the satirist ways to use the novelette for his own purposes.

In choosing typical twentieth-century novelettes I have had to rule out those that are contained in larger novels, though they include some of the best (they are the most penetrative because they find support in the other parts of the novel). I have tried to steer a middle course between the undeniably great but overexposed and the deserving but less well-known novelettes. My main aim, however, has been to represent the classic examples or the typical novelettes by the masters of the genre. A few masters, like Faulkner, Camus, and Gide had to be omitted because they are no longer available for reprint except by the publisher who owns the copyright. Because of the enormous volume of novelettes in our century, and because many are too near us in time for a detached judgment, I have reached only as far as the early 1940s. I shall only mention the brilliant work that has been done since World War II in Germany by Heinrich Böll and others, and in America by novelists who have concentrated talents that were diffused in their novels on the shorter form to produce perhaps their best single works: William Styron's *The Long March,* James Jones' *The Pistol,* and Saul Bellows' *Seize the Day.* The post-Flaubertian novel I have discussed has by this time passed into history, but some of its virtues are recalled when a novelist returns to the discipline of the novelette. The present volume then is only a sampling that should suggest to the reader an area of greater riches that can be explored at his leisure.

The Modern Novelette

A Woman's Kingdom

(1894)

Anton Chekhov

Constance Garnett, translator

Anton Pavlovich Chekhov (1860–1904) was born in Taganrog in South Russia, son of a tradesman, grandson of a serf. He studied medicine at the University of Moscow, supporting himself by contributing sketches to comic papers. He took a degree in 1884 but practiced little except during a cholera epidemic in 1892–1893. In 1886 some of his comic sketches were published as a book (*Particolored Stories*), and in the next year his first play, *Ivanov,* was produced. The remainder of his life was spent writing plays and short fiction. After 1897 tuberculosis forced him to spend most of the year in the Crimea and abroad, and he died in Baden-weiler in the Black Forest.

His first important play, *The Seagull,* was a failure in St. Petersburg (1896) but a success when produced by the Moscow Art Theatre (1898), with which he collaborated on his subsequent plays: *Uncle Vanya* (1899), *The Three Sisters* (1901), and *The Cherry Orchard* (1904). He wrote over a thousand stories, the best of them classic examples of the modern short story, but others that show his interest in the longer forms of the novelette and the novel. For further information see R. Hingley, *Chekhov, A Biographical and Critical Study* (London, 1950); E. J. Simmons, *Chekhov* (London, 1962); *Letters,* trans. Constance Garnett (London, 1920); and *The Notebooks,* trans. S. S. Koteliansky and Leonard Woolf (London, 1921).

A Woman's Kingdom (*Babye tsarstvo*) was first published in 1894 and was reprinted in a collected edition of Chekhov's stories published in 1899–1901. Constance Garnett included it in her translation of his stories (13 vols., 1916–22). The Garnett translation is reprinted with permission of The Macmillan Company and Chatto & Windus, Ltd., from *The Party and Other Stories* by Anton Chekhov. Copyright 1917 by The Macmillan Company, renewed 1945 by Constance Garnett.

I

Christmas Eve

Here was a thick roll of notes. It came from the bailiff at the forest villa; he wrote that he was sending fifteen hundred roubles, which he had been awarded as damages, having won an appeal. Anna Akimovna disliked and feared such words as "awarded damages" and "won the suit." She knew that it was impossible to do without the law, but for some reason, whenever Nazaritch, the manager of the factory, or the bailiff of her villa in the country, both of whom frequently went to law, used to win lawsuits of some sort for her benefit, she always felt uneasy and, as it were, ashamed. On this occasion, too, she felt uneasy and awkward, and wanted to put that fifteen hundred roubles further away that it might be out of her sight.

She thought with vexation that other girls of her age—she was in her twenty-sixth year—were now busy looking after their households, were weary and would sleep sound, and would wake up to-morrow morning in holiday mood; many of them had long been married and had children. Only she, for some reason, was compelled to sit like an old woman over these letters, to make notes upon them, to write answers, then to do nothing the whole evening till midnight, but wait till she was sleepy; and to-morrow they would all day long be coming with Christmas greetings and asking for favours; and the day after to-morrow there would certainly be some scandal at the factory—someone would be beaten or would die of drinking too much vodka, and she would be fretted by pangs of conscience; and after the holidays Nazaritch would turn off some twenty of the workpeople for absence from work, and all of the twenty would hang about at the front door, without their caps on, and she would be ashamed to go out to them, and they would be driven away like dogs. And all her acquaintances would say behind her back, and write to her in anonymous letters, that she was a millionaire and an exploiter—that she was devouring other men's lives and sucking the blood of the workers.

Here there lay a heap of letters read through and laid aside already. They were all begging letters. They were from people who were hungry, drunken, dragged down by large families, sick, degraded, despised. . . . Anna Akimovna had already noted on each letter, three roubles to be paid to one, five to another; these letters would go the same day to the office, and next the distribution of assistance would take place, or, as the clerks used to say, the beasts would be fed.

They would distribute also in small sums four hundred and seventy roubles—the interest on a sum bequeathed by the late Akim Ivanovitch for the relief of the poor and needy. There would be a hideous crush. From the gates to the doors of the office there would stretch a long file of strange people with brutal faces, in rags, numb with cold, hungry and already drunk, in husky voices calling down blessings upon Anna Akimovna, their benefactress, and her parents: those at the back would press upon those in front, and those in front would abuse them with bad language. The clerk would get tired of the noise, the swearing, and the sing-song whining and blessing; would fly out and give someone a box on the ear to the delight of all. And her own people, the factory hands, who received nothing at Christmas but their wages, and had already spent every farthing of it, would stand in the middle of the yard, looking on and laughing—some enviously, others ironically.

"Merchants, and still more their wives, are fonder of beggars than they are of their own workpeople," thought Anna Akimovna. "It's always so."

Her eye fell upon the roll of money. It would be nice to distribute that hateful, useless money among the workpeople to-morrow, but it did not do to give the workpeople anything for nothing, or they would demand it again next time. And what would be the good of fifteen hundred roubles when there were eighteen hundred workmen in the factory besides their wives and children? Or she might, perhaps, pick out one of the writers of those begging letters—some luckless man who had long ago lost all hope of anything better, and give him the fifteen hundred. The money would come upon the poor creature like a thunderclap, and perhaps for the first time in his life he would feel happy. This idea struck Anna Akimovna as original and amusing, and it fascinated her. She took one letter at random out of the pile and read it. Some petty official called Tchalikov had long been out of a situation, was ill, and living in Gushtchin's Buildings; his wife was in consumption, and he had five little girls. Anna Akimovna knew well the four-storeyed house, Gushtchin's Buildings, in which Tchalikov lived. Oh, it was a horrid, foul, unhealthy house!

"Well, I will give it to that Tchalikov," she decided. "I won't send it; I had better take it myself to prevent unnecessary talk. Yes," she reflected, as she put the fifteen hundred roubles in her pocket, "and I'll have a look at them, and perhaps I can do something for the little girls."

She felt light-hearted; she rang the bell and ordered the horses to be brought round.

When she got into the sledge it was past six o'clock in the evening. The windows in all the blocks of buildings were brightly lighted up, and that made the huge courtyard seem very dark: at the gates, and at the far end of the yard near the warehouses and the workpeople's barracks, electric lamps were gleaming.

Anna Akimovna disliked and feared those huge dark buildings, warehouses, and barracks where the workmen lived. She had only once been in the main building since her father's death. The high ceilings with iron girders; the multitude of huge, rapidly turning wheels, connecting straps and levers; the shrill hissing; the clank of steel; the rattle of the trolleys; the harsh puffing of steam; the faces—pale, crimson, or black with coal-dust; the shirts soaked with sweat; the gleam of steel, of copper, and of fire; the smell of oil and coal; and the draught, at times very hot and at times very cold—gave her an impression of hell. It seemed to her as though the wheels, the levers, and the hot hissing cylinders were trying to tear themselves away from their fastenings to crush the men, while the men, not hearing one another, ran about with anxious faces, and busied themselves about the machines, trying to stop their terrible movement. They showed Anna Akimovna something and respectfully explained it to her. She remembered how in the forge a piece of red-hot iron was pulled out of the furnace; and how an old man with a strap round his head, and another, a young man in a blue shirt with a chain on his breast, and an angry face, probably one of the foremen, struck the piece of iron with hammers; and how the golden sparks had been scattered in all directions; and how, a little afterwards, they had dragged out a huge piece of sheet-iron with a clang. The old man had stood erect and smiled, while the young man had wiped his face with his sleeve and explained something to her. And she remembered, too, how in another department an old man with one eye had been filing a piece of iron, and how the iron filings were scattered about; and how a red-haired man in black spectacles, with holes in his shirt, had been working at a lathe, making something out of a piece of steel: the lathe roared and hissed and squeaked, and Anna Akimovna felt sick at the sound, and it seemed as though they were boring into her ears. She looked, listened, did not understand, smiled graciously, and felt ashamed. To get hundreds of thousands of roubles from a business which one does not understand and cannot like— how strange it is!

And she had not once been in the workpeople's barracks. There, she was told, it was damp; there were bugs, debauchery, anarchy. It was an astonishing thing: a thousand roubles were spent annually on keeping the barracks in good order, yet, if she were to believe the anonymous letters, the condition of the workpeople was growing worse and worse every year.

"There was more order in my father's day," thought Anna Akimovna, as she drove out of the yard, "because he had been a workman himself. I know nothing about it and only do silly things."

She felt depressed again, and was no longer glad that she had come, and the thought of the lucky man upon whom fifteen hundred roubles would drop from heaven no longer struck her as original and amusing. To go to some Tchalikov or other, when at home a business worth a million was gradually going to pieces and being ruined, and the workpeople in the barracks were living worse than convicts, meant doing something silly and cheating her conscience. Along the highroad and across the fields near it, workpeople from the neighbouring cotton and paper factories were walking towards the lights of the town. There was the sound of talk and laughter in the frosty air. Anna Akimovna looked at the women and young people, and she suddenly felt a longing for a plain rough life among a crowd. She recalled vividly that far-away time when she used to be called Anyutka, when she was a little girl and used to lie under the same quilt with her mother, while a washerwoman who lodged with them used to wash clothes in the next room; while through the thin walls there came from the neighbouring flats sounds of laughter, swearing, children's crying, the accordion, and the whirr of carpenters' lathes and sewing-machines; while her father, Akim Ivanovitch, who was clever at almost every craft, would be soldering something near the stove, or drawing or planing, taking no notice whatever of the noise and stuffiness. And she longed to wash, to iron, to run to the shop and the tavern as she used to do every day when she lived with her mother. She ought to have been a work-girl and not the factory owner! Her big house with its chandeliers and pictures; her footman Mishenka, with his glossy moustache and swallow-tail coat; the devout and dignified Varvarushka, and smooth-tongued Agafyushka; and the young people of both sexes who came almost every day to ask her for money, and with whom she always for some reason felt guilty; and the clerks, the doctors, and the ladies who were charitable at her expense, who flattered her and secretly despised her for her humble origin—how wearisome and alien it all was to her!

Here was the railway crossing and the city gate; then came houses alternating with kitchen gardens; and at last the broad street where stood the renowned

Gushtchin's Buildings. The street, usually quiet, was now on Christmas Eve full of life and movement. The eating-houses and beer-shops were noisy. If someone who did not belong to that quarter but lived in the centre of the town had driven through the street now, he would have noticed nothing but dirty, drunken, and abusive people; but Anna Akimovna, who had lived in those parts all her life, was constantly recognizing in the crowd her own father or mother or uncle. Her father was a soft fluid character, a little fantastical, frivolous, and irresponsible. He did not care for money, respectability, or power; he used to say that a working man had no time to keep the holy-days and go to church;. and if it had not been for his wife, he would probably never have gone to confession, taken the sacrament or kept the fasts.   While her uncle, Ivan Ivanovitch, on the contrary, was like flint; in everything relating to religion, politics, and morality, he was harsh and relentless, and kept a strict watch, not only over himself, but also over all his servants and acquaintances. God forbid that one should go into his room without crossing oneself before the ikon! The luxurious mansion in which Anna Akimovna now lived he had always kept locked up, and only opened it on great holidays for important visitors, while he lived himself in the office, in a little room covered with ikons. He had leanings towards the Old Believers, and was continually entertaining priests and bishops of the old ritual, though he had been christened, and married, and had buried his wife in accordance with the Orthodox rites. He disliked Akim, his only brother and his heir, for his frivolity, which he called simpleness and folly, and for his indifference to religion. He treated him as an inferior, kept him in the position of a workman, paid him sixteen roubles a month. Akim addressed his brother with formal respect, and on the days of asking forgiveness, he and his wife and daughter bowed down to the ground before him. But three years before his death Ivan Ivanovitch had drawn closer to his brother, forgave his shortcomings, and ordered him to get a governess for Anyutka.

There was a dark, deep, evil-smelling archway under Gushtchin's Buildings; there was a sound of men coughing near the walls. Leaving the sledge in the street, Anna Akimovna went in at the gate and there inquired how to get to No. 46 to see a clerk called Tchalikov. She was directed to the furthest door on the right in the third storey. And in the courtyard and near the outer door, and even on the stairs, there was still the same loathsome smell as under the archway. In Anna Akimovna's childhood, when her father was a simple workman, she used to live in a building like that, and afterwards, when their circumstances were different, she had often visited them in the character of a Lady Bountiful. The narrow stone staircase with its steep dirty steps, with landings at every storey; the greasy swinging lanterns; the stench; the troughs, pots, and rags on the landings near the doors—all this had been familiar to her long ago. . . . One door was open, and within could be seen Jewish tailors in caps, sewing. Anna Akimovna met people on the stairs, but it never entered her head that people might be rude to her. She was no more afraid of peasants or workpeople, drunk or sober, than of her acquaintances of the educated class.

There was no entry at No. 46; the door opened straight into the kitchen. As a rule the dwellings of workmen and mechanics smell of varnish, tar, hides, smoke, according to the occupation of the tenant; the dwellings of persons of noble or official class who have come to poverty may be known by a peculiar rancid, sour smell. This disgusting smell enveloped Anna Akimovna on all sides, and as yet she was only on the threshold. A man in a black coat, no doubt Tchalikov himself, was sitting in a corner at the table with his back to the door, and with him were five little girls. The eldest, a broad-faced thin girl with a comb in her hair, looked about fifteen, while the youngest, a chubby child with hair that stood up like a hedgehog, was not more than three. All the six were eating. Near the stove stood a very thin little woman with a yellow face, far gone in pregnancy. She was wearing a skirt and white blouse, and had an oven fork in her hand.

"I did not expect you to be so disobedient, Liza," the man was saying reproach-fully. "Fie, fie, for shame! Do you want papa to whip you—eh?"

Seeing an unknown lady in the doorway, the thin woman started, and put down the fork.

"Vassily Nikititch!" she cried, after a pause, in a hollow voice, as though she could not believe her eyes.

The man looked round and jumped up. He was a flat-chested, bony man with narrow shoulders and sunken temples. His eyes were small and hollow with dark rings round them, he had a wide mouth, and a long nose like a bird's beak—a little bit bent to the right. His beard was parted in the middle, his moustache was shaven, and this made him look more like a hired footman than a government clerk.

"Does Mr. Tchalikov live here?" asked Anna Akimovna.

"Yes, madam," Tchalikov answered severely, but immediately recognizing Anna Akimovna, he cried: "Anna Akimovna!" and all at once he gasped and clasped his hands as though in terrible alarm. "Benefactress!"

With a moan he ran to her, grunting inarticulately as though he were paralyzed —there was cabbage on his beard and he smelt of vodka—pressed his forehead to her muff, and seemed as though he were in a swoon.

"Your hand, your holy hand!" he brought out breathlessly. "It's a dream, a glorious dream! Children, awaken me!"

He turned towards the table and said in a sobbing voice, shaking his fists:

"Providence has heard us! Our saviour, our angel, has come! We are saved! Children, down on your knees! on your knees!"

Madame Tchalikov and the little girls, except the youngest one, began for some reason rapidly clearing the table.

"You wrote that your wife was very ill," said Anna Akimovna, and she felt ashamed and annoyed. "I am not going to give them the fifteen hundred," she thought.

"Here she is, my wife," said Tchalikov in a thin feminine voice, as though his tears had gone to his head. "Here she is, unhappy creature! With one foot in the grave! But we do not complain, madam. Better death than such a life. Better die, unhappy woman!"

"Why is he playing these antics?" thought Anna Akimovna with annoyance. "One can see at once he is used to dealing with merchants."

"Speak to me like a human being," she said. "I don't care for farces."

"Yes, madam; five bereaved children round their mother's coffin with funeral candles—that's a farce? Eh?" said Tchalikov bitterly, and turned away.

"Hold your tongue," whispered his wife, and she pulled at his sleeve. "The place has not been tidied up, madam," she said, addressing Anna Akimovna; "please excuse it...you know what it is where there are children. A crowded hearth, but harmony."

"I am not going to give them the fifteen hundred," Anna Akimovna thought again.

And to escape as soon as possible from these people and from the sour smell, she brought out her purse and made up her mind to leave them twenty-five roubles, not more; but she suddenly felt ashamed that she had come so far and disturbed people for so little.

"If you give me paper and ink, I will write at once to a doctor who is a friend of mine to come and see you," she said, flushing red. "He is a very good doctor. And I will leave you some money for medicine."

Madame Tchalikov was hastening to wipe the table.

"It's messy here! What are you doing?" hissed Tchalikov, looking at her wrathfully. "Take her to the lodger's room! I make bold to ask you, madam, to step into the lodger's room," he said, addressing Anna Akimovna. "It's clean there."

"Osip Ilyitch told us not to go into his room!" said one of the little girls, sternly.

But they had already led Anna Akimovna out of the kitchen, through a narrow passage room between two bedsteads: it was evident from the arrangement of the beds that in one two slept lengthwise, and in the other three slept across the bed. In the lodger's room, that came next, it really was clean. A neat-looking bed with a red woolen quilt, a pillow in a white pillow-case, even a slipper for the watch, a table covered with a hempen cloth and on it, an inkstand of milky-looking glass, pens, paper, photographs in frames—everything as it ought to be; and another table for rough work, on which lay tidily arranged a watchmaker's tools and watches taken to pieces. On the walls hung hammers, pliers, awls, chisels, nippers, and so on, and there were three hanging clocks which were ticking; one was a big clock with thick weights, such as one sees in eating-houses.

As she sat down to write the letter, Anna Akimovna saw facing her on the table the photographs of her father and of herself. That surprised her.

"Who lives here with you?" she asked.

"Our lodger, madam, Pimenov. He works in your factory."

"Oh, I thought he must be a watchmaker."

"He repairs watches privately, in his leisure hours. He is an amateur."

After a brief silence during which nothing could be heard but the ticking of the clocks and the scratching of the pen on the paper, Tchalikov heaved a sigh and said ironically, with indignation:

"It's a true saying: gentle birth and a grade in the service won't put a coat on your back. A cockade in your cap and a noble title, but nothing to eat. To my thinking, if anyone of humble class helps the poor he is much more of a gentleman than any Tchalikov who has sunk into poverty and vice."

To flatter Anna Akimovna, he uttered a few more disparaging phrases about his gentle birth, and it was evident that he was humbling himself because he considered himself superior to her. Meanwhile she had finished her letter and had sealed it up. The letter would be thrown away and the money would not be spent on medicine—that she knew, but she put twenty-five roubles on the table all the same, and after a moment's thought, added two more red notes. She saw the wasted, yellow hand of Madame Tchalikov, like the claw of a hen, dart out and clutch the money tight.

"You have graciously given this for medicine," said Tchalikov in a quivering voice, "but hold out a helping hand to me also. . .and the children!" he added with a sob. "My unhappy children! I am not afraid for myself; it is for my daughters I fear! It's the hydra of vice that I fear!"

Trying to open her purse, the catch of which had gone wrong, Anna Akimovna was confused and turned red. She felt ashamed that people should be standing before her, looking at her hands and waiting, and most likely at the bottom of their hearts laughing at her. At that instant someone came into the kitchen and stamped his feet, knocking the snow off.

"The lodger has come in," said Madame Tchalikov.

Anna Akimovna grew even more confused. She did not want anyone from the factory to find her in this ridiculous position. As ill-luck would have it, the lodger came in at the very moment when, having broken the catch at last, she was giving Tchalikov some notes, and Tchalikov, grunting as though he were paralyzed, was feeling about with his lips where he could kiss her. In the lodger she recognized the workman who had once clanked the sheet-iron before her in the forge, and had explained things to her. Evidently he had come in straight from the factory; his face looked dark and grimy, and on one cheek near his nose was a smudge of soot. His hands were perfectly black, and his unbelted shirt shone with oil and grease. He was a man of thirty, of medium height, with black hair and broad shoulders, and a look of great physical strength. At the first glance Anna Akimovna perceived that he must be a foreman, who must be receiving at least thirty-five roubles a month, and a stern, loud-voiced man who struck the workmen in the face; all this was evident from his manner of standing, from the attitude he involuntarily assumed at once on seeing a lady in his room, and most of all from the fact that he did not wear top-boots, that he had breast pockets, and a pointed, picturesquely clipped beard. Her father, Akim Ivanovitch, had been the brother of the factory owner, and yet he had been afraid of foremen like this lodger and had tried to win their favour.

"Excuse me for having come in here in your absence," said Anna Akimovna.

The workman looked at her in surprise, smiled in confusion and did not speak.

"You must speak a little louder, madam. . ." said Tchalikov softly. "When Mr. Pimenov comes home from the factory in the evenings he is a little hard of hearing."

But Anna Akimovna was by now relieved that there was nothing more for her to do here; she nodded to them and went rapidly out of the room. Pimenov went to see her out.

"Have you been long in our employment?" she asked in a loud voice, without turning to him.

"From nine years old. I entered the factory in your uncle's time."

"That's a long while! My uncle and my father knew all the workpeople, and I know hardly any of them. I had seen you before, but I did not know your name was Pimenov."

Anna Akimovna felt a desire to justify herself before him, to pretend that she had just given the money not seriously, but as a joke.

"Oh, this poverty," she sighed. "We give charity on holidays and working days, and still there is no sense in it. I believe it is useless to help such people as this Tchalikov."

"Of course it is useless," he agreed. "However much you give him, he will drink it all away. And now the husband and wife will be snatching it from one another and fighting all night," he added with a laugh.

"Yes, one must admit that our philanthropy is useless, boring, and absurd. But still, you must agree, one can't sit with one's hands in one's lap; one must do something. What's to be done with the Tchalikovs, for instance?"

She turned to Pimenov and stopped, expecting an answer from him; he, too, stopped and slowly, without speaking, shrugged his shoulders. Obviously he knew what to do with the Tchalikovs, but the treatment would have been so coarse and inhuman that he did not venture to put it into words. And the Tchalikovs were to him so utterly uninteresting and worthless, that a moment later he had forgotten them; looking into Anna Akimovna's eyes, he smiled with pleasure, and his face wore an expression as though he were dreaming about something very pleasant. Only, now standing close to him, Anna Akimovna saw from his face, and especially from his eyes, how exhausted and sleepy he was.

"Here, I ought to give him the fifteen hundred roubles!" she thought, but for some reason this idea seemed to her incongruous and insulting to Pimenov.

"I am sure you are aching all over after your work, and you come to the door with me," she said as they went down the stairs. "Go home."

But he did not catch her words. When they came out into the street, he ran on ahead, unfastened the cover of the sledge, and helping Anna Akimovna in, said:

"I wish you a happy Christmas!"

II

Christmas Morning

"They have left off ringing ever so long! It's dreadful; you won't be there before the service is over! Get up!"

"Two horses are racing, racing..." said Anna Akimovna, and she woke up; before her, candle in hand, stood her maid, red-haired Masha. "Well, what is it?"

"Service is over already," said Masha with despair. "I have called you three times! Sleep till evening for me, but you told me yourself to call you!"

Anna Akimovna raised herself on her elbow and glanced towards the window. It was still quite dark outside, and only the lower edge of the window-frame was white with snow. She could hear a low, mellow chime of bells; it was not the parish church, but somewhere further away. The watch on the little table showed three minutes past six.

"Very well, Masha. . . . In three minutes. . ." said Anna Akimovna in an imploring voice, and she snuggled under the bed-clothes.

She imagined the snow at the front door, the sledge, the dark sky, the crowd in the church, and the smell of juniper, and she felt dread at the thought; but all the same, she made up her mind that she would get up at once and go to early service. And while she was warm in bed and struggling with sleep—which seems, as though to spite one, particularly sweet when one ought to get up—and while she had visions of an immense garden on a mountain and then Gushtchin's Buildings, she was worried all the time by the thought that she ought to get up that very minute and go to church.

But when she got up it was quite light, and it turned out to be half-past nine. There had been a heavy fall of snow in the night; the trees were clothed in white, and the air was particularly light, transparent, and tender, so that when Anna Akimovna looked out of the window her first impulse was to draw a deep, deep breath. And when she had washed, a relic of far-away childish feelings—joy that to-day was Christmas—suddenly stirred within her; after that she felt light-hearted, free and pure in soul, as though her soul, too, had been washed or plunged in the white snow. Masha came in, dressed up and tightly laced, and wished her a happy Christmas; then she spent a long time combing her mistress's hair and helping her to dress. The fragrance and feeling of the new, gorgeous, splendid dress, its faint rustle, and the smell of fresh scent, excited Anna Akimovna.

"Well, it's Christmas," she said gaily to Masha. "Now we will try our fortunes."

"Last year, I was to marry an old man. It turned up three times the same."

"Well, God is merciful."

"Well, Anna Akimovna, what I think is, rather than neither one thing nor the other, I'd marry an old man," said Masha mournfully, and she heaved a sigh. "I am turned twenty; it's no joke."

Everyone in the house knew that red-haired Masha was in love with Mishenka, the footman, and this genuine, passionate, hopeless love had already lasted three years.

"Come, don't talk nonsense," Anna Akimovna consoled her. "I am going on for thirty, but I am still meaning to marry a young man."

While his mistress was dressing, Mishenka, in a new swallow-tail and polished boots, walked about the hall and drawing-room and waited for her to come out, to wish her a happy Christmas. He had a peculiar walk, stepping softly and delicately; looking at his feet, his hands, and the bend of his head, it might be imagined that he was not simply walking, but learning to dance the first figure of the quadrille. In spite of his fine velvety moustache and handsome, rather flashy appearance, he was steady, prudent, and devout as an old man. He said his prayers, bowing down to the ground, and liked burning incense in his room. He respected people of wealth and rank and had a reverence for them; he despised poor people, and all who came to ask favours of any kind, with all the strength of his cleanly flunkey soul. Under his starched shirt he wore a flannel, winter and summer alike, being very careful of his health; his ears were plugged with cotton-wool.

When Anna Akimovna crossed the hall with Masha, he bent his head downwards a little and said in his agreeable, honeyed voice:

"I have the honour to congratulate you, Anna Akimovna, on the most solemn feast of the birth of our Lord."

Anna Akimovna gave him five roubles, while poor Masha was numb with ecstasy. His holiday get-up, his attitude, his voice, and what he said, impressed her by their beauty and elegance; as she followed her mistress she could think of nothing, could see nothing, she could only smile, first blissfully and then bitterly. The upper storey of the house was called the best or visitors' half, while the name of the business part—old people's or simply women's part—was given to the rooms on the lower storey where Aunt Tatyana Ivanovna kept house. In the upper part the gentry and educated visitors were entertained; in the lower storey, simpler folk and the aunt's personal friends. Handsome, plump, and healthy, still young and fresh, and feeling she had on a magnificent dress which seemed to her to diffuse a sort of radiance all about her, Anna Akimovna went down to the lower storey. Here she was met with reproaches for forgetting God now that she was so highly educated, for sleeping too late for the service, and for not coming downstairs to break the fast, and they all clasped their hands and exclaimed with perfect sincerity that she was lovely, wonderful; and she believed it, laughed, kissed them, gave one a rouble, another three or five according to their position. She liked being downstairs. Wherever one looked there were shrines, ikons, little lamps, portraits of ecclesiastical personages—the place smelt of monks; there was a rattle of knives in the kitchen and already a smell of something savoury, exceedingly appetizing, was pervading all the rooms. The yellow-painted floors shone, and from the doors narrow rugs with bright blue stripes ran like little paths to the ikon corner, and the sunshine was simply pouring in at the windows.

In the dining-room some old women, strangers, were sitting; in Varvarushka's room, too, there were old women, and with them a deaf and dumb girl, who seemed abashed about something and kept saying, "Bli, bli!..." Two skinny-looking little girls who had been brought out of the orphanage for Christmas came up to kiss Anna Akimovna's hand, and stood before her transfixed with admiration of her splendid dress; she noticed that one of the girls squinted, and in the midst of her light-hearted holiday mood she felt a sick pang at her heart at the thought that young men would despise the girl, and that she would never marry. In the cook Agafya's room, five huge peasants in new shirts were sitting round the samovar; these were not workmen from the factory, but relations of the cook. Seeing Anna Akimovna, all the peasants jumped up from their seats, and from regard for decorum, ceased munching though their mouths were full. The cook Stepan, in a white cap, with a knife in his hand, came into the room and gave her his greetings; porters in high felt boots came in, and they, too, offered their greetings. The water-carrier peeped in with icicles on his beard, but did not venture to come in.

Anna Akimovna walked through the rooms followed by her retinue—the aunt, Varvarushka, Nikandrovna, the sewing-maid Marfa Petrovna, and the downstairs Masha. Varvarushka—a tall, thin, slender woman, taller than anyone in the house, dressed all in black, smelling of cypress and coffee—crossed herself in each room before the ikon, bowing down from the waist. And whenever one looked at her one was reminded that she had already prepared her shroud and that lottery tickets were hidden away by her in the same box.

"Anyutinka, be merciful at Christmas," she said, opening the door into the kitchen. "Forgive him, bless the man! Have done with it!"

The coachman Panteley, who had been dismissed for drunkenness in November, was on his knees in the middle of the kitchen. He was a good-natured man, but he used to be unruly when he was drunk, and could not go to sleep, but persisted in wandering about the buildings and shouting in a threatening voice, "I know all about it!" Now from his beefy and bloated face and from his bloodshot eyes it could be seen that he had been drinking continually from November till Christmas.

"Forgive me, Anna Akimovna," he brought out in a hoarse voice, striking his forehead on the floor and showing his bull-like neck.

"It was Auntie dismissed you; ask her."

"What about auntie?" said her aunt, walking into the kitchen, breathing heavily; she was very stout, and on her bosom one might have stood a tray of teacups and a samovar. "What about auntie now? You are mistress here, give your own orders; though these rascals might be all dead for all I care. Come, get up, you hog!" she shouted at Panteley, losing patience. "Get out of my sight! It's the last time I forgive you, but if you transgress again—don't ask for mercy!"

Then they went into the dining-room to coffee. But they had hardly sat down, when the downstairs Masha rushed headlong in, saying with horror, "The singers!" And ran back again. They heard someone blowing his nose, a low bass cough, and footsteps that sounded like horses' iron-shod hoofs tramping about the entry near the hall. For half a minute all was hushed. . . . The singers burst out so suddenly and loudly that everyone started. While they were singing, the priest from the almshouses with the deacon and the sexton arrived. Putting on the stole, the priest slowly said that when they were ringing for matins it was snowing and not cold, but that the frost was sharper towards morning, God bless it! and now there must be twenty degrees of frost.

"Many people maintain, though, that winter is healthier than summer," said the deacon; then immediately assumed an austere expression and chanted after the priest. "Thy Birth, O Christ our Lord. . . ."

Soon the priest from the workmen's hospital came with the deacon, then the

Sisters from the hospital, children from the orphanage, and then singing could be heard almost uninterruptedly. They sang, had lunch, and went away.

About twenty men from the factory came to offer their Christmas greetings. They were only the foremen, mechanicians, and their assistants, the pattern-makers, the accountant, and so on—all of good appearance, in new black coats. They were all first-rate men, as it were picked men; each one knew his value—that is, knew that if he lost his berth to-day, people would be glad to take him on at another factory. Evidently they liked Auntie, as they behaved freely in her presence and even smoked, and when they had all trooped in to have something to eat, the accountant put his arm round her immense waist. They were free-and-easy, perhaps, partly also because Varvarushka, who under the old masters had wielded great power and had kept watch over the morals of the clerks, had now no authority whatever in the house; and perhaps because many of them still remembered the time when Auntie Tatyana Ivanovna, whose brothers kept a strict hand over her, had been dressed like a simple peasant woman like Agafya, and when Anna Akimovna used to run about the yard near the factory buildings and everyone used to call her Anyutka.

The foremen ate, talked, and kept looking with amazement at Anna Akimovna, how she had grown up and how handsome she had become! But this elegant girl, educated by governesses and teachers, was a stranger to them; they could not understand her, and they instinctively kept closer to "Auntie," who called them by their names, continually pressed them to eat and drink, and clinking glasses with them, had already drunk two wine-glasses of rowanberry wine with them. Anna Akimovna was always afraid of their thinking her proud, an upstart, or a crow in peacock's feathers; and now while the foremen were crowding round the food, she did not leave the dining-room, but took part in the conversation. She asked Pimenov, her acquaintance of the previous day:

"Why have you so many clocks in your room?"

"I mend clocks," he answered. "I take the work up between times, on holidays, or when I can't sleep."

"So if my watch goes wrong I can bring it to you to be repaired?" Anna Akimovna asked, laughing.

"To be sure, I will do it with pleasure," said Pimenov, and there was an expression of tender devotion in his face, when, not herself knowing why, she unfastened her magnificent watch from its chain and handed it to him; he looked at it in silence and gave it back. "To be sure, I will do it with pleasure," he repeated. "I don't mend watches now. My eyes are weak, and the doctors have forbidden me to do fine work. But for you I can make an exception."

"Doctors talk nonsense," said the accountant. They all laughed. "Don't you believe them," he went on, flattered by the laughing; "last year a tooth flew out of a cylinder and hit old Kalmykov such a crack on the head that you could see his brains, and the doctor said he would die; but he is alive and working to this day, only he has taken to stammering since that mishap."

"Doctors do talk nonsense, they do, but not so much," sighed Auntie. "Pyotr

Andreyitch, poor dear, lost his sight. Just like you, he used to work day in day out at the factory near the hot furnace, and he went blind. The eyes don't like heat. But what are we talking about?" she said, rousing'herself. "Come and have a drink. My best wishes for Christmas, my dears. I never drink with anyone else, but I drink with you, sinful woman as I am. Please God!"

Anna Akimovna fancied that after yesterday Pimenov despised her as a philanthropist, but was fascinated by her as a woman. She looked at him and thought that he behaved very charmingly and was nicely dressed. It is true that the sleeves of his coat were not quite long enough, and the coat itself seemed short-waisted, and his trousers were not wide and fashionable, but his tie was tied carelessly and with taste and was not as gaudy as the others. And he seemed to be a good-natured man, for he ate submissively whatever Auntie put on his plate. She remembered how black he had been the day before, and how sleepy, and the thought of it for some reason touched her.

When the men were preparing to go, Anna Akimovna put out her hand to Pimenov. She wanted to ask him to come in sometimes to see her, without ceremony, but she did not know how to—her tongue would not obey her; and that they might not think she was attracted by Pimenov, she shook hands with his companions, too.

Then the boys from the school of which she was a patroness came. They all had their heads closely cropped and all wore grey blouses of the same pattern. The teacher—a tall, beardless young man with patches of red on his face—was visibly agitated as he formed the boys into rows; the boys sang in tune, but with harsh, disagreeable voices. The manager of the factory, Nazaritch, a bald, sharp-eyed Old Believer, could never get on with the teachers, but the one who was now anxiously waving his hands he despised and hated, though he could not have said why. He behaved rudely and condescendingly to the young man, kept back his salary, meddled with the teaching, and had finally tried to dislodge him by appointing, a fortnight before Christmas, as porter to the school a drunken peasant, a distant relation of his wife's, who disobeyed the teacher and said rude things to him before the boys.

"You always express yourself so tediously and incomprehensibly," said Anna Akimovna, and she walked to the other end of the big drawing-room.

It was only just past eleven. The stillness of the big room, only broken by the singing that floated up from below, made her yawn. The bronzes, the albums, and the pictures on the walls, representing a ship at sea, cows in a meadow, and views of the Rhine, were so absolutely stale that her eyes simply glided over them without observing them. The holiday mood was already growing tedious. As before, Anna Akimovna felt that she was beautiful, good-natured, and wonderful, but now it seemed to her that that was of no use to anyone; it seemed to her that she did not know for whom and for what she had put on this expensive dress, too, and, as always happened on all holidays, she began to be fretted by loneliness and the persistent thought that her beauty, her health, and her wealth, were a mere cheat, since she was not wanted, was of no use to anyone, and nobody loved her. She walked through all the rooms, humming and looking out of windows; stopping in the drawing-room, she could not resist beginning to talk to Mishenka.

"I don't know what you think of yourself, Misha," she said, and heaved a sigh. "Really, God might punish you for it."

"What do you mean?"

"You know what I mean. Excuse my meddling in your affairs. But it seems you are spoiling your own life out of obstinacy. You'll admit that it is high time you got married, and she is an excellent and deserving girl. You will never find anyone better. She's a beauty, clever, gentle, and devoted. . . . And her appearance! . . . If she belonged to our circle or a higher one, people would be falling in love with her for her red hair alone. See how beautifully her hair goes with her complexion. Oh, goodness! You don't understand anything, and don't know what you want," Anna Akimovna said bitterly, and tears came into her eyes. "Poor girl, I am so sorry for her! I know you want a wife with money, but I have told you already I will give Masha a dowry."

Mishenka could not picture his future spouse in his imagination except as a tall, plump, substantial, pious woman, stepping like a peacock, and, for some reason, with a long shawl over her shoulders; while Masha was thin, slender, tightly laced, and walked with little steps, and, worst of all, she was too fascinating and at times extremely attractive to Mishenka, and that, in his opinion, was incongruous with matrimony and only in keeping with loose behaviour. When Anna Akimovna had promised to give Masha a dowry, he had hesitated for a time; but once a poor student in a brown overcoat over his uniform, coming with a letter for Anna Akimovna, was fascinated by Masha, and could not resist embracing her near the hat-stand, and she had uttered a faint shriek; Mishenka, standing on the stairs above, had seen this, and from that time had begun to cherish a feeling of disgust for Masha. A poor student! Who knows, if she had been embraced by a rich student or an officer the consequences might have been different.

"Why don't you wish it?" Anna Akimovna asked. "What more do you want?"

Mishenka was silent and looked at the arm-chair fixedly, and raised his eyebrows.

"Do you love someone else?"

Silence. The red-haired Masha came in with letters and visiting cards on a tray. Guessing that they were talking about her, she blushed to tears.

"The postmen have come," she muttered. "And there is a clerk called Tchalikov waiting below. He says you told him to come to-day for something."

"What insolence!" said Anna Akimovna, moved to anger. "I gave him no orders. Tell him to take himself off; say I am not at home!"

A ring was heard. It was the priests from her parish. They were always shown into the aristocratic part of the house—that is, upstairs. After the priests, Nazaritch, the manager of the factory, came to pay his visit, and then the factory doctor; then Mishenka announced the inspector of the elementary schools. Visitors kept arriving.

When there was a moment free, Anna Akimovna sat down in a deep arm-chair in the drawing-room, and shutting her eyes, thought that her loneliness was quite natural because she had not married and never would marry.... But that was not her fault. Fate itself had flung her out of the simple working-class surroundings in which, if she could trust her memory, she had felt so snug and at home, into these immense rooms, where she could never think what to do with herself, and could not understand why so many people kept passing before her eyes. What was happening now seemed to her trivial, useless, since it did not and could not give her happiness for one minute.

"If I could fall in love," she thought, stretching; the very thought of this sent a rush of warmth to her heart. "And if I could escape from the factory..." she mused, imagining how the weight of those factory buildings, barracks, and schools would roll off her conscience, roll off her mind.... Then she remembered her father, and thought if he had lived longer he would certainly have married her to a working-man—to Pimenov, for instance. He would have told her to marry, and that would have been all about it. And it would have been a good thing; then the factory would have passed into capable hands.

She pictured his curly head, his bold profile, his delicate, ironical lips and the strength, the tremendous strength, in his shoulders, in his arms, in his chest, and the tenderness with which he had looked at her watch that day.

"Well," she said, "it would have been all right.... I would have married him."

"Anna Akimovna," said Mishenka, coming noiselessly into the drawing-room.

"How you frightened me!" she said, trembling all over. "What do you want?"

"Anna Akimovna," he said, laying his hand on his heart and raising his eyebrows, "you are my mistress and my benefactress, and no one but you can tell me what I ought to do about marriage, for you are as good as a mother to me.... But kindly forbid them to laugh and jeer at me downstairs. They won't let me pass without it."

"How do they jeer at you?"

"They call me Mashenka's Mishenka."

"Pooh, what nonsense!" cried Anna Akimovna indignantly. "How stupid you all are! What a stupid you are, Misha! How sick I am of you! I can't bear the sight of you."

III

Dinner

Just as the year before, the last to pay her visits were Krylin, an actual civil councillor, and Lysevitch, a well-known barrister. It was already dark when they arrived. Krylin, a man of sixty, with a wide mouth and with grey whiskers close to his ears, with a face like a lynx, was wearing a uniform with an Anna ribbon, and white trousers. He held Anna Akimovna's hand in both of his for a long while, looked intently in her face, moved his lips, and at last said, drawling upon one note:

"I used to respect your uncle...and your father, and enjoyed the privilege of their friendship. Now I feel it an agreeable duty, as you see, to present my

Christmas wishes to their honoured heiress...in spite of my infirmities and the distance I have to come.... And I am very glad to see you in good health."

The lawyer Lysevitch, a tall, handsome fair man, with a slight sprinkling of grey on his temples and beard, was distinguished by exceptionally elegant manners; he walked with a swaying step, bowed as it were reluctantly, and shrugged his shoulders as he talked, and all this with an indolent grace, like a spoiled horse fresh from the stable. He was well fed, extremely healthy, and very well off; on one occasion he had won forty thousand roubles, but concealed the fact from his friends. He was fond of good fare, especially cheese, truffles, and grated radish with hemp oil; while in Paris he had eaten, so he said, baked but unwashed guts. He spoke smoothly, fluently, without hesitation, and only occasionally, for the sake of effect, permitted himself to hesitate and snap his fingers as if picking up a word. He had long ceased to believe in anything he had to say in the law courts, or perhaps he did believe in it, but attached no kind of significance to it; it had all so long been familiar, stale, ordinary.... He believed in nothing but what was original and unusual. A copy-book moral in an original form would move him to tears. Both his notebooks were filled with extraordinary expressions which he had read in various authors; and when he needed to look up any expression, he would search nervously in both books, and usually failed to find it. Anna Akimovna's father had in a good-humoured moment ostentatiously appointed him legal adviser in matters concerning the factory, and had assigned him a salary of twelve thousand roubles. The legal business of the factory had been confined to two or three trivial actions for recovering debts, which Lysevitch handed to his assistants.

Anna Akimovna knew that he had nothing to do at the factory, but she could not dismiss him—she had not the moral courage; and besides, she was used to him. He used to call himself her legal adviser, and his salary, which he invariably sent for on the first of the month punctually, he used to call "stern prose." Anna Akimovna knew that when, after her father's death, the timber of her forest was sold for railway sleepers, Lysevitch had made more than fifteen thousand out of the transaction, and had shared it with Nazaritch. When first she found out they had cheated her she had wept bitterly, but afterwards she had grown used to it.

Wishing her a happy Christmas, and kissing both her hands, he looked her up and down, and frowned.

"You mustn't" he said with genuine disappointment. "I have told you, my dear, you mustn't"!

"What do you mean, Viktor Nikolaitch?"

"I have told you you mustn't get fat. All your family have an unfortunate tendency to grow fat. You mustn't," he repeated in an imploring voice, and kissed her hand. "You are so handsome! You are so splendid! Here, your Excellency, let me introduce the one woman in the world whom I have ever seriously loved."

"There is nothing surprising in that. To know Anna Akimovna at your age and not to be in love with her, that would be impossible."

"I adore her," the lawyer continued with perfect sincerity, but with his usual indolent grace. "I love her, but not because I am a man and she is a woman. When I am with her I always feel as though she belongs to some third sex, and I to a fourth, and we float away together into the domain of the subtlest shades, and there we blend into the spectrum. Leconte de Lisle defines such relations better than anyone. He had a superb passage, a marvellous passage. . . ."

Lysevitch rummaged in one notebook, then in the other, and not finding the quotation, subsided. They began talking of the weather, of the opera, of the arrival, expected shortly, of Duse. Anna Akimovna remembered that the year before Lysevitch and, she fancied, Krylin had dined with her, and now when they were getting ready to go away, she began with perfect sincerity pointing out to them in an imploring voice that as they had no more visits to pay, they ought to remain to dinner with her. After some hesitation the visitors agreed.

In addition to the family dinner, consisting of cabbage soup, sucking pig, goose with apples, and so on, a so-called "French" or "chef's" dinner used to be prepared in the kitchen on great holidays, in case any visitor in the upper storey wanted a meal. When they heard the clatter of crockery in the dining-room, Lysevitch began to betray a noticeable excitement; he rubbed his hands, shrugged his shoulders, screwed up his eyes, and described with feeling what dinners her father and uncle used to give at one time, and a marvellous *matelote* of turbots the cook here could make: it was not a *matelote,* but a veritable revelation! He was already gloating over the dinner, already eating it in imagination and enjoying it. When Anna Akimovna took his arm and led him to the dining-room, he tossed off a glass of vodka and put a piece of salmon in his mouth; he positively purred with pleasure. He munched loudly, disgustingly, emitting sounds from his nose, while his eyes grew oily and rapacious.

The *hors d'œuvres* were superb; among other things, there were fresh white mushrooms stewed in cream, and *sauce provençale* made of fried oysters and crayfish, strongly flavoured with some bitter pickles. The dinner, consisting of elaborate holiday dishes, was excellent, and so were the wines. Mishenka waited at table with enthusiasm. When he laid some new dish on the table and lifted the shining cover, or poured out the wine, he did it with the solemnity of a professor of black magic, and, looking at his face and his movements suggesting the first figure of a quadrille, the lawyer thought several times, "What a fool!"

After the third course Lysevitch said, turning to Anna Akimovna:

"The *fin de siècle* woman—I mean when she is young, and of course wealthy— must be independent, clever, elegant, intellectual, bold, and a little depraved. Depraved within limits, a little; for excess, you know, is wearisome. You ought not to vegetate, my dear; you ought not to live like everyone else, but to get the full savour of life, and a slight flavour of depravity is the sauce of life. Revel among flowers of intoxicating fragrance, breathe the perfume of musk, eat hashish, and best of all, love, love, love. . . . To begin with, in your place I would set up seven lovers—one for each day of the week; and one I would call Monday, one Tuesday, the third Wednesday, and so on, so that each might know his day."

This conversation troubled Anna Akimovna; she ate nothing and only drank a glass of wine.

"Let me speak at last," she said. "For myself personally, I can't conceive of love without family life. I am lonely, lonely as the moon in the sky, and a waning moon, too; and whatever you may say, I am convinced, I feel that this waning can only be restored by love in its ordinary sense. It seems to me that such love would define my duties, my work, make clear my conception of life. I want from love peace of soul, tranquillity; I want the very opposite of musk, and spiritualism, and *fin de siècle*...in short"—she grew embarrassed— "a husband and children."

"You want to be married? Well, you can do that, too," Lysevitch assented. "You ought to have all experiences: marriage, and jealousy, and the sweetness of the first infidelity, and even children....But make haste and live—make haste, my dear: time is passing; it won't wait."

"Yes, I'll go and get married!" she said, looking angrily at his well-fed, satisfied face. "I will marry in the simplest, most ordinary way and be radiant with happiness. And, would you believe it, I will marry some plain working man, some mechanic or draughtsman."

"There is no harm in that, either. The Duchess Josiana loved Gwinplin, and that was permissible for her because she was a grand duchess. Everything is permissible for you, too, because you are an exceptional woman: if, my dear, you want to love a negro or an Arab, don't scruple; send for a negro. Don't deny yourself anything. You ought to be as bold as your desires; don't fall short of them."

"Can it be so hard to understand me?" Anna Akimovna asked with amazement, and her eyes were bright with tears. "Understand, I have an immense business on my hands—two thousand workmen, for whom I must answer before God. The men who work for me grow blind and deaf. I am afraid to go on like this; I am afraid! I am wretched, and you have the cruelty to talk to me of negroes and...and you smile!" Anna Akimovna brought her fist down on the table. "To go on living the life I am living now, or to marry someone as idle and incompetent as myself, would be a crime. I can't go on living like this," she said hotly, "I cannot!"

"How handsome she is!" said Lysevitch, fascinated by her. "My God, how handsome she is! But why are you angry, my dear? Perhaps I am wrong; but surely you don't imagine that if, for the sake of ideas for which I have the deepest respect, you renounce the joys of life and lead a dreary existence, your workmen will be any the better for it? Not a scrap! No, frivolity, frivolity!" he said decisively. "It's essential for you; it's your duty to be frivolous and depraved! Ponder that, my dear, ponder it."

Anna Akimovna was glad she had spoken out, and her spirits rose. She was pleased she had spoken so well, and that her ideas were so fine and just, and she was already convinced that if Pimenov, for instance, loved her, she would marry him with pleasure.

Mishenka began to pour out champagne.

"You make me angry, Viktor Nikolaitch," she said, clinking glasses with the lawyer. "It seems to me you give advice and know nothing of life yourself. According to you, if a man be a mechanic or a draughtsman, he is bound to be a peasant and an ignoramus! But they are the cleverest people! Extraordinary people!"

"Your uncle and father...I knew them and respected them..." Krylin said, pausing for emphasis (he had been sitting upright as a post, and had been eating steadily the whole time), "were people of considerable intelligence and...of lofty spiritual qualities."

"Oh, to be sure, we know all about their qualities," the lawyer muttered, and asked permission to smoke.

When dinner was over Krylin was led away for a nap. Lysevitch finished his cigar, and, staggering from repletion, followed Anna Akimovna into her study. Cosy corners with photographs and fans on the walls, and the inevitable pink or pale blue lanterns in the middle of the ceiling, he did not like, as the expression of an insipid and unoriginal character; besides, the memory of certain of his love affairs of which he was now ashamed was associated with such lanterns. Anna Akimovna's study with its bare walls and tasteless furniture pleased him exceedingly. It was snug and comfortable for him to sit on a Turkish divan and look at Anna Akimovna, who usually sat on the rug before the fire, clasping her knees and looking into the fire and thinking of something; and at such moments it seemed to him that her peasant Old Believer blood was stirring within her.

Every time after dinner when coffee and liqueurs were handed, he grew livelier and began telling her various bits of literary gossip. He spoke with eloquence and inspiration, and was carried away by his own stories; and she listened to him and thought every time that for such enjoyment it was worth paying not only twelve thousand, but three times that sum, and forgave him everything she disliked in him. He sometimes told her the story of some tale or novel he had been reading, and then two or three hours passed unnoticed like a minute. Now he began rather dolefully in a failing voice with his eyes shut.

"It's ages, my dear, since I have read anything," he said when she asked him to tell her something. "Though I do sometimes read Jules Verne."

"I was expecting you to tell me something new."

"H'm!...new," Lysevitch muttered sleepily, and he settled himself further back in the corner of the sofa. "None of the new literature, my dear, is any use for you or me. Of course, it is bound to be such as it is, and to refuse to recognize it is to refuse to recognize—would mean refusing to recognize the natural order of things, and I do recognize it, but..." Lysevitch seemed to have fallen asleep. But a minute later his voice was heard again:

"All the new literature moans and howls like the autumn wind in the chimney. 'Ah, unhappy wretch! Ah, your life may be likened to a prison! Ah, how damp and dark it is in your prison! Ah, you will certainly come to ruin, and there is no chance of escape for you!' That's very fine, but I should prefer a literature that would tell us how to escape from prison. Of all contemporary writers, however, I prefer Maupassant." Lysevitch opened his eyes. "A fine writer, a perfect writer!" Lysevitch shifted in his seat. "A wonderful artist! A terrible, prodigious, supernatural artist!" Lysevitch got up from the sofa and raised his right arm. "Maupassant!" he said rapturously. "My dear, read Maupassant! one page of his gives you more than all the riches of the earth! Every line is a new horizon. The softest, tenderest impulses of the soul alternate with violent tempestuous sensations; your soul, as though under the weight of forty thousand atmospheres, is transformed into the most insignificant little bit of some great thing of an undefined rosy hue which I fancy, if one could put it on one's tongue, would yield a pungent, voluptuous taste. What a fury of transitions, of motives, of melodies! You rest peacefully on the lilies and the roses, and suddenly a thought—a terrible, splendid, irresistible thought—swoops down upon you like a locomotive, and bathes you in hot steam and deafens you with its whistle. Read Maupassant, dear girl; I insist on it."

Lysevitch waved his arms and paced from corner to corner in violent excitement.

"Yes, it is inconceivable," he pronounced, as though in despair; "his last thing overwhelmed me, intoxicated me! But I am afraid you will not care for it. To be carried away by it you must savour it, slowly suck the juice from each line, drink it in. . . . You must drink it in!. . . ."

After a long introduction, containing many words such as dæmonic sensuality, a network of the most delicate nerves, simoom, crystal, and so on, he began at last telling the story of the novel. He did not tell the story so whimsically, but told it in minute detail, quoting from memory whole descriptions and conversations; the characters of the novel fascinated him, and to describe them he threw himself into attitudes, changed the expression of his face and voice like a real actor. He laughed with delight at one moment in a deep bass, and at another, on a high shrill note, clasped his hands and clutched at his head with an expression which suggested that it was just going to burst. Anna Akimovna listened enthralled, though she had already read the novel, and it seemed to her ever so much finer and more subtle in the lawyer's version than in the book itself. He drew her attention to various subtleties, and emphasized the felicitous expressions and the profound thoughts, but she saw in it, only life, life, life and herself, as though she had been a character in the novel. Her spirits rose, and she, too, laughing and clasping her hands, thought that she could not go on living such a life, that there was no need to have a wretched life when one might have a splendid one. She remembered her words and thoughts at dinner, and was proud of them; and when Pimenov suddenly rose up in her imagination, she felt happy and longed for him to love her.

When he had finished the story, Lysevitch sat down on the sofa, exhausted.

"How splendid you are! How handsome!" he began, a little while afterwards in a faint voice as if he were ill. "I am happy near you, dear girl, but why am I forty-two instead of thirty? Your tastes and mine do not coincide: you ought to be depraved, and I have long passed that phase, and want a love as delicate and immaterial as a ray of sunshine—that is, from the point of view of a woman of your age, I am of no earthly use."

In his own words, he loved Turgenev, the singer of virginal love and purity, of youth, and of the melancholy Russian landscape; but he loved virginal love, not from knowledge but from hearsay, as something abstract, existing outside real life. Now he assured himself that he loved Anna Akimovna platonically, ideally, though he did not know what those words meant. But he felt comfortable, snug, warm. Anna Akimovna seemed to him enchanting, original, and he imagined that the pleasant sensation that was aroused in him by these surroundings was the very thing that was called platonic love.

He laid his cheek on her hand and said in the tone commonly used in coaxing little children:

"My precious, why have you punished me?"

"How? When?"

"I have had no Christmas present from you."

Anna Akimovna had never heard before of their sending a Christmas box to the lawyer, and now she was at a loss how much to give him. But she must give him something, for he was expecting it, though he looked at her with eyes full of love.

"I suppose Nazaritch forgot it," she said, "but it is not too late to set it right."

She suddenly remembered the fifteen hundred she had received the day before, which was now lying in the toilet drawer in her bedroom. And when she brought that ungrateful money and gave it to the lawyer, and he put it in his coat pocket with indolent grace, the whole incident passed off charmingly and naturally. The sudden reminder of a Christmas box and this fifteen hundred was not unbecoming in Lysevitch.

"Merci," he said, and kissed her finger.

Krylin came in with blissful, sleepy face, but without his decorations.

Lysevitch and he stayed a little longer and drank a glass of tea each, and began to get ready to go. Anna Akimovna was a little embarrased.... She had utterly forgotten in what department Krylin served, and whether she had to give him money or not; and if she had to, whether to give it now or send it afterwards in an envelope.

"Where does he serve?" she whispered to Lysevitch.

"Goodness knows," muttered Lysevitch, yawning.

She reflected that if Krylin used to visit her father and her uncle and respected them, it was probably not for nothing: apparently he had been charitable at their expense, serving in some charitable institution. As she said good-bye she slipped three hundred roubles into his hand; he seemed taken aback, and looked at her for a minute in silence with his pewtery eyes, but then seemed to understand and said:

"The receipt, honoured Anna Akimovna, you can only receive on the New Year."

Lysevitch had become utterly limp and heavy, and he staggered when Mishenka put on his overcoat.

As he went downstairs he looked like a man in the last stage of exhaustion, and it was evident that he would drop asleep as soon as he got into his sledge.

"Your Excellency," he said languidly to Krylin, stopping in the middle of the staircase, "has it ever happened to you to experience a feeling as though some unseen force were drawing you out longer and longer? You are drawn out and turn into the finest wire. Subjectively this finds expression in a curious voluptuous feeling which is impossible to compare with anything."

Anna Akimovna, standing at the top of the stairs, saw each of them give Mishenka a note.

"Good-bye! Come again!" she called to them, and ran into her bedroom.

She quickly threw off her dress, that she was weary of already, put on a dressing-gown, and ran downstairs; and as she ran downstairs she laughed and thumped with her feet like a schoolboy; she had a great desire for mischief.

IV

Evening

Auntie, in a loose print blouse, Varvarushka and two old women, were sitting in the dining-room having supper. A big piece of salt meat, a ham, and various savouries, were lying on the table before them, and clouds of steam were rising from the meat, which looked particularly fat and appetizing. Wine was not served on the lower storey, but they made up for it with a great number of spirits and home-made liqueurs. Agafyushka, the fat, white-skinned, well-fed cook, was standing with her arms crossed in the doorway and talking to the old women, and the dishes were being handed by the downstairs Masha, a dark girl with a crimson ribbon in her hair. The old women had had enough to eat before the morning was over, and an hour before supper had had tea and buns, and so they were now eating with effort—as if it were, from a sense of duty.

"Oh, my girl!" sighed Auntie, as Anna Akimovna ran into the dining-room and sat down beside her. "You've frightened me to death!"

Everyone in the house was pleased when Anna Akimovna was in good spirits and played pranks; this always reminded them that the old men were dead and that the old women had no authority in the house, and anyone could do as he liked without any fear of being sharply called to account for it. Only the two old women glanced askance at Anna Akimovna with amazement: she was humming, and it was a sin to sing at table.

"Our mistress, our beauty, our picture," Agafyushka began chanting with sugary sweetness. "Our precious jewel! The people, the people that have come to-day to look at our queen. Lord, have mercy upon us! Generals, and officers and gentlemen. . . . I kept looking out of window and counting and counting till I gave it up."

"I'd as soon they did not come at all," said Auntie; she looked sadly at her niece and added: "They only waste the time for my poor orphan girl."

Anna Akimovna felt hungry, as she had eaten nothing since the morning. They poured her out some very bitter liqueur; she drank it off, and tasted the salt meat with mustard, and thought it extraordinarily nice. Then the downstairs Masha brought in the turkey, the pickled apples and the gooseberries. And that pleased her, too. There was only one thing that was disagreeable: there was a draught of hot air from the tiled stove; it was stiflingly close and everyone's cheeks were burning. After supper the cloth was taken off and plates of peppermint biscuits, walnuts, and raisins were brought in.

"You sit down, too...no need to stand there!" said Auntie to the cook.

Agafyushka sighed and sat down to the table; Masha set a wineglass of liqueur before her, too, and Anna Akimovna began to feel as though Agafyushka's white neck were giving out heat like the stove. They were all talking of how difficult it was nowadays to get married, and saying that in old days, if men did not court beauty, they paid attention to money, but now there was no making out what they wanted; and while hunchbacks and cripples used to be left old maids, nowadays men would not have even the beautiful and wealthy. Auntie began to set this down to immorality, and said that people had no fear of God, but she suddenly remembered that Ivan Ivanitch, her brother, and Varvarushka—both people of holy life—had feared God, but all the same had had children on the sly, and had sent them to the Foundling Asylum. She pulled herself up and changed the conversation, telling them about a suitor she had once had, a factory hand, and how she had loved him, but her brothers had forced her to marry a widower, an ikon-painter, who, thank God, had died two years after. The downstairs Masha sat down to the table, too, and told them with a mysterious air that for the last week some unknown man with a black moustache, in a great-coat with an astrachan collar, had made his appearance every morning in the yard, had stared at the windows of the big house, and had gone on further—to the buildings; the man was all right, nice-looking. . . .

All this conversation made Anna Akimovna suddenly long to be married— long intensely, painfully; she felt as though she would give half her life and all her fortune only to know that upstairs there was a man who was closer to her than anyone in the world, that he loved her warmly and was missing her; and the thought of such closeness, ecstatic and inexpressible in words, troubled her soul. And the instinct of youth and health flattered her with lying assurances that the real poetry of life was not over but still to come, and she believed it, and leaning back in her chair (her hair fell down as she did so), she began laughing, and, looking at her, the others laughed, too. And it was a long time before this causeless laughter died down in the dining-room.

She was informed that the Stinging Beetle had come. This was a pilgrim woman called Pasha or Spiridonovna—a thin little woman of fifty, in a black dress with a white kerchief, with keen eyes, sharp nose, and a sharp chin; she had sly, viperish eyes and she looked as though she could see right through everyone. Her lips were shaped like a heart. Her viperishness and hostility to everyone had earned her the nickname of the Stinging Beetle.

Going into the dining-room without looking at anyone, she made for the ikons and chanted in a high voice "Thy Holy Birth," then she sang, "The Virgin to-day gives birth to the Son," then "Christ is born," then she turned round and bent a piercing gaze upon all of them.

"A happy Christmas," she said, and she kissed Anna Akimovna on the shoulder.

"It's all I could do, all I could do to get to you, my kind friends." She kissed Auntie on the shoulder. "I should have come to you this morning, but I went in to some good people to rest on the way. 'Stay, Spiridonovna, stay,' they said, and I did not notice that evening was coming on."

As she did not eat meat, they gave her salmon and caviare. She ate looking from under her eyelids at the company, and drank three glasses of vodka. When she had finished she said a prayer and bowed down to Anna Akimovna's feet.

They began to play a game of "kings," as they had done the year before, and the year before that, and all the servants in both storeys crowded in at the doors to watch the game. Anna Akimovna fancied she caught a glimpse once or twice of Mishenka, with a patronizing smile on his face, among the crowd of peasant men and women. The first to be king was Stinging Beetle, and Anna Akimovna as the soldier paid her tribute; and then Auntie was king and Anna Akimovna was peasant, which excited general delight, and Agafyushka was prince, and was quite abashed with pleasure. Another game was got up at the other end of the table—played by the two Mashas, Varvarushka, and the sewing-maid Marfa Petrovna, who was waked on purpose to play "kings," and whose face looked cross and sleepy.

While they were playing they talked of men, and of how difficult it was to get a good husband nowadays, and which state was to be preferred—that of an old maid or a widow.

"You are a handsome, healthy, sturdy lass," said Stinging Beetle to Anna Akimovna. "But I can't make out for whose sake you are holding back."

"What's to be done if nobody will have me?"

"Or maybe you have taken a vow to remain a maid?" Stinging Beetle went on, as though she did not hear. "Well, that's a good deed.... Remain one," she repeated, looking intently and maliciously at her cards. "All right, my dear, remain one....Yes...only maids, these saintly maids, are not all alike." She heaved a sigh and played the king. "Oh no, my girl, they are not all alike! Some really watch over themselves like nuns, and butter would not melt in their mouths; and if such a one does sin in an hour of weakness, she is worried to death, poor thing! so it would be a sin to condemn her. While others will go dressed in black and sew their shroud, and yet love rich old men on the sly. Yes, y-es, my canary birds, some hussies will bewitch an old man and rule over him, my doves, rule over him and turn his head; and when they've saved up money and lottery tickets enough, they will bewitch him to his death."

Varvarushka's only response to these hints was to heave a sigh and look towards the ikons. There was an expression of Christian meekness on her countenance.

"I know a maid like that, my bitterest enemy," Stinging Beetle went on, looking round at everyone in triumph; "she is always sighing, too, and looking at the ikons, the she-devil. When she used to rule in a certain old man's house, if one went to her she would give one a crust, and bid one bow down to the ikons while she would sing: 'In conception Thou dost abide a Virgin...!' On holidays she will give one a bite, and on working days she will reproach one for it. But nowadays I will make merry over her! I will make as merry as I please, my jewel."

Varvarushka glanced at the ikons again and crossed herself.

"But no one will have me, Spiridonovna," said Anna Akimovna to change the conversation. "What's to be done?"

"It's your own fault. You keep waiting for highly educated gentlemen, but you ought to marry one of your own sort, a merchant."

"We don't want a merchant," said Auntie, all in a flutter. "Queen of Heaven, preserve us! A gentleman will spend your money, but then he will be kind to you, you poor little fool. But a merchant will be so strict that you won't feel at home in your own house. You'll be wanting to fondle him and he will be counting his money, and when you sit down to meals with him, he'll grudge you every mouthful, though it's your own, the lout!...Marry a gentleman."

They all talked at once, loudly interrupting one another, and Auntie tapped on the table with the nutcrackers and said, flushed and angry:

"We won't have a merchant; we won't have one! If you choose a merchant I shall go to an almshouse."

"Sh!...Sh!...Hush!" cried Stinging Beetle; when all were silent she screwed up one eye and said: "Do you know what, Annushka, my birdie...? There is no need for you to get married really like everyone else. You're rich and free, you are your own mistress; but yet, my child, it doesn't seem the right thing for you to be an old maid. I'll find you, you know, some trumpery and simple-witted man. You'll marry him for appearances and then have your fling, bonny lass! You can hand him five thousand or ten maybe, and pack kim off where he came from, and you will be mistress in your own house—you can love whom you like and no one can say anything to you. And then you can love your highly educated gentlemen. You'll have a jolly time!" Stinging Beetle snapped her fingers and gave a whistle.

"It's sinful," said Auntie.

"Oh, sinful," laughed Stinging Beetle. "She is educated, she understands. To cut someone's throat or bewitch an old man—that's a sin, that's true; but to love some charming young friend is not a sin at all. And what is there in it, really? There's no sin in it at all! The old pilgrim women have invented all that to make fools of simple folk. I, too, say everywhere it's a sin; I don't know myself why it's a sin." Stinging Beetle emptied her glass and cleared her throat. "Have your fling, bonny lass," this time evidently addressing herself. "For thirty years, wenches, I have thought of nothing but sins and been afraid, but now I see I have wasted my time, I've let it slip by like a ninny! Ah, I have been a fool, a fool!" She sighed. "A woman's time is short and every day is precious. You are handsome, Annushka, and very rich; but as soon as thirty-five or forty strikes for you your time is up. Don't listen to anyone, my girl; live, have your fling till you are forty, and then you will have time to pray forgiveness—there will be plenty of time to bow down and to sew your shroud. A candle to God and a poker to the devil! You can do both at once! Well, how is it to be? Will you make some little man happy?"

"I will," laughed Anna Akimovna. "I don't care now; I would marry a working man."

"Well, that would do all right! Oh, what a fine fellow you would choose then!" Stinging Beetle screwed up her eyes and shook her head. "O—o—oh!"

"I tell her myself," said Auntie, "it's no good waiting for a gentleman, so she had better marry, not a gentleman, but someone humbler; anyway we should have a man in the house to look after things. And there are lots of good men. She might have someone out of the factory. They are all sober, steady men. . . ."

"I should think so," Stinging Beetle agreed. "They are capital fellows. If you like, Aunt, I will make a match for her with Vassily Lebedinsky?"

"Oh, Vasya's legs are so long," said Auntie seriously. "He is so lanky. He has no looks."

There was laughter in the crowd by the door.

"Well, Pimenov? Would you like to marry Pimenov?" Stinging Beetle asked Anna Akimovna.

"Very good. Make a match for me with Pimenov."

"Really?"

"Yes, do!" Anna Akimovna said resolutely, and she struck her fist on the table. "On my honour, I will marry him."

"Really?"

Anna Akimovna suddenly felt ashamed that her cheeks were burning and that everyone was looking at her; she flung the cards together on the table and ran out of the room. As she ran up the stairs and, reaching the upper storey, sat down to the piano in the drawing-room, a murmur of sound reached her from below like the roar of the sea; most likely they were talking of her and of Pimenov, and perhaps Stinging Beetle was taking advantage of her absence to insult Varvarushka and was putting no check on her language.

The lamp in the big room was the only light burning in the upper storey, and it sent a glimmer through the door into the dark drawing-room. It was between nine and ten, not later. Anna Akimovna played a waltz, then another, then a third; she went on playing without stopping. She looked into the dark corner beyond the piano, smiled, and inwardly called to it, and the idea occurred to her that she might drive off to the town to see someone, Lysevitch for instance, and tell him what was passing in her heart. She wanted to talk without ceasing, to laugh, to play the fool, but the dark corner was sullenly silent, and all round in all the rooms of the upper storey it was still and desolate.

She was fond of sentimental songs, but she had a harsh, untrained voice, and so she only played the accompaniment and sang hardly audibly, just above her breath. She sang in a whisper one song after another, for the most part about love, separation, and frustrated hopes, and she imagined how she would hold out her hands to him and say with entreaty, with tears, "Pimenov, take this burden from me!" And then, just as though her sins had been forgiven, there would be joy and comfort in her soul, and perhaps a free, happy life would begin. In an anguish of anticipation she leant over the keys, with a passionate longing for the change in her life to come at once without delay, and was terrified at the thought that her old life would go on for some time longer. Then she played again and sang hardly above her breath, and all was stillness about her. There was no noise coming from downstairs now, they must have gone to bed. It had struck ten some time before. A long, solitary, wearisome night was approaching.

Anna Akimovna walked through all the rooms, lay down for a while on the sofa, and read in her study the letters that had come that evening; there were twelve letters of Christmas greetings and three anonymous letters. In one of them some workman complained in a horrible, almost illegible handwriting that Lenten oil sold in the factory shop was rancid and smelt of paraffin; in another, someone respectfully informed her that over a purchase of iron Nazaritch had lately taken a bribe of a thousand roubles from someone; in a third she was abused for her inhumanity.

The excitement of Christmas was passing off, and to keep it up Anna Akimovna sat down at the piano again and softly played one of the new waltzes, then she remembered how cleverly and creditably she had spoken at dinner to-day. She looked round at the dark windows, at the walls with the pictures, at the faint light that came from the big room, and all at once she began suddenly crying, and she felt vexed that she was so lonely, and that she had no one to talk to and consult. To cheer herself she tried to picture Pimenov in her imagination, but it was unsuccessful.

It struck twelve. Mishenka, no longer wearing his swallowtail but in his reefer jacket, came in, and without speaking lighted two candles; then he went out and returned a minute later with a cup of tea on a tray.

"What are you laughing at?" she asked, noticing a smile on his face.

"I was downstairs and heard the jokes you were making about Pimenov..." he said, and put his hand before his laughing mouth. "If he were sat down to dinner to-day with Viktor Nikolaitch and the general, he'd have died of fright." Mishenka's shoulders were shaking with laughter. "He doesn't know even how to hold his fork, I bet."

The footman's laughter and words, his reefer jacket and moustache, gave Anna Akimovna a feeling of uncleanness. She shut her eyes to avoid seeing him, and, against her own will, imagined Pimenov dining with Lysevitch and Krylin, and his timid, unintellectual figure seemed to her pitiful and helpless, and she felt repelled by it. And only now, for the first time in the whole day, she realized clearly that all she had said and thought about Pimenov and marrying a workman was nonsense, folly, and wilfulness. To convince herself of the opposite, to overcome her repulsion, she tried to recall what she had said at dinner, but now she could not see anything in it: shame at her own thoughts and actions, and the fear that she had said something improper during the day, and disgust at her own lack of spirit, overwhelmed her completely. She took up a candle and, as rapidly as if someone were pursuing her, ran downstairs, woke Spiridonovna, and began assuring her she had been joking. Then she went to her bedroom. Red-haired Masha, who was dozing in an arm-chair near the bed, jumped up and began shaking up the pillows. Her face was exhausted and sleepy, and her magnificent hair had fallen on one side.

"Tchalikov came again this evening," she said, yawning, "but I did not dare to announce him; he was very drunk. He says he will come again to-morrow."

"What does he want with me?" said Anna Akimovna, and she flung her comb on the floor. "I won't see him, I won't."

She made up her mind she had no one left in life but this Tchalikov, that he would never leave off persecuting her, and would remind her every day how uninteresting and absurd her life was. So all she was fit for was to help the poor. Oh, how stupid it was!

She lay down without undressing, and sobbed with shame and depression: what seemed to her most vexatious and stupid of all was that her dreams that day about Pimenov had been right, lofty, honourable, but at the same time she felt that Lysevitch and even Krylin were nearer to her than Pimenov and all the work-people taken together. She thought that if the long day she had just spent could have been represented in a picture, all that had been bad and vulgar—as, for instance, the dinner, the lawyer's talk, the game of "kings"—would have been true, while her dreams and talk about Pimenov would have stood out from the whole as something false, as out of drawing; and she thought, too, that it was too late to dream of happiness, that everything was over for her, and it was impossible to go back to the life when she had slept under the same quilt with her mother, or to devise some new special sort of life.

Red-haired Masha was kneeling before the bed, gazing at her in mournful perplexity; then she, too, began crying, and laid her face against her mistress's arm, and without words it was clear why she was so wretched.

"We are fools!" said Anna Akimovna, laughing and crying. "We are fools! Oh, what fools we are!"

Youth

(1898)

Joseph Conrad

Joseph Conrad (1857–1924) was born Józef Teodor Konrad Nalęcz Korzeniowski in Berdichev, Polish Ukraine. His father was exiled to Siberia for involvement in revolutionary activity, and the young Conrad accompanied his parents. From 1874 to 1894 he followed the sea, traveling widely, especially in the East. He became a British seaman in 1878, and in 1886 he obtained his first command and became a British citizen. In 1889 he began writing fiction, using his adopted language, English, and he shortened his name to Joseph Conrad. In 1895, having ended his seaman's career, he published his first novel, *Almayer's Folly*. Among the many novels that followed were *The Nigger of the Narcissus* (1897), *Lord Jim* (1900), *Nostromo* (1904), *The Secret Agent* (1907), and *Victory* (1915). He also wrote short stories and cultivated the *nouvelle*, the best of which were *Youth, Heart of Darkness,* and *The End of the Tether* (1902); *Typhoon, Falk* (1903), and *The Shadow Line* (1917).

For further information on Conrad's life, see Ford Madox Ford, *Joseph Conrad, a Personal Remembrance* (Boston, 1924); Jessie Conrad, *Joseph Conrad and His Circle* (London, 1935); Georges Jean-Aubry, *The Sea-Dreamer* (Garden City, N.Y., 1957); and Jocelyn Baines, *Joseph Conrad* (London, 1960); for criticism, see Albert Guerard, *Joseph Conrad* (New York, 1947).

Youth was first published in *Blackwood's Magazine* in September 1898. It was published in book form in 1902 with *Heart of Darkness* and *The End of the Tether* in a volume entitled *Youth*. The text, from the collected edition of Conrad's novels (1920ff.) with the author's final revisions, is reprinted by permission of J. M. Dent & Sons Ltd.

This could have occurred nowhere but in England, where men and sea interpenetrate, so to speak—the sea entering into the life of most men, and the men knowing something or everything about the sea, in the way of amusement, of travel, or of bread-winning.

We were sitting round a mahogany table that reflected the bottle, the claret-glasses, and our faces as we leaned on our elbows. There was a director of companies, an accountant, a lawyer, Marlow, and myself. The director had been a *Conway* boy, the accountant had served four years at sea, the lawyer—a fine crusted Tory, High Churchman, the best of old fellows, the soul of honor—had been chief officer in the P. & O. service in the good old days when mail-boats were square-rigged at least on two masts, and used to come down the China Sea before a fair monsoon with stun'-sails set alow and aloft. We all began life in the merchant service. Between the five of us there was the strong bond of the sea, and also the fellowship of the craft, which no amount of enthusiasm for yachting, cruising, and so on can give, since one is only the amusement of life and the other is life itself.

Marlow (at least I think that is how he spelt his name) told the story, or rather the chronicle, of a voyage:

"Yes, I have seen a little of the Eastern seas; but what I remember best is my first voyage there. You fellows know there are those voyages that seem ordered for the illustration of life, that might stand for a symbol of existence. You fight, work, sweat, nearly kill yourself, sometimes do kill yourself, trying to accomplish something—and you can't. Not from any fault of yours. You simply can do nothing, neither great nor little—not a thing in the world—not even marry an old maid, or get a wretched 600-ton cargo of coal to its port of destination.

"It was altogether a memorable affair. It was my first voyage to the East, and my first voyage as second mate; it was also my skipper's first command. You'll admit it was time. He was sixty if a day; a little man, with a broad, not very straight back, with bowed shoulders and one leg more bandy than the other, he had that queer twisted-about appearance you see so often in men who work in the fields. He had a nut-cracker face—chin and nose trying to come together over a sunken mouth—and it was framed in iron-gray fluffy hair, that looked like a chin strap of cotton-wool sprinkled with coal-dust. And he had blue eyes in that old face of his, which were amazingly like a boy's, with that candid expression some quite common men preserve to the end of their days by a rare internal gift of simplicity of heart and rectitude of soul. What induced him to accept me was a wonder. I had come out of a crack Australian clipper, where I had been third officer, and he seemed to have a prejudice against crack clippers as aristocratic and high-toned. He said to me, 'You know, in this ship you will have to work.' I said I had to work in every ship I had ever been in. 'Ah, but this is different, and you gentlemen out of them big ships; . . . but there! I dare say you will do. Join to-morrow.'

"I joined to-morrow. It was twenty-two years ago; and I was just twenty. How time passes! It was one of the happiest days of my life. Fancy! Second mate for the first time—a really responsible officer! I wouldn't have thrown up my new billet for a fortune. The mate looked me over carefully. He was also an old chap, but of another stamp. He had a Roman nose, a snow-white, long beard, and his name was Mahon, but he insisted that it should be pronounced Mann. He was well connected; yet there was something wrong with his luck, and he had never got on.

"As to the captain, he had been for years in coasters, then in the Mediterranean, and last in the West Indian trade. He had never been round the Capes. He could just write a kind of sketchy hand, and didn't care for writing at all. Both were thorough good seamen of course, and between those two old chaps I felt like a small boy between two grandfathers.

"The ship also was old. Her name was the *Judea*. Queer name, isn't it? She belonged to a man Wilmer, Wilcox—some name like that; but he has been bankrupt and dead these twenty years or more, and his name don't matter. She had been laid up in Shadwell basin for ever so long. You can imagine her state. She was all rust, dust, grime—soot aloft, dirt on deck. To me it was like coming out of a palace into a ruined cottage. She was about 400 tons, had a primitive windlass, wooden latches to the doors, not a bit of brass about her, and a big square stern. There was on it, below her name in big letters, a lot of scroll work, with the gilt off, and some sort of a coat of arms, with the motto 'Do or Die' underneath. I remember it took my fancy immensely. There was a touch of romance in it, something that made me love the old thing—something that appealed to my youth!

"We left London in ballast—sand ballast—to load a cargo of coal in a northern port for Bankok. Bankok! I thrilled. I had been six years at sea, but had only seen Melbourne and Sydney, very good places, charming places in their way—but Bankok!

"We worked out of the Thames under canvas, with a North Sea pilot on board. His name was Jermyn, and he dodged all day long about the galley drying his handkerchief before the stove. Apparently he never slept. He was a dismal man, with a perpetual tear sparkling at the end of his nose, who either had been in trouble, or was in trouble, or expected to be in trouble—couldn't be happy unless something went wrong. He mistrusted my youth, my common-sense, and my seamanship, and made a point of showing it in a hundred little ways. I dare say he was right. It seems to me I knew very little then, and I know not much more now; but I cherish a hate for that Jermyn to this day.

"We were a week working up as far as Yarmouth Roads, and then we got into a gale—the famous October gale of twenty-two years ago. It was wind, lightning, sleet, snow, and a terrific sea. We were flying light, and you may imagine how bad it was when I tell you we had smashed bulwarks and a flooded deck. On the second night she shifted her ballast into the lee bow, and by that time we had been blown off somewhere on the Dogger Bank. There was nothing for it but go below with shovels and try to right her, and there we were in that vast hold, gloomy like a cavern, the tallow dips stuck and flickering on the beams, the gale howling above, the ship tossing about like mad on her side; there we all were, Jermyn, the captain, everyone, hardly able to keep our feet, engaged on that gravedigger's work, and trying to toss shovelfuls of wet sand up to windward. At every tumble of the ship you could see vaguely in the dim light men falling down with a great flourish of shovels. One of the ship's boys (we had two), impressed by the weirdness of the scene, wept as if his heart would break. We could hear him blubbering somewhere in the shadows.

"On the third day the gale died out, and by-and-by a north-country tug picked us up. We took sixteen days in all to get from London to the Tyne! When we got into dock we had lost our turn for loading, and they hauled us off to a tier where we remained for a month. Mrs. Beard (the captain's name was Beard) came from Colchester to see the old man. She lived on board. The crew of runners had left, and there remained only the officers, one boy, and the steward, a mulatto who answered to the name of Abraham. Mrs. Beard was an old woman, with a face all wrinkled and ruddy like a winter apple, and the figure of a young girl. She caught sight of me once, sewing on a button, and insisted on having my shirts to repair. This was something different from the captains' wives I had known on board crack clippers. When I brought her the shirts, she said: 'And the socks? They want mending, I am sure, and John's—Captain Beard's—things are all in order now. I would be glad of something to do.' Bless the old woman. She overhauled my outfit for me, and meantime I read for the first time 'Sartor Resartus' and Burnaby's 'Ride to Khiva.' I didn't understand much of the first then; but I remember I preferred the soldier to the philosopher at the time; a preference which life has only confirmed. One was a man, and the other was either more—or less. However, they are both dead, and Mrs. Beard is dead, and youth, strength, genius, thoughts, achievements, simple hearts—all die. . . . No matter.

"They loaded us at last. We shipped a crew. Eight able seamen and two boys. We hauled off one evening to the buoys at the dock-gates, ready to go out, and with a fair prospect of beginning the voyage next day. Mrs. Beard was to start for home by a late train. When the ship was fast we went to tea. We sat rather silent through the meal—Mahon, the old couple, and I. I finished first, and slipped away for a smoke, my cabin being in a deck-house just against the poop. It was high water, blowing fresh with a drizzle; the double dock-gates were opened, and the steam colliers were going in and out in the darkness with their lights burning bright, a great plashing of propellers, rattling of winches, and a lot of hailing on the pier-heads. I watched the procession of head-lights gliding high and of green lights gliding low in the night, when suddenly a red gleam flashed at me, vanished, came into view again, and remained. The fore-end of a steamer loomed up close. I shouted down the cabin, 'Come up, quick!' and then heard a startled voice saying afar in the dark, 'Stop her, sir.' A bell jingled. Another voice cried warningly, 'We are going right into that bark, sir.' The answer to this was a gruff 'All right,' and the next thing was a heavy crash as the steamer struck a glancing blow with the bluff of her bow about our fore-rigging. There was a moment of confusion, yelling, and running about. Steam roared. Then somebody was heard saying, 'All clear, sir.' . . . 'Are you all right?' asked the gruff voice. I had jumped forward to see the damage, and hailed back, 'I think so.' 'Easy astern,' said the gruff voice. A bell jingled. 'What steamer is that?' screamed Mahon. By that time she was no more to us than a bulky shadow maneuvering a little way off. They shouted at us some name—a woman's name, Miranda or Melissa—or some such thing. 'This means another month in this beastly hole,' said Mahon to me, as we peered with lamps about the splintered bulwarks and broken braces. 'But where's the captain?'

"We had not heard or seen anything of him all that time. We went aft to look. A doleful voice arose hailing somewhere in the middle of the dock. *'Judea* ahoy!'...How the devil did he get there?...'Hallo!' we shouted. 'I am adrift in our boat without oars,' he cried. A belated waterman offered his services, and Mahon struck a bargain with him for half-a-crown to tow our skipper alongside; but it was Mrs. Beard that came up the ladder first. They had been floating about the dock in that mizzly cold rain for nearly an hour. I was never so surprised in my life.

"It appears that when he heard my shout 'Come up,' he understood at once what was the matter, caught up his wife, ran on deck, and across, and down into our boat, which was fast to the ladder. Not bad for a sixty-year-old. Just imagine that old fellow saving heroically in his arms that old woman—the woman of his life. He set her down on a thwart, and was ready to climb back on board when the painter came adrift somehow, and away they went together. Of course in the confusion we did not hear him shouting. He looked abashed. She said cheerfully, 'I suppose it does not matter my losing the train now?' 'No, Jenny—you go below and get warm,' he growled. Then to us: 'A sailor has no business with a wife—I say. There I was, out of the ship. Well, no harm done this time. Let's go and look at what that fool of a steamer smashed.'

"It wasn't much, but it delayed us three weeks. At the end of that time, the captain being engaged with his agents, I carried Mrs. Beard's bag to the railway-station and put her all comfy into a third-class carriage. She lowered the window to say, 'You are a good young man. If you see John—Captain Beard—without his muffler at night, just remind him from me to keep his throat well wrapped up.' 'Certainly, Mrs. Beard,' I said. 'You are a good young man; I noticed how attentive you are to John—to Captain——' The train pulled out suddenly; I took my cap off to the old woman: I never saw her again.... Pass the bottle.

"We went to sea next day. When we made that start for Bankok we had been already three months out of London. We had expected to be a fortnight or so—at the outside.

"It was January, and the weather was beautiful—the beautiful sunny winter weather that has more charm than in the summer-time, because it is unexpected, and crisp, and you know it won't, it can't, last long. It's like a windfall, like a godsend, like an unexpected piece of luck.

"It lasted all down the North Sea, all down Channel; and it lasted till we were three hundred miles or so to the westward of the Lizards: then the wind went round to the sou'west and began to pipe up. In two days it blew a gale. The *Judea,* hove to, wallowed on the Atlantic like an old candlebox. It blew day after day: it blew with spite, without interval, without mercy, without rest. The world was nothing but an immensity of great foaming waves rushing at us, under a sky low enough to touch with the hand and dirty like a smoked ceiling. In the stormy space surrounding us there was as much flying spray as air. Day after day and night after night there was nothing round the ship but the howl of the wind, the tumult of the sea, the noise of water pouring over the deck. There was no rest for her and no rest for us. She tossed, she pitched, she stood on her head, she sat on her tail, she rolled, she groaned, and we had to hold on while on deck and cling to our bunks when below, in a constant effort of body and worry of mind.

"One hight Mahon spoke through the small window of my berth. It opened right into my very bed, and I was lying there sleepless, in my boots, feeling as though I had not slept for years, and could not if I tried. He said excitedly—

" 'You got the sounding-rod in here, Marlow? I can't get the pumps to suck. By God! it's no child's play.'

"I gave him the sounding-rod and lay down again, trying to think of various things—but I thought only of the pumps. When I came on deck they were still at it, and my watch relieved at the pumps. By the light of the lantern brought on deck to examine the sounding-rod I caught a glimpse of their weary, serious faces. We pumped all the four hours. We pumped all night, all day, all the week,—watch and watch. She was working herself loose, and leaked badly—not enough to drown us at once, but enough to kill us with the work at the pumps. And while we pumped the ship was going from us piecemeal: the bulwarks went, the stanchions were torn out, the ventilators smashed, the cabin-door burst in. There was not a dry spot in the ship. She was being gutted bit by bit. The long-boat changed, as if by magic, into matchwood where she stood in her gripes. I had lashed her myself, and was rather proud of my handiwork, which had withstood so long the malice of the sea. And we pumped. And there was no break in the weather. The sea was white like a sheet of foam, like a caldron of boiling milk; there was not a break in the clouds, no—not the size of a man's hand—no, not for so much as ten seconds. There was for us no sky, there were for us no stars, no sun, no universe—nothing but angry clouds and an infuriated sea. We pumped watch and watch, for dear life; and it seemed to last for months, for years, for all eternity, as though we had been dead and gone to a hell for sailors. We forgot the day of the week, the name of the month, what year it was, and whether we had ever been ashore. The sails blew away, she lay broadside on under a weather-cloth, the ocean poured over her, and we did not care. We turned those handles, and had the eyes of idiots. As soon as we had crawled on deck I used to take a round turn with a rope about the men, the pumps, and the mainmast, and we turned, we turned incessantly, with the water to our waists, to our necks, over our heads. It was all one. We had forgotten how it felt to be dry.

"And there was somewhere in me the thought: By Jove! this is the deuce of an adventure—something you read about; and it is my first voyage as second mate —and I am only twenty—and here I am lasting it out as well as any of these men, and keeping my chaps up to the mark. I was pleased. I would not have given up the experience for worlds. I had moments of exultation. Whenever the old dismantled craft pitched heavily with her counter high in the air, she seemed to me to throw up, like an appeal, like a defiance, like a cry to the clouds without mercy, the words written on her stern: '*Judea*, London. Do or Die.'

"O youth! The strength of it, the faith of it, the imagination of it! To me she was not an old rattle-trap carting about the world a lot of coal for a freight— to me she was the endeavor, the test, the trial of life. I think of her with pleasure, with affection, with regret—as you would think of someone dead you have loved. I shall never forget her. . . . Pass the bottle.

"One night when tied to the mast, as I explained, we were pumping on, deafened with the wind, and without spirit enough in us to wish ourselves dead, a heavy sea crashed aboard and swept clean over us. As soon as I got my breath I shouted, as in duty bound, 'Keep on, boys!' when suddenly I felt something hard floating on deck strike the calf of my leg. I made a grab at it and missed. It was so dark we could not see each other's faces within a foot—you understand.

"After that thump the ship kept quiet for a while, and the thing, whatever it was, struck my leg again. This time I caught it—and it was a sauce-pan. At first, being stupid with fatigue and thinking of nothing but the pumps, I did not understand what I had in my hand. Suddenly it dawned upon me, and I shouted, 'Boys, the house on deck is gone. Leave this, and let's look for the cook.'

"There was a deck-house forward, which contained the galley, the cook's berth, and the quarters of the crew. As we had expected for days to see it swept away, the hands had been ordered to sleep in the cabin—the only safe place in the ship. The steward, Abraham, however, persisted in clinging to his berth, stupidly, like a mule—from sheer fright I believe, like an animal that won't leave a stable falling in an earthquake. So we went to look for him. It was chancing death, since once out of our lashings we were as exposed as if on a raft. But we went. The house was shattered as if a shell had exploded inside. Most of it had gone overboard—stove, men's quarters, and their property, all was gone; but two posts, holding a portion of the bulkhead to which Abraham's bunk was attached, remained as if by a miracle. We groped in the ruins and came upon this, and there he was, sitting in his bunk, surrounded by foam and wreckage, jabbering cheerfully to himself. He was out of his mind; completely and for ever mad, with this sudden shock coming upon the fag-end of his endurance. We snatched him up, lugged him aft, and pitched him head-first down the cabin companion. You understand there was no time to carry him down with infinite precautions and wait to see how he got on. Those below would pick him up at the bottom of the stairs all right. We were in a hurry to go back to the pumps. That business could not wait. A bad leak is an inhuman thing.

"One would think that the sole purpose of that fiendish gale had been to make a lunatic of that poor devil of a mulatto. It eased before morning, and next day the sky cleared, and as the sea went down the leak took up. When it came to bending a fresh set of sails the crew demanded to put back—and really there was nothing else to do. Boats gone, decks swept clean, cabin gutted, men without a stitch but what they stood in, stores spoiled, ship strained. We put her head for home, and—would you believe it? The wind came east right in our teeth. It blew fresh, it blew continuously. We had to beat up every inch of the way, but she did not leak so badly, the water keeping comparatively smooth. Two hours' pumping in every four is no joke—but it kept her afloat as far as Falmouth.

"The good people there live on casualties of the sea, and no doubt were glad to see us. A hungry crowd of shipwrights sharpened their chisels at the sight of that carcass of a ship. And, by Jove! they had pretty pickings off us before they were done. I fancy the owner was already in a tight place. There were delays. Then it was decided to take part of the cargo out and calk her topsides. This was done, the repairs finished, cargo re-shipped; a new crew came on board, and we went out—for Bankok. At the end of a week we were back again. The crew said they weren't going to Bankok—a hundred and fifty days' passage—in a something hooker that wanted pumping eight hours out of the twenty-four; and the nautical papers inserted again the little paragraph: '*Judea*. Bark. Tyne to Bankok; coals; put back to Falmouth leaky and with crew refusing duty.'

"There were more delays—more tinkering. The owner came down for a day, and said she was as right as a little fiddle. Poor old Captain Beard looked like the ghost of a Geordie skipper—through the worry and humiliation of it. Remember he was sixty, and it was his first command. Mahon said it was a foolish business, and would end badly. I loved the ship more than ever, and wanted awfully to get to Bankok. To Bankok! Magic name, blessed name. Mesopotamia wasn't a patch on it. Remember I was twenty, and it was my first second mate's billet, and the East was waiting for me.

"We went out and anchored in the outer roads with a fresh crew—the third. She leaked worse than ever. It was as if those confounded shipwrights had actually made a hole in her. This time we did not even go outside. The crew simply refused to man the windlass.

"They towed us back to the inner harbor, and we became a fixture, a feature, an institution of the place. People pointed us out to visitors as 'That 'ere bark that's going to Bankok—has been here six months—put back three times.' On holidays the small boys pulling about in boats would hail, '*Judea*, ahoy!' and if a head showed above the rail shouted, 'Where you bound to?—Bankok?' and jeered. We were only three on board. The poor old skipper mooned in the cabin. Mahon undertook the cooking, and unexpectedly developed all a Frenchman's genius for preparing nice little messes. I looked languidly after the rigging. We became citizens of Falmouth. Every shopkeeper knew us. At the barber's or tobacconist's they asked familiarly, 'Do you think you will ever get to Bankok?' Meantime the owner, the underwriters, and the charterers squabbled amongst themselves in London, and our pay went on. . . . Pass the bottle.

"It was horrid. Morally it was worse than pumping for life. It seemed as though we had been forgotten by the world, belonged to nobody, would get nowhere; it seemed that, as if bewitched, we would have to live for ever and ever in that inner harbor, a derision and a by-word to generations of long-shore loafers and dishonest boatmen. I obtained three months' pay and a five days' leave, and made a rush for London. It took me a day to get there and pretty well another to come back—but three months' pay went all the same. I don't know what I did with it. I went to a music-hall, I believe, lunched, dined, and supped in a swell place in Regent Street, and was back to time, with nothing but a complete set of Byron's works and a new railway rug to show for three months' work. The boatman who pulled me off to the ship said: 'Hallo! I thought you had left the old thing. *She* will never get to Bankok.' 'That's all *you* know about it,' I said scornfully—but I didn't like that prophecy at all.

"Suddenly a man, some kind of agent to somebody, appeared with full powers.

He had grog blossoms all over his face, an indomitable energy, and was a jolly soul. We leaped into life again. A hulk came alongside, took our cargo, and then we went into dry dock to get our copper stripped. No wonder she leaked. The poor thing, strained beyond endurance by the gale, had, as if in disgust spat, out all the oakum of her lower seams. She was recalked, new coppered, and made as tight as a bottle. We went back to the hulk and re-shipped our cargo.

"Then on a fine moonlight night, all the rats left the ship.

"We had been infested with them. They had destroyed our sails, consumed more stores than the crew, affably shared our beds and our dangers, and now, when the ship was made seaworthy, concluded to clear out. I called Mahon to enjoy the spectacle. Rat after rat appeared on our rail, took a last look over his shoulder, and leaped with a hollow thud into the empty hulk. We tried to count them, but soon lost the tale. Mahon said: 'Well, well! don't talk to me about the intelligence of rats. They ought to have left before, when we had that narrow squeak from foundering. There you have the proof how silly is the superstition about them. They leave a good ship for an old rotten hulk, where there is nothing to eat, too, the fools! . . . I don't believe they know what is safe or what is good for them, any more than you or I.'

"And after some more talk we agreed that the wisdom of rats had been grossly overrated, being in fact no greater than that of men.

"The story of the ship was known, by this, all up the Channel from Land's End to the Forelands, and we could get no crew on the south coast. They sent us one all complete from Liverpool, and we left once more—for Bankok.

"We had fair breezes, smooth water right into the tropics, and the old *Judea* lumbered along in the sunshine. When she went eight knots everything cracked aloft, and we tied our caps to our heads; but mostly she strolled on at the rate of three miles an hour. What could you expect? She was tired—that old ship. Her youth was where mine is—where yours is—you fellows who listen to this yarn; and what friend would throw your years and your weariness in your face? We didn't grumble at her. To us aft, at least, it seemed as though we had been born in her, reared in her, had lived in her for ages, had never known any other ship. I would just as soon have abused the old village church at home for not being a cathedral.

"And for me there was also my youth to make me patient. There was all the East before me, and all life, and the thought that I had been tried in that ship and had come out pretty well. And I thought of men of old who, centuries ago, went that road in ships that sailed no better, to the land of palms, and spices, and yellow sands, and of brown nations ruled by kings more cruel than Nero the Roman and more splendid than Solomon the Jew. The old bark lumbered on, heavy with her age and the burden of her cargo, while I lived the life of youth in ignorance and hope. She lumbered on through an interminable procession of days; and the fresh gilding flashed back at the setting sun, seemed to cry out over the darkening sea the words painted on her stern, '*Judea,* London. Do or Die.'

"Then we entered the Indian Ocean and steered northerly for Java Head. The winds were light. Weeks slipped by. She crawled on, do or die, and people at home began to think of posting us as overdue.

"One Saturday evening, I being off duty, the men asked me to give them an extra bucket of water or so—for washing clothes. As I did not wish to screw on the fresh-water pump so late, I went forward whistling, and with a key in my hand to unlock the forepeak scuttle, intending to serve the water out of a spare tank we kept there.

"The small down below was as unexpected as it was frightful. One would have thought hundreds of paraffin-lamps had been flaring and smoking in that hole for days. I was glad to get out. The man with me coughed and said, 'Funny smell, sir.' I answered negligently, 'It's good for the health, they say,' and walked aft.

"The first thing I did was to put my head down the square of the midship ventilator. As I lifted the lid a visible breath, something like a thin fog, a puff of faint haze, rose from the opening. The ascending air was hot, and had a heavy, sooty, paraffiny smell. I gave one sniff, and put down the lid gently. It was no use choking myself. The cargo was on fire.

"Next day she began to smoke in earnest. You see it was to be expected, for though the coal was of a safe kind, that cargo had been so handled, so broken up with handling, that it looked more like smithy coal than anything else. Then it had been wetted—more than once. It rained all the time we were taking it back from the hulk, and now with this long passage it got heated, and there was another case of spontaneous combustion.

"The captain called us into the cabin. He had a chart spread on the table, and looked unhappy. He said, 'The coast of West Australia is near, but I mean to proceed to our destination. It is the hurricane month too; but we will just keep her head for Bankok, and fight the fire. No more putting back anywhere, if we all get roasted. We will try first to stifle this 'ere damned combustion by want of air.'

"We tried. We battened down everything, and still she smoked. The smoke kept coming out through imperceptible crevices; it forced itself through bulkheads and covers; it oozed here and there and everywhere in slender threads, in an invisible film, in an incomprehensible manner. It made its way into the cabin, into the forecastle; it poisoned the sheltered places on the deck, it could be sniffed as high as the mainyard. It was clear that if the smoke came out the air came in. This was disheartening. This combustion refused to be stifled.

"We resolved to try water, and took the hatches off. Enormous volumes of smoke, whitish, yellowish, thick, greasy, misty, choking, ascended as high as the trucks. All hands cleared out aft. Then the poisonous cloud blew away, and we went back to work in a smoke that was no thicker now than that of an ordinary factory chimney.

"We rigged the force pump, got the hose along, and by-and-by it burst. Well, it was as old as the ship—a prehistoric hose, and past repair. Then we pumped with the feeble head-pump, drew water with buckets, and in this way managed in time to pour lots of Indian Ocean into the main hatch. The bright stream flashed in sunshine, fell into a layer of white crawling smoke, and vanished on the black surface of coal. Steam ascended mingling with the smoke. We poured salt water as into a barrel without a bottom. It was our fate to pump in that ship, to pump out of her, to pump into her; and after keeping water out of her to save ourselves from being drowned, we frantically poured water into her to save ourselves from being burnt.

"And she crawled on, do or die, in the serene weather. The sky was a miracle of purity, a miracle of azure. The sea was polished, was blue, was pellucid, was sparkling like a precious stone, extending on all sides, all round to the horizon— as if the whole terrestrial globe had been one jewel, one colossal sapphire, a single gem fashioned into a planet. And on the luster of the great calm waters the *Judea* glided imperceptibly, enveloped in languid and unclean vapors, in a lazy cloud that drifted to leeward, light and slow: a pestiferous cloud defiling the splendor of sea and sky.

"All this time of course we saw no fire. The cargo smoldered at the bottom somewhere. Once Mahon, as we were working side by side, said to me with a queer smile: 'Now, if she only would spring a tidy leak—like that time when we first left the Channel—it would put a stopper on this fire. Wouldn't it?' I remarked irrelevantly, 'Do you remember the rats?'

"We fought the fire and sailed the ship too as carefully as though nothing had been the matter. The steward cooked and attended on us. Of the other twelve men, eight worked while four rested. Everyone took his turn, captain included. There was equality, and if not exactly fraternity, then a deal of good feeling. Sometimes a man, as he dashed a bucketful of water down the hatchway, would yell out, 'Hurrah for Bankok!' and the rest laughed. But generally we were taciturn and serious—and thirsty. Oh! how thirsty! And we had to be careful with the water. Strict allowance. The ship smoked, the sun blazed....
Pass the bottle.

"We tried everything. We even made an attempt to dig down to the fire. No good, of course. No man could remain more than a minute below. Mahon, who went first, fainted there, and the man who went to fetch him out did likewise. We lugged them out on deck. Then I leaped down to show how easily it could be done. They had learned wisdom by that time, and contented themselves by fishing for me with a chain-hook tied to a broom-handle, I believe. I did not offer to go and fetch up my shovel, which was left down below.

"Things began to look bad. We put the long-boat into the water. The second boat was ready to swing out. We had also another, a fourteen-foot thing, on davits aft, where it was quite safe.

"Then behold, the smoke suddenly decreased. We re-doubled our efforts to flood the bottom of the ship. In two days there was no smoke at all. Everybody was on the broad grin. This was on a Friday. On Saturday no work, but sailing the ship of course was done. The men washed their clothes and their faces for the first time in a fortnight, and had a special dinner given them. They spoke of spontaneous combustion with contempt, and implied *they* were the boys to put out combustions. Somehow we all felt as though we each had inherited a large fortune. But a beastly smell of burning hung about the ship. Captain Beard had hollow eyes and sunken cheeks. I had never noticed so much before how twisted and bowed he was. He and Mahon prowled soberly about hatches and ventilators, sniffing. It struck me suddenly poor Mahon was a very, very old chap. As to me, I was as pleased and proud as though I had helped to win a great naval battle. O! Youth!

"The night was fine. In the morning a homeward-bound ship passed us hull down,—the first we had seen for months; but we were nearing the land at last, Java Head being about 190 miles off, and nearly due north.

"Next day it was my watch on deck from eight to twelve. At breakfast the captain observed, 'It's wonderful how that smell hangs about the cabin.' About ten, the mate being on the poop, I stepped down on the main-deck for a moment. The carpenter's bench stood abaft the mainmast: I leaned against it sucking at my pipe, and the carpenter, a young chap, came to talk to me. He remarked, 'I think we have done very well, haven't we?' and then I perceived with annoyance the fool was trying to tilt the bench. I said curtly, 'Don't, Chips,' and immediately became aware of a queer sensation, of an absurd delusion,—I seemed somehow to be in the air. I heard all round me like a pent-up breath released— as if a thousand giants simultaneously had said Phoo!—and felt a dull concussion which made my ribs ache suddenly. No doubt about it—I was in the air, and my body was describing a short parabola. But short as it was, I had the time to think several thoughts in, as far as I can remember, the following order: 'This can't be the carpenter—What is it?—Some accident—Submarine volcano?— Coals, gas!—By Jove! we are being blown up—Everybody's dead—I am falling into the after-hatch—I see fire in it.'

"The coal-dust suspended in the air of the hold had glowed dull-red at the moment of the explosion. In the twinkling of an eye, in an infinitesimal fraction of a second since the first tilt of the bench, I was sprawling full length on the cargo. I picked myself up and scrambled out. It was quick like a rebound. The deck was a wilderness of smashed timber, lying crosswise like trees in a wood after a hurricane; an immense curtain of soiled rags waved gently before me— it was the mainsail blown to strips. I thought, The masts will be toppling over directly; and to get out of the way bolted on all-fours towards the poop-ladder. The first person I saw was Mahon, with eyes like saucers, his mouth open, and the long white hair standing straight on end round his head like a silver halo. He was just about to go down when the sight of the main-deck stirring, heaving up, and changing into splinters before his eyes, petrified him on the top step. I stared at him in unbelief, and he stared at me with a queer kind of shocked curiosity. I did not know that I had no hair, no eyebrows, no eyelashes, that my young mustache was burnt off, that my face was black, one cheek laid open, my nose cut, and my chin bleeding. I had lost my cap, one of my slippers, and my shirt was torn to rags. Of all this I was not aware. I was amazed to see the ship still afloat, the poop-deck whole—and, most of all, to see anybody alive. Also the peace of the sky and the serenity of the sea were distinctly surprising. I suppose I expected to see them convulsed with horror. . . . Pass the bottle.

"There was a voice hailing the ship from somewhere—in the air, in the sky— I couldn't tell. Presently I saw the captain—and he was mad. He asked me eagerly, 'Where's the cabin-table?' and to hear such a question was a frightful shock. I had just been blown up, you understand, and vibrated with that experience,—I wasn't quite sure whether I was alive. Mahon began to stamp with both feet and yelled at him, 'Good God! don't you see the deck's blown out of her?' I found my voice, and stammered out as if conscious of some gross neglect of duty, 'I don't know where the cabin-table is.' It was like an absurd dream.

"Do you know what he wanted next? Well, he wanted to trim the yards. Very placidly, and as if lost in thought, he insisted on having the foreyard squared. 'I don't know if there's anybody alive,' said Mahon, almost tearfully. 'Surely,' he said, gently, 'there will be enough left to square the foreyard.'

"The old chap, it seems, was in his own berth, winding up the chronometers, when the shock sent him spinning. Immediately it occurred to him—as he said afterwards—that the ship had struck something, and he ran out into the cabin. There, he saw, the cabin-table had vanished somewhere. The deck being blown up, it had fallen down into the lazarette of course. Where we had our breakfast that morning he saw only a great hole in the floor. This appeared to him so awfully mysterious, and impressed him so immensely, that what he saw and heard after he got on deck were mere trifles in comparison. And, mark, he noticed directly the wheel deserted and his bark off her course—and his only thought was to get that miserable, stripped, undecked, smoldering shell of a ship back again with her head pointing at her port of destination. Bankok! That's what he was after. I tell you this quiet, bowed, bandy-legged, almost deformed little man was immense in the singleness of his idea and in his placid ignorance of our agitation. He motioned us forward with a commanding gesture, and went to take the wheel himself.

"Yes; that was the first thing we did—trim the yards of that wreck! No one was killed, or even disabled, but everyone was more or less hurt. You should have seen them! Some were in rags, with black faces, like coal-heavers, like sweeps, and had bullet heads that seemed closely cropped, but were in fact singed to the skin. Others, of the watch below, awakened by being shot out from their collapsing bunks, shivered incessantly, and kept on groaning even as we went about our work. But they all worked. That crew of Liverpool hard cases had in them the right stuff. It's my experience they always have. It is the sea that gives it—the vastness, the loneliness surrounding their dark stolid souls. Ah! Well! we stumbled, we crept, we fell, we barked our shins on the wreckage, we hauled. The masts stood, but we did not know how much they might be charred down below. It was nearly calm, but a long swell ran from the west and made her roll. They might go at any moment. We looked at them with apprehension. One could not foresee which way they would fall.

"Then we retreated aft and looked about us. The deck was a tangle of planks on edge, of planks on end, of splinters, of ruined woodwork. The masts rose from that chaos like big trees above a matted undergrowth. The interstices of that mass of wreckage were full of something whitish, sluggish, stirring—of something that was like a greasy fog. The smoke of the invisible fire was coming up again, was trailing, like a poisonous thick mist in some valley choked with dead wood. Already lazy wisps were beginning to curl upwards amongst the mass of splinters. Here and there a piece of timber, stuck upright, resembled a post. Half of a fife-rail had been shot through the foresail, and the sky made a patch of glorious blue in the ignobly soiled canvas. A portion of several boards holding together had fallen across the rail, and one end protruded overboard, like a gangway leading upon nothing, like a gangway leading over the deep sea, leading to death—as if inviting us to walk the plank at once and be done with our ridiculous troubles. And still the air, the sky—a ghost, something invisible was hailing the ship.

"Someone had the sense to look over, and there was the helmsman, who had impulsively jumped overboard, anxious to come back. He yelled and swam lustily like a merman, keeping up with the ship. We threw him a rope, and presently he stood amongst us streaming with water and very crest-fallen. The captain had surrendered the wheel, and apart, elbow on rail and chin in hand, gazed at the sea wistfully. We asked ourselves, What next? I thought, Now, this is something like. This is great. I wonder what will happen. O youth!

"Suddenly Mahon sighted a steamer far astern. Captain Beard said, 'We may do something with her yet.' We hoisted two flags, which said in the international language of the sea, 'On fire. Want immediate assistance.' The steamer grew bigger rapidly, and by-and-by spoke with two flags on her foremast, 'I am coming to your assistance.'

"In half an hour she was abreast, to windward, within hail, and rolling slightly, with her engines stopped. We lost our composure, and yelled all together with excitement, 'We've been blown up.' A man in a white helmet, on the bridge, cried, 'Yes! All right! all right!' and he nodded his head, and smiled, and made soothing motions with his hand as though at a lot of frightened children. One of the boats dropped in the water, and walked towards us upon the sea with her long oars. Four Calashes pulled a swinging stroke. This was my first sight of Malay seamen. I've known them since, but what struck me then was their unconcern: they came alongside, and even the bowman standing up and holding to our main-chains with the boat-hook did not deign to lift his head for a glance. I thought people who had been blown up deserved more attention.

"A little man, dry like a chip and agile like a monkey, clambered up. It was the mate of the steamer. He gave one look, and cried, 'O boys—you had better quit.'

"We were silent. He talked apart with the captain for a time,—seemed to argue with him. Then they went away together to the steamer.

"When our skipper came back we learned that the steamer was the *Sommerville*, Captain Nash, from West Australia to Singapore *via* Batavia with mails, and that the agreement was she should tow us to Anjer or Batavia, if possible, where we could extinguish the fire by scuttling, and then proceed on our voyage— to Bankok! The old man seemed excited. 'We will do it yet,' he said to Mahon, fiercely. He shook his fist at the sky. Nobody else said a word.

"At noon the steamer began to tow. She went ahead slim and high, and what was left of the *Judea* followed at the end of seventy fathom of tow-rope,—followed her swiftly like a cloud of smoke with mastheads protruding above. We went aloft to furl the sails. We coughed on the yards, and were careful about the bunts. Do you see the lot of us there, putting a neat furl on the sails of that ship doomed to arrive nowhere? There was not a man who didn't think that at any moment the masts would topple over. From aloft we could not see the ship for smoke, and they worked carefully, passing the gaskets with even turns. 'Harbor furl—aloft there!' cried Mahon from below.

"You understand this? I don't think one of those chaps expected to get down in the usual way. When we did I heard them saying to each other, 'Well, I thought we would come down overboard, in a lump—sticks and all—blame me if I didn't.' 'That's what I was thinking to myself,' would answer wearily another battered and bandaged scarecrow. And, mind, these were men without the drilled-in habit of obedience. To an onlooker they would be a lot of profane scallywags without a redeeming point. What made them do it—what made them obey me when I, thinking consciously how fine it was, made them drop the bunt of the foresail twice to try and do it better? What? They had no professional reputation —no examples, no praise. It wasn't a sense of duty; they all knew well enough how to shirk, and laze, and dodge—when they had a mind to it—and mostly they had. Was it the two pounds ten a month that sent them there? They didn't think their pay half good enough. No; it was something in them, something inborn and subtle and everlasting. I don't say positively that the crew of a French or German merchantman wouldn't have done it, but I doubt whether it would have been done in the same way. There was a completeness in it, something solid like a principle, and masterful like an instinct—a disclosure of something secret—of that hidden something, that gift, of good or evil that makes racial difference, that shapes the fate of nations.

"It was that night at ten that, for the first time since we had been fighting it, we saw the fire. The speed of the towing had fanned the smoldering destruction. A blue gleam appeared forward, shining below the wreck of the deck. It wavered in patches, it seemed to stir and creep like the light of a glowworm. I saw it first, and told Mahon. 'Then the game's up,' he said. 'We had better stop this towing, or she will burst out suddenly fore and aft before we can clear out.' We set up a yell; rang bells to attract their attention; they towed on. At last Mahon and I had to crawl forward and cut the rope with an ax. There was no time to cast off the lashings. Red tongues could be seen licking the wilderness of splinters under our feet as we made our way back to the poop.

"Of course they very soon found out in the steamer that the rope was gone. She gave a loud blast of her whistle, her lights were seen sweeping in a wide circle, she came up ranging close alongside, and stopped. We were all in a tight group on the poop looking at her. Every man had saved a little bundle or a bag. Suddenly a conical flame with a twisted top shot up forward and threw upon the black sea a circle of light, with the two vessels side by side and heaving gently in its center. Captain Beard had been sitting on the gratings still and mute for hours, but now he rose slowly and advanced in front of us, to the mizzen-shrouds. Captain Nash hailed: 'Come along! Look sharp. I have mail-bags on board. I will take you and your boats to Singapore.'

" 'Thank you! No!' said our skipper. 'We must see the last of the ship.'

" 'I can't stand by any longer,' shouted the other. 'Mails—you know.'

" 'Ay! ay! We are all right.'

" 'Very well! I'll report you in Singapore. . . . Good-by!'

"He waved his hand. Our men dropped their bundles quietly. The steamer moved ahead, and passing out of the circle of light, vanished at once from our sight, dazzled by the fire which burned fiercely. And then I knew that I would see the East first as commander of a small boat. I thought it fine; and the fidelity to the old ship was fine. We should see the last of her. Oh the glamour of youth! Oh the fire of it, more dazzling than the flames of the burning ship, throwing a magic light on the wide earth, leaping audaciously to the sky, presently to be quenched by time, more cruel, more pitiless, more bitter than the sea—and like the flames of the burning ship surrounded by an impenetrable night.

. . . . .

"The old man warned us in his gentle and inflexible way that it was part of our duty to save for the underwriters as much as we could of the ship's gear. According we went to work aft, while she blazed forward to give us plenty of light. We lugged out a lot of rubbish. What didn't we save? An old barometer fixed with an absurd quantity of screws nearly cost me my life: a sudden rush of smoke came upon me, and I just got away in time. There were various stores, bolts of canvas, coils of rope; the poop looked like a marine bazaar, and the boats were lumbered to the gunwales. One would have thought the old man wanted to take as much as he could of his first command with him. He was very, very quiet, but off his balance evidently. Would you believe it? He wanted to take a length of old stream-cable and a kedge-anchor with him in the long-boat. We said, 'Ay, ay, sir,' deferentially, and on the quiet let the thing slip overboard. The heavy medicine-chest went that way, two bags of green coffee, tins of paint—fancy, paint!—a whole lot of things. Then I was ordered with two hands into the boats to make a stowage and get them ready against the time it would be proper for us to leave the ship.

"We put everything straight, stepped the long-boat's mast for our skipper, who was in charge of her, and I was not sorry to sit down for a moment. My face felt raw, every limb ached as if broken, I was aware of all my ribs, and would have sworn to a twist in the backbone. The boats, fast astern, lay in a deep shadow, and all around I could see the circle of the sea lighted by the fire. A gigantic flame arose forward straight and clear. It flared fierce, with noises like the whir of wings, with rumbles as of thunder. There were cracks, detonations, and from the cone of flame the sparks flew upwards, as man is born to trouble, to leaky ships, and to ships that burn.

"What bothered me was that the ship, lying broadside to the swell and to such wind as there was—a mere breath—the boats would not keep astern where they were safe, but persisted, in a pig-headed way boats have, in getting under the counter and then swinging alongside. They were knocking about dangerously and coming near the flame, while the ship rolled on them, and, of course, there was always the danger of the masts going over the side at any moment. I and my two boat-keepers kept them off as best we could with oars and boat-hooks; but to be constantly at it became exasperating, since there was no reason why we should not leave at once. We could not see those on board, nor could we imagine what caused the delay. The boat-keepers were swearing feebly, and I had not only my share of the work, but also had to keep at it two men who showed a constant inclination to lay themselves down and let things slide.

"At last I hailed 'On deck there,' and someone looked over. 'We're ready here,' I said. The head disappeared, and very soon popped up again. 'The captain says, All right, sir, and to keep the boats well clear of the ship.'

"Half an hour passed. Suddenly there was a frightful racket, rattle, clanking of chain, hiss of water, and millions of sparks flew up into the shivering column of smoke that stood leaning slightly above the ship. The catheads had burned away, and the two red-hot anchors had gone to the bottom, tearing out after them two hundred fathom of red-hot chain. The ship trembled, the mass of flame swayed as if ready to collapse, and the fore top-gallant-mast fell. It darted down like an arrow of fire, shot under, and instantly leaping up within an oar's-length of the boats, floated quietly, very black on the luminous sea. I hailed the deck again. After some time a man in an unexpectedly cheerful but also muffled tone, as though he had been trying to speak with his mouth shut, informed me, 'Coming directly, sir,' and vanished. For a long time I heard nothing but the whir and roar of the fire. There were also whistling sounds. The boats jumped, tugged at the painters, ran at each other playfully, knocked their sides together, or, do what we would, swung in a bunch against the ship's side. I couldn't stand it any longer, and swarming up a rope, clambered aboard over the stern.

"It was as bright as day. Coming up like this, the sheet of fire facing me, was a terrifying sight, and the heat seemed hardly bearable at first. On a settee cushion dragged out of the cabin, Captain Beard, with his legs drawn up and one arm under his head, slept with the light playing on him. Do you know what the rest were busy about? They were sitting on deck right aft, round an open case, eating bread and cheese and drinking bottled stout.

"On the background of flames twisting in fierce tongues above their heads they seemed at home like salamanders, and looked like a band of desperate pirates. The fire sparkled in the whites of their eyes, gleamed on patches of white skin seen through the torn shirts. Each had the marks as of a battle about him—bandaged heads, tied-up arms, a strip of dirty rag round a knee—and each man had a bottle between his legs and a chunk of cheese in his hand. Mahon got up. With his handsome and disreputable head, his hooked profile, his long white beard, and with an uncorked bottle in his hand, he resembled one of those reckless sea-robbers of old making merry amidst violence and disaster. 'The last meal on board,' he explained solemnly. 'We had nothing to eat all day, and it was no use leaving all this.' He flourished the bottle and indicated the sleeping skipper. 'He said he couldn't swallow anything, so I got him to lie down,' he went on; and as I stared, 'I don't know whether you are aware, young fellow, the man had no sleep to speak of for days—and there will be dam' little sleep in the boats.' 'There will be no boats by-and-by if you fool about much longer,' I said, indignantly. I walked up to the skipper and shook him by the shoulder. At last he opened his eyes, but did not move. 'Time to leave her, sir,' I said, quietly.

"He got up painfully, looked at the flames, at the sea sparkling round the ship, and black, black as ink farther away; he looked at the stars shining dim through a thin veil of smoke in a sky black, black as Erebus.

" 'Youngest first,' he said.

"And the ordinary seaman, wiping his mouth with the back of his hand, got up, clambered over the taffrail, and vanished. Others followed. One, on the point of going over, stopped short to drain his bottle, and with a great swing of his arm flung it at the fire. 'Take this!' he cried.

"The skipper lingered disconsolately, and we left him to commune alone for awhile with his first command. Then I went up again and brought him away at last. It was time. The ironwork on the poop was hot to the touch.

"Then the painter of the long-boat was cut, and the three boats, tied together, drifted clear of the ship. It was just sixteen hours after the explosion when we abandoned her. Mahon had charge of the second boat, and I had the smallest— the 14-foot thing. The long-boat would have taken the lot of us; but the skipper said we must save as much property as we could—for the underwriters—and so I got my first command. I had two men with me, a bag of biscuits, a few tins of meat, and a breaker of water. I was ordered to keep close to the long-boat, that in case of bad weather we might be taken into her.

"And do you know what I thought? I thought I would part company as soon as I could. I wanted to have my first command all to myself. I wasn't going to sail in a squadron if there were a chance for independent cruising. I would make land by myself. I would beat the other boats. Youth! All youth! The silly, charming, beautiful youth.

"But we did not make a start at once. We must see the last of the ship. And so the boats drifted about that night, heaving and setting on the swell. The men dozed, waked, sighed, groaned. I looked at the burning ship.

"Between the darkness of earth and heaven she was burning fiercely upon a disc of purple sea shot by the blood-red play of gleams; upon a disc of water glittering and sinister. A high, clear flame, an immense and lonely flame, ascended from the ocean, and from its summit the black smoke poured continuously at the sky. She burned furiously, mournful and imposing like a funeral pile kindled in the night, surrounded by the sea, watched over by the stars. A magnificent death had come like a grace, like a gift, like a reward to that old ship at the end of her laborious days. The surrender of her weary ghost to the keeping of stars and sea was stirring like the sight of a glorious triumph. The masts fell just before daybreak, and for a moment there was a burst and turmoil of sparks that seemed to fill with flying fire the night patient and watchful, the vast night lying silent upon the sea. At daylight she was only a charred shell, floating still under a cloud of smoke and bearing a glowing mass of coal within.

"Then the oars were got out, and the boats forming in a line moved round her remains as if in procession—the long-boat leading. As we pulled across her stern a slim dart of fire shot out viciously at us, and suddenly she went down, head first, in a great hiss of steam. The unconsumed stern was the last to sink; but the paint had gone, had cracked, had peeled off, and there were no letters, there was no word, no stubborn device that was like her soul, to flash at the rising sun her creed and her name.

"We made our way north. A breeze sprang up, and about noon all the boats came together for the last time. I had no mast or sail in mine, but I made a mast out of a spare oar and hoisted a boat-awning for a sail, with a boat-hook for a yard. She was certainly over-masted, but I had the satisfaction of knowing that with the wind aft I could beat the other two. I had to wait for them. Then we all had a look at the captain's chart, and, after a sociable meal of hard bread and water, got our last instructions. These were simple: steer north, and keep together as much as possible. 'Be careful with that jury rig, Marlow,' said the captain; and Mahon, as I sailed proudly past his boat, wrinkled his curved nose and hailed, 'You will sail that ship of yours under water, if you don't look out, young fellow.' He was a malicious old man—and may the deep sea where he sleeps now rock him gently, rock him tenderly to the end of time!

"Before sunset a thick rain-squall passed over the two boats, which were far astern, and that was the last I saw of them for a time. Next day I sat steering my cockle-shell—my first command—with nothing but water and sky around me. I did sight in the afternoon the upper sails of a ship far away, but said nothing, and my men did not notice her. You see I was afraid she might be homeward bound, and I had no mind to turn back from the portals of the East. I was steering for Java—another blessed name—like Bankok, you know. I steered many days.

"I need not tell you what it is to be knocking about in an open boat. I remember nights and days of calm when we pulled, we pulled, and the boat seemed to stand still, as if bewitched within the circle of the sea horizon. I remember the heat, the deluge of rain-squalls that kept us baling for dear life (but filled our water-cask), and I remember sixteen hours on end with a mouth dry as a cinder and a steering-oar over the stern to keep my first command head on to a breaking sea. I did not know how good a man I was till then. I remember the drawn faces, the dejected figures of my two men, and I remember my youth and the feeling that will never come back any more—the feeling that I could last for ever, outlast the sea, the earth, and all men; the deceitful feeling that lures us on to joys, to perils, to love, to vain effort—to death; the triumphant conviction of strength, the heat of life in the handful of dust, the glow in the heart that with every year grows dim, grows cold, grows small, and expires—and expires, too soon—before life itself.

"And this is how I see the East. I have seen its secret places and have looked into its very soul; but now I see it always from a small boat, a high outline of mountains, blue and afar in the morning; like faint mist at noon; a jagged wall of purple at sunset. I have the feel of the oar in my hand, the vision of a scorching blue sea in my eyes. And I see a bay, a wide bay, smooth as glass and polished like ice, shimmering in the dark. A red light burns far off upon the gloom of the land, and the night is soft and warm. We drag at the oars with aching arms, and suddenly a puff of wind, a puff faint and tepid and laden with strange odors of blossoms, of aromatic wood, comes out of the still night—the first sigh of the East on my face. That I can never forget. It was impalpable and enslaving, like a charm, like a whispered promise of mysterious delight.

"We had been pulling this finishing spell for eleven hours. Two pulled, and he whose turn it was to rest sat at the tiller. We had made out the red light in that bay and steered for it, guessing it must mark some small coasting port. We passed two vessels, outlandish and high-sterned, sleeping at anchor, and, approaching the light, now very dim, ran the boat's nose against the end of a jutting wharf. We were blind with fatigue. My men dropped the oars and fell off the thwarts as if dead. I made fast to a pile. A current rippled softly. The scented obscurity of the shore was grouped into vast masses, a density of colossal clumps of vegetation, probably—mute and fantastic shapes. And at their foot the semicircle of a beach gleamed faintly, like an illusion. There was not a light, not a stir, not a sound. The mysterious East faced me, perfumed like a flower, silent like death, dark like a grave.

"And I sat weary beyond expression, exulting like a conqueror, sleepless and entranced as if before a profound, a fateful enigma.

"A splashing of oars, a measured dip reverberating on the level of water, intensified by the silence of the shore into loud claps, made me jump up. A boat, a European boat, was coming in. I invoked the name of the dead; I hailed: *Judea* ahoy! A thin shout answered.

"It was the captain. I had beaten the flagship by three hours, and I was glad to hear the old man's voice, tremulous and tired. 'Is it you, Marlow?' 'Mind the end of that jetty, sir,' I cried.

"He approached cautiously, and brought up with the deep-sea lead-line which we had saved—for the underwriters. I eased my painter and fell alongside. He sat, a broken figure at the stern, wet with dew, his hands clasped in his lap. His men were asleep already. 'I had a terrible time of it,' he murmured. 'Mahon is behind—not very far.' We conversed in whispers, in low whispers, as if afraid to wake up the land. Guns, thunder, earthquakes would not have awakened the men just then.

"Looking around as we talked, I saw away at sea a bright light traveling in the night. 'There's a steamer passing the bay,' I said. She was not passing, she was entering, and she even came close and anchored. 'I wish,' said the old man, 'you would find out whether she is English. Perhaps they could give us a passage somewhere.' He seemed nervously anxious. So by dint of punching and kicking I started one of my men into a state of somnambulism, and giving him an oar, took another and pulled towards the lights of the steamer.

"There was a murmur of voices in her, metallic hollow clangs of the engine-room, footsteps on the deck. Her ports shone, round like dilated eyes. Shapes moved about, and there was a shadowy man high up on the bridge. He heard my oars.

"And then, before I could open my lips, the East spoke to me, but it was in a Western voice. A torrent of words was poured into the enigmatical, the fateful silence; outlandish, angry words, mixed with words and even whole sentences of good English, less strange but even more surprising. The voice swore and cursed violently; it riddled the solemn peace of the bay by a volley of abuse. It began by calling me Pig, and from that went crescendo into unmentionable adjectives—in English. The man up there raged aloud in two languages, and with a sincerity in his fury that almost convinced me I had, in some way, sinned against the harmony of the universe. I could hardly see him, but began to think he would work himself into a fit.

"Suddenly he ceased, and I could hear him snorting and blowing like a porpoise. I said—

" 'What steamer is this, pray?'

" 'Eh? What's this? And who are you?'

" 'Castaway crew of an English bark burnt at sea. We came here to-night. I am the second mate. The captain is in the long-boat, and wishes to know if you would give us a passage somewhere.'

" 'Oh, my goodness! I say.... This is the *Celestial* from Singapore on her return trip. I'll arrange with your captain in the morning,... and,... I say,... did you hear me just now?'

" 'I should think the whole bay heard you.'

" 'I thought you were a shore-boat. Now, look here—this infernal lazy scoundrel of a caretaker has gone to sleep again—curse him. The light is out, and I nearly ran foul of the end of this damned jetty. This is the third time he plays me this trick. Now, I ask you, can anybody stand this kind of thing? It's enough to drive a man out of his mind. I'll report him.... I'll get the Assistant Resident to give him the sack, by ... See—there's no light. It's out, isn't it? I take you to witness the light's out. There should be a light, you know. A red light on the——'

" 'There was a light,' I said, mildly.

" 'But it's out, man! What's the use of talking like this? You can see for yourself it's out—don't you? If you had to take a valuable steamer along this God-forsaken coast you would want a light too. I'll kick him from end to end of his miserable wharf. You'll see if I don't. I will——'

" 'So I may tell my captain you'll take us?' I broke in.

" 'Yes, I'll take you. Good night,' he said, brusquely.

"I pulled back, made fast again to the jetty, and then went to sleep at last. I had faced the silence of the East. I had heard some of its languages. But when I opened my eyes again the silence was as complete as though it had never been broken. I was lying in a flood of light, and the sky had never looked so far, so high, before. I opened my eyes and lay without moving.

"And then I saw the men of the East—they were looking at me. The whole length of the jetty was full of people. I saw brown, bronze, yellow faces, the black eyes, the glitter, the color of an Eastern crowd. And all these beings stared without a murmur, without a sigh, without a movement. They stared down at the boats, at the sleeping men who at night had come to them from the sea. Nothing moved. The fronds of palms stood still against the sky. Not a branch stirred along the shore, and the brown roofs of hidden houses peeped through the green foliage, through the big leaves that hung shining and still like leaves forged of heavy metal. This was the East of the ancient navigators, so old, so mysterious, resplendent and somber, living and unchanged, full of danger and promise. And these were the men. I sat up suddenly. A wave of movement passed through the crowd from end to end, passed along the heads, swayed the bodies, ran along the jetty like a ripple on the water, like a breath of wind on a field—and all was still again. I see it now—the wide sweep of the bay, the glittering sands, the wealth of green infinite and varied, the sea blue like the sea of a dream, the crowd of attentive faces, the blaze of vivid color—the water reflecting it all, the curve of the shore, the jetty, the high-sterned outlandish craft floating still, and the three boats with tired men from the West sleeping unconscious of the land and the people and of the violence of sunshine. They slept thrown across the thwarts, curled on bottom-boards, in the careless attitudes of death. The head of the old skipper, leaning back in the stern of the long-boat, had fallen on his breast, and he looked as though he would never wake. Farther out old Mahon's face was upturned to the sky, with the long white beard spread out on his breast, as though he been shot where he sat at the tiller; and a man, all in a heap in the bows of the boat, slept with both arms embracing the stem-head and with his cheek laid on the gunwale. The East looked at them without a sound.

"I have known its fascinations since: I have seen the mysterious shores, the still water, the lands of brown nations, where a stealthy Nemesis lies in wait, pursues, overtakes so many of the conquering race, who are proud of their wisdom, of their knowledge, of their strength. But for me all the East is contained in that vision of my youth. It is all in that moment when I opened my young eyes on it. I came upon it from a tussle with the sea—and I was young—and I saw it looking at me. And this is all that is left of it! Only a moment; a moment of strength, of romance, of glamour—of youth! . . . A flick of sunshine upon a strange shore, the time to remember, the time for a sigh, and—good-by!—Night—Good-by . . . !"

He drank.

"Ah! The good old time—the good old time. Youth and the sea. Glamour and the sea! The good, strong sea, the salt, bitter sea, that could whisper to you and roar at you and knock your breath out of you."

He drank again.

"By all that's wonderful, it is the sea, I believe, the sea itself—or is it youth alone? Who can tell? But you here—you all had something out of life: money, love—whatever one gets on shore—and, tell me, wasn't that the best time, that time when we were young at sea; young and had nothing, on the sea that gives nothing, except hard knocks—and sometimes a chance to feel your strength—that only—what you all regret?"

And we all nodded at him: the man of finance, the man of accounts, the man of law, we all nodded at him over the polished table that like a still sheet of brown water reflected our faces, lined, wrinkled; our faces marked by toil, by deceptions, by success, by love; our weary eyes looking still, looking always, looking anxiously for something out of life, that while it is expected is already gone—has passed unseen, in a sigh, in a flash—together with the youth, with the strength, with the romance of illusions.

Tonio Kröger

(1903)

Thomas Mann

H. T. Lowe-Porter, translator

German novelist and man of letters, Thomas Mann (1875–1955) was born in Lübeck to a wealthy family of burghers. At twenty-three he published his first book of short stories, *Little Herr Friedemann* (1898), and three years later his first novel, *Buddenbrooks* (1901). Thereafter he published a continuous stream of novels, stories, literary essays, and political pamphlets until his death, consciously making of himself a twentieth-century Goethe. His best-known novels are *The Magic Mountain* (1924), the *Joseph and His Brothers* tetralogy (1935–44), *Doctor Faustus* (1947), *The Holy Sinner* (1951), and *The Confessions of Felix Krull* (1954). His *novellen* include, besides *Tonio Kröger, Death in Venice* (1912), *Mario and the Magician* (1930), and others collected in *Stories of Three Decades* (1936). Mann won the Nobel Prize for literature in 1929. With the rise of Hitler he moved to Switzerland (1933), and in 1936 he broke openly with nazism and was deprived of his German citizenship; in 1938 he immigrated to the United States and became an American citizen. After the war, however, he returned to Europe, spending his last years in Switzerland.

For more biographical information, see Joseph Gerard Brennan, *Thomas Mann's World* (New York, 1942); for criticism, see *The Stature of Thomas Mann: A Critical Anthology,* ed. Charles Neider (New York, 1947); Henry Hatfield, *Thomas Mann* (Norfolk, Conn., 1951); and Erich Heller, *The Ironic German* (Boston, 1958), especially pp. 68–75.

Tonio Kröger was begun in late 1900, even before *Buddenbrooks* was accepted for publication. This "elegiac *novelle,*" originally called simply "Literature," deals with the same partly autobiographical problem as *Buddenbrooks,* the conflict between art and middle-class society. Tonio is another Hanno Buddenbrooks, torn between the romance of his mother (southern temperament and his name, "Tonio") and the mercantile world of his father. As his painter friend Lisaveta says, "You are a burgher who has lost his way."

Tonio Kröger, copyright, 1936 by Alfred A. Knopf, Inc., is reprinted from *Stories of Three Decades* by Thomas Mann, translated by H. T. Lowe-Porter, by permission of Alfred A. Knopf, Inc.

The winter sun, poor ghost of itself, hung milky and wan behind layers of cloud above the huddled roofs of the town. In the gabled streets it was wet and windy and there came in gusts a sort of soft hail, not ice, not snow.

School was out. The hosts of the released streamed over the paved court and out at the wrought-iron gate, where they broke up and hastened off right and left. Elder pupils held their books in a strap high on the left shoulder and rowed, right arm against the wind, towards dinner. Small people trotted gaily off, splashing the slush with their feet, the tools of learning rattling amain in their walrus-skin satchels. But one and all pulled off their caps and cast down their eyes in awe before the Olympian hat and ambrosial beard of a master moving homewards with measured stride. . . .

"Ah, there you are at last, Hans," said Tonio Kröger. He had been waiting a long time in the street and went up with a smile to the friend he saw coming out of the gate in talk with other boys and about to go off with them. . . . "What?" said Hans, and looked at Tonio. "Right-oh! We'll take a little walk, then."

Tonio said nothing and his eyes were clouded. Did Hans forget, had he only just remembered that they were to take a walk together today? And he himself had looked forward to it with almost incessant joy.

"Well, good-bye, fellows," said Hans Hansen to his comrades. "I'm taking a walk with Kröger." And the two turned to their left, while the others sauntered off in the opposite direction.

Hans and Tonio had time to take a walk after school because in neither of their families was dinner served before four o'clock. Their fathers were prominent business men, who held public office and were of consequence in the town. Hans's people had owned for some generations the big wood-yards down by the river, where powerful machine-saws hissed and spat and cut up timber; while Tonio was the son of Consul Kröger, whose grain-sacks with the firm name in great black letters you might see any day.

Tonio loved his dark, fiery mother, who played the piano and mandolin so wonderfully, and he was glad his doubtful standing among men did not distress her. Though at the same time he found his father's annoyance a more dignified and respectable attitude and despite his scoldings understood him very well, whereas his mother's blithe indifference always seemed just a little wanton. His thoughts at times would run something like this: "It is true enough that I am what I am and will not and cannot alter: heedless, self-willed, with my mind on things nobody else thinks of. And so it is right they should scold and punish me and not smother things all up with kisses and music. After all, we are not gypsies living in a green wagon; we're respectable people, the family of Consul Kröger." And not seldom he would think: "Why is it I am different, why do I fight everything, why am I at odds with the masters and like a stranger among the other boys? The good scholars, and the solid majority—they don't find the masters funny, they don't write verses, their thoughts are all about things that people do think about and can talk about out loud. How regular and comfortable they must feel, knowing that everybody knows just where they stand! It must be nice! But what is the matter with me, and what will be the end of it all?"

These thoughts about himself and his relation to life played an important part in Tonio's love for Hans Hansen. He loved him in the first place because he was handsome; but in the next because he was in every respect his own opposite and foil. Hans Hansen was a capital scholar, and a jolly chap to boot, who was head at drill, rode and swam to perfection, and lived in the sunshine of popularity. The masters were almost tender with him, they called him Hans and were partial to him in every way; the other pupils curried favour with him; even grown people stopped him on the street, twitched the shock of hair beneath his Danish sailor cap, and said: "Ah, here you are, Hans Hansen, with your pretty blond hair! Still head of the school? Remember me to your father and mother, that's a fine lad!"

Such was Hans Hansen; and ever since Tonio Kröger had known him, from the very minute he set eyes on him, he had burned inwardly with a heavy, envious longing. "Who else has blue eyes like yours, or lives in such friendliness and harmony with all the world? You are always spending your time with some right and proper occupation. When you have done your prep you take your riding-lesson, or make things with a fret-saw; even in the holidays, at the seashore, you row and sail and swim all the time, while I wander off somewhere and lie down in the sand and stare at the strange and mysterious changes that whisk over the face of the sea. And all that is why your eyes are so clear. To be like you. . . ."

He made no attempt to be like Hans Hansen, and perhaps hardly even seriously wanted to. What he did ardently, painfully want was that just as he was, Hans Hansen should love him; and he wooed Hans Hansen in his own way, deeply, lingeringly, devotedly, with a melancholy that gnawed and burned more terribly than all the sudden passion one might have expected from his exotic looks.

And he wooed not in vain. Hans respected Tonio's superior power of putting certain difficult matters into words; moreover, he felt the lively presence of an uncommonly strong and tender feeling for himself; he was grateful for it, and his response gave Tonio much happiness—though also many pangs of jealousy and disillusion over his futile efforts to establish a communion of spirit between them. For the queer thing was that Tonio, who after all envied Hans Hansen for being what he was, still kept on trying to draw him over to his own side; though of course he could succeed in this at most only at moments and superficially. . . .

"I have just been reading something so wonderful and splendid . . ." he said. They were walking and eating together out of a bag of fruit toffees they had bought at Iverson's sweet-shop in Mill Street for ten pfennigs. "You must read it, Hans, it is Schiller's *Don Carlos* . . . I'll lend it you if you like. . . ."

"Oh, no," said Hans Hansen, "you needn't, Tonio, that's not anything for me. I'll stick to my horse books. There are wonderful cuts in them, let me tell you. I'll show them to you when you come to see me. They are instantaneous photography—the horse in motion; you can see him trot and canter and jump, in all positions, that you never can get to see in life, because they happen so fast. . . ."

"In all positions?" asked Tonio politely. "Yes, that must be great. But about

Don Carlos—it is beyond anything you could possibly dream of. There are places in it that are so lovely they make you jump . . . as though it were an explosion—"

"An explosion?" asked Hans Hansen. "What sort of an explosion?"

"For instance, the place where the king has been crying because the marquis betrayed him . . . but the marquis did it only out of love for the prince, you see, he sacrifices himself for his sake. And the word comes out of the cabinet into the antechamber that the king has been weeping. 'Weeping? The king been weeping?' All the courtiers are fearfully upset, it goes through and through you, for the king has always been so frightfully stiff and stern. But it is so easy to understand why he cried, and I feel sorrier for him than for the prince and the marquis put together. He is always so alone, nobody loves him, and then he thinks he has found one man, and then *he* betrays him. . . ."

Hans Hansen looked sideways into Tonio's face, and something in it must have won him to the subject, for suddenly he shoved his arm once more into Tonio's and said:

"How had he betrayed him, Tonio?"

Tonio went on.

"Well," he said, "you see all the letters for Brabant and Flanders—"

"There comes Irwin Immerthal," said Hans.

Tonio stopped talking. If only the earth would open and swallow Immerthal up! "Why does he have to come disturbing us? If he only doesn't go with us all the way and talk about the riding-lessons!" For Irwin Immerthal had riding-lessons too. He was the son of the bank president and lived close by, outside the city wall. He had already been home and left his bag, and now he walked towards them through the avenue. His legs were crooked and his eyes like slits.

" 'lo, Immerthal," said Hans. "I'm taking a little walk with Kröger. . . ."

"I have to go into town on an errand," said Immerthal. "But I'll walk a little way with you. Are those fruit toffees you've got? Thanks, I'll have a couple. Tomorrow we have our next lesson, Hans." He meant the riding-lesson.

"What larks!" said Hans. "I'm going to get the leather gaiters for a present, because I was top lately in our papers."

"You don't take riding-lessons, I suppose, Kröger?" asked Immerthal, and his eyes were only two gleaming cracks.

"No . . ." answered Tonio, uncertainly.

"You ought to ask your father," Hans Hansen remarked, "so you could have lessons too, Kröger."

"Yes . . ." said Tonio. He spoke hastily and without interest; his throat had suddenly contracted, because Hans had called him by his last name. Hans seemed conscious of it too, for he said by way of explanation: "I call you Kröger because your first name is so crazy. Don't mind my saying so, I can't do with it at all. Tonio —why, what sort of name is that? Though of course I know it's not your fault in the least."

"No, they probably called you that because it sounds so foreign and sort of something special," said Immerthal, obviously with intent to say just the right thing.

Tonio's mouth twitched. He pulled himself together and said:

"Yes, it's a silly name—Lord knows I'd rather be called Heinrich or Wilhelm. It's all because I'm named after my mother's brother Antonio. She comes from down there, you know. . . ."

There he stopped and let the others have their say about horses and saddles. Hans had taken Immerthal's arm; he talked with a fluency that *Don Carlos* could never have roused in him. . . . Tonio felt a mounting desire to weep pricking his nose from time to time; he had hard work to control the trembling of his lips.

Hans could not stand his name—what was to be done? He himself was called Hans, and Immerthal was called Irwin; two good, sound, familiar names, offensive to nobody. And Tonio was foreign and queer. Yes, there was always something queer about him, whether he would or no, and he was alone, the regular and usual would none of him; although after all he was no gypsy in a green wagon, but the son of Consul Kröger, a member of the Kröger family. But why did Hans call him Tonio as long as they were alone and then feel ashamed as soon as anybody else was by? Just now he had won him over, they had been close together, he was sure. "How had he betrayed him, Tonio?" Hans asked, and took his arm. But he had breathed easier directly Immerthal came up, he had dropped him like a shot, even gratuitously taunted him with his outlandish name. How it hurt to have to see through all this! . . . Hans Hansen did like him a little, when they were alone, that he knew. But let a third person come, he was ashamed, and offered up his friend. And again he was alone. He thought of King Philip. The king had wept. . . .

"Goodness, I have to go," said Irwin Immerthal. "Good-bye, and thanks for the toffee." He jumped upon a bench that stood by the way, ran along it with his crooked legs, jumped down, and trotted off.

"I like Immerthal," said Hans, with emphasis. He had a spoilt and arbitrary was of announcing his likes and dislikes, as though graciously pleased to confer them like an order on this person and that. . . . He went on talking about the riding-lessons where he had left off. Anyhow, it was not very much farther to his house; the walk over the walls was not a long one. They held their caps and bent their heads before the strong, damp wind that rattled and groaned in the leafless trees. And Hans Hansen went on talking, Tonio throwing in a forced yes or no from time to time. Hans talked eagerly, had taken his arm again; but the contact gave Tonio no pleasure. The nearness was only apparent, not real; it meant nothing. . . .

They struck away from the walls close to the station, where they saw a train puff busily past, idly counted the coaches, and waved to the man who was perched on top of the last one bundled in a leather coat. They stopped in front of the Hansen villa on the Lindenplatz, and Hans went into detail about what fun it was to stand on the bottom rail of the garden gate and let it swing on its creaking hinges. After that they said good-bye.

"I must go in now," said Hans. "Good-bye, Tonio. Next time I'll take you home, see if I don't."

"Good-bye, Hans," said Tonio. "It was a nice walk."

They put out their hands, all wet and rusty from the garden gate. But as Hans looked into Tonio's eyes, he bethought himself, a look of remorse came over his charming face.

"And I'll read *Don Carlos* pretty soon, too," he said quickly. "That bit about the king in his cabinet must be nuts." Then he took his bag under his arm and ran off through the front garden. Before he disappeared he turned and nodded once more.

And Tonio went off as though on wings. The wind was at his back; but it was not the wind alone that bore him along so lightly.

Hans would read *Don Carlos,* and then they would have something to talk about, and neither Irwin Immerthal nor another could join in. How well they understood each other! Perhaps—who knew?—some day he might even get Hans to write poetry! . . . No, no, that he did not ask. Hans must not become like Tonio, he must stop just as he was, so strong and bright, everybody loved him as he was, and Tonio most of all. But it would do him no harm to read *Don Carlos. . . .* Tonio passed under the squat old city gate, along by the harbour, and up the steep, wet, windy, gabled street to his parents' house. His heart beat richly: longing was awake in it, and a gentle envy; a faint contempt, and no little inno-cent bliss.

Ingeborg Holm, blonde little Inge, the daughter of Dr. Holm, who lived on Market Square opposite the tall old Gothic fountain with its manifold spires—she it was Tonio Kröger loved when he was sixteen years old.

Strange how things come about! He had seen her a thousand times; then one evening he saw her again; saw her in a certain light, talking with a friend in a certain saucy way, laughing and tossing her head; saw her lift her arm and smooth her back hair with her schoolgirl hand, that was by no means particularly fine or slender, in such a way that the thin white sleeve slipped down from her elbow; heard her speak a word or two, a quite indifferent phrase, but with a certain intonation, with a warm ring in her voice; and his heart throbbed with ecstasy, far stronger than that he had once felt when he looked at Hans Hansen long ago, when he was still a little, stupid boy.

That evening he carried away her picture in his eye: the thick blond plait, the longish, laughing blue eyes, the saddle of pale freckles across the nose. He could not go to sleep for hearing that ring in her voice; he tried in a whisper to imitate the tone in which she had uttered the commonplace phrase, and felt a shiver run through and through him. He knew by experience that this was love. And he was accurately aware that love would surely bring him much pain, affliction, and sadness, that it would certainly destroy his peace, filling his heart to overflowing with melodies which would be no good to him because he would never have the time or tranquillity to give them permanent form. Yet he received this love with joy, surrendered himself to it, and cherished it with all the strength of his being; for he knew that love made one vital and rich, and he longed to be vital and rich, far more than he did to work tranquilly on anything to give it permanent form.

Tonio Kröger fell in love with merry Ingeborg Holm in Frau Consul Hustede's drawing-room on the evening when it was emptied of furniture for the weekly dancing-class. It was a private class, attended only by members of the first families; it met by turns in the various parental houses to receive instruction from Knaak, the dancing-master, who came from Hamburg expressly for the purpose.

François Knaak was his name, and what a man he was! "*J'ai l'honneur de me vous représenter*," he would say, "*mon nom est Knaak. . . .* This is not said during the bowing, but after you have finished and are standing up straight again. In a low voice, but distinctly. Of course one does not need to introduce oneself in French every day in the week, but if you can do it correctly and faultlessly in French you are not likely to make a mistake when you do it in German." How marvellously the silky black frock-coat fitted his chubby hips! His trouser-legs fell down in soft folds upon his patent-leather pumps with their wide satin bows, and his brown eyes glanced about him with languid pleasure in their own beauty.

All this excess of self-confidence and good form was positively overpowering. He went trippingly—and nobody tripped like him, so elastically, so weavingly, rockingly, royally—up to the mistress of the house, made a bow, waited for a hand to be put forth. This vouchsafed, he gave murmurous voice to his gratitude, stepped buoyantly back, turned on his left foot, swiftly drawing the right one backwards on its toe-tip, and moved away, with his hips shaking.

When you took leave of a company you must go backwards out at the door; when you fetched a chair, you were not to shove it along the floor or clutch it by one leg; but gently, by the back, and set it down without a sound. When you stood, you were not to fold your hands on your tummy or seek with your tongue the corners of your mouth. If you did, Herr Knaak had a way of showing you how it looked that filled you with disgust for that particular gesture all the rest of your life.

This was deportment. As for dancing, Herr Knaak was, if possible, even more of a master at that. The salon was emptied of furniture and lighted by a gas-chandelier in the middle of the ceiling and candles on the mantel-shelf. The floor was strewn with talc, and the pupils stood about in a dumb semicircle. But in the next room, behind the portières, mothers and aunts sat on plush-upholstered chairs and watched Herr Knaak through their lorgnettes, as in little springs and hops, curtsying slightly, the hem of his frock-coat held up on each side by two fingers, he demonstrated the single steps of the mazurka. When he wanted to dazzle his audience completely he would suddenly and unexpectedly spring from the ground, whirling his two legs about each other with bewildering swiftness in the air, as it were trilling with them, and then, with a subdued bump, which nevertheless shook everything within him to its depths, returned to earth.

"What an unmentionable monkey!" thought Tonio Kröger to himself. But he saw the absorbed smile on jolly little Inge's face as she followed Herr Knaak's movements; and that, though not that alone, roused in him something like admiration of all this wonderfully controlled corporeality. How tranquil, how imperturbable was Herr Knaak's gaze! His eyes did not plumb the depth of things to the place where life becomes complex and melancholy; they knew nothing save that they were beautiful brown eyes. But that was just why his bearing was so proud. To be able to walk like that, one must be stupid; then one was loved, then one was lovable. He could so well understand how it was that Inge, blonde, sweet little Inge, looked at Herr Knaak as she did. But would never a girl look at him like that?

Oh, yes, there would, and did. For instance, Magdalena Vermehren, Attorney Vermehren's daughter, with the gentle mouth and the great, dark, brilliant eyes, so serious and adoring. She often fell down in the dance; but when it was "ladies' choice" she came up to him; she knew he wrote verses and twice she had asked him to show them to her. She often sat at a distance, with drooping head, and gazed at him. He did not care. It was Inge he loved, blonde, jolly Inge, who most assuredly despised him for his poetic effusions . . . he looked at her, looked at her narrow blue eyes full of fun and mockery, and felt an envious longing; to be shut away from her like this, to be forever strange—he felt it in his breast, like a heavy, burning weight.

"First couple *en avant*," said Herr Knaak; and no words can tell how marvellously he pronounced the nasal. They were to practise the quadrille, and to Tonio Kröger's profound alarm he found himself in the same set with Inge Holm. He avoided her where he could, yet somehow was forever near her; kept his eyes away from her person and yet found his gaze ever on her. There she came, tripping up hand-in-hand with red-headed Ferdinand Matthiessen; she flung back her braid, drew a deep breath, and took her place opposite Tonio. Herr Heinzelmann, at the piano, laid bony hands upon the keys, Herr Knaak waved his arm, the quadrille began.

She moved to and fro before his eyes, forwards and back, pacing and swinging; he seemed to catch a fragrance from her hair or the folds of her thin white frock, and his eyes grew sadder and sadder. "I love you, dear, sweet Inge," he said to himself, and put into his words all the pain he felt to see her so intent upon the dance with not a thought of him. Some lines of an exquisite poem by Storm came into his mind: "I would sleep, but thou must dance." It seemed against all sense, and most depressing, that he must be dancing when he was in love. . . .

"First couple *en avant*," said Herr Knaak; it was the next figure. "*Compliment! Moulinet des dames! Tour de main!*" and he swallowed the silent *e* in the "*de*," with quite indescribable ease and grace.

"Second couple *en avant!*" This was Tonio Kröger and his partner. "*Compliment!*" And Tonio Kröger bowed. "*Moulinet des dames!*" And Tonio Kröger, with bent head and gloomy brows, laid his hand on those of the four ladies, on Ingeborg Holm's hand, and danced the *moulinet*.

Roundabout rose a tittering and laughing. Herr Knaak took a ballet pose conventionally expressive of horror. "Oh, dear! Oh, dear!" he cried. "Stop! Stop! Kröger among the ladies! *En arrière*, Fräulein Kröger, step back, *fi donc!* Everybody else understood it but you. Shoo! Get out! Get away!" He drew out his yellow silk handkerchief and flapped Tonio Kröger back to his place.

Everyone laughed, the girls and the boys and the ladies beyond the portières;

Herr Knaak had made something too utterly funny out of the little episode, it was as amusing as a play. But Herr Heinzelmann at the piano sat and waited, with a dry, business-like air, for a sign to go on; he was hardened against Herr Knaak's effects.

Then the quadrille went on. And the intermission followed. The parlourmaid came clinking in with a tray of wine-jelly glasses, the cook followed in her wake with a load of plum-cake. But Tonio Kröger stole away. He stole out into the corridor and stood there, his hands behind his back, in front of a window with the blind down. He never thought that one could not see through the blind and that it was absurd to stand there as though one were looking out.

For he was looking within, into himself, the theatre of so much pain and long-ing. Why, why was he here? Why was he not sitting by the window in his own room, reading Storm's *Immensee* and lifting his eyes to the twilight garden out-side, where the old walnut tree moaned? That was the place for him! Others might dance, others bend their fresh and lively minds upon the pleasure in hand!...But no, no, after all, his place was here, where he could feel near Inge, even although he stood lonely and aloof, seeking to distinguish the warm notes of her voice amid the buzzing, clattering, and laughter within. Oh, lovely Inge, blonde Inge of the narrow, laughing blue eyes! So lovely and laughing as you are one can only be if one does not read *Immensee* and never tries to write things like it. And that was just the tragedy!

Ah, she *must* come! She *must* notice where he had gone, must feel how he suffered! She must slip out to him, even pity must bring her, to lay her hand on his shoulder and say: "Do come back to us, ah, don't be sad—I love you, Tonio." He listened behind him and waited in frantic suspense. But not in the least. Such things did not happen on this earth.

Had she laughed at him too like all the others? Yes, she had, however gladly he would have denied it for both their sakes. And yet it was only because he had been so taken up with her that he had danced the *moulinet des dames*. Suppose he had—what did that matter? Had not a magazine accepted a poem of his a little while ago—even though the magazine had failed before his poem could be printed? The day was coming when he would be famous, when they would print everything he wrote; and *then* he would see if that made any impres-sion on Inge Holm! No, it would make no impression at all; that was just it. Magdalena Vermehren, who was always falling down in the dances, yes, she would be impressed. But never Ingeborg Holm, never blue-eyed, laughing Inge. So what was the good of it?

Tonio Kröger's heart contracted painfully at the thought. To feel stirring within you the wonderful and melancholy play of strange forces and to be aware that those others you yearn for are blithely inaccessible to all that moves you—what a pain is this! And yet! He stood there aloof and alone, staring hopelessly at a drawn blind and making, in his distraction, as though he could look out. But yet he was happy. For he lived. His heart was full; hotly and sadly it beat for thee, Ingeborg Holm, and his soul embraced thy blonde, simple, pert, com-monplace little personality in blissful self-abnegation.

Often after that he stood thus, with burning cheeks, in lonely corners, whither the sound of the music, the tinkling of glasses and fragrance of flowers came but faintly, and tried to distinguish the ringing tones of thy voice amid the distant happy din; stood suffering for thee—and still was happy! Often it angered him to think that he might talk with Magdalena Vermehren, who always fell down in the dance. She understood him, she laughed or was serious in the right places; while Inge the fair, let him sit never so near her, seemed remote and estranged, his speech not being her speech. And still—he was happy. For happiness, he told himself, is not in being loved—which is a satisfaction of the vanity and mingled with disgust. Happiness is in loving, and perhaps in snatching fugitive little approaches to the beloved object. And he took inward note of this thought, wrote it down in his mind; followed out all its implications and felt it to the depths of his soul.

"Faithfulness," thought Tonio Kröger. "Yes, I will be faithful, I will love thee, Ingeborg, as long as I live!" He said this in the honesty of his intentions. And yet a still small voice whispered misgivings in his ear: after all, he had forgotten Hans Hansen utterly, even though he saw him every day! And the hateful, the pitiable fact was that this still, small, rather spiteful voice was right: time passed and the day came when Tonio Kröger was no longer so unconditionally ready as once he had been to die for the lively Inge, because he felt in himself desires and powers to accomplish in his own way a host of wonderful things in this world.

And he circled with watchful eye the sacrificial altar, where flickered the pure, chaste flame of his love; knelt before it and tended and cherished it in every way, because he so wanted to be faithful. And in a little while, unobservably, without sensation or stir, it went out after all.

But Tonio Kröger still stood before the cold altar, full of regret and dismay at the fact that faithfulness was impossible upon this earth. Then he shrugged his shoulders and went his way.

He went the way that go he must, a little idly, a little irregularly, whistling to himself, gazing into space with his head on one side; and if he went wrong it was because for some people there is no such thing as a right way. Asked what in the world he meant to become, he gave various answers, for he was used to say (and had even already written it) that he bore within himself the possibility of a thousand ways of life, together with the private conviction that they were all sheer impossibilities.

Even before he left the narrow streets of his native city, the threads that bound him to it had gently loosened. The old Kröger family gradually declined, and some people quite rightly considered Tonio Kröger's own existence and way of life as one of the signs of decay. His father's mother, the head of the family, had died, and not long after his own father followed, the tall, thoughtful, carefully dressed gentleman with the field-flower in his buttonhole. The great Kröger house, with all its stately tradition, came up for sale, and the firm was dissolved. Tonio's mother, his beautiful, fiery mother, who played the piano and mandolin so wonderfully and to whom nothing mattered at all, she married again after a year's time; married a musician, moreover, a virtuoso with an Italian name, and went away with him into remote blue distances. Tonio Kröger found this a little irregular, but who was he to call her to order, who wrote poetry himself and could not even give an answer when asked what he meant to do in life?

And so he left his native town and its tortuous, gabled streets with the damp wind whistling through them; left the fountain in the garden and the ancient walnut tree, familiar friends of his youth; left the sea too, that he loved so much, and felt no pain to go. For he was grown up and sensible and had come to realize how things stood with him; he looked down on the lowly and vulgar life he had led so long in these surroundings.

He surrendered utterly to the power that to him seemed the highest on earth, to whose service he felt called, which promised him elevation and honours: the power of intellect, the power of the Word, that lords it with a smile over the unconscious and inarticulate. To this power he surrendered with all the passion of youth, and it rewarded him with all it had to give, taking from him inexorably, in return, all that it is wont to take.

It sharpened his eyes and made him see through the large words which puff out the bosoms of mankind; it opened for him men's souls and his own, made him clairvoyant, showed him the inwardness of the world and the ultimate behind men's words and deeds. And all that he saw could be put in two words: the comedy and the tragedy of life.

And then, with knowledge, its torment and its arrogance, came solitude; because he could not endure the blithe and innocent with their darkened understanding, while they in turn were troubled by the sign on his brow. But his love of the word kept growing sweeter and sweeter, and his love of form; for he used to say (and had already said it in writing) that knowledge of the soul would unfailingly make us melancholy if the pleasures of expression did not keep us alert and of good cheer.

He lived in large cities and in the south, promising himself a luxuriant ripening of his art by southern suns; perhaps it was the blood of his mother's race that drew him thither. But his heart being dead and loveless, he fell into adventures of the flesh, descended into the depths of lust and searing sin, and suffered unspeakably thereby. It might have been his father in him, that tall, thoughtful, fastidiously dressed man with the wild flower in his buttonhole, that made him suffer so down there in the south; now and again he would feel a faint, yearning memory of a certain joy that was of the soul; once it had been his own, but now, in all his joys, he could not find it again.

Then he would be seized with disgust and hatred of the senses; pant after purity and seemly peace, while still he breathed the air of art, the tepid, sweet air of permanent spring, heavy with fragrance where it breeds and brews and burgeons in the mysterious bliss of creation. So for all result he was flung to and fro forever between two crass extremes: between icy intellect and scorching sense, and what with his pangs of conscience led an exhausing life, rare, extraordinary, excessive, which at bottom he, Tonio Kröger, despised. "What a labyrinth!" he sometimes thought. "How could I possibly have got into all these fantastic adventures? As though I had a wagonful of travelling gypsies for my ancestors!"

But as his health suffered from these excesses, so his artistry was sharpened; it grew fastidious, precious, *raffiné*, morbidly sensitive in questions of tact and taste, rasped by the banal. His first appearance in print elicited much applause; there was joy among the elect, for it was a good and workmanlike performance, full of humour and acquaintance with pain. In no long time his name—the same by which his masters had reproached him, the same he had signed to his earliest verses on the walnut tree and the fountain and the sea, those syllables compact of the north and the south, that good middle-class name with the exotic twist to it—became a synonym for excellence; for the painful thoroughness of the experiences he had gone through, combined with a tenacious ambition and a persistent industry, joined battle with the irritable fastidiousness of his taste and under grinding torments issued in work of a quality quite uncommon.

He worked, not like a man who works that he may live; but as one who is bent on doing nothing but work; having no regard for himself as a human being but only as a creator; moving about grey and unobtrusive among his fellows like an actor without his make-up, who counts for nothing as soon as he stops representing something else. He worked withdrawn out of sight and sound of the small fry, for whom he felt nothing but contempt, because to them a talent was a social asset like another; who, whether they were poor or not, went about ostentatiously shabby or else flaunted startling cravats, all the time taking jolly good care to amuse themselves, to be artistic and charming without the smallest notion of the fact that good work only comes out under pressure of a bad life; that he who lives does not work; that one must die to life in order to be utterly a creator.

"Shall I disturb you?" asked Tonio Kröger on the threshold of the atelier. He held his hat in his hand and bowed with some ceremony, although Lisabeta Ivanovna was a good friend of his, to whom he told all his troubles.

"Mercy on you, Tonio Kröger! Don't be so formal," answered she, with her lilting intonation. "Everybody knows you were taught good manners in your nursery." She transferred her brush to her left hand, that held the palette, reached him her right, and looked him in the face, smiling and shaking her head.

"Yes, but you are working," he said. "Let's see. Oh, you've been getting on," and he looked at the colour-sketches leaning against chairs at both sides of the easel and from them to the large canvas covered with a square linen mesh, where the first patches of colour were beginning to appear among the confused and schematic lines of the charcoal sketch.

This was in Munich, in a back building in Schellingstrasse, several storeys up. Beyond the wide window facing the north were blue sky, sunshine, birds twittering; the young sweet breath of spring streaming through an open pane mingled with the smells of paint and fixative. The afternoon light, bright golden, flooded the spacious emptiness of the atelier; it made no secret of the bad flooring or the rough table under the window, covered with little bottles, tubes, and brushes; it illumined the unframed studies on the unpapered walls, the torn silk screen that shut off a charmingly furnished little living-corner near the door; it shone upon the inchoate work on the easel, upon the artist and the poet there before it.

She was about the same age as himself—slightly past thirty. She sat there on a low stool, in her dark-blue apron, and leant her chin in her hand. Her brown hair, compactly dressed, already a little grey at the sides, was parted in the middle and waved over the temples, framing a sensitive, sympathetic, dark-skinned face, which was Slavic in its facial structure, with flat nose, strongly accentuated cheekbones, and little bright black eyes. She sat there measuring her work with her head on one side and her eyes screwed up; her features were drawn with a look of misgiving, almost of vexation.

He stood beside her, his right hand on his hip, with the other furiously twirling his brown moustache. His dress, reserved in cut and a soothing shade of grey, was punctilious and dignified to the last degree. He was whistling softly to himself, in the way he had, and his slanting brows were gathered in a frown. The darkbrown hair was parted with severe correctness, but the laboured forehead beneath showed a nervous twitching, and the chiselled southern features were sharpened as though they had been gone over again with a graver's tool. And yet the mouth —how gently curved it was, the chin how softly formed!...After a little he drew his hand across his brow and eyes and turned away.

"I ought not to have come," he said.

"And why not, Tonio Kröger?"

"I've just got up from my desk, Lisabeta, and inside my head it looks just the way it does on this canvas. A scaffolding, a faint first draft smeared with corrections and a few splotches of colour; yes, and I come up here and see the same thing. And the same conflict and contradiction in the air," he went on, sniffing, "that has been torturing me at home. It's extraordinary. If you are possessed by an idea, you find it expressed everywhere, you even *smell* it. Fixative and the breath of spring; art and—what? Don't say nature, Lisabeta, 'nature' isn't exhausting. Ah, no, I ought to have gone for a walk, though it's doubtful if it would have made me feel better. Five minutes ago, not far from here, I met a man I know, Adalbert, the novelist. 'God damn the spring!' says he in the aggressive way he has. 'It is and always has been the most ghastly time of the year. Can you get hold of a single sensible idea, Kröger? Can you sit still and work out even the smallest effect, when your blood tickles till it's positively indecent and you are teased by a whole host of irrelevant sensations that when you look at them turn out to be unworkable trash? For my part, I am going to a café. A café is neutral territory, the change of the seasons doesn't affect it; it represents, so to speak, the detached and elevated sphere of the literary man, in which one is only capable of refined ideas.' And he went into the café...and perhaps I ought to have gone with him."

Lisabeta was highly entertained.

"I like that, Tonio Kröger. That part about the indecent tickling is good. And he is right too, in a way, for spring is really not very conducive to work. But now listen. Spring or no spring, I will just finish this little place—work out this little effect, as your friend Adalbert would say. Then we'll go into the 'salon' and have tea, and you can talk yourself out, for I can perfectly well see you are too full for utterance. Will you just compose yourself somewhere—on that chest, for instance, if you are not afraid for your aristocratic garments—"

"Oh, leave my clothes alone, Lisabeta Ivanovna! Do you want me to go about in a ragged velveteen jacket or a red waistcoat? Every artist is as bohemian as the deuce, inside! Let him at least wear proper clothes and behave outwardly like a respectable being. No, I am not too full for utterance," he said as he watched her mixing her paints. "I've told you, it is only that I have a problem and a conflict, that sticks in my mind and disturbs me at my work. . . . Yes, what was it we were just saying? We were talking about Adalbert, the novelist, that stout and forthright man. 'Spring is the most ghastly time of the year,' says he, and goes into a café. A man has to know what he needs, eh? Well, you see he's not the only one; the spring makes me nervous, too; I get dazed with the triflingness and sacredness of the memories and feelings it evokes; only that I don't succeed in looking down on it; for the truth is it makes me ashamed; I quail before its sheer naturalness and triumphant youth. And I don't know whether I should envy Adalbert or despise him for his ignorance. . . .

"Yes, it is true; spring is a bad time for work; and why? Because we are feeling too much. Nobody but a beginner imagines that he who creates must feel. Every real and genuine artist smiles at such naïve blunders as that. A melancholy enough smile, perhaps, but still a smile. For what an artist talks about is never the main point; it is the raw material, in and for itself indifferent, out of which, with bland and serene mastery, he creates the work of art. If you care too much about what you have to say, if your heart is too much in it, you can be pretty sure of making a mess. You get pathetic, you wax sentimental; something dull and doddering, without roots or outlines, with no sense of humour—something tiresome and banal grows under your hand, and you get nothing out of it but apathy in your audience and disappointment and misery in yourself. For so it is, Lisabeta; feeling, warm, heartfelt feeling, is always banal and futile; only the irritations and icy ecstasies of the artist's corrupted nervous system are artistic. The artist must be unhuman, extra-human; he must stand in a queer aloof relationship to our humanity; only so is he in a position, I ought to say only so would he be tempted, to represent it, to present it, to portray it to good effect. The very gift of style, of form and expression, is nothing else than this cool and fastidious attitude towards humanity; you might say there has to be this impoverishment and devastation as a preliminary condition. For sound natural feeling, say what you like, has no taste. It is all up with the artist as soon as he becomes a man and begins to feel. Adalbert knows that; that's why he betook himself to the café, the neutral territory—God help him!"

"Yes, God help him, Batuschka," said Lisabeta, as she washed her hands in a tin basin. "You don't need to follow his example."

"No, Lisabeta, I am not going to; and the only reason is that I am now and again in a position to feel a little ashamed of the springtime of my art. You see sometimes I get letters from strangers, full of praise and thanks and admiration from people whose feelings I have touched. I read them and feel touched myself at these warm if ungainly emotions I have called up; a sort of pity steals over me at this naïve enthusiasm; and I positively blush at the thought of how these good people would freeze up if they were to get a look behind the scenes. What they, in their innocence, cannot comprehend is that a properly constituted, healthy, decent man never writes, acts, or composes—all of which does not hinder me from using his admiration for my genius to goad myself on; nor from taking it in deadly earnest and aping the airs of a great man. Oh, don't talk to me, Lisabeta. I tell you I am sick to death of depicting humanity without having any part or lot in it.... Is an artist a male, anyhow? Ask the females! It seems to me we artists are all of us something like those unsexed papal singers ... we sing like angels; but—"

"Shame on you, Tonio Kröger. But come to tea. The water is just on the boil, and here are some *papyros*. You were talking about singing soprano, do go on. But really you ought to be ashamed of yourself. If I did not know your passionate devotion to your calling and how proud you are of it—"

"Don't talk about 'calling,' Lisabeta Ivanovna. Literature is not a calling, it is a curse, believe me! When does one begin to feel the curse? Early, horribly early. At a time when one ought by rights still to be living in peace and harmony with God and the world. It begins by your feeling yourself set apart, in a curious sort of opposition to the nice, regular people; there is a gulf of ironic sensibility, of knowledge, scepticism, disagreement, between you and the others; it grows deeper and deeper, you realize that you are alone; and from then on any *rapprochement* is simply hopeless! What a fate! That is, if you still have enough heart, enough warmth of affections, to feel how frightful it is! ... Your self-consciousness is kindled, because you among thousands feel the sign on your brow and know that everyone else sees it. I once knew an actor, a man of genius, who had to struggle with a morbid self-consciousness and instability. When he had no rôle to play, nothing to represent, this man, consummate artist but impoverished human being, was overcome by an exaggerated consciousness of his ego. A genuine artist—not one who has taken up art as a profession like another, but artist foreordained and damned—you can pick out, without boasting very sharp perceptions, out of a group of men. The sense of being set apart and not belonging, of being known and observed, something both regal and incongruous shows in his face. You might see something of the same sort on the features of a prince walking through a crowd in ordinary clothes. But no civilian clothes are any good here, Lisabeta. You can disguise yourself, you can dress up like an attaché or a lieutenant of the guard on leave; you hardly need to give a glance or speak a word before everyone knows you are not a human being, but something else: something queer, different, inimical.

"But what is it, to be an artist? Nothing shows up the general human dislike of thinking, and man's innate craving to be comfortable, better than his attitude to this question. When these worthy people are affected by a work of art, they say humbly that that sort of thing is a 'gift.' And because in their innocence they assume that beautiful and uplifting results must have beautiful and uplifting causes, they never dream that the 'gift' in question is a very dubious affair and rests upon extremely sinister foundations. Everybody knows that artists are 'sensitive' and easily wounded; just as everybody knows that ordinary people, with a normal bump of self-confidence, are not. Now you see, Lisabeta, I cherish at the bottom of my soul all the scorn and suspicion of the artist gentry—translated into terms of the intellectual—that my upright old forbears there on the Baltic would have felt for any juggler or mountebank that entered their houses. Listen to this. I know a banker, grey-haired business man, who has a gift for writing stories. He employs this gift in his idle hours, and some of his stories are of the first rank. But despite—I say despite—this excellent gift his withers are by no means unwrung: on the contrary, he has had to serve a prison sentence, on anything but trifling grounds. Yes, it was actually first *in prison* that he became conscious of his gift, and his experiences as a convict are the main theme in all his works. One might be rash enough to conclude that a man has to be at home in some kind of jail in order to become a poet. But can you escape the suspicion that the source and essence of his being an artist had less to do with his life in prison than they had with the reasons that *brought him there?* A banker who writes—that is a rarity, isn't it? But a banker who isn't a criminal, who is irreproachably respectable, and yet writes—he doesn't exist. Yes, you are laughing, and yet I am more than half serious. No problem, none in the world, is more tormenting than this of the artist and his human aspect. Take the most miraculous case of all, take the most typical and therefore the most powerful of artists, take such a morbid and profoundly equivocal work as *Tristan and Isolde,* and look at the effect it has on a healthy young man of thoroughly normal feelings. Exaltation, encouragement, warm, downright enthusiasm, perhaps incitement to 'artistic' creation of his own. Poor young dilettante! In us artists it looks fundamentally different from what he wots of, with his 'warm heart' and 'honest enthusiasm.' I've seen women and youths go mad over artists . . . and I *knew* about them . . . ! The origin, the accompanying phenomena, and the conditions of the artist life—good Lord, what I haven't observed about them, over and over!"

"Observed, Tonio Kröger? If I may ask, only 'observed'?"

He was silent, knitting his oblique brown brows and whistling softly to himself.

"Let me have your cup, Tonio. The tea is weak. And take another cigarette. Now, you perfectly know that you are looking at things as they do not necessarily have to be looked at. . . ."

"That is Horatio's answer, dear Lisabeta. ' 'Twere to consider too curiously, to consider so.' "

"I mean, Tonio Kröger, that one can consider them just exactly as well from another side. I am only a silly painting female, and if I can contradict you at all, if I can defend your own profession a little against you, it is not by saying anything new, but simply by reminding you of some things you very well know yourself: of the purifying and healing influence of letters, the subduing of the passions by knowledge and eloquence; literature as the guide to understanding, forgiveness, and love, the redeeming power of the word, literary art as the noblest manifestation of the human mind, the poet as the most highly developed of human beings, the poet as saint. Is it to consider things not curiously enough, to consider them so?"

"You may talk like that, Lisabeta Ivanovna, you have a perfect right. And with reference to Russian literature, and the works of your poets, one can really worship them; they really come close to being that elevated literature you are talking about. But I am not ignoring your objections, they are part of the things I have in my mind today.... Look at me, Lisabeta. I don't look any too cheerful, do I? A little old and tired and pinched, eh? Well, now to come back to the 'knowledge.' Can't you imagine a man, born orthodox, mild-mannered, well-meaning, a bit sentimental, just simply over-stimulated by his psychological clairvoyance, and going to the dogs? Not to let the sadness of the world unman you; to read, mark, learn, and put to account even the most torturing things and to be of perpetual good cheer, in the sublime consciousness of moral superiority over the horrible invention of existence—yes, thank you! But despite all the joys of expression once in a while the thing gets on your nerves. 'Tout comprendre c'est tout pardonner.' I don't know about that. There is something I call being sick of knowledge, Lisabeta: when it is enough for you to see through a thing in order to be sick to death of it, and not in the least in a forgiving mood. Such was the case of Hamlet the Dane, that typical literary man. He knew what it meant to be called to knowledge without being born to it. To see things clear, if even through your tears, to recognize, notice, observe—and have to put it all down with a smile, at the very moment when hands are clinging, and lips meeting, and the human gaze is blinded with feeling—it is infamous, Lisabeta, it is indecent, outrageous—but what good does it do to be outraged?

"Then another and no less charming side of the thing, of course, is your ennui, your indifferent and ironic attitude towards truth. It is a fact that there is no society in the world so dumb and hopeless as a circle of literary people who are hounded to death as it is. All knowledge is old and tedious to them. Utter some truth that it gave you considerable youthful joy to conquer and possess—and they will all chortle at you for your naïveté. Oh, yes, Lisabeta, literature is a wearing job. In human society, I do assure you, a reserved and sceptical man can be taken for stupid, whereas he is really only arrogant and perhaps lacks courage. So much for 'knowledge.' Now for the 'Word.' It isn't so much a matter of the 'redeeming power' as it is of putting your emotions on ice and serving them up chilled! Honestly, don't you think there's a good deal of cool cheek in the prompt and superficial way a writer can get rid of his feelings by turning them into literature? If your heart is too full, if you are overpowered with the emotions of some sweet or exalted moment—nothing simpler! Go to the literary man, he will put it all straight for you instanter. He will analyse and formulate your affair, label it and express it and discuss it and polish it off and make you indifferent to it for time and eternity—and not charge you a farthing. You will go home quite relieved, cooled off, enlightened; and wonder what it was all about and why you were so mightily moved. And will you seriously enter the lists in behalf of this vain and frigid charlatan? What is uttered, so runs this credo, is finished and done with. If the whole world could be expressed, it would be saved, finished and done.... Well and good. But I am not a nihilist—"

"You are not a—" said Lisabeta.... She was lifting a teaspoonful of tea to her mouth and paused in the act to stare at him.

"Come, come, Lisabeta, what's the matter? I say I am not a nihilist, with respect that is, to lively feeling. You see, the literary man does not understand that life may go on living, unashamed, even after it has been expressed and therewith finished. No matter how much it has been redeemed by becoming literature, it keeps right on sinning—for all action is sin in the mind's eye—

"I'm nearly done, Lisabeta. Please listen. I love life—this is an admission. I present it to you, you may have it. I have never made it to anyone else. People say—people have even written and printed—that I hate life, or fear or despise or abominate it. I liked to hear this, it has always flattered me; but that does not make it true. I love life. You smile; and I know why, Lisabeta. But I implore you not to take what I am saying for literature. Don't think of Cæsar Borgia or any drunken philosophy that has him for a standard-bearer. He is nothing to me, your Cæsar Borgia. I have no opinion of him, and I shall never comprehend how one can honour the extraordinary and dæmonic as an ideal. No, life as the eternal antinomy of mind and art does not represent itself to us as a vision of savage greatness and ruthless beauty; we who are set apart and different do not conceive it as, like us, unusual; it is the normal, respectable, and admirable that is the kingdom of our longing: life, in all its seductive banality! That man is very far from being an artist, my dear, whose last and deepest enthusiasm is the *raffiné*, the eccentric and satanic; who does not know a longing for the innocent, the simple, and the living, for a little friendship, devotion, familiar human happiness—the gnawing, surreptitious hankering, Lisabeta, for the bliss of the commonplace. . . .

"A genuine human friend. Believe me, I should be proud and happy to possess a friend among men. But up to now all the friends I have had have been dæmons, kobolds, impious monsters, and spectres dumb with excess of knowledge —that is to say, literary men.

"I may be standing upon some platform, in some hall in front of people who have come to listen to me. And I find myself looking round among my hearers, I catch myself secretly peering about the auditorium, and all the while I am thinking who it is that has come here to listen to me, whose grateful applause is in my ears, with whom my art is making me one. . . . I do not find what I seek, Lisabeta, I find the herd. The same old community, the same old gathering of early Christians, so to speak: people with fine souls in uncouth bodies, people who are always falling down in the dance, if you know what I mean; the kind to whom poetry serves as a sort of mild revenge on life. Always and only the poor and suffering, never any of the others, the blue-eyed ones, Lisabeta—they do not need mind. . . .

"And, after all, would it not be a lamentable lack of logic to want it otherwise? It is against all sense to love life and yet bend all the powers you have to draw it over to your own side, to the side of finesse and melancholy and the whole sickly aristocracy of letters. The kingdom of art increases and that of health and innocence declines on this earth. What there is left of it ought to be carefully preserved; one ought not to tempt people to read poetry who would much rather read books about the instantaneous photography of horses.

"For, after all, what more pitiable sight is there than life led astray by art?

We artists have a consummate contempt for the dilettante, the man who is leading a living life and yet thinks he can be an artist too if he gets the chance. I am speaking from personal experience, I do assure you. Suppose I am in a company in a good house, with eating and drinking going on, and plenty of conversation and good feeling; I am glad and grateful to be able to lose myself among good regular people for a while. Then all of a sudden—I am thinking of something that actually happened—an officer gets up, a lieutenant, a stout, good-looking chap, whom I could never have believed guilty of any conduct unbecoming his uniform, and actually in good set terms asks the company's permission to read some verses of his own composition. Everybody looks disconcerted, they laugh and tell him to go on, and he takes them at their word and reads from a sheet of paper he has up to now been hiding in his coat-tail pocket —something about love and music, as deeply felt as it is inept. But I ask you: a lieutenant! A man of the world! He surely did not need to.... Well, the inevitable result is long faces, silence, a little artificial applause, everybody thoroughly uncomfortable. The first sensation I am conscious of is guilt—I feel partly responsible for the disturbance this rash youth has brought upon the company; and no wonder, for I, as a member of the same guild, am a target for some of the unfriendly glances. But next minute I realize something else: this man for whom just now I felt the greatest respect has suddenly sunk in my eyes. I feel a benevolent pity. Along with some other brave and good-natured gentlemen I go up and speak to him. 'Congratulations, Herr Lieutenant,' I say, 'that is a very pretty talent you have. It was charming.' And I am within an ace of clapping him on the shoulder. But is that the way one is supposed to feel towards a lieutenant— benevolent? ... It was his own fault. There he stood, suffering embarrassment for the mistake of thinking that one may pluck a single leaf from the laurel tree of art without paying for it with his life. No, there I go with my colleague, the convict banker—but don't you find, Lisabeta, that I have quite a Hamlet-like flow of oratory today?"

"Are you done, Tonio Kröger?"

"No. But there won't be any more."

"And quite enough too. Are you expecting a reply?"

"Have you one ready?"

"I should say. I have listened to you faithfully, Tonio, from beginning to end, and I will give you the answer to everything you have said this afternoon and the solution of the problem that has been upsetting you. Now: the solution is that you, as you sit there, are, quite simply, a bourgeois."

"Am I?" he asked a little crestfallen.

"Yes; that hits you hard, it must. So I will soften the judgment just a little. You are a bourgeois on the wrong path, a bourgeois *manqué*."

Silence. Then he got up resolutely and took his hat and stick.

"Thank you, Lisabeta Ivanovna; now I can go home in peace. I am expressed."

Towards autumn Tonio Kröger said to Lisabeta Ivanovna:

"Well, Lisabeta, I think I'll be off. I need a change of air. I must get away, out into the open."

"Well, well, well, little Father! Does it please your Highness to go down to Italy again?"

"Oh, get along with your Italy, Lisabeta. I'm fed up with Italy, I spew it out of my mouth. It's a long time since I imagined I could belong down there. Art, eh? Blue-velvet sky, ardent wine, the sweets of sensuality. In short, I don't want it—I decline with thanks. The whole *bellezza* business makes me nervous. All those frightfully animated people down there with their black animal-like eyes; I don't like them either. These Romance peoples have no soul in their eyes. No, I'm going to take a trip to Denmark."

"To Denmark?"

"Yes. I'm quite sanguine of the results. I happen never to have been there, though I lived all my youth so close to it. Still I have always known and loved the country. I suppose I must have this northern tendency from my father, for my mother was really more for the *bellezza*, in so far, that is, as she cared very much one way or the other. But just take the books that are written up there, that clean, meaty, whimsical Scandinavian literature, Lisabeta, there's nothing like it, I love it. Or take the Scandinavian meals, those incomparable meals, which can only be digested in strong sea air (I don't know whether I can digest them in any sort of air); I know them from my home too, because we ate that way up there. Take even the names, the given names that people rejoice in up north; we have a good many of them in my part of the country too: Ingeborg, for instance, isn't it the purest poetry—like a harp-tone? And then the sea—up there it's the Baltic! . . . In a word, I am going, Lisabeta. I want to see the Baltic again and read the books and hear the names on their native heath; I want to stand on the terrace at Kronberg, where the ghost appeared to Hamlet, bringing despair and death to that poor, noble-souled youth. . . ."

"How are you going, Tonio, if I may ask? What route are you taking?"

"The usual one," he said, shrugging his shoulders, and blushed perceptibly. "Yes, I shall touch my—my point of departure, Lisabeta, after thirteen years, and that may turn out rather funny."

She smiled.

"That is what I wanted to hear, Tonio Kröger. Well, be off, then, in God's name. Be sure to write to me, do you hear? I shall expect a letter full of your experiences in—Denmark."

And Tonio Kröger travelled north. He travelled in comfort (for he was wont to say that anyone who suffered inwardly more than other people had a right to a little outward ease); and he did not stay until the towers of the little town he had left rose up in the grey air. Among them he made a short and singular stay.

The dreary afternoon was merging into evening when the train pulled into the narrow, reeking shed, so marvellously familiar. The volumes of thick smoke rolled up to the dirty glass roof and wreathed to and fro there in long tatters, just as they had, long ago, on the day when Tonio Kröger, with nothing but derision in his heart, had left his native town.—He arranged to have his luggage sent to his hotel and walked out of the station.

There were the cabs, those enormously high, enormously wide black cabs drawn by two horses, standing in a rank. He did not take one, he only looked at them, as he looked at everything: the narrow gables, and the pointed towers peering above the roofs close at hand; the plump, fair, easy-going populace, with their broad yet rapid speech. And a nervous laugh mounted in him, mysteriously akin to a sob.—He walked on, slowly, with the damp wind constantly in his face, across the bridge, with the mythological statues on the railings, and some distance along the harbour.

Good Lord, how tiny and close it all seemed! The comical little gabled streets were climbing up just as of yore from the port to the town! And on the ruffled waters the smoke-stacks and masts of the ships dipped gently in the wind and twilight. Should he go up that next street, leading, he knew, to a certain house? No, to-morrow. He was too sleepy. His head was heavy from the journey, and slow, vague trains of thought passed through his mind.

Sometimes in the past thirteen years, when he was suffering from indigestion, he had dreamed of being back home in the echoing old house in the steep, narrow street. His father had been there too, and reproached him bitterly for his dissolute manner of life, and this, each time, he had found quite as it should be. And now the present refused to distinguish itself in any way from one of those tantalizing dream-fabrications in which the dreamer asks himself if this be delusion or reality and is driven to decide for the latter, only to wake up after all in the end. ...He paced through the half-empty streets with his head inclined against the wind, moving as though in his sleep in the direction of the hotel, the first hotel in the town, where he meant to sleep. A bow-legged man, with a pole at the end of which burned a tiny fire, walked before him with a rolling, seafaring gait and lighted the gas-lamps.

What was at the bottom of this? What was it burning darkly beneath the ashes of his fatigue, refusing to burst out into a clear blaze? Hush, hush, only no talk. Only don't make words! He would have liked to go on so, for a long time, in the wind, through the dusky, dreamily familiar streets—but everything was so little and close together here. You reached your goal at once.

In the upper town there were arc-lamps, just lighted. There was the hotel with the two black lions in front of it; he had been afraid of them as a child. And there they were, still looking at each other as though they were about to sneeze; only they seemed to have grown much smaller. Tonio Kröger passed between them into the hotel.

As he came on foot, he was received with no great ceremony. There was a porter, and a lordly gentleman dressed in black, to do the honours; the latter, shoving back his cuffs with his little fingers, measured him from the crown of his head to the soles of his boots, obviously with intent to place him, to assign him to his proper category socially and hierarchically speaking and then mete out the suitable degree of courtesy. He seemed not to come to any clear decision and compromised on a moderate display of politeness. A mild-mannered waiter with yellow-white side-whiskers, in a dress suit shiny with age, and rosettes on his soundless shoes, led him up two flights into a clean old room furnished in patriarchal style. Its windows gave on a twilit view of courts and gables, very mediæval and picturesque, with the fantastic bulk of the old church close by. Tonio Kröger stood awhile before this window; then he sat down on the wide sofa, crossed his arms, drew down his brows, and whistled to himself.

Lights were brought and his luggage came up. The mild-mannered waiter laid the hotel register on the table, and Tonio Kröger, his head on one side, scrawled something on it that might be taken for a name, a station, and a place of origin. Then he ordered supper and went on gazing into space from his sofa-corner. When it stood before him he let it wait long untouched, then took a few bites and walked up and down an hour in his room, stopping from time to time and closing his eyes. Then he very slowly undressed and went to bed. He slept long and had curiously confused and ardent dreams.

It was broad day when he woke. Hastily he recalled where he was and got up to draw the curtains; the pale-blue sky, already with a hint of autumn, was streaked with frayed and tattered cloud; still, above his native city the sun was shining.

He spent more care than usual upon his toilette, washed and shaved and made himself fresh and immaculate as though about to call upon some smart family where a well-dressed and flawless appearance was *de rigueur;* and while occupied in this wise he listened to the anxious beating of his heart.

How bright it was outside! He would have liked better a twilight air like yesterday's, instead of passing through the streets in the broad sunlight, under everybody's eye. Would he meet people he knew, be stopped and questioned and have to submit to be asked how he had spent the last thirteen years? No, thank goodness, he was known to nobody here; even if anybody remembered him, it was unlikely he would be recognized—for certainly he had changed in the meantime! He surveyed himself in the glass and felt a sudden sense of security behind his mask, behind his work-worn face, that was older than his years. . . . He sent for breakfast, and after that he went out; he passed under the disdainful eye of the porter and the gentleman in black, through the vestibule and between the two lions, and so into the street.

Where was he going? He scarcely knew. It was the same as yesterday. Hardly was he in the midst of this long-familiar scene, this stately conglomeration of gables, turrets, arcades, and fountains, hardly did he feel once more the wind in his face, that strong current wafting a faint and pungent aroma from far-off dreams, than the same mistiness laid itself like a veil about his senses. . . . The muscles of his face relaxed, and he looked at men and things with a look grown suddenly calm. Perhaps right there, on that street corner, he might wake up after all. . . .

Where was he going? It seemed to him the direction he took had a connection with his sad and strangely rueful dreams of the night. . . . He went to Market

Square, under the vaulted arches of the Rathaus, where the butchers were weighing out their wares red-handed, where the tall old Gothic fountain stood with its manifold spires. He paused in front of a house, a plain narrow building, like many another, with a fretted baroque gable; stood there lost in contemplation. He read the plate on the door, his eyes rested a little while on each of the windows. Then slowly he turned away.

Where did he go? Towards home. But he took a roundabout way outside the walls—for he had plenty of time. He went over the Millwall and over the Holstenwall, clutching his hat, for the wind was rushing and moaning through the trees. He left the wall near the station, where he saw a train puffing busily past, idly counted the coaches, and looked after the man who sat perched upon the last. In the Lindenplatz he stopped at one of the pretty villas, peered long into the garden and up at the windows, lastly conceived the idea of swinging the gate to and fro upon its hinges till it creaked. Then he looked awhile at his moist, rust-stained hand and went on, went through the squat old gate, along the harbour, and up the steep, windy street to his parents' house.

It stood aloof from its neighbours, its gable towering above them; grey and sombre, as it had stood these three hundred years; and Tonio Kröger read the pious, half-illegible motto above the entrance. Then he drew a long breath and went in.

His heart gave a throb of fear, lest his father might come out of one of the doors on the ground floor, in his office coat, with the pen behind his ear, and take him to task for his excesses. He would have found the reproach quite in order; but he got past unchidden. The inner door was ajar, which appeared to him reprehensible though at the same time he felt as one does in certain broken dreams, where obstacles melt away of themselves, and one presses onward in marvellous favour with fortune. The wide entry, paved with great square flags, echoed to his tread. Opposite the silent kitchen was the curious projecting structure, of rough boards, but cleanly varnished, that had been the servants' quarters. It was quite high up and could only be reached by a sort of ladder from the entry. But the great cupboards and carven presses were gone. The son of the house climbed the majestic staircase, with his hand on the white-enamelled, fret-work balustrade. At each step he lifted his hand, and put it down again with the next as though testing whether he could call back his ancient familiarity with the stout old railing. . . . But at the landing of the entresol he stopped. For on the entrance door was a white plate; and on it in black letters he read: "Public Library."

"Public Library?" thought Tonio Kröger. What were either literature or the public doing here? He knocked. . .heard a "Come in," and obeying it with gloomy suspense gazed upon a scene of most unhappy alteration.

The storey was three rooms deep, and all the doors stood open. The walls were covered nearly all the way up with long rows of books in uniform bindings, standing in dark-coloured bookcases. In each room a poor creature of a man sat writing behind a sort of counter. The farthest two just turned their heads, but the nearest got up in haste and, leaning with both hands on the table, stuck out his head, pursed his lips, lifted his brows, and looked at the visitor with eagerly blinking eyes.

"I beg pardon," said Tonio Kröger without turning his eyes from the bookshelves. "I am a stranger here, seeing the sights. So this is your Public Library? May I examine your collection a little?"

"Certainly, with pleasure," said the official, blinking still more violently. "It is open to everybody.... Pray look about you. Should you care for a catalogue?

"No, thanks," answered Tonio Kröger, "I shall soon find my way about." And he began to move slowly along the walls, with the appearance of studying the rows of books. After a while he took down a volume, opened it, and posted himself at the window.

This was the breakfast-room. They had eaten here in the morning instead of in the big dining-room upstairs, with its white statues of gods and goddesses standing out against the blue walls. ...Beyond there had been a bedroom, where his father's mother had died—only after a long struggle, old as she was, for she had been of a pleasure-loving nature and clung to life. And his father too had drawn his last breath in the same room: that tall, correct, slightly melancholy and pensive gentleman with the wild flower in his buttonhole.... Tonio had sat at the foot of his death-bed, quite given over to unutterable feelings of love and grief. His mother had knelt at the bedside, his lovely, fiery mother, dissolved in hot tears; and after that she had withdrawn with her artist into the far blue south.... And beyond still, the small third room, likewise full of books and presided over by a shabby man—that had been for years on end his own. Thither he had come after school and a walk—like today's; against that wall his table had stood with the drawer where he had kept his first clumsy, heart-felt attempts at verse.... The walnut tree...a pang went through him. He gave a sidewise glance out at the window. The garden lay desolate, but there stood the old walnut tree where it used to stand, groaning and creaking heavily in the wind. And Tonio Kröger let his gaze fall upon the book he had in his hands, an excellent piece of work, and very familiar. He followed the black lines of print, the paragraphs, the flow of words that flowed with so much art, mounting in the ardour of creation to a certain climax and effect and then as artfully breaking off....

"Yes, that was well done," he said; put back the book and turned away. Then he saw that the functionary still stood bolt-upright, blinking with a mingled expression of zeal and misgiving.

"A capital collection, I see," said Tonio Kröger. "I have already quite a good idea of it. Much obliged to you. Good-bye." He went out; but it was a poor exit, and he felt sure the official would stand there perturbed and blinking for several minutes.

He felt no desire for further researches. He had been home. Strangers were living upstairs in the large rooms behind the pillared hall; the top of the stairs was shut off by a glass door which used not to be there, and on the door was a plate. He went away, down the steps, across the echoing corridor, and left his parental home. He sought a restaurant, sat down in a corner, and brooded over a heavy, greasy meal. Then he returned to his hotel.

"I am leaving," he said to the fine gentleman in black. "This afternoon." And he asked for his bill, and for a carriage to take him down to the harbour where he should take the boat for Copenhagen. Then he went up to his room and sat there stiff and still, with his cheek on his hand, looking down on the table before him with absent eyes. Later he paid his bill and packed his things. At the appointed hour the carriage was announced and Tonio Kröger went down in travel array.

At the foot of the stairs the gentleman in black was waiting.

"Beg pardon," he said, shoving back his cuffs with his little fingers.... "Beg pardon, but we must detain you just a moment. Herr Seehaase, the proprietor, would like to exchange two words with you. A matter of form.... He is back there.... If you will have the goodness to step this way.... It is *only* Herr Seehaase, the proprietor."

And he ushered Tonio Kröger into the background of the vestibule.... There, in fact, stood Herr Seehaase. Tonio Kröger recognized him from old time. He was small, fat, and bow-legged. His shaven side-whisker was white, but he wore the same old low-cut dress coat and little velvet cap embroidered in green. He was not alone. Beside him, at a little high desk fastened into the wall, stood a policeman in a helmet, his gloved right hand resting on a document in coloured inks; he turned towards Tonio Kröger with his honest, soldierly face as though he expected Tonio to sink into the earth at his glance.

Tonio Kröger looked at the two and confined himself to waiting.

"You came from Munich?" the policeman asked at length in a heavy, good-natured voice.

Tonio Kröger said he had.

"You are going to Copenhagen?"

"Yes, I am on the way to a Danish seashore resort."

"Seashore resort? Well, you must produce your papers," said the policeman. He uttered the last word with great satisfaction.

"Papers...?" He had no papers. He drew out his pocket-book and looked into it; but aside from notes there was nothing there but some proof-sheets of a story which he had taken along to finish reading. He hated relations with officials and had never got himself a passport....

"I am sorry," he said, "but I don't travel with papers."

"Ah!" said the policeman. "And what might be your name?"

Tonio replied.

"It that a fact?" asked the policeman, suddenly erect, and expanding his nostrils as wide as he could....

"Yes, that is a fact," answered Tonio Kröger.

"And what are you, anyhow?"

Tonio Kröger gulped and gave the name of his trade in a firm voice. Herr Seehaase lifted his head and looked him curiously in the face.

"H'm," said the policeman. "And you give out that you are not identical with an individdle named"—he said "individdle" and then, referring to his document in coloured inks, spelled out an involved, fantastic name which mingled all the sounds of all the races—Tonio Kröger forgot it next minute—"of unknown parentage and unspecified means," he went on, "wanted by the Munich police for various shady transactions, and probably in flight towards Denmark?

"Yes, I give out all that, and more," said Tonio Kröger, wriggling his shoulders. The gesture made a certain impression.

"What? Oh, yes, of course," said the policeman. "You say you can't show any papers—"

Herr Seehaase threw himself into the breach.

"It is only a formality," he said pacifically, "nothing else. You must bear in mind the official is only doing his duty. If you could only identify yourself somehow—some document. . . ."

They were all silent. Should he make an end of the business, by revealing to Herr Seehaase that he was no swindler without specified means, no gypsy in a green wagon, but the son of the late Consul Kröger, a member of the Kröger family? No, he felt no desire to do that. After all, were not these guardians of civic order within their right? He even agreed with them—up to a point. He shrugged his shoulders and kept quiet.

"What have you got, then?" asked the policeman. "In your portfoly, I mean?"

"Here? Nothing. Just a proof-sheet," answered Tonio Kröger.

"Proof-sheet? What's that? Let's see it."

And Tonio Kröger handed over his work. The policeman spread it out on the shelf and began reading. Herr Seehaase drew up and shared it with him. Tonio Kröger looked over their shoulders to see what they read. It was a good moment, a little effect he had worked out to a perfection. He had a sense of self-satisfaction.

"You see," he said, "there is my name. I wrote it, and it is going to be published, you understand."

"All right, that will answer," said Herr Seehaase with decision, gathered up the sheets and gave them back. "That will have to answer, Peterson," he repeated crisply, shutting his eyes and shaking his head as though to see and hear no more. "We must not keep the gentleman any longer. The carriage is waiting. I implore you to pardon the little inconvenience, sir. The officer has only done his duty, but I told him at once he was on the wrong track. . . ."

"Indeed!" thought Tonio Kröger.

The officer seemed still to have his doubts; he muttered something else about individdle and document. But Herr Seehaase, overflowing with regrets, led his guest through the vestibule, accompanied him past the two lions to the carriage, and himself, with many respectful bows, closed the door upon him. And then the funny, high, wide old cab rolled and rattled and bumped down the steep, narrow street to the quay.

And such was the manner of Tonio Kröger's visit to his ancestral home.

Night fell and the moon swam up with silver gleam as Tonio Kröger's boat reached the open sea. He stood at the prow wrapped in his cloak against a mounting wind, and looked beneath into the dark going and coming of the waves as they hovered and swayed and came on, to meet with a clap and shoot erratically away in a bright gush of foam.

He was lulled in a mood of still enchantment. The episode at the hotel, their wanting to arrest him for a swindler in his own home, had cast him down a little, even although he found it quite in order—in a certain way. But after he came on board he had watched, as he used to do as a boy with his father, the lading of goods into the deep bowels of the boat, amid shouts of mingled Danish and Plattdeutsch; not only boxes and bales, but also a Bengal tiger and a polar bear were lowered in cages with stout iron bars. They had probably come from Hamburg and were destined for a Danish menagerie. He had enjoyed these distractions. And as the boat glided along between flat river-banks he quite forgot Officer Peterson's inquisition; while all the rest—his sweet, sad, rueful dreams of the night before, the walk he had taken, the walnut tree—had welled up again in his soul. The sea opened out and he saw in the distance the beach where he as a lad had been let to listen to the ocean's summer dreams; saw the flashing of the lighthouse tower and the lights of the Kurhaus where he and his parents had lived. . . . The Baltic! He bent his head to the strong salt wind; it came sweeping on, it enfolded him, made him faintly giddy and a little deaf; and in that mild confusion of the senses all memory of evil, of anguish and error, effort and exertion of the will, sank away into joyous oblivion and were gone. The roaring, foaming, flapping, and slapping all about him came to his ears like the groan and rustle of an old walnut tree, the creaking of a garden gate. . . . More and more the darkness came on.

"The stars! Oh, by Lord, look at the stars!" a voice suddenly said, with a heavy singsong accent that seemed to come out of the inside of a tun. He recognized it. It belonged to a young man with red-blond hair who had been Tonio Kröger's neighbour at dinner in the salon. His dress was very simple, his eyes were red, and he had the moist and chilly look of a person who has just bathed. With nervous and self-conscious movements he had taken unto himself an astonishing quantity of lobster omelet. Now he leaned on the rail beside Tonio Kröger and looked up at the skies, holding his chin between thumb and forefinger. Beyond a doubt he was in one of those rare and festal and edifying moods that cause the barriers between man and man to fall; when the heart opens even to the stranger, and the mouth utters that which otherwise it would blush to speak. . . .

"Look, by dear sir, just look at the stars. There they stahd and glitter; by goodness, the whole sky is full of theb! And I ask you, when you stahd ahd look up at theb, ahd realize that bany of theb are a huddred tibes larger thad the earth, how does it bake you feel? Yes, we have idvehted the telegraph and the telephode and all the triuphs of our bodern tibes. But whed we look up there, after all we have to recogdize and uhderstad that we are worbs, biserable worbs, ahd dothing else. Ab I right, sir, or ab I wrog? Yes, we are worbs," he answered himself, and nodded meekly and abjectly in the direction of the firmament.

"Ah, no, he has no literature in his belly," thought Tonio Kröger. And he recalled something he had lately read, an essay by a famous French writer on cosmological and psychological philosophies, a very delightful *causerie*.

He made some sort of reply to the young man's feeling remarks, and they went on talking, leaning over the rail, and looking into the night with its movement and fitful lights. The young man, it seemed, was a Hamburg merchant on his holiday.

"Y'ought to travel to Copedhagen on the boat, thigks I, and so here I ab, and so far it's been fide. But they shouldn't have given us the lobster obelet, sir, for it's going to be storby—the captain said so hibself—and that's do joke with indigestible food like that in your stobach...."

Tonio Kröger listed to all this engaging artlessness and was privately drawn to it.

"Yes," he said, "all the food up here is too heavy. It makes one lazy and melancholy."

"Belancholy?" repeated the young man, and looked at him, taken aback. Then he asked, suddenly: "You are a stradger up here, sir?"

"Yes, I come from a long way off," answered Tonio Kröger vaguely, waving his arm.

"But you're right," said the youth; "Lord kdows you are right about the belancholy. I am dearly always belancholy, but specially on evedings like this when there are stars in the sky." And he supported his chin again with thumb and forefinger.

"Surely this man writes verses," thought Tonio Kröger; "business man's verses, full of deep feeling and single-mindedness."

Evening drew on. The wind had grown so violent as to prevent them from talking. So they thought they would sleep a bit, and wished each other good-night.

Tonio Kröger stretched himself out on the narrow cabin bed, but he found no repose. The strong wind with its sharp tang had power to rouse him; he was strangely restless with sweet anticipations. Also he was violently sick with the motion of the ship as she glided down a steep mountain of wave and her screw vibrated as in agony, free of the water. He put on all his clothes again and went up to the deck.

Clouds raced across the moon. The sea danced. It did not come on in full-bodied, regular waves; but far out in the pale and flickering light the water was lashed, torn, and tumbled; leaped upward like great licking flames; hung in jagged and fantastic shapes above dizzy abysses, where the foam seemed to be tossed by the playful strength of colossal arms and flung upward in all directions. The ship had a heavy passage; she lurched and stamped and groaned through the welter; and far down in her bowels the tiger and the polar bear voiced their acute discomfort. A man in an oilskin, with the hood drawn over his head and a lantern strapped to his chest, went straddling painfully up and down the deck. And at the stern, leaning far out, stood the young man from Hamburg suffering the worst. "Lord!" he said, in a hollow, quavering voice, when he saw Tonio Kröger. "Look at the uproar of the elebents, sir!" But he could say no more—he was obliged to turn hastily away.

Tonio Kröger clutched at a taut rope and looked abroad into the arrogance of the elements. His exultation outvied storm and wave; within himself he chanted a song to the sea, instinct with love of her: "O thou wild friend of my youth, Once more I behold thee—" But it got no further, he did not finish it. It was not fated to receive a final form nor in tranquillity to be welded to a perfect whole. For his heart was too full. . . .

Long he stood; then stretched himself out on a bench by the pilot-house and looked up at the sky, where stars were flickering. He even slept a little. And when the cold foam splashed his face it seemed in his half-dreams like a caress.

Perpendicular chalk-cliffs, ghostly in the moonlight, came in sight. They were nearing the island of Möen. Then sleep came again, broken by salty showers of spray that bit into his face and made it stiff. . . . When he really roused, it was broad day, fresh and palest grey, and the sea had gone down. At breakfast he saw the young man from Hamburg again, who blushed rosy-red for shame of the poetic indiscretions he had been betrayed into by the dark, ruffled up his little red-blond moustache with all five fingers, and called out a brisk and soldierly good-morning—after that he studiously avoided him.

And Tonio Kröger landed in Denmark. He arrived in Copenhagen, gave tips to everybody who laid claim to them, took a room at a hotel, and roamed the city for three days with an open guide-book and the air of an intelligent foreigner bent on improving his mind. He looked at the king's New Market and the "Horse" in the middle of it, gazed respectfully up the columns of the Frauenkirch, stood long before Thorwaldsen's noble and beautiful statuary, climbed the round tower, visited castles, and spent two lively evenings in the Tivoli. But all this was not exactly what he saw.

The doors of the houses—so like those in his native town, with open-work gables of baroque shape—bore names known to him of old; names that had a tender and precious quality, and withal in their syllables an accent of plaintive reproach, of repining after the lost and gone. He walked, he gazed, drawing deep, lingering draughts of moist sea air; and everywhere he saw eyes as blue, hair as blond, faces as familiar, as those that had visited his rueful dreams the night he had spent in his native town. There in the open street it befell him that a glance, a ringing word, a sudden laugh would pierce him to his marrow.

He could not stand the bustling city for long. A restlessness, half memory and half hope, half foolish and half sweet, possessed him; he was moved to drop this rôle of ardently inquiring tourist and lie somewhere, quite quietly, on a beach. So he took ship once more and travelled under a cloudy sky, over a black water, northwards along the coast of Seeland towards Helsingör. Thence he drove, at once, by carriage, for three-quarters of an hour, along and above the sea, reaching at length his ultimate goal, the little white "bath-hotel" with green blinds. It stood surrounded by a settlement of cottages, and its shingled turret tower looked out on the beach and the Swedish coast. Here he left the carriage, took possession of the light room they had ready for him, filled shelves and presses with his kit, and prepared to stop awhile.

It was well on in September; not many guests were left in Aalsgaard. Meals were served on the ground floor, in the great beamed dining-room, whose lofty windows led out upon the veranda and the sea. The landlady presided, an elderly spinster with white hair and faded eyes, a faint colour in her check and a feeble twittering voice. She was forever arranging her red hands to look well upon the table-cloth. There was a short-necked old gentleman, quite blue in the face, with a grey sailor beard; a fish-dealer he was, from the capital, and strong at the German. He seemed entirely congested and inclined to apoplexy; breathed in short gasps, kept putting his beringed first finger to one nostril, and snorting violently to get a passage of air through the other. Notwithstanding, he addressed himself constantly to the whisky-bottle, which stood at his place at luncheon and dinner, and breakfast as well. Besides him the company consisted only of three tall American youths with their governor or tutor, who kept adjusting his glasses in unbroken silence. All day long he played football with his charges, who had narrow, taciturn faces and reddish-yellow hair parted in the middle. "Please pass the *wurst*," said one. "That's not *wurst*, it's *schinken*," said the other, and this was the extent of their conversation, as the rest of the time they sat there dumb, drinking hot water.

Tonio Kröger could have wished himself no better table-companions. He revelled in the peace and quiet, listened to the Danish palatals, the clear and the clouded vowels in which the fish-dealer and the landlady desultorily conversed; modestly exchanged views with the fish-dealer on the state of the barometer, and then left the table to go through the veranda and onto the beach once more, where he had already spent long, long morning hours.

Sometimes it was still and summery there. The sea lay idle and smooth, in stripes of blue and russet and bottle-green, played all across with glittering silvery lights. The seaweed shrivelled in the sun and the jelly-fish lay steaming. There was a faintly stagnant smell and a whiff of tar from the fishing-boat against which Tonio Kröger leaned, so standing that he had before his eyes not the Swedish coast but the open horizon, and in his face the pure, fresh breath of the softly breathing sea.

Then grey, stormy days would come. The waves lowered their heads like bulls and charged against the beach; they ran and ramped high up the sands and left them strewn with shining wet sea-grass, driftwood, and mussels. All abroad beneath an overcast sky extended ranges of billows, and between them foaming valleys palely green; but above the spot where the sun hung behind the cloud a patch like white velvet lay on the sea.

Tonio Kröger stood wrapped in wind and tumult, sunk in the continual dull, drowsy uproar that he loved. When he turned away it seemed suddenly warm and silent all about him. But he was never unconscious of the sea at his back; it called, it lured, it beckoned him. And he smiled.

He went landward, by lonely meadow-paths, and was swallowed up in the beech-groves that clothed the rolling landscape near and far. Here he sat down on the moss, against a tree, and gazed at the strip of water he could see between the trunks. Sometimes the sound of surf came on the wind—a noise like boards collapsing at a distance. And from the tree-tops over his head a cawing—hoarse, desolate, forlorn. He held a book on his knee, but did not read a line. He enjoyed profound forgetfulness, hovered disembodied above space and time; only now and again his heart would contract with a fugitive pain, a stab of longing and regret, into whose origin he was too lazy to inquire.

Thus passed some days. He could not have said how many and had no desire to know. But then came one on which something happened; happened while the sun stood in the sky and people were about; and Tonio Kröger, even, felt no vast surprise.

The very opening of the day had been rare and festal. Tonio Kröger woke early and suddenly from his sleep, with a vague and exquisite alarm; he seemed to be looking at a miracle, a magic illumination. His room had a glass door and balcony facing the sound; a thin white gauze curtain divided it into living- and sleeping-quarters, both hung with delicately tinted paper and furnished with an airy good taste that gave them a sunny and friendly look. But now to his sleep-drunken eyes it lay bathed in a serene and roseate light, an unearthly brightness that gilded walls and furniture and turned the gauze curtain to radiant pink cloud. Tonio Kröger did not at once understand. Not until he stood at the glass door and looked out did he realize that this was the sunrise.

For several days there had been clouds and rain; but now the sky was like a piece of pale-blue silk, spanned shimmering above sea and land, and shot with light from red and golden clouds. The sun's disk rose in splendour from a crisply glittering sea that seemed to quiver and burn beneath it. So began the day. In a joyous daze Tonio Kröger flung on his clothes, and breakfasting in the veranda before everybody else, swam from the little wooden bath-house some distance out into the sound, then walked for an hour along the beach. When he came back, several omnibuses were before the door, and from the dining-room he could see people in the parlour next door where the piano was, in the veranda, and on the terrace in front; quantities of people sitting at little tables enjoying beer and sandwiches amid lively discourse. There were whole families, there were old and young, there were even a few children.

At second breakfast—the table was heavily laden with cold viands, roast, pickled, and smoked—Tonio Kröger inquired what was going on.

"Guests," said the fish-dealer. "Tourists and ball-guests from Helsingör. Lord help us, we shall get no sleep this night! There will be dancing and music, and I fear me it will keep up till late. It is a family reunion, a sort of celebration and excursion combined; they all subscribe to it and take advantage of the good weather. They came by boat and bus and they are having breakfast. After that they go on with their drive, but at night they will all come back for a dance here in the hall. Yes, damn it, you'll see we shan't get a wink of sleep."

"Oh, it will be a pleasant change," said Tonio Kröger.

After that there was nothing more said for some time. The landlady arranged her red fingers on the cloth, the fish-dealer blew through his nostril, the Americans drank hot water and made long faces.

Then all at once a thing came to pass: *Hans Hansen and Ingeborg Holm walked through the room.*

Tonio Kröger, pleasantly fatigued after his swim and rapid walk, was leaning back in his chair and eating smoked salmon on toast; he sat facing the veranda and the ocean. All at once the door opened and the two entered hand-in-hand— calmly and unhurried. Ingeborg, blonde Inge, was dressed just as she used to be at Herr Knaak's dancing-class. The light flowered frock reached down to her ankles and it had a tulle fichu draped with a pointed opening that left her soft throat free. Her hat hung by its ribbons over her arm. She, perhaps, was a little more grown up than she used to be, and her wonderful plait of hair was wound round her head; but Hans Hansen was the same as ever. He wore his sailor over-coat with gilt buttons, and his wide blue sailor collar lay across his shoulders and back; the sailor cap with its short ribbons he was dangling carelessly in his hand. Ingeborg's narrow eyes were turned away; perhaps she felt shy before the company at table. But Hans Hansen turned his head straight towards them, and measured one after another defiantly with his steel-blue eyes; challengingly, with a sort of contempt. He even dropped Ingeborg's hand and swung his cap harder than ever, to show what manner of man he was. Thus the two, against the silent, blue-dyed sea, measured the length of the room and passed through the opposite door into the parlour.

This was at half past eleven in the morning. While the guests of the house were still at table the company in the veranda broke up and went away by the side door. No one else came into the dining-room. The guests could hear them laughing and joking as they got into the omnibuses, which rumbled away one by one.... "So they are coming back?" asked Tonio Kröger.

"That they are," said the fish-dealer. "More's the pity. They have ordered music, let me tell you—and my room is right above the dining-room."

"Oh, well, it's a pleasant change," repeated Tonio Kröger. Then he got up and went away.

That day he spent as he had the others, on the beach and in the wood, holding a book on his knee and blinking in the sun. He had but one thought; they were coming back to have a dance in the hall, the fish-dealer had promised they would; and he did nothing but be glad of this, with a sweet and timorous gladness such as he had not felt through all these long dead years. Once he happened, by some chance association, to think of his friend Adalbert, the novelist, the man who had known what he wanted and betaken himself to the café to get away from the spring. Tonio Kröger shrugged his shoulders at the thought of him.

Luncheon was served earlier than usual, also supper, which they ate in the parlour because the dining-room was being got ready for the ball, and the whole house flung in disorder for the occasion. It grew dark; Tonio Kröger sitting in his room heard on the road and in the house the sounds of approaching festivity. The picnickers were coming back; from Helsingör, by bicycle and car-riage, new guests were arriving; a fiddle and a nasal clarinet might be heard practising down in the dining-room. Everything promised a brilliant ball....

Now the little orchestra struck up a march; he could hear the notes, faint but lively. The dancing opened with a polonaise. Tonio Kröger sat for a while and listened. But when he heard the march-time go over into a waltz he got up and slipped noiselessly out of his room.

From his corridor it was possible to go by the side stairs to the side entrance of the hotel and thence to the veranda without passing through a room. He took this route, softly and stealthily as though on forbidden paths, feeling along through the dark, relentlessly drawn by this stupid jigging music, that now came up to him loud and clear.

The veranda was empty and dim, but the glass door stood open into the hall, where shone two large oil lamps, furnished with bright reflectors. Thither he stole on soft feet; and his skin prickled with the thievish pleasure of standing unseen in the dark and spying on the dancers there in the brightly lighted room. Quickly and eagerly he glanced about for the two whom he sought. . . .

Even though the ball was only half an hour old, the merriment seemed in full swing; however, the guests had come hither already warm and merry, after a whole day of carefree, happy companionship. By bending forward a little, Tonio Kröger could see into the parlour from where he was. Several old gentlemen sat there smoking, drinking, and playing cards; others were with their wives on the plush-upholstered chairs in the foreground watching the dance. They sat with their knees apart and their hands resting on them, puffing out their cheeks with a prosperous air; the mothers, with bonnets perched on their parted hair, with their hands folded over their stomachs and their heads on one side, gazed into the whirl of dancers. A platform had been erected on the long side of the hall, and on it the musicians were doing their utmost. There was even a trumpet, that blew with a certain caution, as though afraid of its own voice, and yet after all kept breaking and cracking. Couples were dipping and circling about, others walked arm-in-arm up and down the room. No one wore ballroom clothes; they were dressed as for an outing in the summertime: the men in countrified suits which were obviously their Sunday wear; the girls in light-coloured frocks with bunches of field-flowers in their bodices. Even a few children were there, dancing with each other in their own way, even after the music stopped. There was a long-legged man in a coat with a little swallow-tail, a provincial lion with an eye-glass and frizzed hair, a post-office clerk or some such thing; he was like a comic figure stepped bodily out of a Danish novel; and he seemed to be the leader and manager of the ball. He was everywhere at once, bustling, perspiring, officious, utterly absorbed; setting down his feet, in shiny, pointed, military half-boots, in a very artificial and involved manner, toes first; waving his arms to issue an order, clapping his hands for the music to begin; here, there, and everywhere, and glancing over his shoulder in pride at his great bow of office, the streamers of which fluttered grandly in his rear.

Yes, there they were, those two, who had gone by Tonio Kröger in the broad light of day; he saw them again—with a joyful start he recognized them almost at the same moment. Here was Hans Hansen by the door, quite close; his legs apart, a little bent over, he was eating with circumspection a large piece of sponge-cake, holding his hand cupwise under his chin to catch the crumbs. And there by the wall sat Ingeborg Holm, Inge the fair; the post-office clerk was just mincing up to her with an exaggerated bow and asking her to dance. He laid one hand on his back and gracefully shoved the other into his bosom. But she was shaking her head in token that she was a little out of breath and must rest awhile, whereat the post-office clerk sat down by her side.

Tonio Kröger looked at them both, these two for whom he had in time past suffered love—at Hans and Ingeborg. They were Hans and Ingeborg not so much by virtue of individual traits and similarity of costume as by similarity of race and type. This was the blond, fair-haired breed of the steel-blue eyes, which stood to him for the pure, the blithe, the untroubled in life; for a virginal aloofness that was at once both simple and full of pride. . . . He looked at them. Hans Hansen was standing there in his sailor suit, lively and well built as ever, broad in the shoulders and narrow in the hips; Ingeborg was laughing and tossing her head in a certain high-spirited way she had; she carried her hand, a schoolgirl hand, not at all slender, not at all particularly aristocratic, to the back of her head in a certain manner so that the thin sleeve fell away from her elbow—and suddenly such a pang of home-sickness shook his breast that involuntarily he drew farther back into the darkness lest someone might see his features twitch.

"Had I forgotten you?" he asked. "No, never. Not thee, Hans, not thee, Inge the fair! It was always you I worked for; when I heard applause I always stole a look to see if you were there. . . . Did you read *Don Carlos*, Hans Hansen, as you promised me at the garden gate? No, don't read it! I do not ask it any more. What have you to do with a king who weeps for loneliness? You must not cloud your clear eyes or make them dreamy and dim by peering into melancholy poetry. . . . To be like you! To begin again, to grow up like you, regular like you, simple and normal and cheerful, in conformity and understanding with God and man, beloved of the innocent and happy. To take you, Ingeborg Holm, to wife, and have a son like you, Hans Hansen—to live free from the curse of knowledge and the torment of creation, live and praise God in blessed mediocrity! Begin again? But it would do no good. It would turn out the same—everything would turn out the same as it did before. For some go of necessity astray, because for them there is no such thing as a right path."

The music ceased; there was a pause in which refreshments were handed round. The post-office assistant tripped about in person with a trayful of herring salad and served the ladies; but before Ingeborg Holm he even went down on one knee as he passed her the dish, and she blushed for pleasure.

But now those within began to be aware of a spectator behind the glass door; some of the flushed and pretty faces turned to measure him with hostile glances; but he stood his ground. Ingeborg and Hans looked at him too, at almost the same time, both with that utter indifference in their eyes that looks so like contempt. And he was conscious too of a gaze resting on him from a different quarter; turned his head and met with his own the eyes that had sought him out. A girl stood not far off, with a fine, pale little face—he had already noticed her. She had not danced much, she had few partners, and he had seen her sitting there against the wall, her lips closed in a bitter line. She was standing alone now too; her dress was a thin light stuff, like the others, but beneath the transparent frock her shoulders showed angular and poor, and the thin neck was thrust down so deep between those meagre shoulders that as she stood there motionless she might almost be thought a little deformed. She was holding her hands in their thin mitts across her flat breast, with the finger-tips touching; her head was drooped, yet she was looking up at Tonio Kröger with black swimming eyes. He turned away. . . .

Here, quite close to him, were Ingeborg and Hans. He had sat down beside her—she was perhaps his sister—and they ate and drank together surrounded by other rosy-cheeked folk; they chattered and made merry, called to each other in ringing voices, and laughed aloud. Why could he not go up and speak to them? Make some trivial remark to him or her, to which they might at least answer with a smile? It would make him happy—he longed to do it; he would go back more satisfied to his room if he might feel he had established a little contact with them. He thought out what he might say; but he had not the courage to say it. Yes, this too was just as it had been: they would not understand him, they would listen like strangers to anything he was able to say. For their speech was not his speech.

It seemed the dance was about to begin again. The leader developed a comprehensive activity. He dashed hither and thither, adjuring everybody to get partners; helped the waiters to push chairs and glasses out of the way, gave orders to the musicians, even took some awkward people by the shoulders and shoved them aside. . . . What was coming? They formed squares of four couples each. . . . A frightful memory brought the colour to Tonio Kröger's cheeks. They were forming for a quadrille.

The music struck up, the couples bowed and crossed over. The leader called off; he called off—Heaven save us—in French! And pronounced the nasals with great distinction. Ingeborg Holm danced close by, in the set nearest the glass door. She moved to and fro before him, forwards and back, pacing and turning; he caught a waft from her hair or the thin stuff of her frock, and it made him close his eyes with the old, familiar feeling, the fragrance and bitter-sweet enchantment he had faintly felt in all these days, that now filled him utterly with irresistible sweetness. And what was the feeling? Longing, tenderness? Envy? Self-contempt?. . . *Moulinet des dames!* "Did you laugh, Ingeborg the blonde, did you laugh at me when I disgraced myself by dancing the *moulinet?* And would you still laugh today even after I have become something like a famous man? Yes, that you would, and you would be right to laugh. Even if I in my own person had written the nine symphonies and *The World as Will and Idea* and painted the Last Judgment, you would still be eternally right to laugh. . . ." As he looked at her he thought of a line of verse once so familiar to him, now long forgotten: "I would sleep, but thou must dance." How well he knew it, that melancholy northern mood it evoked—its heavy inarticulateness. To sleep. . . . To long to be allowed to live the life of simple feeling, to rest sweetly and passively in feeling alone, without compulsion to act and achieve—and yet to be forced to dance, dance the cruel and perilous sword-dance of art; without even being allowed to forget the melancholy conflict within oneself; to be forced to dance, the while one loved. . . .

A sudden wild extravagance had come over the scene. The sets had broken up, the quadrille was being succeeded by a galop, and all the couples were leaping and gliding about. They flew past Tonio Kröger to a maddeningly quick tempo, crossing, advancing, retreating, with quick, breathless laughter. A couple came rushing and circling towards Tonio Kröger; the girl had a pale, refined face and lean, high shoulders. Suddenly, directly in front of him, they tripped and slipped and stumbled.... The pale girl fell, so hard and violently it almost looked dangerous; and her partner with her. He must have hurt himself badly, for he quite forgot her, and, half rising, began to rub his knee and grimace; while she, quite dazed, it seemed, still lay on the floor. Then Tonio Kröger came forward, took her gently by the arms, and lifted her up. She looked dazed, bewildered, wretched; then suddenly her delicate face flushed pink.

"*Tak, O, mange tak!*" she said, and gazed up at him with dark, swimming eyes.

"You should not dance any more, Fräulein," he said gently. Once more he looked round at *them,* at Ingeborg and Hans, and then he went out, left the ball and the veranda and returned to his own room.

He was exhausted with jealousy, worn out with the gaiety in which he had had no part. Just the same, just the same as it had always been. Always with burning cheeks he had stood in his dark corner and suffered for you, you blond, you living, you happy ones! And then quite simply gone away. Somebody *must* come now! Ingeborg *must* notice he had gone, must slip after him, lay a hand on his shoulder and say: "Come back and be happy. I love you!" But she came not at all. No, such things did not happen. Yes, all was as it had been, and he too was happy, just as he had been. For his heart was alive. But between that past and this present what had happened to make him become that which he now was? Icy desolation, solitude: mind, and art, forsooth!

He undressed, lay down, put out the light. Two names he whispered into his pillow, the few chaste northern syllables that meant for him his true and native way of love, of longing and happiness; that meant to him life and home, meant simple and heartfelt feeling. He looked back on the years that had passed. He thought of the dreamy adventures of the senses, nerves, and mind in which he had been involved; saw himself eaten up with intellect and introspection, ravaged and paralysed by insight, half worn out by the fevers and frosts of creation, helpless and in anguish of conscience between two extremes, flung to and fro between austerity and lust; *raffiné,* impoverished, exhausted by frigid and artificially heightened ecstasies; erring, forsaken, martyred, and ill—and sobbed with nostalgia and remorse.

Here in his room it was still and dark. But from below life's lulling, trivial waltz-rhythm came faintly to his ears.

Tonio Kröger sat up in the north, composing his promised letter to his friend Lisabeta Ivanovna.

"Dear Lisabeta down there in Arcady, whither I shall shortly return," he wrote: "Here is something like a letter, but it will probably disappoint you, for I mean to keep it rather general. Not that I have nothing to tell; for indeed, in my way, I have had experiences; for instance, in my native town they were even going to arrest me...but of that by word of mouth. Sometimes now I have days when I would rather state things in general terms than go on telling stories.

"You probably still remember, Lisabeta, that you called me a *bourgeois,* a *bourgeois manqué?* You called me that in an hour when, led on by other confessions I had previously let slip, I confessed to you my love of life, or what I call life. I ask myself if you were aware how very close you came to the truth, how much my love of 'life' is one and the same thing as my being a *bourgeois.* This journey of mine has given me much occasion to ponder the subject.

"My father, you know, had the temperament of the north: solid, reflective, puritanically correct, with a tendency to melancholia. My mother, of indeterminate foreign blood, was beautiful, sensuous, naïve, passionate, and careless at once, and, I think, irregular by instinct. The mixture was no doubt extraordinary and bore with it extraordinary dangers. The issue of it, a *bourgeois* who strayed off into art, a bohemian who feels nostalgic yearnings for respectability, an artist with a bad conscience. For surely it is my *bourgeois* conscience makes me see in the artist life, in all irregularity and all genius, something profoundly suspect, profoundly disreputable; that fills me with this lovelorn *faiblesse* for the simple and good, the comfortably normal, the average unendowed respectable human being.

"I stand between two worlds. I am at home in neither, and I suffer in consequence. You artists call me a *bourgeois,* and the *bourgeois* try to arrest me.... I don't know which makes me feel worse. The *bourgeois* are stupid; but you adorers of the beautiful, who call me phlegmatic and without aspirations, you ought to realize that there is a way of being an artist that goes so deep and is so much a matter of origins and destinies that no longing seems to it sweeter and more worth knowing than longing after the bliss of the commonplace.

"I admire those proud, cold beings who adventure upon the paths of great and dæmonic beauty and despise 'mankind'; but I do not envy them. For if anything is capable of making a poet of a literary man, it is my *bourgeois* love of the human, the living and usual. It is the source of all warmth, goodness, and humour; I even almost think it is itself that love of which it stands written that one may speak with the tongues of men and of angels and yet having it not is as sounding brass and tinkling cymbals.

"The work I have so far done is nothing or not much—as good as nothing. I will do better, Lisabeta—this is a promise. As I write, the sea whispers to me and I close my eyes. I am looking into a world unborn and formless, that needs to be ordered and shaped; I see into a whirl of shadows of human figures who beckon to me to weave spells to redeem them: tragic and laughable figures and some that are both together—and to these I am drawn. But my deepest and secretest love belongs to the blond and blue-eyed, the fair and living, the happy, lovely, and commonplace.

"Do not chide this love, Lisabeta; it is good and fruitful. There is longing in it, and gentle envy; a touch of contempt and no little innocent bliss."

The Seven That Were Hanged

(1908)

Leonid Andreyev

Anonymous Translation

Leonid Nicolaievich Andreyev (1871–1919) was born to poor, middle-class parents in the Orel region of central Russia. He studied law at the University of Petrograd and later transferred to the University of Moscow, receiving a law degree in 1897. After a single case, which he lost, he gave up the law and became a court reporter. He graduated from court-reporting to writing features for newspapers and thence to short stories, publishing his first collection in 1901. The Revolution of 1905 led him to write *The Governor,* a story of a governor who orders his troops to fire upon an orderly crowd marching in protest and then realizes that he has assured his own assassination. *The Seven That Were Hanged* (1908) was another response to those turbulent days and to the ruthless procedures adopted by the government to stop bombings and assassinations. The slow, regular court procedures had been replaced by twenty-four-hour trials with foregone verdicts. The story was immediately popular and went through many editions.

Andreyev moved to Finland in 1908. He was opposed to the Bolshevik Revolution of 1917, and *S.O.S.,* an attack on Bolshevism, was published in the year of his death. He died just before a scheduled trip to the United States to lecture against the new government in Russia. In addition to his novelettes and short stories, he wrote a number of plays: *Anathema* (1904), *The Life of Man* (1907), and *King Hunger* (1909).

For additional information, see Alexander Kaun, *Leonid Andreyev* (New York, 1924) and S. Persky, *Contemporary Russian Novelists* (New York, 1913), pp. 199–245. This anonymous translation is from *The Seven That Were Hanged and Other Stories,* by Leonid Andreyev. Copyright 1958 by Random House, Inc. Reprinted by permission of Random House, Inc.

I

"At One O'Clock in the Afternoon, Your Excellency!"

As the Minister was a very fat man, predisposed to apoplexy, and as it was necessary therefore to spare him every dangerous emotion, they took the minutest precautions in warning him that a serious attempt upon his life had been planned. When they saw that he received the news calmly, they gave him the details: the attempt was to be made the next day, at the moment when His Excellency was to leave the house to go to make his report. A few terrorists, armed with revolvers and bombs, whom a police spy had betrayed and who were now being watched by the police, were to meet near the steps at one o'clock in the afternoon, and await the Minister's exit. There the criminals would be arrested.

"Pardon me," interrupted the Minister in surprise. "How do they know that I am to go to present my report at one o'clock in the afternoon, when I learned it myself only two days ago?"

The commander of the body-guard made a vague gesture signifying ignorance.

"At one o'clock in the afternoon, Your Excellency!"

Astonished, and at the same time satisfied with the police who had managed the affair so well, the Minister shook his head; a disdainful smile appeared on his thick red lips; quickly he made all the necessary preparations to pass the night in another palace; in no way did he wish to embarrass the police. His wife and children also were removed from the dangerous premises.

As long as the lights gleamed in this new residence, and while his familiars bustled about him expressing their indignation, the Minister felt a sensation of agreeable excitement. It seemed to him that he had just received, or was about to receive, a great and unexpected reward. But the friends went away, and the lights were put out. The intermittent and fantastic glare of the arc-lights in the street fell upon the ceiling and the walls, penetrating through the high windows, symbolizing, as it were, the fragility of all bolts and walls, the vanity of all supervision. Then, in the silence and the solitude of a strange chamber, the dignitary was seized with an unspeakable terror.

He was afflicted with a kidney trouble. Every violent emotion caused his face, feet, and hands to swell, and made him appear heavier, more massive. Now, like a heap of bloated flesh that made the bed-springs bend, he suffered the anguish of the sick as he felt his face puff up and become, as it were, something foreign to his body. His thought recurred obstinately to the cruel fate that his enemies were preparing for him. He evoked one after the other all the horrible attempts of recent date, in which bombs had been thrown against persons as noble as himself and bearing even higher titles, tearing their bodies into a thousand shreds, hurling their brains against foul brick walls, and knocking their teeth from their jaws. And, at these recollections, it seemed to him that his diseased body was another man's body suffering from the fiery shock of the explosion. He pictured to himself his arms detached from his shoulders, his teeth broken, his brain crushed. His legs, stretched out in the bed, grew numb and motionless, the feet pointing upward, like those of a dead man. He breathed noisily, coughing occasionally, to avoid all resemblance to a corpse: he moved about, that he might hear the sound of the metallic springs, the rustling of the silk coverlet. And, to prove that he was really alive, he exclaimed in a loud and clear voice:

"Brave fellows! Brave fellows!"

These words of praise were for the police, the gendarmes, the soldiers, all those who protected his life and had prevented the assassination. But in vain did he stir about, lavish his praise, and smile at the discomfiture of the terrorists; he could not yet believe that he was saved. It seemed to him that the death evoked for him by the anarchists, and which existed in their thought, was already there and would remain there, refusing to go away until the assassins should be seized, deprived of their bombs, and lodged safely in prison. There it stood, in the corner yonder, declining to leave, and unable to leave, like an obedient soldier placed on guard by an unknown will.

"At one o'clock in the afternoon, Your Excellency!" This phrase came back to him continually, uttered in all tones, now joyously and ironically, now irritably, now obstinately and stupidly. One would have said that a hundred phonographs had been placed in the chamber, and were crying one after the other, with the idiotic persistence of machines:

"At one o'clock in the afternoon, Your Excellency!"

And this "one o'clock in the afternoon" of the next day, which so short a time before was in no way to be distinguished from other hours, had taken on a menacing importance; it had stepped out of the clock-dial, and was beginning to live a distinct life, stretching itself like an immense black curtain, to divide life into two parts. Before it and after it no other hour existed; it alone, presumptuous and obsessing, was entitled to a special life.

Grinding his teeth, the Minister raised himself in his bed to a sitting posture. It was positively impossible for him to sleep.

Pressing his bloated hands against his face, he pictured to himself with terrifying clearness how he would have risen on the morrow if he had been left in ignorance; he would have taken coffee, and dressed. And neither he, or the Swiss who would have helped him on with his fur coat, or the valet who would have served his coffee, would have understood the uselessness of breakfasting and dressing, when a few moments later everything would be annihilated by the explosion. . . . The Swiss opens the door. . . . And it is he, this good and thoughtful Swiss, with the blue eyes, and the open countenance, and the numerous military decorations—he it is who opens the terrible door with his own hands. . . .

"Ah!" suddenly exclaimed the Minister aloud; slowly he removed his hands from his face. Gazing far before him into the darkness with a fixed and attentive look, he stretched out his hand to turn on the light. Then he arose, and in his bare feet walked around the strange chamber so unfamiliar to him; finding another light, he turned that on also. The room became bright and agreeable; there was only the disordered bed and the fallen coverlet to indicate a terror that had not yet completely disappeared.

Clad in a night-shirt, his beard in a tangle, a look of irritation on his face, the Minister resembled those old people who are tormented by asthma and insomnia. One would have said that the death prepared for him by others had stripped him bare, had torn him from the luxury with which he was surrounded. Without dressing he threw himself into an arm-chair, his eyes wandered to the ceiling.

"Imbeciles!" he cried in a contemptuous tone of conviction.

"Imbeciles!" And he was speaking of the policemen whom but a few moments before he had called "brave fellows," and who, through excess of zeal, had told him all the details of the attack that had been planned.

"Evidently," he thought with lucidity, "I am afraid now because I have been warned and because I know. But, if I had been left in ignorance, I should have taken my coffee quietly. And then, evidently, this death. . . . But am I then so afraid of death? I have a kidney trouble; some day I must die of it, and yet I am not afraid, because I don't know when. And these imbeciles say to me: 'At one o'clock in the afternoon, Your Excellency!' They thought that I would be glad to know about it! . . . Instead of that, death has placed himself in the corner yonder, and does not go away! He does not go away, because I have that fixed idea! To die is not so terrible; the terrible thing is to know that one is going to die. It would be quite impossible for a man to live if he knew the hour and day of his death with absolute certainty. And yet these idiots warn me: 'At one o'clock in the afternoon, Your Excellency!' "

Recently he had been ill, and the doctors had told him that he was going to die and should make his final arrangements. He had refused to believe them; and, in fact, he did not die. Once, in his youth, it had happened to him to get beyond his depth; he had decided to put an end to his existence; he had loaded his revolver, written some letters, and even fixed the hour of his suicide; then, at the last moment, he had reconsidered. And always, at the supreme moment, something unexpected may happen; consequently no man can know when he will die.

"At one o'clock in the afternoon, Your Excellency!" these amiable idiots had said to him. They had informed him only because his death had been plotted; and yet he was terrified simply to learn the hour when it might have occurred. He admitted that they would kill him some day or other, but it would not be the next day. . . . it would not be the next day, and he could sleep quietly, like an immortal being. . . . The imbeciles! They did not know what a gulf they had dug in saying, with stupid amiability: "At one o'clock in the afternoon, Your Excellency!"

From the bitter anguish that shot through his heart, the Minister understood that he would know neither sleep, nor rest, nor joy, until this black and accursed hour, thus detached from the course of time, had passed. It was enough in itself to annihilate the light and enwrap the man in the opaque darkness of fear. Now that he was awake, the fear of death permeated his entire body, filtered into his bones, exuded from every pore.

Already the Minister had ceased to think of the assassins of the morrow: they had disappeared, forgotten in the multitude of inauspicious things that surrounded his life. He feared the unexpected, the inevitable: an attack of apoplexy, a laceration of the heart, the rupture of a little artery suddenly made powerless to resist the flow of blood and splitting like a glove on swollen hands.

His thick, short neck frightened him; he dared not look at his swollen fingers, full of some fatal fluid. And though, just before, in the darkness, he had been compelled to stir in order to avoid resemblance to a corpse, now, under this bright, cold, hostile, frightful light, it seemed to him horrible, impossible, to move even to light a cigarette or ring for a servant. His nerves were at a tension. With red and upturned eyes and burning head, he stifled.

Suddenly, in the darkness of the sleeping house, the electric bell just under the ceiling, among the dust and spiders' webs, became animate. Its little metallic tongue beat hurriedly against its sonorous edge. It stopped for a moment, and then began to ring again in a continuous and terrifying fashion.

People came running. Here and there lamps were lighted on the walls and chandeliers—too few of them for intense illumination, but enough to create shadows. On every hand appeared these shadows: they arose in the corners and stretched out upon the ceiling, fastening upon all projections and running along the walls. It was difficult to understand where all these taciturn, monstrous, and innumerable shadows could have kept themselves before—mute souls of mute things.

A thick and trembling voice said something indistinguishable. Then they telephoned to the doctor: the Minister was ill. His Excellency's wife was summoned also.

II

Sentenced to Be Hanged

The predictions of the police were realized. Four terrorists, three men and one woman, carrying bombs, revolvers, and infernal machines, were taken in front of the steps of the residence; a fifth accomplice was arrested at her dwelling, where the implements had been manufactured and the conspiracy planned. A large quantity of dynamite and many weapons were found there. All five were very young: the eldest of the men was twenty-eight, the younger of the women nineteen. They were tried in the fortress where they had been imprisoned after their arrest; they were tried quickly and secretly, as was the custom at that merciless epoch.

Before the court all five were calm, but serious and thoughtful; their contempt for the judges was so great that they did not care to emphasize their fearlessness by a useless smile or a pretence of gaiety. They were just tranquil enough to protect their souls and the deep gloom of their agony from the malevolent gaze of strangers. Some questions they refused to answer, some they answered simply, briefly, precisely, as if they were speaking, not to judges, but to statisticians desirous of completing tables of figures. Three of them, one woman and two men, gave their real names; two refused to disclose their identity, which remained unknown to the court. In everything that happened they manifested that distant and attenuated curiosity peculiar to people seriously ill or possessed by a single all-powerful idea. They cast swift glances, seized upon an interesting word in its flight, and went back to their thoughts, resuming them at the exact point where they had dropped them.

The accused placed nearest the judges had given his name as Sergey Golovin, a former officer, son of a retired colonel. He was very young, with broad shoulders, and so robust that neither the prison or the expectation of certain death had been able to dim the color of his cheeks or the expression of happy innocence in his blue eyes. Throughout the trial he twisted his thick blond beard, to which he had not yet become accustomed, and gazed steadily at the window, knitting his brows.

It was the latter part of winter, that period into which, among snowstorms and gray, cold days, the approaching spring projects sometimes, as a forerunner, a warm and luminous day, or even a single hour, so passionately young and sparkling that the sparrows in the street become mad with joy and men seem intoxicated. Now, through the upper window, still covered with the dust of the previous summer, a very odd and beautiful sky was to be seen; at the first glance it seemed a thick and milky gray; then, upon a second examination, it appeared to be covered with azure stains, of an ever-deepening blue, a blue pure and infinite. And because it did not strip itself suddenly, but modestly draped itself in the transparent veil of clouds, it became charming, like one's *fiancée*. Sergey Golovin looked at the sky, pulled at his mustache, winked now one and now the other of his eyes behind the long, heavy eyelashes, and reflected profoundly on nobody knows what. Once, even, his fingers moved rapidly, and an expression of naïve joy appeared upon his face; but he looked around him, and his joy was extinguished like a live coal upon which one steps. Almost instantaneously, almost without transition, the redness of his cheeks gave place to a corpse-like pallor; a fine hair painfully pulled out was pressed as in a vice between his bloodless finger-ends. But the joy of life and of the spring was still stronger. A few minutes later the young face resumed its naïve expression and sought again the sky of spring.

Toward the sky also looked an unknown young girl, surnamed Musya. She was younger than Golovin, but seemed his elder because of the severity, the gravity, of her proud and loyal eyes. The delicate neck and slender arms alone revealed that intangible something which is youth itself, and which sounded so distinctly in the pure harmonious voice that resembled a costly instrument in perfect tune. Musya was very pale, of that passionate pallor peculiar to those who burn with an inner, radiant, and powerful fire. She scarcely stirred; from time to time only, with a gesture that was hardly visible, she felt for a deep trace in the third finger of her right hand—the trace of a ring recently removed. She looked at the sky with calmness and indifference; she looked at it simply because everything in this commonplace and dirty hall was hostile to her and seemed to scrutinize her face. This bit of blue sky was the only pure and true thing upon which she could look with confidence.

The judges pitied Sergey Golovin and hated Musya.

Musya's neighbor, motionless also, with hands folded between his knees and somewhat of affectation in his pose, was an unknown surnamed Werner. If one can bolt a face as one bolts a heavy door, the unknown had bolted his as if it were a door of iron. He gazed steadily at the floor, and it was impossible to tell whether he was calm or deeply moved, whether he was thinking of something or listening to the testimony of the policemen. He was rather short of stature; his features were fine and noble. He gave the impression of an immense and calm force, of a cold and audacious valor. The very politeness with which he uttered his clear and curt replies seemed dangerous on his lips. On the backs of the other prisoners the customary cloak seemed a ridiculous costume; on him it was not even noticeable, so foreign was the garment to the man. Although Werner had been armed only with a poor revolver, while the others carried bombs and infernal machines, the judges looked upon him as the leader, and treated him with a certain respect, with the same brevity which he employed toward them.

In his neighbor, Vasily Kashirin, a frightful moral struggle was going on between the intolerable terror of death and the desperate desire to subdue this fear and conceal it from the judges. Ever since the prisoners had been taken to court in the morning, he had been stifling under the hurried beating of his heart. Drops of sweat appeared continually on his brow; his hands were moist and cold; his damp and icy shirt, sticking to his body, hindered his movements. By a super-human effort of the will he kept his fingers from trembling, and maintained the firmness and moderation of his voice and the tranquillity of his gaze. He saw nothing around him; the sound of the voice that he heard seemed to reach him through a fog, and it was in a fog also that he stiffened himself in a desperate effort to answer firmly and aloud. But, as soon as he had spoken, he forgot the questions, as well as his own phrases; the silent and terrible struggle began again. And upon his person death was so in evidence that the judges turned their eyes away from him. It was as difficult to determine his age as that of a rotting corpse. According to his papers he was only twenty-three. Once or twice Werner touched him gently on the knee, and each time he answered briefly:

"It's nothing."

His hardest moment was when he suddenly felt an irresistible desire to utter inarticulate cries, like a hunted beast. Then he gave Werner a slight push; without raising his eyes, the latter answered in a low voice:

"It's nothing, Vasya. It will soon be over!"

Consumed by anxiety, Tanya Kovalchuk, the fifth terrorist, sheltered her comrades with a maternal look. She was still very young; her cheeks seemed as highly colored as those of Sergey Golovin; and yet she seemed to be the mother of all the accused, so full of tender anxiety and infinite love were her looks, her smile, her fear. The progress of the trial did not interest her. She listened to her comrades simply to see if their voices trembled, if they were afraid, if they needed water.

But she could not look at Vasya; his anguish was too intense; she contented herself with cracking her plump fingers. At Musya and Werner she gazed with proud and respectful admiration, her face then wearing a grave and serious expression. As for Sergey Golovin, she continually tried to attract his attention by her smile.

"The dear comrade, he is looking at the sky. Look, look!" thought she, as she observed the direction of his eyes.

"And Vasya? My God! My God!...What can be done to comfort him? If I speak to him, perhaps it will make matters worse; suppose he should begin to weep?"

Like a peaceful pool reflecting every wandering cloud, her amiable and clear countenance showed all the feelings and all the thoughts, however fleeting, of her four comrades. She forgot that she was on trial too and would be hanged; her indifference to this was absolute. It was in her dwelling that the bombs and dynamite had been found; strange as it may seem, she had received the police with pistol shots, and had wounded one of them in the head.

The trial ended toward eight o'clock, just as the day was drawing to its close. Little by little in the eyes of Sergey and Musya, the blue sky disappeared; without reddening, without smiling, it grew dim gently as on a summer evening, becoming grayish, and suddenly cold and wintry. Golovin heaved a sigh, stretched himself, and raised his eyes toward the window, where the chilly darkness of the night was already making itself manifest; still pulling his beard, he began to examine the judges, the soldiers, and their weapons, exchanging a smile with Tanya Koval-chuk. As for Musya, when the sun had set completely, she did not lower her gaze to the ground, but directed it toward a corner where a spider's web was swaying gently in the invisible current of warm air from the stove; and thus she remained until the sentence had been pronounced.

After the verdict, the condemned said their farewells to their lawyers, avoiding their disconcerted, pitying, and confused looks; then they grouped themselves for a moment near the door, and exchanged short phrases.

"It's nothing, Vasya! All will soon be over!" said Werner.

"But there is nothing the matter with me, brother!" answered Kashirin, in a strong, quiet, and almost joyous voice. In fact, his face had taken on a slight color, no longer resembling that of a corpse.

"The devil take them! They have hanged us all just the same!" swore Golovin naïvely.

"It was to have been expected," answered Werner, without agitation.

"To-morrow the final judgment will be rendered, and they will put us all in the same cell," said Tanya, to console her comrades. "We shall remain together until the execution."

Silently, and with a resolute air, Musya started off.

III

"I Must Not Be Hanged"

A fortnight before the affair of the terrorists, in the same court, but before other judges, Ivan Yanson, a peasant, had been tried and sentenced to be hanged.

Ivan Yanson had been hired as a farm-hand by a well-to-do farmer, and was distinguished in no way from the other poor devils of his class. He was a native of Wesenberg, in Esthonia; for some years he had been advancing gradually toward the capital, passing from one farm to another. He had very little knowledge of Russian. As there were none of his countrymen living in the neighborhood, and as his employer was a Russian, named Lazaref, Yanson remained silent for almost two years. He said hardly a word to either man or beast. He led the horse to water and harnessed it without speaking to it, walking about it lazily, with short hesitating steps. When the horse began to run, Yanson did not say a word, but beat it cruelly with his enormous whip. Drink transformed his cold and wicked obstinacy into fury. The hissing of the lash and the regular and painful sound of his wooden shoes on the floor of the shed could be heard even at the farm-house. To punish him for torturing the horse the farmer at first beat Yanson, but, not succeeding in correcting him, he gave it up.

Once or twice a month Yanson got drunk, especially when he took his master to the station. His employer once on board the train, Yanson drove a short distance away, and waited until the train had started.

Then he returned to the station, and got drunk at the buffet. He came back to the farm on the gallop, a distance of seven miles, beating the unfortunate beast unmercifully, giving it its head, and singing and shouting incomprehensible phrases in Esthonian. Sometimes silent, with set teeth, impelled by a whirlwind of indescribable fury, suffering, and enthusiasm, he was like a blind man in his mad career; he did not see the passers-by, he did not insult them, uphill and down he maintained his furious gait.

His master would have discharged him, but Yanson did not demand high wages, and his comrades were no better than he.

One day he received a letter written in Esthonian; but, as he did not know how to read or write, and as no one about him knew this language, Yanson threw it into the muck-heap with savage indifference, as if he did not understand that it brought him news from his native country. Probably needing a woman, he tried also to pay court to the girl employed on the farm. She repulsed him, for he was short and puny, and covered with hideous freckles; after that, he let her alone.

But, though he spoke little, Yanson listened continually. He listened to the desolate snow-covered fields, containing hillocks of frozen manure that resembled a series of little tombs heaped up by the snow; he listened to the bluish and limpid distance, the sonorous telegraph-poles. He alone knew what the fields and telegraph-poles were saying. He listened also to the conversations of men, the stories of murder, pillage, fire.

One night, in the village, the little church-bell began to ring in a feeble and lamentable way; flames appeared. Malefactors from nobody knew where were pillaging the neighboring farm. They killed the owner and his wife, and set fire to the house. This caused a feeling of anxiety on the farm where Yanson lived: day and night the dogs were loose; the master kept a gun within reach of his bed. He wished also to give an old weapon to Yanson, but the latter, after examining it, shook his head and refused it. The farmer did not understand that Yanson had more confidence in the efficacy of his Finnish knife than in this rusty old machine.

"It would kill me myself!" said he.

"You are only an imbecile, Ivan!"

And one winter evening, when the other farm-hand had gone to the station, this same Ivan Yanson, who was afraid of a gun, committed robbery and murder, and made an attempt at rape. He did it with an astonishing simplicity. After shutting the servant in the kitchen, lazily, like a man almost dead with sleep, he approached his master from behind, and stabbed him several times in the back. The master fell unconscious; his wife began to cry and to run about the chamber. Showing his teeth, and holding his knife in his hand, Yanson began to ransack trunks and drawers. He found the money; then, as if he had just seen the master's wife for the first time, he threw himself upon her to rape her, without the slightest premeditation. But he happened to drop his knife; and, as the woman was the stronger, she not only resisted Yanson, but half strangled him. At this moment the farmer recovered his senses, and the servant broke in the kitchen-door and came in. Yanson fled. They took him an hour later, squatting in the corner of the shed, and scratching matches which continually went out. He was trying to set fire to the farm.

A few days later the farmer died. Yanson was tried and sentenced to death. In the court one would have said that he did not understand what was going on; he viewed the large imposing hall without curiosity, and explored his nose with a shrunken finger that nothing disgusted. Only those who had seen him at church on Sunday could have guessed that he had done something in the way of making a toilet; he wore a knitted cravat of dirty red; in spots his hair was smooth and dark; in others it consisted of light thin locks, like wisps of straw on an unculti-vated and devastated field.

When the sentence of death by hanging was pronounced, Yanson suddenly showed emotion. He turned scarlet, and began to untie and tie his cravat, as if it were choking him. Then he waved his arms without knowing why, and declared to the presiding judge, who had read the sentence:

"She has said that I must be hanged."

" 'She'? Who?" asked the presiding judge, in a deep bass voice.

Yanson pointed at the presiding judge with his finger, and, looking at him furtively, answered angrily:

"You!"

"Well?"

Again Yanson turned his eyes toward one of the judges, in whom he divined a friend, and repeated:

"She has said that I must be hanged. I must not be hanged."

"Take away the accused."

But Yanson still had time to repeat, in a grave tone of conviction:

"I must not be hanged."

And with his outstretched finger and irritated face, to which he tried in vain to give an air of gravity, he seemed so stupid that the guard, in violation of orders, said to him in an undertone as he led him away:

"Well, you are a famous imbecile, you are!"

"I must not be hanged!" repeated Yanson, obstinately.

They shut him up again in the cell in which he had passed a month, and to which he had become accustomed, as he had become accustomed to everything: to blows, to brandy, to the desolate and snow-covered country sown with rounded hillocks resembling tombs. It even gave him pleasure to see his bed again, and his grated window, and to eat what they gave him; he had taken nothing since morning. The disagreeable thing was what had happened in court, about which he knew not what to think. He had no idea at all of what death by hanging was like.

The guard said to him, in a tone of remonstrance:

"Well, brother, there you are, hanged!"

"And when will they hang me?" asked Yanson, in a tone of incredulity. The guard reflected.

"Ah! wait, brother; you must have companions; they do not disturb themselves for a single individual, and especially for a little fellow like you."

"Then, when?" insisted Yanson.

He was not offended that they did not want to take the trouble to hang him all alone; he did not believe in this excuse, and thought they simply wanted to put off the execution, and then pardon him.

"When? When?" resumed the guard. "It is not a question of hanging a dog, which one takes behind a shed and dispatches with a single blow! Is that what you would like, imbecile?"

"Why, no, I would not like it!" said Yanson suddenly, with a joyous grimace. "'Twas she that said I must be hanged, but I, I do not want to be hanged!"

And, for the first time in his life perhaps, he began to laugh—a grinning and stupid laugh, but terribly gay. He seemed like a goose beginning to quack. The guard looked at Yanson in astonishment, and then knitted his brows: this stupid gaiety on the part of a man who was to be executed insulted the prison, the gallows itself, and made them ridiculous. And suddenly it seemed to the old guard, who had passed all his life in prison and considered the laws of the gaol as those of nature, that the prison and all of life were a sort of mad-house in which he, the guard, was the chief madman.

"The devil take you!" said he, spitting on the ground. "Why do you show your teeth? This is no wine-shop!"

"And I, I do not want to be hanged! Ha! ha! ha!"

Yanson laughed always.

"Satan!" replied the guard, crossing himself.

All the evening Yanson was calm, and even joyous. He repeated the phrase that he had uttered: "I must not be hanged," and so convincing, so irrefutable was it that he had no occasion for anxiety. He had long since forgotten his crime; sometimes he simply regretted that he had not succeeded in raping the woman. Soon he thought no more about the matter.

Every morning Yanson asked when he would be hanged, and every morning the guard answered him angrily:

"You have time enough." And he went out quickly, before Yanson began to laugh.

Thanks to this invariable exchange of words, Yanson persuaded himself that the execution would never take place; for whole days he lay upon his bed, dreaming vaguely of the desolate and snow-covered fields, of the buffet at the railway station, and also of things farther away and more luminous. He was well fed in prison, he took on flesh.

"She would love me now," he said to himself, thinking of his master's wife. "Now I am as big as her husband."

He had only one desire—to drink brandy and course madly over the roads with his horse at full gallop.

When the terrorists were arrested, the whole prison learned of it. One day, when Yanson put his customary question, the guard answered him abruptly, in an irritated voice:

"It will be soon. In a week, I think."

Yanson turned pale; the gaze of his glassy eyes became so thick that he seemed as if asleep.

"You are joking?" he asked.

"Formerly you could not await the time, to-day you say that I am joking. No jokes are tolerated here. It is you who like jokes, but we do not tolerate them," replied the guard with dignity; then he went out.

When evening came, Yanson had grown thin. His skin, which had become smooth again for a few days, was contracted into a thousand little wrinkles. He took no notice of anything; his movements were made slowly, as if every toss of the head, every gesture of the arm, every step, were a difficult undertaking, that must first be deeply studied. During the night Yanson lay on his camp-bed, but his eyes did not close; they remained open until morning.

"Ah!" exclaimed the guard, on seeing him the next day.

With the satisfaction of the *savant* who has made a new and a successful experiment, he examined the condemned man attentively and without haste; now everything was proceeding in the usual fashion. Satan was covered with shame, the sanctity of the prison and of the gallows was re-established. Indulgent, and even full of sincere pity, the old man asked:

"Do you want to see someone?"

"Why?"

"To say good-bye, of course...to your mother, for instance, or to your brother."

"I must not be hanged," said Yanson in a low voice, casting a glance sidewise at the gaoler. "I do not want to be hanged."

The guard looked at him, without saying a word.

Yanson was a little calmer in the evening. The day was so ordinary, the cloudy winter sky shone in so usual a fashion, so familiar was the sound of steps and conversations in the corridor, that he ceased to believe in the execution. Formerly the night had been to him simply the moment of darkness, the time for sleep. But now he was conscious of its mysterious and menacing essence. To disbelieve in death one must see and hear about one the customary course of life: steps, voices, light. And now everything seemed extraordinary to him; this silence, these shades, that seemed to be already the shades of death; already he felt the approach of inevitable death; in bewilderment he climbed the first steps of the gibbet.

The day, the night, brought him alternations of hope and fear; and so things went until the evening when he felt, or understood, that the inevitable death would come three days later, at sunrise.

He had never thought of death; for him it had no shape. But now he felt plainly that it had entered his cell, and was groping about in search of him. To escape it he began to run.

The room was so small that the corners seemed to push him back toward the centre. He could not hide himself anywhere. Several times he struck the walls with his body; once he hurled himself against the door. He staggered and fell, with his face upon the ground; he felt the grasp of death upon him. Glued to the floor, his face touching the dirty black asphalt, Yanson screamed with terror until help came. When they had lifted him up, seated him on his bed, and sprinkled him with cold water, he did not dare to open both eyes. He half opened one, perceived an empty and luminous corner of his cell, and began again to scream.

But the cold water had its effect. The guard, moreover, always the same old man, slapped Yanson several times on the head in a fatherly fashion. This sensation of life drove out the thought of death. Yanson slept deeply the rest of the night. He lay on his back, with mouth open, snoring loud and long. Between his half-closed eyelids appeared a whitish, flat, and dead eye, without a pupil.

Then day, night, voices, steps, the cabbage soup, everything became for him one continuous horror that plunged him into a state of wild astonishment. His weak mind could not reconcile the monstrous contradiction between, on the one hand, the bright light and the odor of the cabbage, and, on the other, the fact that two days later he must die. He thought of nothing; he did not even count the hours; he was simply the prey of a dumb terror in presence of this contradiction that bewildered his brain: today life, tomorrow death. He ate nothing, he slept no more; he sat timidly all night long on a stool, with his legs crossed under him, or else he walked up and down his cell with furtive steps. He appeared to be in a state of open-mouthed astonishment; before taking the most common-place article into his hands he would examine it suspiciously.

The gaolers ceased to pay attention to him. His was the ordinary condition of the condemned man, resembling, according to his gaoler who had not experienced it himself, that of an ox felled by a club.

"He is stunned; now he will feel nothing more until the moment of death," said the guard, examining him with his experienced eye. "Ivan, do you hear? Ho there, Ivan!"

"I must not be hanged!" answered Yanson, in a colorless voice; his lower jaw had dropped.

"If you had not killed, they would not hang you," reproachfully said the chief gaoler, a highly important young man, wearing a decoration. "To steal, you have killed and you do not want to be hanged!"

"I do not want to be hanged!" replied Yanson.

"Well, you don't have to want to; that's your affair. But, instead of talking nonsense, you would do better to dispose of your possessions. You surely must have something."

"He has nothing at all! A shirt and a pair of plantaloons! And a fur cap!"

Thus time passed until Thursday. And Thursday, at midnight, a large number of people entered Yanson's cell; a man with cloth epaulets said to him:

"Get ready! it is time to start."

Always with the same slowness and the same indolence Yanson dressed himself in all that he possessed, and tied his dirty shawl around his neck. While watching him dress, the man with the epaulets, who was smoking a cigarette, said to one of the assistants:

"How warm it is today! It is spring!"

Yanson's eyes closed; he was in a complete drowse. The guard shouted:

"Come, come! Make haste! You are going to sleep!"

Suddenly Yanson ceased to move.

"I must not be hanged," said he, with indolence.

He began to walk submissively, shrugging his shoulders. In the courtyard the moist spring air had a sudden effect upon him; his nose began to run; it was thawing; close by, drops of water were falling with a joyous sound. While the gendarmes were getting into the unlighted vehicle, bending over and rattling their swords, Yanson lazily passed his finger under his running nose, or arranged his badly tied shawl.

IV

We of Orel

The court that had tried Yanson sentenced to death at the same session Michael Goloubetz, known as Michka the Tzigane, a peasant of the department of Orel, district of Eletz. The last crime of which they accused him, with evidence in support of the charge, was robbery, followed by the assassination of three persons. As for his past, it was unknown. There were vague indications to warrant the belief that the Tzigane had taken part in a whole series of other murders. With absolute sincerity and frankness he termed himself a brigand, and overwhelmed with his irony those who, to follow the fashion, pompously styled themselves "expropriators"; his last crime he described willingly in all its details. But, at the slightest reference to the past, he answered:

"Go ask the wind that blows over the fields!"

And, if they persisted in questioning him, the Tzigane assumed a dignified and serious air.

"We of Orel are all hot-heads, the fathers of all the robbers of the world," said he, in a sedate and judicial tone.

They had nicknamed him Tzigane because of his physiognomy and his thieving habits. He was thin and strangely dark; yellow spots outlined themselves upon his cheekbones which were as prominent as those of a Tartar. He had a way of rolling the whites of his eyes, that reminded one of a horse. His gaze was quick and keen, full of curiosity, terrifying. The things over which his swift glance passed seemed to lose something or other, and to become transformed by surrendering to him part of themselves. One hesitated to take a cigarette that he had looked at, as if it had already been in his mouth. His extraordinarily mobile nature made him seem now to coil and concentrate himself like a twisted handkerchief, now to scatter himself like a sheaf of sparks. He drank water almost by the pailful, like a horse.

When the judges questioned him, he raised his head quickly, and answered without hesitation, even with satisfaction:

"It is true!"

Sometimes, to lend emphasis, he rolled his "r's" vigorously.

Suddenly he jumped to his feet, and said to the presiding judge:

"Permit me to whistle?"

"Why?" exclaimed the judge, in astonishment.

"The witnesses say that I gave the signal to my comrades; I will show you how I did it. It is very interesting."

A little disconcerted, the judge granted the desired permission. The Tzigane quickly placed four fingers in his mouth, two of each hand; he rolled his eyes furiously. And the inanimate air of the court-room was rent by a truly savage whistle. There was everything in the piercing sound, partly human, partly animal; the mortal anguish of the victim, and the savage joy of the assassin; a threat, a call, and the tragic solitude, the darkness, of a rainy autumn night.

The judge shook his hand; with docility the Tzigane stopped. Like an artist who has just played a difficult air with assured success, he sat down, wiped his wet fingers on his cloak, and looked at the spectators with a satisfied air.

"What a brigand!" exclaimed one of the judges, rubbing his ear. But another, who had Tartar eyes, like the Tzigane's, was looking dreamily into the distance, over the brigand's head; he smiled, and replied:

"It was really interesting."

Without remorse, the judges sentenced the Tzigane to death.

"It is just!" said the Tzigane, when the sentence had been pronounced.

And, turning to a soldier of the guard, he added with an air of bravado:

"Well, let us be off, imbecile! And keep a good hold of your gun, lest I snatch it from you!"

The soldier looked at him seriously and timidly; he exchanged a glance with his comrade, and tested his weapon to see if it was in working order. The other did the same. And all the way to the prison it seemed to the soldiers that they did not walk, but flew; they were so absorbed by the condemned man that they were unconscious of the route, of the weather, and of themselves.

Like Yanson, Michka the Tzigane remained seventeen days in prison before being executed. And the seventeen days passed as rapidly as a single day, filled with a single thought, that of flight, of liberty, of life. The turbulent and incoercible spirit of the Tzigane, stifled by the walls, the gratings, and the opaque window through which nothing could be seen, employed all its force in setting Michka's brain on fire. As in a vapor of intoxication, bright but incomplete images whirled, clashed, and mingled in his head; they passed with a blinding and irresistible rapidity, and they all tended to the same end: flight, liberty, life. For entire hours, with nostrils distended like those of a horse, the Tzigane sniffed the air; it seemed to him that he inhaled the odor of hemp and flame, of dense smoke. Or else he turned in his cell like a top, examining the walls, feeling them with his fingers, measuring them, piercing the ceiling with his gaze, sawing the bars in his mind. His agitation was a source of torture to the soldier who watched him through the window; several times he threatened to fire on him.

During the night the Tzigane slept deeply, almost without stirring, in an invariable but living immobility, like a temporarily inactive spring. But, as soon as he jumped to his feet, he began again to plan, to grope, to study. His hands were always dry and hot. Sometimes his heart suddenly congealed, as if they had placed in his breast a new block of ice which did not melt, and which caused a continuous shiver to run over his skin. At these times his naturally dark complexion became darker still, taking on the blue-black shade of bronze. Then a queer tic seized him; he constantly licked his lips, as if he had eaten a dish that was much too sweet; then, with a hiss, and with set teeth, he spat upon the ground the saliva that had thus accumulated in his mouth. He left his words unfinished; his thoughts ran so fast that his tongue could no longer keep up with them.

One day the chief of the guards entered his cell, accompanied by a soldier. He squinted at the spittle with which the ground was spattered, and said rudely:

"See how he has dirtied his cell!"

The Tzigane replied quickly:

"And you, you ugly mug, you have soiled the whole earth, and I haven't said a word to you. Why do you annoy me?"

With the same rudeness the chief of the guards offered him the post of hangman. The Tzigane showed his teeth, and began to laugh:

"So they can find none! That's not bad! Go on then hanging people! Ah! Ah! There are necks and ropes, and nobody to do the hanging! My God, that's not bad."

"They will give your life as a reward!"

"I should say so: I could hardly play the hangman after I am dead!"

"Well, what do you say, yes or no?"

"And how do they hang here? They probably choke people secretly."

"No, they hang them to music!" retorted the chief.

"Imbecile! Of course there must be music...like this...."

And he began to sing a captivating air.

"You have gone completely mad, my friend!" said the guard. "Come, speak seriously, what is your decision?"

The Tzigane showed his teeth.

"Are you in a hurry? Come back later, and I will tell you!"

And to the chaos of unfinished images which overwhelmed the Tzigane was added a new idea: how agreeable it would be to be the headsman! He clearly pictured to himself the square black with people, and the scaffold on which he, the Tzigane, walked back and forth, in a red shirt, with axe in hand. The sun illuminates the heads, plays gaily on the axe blade; everything is so joyous, so sumptuous, that even he whose head is to be cut off smiles. Behind the crowd are to be seen the carts and the noses of the horses; the peasants have come to town for the occasion. Still farther away fields. The Tzigane licked his lips, and spat upon the ground. Suddenly it seemed to him that his fur cap had just been pulled down over his mouth; everything became dark; he gasped for breath; and his heart changed into a block of ice, while little shivers ran through his body.

Twice more the chief came back; the Tzigane, showing his teeth again, answered:

"What a hurry you are in! Come back another time!"

Finally, one day, the gaoler cried to him, as he was passing by the window:

"You have lost your chance, my ill-favoured raven. They have found another."

"The devil take you! Go, be the hangman yourself!" replied the Tzigane. And he ceased to dream of the splendors of his trade.

But toward the end, the nearer drew the day of execution, the more intolerable became the impetousity of the torn images. The Tzigane would have liked to wait, to halt, but the furious torrent carried him on, giving him no chance to get a hold on anything; for everything was in a whirl. And his sleep became agitated; he had new and shapeless visions, as badly squared as painted blocks, and even more impetuous than his thoughts had been. It was no longer a torrent, but a continual fall from an infinite height, a whirling flight through the whole world of colors. Formerly the Tzigane had worn only a mustache tolerably well cared for; in prison he had been obliged to grow his beard, which was short, black, and stubbly, giving him a crazy look. There were moments, in fact, when the Tzigane lost his mind. He turned about in his cell all unconscious of his movements, continuing to feel for the rough and uneven walls. And he always drank great quantities of water, like a horse.

One evening, when they were lighting the lamps, the Tzigane dropped on all fours in the middle of his cell, and began to howl like a wolf. He did this very seriously, as if performing an indispensable and important act. He filled his lungs with air, and then expelled it slowly in a prolonged and trembling howl. With knit brows, he listened to himself attentively. The very trembling of the voice seemed a little affected; he did not shout indistinctly; he made each note in this wild beast's cry sound separately, full of unspeakable suffering and terror.

Suddenly he stopped, and remained silent for a few minutes, without getting up. He began to whisper, as if speaking to the ground:

"Dear friends, good friends. . .dear friends. . .good friends. . .have pit. . .friends! My friends!"

He said a word, and listened to it.

He jumped to his feet, and for a whole hour poured forth a steady stream of the worst curses.

"Go to the devil, you scoundrels!" he screamed, rolling his bloodshot eyes. "If I must be hanged, hang me, instead of . . . Ah, you blackguards!"

The soldier on guard, as white as chalk, wept with anguish and fear; he pounded the door with the muzzle of his gun, and cried in a lamentable voice:

"I will shoot you! By God, do you hear? I will shoot you!"

But he did not dare to fire; they never fire on prisoners sentenced to death, except in case of revolt. And the Tzigane ground his teeth, swore, and spat. His brain, placed on the narrow frontier that separates life from death, crumbled like a lump of dried clay.

When they came, during the night, to take him to the gallows, he regained a little of his animation. His cheeks took on some color; in his eyes the usual strategy, a little savage, sparkled again, and he asked of one of the functionaries:

"Who will hang us? The new one? Is he accustomed to it yet?"

"You needn't disturb yourself about that," answered the personage thus appealed to.

"What? Not disturb myself! It is not Your Highness that is going to be hanged, but I! At least don't spare the soap on the slip-noose; the State pays for it!"

"I beg you to hold your tongue!"

"This fellow, you see, consumes all the soap in the prison; see how his face shines," continued the Tzigane, pointing to the chief of the guards.

"Silence!"

"Don't spare the soap!"

Suddenly he began to laugh, and his legs became numb. Yet, when he arrived in the court-yard, he could still cry:

"Say, there! you fellows yonder, come forward with my carriage!"

V

"Kiss Him and Be Silent"

The verdict against the five terrorists was pronounced in its final form and confirmed the same day. The condemned were not notified of the day of execution. But they foresaw that they would be hanged, according to custom, the same night, or, at the latest, the night following. When they were offered the opportunity of seeing their families the next day, they understood that the execution was fixed for Friday at daybreak.

Tanya Kovalchuk had no near relatives. She knew only of some distant relatives living in Little Russia, who probably knew nothing of the trial or the verdict. Musya and Werner, not having revealed their identity, did not insist on seeing any of their people. Only Sergey Golovin and Vasily Kashirin were to see their families. The thought of this approaching interview was frightful to both of them, but they could not make up their minds to refuse a final conversation, a last kiss.

Sergey Golovin thought sadly of this visit. He was fond of his father and mother; he had seen them very recently, and he was filled with terror at the thought of what was going to happen. The hanging itself, in all its monstrosity, in its disconcerting madness, outlined itself more readily in his imagination than these few short, incomprehensible minutes, that seemed apart from time, apart from life. What to do? What to say? The most simple and customary gestures—to shake hands, embrace, and say "How do you do, father?"—seemed to him frightful in their monstrous, inhuman, insane insignificance.

After the verdict they did not put the condemned in the same cell, as Tanya expected them to do. All the morning, up to the time when he received his parents, Sergey Golovin walked back and forth in his cell, twisting his short beard, his features pitiably contracted. Sometimes he stopped suddenly, filled his lungs with air, and puffed like a swimmer who has remained too long under water. But, as he was in good health, and as his young life was solidly implanted

within him, even in these minutes of atrocious suffering, the blood coursed under
his skin, coloring his cheeks; his blue eyes preserved their usual brilliancy.

Everything went off better than Sergey expected; his father, Nicolas Sergiévitch
Golovin, a retired colonel, was the first to enter the room where the visitors were
received. Everything about him was white and of the same whiteness: face, hair,
beard, hands. His old and well-brushed garment smelt of benzine; his epaulets
seemed new. He entered with a firm and measured step, straightening himself
up. Extending his dry, white hand, he said aloud:

"How do you do, Sergey?"

Behind him came the mother, with short steps; she wore a strange smile. But
she too shook hands with her son, and repeated aloud:

"How do you do, my little Sergey?"

She kissed him and sat down without saying a word. She did not throw herself
upon her son, she did not begin to weep or cry, as Sergey expected her to do.
She kissed him and sat down without speaking. With a trembling hand she even
smoothed the wrinkles in her black silk gown.

Sergey did not know that the colonel had spent the entire previous night in
rehearsing this interview. "We must lighten the last moments of our son's life, and
not make them more painful for him," the colonel had decided; and he had
carefully weighed each phrase, each gesture, of the morrow's visit. But sometimes,
in the course of the rehearsal, he became confused, he forgot what he had prepared himself to say, and he wept bitterly, sunk in the corner of his sofa. The
next morning he had explained to his wife what she was to do.

"Above all, kiss him and be silent," he repeated. "You will be able to speak
later, a little later; but, after kissing him, be silent. Do not speak immediately
after kissing him, do you understand? Otherwise you will say what you should
not."

"I understand, Nicolas Sergiévitch!" answered the mother, with tears.

"And do not weep! May God keep you from that! Do not weep! You will
kill him if you weep, mother!"

"And why do you weep yourself?"

"Why should one not weep here with the rest of you? You must not weep,
do you hear?"

"All right, Nicolas Sergiévitch."

They got into a cab and started off, silent, bent, old; they were plunged in
their thoughts amid the gay roar of the city; it was the carnival season, and the
streets were filled with a noisy crowd.

They sat down. The colonel assumed a suitable attitude, his right hand thrust
in the front of his frock-coat. Sergey remained seated a moment; his look met
his mother's wrinkled face; he rose suddenly.

"Sit down, my little Sergey!" begged the mother.

"Sit down, Sergey!" repeated the father.

They kept silence. The mother wore a strange smile.

"How many moves we have made in your behalf, Sergey! Your father. . ."

"It was useless, my little mother!"

The colonel said, firmly:

"We were in duty bound to do it that you might not think that your parents had abandoned you."

Again they became silent. They were afraid to utter a syllable, as if each word of the language had lost its proper meaning and now meant but one thing: death. Sergey looked at the neat little frock-coat smelling of benzine, and thought: "He has no orderly now; then he must have cleaned his coat himself. How is it that I have never seen him clean his coat? Probably he does it in the morning." Suddenly he asked:

"And my sister? Is she well?"

"Ninotchka knows nothing!" answered the mother, quickly.

But the colonel sternly interrupted her:

"What is the use of lying? She has read the newspaper . . . let Sergey know that . . . all . . . his own . . . have thought . . . and . . ."

Unable to continue, he stopped. Suddenly the mother's face contracted, her features became confused and wild. Her colorless eyes were madly distended; more and more she panted for breath.

"Se . . . Ser . . . Ser . . . Ser . . ." she repeated, without moving her lips; "Ser . . ."

"My little mother!"

The colonel took a step; trembling all over, without knowing how frightful he was in his corpse-like pallor, in his desperate and forced firmness, he said to his wife:

"Be silent! Do not torture him! Do not torture him! Do not torture him! He must die! Do not torture him!"

Frightened, she was silent already, and he continued to repeat, with his trembling hands pressed against his breast:

"Do not torture him!"

Then he took a step backward, and again thrust his hand into the front of his frock-coat; wearing an expression of forced calmness, he asked aloud, with pallid lips:

"When?"

"To-morrow morning," answered Sergey.

The mother looked at the ground, biting her lips, as if she heard nothing. And she seemed to continue to bite her lips as she let fall these simple words:

"Ninotchka told me to kiss you, my little Sergey!"

"Kiss her for me!" said the condemned man.

"Good! The Chvostofs send their salutations. . . ."

"Who are they? Ah! yes. . . ."

The colonel interrupted him:

"Well, we must start. Rise, mother, it is necessary!"

The two men lifted the swooning woman.

"Bid him farewell!" ordered the colonel. "Give him your blessing!"

She did everything that she was told. But, while giving her son a short kiss and making on his person the sign of the cross, she shook her head and repeated distractedly:

"No, it is not that! No, it is not that!"

"Adieu, Sergey!" said the father. They shook hands, and exchanged a short, but earnest, kiss.

"You. . ." began Sergey.

"Well?" asked the father, spasmodically.

"No, not like that. No, no! What shall I say?" repeated the mother, shaking her head.

She had sat down again, and was tottering.

"You. . ." resumed Sergey. Suddenly his face took on a lamentable expression, and he grimaced like a child, tears filling his eyes. Through their sparkling facets he saw beside him the pale face of his father, who was weeping also.

"Father, you are a strong man!"

"What do you say? What do you say?" said the bewildered colonel. Suddenly, as if completely broken, he fell, with his head on his son's shoulder. And the two covered each other with ardent kisses, the father receiving them on his light hair, the prisoner on his cloak.

"And I?" asked suddenly a hoarse voice.

They looked: the mother was on her feet again, and, with her head thrown back, was watching them wrathfully, almost hatefully.

"What is the matter with you, mother?" cried the colonel.

"And I?" she repeated, shaking her head with an insane energy. "You embrace each other, and I? You are men, are you not? And I? and I?. . ."

"Mother!" and Sergey threw himself into her arms.

The last words of the colonel were:

"My blessing for your death, Sergey! Die with courage, like an officer!"

And they went away. . . . On returning to his cell Sergey lay upon his camp-bed, with face turned toward the wall that the soldiers might not see him, and wept a long time.

•   •   •   •   •

Vasily Kashirin's mother came alone to visit him. The father, a rich merchant, had refused to accompany her. When the old woman entered, Vasily was walking in his cell. In spite of the heat, he was trembling with cold. The conversation was short and painful.

"You ought not to have come, mother. Why should we two torment each other?"

"Why all this, Vasya? Why have you done this, my son? God! God!"

The old woman began to weep, drying her tears with her black silk neckerchief.

Accustomed as they were, his brothers and he, to treat their mother roughly, she being a simple woman who did not understand them, he stopped, and, in the midst of his shivering, said to her, harshly:

"That's it, I knew how it would be. You understand nothing, mama, nothing!"

"Very well, my son. What is the matter with you? Are you cold?"

"I am cold," answered Vasily, and he began to walk again, looking sidewise now and then at the old woman with the same air of irritation.

"You are cold, my son. . ."

"Ah! You speak of cold, but soon. . ." He made a gesture of desperation.

Again the mother began to sob.

"I said to your father: 'Go to see him, he is your son your flesh; give him a last farewell.' He would not."

"The devil take him! He is not a father. All his life he has been a scoundrel. He remains one!"

"Yet, Vasya, he is your father. . . ."

And the old woman shook her head reproachfully.

It was ridiculous and terrible. This paltry and useless conversation engaged them when face to face with death. While almost weeping, so sad was the situation, Vasily cried out:

"Understand then, mother. They are going to hang me, to hang me! Do you understand, yes or no?"

"And why did you kill?" she cried.

"My God! What are you saying? Even the beasts have feelings. Am I your son or not?"

He sat down and wept. His mother wept also; but, in their incapability of communicating in the same affection in order to face the terror of the approaching death, they wept cold tears that did not warm the heart.

"You ask me if I am your mother? You heap reproaches on me; and yet I have turned completely white these last few days."

"All right, all right, forgive me. Adieu! Embrace my brothers for me."

"Am I not your mother? Do I not suffer for you?"

At last she departed. She was weeping so that she could not see her way. And, the farther she got from the prison, the more abundant became her tears. She retraced her steps, losing herself in this city in which she was born, in which she had grown up, in which she had grown old. She entered a little abandoned garden, and sat down on a damp bench.

And suddenly she understood: to-morrow they would hang her son! She sprang to her feet, and tried to shout and run, but suddenly her head turned, and she sank to the earth. The path, white with frost, was wet and slippery; the old woman could not rise again. She rested her weight on her wrists, and then fell back again. The black neckerchief slipped from her head, uncovering her dirty gray hair. It seemed to her that she was celebrating her son's wedding. Yes, they had just married him, and she had drunk a little wine; she was slightly intoxicated.

"I cannot help myself! My God, I cannot help myself!"

And, with swinging head, she said to herself that she had drunk too much, and was crawling around on the wet ground, . . . but they gave her wine to drink, and wine again, and still more wine. And from her heart arose the laugh of the drunkard and the desire to abandon herself to a wild dance; . . . but they kept on lifting cups to her lips, one after another, one after another.

VI

The Hours Fly

In the fortress where the condemned terrorists were confined there was a steeple with an old clock. Every hour, every half-hour, every quarter of an hour, this clock struck in a tone of infinite sadness, like the distant and plaintive cry of birds of passage. In the daytime this odd and desolate music was lost in the noise of the city, of the broad and animated street that passed the fortress. The tramways rumbled, the shoes of the horses rattled, the trembling automobiles sounded their hoarse horns far into the distance. As the carnival was approaching, the peasants of the suburbs had come to town to earn some money as cab-drivers; the bells of the little Russian horses tinkled noisily. The conversations were gay, and had a flavor of intoxication, real holiday conversations. The weather harmonized with the occasion; the spring had brought a thaw, and the road was wet with dirty puddles. The trees on the squares had suddenly darkened. A slightly warm wind was blowing from the sea in copious moist puffs—a light, fresh air that seemed to have started on a joyous flight toward the infinite.

By night the street was silent under the brilliancy of the large electric suns. The immense fortress with its smooth walls was plunged in darkness and silence; a barrier of calm and shadow separated it from the ever-living city. Then they heard the striking of the hours, the slow, sad birth and death of a strange melody, foreign to the land. Like big drops of transparent glass, the hours and the minutes fell from an immeasurable height into a metallic basin that was vibrating gently. Sometimes they were like birds that passed.

Into the cells came, day and night, this single sound. It penetrated through the roof, through the thick stone walls; it alone broke the silence. Sometimes they forgot it, or did not hear it. Sometimes they awaited it with despair; they lived only by and for this sound, having learned to be distrustful of silence. The prison was reserved for criminals of note; its special, rigorous regulations were as rigid and sharp as the corners of the walls. If there is nobility in cruelty, then the solemn, deaf, dead silence that caught up every breath and every rustle was noble.

In this silence, penetrated by the desolate striking of the flying minutes, three men and two women, separated from the world, were awaiting the coming of the night, of the dawn, and of the execution; and each was preparing for it in his own fashion.

Throughout her life Tanya Kovalchuk had thought only of others, and now also it was for her comrades that she underwent suffering and torture. She pictured death to herself only because it threatened Sergey Golovin, Musya, and the others; but her thoughts did not dwell on the fact that she too would be executed.

As if to reward herself for the artificial firmness that she had shown before the judges, she wept for hours altogether. This is characteristic of old women who have suffered much. When it occurred to her that Sergey might be unprovided with tobacco, or that Werner possibly was deprived of the tea of which he was so fond—and this at the moment that they were about to die—she suffered perhaps as much as at the idea of the execution. The execution was something inevitable, even incidental, not worthy of consideration; but that an imprisoned man should be without tobacco on the very eve of his execution was an idea absolutely intolerable. Evoking the pleasant memories of their common life, she lamented over the interview between Sergey and his parents.

For Musya she felt a special pity. For a long time it had seemed to her, mistakenly, however, that Musya was in love with Werner; she had beautiful and luminous dreams for their future. Before her arrest Musya wore a silver ring on which were engraved a skull and crossbones surrounded with a crown of thorns. Often Tanya Kovalchuk had looked at this ring sorrowfully, viewing it as a symbol of renunciation; half serious, half joking, she had asked Musya to take it off.

"No, Tanya, I will not give it to you. You will soon have another on your finger!"

Her comrades always thought that she would soon be married, which much offended her. She wanted no husband. And, as she recalled these conversations with Musya and reflected that Musya was indeed sacrificed, Tanya, full of motherly pity, felt the tears choking her. Every time the clock struck, she lifted her face, covered with tears, and listened, wondering how this plaintive and persistent summons of death was being received in the other cells.

VII

There Is No Death

And Musya was happy!

With arms folded behind her back, dressed in a prisoner's gown that was too large for her and that made her look like a youth wearing a borrowed costume, she walked back and forth in her cell, at a regular pace, never wearying. She had tucked up the long sleeves of her gown, and her thin and emaciated arms, the arms of a child, emerged from the flaring breadths like flower-stems from a coarse and unclean pitcher. The roughness of the stuff irritated the skin of her white and slender neck; sometimes, with her two hands, she released her throat, and felt cautiously for the spot where her skin was burning.

Musya walked with a long stride, and tried blushingly to justify to herself the fact that the finest of deaths, reserved hitherto for martyrs, had been assigned to her, so young, so humble, and who had done so little. It seemed to her that, in dying upon the scaffold, she was making a pretentious show that was in bad taste.

At her last interview with her lawyer she had asked him to procure poison for her, but immediately had given up the idea: would not people think that she was actuated by fear or by ostentation? Instead of dying modestly and unnoticed, would she not cause still further scandal? And she had added, quickly:

"No, no, it is useless!"

Now her sole desire was to explain, to prove, that she was not a heroine, that it was not a frightful thing to die, and that no one need pity her or worry on her account.

Musya sought excuses, pretexts of such a nature as to exalt her sacrifice and give it a real value, as if it had actually been called in question.

"In fact," she said to herself, "I am young; I might have lived for a long time. But. . ."

Just as the gleam of a candle is effaced by the radiance of the rising sun, youth and life seem to her dull and sombre beside the magnificent and luminous halo that is about to crown her modest person.

"Is it possible?" Musya asks herself, in great confusion. "Is it possible that I am worth anybody's tears?"

And she is seized with an unspeakable joy. There is no more doubt; she has been taken into the pale. She has a right to figure among the heroes who from all countries go to heaven through flames and executions. What serene peace, what infinite happiness! An immaterial being, she believes herself hovering in a divine light.

Of what else was Musya thinking? Of many things, since for her the thread of life was not severed by death but continued to unroll in a calm and regular fashion. She was thinking of her comrades, of those who at a distance were filled with anguish at the idea of her approaching execution, of those who nearer at hand would go with her to the gallows. She was astonished that Vasily should be a prey to terror, he who had always been brave. On Tuesday morning, when they had prepared themselves to kill, and then to die themselves, Tanya Koval-chuk had trembled with emotion; they had been obliged to send her away, whereas Vasily joked and laughed and moved about amid the bombs with so little caution that Werner had said to him severely:

"One should not play with death!"

Why, then, was Vasily afraid now? And this incomprehensible terror was so foreign to Musya's soul that she soon ceased to think about it and to inquire into its cause. Suddenly she felt a mad desire to see Sergey Golovin and laugh with him.

Perhaps too her thought was unwilling to dwell long on the same subject, resembling therein a light bird that hovers before infinite horizons, all space, the caressing and tender azure, being accessible to it. The hours continued to strike. Thoughts blended in this harmonious and distant symphony; fleeting images became a sort of music. It seemed to Musya that she was travelling on a broad and easy road in a quiet night; the carriage rode easily on its springs. All care had vanished; the tired body was dissolved in the darkness; joyous and weary, the thought peacefully created vivid images, and became intoxicated on their beauty. Musya recalled three comrades who had been hanged lately; their faces were illuminated and near, nearer than those of the living. . . . So in the morning one thinks gaily of the hospitable friends who will receive you in the evening with smiles on their lips.

At last Musya became weary from walking. She lay down cautiously on the camp-bed, and continued to dream, with half-closed eyes.

"Is this really death? My God, how beautiful it is! Or is it life? I do not know, I do not know! I am going to see and hear. . . ."

From the first days of her imprisonment she had been a prey to hallucinations. She had a very musical ear; her sense of hearing, sharpened by the silence, gathered in the slightest echoes of life; the footsteps of the sentinels in the corridor, the striking of the clock, the whispering of the wind over the zinc roof, the creaking of a lantern, all blended for her in a vast and mysterious symphony. At first the hallucinations frightened Musya, and she drove them away as morbid manifestations; then, perceiving that she was in good health and had no pathological symptoms, she ceased to resist.

But now she hears very plainly the sound of the military band. She opens her eyes in astonishment, and raises her head. Through the windows she sees the night; the clock strikes. "Again!" she thought, as she closed her eyes without disturbing herself. Again the music begins. Musya clearly distinguishes the steps of the soldiers as they turn the corner of the prison; a whole regiment is passing before her windows. The boots keep time to the music on the frozen ground; one! two! one! two! Sometimes a boot squeaks; a foot slips and then recovers itself. The music draws nearer; it is playing a noisy and stirring triumphal march which Musya does not know. There is probably some festival in the fortress.

The soldiers are under her windows, and the cell is filled with joyous, regular, and harmonious sounds. A big brass trumpet emits false notes: it is not in time; now it is in advance, now it lags behind in a ridiculous fashion. Musya pictures to herself a little soldier playing this trumpet assiduously, and she laughs.

The regiment has passed; the sound of the footsteps grows fainter and fainter; one! two! one! two! In the distance the music becomes gayer and more beautiful. Several times more the trumpet sounds out of time, with its metallic, sonorous, and gay voice, and then all is quiet. Again the clock in the steeple strikes the hours.

New forms come and lean over her, surrounding her with transparent clouds and lifting her to a great height, where birds of prey are hovering. At left and right, above and below, everywhere birds are crying like heralds; they call, they warn. They spread their wings, and immensity sustains them. And on their inflated breasts that split the air is reflected the sparkling azure. The beating of Musya's heart becomes more and more regular, her respiration more and more calm and peaceful. She sleeps; her face is pale; her features are drawn; there are dark rings around her eyes. On her lips a smile. To-morrow, when the sun shall rise, this intelligent and fine face will be deformed by a grimace in which no trace of the human will be left; the brain will be inundated with thick blood; the glassy eyes will protrude from their orbits. But to-day Musya sleeps quietly, and smiles in her immortality.

Musya sleeps.

And the prison continues to live its special, blind, vigilant life, a sort of perpetual anxiety. They walk. They whisper. A gun rings out. It seems as if someone cries out. Is this reality or hallucination?

The grating in the door lowers noiselessly. In the dark opening appears a sinister bearded face. For a long time the widely opened eyes view with astonishment the sleeping Musya; then the face disappears as quietly as it came.

The bells in the steeple ring and sing interminably. One would say that the weary hours were climbing a high mountain toward midnight. The ascent grows more and more painful. They slip, fall back with a groan, and begin again to toil painfully toward the black summit.

There is a sound of footsteps. Whispering voices are heard. Already they are harnessing the horses to the sombre, unlighted vehicle.

VIII

Death Exists, and Life Also

Sergey Golovin never thought of death. It seemed to him something incidental and foreign. He was robust, endowed with that serenity in the joy of living which causes all evil thoughts, all thoughts fatal to life, to disappear rapidly, leaving the organism intact. Just as, with him, physical wounds healed quickly, so all injuries to his soul were immediately nullified. He brought into all his acts, into his pleasures and into his preparations for crime, the same happy and tranquil gravity: everything in life was gay, everything was important, worthy of being well done.

And he did everything well; he sailed a boat admirably, he was an excellent marksman. He was as faithful in friendship as in love, and had an unshakeable confidence in the "word of honor." His comrades declared laughingly that, if one who had been proved a spy should swear to Sergey that he was not a spy, Sergey would believe him and shake hands with him. A single fault: he thought himself a good singer, whereas he sang atrociously false, even in the case of revolutionary hymns. He got angry when they laughed at him.

"Either you are all asses, or else I am an ass!" he said in a serious and offended tone. And, after a moment's reflection, the comrades declared, in a tone quite as serious:

"It is you who are an ass. You show it in your voice!"

And, as is sometimes the case with worthy people, they loved him perhaps more for his eccentricities than for his virtues.

He thought so little of death, he feared it so little, that on the fatal morning, before leaving the dwelling of Tanya Kovalchuk, he alone had breakfasted with appetite, as usual. He had taken two glasses of tea, and eaten a whole two-cent loaf. Then, looking with sadness at Werner's untouched bread, he said to him:

"Why don't you eat? Eat; it is necessary to get strength!"

"I am not hungry."

"Well, I will eat your bread! Shall I?"

"What an appetite you have, Sergey!"

By way of reply, Sergey, with his mouth full, began to sing, in a false and hollow voice:

"A hostile wind is blowing o'er our heads."

After the arrest Sergey had a moment of sadness; the plot had been badly planned. But he said to himself: "Now there is something else that must be done well: to die." And his gaiety returned. On his second day in the fortress he began gymnastic exercises, according to the extremely rational system of a German named Müller, which interested him much. He undressed himself completely; and, to the amazement of the anxious sentinel, he went carefully through the eighteen prescribed exercises.

As a propagander of the Müller system, it gave him much satisfaction to see the soldier follow his movements. Although he knew that he would get no answer, he said to the eye that appeared at the grating:

"That is the kind of thing that does you good, brother; that gives you strength! That is what they ought to make you do in the regiment," he added, in a gentle and persuasive voice, that he might not frighten the soldier, not suspecting that his guardian took him for a madman.

The fear of death showed itself in him progressively, seemingly by shocks: it seemed to him that someone was thumping him violently in the heart from below. Then the sensation disappeared, but came back a few hours later, each time more intense and prolonged. It was beginning already to take on the vague outlines of an unendurable anguish.

"Is it possible that I am afraid?" thought Sergey, in astonishment. "How stupid!"

It was not he who was afraid; it was his young, robust, and vigorous body, which neither the gymnastics of Müller or the cold shower-baths could deceive. The stronger and fresher he became after his cold-water ablutions, the more acute and unendurable was his sensation of temporary fear. And it was in the morning, after his deep sleep and physical exercises, that this atrocious fear like something foreign appeared—exactly at the moment when formerly he had been particularly conscious of his strength and his joy in living. He noticed this, and said to himself:

"You are stupid, my friend. In order that the body may die more easily, it should be weakened, not fortified."

From that time he gave up his gymnastics and his massage. And, to explain this right-about-face, he cried to the soldier:

"Brother, the method is a good one. It is only for those who are going to be hanged that it is good for nothing."

In fact, he felt a sort of relief. He tried also to eat less in order to further weaken himself, but, in spite of the lack of air and exercise, his appetite remained excellent. Sergey could not resist it, and ate everything that they brought him. Then he resorted to a subterfuge; before sitting down to table, he poured half of his soup into his bucket. And this method succeeded; a great weariness, a vague numbness, took possession of him.

"I will teach you!" he said, threatening his body; and he caressed his softening muscles sadly.

But soon the body became accustomed to this régime, and the fear of death appeared again, not in so acute a form, but as a vague sensation of nausea, still harder to bear. "It is because this lasts so long," thought Sergey "If only I could sleep all the time until the day of execution!" He tried to sleep as much as possible.

His first efforts were not altogether fruitless; then insomnia set in, accompanied with obsessing thoughts and, with these, a regret that he must part with life.

"Am I then afraid of it?" he asked himself, thinking of death. "It is the loss of life that I regret. Life is an admirable thing, whatever the pessimists may say. What would a pessimist say if they were to hang him? Ah! I regret to lose my life, I regret it much."

When he clearly understood that for him all was over, that he had before him only a few hours of empty waiting and then death, he had a queer feeling. It seemed to him that they had stripped him naked in an extraordinary fashion. Not only had they taken away his clothes, but also sun, air sound and light, speech and the power of action. Death had not yet arrived, and yet life seemed already absent; he felt a strange sensation, sometimes incomprehensible, sometimes intelligible, but very subtle and mysterious.

"What is it then?" wondered Sergey, in his torment. "And I, where am I?... What I?"

He examined himself attentively, with interest, beginning with his loose slippers, such as the prisoners wore, and stopping with his belly, over which hung his ample cloak. He began to walk back and forth in his cell, with arms apart, and continued to look at himself as a woman does when trying on a gown that is too long. He tried to turn his head: it turned. And what seemed to him a little terrifying was he himself, Sergey Golovin, who soon would be no more!

Everything became strange.

He tried to walk, and it seemed queer to him to walk. He tried to sit down, and he was surprised that he could do so. He tried to drink water, and it seemed queer to him to drink, to swallow, to hold the goblet, to see his fingers, his trembling fingers. He began to cough, and thought: "How curious it is! I cough."

"What is the matter? Am I going mad?" he asked himself. "That would be the last straw, indeed!"

He wiped his brow, and this gesture seemed to him equally surprising. Then he fixed himself in a motionless posture, without breathing—for entire hours, it seemed to him, extinguishing all thought, holding his breath, avoiding all motion; for every thought was madness, every gesture an aberration. Time disappeared as if transformed into space, into a transparent space in which there was no air, into an immense place containing everything—land and life and men. And one could take in everything at a glance, to the very extremity, to the edge of the unknown gulf, to death. And it was not because he saw death that Sergey suffered, but because he saw life and death at the same time. A sacrilegious hand had lifted the curtain which from all eternity had hidden the mystery of life and the mystery of death; they had ceased to be mysteries, but they were no more comprehensible than truth written in a foreign language.

"And here we are back to Müller again!" he suddenly declared aloud, in a voice of deep conviction. He shook his head, and began to laugh gaily, sincerely:

"Ah, my good Müller! My dear Müller! My worthy German! You are right, after all, Müller; as for me, brother Müller, I am only an ass!"

He quickly made the round of his cell; and, to the great astonishment of the soldier who was watching him through the grating, he entirely undressed and went through the eighteen exercises with scrupulous exactness. He bent and straightened up his young body which had grown a little thin; he stooped, inhaling and exhaling the air; he raised himself on tiptoe, and moved his arms and legs.

"Yes, but, you know, Müller," reasoned Sergey, throwing out his chest, his ribs outlining themselves plainly under his thin, distended skin—"you know, Müller, there is still a nineteenth exercise—suspension by the neck in a fixed position. And that is called hanging. Do you understand, Müller? They take a living man, Sergey Golovin, for example, they wrap him up like a doll, and they hang him by the neck until he is dead. It is stupid, Müller, but that is the way it is; one must be resigned!"

He leaned on his right side, and repeated:

"One must be resigned, Müller!"

IX

The Horrible Solitude

Under the same roof and to the same melodious chant of the indifferent hours, separated from Sergey and from Musya by a few empty cells, but as isolated as if he alone had existed in the whole universe, the unhappy Vasily Kashirin was finishing his life in anguish and terror.

Covered with sweat, his shirt adhering to his body, his formerly curly hair now falling in straight locks, he went back and forth in his cell with the jerky and lamentable gait of one suffering atrociously with the toothache. He sat down for a moment, and then began to run again; then he rested his forehead against the wall, stopped, and looked about as if in search of a remedy. He had so changed that one might think that he possessed two different faces, one of which, the younger, had gone nobody knows where, to give place to the second, a terrible face, that seemed to have come from darkness.

Fear had shown itself suddenly to him, and had seized upon his person as an exclusive and sovereign mistress. On the fatal morning, when he was marching to certain death, he had played with it; but that evening, confined in his cell, he had been carried away and lashed by a wave of mad terror. As long as he had gone freely forward to meet danger and death, as long as he had held his fate in his own hands, however terrible it might be, he had appeared tranquil and even joyous, the small amount of shameful and decrepit fear that he had felt having disappeared in a consciousness of infinite liberty, in the firm and audacious affirmation of his intrepid will, leaving no trace behind. With an infernal machine strapped around his waist, he had transformed himself into an instrument of death, he had borrowed from the dynamite its cruel reason and its flashing and homicidal power. In the street, among the busy people preoccupied with their affairs and quickly dodging the tramcars and the cabs, it seemed to him as if he came from another and an unknown world, where there was no such thing as death or fear.

Suddenly a brutal, bewildering change had taken place. Vasily no longer went where he wanted to go, but was led where others wanted him to go. He no longer chose his place; they placed him in a stone cage and locked him in, as if he were a thing. He could no longer choose between life and death; they led him to death, certainly and inevitably. He who had been for a moment the incarnation of will, of life, and of force, had become a lamentable specimen of impotence; he was nothing but an animal destined for the slaughter. Whatever he might say, they would not listen; if he started to cry out, they would stuff a rag in his mouth; and, if he even tried to walk, they would take him away and hang him. If he resisted, if he struggled, if he lay down on the ground, they would be stronger than he; they would pick him up, they would tie him, and thus they would carry him to the gallows. And his imagination gave to the men charged with this execution, men like himself, the new, extraordinary, and terrifying aspect of unthinking automata, whom nothing in the world could stop, and who seized a man, overpowered him, hanged him, pulled him by the feet, cut the rope, put the body in a coffin, carried it away, and buried it.

From the first day of his imprisonment, people and life had tranformed themselves for him into an unspeakably frightful world filled with mechanical dolls. Almost mad with fear, he tried to fancy to himself that these people had tongues and spoke, but he did not succeed. Their mouths opened, something like a sound came from them; then they separated with movements of their legs, and all was over. He was in the situation of a man who, left alone in a house at night, should see all things become animate, move, and assume over him an unlimited power; suddenly the wardrobe, the chair, the sofa, the writing-table would sit in judgment upon him. He would cry out, call for help, beg, and rove from room to room; and the things would speak to each other in their own tongue; and then the wardrobe, the chair, the sofa, and the writing-table would start to hang him, the other things looking on.

In the eyes of Vasily Kashirin, sentenced to be hanged, everything took on a puerile aspect; the cell, the grated door, the striking apparatus of the clock, the fortress with its carefully modelled ceilings, and, above, the mechanical doll equipped with a musket, who walked up and down in the corridor, and the other dolls who frightened him by looking through the grating and handing him his food without a word.

A man had disappeared from the world.

In court the presence of the comrades had brought Kashirin back to himself. Again for a moment he saw people; they were there, judging him, speaking the language of men, listening, and seeming to understand. But, when he saw his mother, he felt clearly, with the terror of a man who is going mad and he knows it, that this old woman in a black neckerchief was a simple mechanical doll. He was astonished at not having suspected it before, and at having awaited this visit as something infinitely sorrowful in its distressing gentleness. While forcing himself to speak, he thought with a shudder:

"My God! But it is a doll! A doll-mother! And yonder is a doll-soldier; at home there is a doll-father, and this is the doll Vasily Kashirin."

When the mother began to weep, Vasily again saw something human in her, but this disappeared with the first words that she uttered. With curiosity and terror he watched the tears flow from the doll's eyes.

When his fear became intolerable, Vasily Kashirin tried to pray. There remained with him only a bitter, detestable, and enervating rancor against all the religious principles upon which his youth had been nourished, in the house of his father, a large merchant. He had no faith. But one day, in his childhood, he had heard some words that had made an impression upon him and that remained surrounded forever with a gentle poesy: These words were:

"Joy of all the afflicted!"

Sometimes, in painful moments, he whispered, without praying, without even accounting to himself for what he was doing: "Joy of all the afflicted!" And then he suddenly felt relieved; he had a desire to approach someone who was dear to him and complain gently:

"Our life!...but is it really a life? Say, my dear, is it really a life?"

And then suddenly he felt himself ridiculous; he would have liked to bare his breast and ask someone to beat it.

He had spoken to no one, not even to his best comrades, of his "Joy of all the afflicted!" He seemed to know nothing of it himself, so deeply hidden was it in his soul. And he evoked it rarely, with precaution.

Now that the fear of the unfathomable mystery which was rising before him completely covered him, as the water covers the plants on the bank when the tide is rising, he had a desire to pray. He wanted to fall upon his knees, but was seized with shame before the sentinel; so, with hands clasped upon his breast, he murmured in a low voice:

"Joy of all the afflicted!"

And he repeated with anxiety, in a tone of supplication;

"Joy of all the afflicted, descend into me, sustain me!"

Something moved softly. It seemed to him that a sorrowful and gentle force hovered in the distance and then vanished, without illuminating the shades of the agony. In the steeple the hour struck. The soldier yawned longer and repeatedly.

"Joy of all the afflicted! You are silent! And you will say nothing to Vasily Kashirin!"

He wore an imploring smile, and waited. But in his soul there was the same void as around him. Useless and tormenting thoughts came to him; again he saw the lighted candles, the priest in his robe, the holy image painted on the wall, his father bending and straightening up again, praying and kneeling, casting furtive glances at Vasily to see if he too was praying or was simply amusing himself. And Kashirin was in still deeper anguish than before.

Everything disappeared.

His consciousness went out like the dying embers that one scatters on the hearth; it froze, like the body of a man just dead in which the heart is still warm while the hands and feet are already cold.

Vasily had a moment of wild terror when they came into his cell to get him. He did not even suspect that the hour of the execution had arrived; he simply saw the people and took fright, almost like a child.

"I will not do it again! I will not do it again!" he whispered, without being heard; and his lips became icy as he recoiled slowly toward the rear of his cell, just as in childhood he had tried to escape the punishments of his father.

"You will have to go. . ."

They talked, they walked around him, they gave him he knew not what. He closed his eyes, staggered, and began to prepare himself painfully. Undoubtedly he had recovered consciousness; he suddenly asked a cigarette of one of the officials, who amiably extended his cigarette-case.

X

The Walls Crumble

The unknown, surnamed Werner, was a man fatigued by struggle. He had loved life, the theatre, society, art, literature, passionately. Endowed with an excellent memory, he spoke several languages perfectly. He was fond of dress, and had excellent manners. Of the whole group of terrorists he was the only one who was able to appear in society without risk of recognition.

For a long time already, and without his comrades having noticed it, he had entertained a profound contempt for men. More of a mathematician than a poet, ecstasy and inspiration had remained so far things unknown to him; at times he would look upon himself as a madman seeking to square the circle in seas of human blood. The enemy against which he daily struggled could not inspire him with respect; it was nothing but a compact network of stupidities, treasons, false-hoods, base deceits. The thing that had finally destroyed in him forever, it seemed to him, the desire to live, was his execution of a police-spy in obedience to the order of his party. He had killed him tranquilly, but at sight of this human counte-nance, inanimate, calm, but still false, pitiable in spite of everything, he suddenly lost his esteem for himself and his work. He considered himself as the most indifferent, the least interesting, of beings. Being a man of will, he did not leave his party; apparently he remained the same; but from that time there was some-thing cold and terrifying in his eyes. He said nothing to anyone.

He possessed also a very rare quality: he knew not fear. He pitied those of his comrades who had this feeling, especially Vasily Kashirin. But his pity was cold, almost official.

Werner understood that the execution was not simply death, but also something more. In any case, he was determined to meet it calmly, to live until the end as if nothing had happened or would happen. Only in this way could he express the profoundest contempt for the execution and preserve his liberty of mind. In the courtroom—his comrades, although knowing well his cold and haughty intrepidity, perhaps would not have believed it themselves—he thought not of life or of death: he played in his mind a difficult game of chess, giving it his deepest and quietest attention. And excellent player, he had begun this game on the very day of his imprisonment, and he kept it up continually. And the verdict that condemned him did not displace a single piece on the invisible board.

The idea that he probably would not finish the game did not stop Werner. On the morning of the last day he began by correcting a plan that had failed the night before. With hands pressed between his knees, he sat a long time motionless; then he arose, and began to walk, reflecting. He had a gait of his own; the upper part of his body inclined a little forward, and he brought down his heels forcibly; even when the ground was dry, he left clear foot-prints behind him. He whistled softly a rather simple Italian melody, which helped him to reflect.

But now he was shrugging his shoulders and feeling his pulse. His heart beat fast, but tranquilly and regularly, with a sonorous force. Like a novice thrown into prison for the first time, he examined attentively the cell, the bolts, the chair screwed to the wall, and said to himself:

"Why have I such a sensation of joy, of liberty? Yes, of liberty; I think of to-morrow's execution, and it seems to me that it does not exist. I look at the walls, and they seem to me not to exist either. And I feel as free as if instead of being in prison, I had just come out of another cell in which I had been confined all my life."

Werner's hands began to tremble, a thing unknown to him. His thought became more and more vibrant. It seemed to him that tongues of fire were moving in his head, trying to escape from his brain to lighten the still obscure distance. Finally the flame darted forth, and the horizon was brilliantly illuminated.

The vague lassitude that had tortured Werner during the last two years had disappeared at the sight of death; his beautiful youth came back as he played. It was even something more than beautiful youth. With the astonishing clearness of mind that sometimes lifts man to the supreme heights of meditation, Werner saw suddenly both life and death; and the majesty of this new spectacle struck him. He seemed to be following a path as narrow as the edge of a blade, on the crest of the loftiest mountain. On one side he saw life, and on the other he saw death; and they were like two deep seas, sparkling and beautiful, melting into each other at the horizon in a single infinite extension.

"What is this, then? What a divine spectacle!" said he slowly.

He arose involuntarily and straightened up, as if in presence of the Supreme Being. And, annihilating the walls, annihilating space and time, by the force of his all-penetrating look, he cast his eyes into the depths of the life that he had quitted.

And life took on a new aspect. He no longer tried, as of old, to translate into words what he was; moreover, in the whole range of human language, still so poor and miserly, he found no words adequate. The paltry, dirty, and evil things that suggested to him contempt and sometimes even disgust at the sight of men had completely disappeared, just as, to people rising in a balloon, the mud and filth of the narrow streets become invisible and ugliness changes into beauty.

With an unconscious movement Werner walked toward the table and leaned upon it with his right arm. Haughty and authoritarian by nature, he had never been seen in a prouder, freer, and more imperious attitude; never had his face worn such a look, never had he so lifted up his head, for at no previous time had he been as free and powerful as now, in this prison, on the eve of execution, at the threshold of death.

In his illuminated eyes men wore a new aspect, an unknown beauty and charm.

He hovered above time, and never had this humanity, which only the night before was howling like a wild beast in the forests, appeared to him so young. What had heretofore seemed to him terrible, unpardonable, and base became suddenly touching and naïve, just as we cherish in the child the awkwardness of its behaviour, the incoherent stammerings in which its unconscious genius glimmers, its laughable errors and blunders, its cruel bruises.

"My dear friends!"

Werner smiled suddenly, and his attitude lost its haughty and imposing force. Again he became the prisoner suffering in his narrow cell, weary of seeing a curious eye steadily fixed upon him through the door. He sat down, but not in his usual stiff position, and looked at the walls and the gratings with a weak and gentle smile such as his face had never worn. And something happened which had never happened to him before: he wept.

"My dear comrades!" he whispered, shedding bitter tears. "My dear comrades!"

What mysterious path had he followed to pass from a feeling of unlimited and haughty liberty to this passionate and moving pity? He did not know. Did he really pity his comrades, or did his tears hide something more passionate, something really greater? His heart, which had suddenly revived and reblossomed, could not tell him. Werner wept, and whispered:

"My dear comrades! My dear comrades!"

And in this man who wept, and who smiled through his tears, no one—not the judges, or his comrades, or himself—would have recognized the cold and haughty Werner, sceptical and insolent.

XI

On the Way to the Gallows

Before getting into the vehicles, all five of the condemned were gathered in a large cold room with an arched ceiling, resembling an abandoned office or an unused reception-room. They were permitted to talk with each other.

Only Tanya Kovalchuk took immediate advantage of the permission. The others pressed in silence hands as cold as ice or as hot as fire; dumb, trying to avoid each other's gaze, they formed a confused and distracted group. Now that they were reunited, they seemed to be ashamed of what they had felt individually in the solitude. They were afraid to look at each other, afraid to show the new, special, somewhat embarrassing thing that they felt or suspected in each other.

Nevertheless, they did look, and, after a smile or two, all found themselves at ease, as before; no change revealed itself, or, if something had happened, all had taken an equal share in it, so that nothing special was noticeable in any one of them. All talked and moved in a queer and jerky fashion, impulsively, either too slowly or too quickly. Sometimes one of them quickly repeated the same words, or else failed to finish a phrase that he had begun or thought he had already spoken. But nothing of all this did they notice. All blinkingly examined the familiar objects without recognizing them, like people who have suddenly taken off their glasses. They often turned around quickly, as if someone were calling them from the rear. But they did not notice this. The cheeks and ears of Musya and Tanya were burning. At first Sergey was a little pale; he soon recovered, and appeared as usual.

Vasily alone attracted attention. Even in such a group he was extraordinary and dreadful. Werner was moved, and said in a low voice to Musya, with deep anxiety:

"What is the matter with him, Musya? Is it possible that he has...? Really, we must speak to him."

Vasily looked at Werner from a distance, as if he had not recognized him; then he lowered his eyes.

"But, Vasily, what is the matter with your hair? What is the matter with you? It is nothing, brother, it will soon be over! We must control ourselves! We really must!"

Vasily did not break the silence. But, when they had already concluded that he would say absolutely nothing, there came a hollow, tardy, terribly distant reply, such as the grave might give up after a long appeal:

"But there is nothing the matter with me. I am in control of myself!"

He repeated:

"I am in control of myself!"

Werner was delighted.

"Good, good! You are a brave fellow! All is well!"

But, when his eyes met the dark and heavy gaze of Vasily, he felt a momentary anguish, asking himself: "But whence does he look? whence does he speak?" In a tone of deep tenderness, he said:

"Vasily, do you hear? I love you much!"

"And I too, I love you much!" replied a tongue that moved painfully.

Suddenly Musya seized Werner by the arm, and, expressing her astonishment forcibly, like an actress on the stage, she said:

"Werner, what is the matter with you? You said: 'I love you'? You never said that to anyone before. And why is your face so sparkling and your voice so tender? What is it? What is it?"

And Werner, also in the manner of an actor dwelling upon his words, answered, as he pressed the young girl's hand:

"Yes, I love, now! Do not tell the others. I am ashamed of it, but I love my brothers passionately!"

Their eyes met and burst into flame: everything about them became extinct, just as all other lights pale in the fugitive flash of the lightning.

"Yes!" said Musya. "Yes, Werner!"

"Yes!" he answered. "Yes, Musya, yes!"

They had understood something and ratified it forever. With sparkling eyes and quick steps Werner moved on again in the direction of Sergey.

"Sergey!"

But it was Tanya Kovalchuk that answered. Full of joy, almost weeping with maternal pride, she pulled Sergey violently by the sleeve.

"Just listen, Werner! I weep on his account. I torment myself, and he, he does gymnastics!"

"The Müller system?" asked Werner, with a smile.

Sergey, somewhat confused, knit his brows.

"You do wrong to laugh, Werner! I have absolutely convinced myself. . ."

Everybody began to laugh. Gaining strength and firmness from their mutual communion, they gradually became again what they used to be; they did not notice it, and thought that they were always the same. Suddenly Werner stopped laughing; with perfect gravity he said to Sergey:

"You are right, Sergey! You are perfectly right!"

"Understand this then!" rejoined Sergey, satisfied. "Of course we. . ."

Just then they were asked to get into the vehicles. The officials even had the amiability to allow them to place themselves in their own fashion, in pairs. In general, they were very amiable with them, even too much so; were they trying to give evidence of a little humanity, or to show that they were not responsible for what was taking place and that everything was happening of itself? It is impossible to say, but all those taking part were pale.

"Go with him, Musya!" said Werner, pointing the young girl to Vasily, who stood motionless.

"I understand!" she answered, nodding her head. "And you?"

"I? Tanya will go with Sergey, you with Vasily. As for me, I shall be alone! What matters it? I can stand it, you know!"

When they had reached the courtyard, the damp and slightly warm air fell softly upon their faces and eyes, cut their breathing, and penetrated their shivering bodies, purifying them. It was hard to believe that this stimulant was simply the wind, a spring wind, gentle and moist.

The astonishing spring night had a flavor of melted snow, of infinite space; it made the stones resound. Brisk and busy little drops of water fell rapidly, one after another, making a sonorous song. But, if one of them delayed a little or fell too soon, the song changed into a joyous splash, an animated confusion. Then a big drop fell heavily, and again the spring-like song began, rhythmical and sonorous. Above the city, higher than the walls of the fortress, was the pale halo formed by the electric lights.

Sergey Golovin heaved a deep sigh, and then held his breath, as if regretting to expel from his lungs air so pure and fresh.

"Have we had this fine weather long?" Werner inquired. "It is spring!"

"Only since yesterday!" they answered politely and promptly. "There have been many cold days."

One after another the black vehicles came up, took in two persons, and went away in the darkness, toward the spot where a lantern was swinging in the gateway. Around each vehicle were moving the gray outlines of soldiers; their horses' shoes resounded loudly; often the beasts slipped on the wet snow.

When Werner bent to get into the vehicle, a gendarme said to him, in a vague way:

"There is another in there who *goes* with you!"

Werner was astonished.

"Who *goes* where? Ah! Yes! Another one! Who is it?"

The soldier said nothing. In a dark corner something small and motionless, but alive, lay rolled up; an open eye shone under an oblique ray of the lantern. As he sat down, Werner brushed against a knee with his foot.

"Pardon me, comrade!"

There was no answer. Not until the vehicle had started did the man ask hesitatingly, in bad Russian:

"Who are you?"

"My name is Werner, sentenced to be hanged for an attempt upon the life of XX. And you?"

"I am Yanson. . . . I must not be hanged. . . ."

In two hours they would be face to face with the great mystery as yet unsolved; in two hours they would leave life for death; thither both were going, and yet they became acquainted. Life and death were marching simultaneously on two different planes, and to the very end, even in the most laughable and most stupid details, life remained life.

"What did you do, Yanson?"

"I stuck a knife into my boss. I stole money."

From the sound of his voice it seemed as if Yanson were asleep. Werner found his limp hand in the darkness, and pressed it. Yanson lazily withdrew it.

"You are afraid?" asked Werner.

"I do not want to be hanged."

They became silent. Again Werner found the Esthonian's hand, and pressed it tightly between his dry and burning palms. It remained motionless, but Yanson did not try again to release it.

They stifled in the cramped vehicle, whose musty smell mingled with the odors of the soldiers' uniform, of the muck-heap, and of wet leather. The breath of a young gendarme, redolent of garlic and bad tobacco, streamed continually into the face of Werner, who sat opposite. But the keen fresh air came in at the windows, and thanks to this the presence of spring was felt in the little moving box even more plainly than outside. The vehicle turned now to the right, now to the left; sometimes it seemed to turn around and go back. There were moments when it appeared to the prisoners as if they had been going in a circle for hours. At first the bluish electric light came in between the heavy lowered curtains; then suddenly, after a turn, darkness set in; it was from this that the travellers gathered that they had reached the suburbs and were approaching the station of S——. Sometimes, at a sudden turn, Werner's bent and living knee brushed in a friendly way against the bent and living knee of the gendarme, and it was hard to believe in the approaching execution.

"Where are we going?" asked Yanson, suddenly. The continuous and prolonged shaking of the sombre vehicle gave him vertigo and a little nausea.

Werner answered, and pressed the Esthonian's hand more tightly than before. He would have liked to say specially friendly and kind words to this little sleeping man, whom already he loved more than anyone in the world.

"Dear friend! I think that you are in an uncomfortable position! Draw nearer to me!"

At first Yanson said nothing, but after a moment he replied:

"Thank you! I am comfortable! And you, they are going to hang you too?"

"Yes!" replied Werner, with an unlooked-for gaiety, almost laughing. He made a free-and-easy gesture, as if they were speaking of some futile and stupid prank that a band of affectionate practical jokers were trying to play upon them.

"You have a wife?" asked Yanson.

"No! A wife! I! No, I am alone!"

"So am I! I am alone."

Werner, too, was beginning to feel the vertigo. At times it seemed to him that he was on his way to some festivity. A queer thing; almost all those who were going to the execution had the same feeling; although a prey to fear and anguish, they rejoiced vaguely in the extraordinary thing that was about to happen. Reality became intoxicated on madness, and death, coupling with life, gave birth to phantoms.

"Here we are at last!" said Werner, gay and curious, when the vehicle stopped; and he leaped lightly to the ground. Not so with Yanson, who resisted, without saying a word, very lazily it seemed, and who refused to descend. He clung to the handle of the door; the gendarme loosened his weak fingers, and grasped his arm. Ivan caught at the corner, at the door, at the high wheel, but yielded at every intervention of the gendarme. He adhered to things rather than gripped them. And it was not necessary to use much force to loosen his grasp. In short, they prevailed over him.

As always at night, the station was dark, deserted, and inanimate. The passenger trains had already passed, and for the train that was waiting on the track for the prisoners there was no need of light or activity. Werner was seized with ennui. He was not afraid, he was not in distress, but he was bored; an immense, heavy, fatiguing ennui filled him with a desire to go away no matter where, lie down, and close his eyes. He stretched himself, and yawned repeatedly.

"If only they did these things more quickly!" said he, wearily.

Yanson said nothing, and shuddered.

When the condemned passed over the deserted platform surrounded with soldiers, on their way to the poorly lighted railway carriages, Werner found himself placed beside Sergey Golovin. The latter designated something with his hand, and began to speak; his neighbor clearly understood only the word "lamp"; the rest of the phrase was lost in a weary and prolonged yawn.

"What did you say?" asked Werner, yawning also.

"The reflector...the lamp of the reflector is smoking," said Sergey.

Werner turned around. It was true; the glass shades were already black.

"Yes, it is smoking!"

Suddenly he thought: "What matters it to me whether the lamp is smoking, when...?" Sergey undoubtedly had the same idea. He threw a quick glance at Werner, and turned away his head. But both stopped yawning.

All walked to the train without difficulty; Yanson alone had to be led. At first he stiffened his legs, and glued the soles of his feet to the platform; then he bent his knees. The entire weight of his body fell upon the arms of the policemen; his legs dragged like those of a drunken man; and the toes of his boots ground against the wooden platform. With a thousand difficulties, but in silence, they lifted him into the railway-carriage.

Vasily Kashirin himself walked unsupported; unconsciously he imitated the movements of his comrades. After mounting the steps of the carriage, he drew back; a policeman took him by the elbow to sustain him. Then Vasily began to tremble violently and uttered a piercing cry, pushing away the policeman!

"Aie!"

"Vasily, what is the matter with you?" asked Werner rushing toward him.

Vasily kept silence, shivering the while. The policeman, vexed and even chagrined, explained:

"I wanted to sustain him, and he—he..."

"Come, Vasily, I will sustain you," said Werner.

"He tried to take his comrade's arm. But the latter repulsed him, and cried louder than ever.

"Vasily, it is I, Werner!"

"I know! Don't touch me! I want to walk alone!"

And, still trembling, he entered the carriage and sat down in a corner. Werner leaned toward Musya, and asked in a low voice, designating Vasily with his eyes:

"Well, how are things with him?"

"Badly!" answered Musya, in a whisper. "He is already dead. Tell me, Werner, does death really exist?"

"I don't know, Musya; but I think not!" answered Werner in a serious and thoughtful tone.

"That is what I thought! And he? I suffered on his account during the whole ride; it seemed to me that I was travelling beside a dead man."

"I don't know, Musya. Perhaps death still exists for some. Later it will not exist at all. For me, for instance, death has existed, but now it exists no more."

The slightly pallid cheeks of Musya reddened.

"It has existed for you, Werner? For you?"

"Yes, but no more. As for you!"

They heard a sound at the door of the railway carriage; Michka the Tzigane entered spitting, breathing noisily, and making a racket with his boot-heels. He glanced about him, and stopped short.

"There is no room left, officer!" he declared to the fatigued and irritated policeman. "See to it that I travel comfortably, otherwise I will not go with you! Rather hang me right here, to the lamp-post! Oh, the scoundrels, what a carriage they have given me! Do you call this a carriage? The devil's guts, yes, but not a carriage!"

But suddenly he lowered his head, stretched out his neck, and advanced towards the other prisoners. From the frame of his bushy hair and beard his black eyes shot a savage, sharp, and rather crazy look.

"Oh, my God!" he cried; "so this is where we are! How do you do, sir!"

He sat down opposite Werner, holding out his hand; then, with a wink, he leaned over and swiftly passed his hand across his companion's neck:

"You too? Eh?"

"Yes!" smiled Werner.

"All?"

"All!"

"Oh! oh!" said the Tzigane, showing his teeth. He examined the other prisoners with a swift glance, which nevertheless dwelt longest on Musya and Yanson.

"On account of the Minister?"

"Yes. And you?"

"Oh, sir, my case is quite another story. I am not so distinguished! I, sir, am a brigand, an assassin. That makes no difference, sir; move up a little to make room for me; it is not my fault that they have put me in your company! In the other world there will be room for all."

He took the measure of all the prisoners with a watchful, distrustful, and savage gaze. But they looked at him without a word, seriously and even with evident compassion. Again he showed his teeth, and slapped Werner several times on the knee.

"So that is how it is, sir! As they say in the song:

" 'Take care to make no sound, O forest of green oaks!' "

"Why do you call me sir, when all of us. . ."

"You are right!" acquiesced the Tzigane, with satisfaction. "Why should you be sir, since you are to be hanged beside me? There sits the real sir!"

He pointed his finger at the silent policeman.

"And your comrade yonder, he doesn't seem to be enjoying himself hugely!" he added, looking at Vasily. "Say there, you are afraid?"

"No!" answered a tongue that moved with difficulty.

"Well, then, don't be so disturbed; there is nothing to be ashamed of. It is only dogs that wag their tails and show their teeth when they are going to be hanged; you are a man. And this marionette, who is he? He certainly is not one of your crowd?"

His eyes danced incessantly; constantly, with a hissing sound, he spat out his abundant and sweetish saliva. Yanson, doubled up motionless in a corner, slightly shook the ears of his bald fur cap, but said nothing. Werner answered for him.

"He killed his employer."

"My God!" exclaimed the Tzigane, in astonishment. "How is it that they permit such birds as that to kill people?"

For a moment he looked at Musya stealthily; then suddenly he turned, and fixed his straight and piercing gaze upon her.

"Miss! Say there, Miss! what is the matter with you? Your cheeks are pink, and you are laughing! Look, she is really laughing! Look! Look!" And he seized Werner's knee with his hooked fingers.

Blushing and somewhat confused, Musya squarely returned the gaze of the attentive and savage eyes that questioned her. All kept silence.

The little cars bounced speedily along the narrow track. At every turn or grade-crossing the whistle blew, the engineer being afraid of crushing somebody. Was it not atrocious to think that so much care and effort, in short all human activity, was being expended in taking men to be hanged? The maddest thing in the world was being done with an air of simplicity and reasonableness. Cars were running; people were sitting in them as usual, travelling as people ordinarily travel. Then there would be a halt as usual: "Five minutes' stop."

And then would come death—eternity—the great mystery.

XII

The Arrival

The train advanced rapidly.

Sergey Golovin remembered to have spent the summer, some years before, in a little country-house along this very line. He had often travelled the road by day and by night, and knew it well. Closing his eyes, he could fancy himself returning by the last train, after staying out late at night with friends.

"I shall arrive soon," thought he, straightening up: and his eyes met the dark grated window. Around him nothing stirred. Only the Tzigane kept on spitting, and his eyes ran the length of the car, seeming to touch the doors and the soldiers.

"It is cold," said Vasily Kashirin between his thin lips, which seemed frozen.

Tanya Kovalchuk bestirred herself in a maternal fashion:

"Here's a very warm kerchief to wrap around your..."

"Neck?" asked Sergey, and he was frightened by his own question.

"What matters it, Vasya? Take it."

"Wrap yourself up. You will be warmer," added Werner.

He turned to Yanson, and asked him tenderly:

"And aren't you cold, too?"

"Werner, perhaps he wants to smoke. Comrade, do you want to smoke?" asked Musya. "We have some tobacco."

"Yes, I want to."

"Give him a cigarette, Sergey," said Werner.

But Sergey was already holding out his cigarette-case.

And all began to watch tenderly Yanson's clumsy fingers as they took the cigarette and struck the match, and the little curl of bluish smoke that issued from his mouth.

"Thank you," said Yanson. "It is good."

"How queer it is," said Sergey.

"How queer what is?" asked Werner.

"The cigarette," answered Sergey, unwilling to say all that he thought.

Yanson held the cigarette between his pale and living fingers. With astonishment he looked at it. And all fixed their gaze on this tiny bit of paper, on this little curl of smoke rising from the gray ashes.

The cigarette went out.

"It is out," said Tanya.

"Yes, it is out."

"The devil take it!" said Werner, looking anxiously at Yanson, whose hand, holding the cigarette, hung as if dead. Suddenly the Tzigane turned, placed his face close to Werner's, and, looking into the whites of his eyes, whispered:

"Suppose, sir, we were to attack the soldiers of the convoy? What do you think about it?"

"No," answered Werner.

"Why? It is better to die fighting. I will strike a blow, they strike back, and I shall die without noticing it."

"No, it is not necessary," said Werner. And he turned to Yanson:

"Why don't you smoke?"

Yanson's dried-up face wrinkled pitifully, as if someone had pulled the threads that moved the creases in his face. As in a nightmare, Yanson sobbed in a color-less voice, shedding no tears:

"I can't smoke. Ah! Ah! Ah! I must not be hanged. Ah! Ah! Ah!"

Everybody turned toward him. Tanya, weeping copiously, stroked his arms and readjusted his fur cap.

"My dear, my friend, don't cry, my friend! My poor friend!"

Suddenly the cars bumped into one another and began to slow up. The prisoners rose, but immediately sat down again.

"Here we are," said Sergey.

It was as if all the air had suddenly been pumped out of the car. It became difficult to breathe. Their swollen hearts became heavy in their breasts, rose to their throats, beat desperately and their blood, in its terror, seemed to revolt. Their eyes looked at the trembling floor, their ears listened to the slowly-turning wheels, which began to turn more slowly still, and gently stopped.

The train halted.

The prisoners were plunged into a strange stupor. They did not suffer. They seemed to live an unconscious life. Their corporeal being was absent; only its phantom moved about, voiceless but speaking, silent but walking. They went out. They arranged themselves in pairs, breathing in the fresh air of the woods. Like one in a dream, Yanson struggled awkwardly: they dragged him from the car.

"Are we to go on foot?" asked someone, almost gaily.

"It isn't far," answered a careless voice.

Without a word they advanced into the forest, along a damp and muddy road. Their feet slipped and sank into the snow, and their hands sometimes clung involuntarily to those of their comrades. Breathing with difficulty the soldiers marched in single file, on either side of the prisoners. An irritated voice complained:

"Could they not have cleared the road? It is difficult to advance."

A deferential voice answered:

"It was cleaned, Your Honour, but it is thawing. There is nothing to be done."

The prisoners began to recover their consciousness. Now they seemed to grasp the idea: "It is true, they could not clean the roads"; now it became obscured again, and there remained only the sense of smell, which perceived with singular keenness the strong and healthy odor of the forest; and now again all became very clear and comprehensible, the forest, and the night, and the road...and the certainty that very soon, in a minute, implacable death would lay its hands upon them. And little by little a whispering began:

"It is almost four o'clock."

"I told you so. We started too early."

"The sun rises at five."

"That's right, at five: we should have waited."

They halted in the twilight. Near by, behind the trees, whose huge shadows were waving on the ground, swung silently two lanterns. There the gallows had been erected.

"I have lost one of my rubbers," said Sergey.

"Well?" asked Werner, not understanding.

"I have lost it. I am cold."

"Where is Vasily?"

"I don't know. There he is."

Vasily was standing close by them, gloomy and motionless.

"Where is Musya?"

"Here I am. Is that you, Werner?"

They looked at each other, their eyes avoiding the silent and terrible significant swaying of the lanterns. At the left the thin forest seemed to be growing lighter. And beyond, something vast and gray and flat appeared, whence came a moist breeze.

"That is the sea," said Sergey, sucking in the damp air. "That is the sea."

Musya answered by a line from the song:

> "My love as broad as is the sea."

"What did you say, Musya?"

> "The shores of life cannot contain
> My love as broad as is the sea."

" 'My love as broad as is the sea,' " repeated Sergey, pensively.

" 'My love as broad as is the sea,' " echoed Werner. And suddenly he exclaimed in astonishment:

"Musya, my little Musya, how young you still are!"

Just then, close to Werner's ear, sounded the breathless and passionate voice of the Tzigane:

"Sir, sir, look at the forest. My God! What is all that? And yonder! The lanterns! My God, is that the scaffold?"

Werner looked at him. The convulsed features of the unfortunate man were frightful to see.

"We must say our farewells," said Tanya.

"Wait! They still have to read the sentence. Where is Yanson?"

Yanson lay stretched in the snow, surrounded by people. A strong smell of ammonia filled the air around him.

"Well, doctor, will you soon be through?" asked someone, impatiently.

"It's nothing. A fainting fit. Rub his ears with snow. He is better already. You can read."

The light of a dark lantern fell upon the paper and the ungloved white hands. Both paper and hands trembled. The voice also.

"Gentlemen, perhaps it is better not to read. You all know the sentence."

"Do not read!" answered Werner for all; and the light immediately went out.

The condemned refused also the services of the priest. Said the Tzigane:

"No nonsense, father; you will forgive me, they will hang me."

The broad dark silhouette of the priest took a few steps backward and disappeared. The day was breaking. The snow became whiter, the faces of the condemned darker, and the forest barer and sadder.

"Gentlemen, you will go in pairs, choosing your companion. But I beg you to make haste."

Werner pointed to Yanson, who now was standing again, sustained by two soldiers.

"I will go with him. You, Sergey, take Vasily. You go first."

"All right."

"I am going with you, Musya," said Tanya. "Come, let us kiss each other!"

Quickly they kissed all round. The Tzigane kissed forcibly; they felt his teeth. Yanson kissed gently and softly, with mouth half open. He did not seem to understand what he was doing. When Sergey and Kashirin had taken a few steps, the latter stopped suddenly, and in a loud voice, which seemed strange and unfamiliar, shouted:

"Good-bye, comrades."

"Good-bye, comrade," they answered him.

The two started off again. All was quiet. The lanterns behind the trees became motionless. They expected to hear a cry, a voice, some sound or other, but there as here all was calm.

"Oh! My God!" exclaimed someone, hoarsely.

They turned around: it was the Tzigane, crying desperately:

"They are going to hang us."

He struggled, clutching the air with his hands, and cried again:

"God! Am I to be hanged alone? My God!"

His convulsive hands gripped the hand of Werner, and he continued:

"Sir, my dear sir, my good sir. You will come with me, won't you?"

Werner, his face drawn with sorrow, answered:

"I cannot; I am with Yanson."

"Oh! My God! then I shall be alone. Why? Why?"

Musya took a step toward him, and said softly:

"I will go with you."

The Tzigane drew back, and fixed his big swollen eyes upon her;

"Will you?"

"Yes."

"But you are so little! You are not afraid of me? No, I don't want you to. I will go alone."

"But I am not afraid of you."

The Tzigane grinned.

"Don't you know that I am a brigand? And you are willing to go with me? Think a moment. I shall not be angry if you refuse."

Musya was silent. And in the faint light of the dawn her face seemed to take on a luminous and mystic pallor. Suddenly she advanced rapidly toward the Tzigane, and, taking his head in her hands, kissed him vigorously. He took her by the shoulders, put her away a little, and then kissed her loudly on her cheeks and eyes.

The soldier nearest them stopped, opened his hands, and let his gun fall. But he did not stoop to pick it up. He stood still for a moment, then turned suddenly, and began to walk into the forest.

"Where are you going?" shouted his comrade, in a frightened voice. "Stay!"

But the other painfully endeavored to advance. Suddenly he clutched the air with his hands, and fell, face downward.

"Milksop, pick up your gun, or I will pick it up for you," cried the Tzigane, firmly. "You don't know your duty. Have you never seen a man die?"

Again the lantern swung. The turn of Werner and Yanson had come.

"Good-bye, sir!" said the Tzigane, in a loud voice. "We shall meet again in the other world. When you see me there, don't turn away from me."

"Good-bye!"

"I must not be hanged," said Yanson again, in a faint voice.

But Werner grasped his hand, and Yanson took a few steps. Then he was seen to sink into the snow. They bent over him, lifted him up, and carried him, while he weakly struggled in the soldiers' arms.

And again the yellow lanterns became motionless.

"And I, Musya? Am I then to go alone?" said Tanya, sadly. "We have lived together, and now..."

"Tanya, my good Tanya!"

The Tzigane hotly interrupted, holding Musya as if he feared that they might tear her from him.

"Miss," he cried, "you are able to go alone. You have a pure soul. You can go alone where you like. But I cannot. I am a bandit. I cannot go alone. 'Where are you going?' they will say to me, 'you who have killed, you who have stolen?' For I have stolen horses, too, Miss. And with her I shall be as if I were with an innocent child. Do you understand?"

"Yes, I understand. Go on then! Let me kiss you once more, Musya."

"Kiss each other! Kiss each other!" said the Tzigane. "You are women. You must say good-bye to each other."

Then came the turn of Musya and the Tzigane. The woman walked carefully, her feet slipping, lifting her skirts by force of habit. Holding her with a strong hand, and feeling the ground with his foot, the man accompanied her to death. The lights became motionless. Around Tanya all was tranquil again, and solitary. The soldiers, gray in the dawn's pale light, were silent.

"I am left alone," said Tanya. And she sighed. "Sergey is dead, Werner and Vasily are dead. And Musya is dying. I am alone. Soldiers, my little soldiers, you see, I am alone, alone..."

The sun appeared above the sea. . . .

They placed the bodies in boxes, and started off with them. With elongated necks, bulging eyes, and blue tongues protruding from their mouths, the dead retraced the road by which, living, they had come.

And the snow was still soft, and the air of the forest was still pure and balmy.

On the white road lay the black rubber that Sergey had lost. . . .

Thus it was that men greeted the rising sun.

The Bench of Desolation

(1910)

Henry James

An American by birth, Henry James (1843–1916) lived most of his life abroad and died a British subject. His novelettes (or *nouvelles* as he called them) reflect the transition from his early to late manner in his novels—from *The American* (1877) and *The Portrait of a Lady* (1881) to *The Wings of the Dove* (1902), *The Ambassadors* (1903), and *The Golden Bowl* (1904). *Daisy Miller* (1878) or even *The Turn of the Screw* (1898) is a very different novelette from *The Beast in the Jungle* (1903) or *The Bench of Desolation* (1910). James' final phase is characterized by an extreme refinement of sensation and moral insight expressed through a more subjective, even poetic medium, rendered "difficult" by the famous Jamesian involution and elaboration of sentence structure.

The Bench of Desolation, next to the last tale James wrote, appeared too late to be included in the New York edition of James' work (1907ff.). It was first published in *Putnam's Magazine,* October 1909 to January 1910, and was reprinted in *The Finer Grain* (1910), James' last book of fiction. For notes on *The Bench of Desolation,* see J. A. Ward, *The Imagination of Disaster* (Lincoln, Nebr., 1961), pp. 161–63; and Charles G. Hoffman, *The Short Novels of Henry James* (New York, 1957), pp. 111–17.

I

She had practically, he believed, conveyed the intimation, the horrid, brutal, vulgar menace, in the course of their last dreadful conversation, when, for whatever was left him of pluck or confidence—confidence in what he would fain have called a little more aggressively the strength of his position—he had judged best not to take it up. But this time there was no question of not understanding, or of pretending he didn't; the ugly, the awful words, ruthlessly formed by her lips,

137

were like the fingers of a hand that she might have thrust into her pocket for extraction of the monstrous object that would serve best for—what should he call it?—a gage of battle.

"If I haven't a very different answer from you within the next three days I shall put the matter into the hands of my solicitor, whom it may interest you to know I've already seen. I shall bring an action for 'breach' against you, Herbert Dodd, as sure as my name's Kate Cookham."

There it was, straight and strong—yet he felt he could say for himself, when once it had come, or even, already just as it was coming, that it turned on, as if she had moved an electric switch, the very brightest light of his own very reasons. There *she* was, in all the grossness of her native indelicacy, in all her essential excess of will and destitution of scruple; and it was the woman capable of that ignoble threat who, his sharper sense of her quality having become so quite deterrent, was now making for him a crime of it that he shouldn't wish to tie himself to her for life. The vivid, lurid thing was the reality, all unmistakable, of her purpose; she had thought her case well out; had measured its odious, specious presentability; had taken, he might be sure, the very best advice obtainable at Properley, where there was always a first-rate promptitude of everything fourth-rate; it was disgustingly certain, in short, that she'd proceed. She was sharp and adroit, moreover—distinctly in certain ways a master-hand; how otherwise, with her so limited mere attractiveness, should she have entangled him? He couldn't shut his eyes to the very probable truth that if she should try it she'd pull it off. She *knew* she would—precisely; and her assurance was thus the very proof of her cruelty. That she had pretended she loved him was comparatively nothing; other women had pretended it, and other women too had really done it; but that she had pretended he could possibly have been right and safe and blest in loving *her,* a creature of the kind who could sniff that squalor of the law-court, of claimed damages and brazen lies and published kisses, of love-letters read amid obscene guffaws, as a positive tonic to resentment, as a high incentive to her course—this was what put him so beautifully in the right. It was what might signify in a woman all through, he said to himself, the mere imagination of such machinery. Truly what a devilish conception and what an appalling nature!

But there was no doubt, luckily, either, that he *could* plant his feet the firmer for his now intensified sense of these things. He was to live, it appeared, abominably worried, he was to live consciously rueful, he was to live perhaps even what a scoffing world would call abjectly exposed; but at least he was to live saved. In spite of his clutch of which steadying truth, however, and in spite of his declaring to her, with many other angry protests and pleas, that the line of conduct she announced was worthy of a vindictive barmaid, a lurking fear in him, too deep to counsel mere defiance, made him appear to keep open a little, till he could somehow turn round again, the door of possible composition. He had scoffed at her claim, at her threat, at her thinking she could hustle and bully him—"Such a way, my eye, to call back to life a dead love!"—yet his instinct was ever, prudentially but helplessly, for gaining time, even if time only more woefully to quake, and he gained it now by not absolutely giving for his ultimatum that he wouldn't think of coming round. He didn't in the smallest degree mean to come round, but it was characteristic of him that he could for three or four days breathe a little easier by having left her under the impression that he perhaps might. At the same time he couldn't not have said—what had conduced to bring out, in retort, her own last word, the word on which they had parted—"Do you mean to say you yourself would now be *willing* to marry and live with a man of whom you could feel, the thing done, that he'd be all the while thinking of you in the light of a hideous coercion?" "Never you mind about *my* willingness," Kate had answered; "you've known what that has been for the last six months. Leave that to me, my willingness—I'll take care of it all right; and just see what conclusion you can come to about your own."

He was to remember afterward how he had wondered whether, turned upon her in silence while her odious lucidity reigned unchecked, his face had shown her anything like the quantity of hate he felt. Probably not at all; no man's face *could* express that immense amount; especially the fair, refined, intellectual, gentleman-like face which had had—and by her own more than once repeated avowal—so much to do with the enormous fancy she had originally taken to him. "Which—frankly now—would you personally *rather* I should do," he had at any rate asked her with an intention of supreme irony: "just sordidly marry you on top of this, or leave you the pleasure of your lovely appearance in court and of your so assured (since that's how you feel it) big haul of damages? Shan't you be awfully disappointed, in fact, if I don't let you get something better out of me than a poor plain ten-shilling gold ring and the rest of the blasphemous rubbish, as we should make it between us, pronounced at the altar? I take it, of course," he had swaggered on, "that your pretension wouldn't be for a moment that I should—after the act of profanity—take up my life with you."

"It's just as much my dream as it ever was, Herbert Dodd, to take up mine with *you!* Remember for me that I can do with it, my dear, that my idea is for even as much as that of you!" she had cried; "remember that for me, Herbert Dodd; remember, remember!"

It was on this she had left him—left him frankly under a mortal chill. There might have been the last ring of an appeal or a show of persistent and perverse tenderness in it, however preposterous any such matter; but in point of fact her large, clean, plain brown face—so much too big for her head, he now more than ever felt it to be, just as her head was so much too big for her body, and just as her hats had an irritating way of appearing to decline choice and conformity in respect to *any* of her dimensions—presented itself with about as much expression as his own shop-window when the broad, blank, sallow blind was down. He was fond of his shop-window with some good show on; he had a fancy for a good show and was master of twenty different schemes of taking arrangement for the old books and prints, "high-class rarities" his modest catalogue called them, in which he dealt and which his maternal uncle, David Geddes, had, as he liked to say, "handed down" to him. His widowed mother had screwed the whole thing, the stock and the connexion and the rather bad little house in the rather bad little street, out of the ancient worthy, shortly before his death, in the name of the youngest and most interesting, the "delicate" one and the literary of her five scattered and struggling children. He could enjoy his happiest collocations and contrasts and effects, his harmonies and varieties of toned and faded leather and cloth, his sought colour-notes and the high clearnesses, here and there, of his white and beautifully figured price-labels, which pleased him enough in themselves almost to console him for not oftener having to break, on a customer's insistence, into the balanced composition. But the dropped expanse of time-soiled canvas, the thing of Sundays and holidays, with just his name, "Herbert Dodd, Successor," painted on below his uncle's antique style, the feeble pen-like flourishes already quite archaic—this ugly vacant mask, which might so easily be taken for the mask of failure, somehow always gave him a chill.

That had been just the sort of chill—the analogy was complete—of Kate Cookham's last look. He supposed people doing an awfully good and sure and steady business, in whatever line, could see a whole front turned to vacancy that way, and merely think of the hours off represented by it. Only for this—nervously to bear it, in other words, and Herbert Dodd, quite with the literary temperament himself, was capable of that amount of play of fancy, or even of morbid analysis—you had to be on some footing, you had to feel some confidence, pretty different from his own up to now. He had never *not* enjoyed passing his show on the other side of the street and taking it in thence with a casual obliquity; but he had never held optical commerce with the drawn blind for a moment longer than he could help. It *always* looked horribly final and as if it never would come up again. Big and bare, with his name staring at him from the middle, it thus offered in its grimness a term of comparison for Miss Cookham's ominous visage. She never wore pretty, dotty, transparent veils, as Nan Drury did, and the words "Herbert Dodd"—save that she had sounded them at him there two or three times more like a Meg Merrilies or the bold bad woman in one of the melodramas of high life given during the fine season in the pavilion at the end of Properley Pier—were dreadfully, were permanently, seated on her lips. *She* was grim, no mistake.

That evening, alone in the back room above the shop, he saw so little what he could do that, consciously demoralised for the hour, he gave way to tears about it. Her taking a stand so incredibly "low," that was what he couldn't get over. The particular bitterness of his cup was his having let himself in for a struggle on such terms—the use, on her side, of the vulgarest process known to the law: the vulgarest, the vulgarest, he kept repeating that, clinging to the help rendered him by this imputation to his terrorist of the vice he sincerely believed he had ever, among difficulties (for oh, he recognised the difficulties!) sought to keep most alien to him. He knew what he was, in a dismal, down-trodden sphere enough—the lean young proprietor of an old business that had itself rather shrivelled with age than ever grown fat, the purchase and sale of second-hand books and prints, with the back street of long-fronted south-coast watering-place (Old Town by good luck) for the dusky field of his life. But he had gone in for all the education he could get—his educated customers would often hang about for more talk by the half-hour at a time, he actually feeling himself, and almost with a scruple, hold them there; which meant that he had had (he couldn't be blind to that) natural taste and had lovingly cultivated and formed it. Thus, from as far back as he could remember, there had been things all round him that he suffered from when other people didn't; and he had kept most of his suffering to himself—which had taught him, in a manner, *how* to suffer, and how almost to like to.

So, at any rate, he had never let go his sense of certain differences, he had done everything he could to keep it up—whereby everything that was vulgar was on the wrong side of his line. He had believed, for a series of strange, oppressed months, that Kate Cookham's manners and tone were on the right side; she had been governess—for young children—in two very good private families, and now had classes in literature and history for bigger girls who were sometimes brought by their mammas; in fact, coming in one day to look over his collection of students' manuals, and drawing it out, as so many did, for the evident sake of his conversation, she had appealed to him that very first time by her apparently pronounced intellectual side—goodness knew she didn't even then by the physical!—which she had artfully kept in view till she had entangled him past undoing. And it had all been but the cheapest of traps—when he came to take the pieces apart a bit—laid over a brazen avidity. What he now collapsed for, none the less—what he sank down on a chair at a table and nursed his weak, scared sobs in his resting arms for—was the fact that, whatever the trap, it held him as with the grip of sharp, murderous steel. There he was, there he was; alone in the brown summer dusk—brown through *his* windows—he cried and he cried. He shouldn't get out without losing a limb. The only question was which of his limbs it should be.

Before he went out, later on—for he at last felt the need to—he could, however, but seek to remove from his face and his betraying eyes, over his wash-stand, the traces of his want of fortitude. He brushed himself up; with which, catching his stricken image a bit spectrally in an old dim toilet-glass, he knew again, in a flash, the glow of righteous resentment. Who should be assured against coarse usage if a man of his really elegant, perhaps in fact a trifle over-refined or "effete" appearance, his absolutely gentlemanlike type, couldn't be? He never went so far as to rate himself, with exaggeration, a gentleman; but he would have maintained against all comers, with perfect candour and as claiming a high advantage, that he was, in spite of that liability to blubber, "like" one; which he *was* no doubt, for that matter, at several points. Like what lady then, who could ever possibly have been taken for one, was Kate Cookham, and therefore how could one have anything—anything of the intimate and private order—out with her fairly and on the plane, the only possible one, of common equality? He might find himself crippled for life; he believed verily, the more he thought, that that was what was before him. But he ended by seeing this doom in the almost redeeming light of the fact that it would all have been because he was, comparatively, too aristocratic. Yes, a man in his station couldn't afford to carry that so far—it must sooner or later, in one way or another, spell ruin. Never mind—it was the only thing he could be. Of course he should exquisitely suffer—but when hadn't he exquisitely suffered? How was he going to get through life by *any* arrangement without that? No wonder such a woman as Kate Cookham had been keen to annex so rare a value. The right thing would have been that the highest price should be paid for it—by such a different sort of logic from this nightmare of *his* having to pay.

II

Which was the way, of course, he talked to Nan Drury—as he had felt the immediate wild need to do; for he should perhaps be able to bear it all somehow or other with *her*—while they sat together, when time and freedom served, on one of the very last, the far westward benches of the interminable sea-front. It wasn't every one who walked so far, especially at that flat season—the only ghost of a bustle now, save for the gregarious, the obstreperous haunters of the fluttering, far-shining Pier, being reserved for the sunny Parade of midwinter. It wasn't every one who cared for the sunsets (which you got awfully well from there, and which were a particular strong point of the lower, the more "sympathetic" as Herbert Dodd liked to call it, Properley horizon) as he had always intensely cared, and as he had found Nan Drury care; to say nothing of his having also observed how little they directly spoke to Miss Cookham. He had taught this oppressive companion to notice them a bit, as he had taught her plenty of other things, but that was a different matter; for the reason that the "land's end" (stretching a point it carried off that name) had been, and had had to be by their lack of more sequestered resorts and conveniences, the scene of so much of what she styled their wooing-time—or, to put it more properly, of the time during which she had made the straightest and most unabashed love to *him*: just as it could henceforth but render possible, under an equal rigour, that he should enjoy there periods of consolation from beautiful, gentle, tender-souled Nan, to whom he was now at last, after the wonderful way they had helped each other to behave, going to make love, absolutely unreserved and abandoned, absolutely reckless and romantic love, a refuge from poisonous reality, as hard as ever he might.

The league-long, paved, lighted, garden-plotted, seated and refuged Marina renounced its more or less celebrated attractions to break off short here; and an inward curve of the kindly westward shore almost made a wide-armed bay, with all the ugliness between town and country, and the further casual fringe of the coast, turning, as the day waned, to rich afternoon blooms of grey and brown and distant—it might fairly have been beautiful Hampshire—blue. Here it was that all that blighted summer, with Nan—from the dreadful May-day on—he gave himself up to the reaction of intimacy with the *kind* of woman, at least, that he liked; even if of everything else that might make life possible he was to be, by what he could make out, for ever starved. Here it was that—as well as on whatever other scraps of occasions they could manage—Nan began to take off and fold up and put away in her pocket her pretty, dotty, becoming veil; as under the logic of his having so tremendously ceased, in the shake of his dark storm-gust, to be engaged to another woman. Her removal of that obstacle to a trusted friend's assuring himself whether the peachlike bloom of her finer facial curves bore the test of such further inquiry into their cool sweetness as might reinforce a mere baffled gaze—her momentous, complete surrender of so much of her charm, let us say, both marked the change in the situation of the pair and established the record of their perfect observance of every propriety for so long before. They afterward, in fact, could have dated it, their full clutch of their freedom and the bliss of their having so little henceforth to consider save their impotence, their poverty, their ruin; dated it from the hour of his recital to her of the—at the first blush—quite appalling upshot of his second and conclusive "scene of violence" with the mistress of his fortune, when the dire terms of his release had had to be formally, and oh! so abjectly, acceded to. She "compromised," the cruel brute, for Four Hundred Pounds down—for not a farthing less would she stay her strength from "proceedings." No jury in the land but would give her six, on the nail ("Oh, she knew quite where she was, thank you!"), and he might feel lucky to get off with so whole a skin. This was the sum, then, for which he had grovellingly compounded—under an agreement sealed by a supreme exchange of remarks.

" 'Where in the name of lifelong ruin are you to *find* Four Hundred?' " Miss Cookham had mockingly repeated after him while he gasped as from the twist of her grip on his collar. "That's *your* look-out, and I should have thought you'd have made sure you knew before you decided on your base perfidy." And then she had mouthed and minced, with ever so false a gentility, her consistent, her sickening conclusion. "Of course—I may mention again—if you too distinctly object to the trouble of looking, you know where to find *me*."

"I had rather starve to death than ever go within a mile of you!" Herbert described himself as having sweetly answered; and that was accordingly where *they* devotedly but desperately were—he and she, penniless Nan Drury. Her father, of Drury & Dean, was like so far too many other of the anxious characters who peered through the dull window-glass of dusty offices at Properley, an Estate and House Agent, Surveyor, Valuer and Auctioneer; she was the prettiest of six, with two brothers, neither of the least use, but, thanks to the manner in which their main natural protector appeared to languish under the accumulation of his attributes, they couldn't be said very particularly or positively to live. Their continued collective existence was a good deal of a miracle even to themselves, though they had fallen into the way of not unnecessarily, or too nervously, exchanging remarks upon it, and had even in a sort, from year to year, got used to it. Nan's brooding pinkness when he talked to her, her so very parted lips, considering her pretty teeth, her so very parted eyelids, considering her pretty eyes, all of which might have been those of some waxen image of uncritical faith, cooled the heat of his helplessness very much as if he were laying his head on a tense silk pillow. She had, it was true, forms of speech, familiar watchwords, that affected him as small scratchy perforations of the smooth surface from within; but his pleasure in her and need of her were independent of such things and really almost altogether determined by the fact of the happy, even if all so lonely, forms and instincts in her which claimed kinship with his own. With her natural elegance stamped on her as by a die, with her dim and disinherited individual refinement of grace, which would have made any one wonder who she was anywhere—hat and veil and feather-boa and smart umbrella-knob and all—with her regular God-given distinction of type, in fine, she couldn't abide vulgarity much more than he could.

Therefore it didn't seem to him, under his stress, to matter particularly for instance, if she *would* keep on referring so many things to the time, as she called it, when she came into his life—his own great insistence and contention being that she hadn't in the least entered there till his mind was wholly made up to eliminate his other friend. What that methodical fury was so fierce to bring home to him was the falsity to herself involved in the later acquaintance; whereas just his precious right to hold up his head to everything—before himself at least—sprang from the fact that she couldn't make dates fit anyhow. He hadn't so much as heard of his true beauty's existence (she had come back but a few weeks before from her two years with her terrible trying deceased aunt at Swindon, previous to which absence she had been an unnoticeable chit) till days and days, ever so many, upon his honour, after he had struck for freedom by his great first backing-out letter—the precious document, the treat for a British jury, in which, by itself, Miss Cookham's firm instructed her to recognise the prospect of a fortune. The way the ruffians had been "her" ruffians—it appeared as if she had posted them behind her from the first of her beginning her game!—and the way "instructions" bounced out, with it, at a touch, larger than life, as if she had arrived with her pocket full of them! The date of the letter, taken with its other connexions, and the date of *her* first give-away for himself, his seeing her get out of the Brighton train with Bill Frankle that day he had gone to make the row at the Station parcels' office about the miscarriage of the box from Wales—those were the facts it sufficed him to point to, as he had pointed to them for Nan Drury's benefit, goodness knew, often and often enough. If he didn't seek occasion to do so for anyone else's—in open court as they said—that was his own affair, or at least his and Nan's.

It little mattered, meanwhile, if on their bench of desolation all that summer— and, it may be added, for summers and summers, to say nothing of winters, there and elsewhere, to come—she did give way to her artless habit of not contradicting him enough, which led to her often trailing up and down before him, too complacently, the untimely shreds and patches of his own glooms and desperations. "Well, I'm glad I *am* in your life, terrible as it is, however or whenever I did come in!" and "*Of course* you'd rather have starved—and it seems pretty well as if we shall, doesn't it?—than have bought her off by a false, abhorrent love, wouldn't you?" and "It isn't as if she hadn't made up to you the way she did before you had so much as looked at her, is it? or as if you hadn't shown her what you felt her really to be before you had so much as looked at *me*, is it either?" and "Yes, how on earth, pawning the shoes on your feet, you're going to raise another shilling—*that's* what you want to know, poor darling, don't you?"

III

His creditor, at the hour it suited her, transferred her base of operations to town, to which impenetrable scene she had also herself retired; and his raising of the first Two Hundred, during five exasperated and miserable months, and then of another Seventy piece-meal, bleedingly, after long delays and under the epistolary whiplash cracked by the London solicitor in his wretched ear even to an effect of the very report of Miss Cookham's tongue—these melancholy efforts formed a scramble up an arduous steep where steps were planted and missed, and bared knees were excoriated, and clutches at wayside tufts succeeded and failed, on a system to which poor Nan could have intelligently entered only if she had been somehow less ladylike. She kept putting into his mouth the sick quaver of where he should find the rest, the always inextinguishable rest, long after he had in silent rage fallen away from any further payment at all—at first, he had but too blackly felt, for himself, to the still quite possible non-exclusion of some penetrating ray of "exposure." He didn't care a tuppenny damn now, and in point of fact, after he had by hook and by crook succeeded in being able to unload to the tune of Two-Hundred-and-Seventy, and then simply returned the newest reminder of his outstanding obligation unopened, this latter belated but real sign of fight, the first he had risked, remarkably caused nothing at all to happen; nothing at least but his being moved to quite tragically rueful wonder as to whether exactly some such demonstration mightn't have served his turn at an earlier stage.

He could by this time at any rate measure his ruin—with three fantastic mortgages on his house, his shop, his stock, and a burden of interest to carry under which his business simply stretched itself inanimate, without strength for a protesting kick, without breath for an appealing groan. Customers lingering for further enjoyment of the tasteful remarks he had cultivated the unobtrusive art of throwing in, would at this crisis have found plenty to repay them, might his wit have strayed a little more widely still, toward a circuitous egotistical outbreak, from the immediate question of the merits of this and that author or of the condition of this and that volume. He had come to be conscious through it all of strangely glaring at people when they tried to haggle—and not, as formerly, with the glare of derisive comment on their overdone humour, but with that of fairly idiotised surrender; as if they were much mistaken in supposing, for the sake of conversation, that he might take himself for saveable by the difference between sevenpence and ninepence. He watched everything impossible and deplorable happen, as in an endless prolongation of his nightmare; watched himself proceed, that is, with the finest, richest incoherence to the due preparation of his catastrophe. Everything came to seem *equally* part of this—in complete defiance of proportion; even his final command of detachment, on the bench of desolation (where each successive fact of his dire case regularly cut itself out black, yet of senseless silhouette, against the red west), in respect to poor Nan's flat infelicities, which for the most part kept no pace with the years or with change, but only shook like hard peas in a child's rattle, the same peas always, of course, so long as the rattle didn't split open with usage or from somebody's act of irritation. They represented, or they had long done so, her contribution to the more superficial of the two branches of intimacy—the intellectual alternative, the one that didn't merely consist in her preparing herself for his putting his arm round her waist.

There were to have been moments, nevertheless, all the first couple of years, when she did touch in him, though to his actively dissimulating it, a more or less sensitive nerve—moments as they were too, to do her justice, when she treated him not to his own wisdom, or even folly, served up cold, but to a certain small bitter fruit of her personal, her unnatural, plucking. "I wonder that since *she* took legal advice so freely, to come down on you, you didn't take it yourself, a little, before being so sure you stood no chance. Perhaps *your* people would have been sure of something quite different—*perhaps,* I only say, you know." She "only" said it, but she said it, none the less, in the early time, about once a fortnight. In the later, and especially after their marriage, it had a way of coming up again to the exclusion, as it seemed to him, of almost everything else; in fact, during the most dismal years, the three of the loss of their two children, the long stretch of sordid embarrassment ending in her death, he was afterward to think of her as having generally said it several times a day. He was then also to remember that his answer, before she had learnt to discount it, had been inveterately at hand: "What would any solicitor have done or wanted to do but drag me just into the hideous public arena"—he had always so put it—"that it has been at any rate my pride and my honour, the one rag of self-respect covering my nakedness, to have loathed and avoided from every point of view?"

That had disposed of it so long as he cared, and by the time he had ceased to care for anything it had also lost itself in the rest of the vain babble of home. After his wife's death, during his year of mortal solitude, it woke again as an echo of far-off things—far-off, very far-off, because he felt then not ten but twenty years older. That was by reason simply of the dead weight with which his load of debt had settled—the persistence of his misery dragging itself out. With all that had come and gone the bench of desolation was still there, just as the immortal flush of the westward sky kept hanging its indestructible curtain. He had never got away—everything had left him, but he himself had been able to turn his back on nothing—and now, his day's labour before a dirty desk at the Gas Works ended, he more often than not, almost any season at temperate Properley serving his turn, took his slow, straight way to the Land's End and, collapsing there to rest, sat often for an hour at a time staring before him. He might in these sessions, with his eyes on the grey-green sea, have been counting again and still recounting the beads, almost all worn smooth, of his rosary of pain—which had for the fingers of memory and the recurrences of wonder the same felt break of the smaller ones by the larger that would have aided a pious mumble in some dusky altar-chapel.

If it has been said of him that when once full submersion, as from far back, had visibly begun to await him, he watched himself, in a cold lucidity, *do* punctually and necessarily each of the deplorable things that were inconsistent with his keeping afloat, so at present again he might have been held agaze just by the presented grotesqueness of that vigil. Such ghosts of dead seasons were all he *had* now to watch—such a recaptured sense, for instance, as that of the dismal unavailing awareness that had attended his act of marriage. He had let submersion final and absolute become the signal for it—a mere minor determinant having been the more or less contemporaneously unfavourable effect on the business of Drury & Dean of the sudden disappearance of Mr. Dean with the single small tin box into which the certificates of the firm's credit had been found to be compressible. That had been his only form—or had at any rate seemed his only one. He couldn't not have married, no doubt, just as he couldn't not have suffered the last degree of humiliation and almost of want, or just as his wife and children couldn't not have died of the little he was able, under dire reiterated pinches, to do for them; but it *was* "rum," for final solitary brooding, that he hadn't appeared to see his way definitely to undertake the support of a family till the last scrap of his little low-browed, high-toned business and the last figment of "property" in the old tiled and timbered shell that housed it had been sacrificed to creditors mustering six rows deep.

Of course what had counted too in the odd order was that, even at the end of the two or three years he had "allowed" her, Kate Cookham, gorged with his unholy tribute, had become the subject of no successful siege on the part either of Bill Frankle or, by what he could make out, of any one else. She had judged decent—he could do her that justice—to take herself personally out of his world, as he called it, for good and all, as soon as he had begun regularly to bleed; and, to whatever lucrative practice she might be devoting her great talents in London or elsewhere, he felt his conscious curiosity about her as cold, with time, as the passion of vain protest that she had originally left him to. He could recall but two direct echoes of her in all the bitter years—both communicated by Bill Frankle, disappointed and exposed and at last quite remarkably ingenuous sneak, who had also, from far back, taken to roaming the world, but who, during a period, used fitfully and ruefully to reappear. Herbert Dodd had quickly seen, at their first meeting—every one met every one sooner or later at Properley, if meeting it could always be called, either in the glare or the gloom of the explodedly attractive Embankment—that no silver stream of which he himself had been the remoter source could have played over the career of this all but repudiated acquaintance. That hadn't fitted with his first, his quite primitive raw vision of the probabilities, and he had further been puzzled when, much later on, it had come to him in a roundabout way that Miss Cookham was supposed to be, or to have been, among them for a few days "on the quiet," and that Frankle, who had seen her and who claimed to know more about it than he said, was cited as authority for the fact. But he hadn't himself at this juncture seen Frankle; he had only wondered, and a degree of mystification had even remained.

That memory referred itself to the dark days of old Drury's smash, the few weeks between his partner's dastardly flight and Herbert's own comment on it in the form of his standing up with Nan for the nuptial benediction of the Vicar of St. Bernard's on a very cold, bleak December morning and amid a circle of seven or eight long-faced, red-nosed, and altogether dowdy persons. Poor Nan herself had come to affect him as scarce other than red-nosed and dowdy by that time, but this only added, in his then, and indeed in his lasting view, to his general and his particular morbid bravery. He had cultivated ignorance, there were small inward immaterial luxuries he could scrappily cherish even among other, and the harshest, destitutions; and one of them was represented by this easy refusal of his mind to render to certain passages of his experience, to various ugly images, names, associations, the homage of continued attention. That served him, that helped him; but what happened when, a dozen dismal years having worn themselves away, he sat single and scraped bare again, as if his long wave of misfortune had washed him far beyond everything and then conspicuously re-treated, was that, thus stranded by tidal action, deposited in the lonely hollow of his fate, he felt even sustaining pride turn to nought and heard no challenge from it when old mystifications, stealing forth in the dusk of the day's work done, scratched at the door of speculation and hung about, through the idle hours, for irritated notice.

The evenings of his squalid clerkship were all leisure now, but there was nothing at all near home, on the other hand, for his imagination, numb and stiff from its long chill, to begin to play with. Voices from far off would quaver to him therefore in the stillness; where he knew for the most recurrent, little by little, the faint wail of his wife. He had become deaf to it in life, but at present, after so great an interval, he listened again, listened and listened, and seemed to hear it sound as by the pressure of some weak broken spring. It phrased for his ear her perpetual question, the one she had come to at the last as under the obsession of a discovered and resented wrong, a wrong withal that had its source much more in his own action than anywhere else. "That you didn't make *sure* she could have done anything, that you didn't make sure and that you were too afraid!"—this commemoration had ended by playing such a part of Nan's finally quite contracted consciousness as to exclude everything else.

At the time, somehow, he had made his terms with it; he had then more urgent questions to meet than that of the poor creature's taste in worrying pain; but actually it struck him—not the question, but the fact itself of the taste—as the one thing left over from all that had come and gone. So it was; nothing remained to him in the world, on the bench of desolation, but the option of taking up that echo—together with an abundance of free time for doing so. That he hadn't made sure of what might and what mightn't have been done to him, that he had been too afraid—had the proposition a possible bearing on his present apprehension of things? To reply indeed he would have had to be able to say what his present apprehension of things, left to itself, amounted to; an uninspiring effort indeed he judged it, sunk to so poor a pitch was his material of thought—though it might at last have been the feat he sought to perform as he stared at the grey-green sea.

IV

It was seldom he was disturbed in any form of sequestered speculation, or that at his times of predilection, especially that of the long autumn blankness between the season of trippers and the season of Bath-chairs, there were westward stragglers enough to jar upon his settled sense of priority. For himself his seat, the term of his walk, was consecrated; it had figured to him for years as the last (though there were others, not immediately near it, and differently disposed, that might have aspired to the title); so that he could invidiously distinguish as he approached, make out from a distance any accident of occupation, and never draw nearer while that unpleasantness lasted. What he disliked was to compromise on his tradition, whether for a man, a woman, or a connoodling couple; it was to idiots of this last composition he most objected, he having sat there, in the past, alone, having sat there interminably with Nan, having sat there with—well, with other women when women, at hours of ease, could still care or count for him, but having never shared the place with any shuffling or snuffling strangers.

It was a world of fidgets and starts, however, the world of his present dreariness; he alone possessed in it, he seemed to make out, of the secret of the dignity of sitting still with one's fate; so that if he took a turn about or rested briefly elsewhere even foolish philanderers—though this would never have been his and Nan's way—ended soon by some adjournment as visibly pointless as their sprawl. Then, their backs turned, he would drop down on it, the bench of desolation—which was what he, and he only, made it, by sad adoption; where, for that matter, moreover, once he had settled at his end, it was marked that nobody else ever came to sit. He saw people, along the Marina, take this liberty with other resting presences; but his own struck them perhaps in general as either of too grim or just of too dingy a vicinage. He might have affected the fellow-lounger as a man evil, unsociable, possibly engaged in working out the idea of a crime; or otherwise, more probably—for on the whole he surely looked harmless—devoted to the worship of some absolutely unpractical remorse.

On a certain October Saturday he had got off as usual, early; but the afternoon light, his pilgrimage drawing to its aim, could still show him, at long range, the rare case of an established usurper. His impulse was then, as by custom, to deviate a little and wait, all the more that the occupant of the bench was a lady, and that ladies, when alone, were—at that austere end of the varied frontal stretch—markedly discontinuous; but he kept on at sight of this person's rising, while he was still fifty yards off, and proceeding, her back turned, to the edge of the broad terrace, the outer line of which followed the interspaced succession of seats and was guarded by an iron rail from the abruptly lower level of the beach. Here she stood before the sea, while our friend on his side, recognising no reason to the contrary, sank into the place she had quitted. There were other benches, eastward and off by the course of the drive, for vague ladies. The lady indeed thus thrust upon Herbert's vision might have struck an observer either as not quite vague or as vague with a perverse intensity suggesting design.

Not that our own observer at once thought of these things; he only took in, and with no great interest, that the obtruded presence was a "real" lady; that she was dressed—he noticed such matters—with a certain elegance of propriety or intention of harmony; and that she remained perfectly still for a good many minutes; so many, in fact, that he presently ceased to heed her, and that as she wasn't straight before him, but as far to the left as was consistent with his missing her profile, he had turned himself to one of his sunsets again (though it wasn't quite one of his best) and let it hold him for a time that enabled her to alter her attitude and present a fuller view. Without other movement, but her back now to the sea and her face to the odd person who had appropriated her corner, she had taken a sustained look at him before he was aware she had stirred. On that apprehension, however, he became also promptly aware of her direct, her applied observation. As his sense of this quickly increased he wondered who she was and what she wanted—what, as it were, was the matter with her; it suggested to him, the next thing, that she had, under some strange idea, actually been waiting for him. Any idea about him to-day on the part of any one could only be strange.

Yes, she stood there with the ample width of the Marina between them, but turned to him, for all the world, as to show frankly that she was concerned with him. And she *was*—oh, yes—a real lady: a middle-aged person, of good appearance and of the best condition, in quiet but "handsome" black, save for very fresh white kid gloves, and with a pretty, dotty, becoming veil, predominantly white, adjusted to her countenance; which through it somehow, even to his imperfect sight, showed strong fine black brows and what he would have called on the spot character. But she was pale; her black brows were the blacker behind the flattering tissue; she still kept a hand, for support, on the terrace rail, while the other, at the end of an extended arm that had an effect of rigidity, clearly pressed hard on the knob of a small and shining umbrella, the lower extremity of whose stick was equally, was sustainingly, firm on the walk. So this mature, qualified, important person stood and looked at the limp, undistinguished—oh, his values of aspect now!—shabby man on the bench.

It was extraordinary, but the fact of her interest, by immensely surprising, by immediately agitating him, blinded him at first to her identity and, for the space of his long stare, diverted him from it; with which even then, when recognition did break, the sense of the shock, striking inward, simply consumed itself in gaping stillness. He sat there motionless and weak, fairly faint with surprise, and there was no instant, in all the succession of so many, at which Kate Cookham could have caught the special sign of his intelligence. Yet that she did catch something he saw—for he saw her steady herself, by her two supported hands, to meet it; while, after she had done so, a very wonderful thing happened, of which he could scarce, later on, have made a clear statement, though he was to think it over again and again. She moved toward him, she reached him, she stood there, she sat down near him, he merely passive and wonderstruck, unresentfully "impressed," gaping and taking it in—and all as with an open allowance on the part of each, so that they positively and quite intimately met in it, of the impertinence for their case, this case that brought them again, after horrible years, face to face, of the vanity, the profanity, the impossibility, of anything between them but silence.

Nearer to him, beside him at a considerable interval (oh, she was immensely considerate!) she presented him, in the sharp terms of her transformed state—but thus the more amply, formally, ceremoniously—with the reasons that would serve him best for not having precipitately known her. She was simply another and a totally different person, and the exhibition of it to which she had proceeded with this solemn anxiety was all, obviously, for his benefit—once he had, as he appeared to be doing, provisionally accepted her approach. He had remembered her as inclined to the massive and disowned by the graceful; but this was a spare, fine, worn, almost wasted lady—who had repaired waste, it was true, however, with something he could only appreciate as a rich accumulation of manner. She was strangely older, so far as that went—marked by experience and as if many things had happened to her; her face had suffered, to its improvement, contraction and concentration; and if he had granted, of old and from the first, that her eyes were remarkable, had they yet ever had for him this sombre glow? Withal, something said, she had flourished—he felt it, wincing at it, as that; she had had a life, a career, a history, something that her present waiting air and nervous consciousness couldn't prevent his noting there as a deeply latent assurance. She had flourished, she had flourished—though to learn it after this fashion was somehow at the same time not to feel she flaunted it. It wasn't thus execration that she revived in him; she made in fact, exhibitively, as he could only have put it, the matter of long ago irrelevant, and these extraordinary minutes of their reconstituted relation—how many? how few?—addressed themselves altogether to new possibilities.

Still it after a little awoke in him as with the throb of a touched nerve that his own very attitude was supplying a connection; he knew presently that he wouldn't have had her go, *couldn't* have made a sign to her for it—which was what she had been uncertain of—without speaking to him; and that therefore he was, as at the other, the hideous time, passive to whatever she might do. She was even yet, she was always, in possession of him; she had known how and where to find him and had appointed that he should see her, and, though he had never dreamed it was again to happen to him, he was meeting it already as if it might have been the only thing that the least humanly *could*. Yes, he had come back there to flop, by long custom, upon the bench of desolation *as* the man in the whole place, precisely, to whom nothing worth more than tuppence could happen; whereupon, in the grey desert of his consciousness, the very earth had suddenly opened and flamed. With this, further, it came over him that he hadn't been prepared and that his wretched appearance must show it. He wasn't fit to receive a visit—any visit; a flush for his felt misery, in the light of her opulence, broke out in his lean cheeks. But if he coloured he sat as he was—she should at least, as a visitor, be satisfied. His eyes only, at last, turned from her and resumed a little their gaze at the sea. That, however, didn't relieve him, and he perpetrated in the course of another moment the odd desperate gesture of raising both his hands to his face and letting them, while he pressed it to them, cover and guard it. It was as he held them there that she at last spoke.

"I'll go away if you wish me to." And then she waited a moment. "I mean now—now that you've seen I'm here. I wanted you to know it, and I thought of writing—I was afraid of our meeting accidentally. Then I was afraid that if I wrote you might refuse. So I thought of this way—as I knew you must come out here." She went on with pauses, giving him a chance to make a sign. "I've waited several days. But I'll do what you wish. Only I should like in that case to come back." Again she stopped; but strange was it to him that he wouldn't have made her break off. She held him in boundless wonder. "I came down— I mean I came from town—on purpose. I'm staying on still, and I've a great patience and will give you time. Only may I say it's important? Now that I do see you," she brought out in the same way, "I see how inevitable it was—I mean that I should have wanted to come. But you must feel about it as you can," she wound up—"till you get used to the idea."

She spoke so for accommodation, for discretion, for some ulterior view already expressed in her manner, that, after taking well in, from behind his hands, that this was her very voice—oh, ladylike!—heard, and heard in deprecation of displeasure, after long years again, he uncovered his face and freshly met her eyes. More than ever he couldn't have known her. Less and less remained of the figure all the facts of which had long ago so hardened for him. She was a handsome, grave, authoritative, but refined and, as it were, physically rearranged person— she, the outrageous vulgarity of whose prime assault had kept him shuddering so long as a shudder was in him. That atrocity in her was what everything had been built on, but somehow, all strangely, it was slipping from him; so that, after the oddest fashion conceivable, when he felt he mustn't let her go, it was as if he were putting out his hand to *save* the past, the hideous, real, unalterable past, exactly as she had been the cause of its being and the cause of his undergoing it. He should have been too awfully "sold" if he wasn't going to have been right about her.

"I don't mind," he heard himself at last say. Not to mind had seemed for the instant the length he was prepared to go; but he was afterward aware of how soon he must have added: "You've come on purpose to see me?" He was on the point of putting to her further: "What, then, do you want of me?" But he would keep —yes, in time—from appearing to show he cared. If he showed he cared, where then would be his revenge? So he was already, within five minutes, thinking his revenge uncomfortably over instead of just comfortably knowing it. What came to him, at any rate, as they actually fell to talk, was that, with such precautions, considerations, reduplications of consciousness, almost avowed feelings of her way on her own part, and light fingerings of his chords of sensibility, she was understanding, she *had* understood, more things than all the years, up to this strange eventide, had given him an inkling of. They talked, they went on—he hadn't let her retreat, to whatever it committed him and however abjectly it did so; yet keeping off and off, dealing with such surface facts as involved ancient acquaintance but kept abominations at bay. The recognition, the attestation that she *had* come down for him, that there would be reasons, that she had even hovered and watched, assured herself a little of his habits (which she managed to speak of as if, on their present ampler development, they were much to be deferred to), held them long enough to make vivid how, listen as stiffly or as serenely as he might, she sat there in fear, just as she had so stood there at first, and that her fear had really to do with her calculation of some sort of chance with him. What chance could it possibly be? Whatever it might have done, on this prodigious showing, with Kate Cookham, it made the present witness to the state of his fortunes simply exquisite: he ground his teeth secretly together as he saw he should have to take *that*. For what did it mean but that she would have liked to pity him if she could have done it with safety? Ah, however, he must give her no measure of safety!

By the time he had remarked, with that idea, that she probably saw few changes about them there that weren't for the worse—the place was going down, down and down, so fast that goodness knew where it would stop—and had also mentioned that in spite of this he himself remained faithful, with all its faults loving it still; by the time he had, after that fashion, superficially indulged her, adding a few further light and just sufficiently dry reflexions on local matters, the disappearance of landmarks and important persons, the frequency of gales, the low policy of the Town Council in playing down to cheap excursionists: by the time he had so acquitted himself, and she had observed, of her own motion, that she was staying at the Royal, which he knew for the time-honoured, the conservative and exclusive hotel, he had made out for himself one thing at least, the amazing fact that he had been landed by his troubles, at the end of time, in a "social relation," of all things in the world, and how of that luxury he was now having unprecedented experience. He had but once in his life had his nose in the Royal, on the occasion of his himself delivering a parcel during some hiatus in his succession of impossible small boys and meeting in the hall the lady who had bought of him, in the morning, a set of Crabbe; largely, he flattered himself, under the artful persuasion of his acute remarks on that author, gracefully associated by him, in this colloquy, he remembered, with a glance at Charles Lamb as well, and who went off, in a day or two, without settling, though he received her cheque from London three or four months later.

That hadn't been a social relation; and truly, deep within his appeal to himself to be remarkable, to be imperturbable and impenetrable, to be in fact quite incomparable now, throbbed the intense vision of his drawing out and draining dry the sensation he had begun to taste. He would do it, moreover—that would be the refinement of his art—not only without the betraying anxiety of a single question, but just even by seeing her flounder (since she must, in a vagueness deeply disconcerting to her) as to her real effect on him. She was distinctly floundering by the time he had brought her—it had taken ten minutes—down to a consciousness of absurd and twaddling topics, to the reported precarious state, for instance, of the syndicate running the Bijou Theatre at the Pierhead—all as an admonition that she might want him to want to know why she was thus waiting on him, might want it for all she was worth, before he had ceased to be so remarkable as not to ask her. He didn't—and this assuredly was wondrous enough—want to do anything worse to her than let her flounder; but he was willing to do that so long as it mightn't prevent his seeing at least where *he* was. He seemed still to see where he was even at the minute that followed her final break-off, clearly intended to be resolute, from make-believe talk.

"I wonder if I might prevail on you to come to tea with me to-morrow at five."

He didn't so much as answer it—though he could scarcely believe his ears. To-morrow was Sunday, and the proposal referred, clearly, to the custom of "five-o'clock" tea, known to him only by the contemporary novel of manners and the catchy advertisements of table linen. He had never in his life been present at any such luxurious rite, but he was offering practical indifference to it as a false mark of his sense that his social relation had already risen to his chin. "I gave up my very modest, but rather interesting little old book business, perhaps you know, ever so long ago."

She floundered so that she could say nothing—meet *that* with no possible word; all the less too that his tone, casual and colourless, wholly defied any apprehension of it as a reverse. Silence only came; but after a moment she returned to her effort. "If you *can* come I shall be at home. To see you otherwise than thus was, in fact, what, as I tell you, I came down for. But I leave it," she returned, "to your feeling."

He had at this, it struck him, an inspiration; which he required, however, a minute or two to decide to carry out; a minute or two during which the shake of his foot over his knee became an intensity of fidget. "Of course I know I still owe you a large sum of money. If it's about *that* you wish to see me," he went on, "I may as well tell you just here that I shall be able to meet my full obligation in the future as little as I've met it in the past. I can never," said Herbert Dodd, "pay up that balance."

He had looked at her while he spoke, but on finishing looked off at the sea again and continued to agitate his foot. He knew now what he had done, and why; and the sense of her fixed dark eyes on him during his speech and after didn't alter his small contentment. Yet even when she still said nothing he didn't turn round; he simply kept his corner as if *that* were his point made, should it even be the last word between them. It might have been, for that matter, from the way in which she presently rose, gathering herself, her fine umbrella and her very small smart reticule, in the construction of which shining gilt much figured, well together, and, after standing another instant, moved across to the rail of the terrace as she had done before and remained, as before, with her back to him, though this time, it well might be, under a different fear. A quarter of an hour ago she hadn't tried him, and had had that anxiety; now that she had tried him it wasn't easier—but she was thinking what she still could do. He left her to think —nothing, in fact, more interesting than the way she might decide had ever happened to him; but it was a part of this also that as she turned round and came nearer again he didn't rise, he gave her no help. If she got any, at least, from his looking up at her only, meeting her fixed eyes once more in silence, that was her own affair. "You must think," she said—"you must take all your time, but I shall be at home." She left it to him thus—she insisted, with her idea, on leaving him somewhere too. And on her side as well she showed an art—which resulted, after another instant, in his having to rise to his feet. He flushed afresh as he did it—it exposed him so shabbily the more; and now if she took him in, with each of his seedy items, from head to foot, he didn't and couldn't and wouldn't know it, attaching his eyes hard and straight to something quite away from them.

It stuck in his throat to say he'd come, but she had so curious a way with her that he still less could say he wouldn't, and in a moment had taken refuge in something that was neither. "Are you married?"—he put it to her with that plainness, though it had seemed before he said it to do more for him than while she waited before replying.

"No, I'm not married," she said; and then had another wait that might have amounted to a question of what this had to do with it.

He surely couldn't have told her; so that he had recourse, a little poorly as he felt, but to an "Oh!" that still left them opposed. He turned away for it—that is for the poorness, which, lingering in the air, had almost a vulgar platitude; and when he presently again wheeled about she had fallen off as for quitting him, only with a pause, once more, for a last look. It was all a bit awkward, but he had another happy thought, which consisted in his silently raising his hat as for a sign of dignified dismissal. He had cultivated of old, for the occasions of life, the right, the discriminated bow, and now, out of the grey limbo of the time when he could care for such things, this flicker of propriety leaped and worked. She might, for that matter, herself have liked it; since, receding further, only with her white face toward him, she paid it the homage of submission. He remained dignified, and she almost humbly went.

V

Nothing in the world, on the Sunday afternoon, could have prevented him from going; he was not after all destitute of three or four such articles of clothing as, if they wouldn't particularly grace the occasion, wouldn't positively dishonour it. That deficiency might have kept him away, but no voice of the spirit, no consideration of pride. It sweetened his impatience, in fact—for he fairly felt it a long time to wait—that his pride would really most find its account in his acceptance of these conciliatory steps. From the moment he could put it in that way—that he couldn't refuse to hear what she might have, so very elaborately, to say for herself—he ought certainly to be at his ease; in illustration of which he whistled odd snatches to himself as he hung about on that cloud-dappled autumn Sunday, a mild private minstrelsy that his lips hadn't known since when? The interval of the twenty-four hours, made longer by a night of many more revivals than oblivious, had, in fact, dragged not a little; in spite of which, however, our extremely brushed-up and trimmed and polished friend knew an unprecedented flutter as he was ushered, at the Royal Hotel, into Miss Cookham's sitting-room. Yes, it was an adventure, and he had never had an adventure in his life; the term, for him, was essentially a term of high appreciation—such as disqualified for that figure, under due criticism, every single passage of his past career.

What struck him at the moment as qualifying in the highest degree this actual passage was the fact that at no great distance from his hostess in the luxurious room, as he apprehended it, in which the close of day had begun to hang a few shadows, sat a gentleman who rose as she rose, and whose name she at once mentioned to him. He had for Herbert Dodd all the air of a swell, the gentleman —rather red-faced and bald-headed, but moustachioed, waistcoated, necktied to the highest pitch, with an effect of chains and rings, of shining teeth in a glassily monocular smile; a wondrous apparition to have been asked to "meet" him, as in contemporary fiction, or for him to have been asked to meet. "Captain Roper, Mr. Herbert Dodd"—their entertainer introduced them, yes; but with a sequel immediately afterward more disconcerting apparently to Captain Roper himself even than to her second and more breathless visitor; a "Well then, good-bye till the next time," with a hand thrust straight out, which allowed the personage so addressed no alternative but to lay aside his teacup, even though Herbert saw there was a good deal left in it, and glare about him for his hat. Miss Cookham had her tea-tray on a small table before her, she had served Captain Roper while waiting for Mr. Dodd; but she simply dismissed him now, with a high sweet un-mistakable decision, a knowledge of what she was about, as our hero would have called it, which enlarged at a stroke the latter's view of the number of different things and sorts of things, in the sphere of the manners and ways of those living at their ease, that a social relation would put before one. Captain Roper would have liked to remain, would have liked more tea, but Kate signified in this direct fashion that she had had enough of him. Herbert had seen things, in his walk of life—rough things plenty; but never things smoothed with that especial smooth-ness, carried out as it were by the fine form of Captain Roper's own retreat, which included even a bright convulsed leave-taking cognisance of the plain, vague individual, of no lustre at all and with the very low-class guard of an old silver watch buttoned away under an ill-made coat, to whom he was sacrificed.

It came to Herbert as he left the place a shade less remarkable—though there was still wonder enough and to spare—that he had been even publicly and designedly sacrificed; exactly so that, as the door closed behind him, Kate Cook-ham, standing there to wait for it, could seem to say, across the room, to the friend of her youth, only by the expression of her fine eyes: "There—see what I do for you!" "For" him—that was the extraordinary thing, and not less so that he was already, within three minutes, after this fashion, taking it in as by the intensity of a new light; a light that was one somehow with this rich inner air of the plush-draped and much-mirrored hotel, where the firelight and the approach of evening confirmed together the privacy and the loose curtains at the wide window were parted for a command of his old lifelong Parade—the field of life so familiar to him from below and in the wind and the wet, but which he had never in all the long years hung over at this vantage.

"He's an acquaintance, but a bore," his hostess explained in respect to Captain Roper. "He turned up yesterday, but I didn't invite him, and I had said to him before you came in that I was expecting a gentleman with whom I should wish to be alone. I go quite straight at my idea that way, as a rule; but you know," she now strikingly went on, "how straight I go. And he had had," she added, "his tea."

Dodd had been looking all round—had taken in, with the rest, the brightness, the distinguished elegance, as he supposed it, of the tea-service with which she was dealing and the variously-tinted appeal of certain savoury edibles on plates. "Oh, but he *hadn't* had his tea!" he heard himself the next moment earnestly reply; which speech had at once betrayed, he was then quickly aware, the candour of his interest, the unsophisticated state that had survived so many troubles. If he was so interested how could he be proud, and if he was proud how could he be so interested?

He had made her at any rate laugh outright, and was further conscious, for this, both that it was the first time of that since their new meeting, and that it didn't affect him as harsh. It affected him, however, as free, for she replied at once, still smiling and as a part of it: "Oh, I think we shall get on!"

This told him he had made some difference for her, shown her the way, or something like it, that she hadn't been sure of yeterday; which, moreover, wasn't what he had intended—he had come armed for showing her nothing; so that after she had gone on, with the same gain of gaiety, "You must at any rate comfortably have yours," there was but one answer for him to make.

His eyes played again over the tea-things—they seemed strangely to help him; but he didn't sit down. "I've come, as you see—but I've come, please, to understand; and if you require to be alone with me, and if I break bread with you, it seems to me I should first know exactly where I am and to what you suppose I so commit myself." He had thought it out and over and over, particularly the turn about breaking bread; though perhaps he didn't give it, in her presence— this was impossible, her presence altered so many things—quite the full sound or the weight he had planned.

But it had none the less come to his aid—it had made her perfectly grave. "You commit yourself to nothing. You're perfectly free. It's only I who commit myself."

On which, while she stood there as if all handsomely and deferentially waiting for him to consider and decide, he would have been naturally moved to ask her what she committed herself then *to*—so moved, that is, if he hadn't, before saying it, thought more sharply still of something better. "Oh, that's another thing."

"Yes, that's another thing," Kate Cookham returned. To which she added, "So *now* won't you sit down?" He sank with deliberation into the seat from which Captain Roper had risen; she went back to her own, and while she did so spoke again. "I'm *not* free. At least," she said over her tea-tray, "I'm free only for this."

Everything was there before them and around them, everything massive and shining, so that he had instinctively fallen back in his chair as for the wondering, the resigned acceptance of it; where her last words stirred in him a sense of odd depreciation. Only for "that"? "That" was everything, at this moment, to his long inanition, and the effect, as if she had suddenly and perversely mocked him, was to press the spring of a protest. "Isn't 'this' then riches?"

"Riches?" she smiled over, handing him his cup—for she had triumphed in having struck from him a question.

"I mean haven't you a lot of money?" He didn't care now that it was out; his cup was in his hand, and what was that but proved interest? He had succumbed to the social relation.

"Yes, I've money. Of course you wonder—but I've wanted you to wonder. It was to make you take that in that I came. So now you know," she said, leaning back where she faced him, but in a straighter chair and with her arms closely folded, after a fashion characteristic of her, as for some control of her nerves.

"You came to show you've money?"

"That's one of the things. Not a lot—not even very much. But enough," said Kate Cookham.

"Enough? I should think so!" he again couldn't help a bit crudely exhaling.

"Enough for what I wanted. I don't always live like this—not at all. But I came to the best hotel on purpose. I wanted to show you I could. Now," she asked, "do you understand?"

"Understand?" He only gaped.

She threw up her loosed arms, which dropped again beside her. "I did it *for* you—I did it *for* you!"

" 'For' me—?"

"What I did—what I did here of old."

He stared, trying to see it. "When you made me pay you?"

"The Two Hundred and Seventy—all I could get from you, as you reminded me yesterday, so that I had to give up the rest. It was my idea," she went on—"it was my idea."

"To bleed me quite to death?" Oh, his ice was broken now!

"To make you raise money—since you could, you *could*. You did, you did—so what better proof?"

His hands fell from what he had touched; he could only state—her own manner for it was different now too. "I did. I did indeed——!" And the woeful weak simplicity of it, which seemed somehow all that was left him, fell even on his own ear.

"Well then, here it is—it isn't lost!" she returned with a graver face.

" 'Here' it is," he gasped, "my poor agonised old money—my blood?"

"Oh, it's *my* blood too, you must know now!" She held up her head as not before—as for her right to speak of the thing to-day most precious to her. "I took it, but this—my being here this way—is what I've made of it! That was the idea I had!"

Her "ideas," as things to boast of, staggered him. "To have everything in the world, like this, at my wretched expense?"

She had folded her arms back again—grasping each elbow she sat firm; she knew he could see, and had known well from the first, what she had wanted to say, difficult, monstrous though it might be. "No more than at my own—but to do something with your money that you'd never do yourself."

"Myself, myself?" he wonderingly wailed. "Do you know—or don't you?—what my life has been?"

She waited, and for an instant, though the light in the room had failed a little more and would soon be mainly that of the flaring lamps on the windy Parade, he caught from her dark eye a silver gleam of impatience. "You've suffered and you've worked—which, God knows, is what I've done! *Of course* you've suf-ered," she said—"you inevitably had to! We have to," she went on, "to do or to be or to get anything."

"And pray what have I done or been or got?" Herbert Dodd found it almost desolately natural to demand.

It made her cover him again as with all she was thinking of. "Can you imagine nothing, or can't you conceive——?" And then as her challenge struck deeper in, deeper down than it had yet reached and with the effect of a rush of the blood to his face, "It was *for* you, it was *for* you!" she again broke out—"and for what or whom else could it have been?"

He saw things to a tune now that made him answer straight: "I thought at one time it might be for Bill Frankle."

"Yes—that was the way you treated me," Miss Cookham as plainly replied. But he let this pass; his thought had already got away from it. "What good then —its having been for me—has that ever done me?"

Doesn't it do you any good *now*?" his friend returned. To which she added, with another dim play of her tormented brightness, before he could speak: "But if you won't even have your tea——!"

He had in fact touched nothing, and if he could have explained, would have pleaded very veraciously that his appetite, keen when he came in, had somehow suddenly failed. It was beyond eating or drinking, what she seemed to want him to take from her. So if he looked, before him, over the array, it was to say, very grave and graceless: "Am I to understand that you offer to repay me?"

"I offer to repay you with interest, Herbert Dodd"—and her emphasis of the great word was wonderful.

It held him in his place a minute, and held his eyes upon her; after which, agitated too sharply to sit still, he pushed back his chair and stood up. It was as if mere distress or dismay at first worked in him, and was in fact a wave of deep and irresistible emotion which made him, on his feet, sway as in a great trouble and then, to correct it, throw himself stiffly toward the window, where he stood and looked out unseeing. The road, the wide terrace beyond, the seats, the eternal sea beyond that, the lighted lamps now flaring in the October night-wind, with the few dispersed people abroad at the tea-hour; these things, meeting and melting into the firelit hospitality at his elbow—or was it that portentous amenity that melted into *them?*—seemed to form round him and to put before him, all together, the strangest of circles and the newest of experiences, in which the unforgettable and the unimaginable were confoundingly mixed. "Oh, oh, oh!" —he could only almost howl for it.

And then, while a thick blur for some moments mantled everything, he knew she had got up, that she stood watching him, allowing for everything, again all "cleverly" patient with him, and he heard her speak again as with studied quiet-ness and clearness. "I wanted to take care of you—it was what I first wanted—and what you first consented to. I'd have done it, oh, I'd have done it, I'd have loved you and helped you and guarded you, and you'd have had no trouble, no bad blighting ruin, in all your easy, yes, just your quite jolly and comfortable life. I showed you and proved to you this—I brought it home to you, as I fondly fancied, and it made me briefly happy. You swore you cared for me, you wrote it and made me believe it—you pledged me your honour and your faith. Then you turned and changed suddenly, from one day to another; everything altered, you broke your vows, you as good as told me you only wanted it off. You faced me with dislike, and in fact tried not to face me at all; you behaved as if you hated me—you had seen a girl, of great beauty, I admit, who made me a fright and a bore."

This brought him straight round. "No, Kate Cookham."

"Yes, Herbert Dodd." She but shook her head, calmly and nobly, in the now gathered dusk, and her memories and her cause and her character—or was it only her arch-subtlety, her line and her "idea"?—gave her an extraordinary large assurance.

She had touched, however, the treasure of his own case—his terrible own case that began to live again at once by the force of her talking of hers, and which could always all cluster about his great asseveration. "No, no, never, never; I had never seen her then and didn't dream of her; so that when you yourself began to be harsh and sharp with me, and to seem to want to quarrel, I could have but one idea—which was an appearance you didn't in the least, as I saw it then, account for or disprove."

"An appearance——?" Kate desired, as with high astonishment, to know which one.

"How *shouldn't* I have supposed you really to care for Bill Frankle?—as, thoroughly believing the motive of your claim for my money to be its help to your marrying him, since you couldn't marry me. I was only surprised when, time passing, I made out that that hadn't happened; and perhaps," he added the next instant, with something of a conscious lapse from the finer style, "hadn't been in question."

She had listened to this only staring, and she was silent after he had said it, so silent for some instants that while he considered her something seemed to fail him, much as if he had thrown out his foot for a step and not found the place to rest it. He jerked round to the window again, and then she answered, but without passion, unless it was that of her weariness for something stupid and forgiven in him, "Oh, the blind, the pitiful folly!"—to which, as it might perfectly have applied to her own behaviour, he returned nothing. She had, moreover, at once gone on. "Put it then that there wasn't much to do—between your finding that you loathed me for another woman, or discovering only, when it came to the point, that you loathed me quite enough for myself."

Which, offered him in that immensely effective fashion, he recognised that he must just unprotestingly and not so very awkwardly—not so *very*!—take from her; since, whatever he had thus come to her for, it wasn't to perjure himself with any pretence that, "another woman" or no other woman, he hadn't, for years and years, abhorred her. Now he was taking tea with her—or rather, literally, seemed not to be; but this made no difference, and he let her express it as she would while he distinguished a man he knew, Charley Coote, outside on the Parade, under favour of the empty hour and one of the flaring lamps, making up to a young woman with whom (it stuck out grotesquely in his manner) he had never before conversed. Dodd's own position was that of acquiescing in this recall of what had so bitterly been—but he hadn't come back to her, of himself, to stir up, to recall or to recriminate, and for *her* it could but be the very lesson of her whole present act that if she touched anything she touched everything. Soon enough she was indeed, and all overwhelmingly, touching everything——with a hand of which the boldness grew.

"But I didn't let *that,* even, make a difference in what I wanted—which was all," she said, "and had only and passionately been, to take care of you. I had *no* money whatever—nothing then of my own, not a penny to come by anyhow; so it wasn't with mine I could do it. But I could do it with yours," she amazingly wound up—"if I could once get yours out of you."

He faced straight about again—his eyebrows higher than they had ever been in his life. "Mine? What penny of it was mine? What scrap beyond a bare, mean little living had I ever pretended to have?"

She held herself still a minute, visibly with force; only her eyes consciously attached to the seat of a chair the back of which her hands, making it tilt toward her a little, grasped as for support. "You pretended to have enough to marry me—and that was all I afterwards claimed of you when you wouldn't." He was on the point of retorting that he had absolutely pretended to nothing—least of all to the primary desire that such a way of putting it fastened on him; he was on the point for ten seconds of giving her full in the face: "I never *had* any such dream till you yourself—infatuated with me as, frankly, you on the whole appeared to be—got round me and muddled me up and made me behave as if in a way that went against the evidence of my senses." But he was to feel as quickly that, whatever the ugly, the spent, the irrecoverable truth, he might better have bitten his tongue off: there beat on him there this strange and other, this so prodigiously different beautiful and dreadful truth that no far remembrance and no abiding ache of his own could wholly falsify, and that was indeed all out with her next words. "That—*using* it for you and using you yourself for your own future—was my motive. I've led my life, which has been an affair, I assure you; and, as I've told you without your quite seeming to understand, I've brought everything fivefold back to you."

The perspiration broke out on his forehead. "Everything's mine?" he quavered as for the deep piercing pain of it.

"Everything!" said Kate Cookham.

So it told him how she had loved him—but with the tremendous effect at once of its only glaring out at him from the whole thing that it was verily she, a thousand times over, who, in the exposure of his youth and his vanity, had, on the bench of desolation, the scene of yesterday's own renewal, left for him no forward step to take. It hung there for him tragically vivid again, the hour she had first found him sequestered and accessible after making his acquaintance at his shop. And from this, by a succession of links that fairly clicked to his ear as with their perfect fitting, the fate and the pain and the payment of others stood together in a great grim order. Everything there then was *his*—to make him ask what had been Nan's, poor Nan's of the constant question of whether he need have collapsed. She was before him, she was between them, his little dead dissatisfied wife; across all whose final woe and whose lowly grave he was to reach out, it appeared, to take gifts. He saw them too, the gifts; saw them—she bristled with them—in his actual companion's brave and sincere and authoritative figure, her strangest of demonstrations. But the other appearance was intenser, as if their ghost had waved wild arms; so that half a minute hadn't passed before the one poor thing that remained of Nan, and that yet thus became a quite mighty and momentous poor thing, was sitting on his lips as for its sole opportunity.

"Can you give me your word of honour that I mightn't, under decent advice, have defied you?"

It made her turn very white; but now that she had said what she *had* said she could still hold up her head. "Certainly you might have defied me, Herbert Dodd."

"They would have told me you had no legal case?"

Well, if she was pale she was bold. "You talk of decent advice——!" She broke off, there was too much to say, and all needless. What she said instead was: "They would have told you I had nothing."

"I didn't so much as ask," her sad visitor remarked.

"Of course you didn't so much as ask."

"I couldn't be so outrageously vulgar," he went on.

"*I* could, by God's help!" said Kate Cookham.

"Thank you." He had found at his command a tone that made him feel more gentlemanlike than he had ever felt in his life or should doubtless ever feel again. It might have been enough—but somehow as they stood there with this immense clearance between them it wasn't. The clearance was like a sudden gap or great bleak opening through which there blew upon them a deadly chill. Too many things had fallen away, too many new rolled up and over him, and they made something within shake him to his base. It upset the full vessel, and though she kept her eyes on him he let that consequence come, bursting into tears, weakly crying there before her even as he had cried to himself in the hour of his youth when she had made him groundlessly fear. She turned away then—*that* she couldn't watch, and had presently flung herself on the sofa and, all responsively waiting, buried her own face on the cushioned arm. So for a minute their smothered sobs only filled the room. But he made out, through this disorder, where he had put down his hat; his stick and his new tan-coloured gloves—they had cost two-and-thruppence and would have represented sacrifices—were on the chair beside it. He picked these articles up and all silently and softly—gasping, that is, but quite on tiptoe—reached the door and let himself out.

VI

Off there on the bench of desolation a week later she made him a more particular statement, which it had taken the remarkably tense interval to render possible. After leaving her at the hotel that last Sunday he had gone forth in his reaggravated trouble and walked straight before him, in the teeth of the west wind, close to the iron rails of the stretched Marina and with his tell-tale face turned from persons occasionally met and toward the surging sea. At the land's end, even in the confirmed darkness and the perhaps imminent big blow, his immemorial nook, small shelter as it yielded, had again received him; and it was in the course of this heedless session, no doubt, where the agitated air had nothing to add to the commotion within him, that he began to look his extraordinary fortune a bit straighter in the face and see it confess itself at once a fairy-tale and a nightmare. That, visibly, confoundingly, she was still attached to him (attached in tact was a mild word!) and that the unquestionable proof of it was in this offered pecuniary salve, of the thickest composition, for his wounds and sores and shames—these things were the fantastic fable, the tale of money in handfuls, that he seemed to have only to stand there and swallow and digest and feel himself full-fed by; but the whole of the rest was nightmare, and most of all nightmare his having thus to thank one through whom Nan and his little girls had known torture.

He didn't care for himself now, and this unextinguished and apparently inextinguishable charm by which he had held her was a fact incredibly romantic; but he gazed with a longer face than he had ever had for anything in the world at his potential acceptance of a great bouncing benefit from the person he intimately, if even in a manner indirectly, associated with the conditions to which his lovely wife and his little girls (who would have been so lovely too) had pitifully succumbed. He had accepted the social relation—which meant he had taken even that on trial—without knowing what it so dazzlingly masked; for a social relation it had become with a vengeance when it drove him about the place as now at his hours of freedom (and he actually and recklessly took, all demoralised and unstrung and unfit either for work or for anything else, other liberties that would get him into trouble) under this queer torment of irreconcilable things, a bewildered consciousness of tenderness and patience and cruelty, of great evident mystifying facts that were as little to be questioned as to be conceived or explained, and that were yet least, withal, to be lost sight of.

On that Sunday night he had wandered wild, incoherently ranging and throbbing, but this became the law of his next days as well, since he lacked more than ever all other resort or refuge and had nowhere to carry, to deposit, or contractedly let loose and lock up, as it were, his swollen consciousness, which fairly split in twain the raw shell of his sordid little boarding-place. The arch of the sky and the spread of sea and shore alone gave him space; he could roam with himself anywhere, in short, far or near—he could only never take himself back. That certitude —that this was impossible to him even should she wait there among her plushes and bronzes ten years—was the thing he kept closest clutch of; it did wonders for what he would have called his self-respect. Exactly as he had left her so he would stand off—even though at moments when he pulled up sharp somewhere to put himself an intensest question his heart almost stood still. The days of the week went by, and as he had left her she stayed; to the extent, that is, of his having neither sight nor sound of her, and of the failure of every sign. It took nerve, he said, not to return to her, even for curiosity—since how, after all, in the name of wonder, had she invested the fruits of her extortion to such advantage, there being no chapter of all the obscurity of the years to beat that for queerness? But he dropped, tired to death, on benches, half a dozen times an evening—exactly on purpose to recognise that the nerve required was just the nerve he had.

As the days without a token from her multiplied he came in as well for hours

—and these indeed mainly on the bench of desolation—of sitting stiff and stark in presence of the probability that he had lost everything for ever. When he passed the Royal he never turned an eyelash, and when he met Captain Roper on the Front, three days after having been introduced to him he "cut him dead"— another privileged consequence of a social relation—rather than seem to himself to make the remotest approach to the question of whether Miss Cookham had left Properly. He had cut people in the days of his life before, just as he had come to being himself cut—since there had been no time for him wholly without one or other face of that necessity—but had never affected such a severance as of this rare connexion, which helped to give him thus the measure of this really precious sincerity. If he had lost what had hovered before him he had lost it, his only tribute to which proposition was to grind his teeth with one of those "scrunches," as he would have said, of which the violence fairly reached his ear. It wouldn't make him lift a finger, and in fact if Kate had simply taken herself off on the Tuesday or the Wednesday she would have been reabsorbed again into the darkness from which she had emerged—and no lifting of fingers, the unspeakable chapter closed, would evermore avail. That at any rate was the kind of man he still was—even after all that had come and gone, and even if for a few dazed hours certain things had seemed pleasant. The dazed hours had passed, the surge of the old bitterness had dished him (shouldn't he have been shamed if it hadn't?) and he might sit there as before, as always, with nothing at all on earth to look to. He had therefore wrongfully believed himself to be degraded; and the last word about him would be that he *couldn't* then, it appeared, sink to vulgarity as he had tried to let his miseries make him.

And yet on the next Sunday morning, face to face with him again at the land's end, what she very soon came to was: "As if I believed you didn't *know* by what cord you hold me!" Absolutely, too, and just that morning in fact, above all, he wouldn't, he quite couldn't have taken his solemn oath that he hadn't a sneaking remnant, as he might have put it to himself—a remnant of faith in tremendous things still to come of their interview. The day was sunny and breezy, the sea of a cold purple; he wouldn't go to church as he mostly went of Sunday mornings, that being in its way too a social relation—and not least when two-and-thruppenny tan-coloured gloves were new; which indeed he had the art of keeping them for ages. Yet he would dress himself as he scarce mustered resources for even to figure on the fringe of Society, local and transient, at St. Bernard's, and in this trim he took his way westward; occupied largely, as he went, it might have seemed to any person pursuing the same course and happening to observe him, in a fascinated study of the motions of his shadow, the more or less grotesque shape projected, in front of him and mostly a bit to the right, over the balanced asphalt of the Parade and dangling and dancing at such a rate, shooting out and then contracting, that, viewed in themselves, its eccentricities might have formed the basis of an interesting challenge: "Find the state of mind, guess the nature of the agitation, possessing the person so remarkably represented!" Herbert Dodd, for that matter, might have been himself attempting to make by the sun's sharp aid some approach to his immediate horoscope.

It had at any rate been thus put before him that the dandling and dancing of his image occasionally gave way to perfect immobility, when he stopped and kept his eyes on it. "Suppose she should come, suppose she *should!*" it is revealed at least to ourselves that he had at these moments audibly breathed—breathed with the intensity of an arrest between hope and fear. It had glimmered upon him from early, with the look of the day, that, given all else that could happen, this would be rather, as he put it, in her line; and the possibility lived for him, as he proceeded, to the tune of a suspense almost sickening. It was, from one small stage of his pilgrimage to another, the "For ever, never!" of the sentimental case the playmates of his youth used to pretend to settle by plucking the petals of a daisy. But it came to his truly turning faint—so "queer" he felt—when, at the gained point of the long stretch from which he could always tell, he arrived within positive sight of his immemorial goal. His seat was taken and she was keeping it for him—it could only be *she* there in possession; whereby it shone out for Herbert Dodd that if he hadn't been quite sure of her recurrence she had at least been quite sure of his. *That* pulled him up to some purpose, where recognition began for them—or to the effect, in other words, of his pausing to judge if he could bear for the sharpest note of their intercourse, this inveterate demonstration of her making him do what she liked. What settled the question for him then— and just while they avowedly watched each other, over the long interval, before closing, as if, on either side, for the major advantage—what settled it was this very fact that what she liked she liked so terribly. If it were simply to "use" him, as she had said the last time, and no matter to the profit of which of them she called it, one might let it go for that; since it could make her wait over, day after day, in that fashion, and with such a spending of money, on the hazard of their meeting again. How could she be the least sure he would ever again consent to it after the proved action on him, a week ago, of her last monstrous honesty? It was indeed positively as if he were now himself putting this influence—and for their common edification—to the supreme, to the finest test. He had a sublime, an ideal flight, which lasted about a minute. "Suppose, now that I see her there and what she has taken so characteristically for granted, suppose I just show her that she *hasn't* only confidently to wait or whistle for me, and that the length of my leash is greater than she measures, and that everything's impossible always?—show it by turning my back on her now and walking straight away. She won't be able not to understand *that!*"

Nothing had passed, across their distance, but the mute apprehension of each on the part of each; the whole expanse, at the church hour, was void of other life (he had scarce met a creature on his way from end to end) and the sun-seasoned gusts kept brushing the air and all the larger prospect clean. It was through this beautiful lucidity that he watched her watch him, as it were—watch him for what he would do. Neither moved at this high tension; Kate Cookham, her face fixed on him, only waited with a stiff appearance of leaving him, not for dignity but— to an effect of even deeper perversity—for kindness, free to choose. It yet somehow affected him at present, this attitude, as a gage of her *knowing too*—knowing, that is, that he wasn't really free, that this was the thinnest of vain parades, the poorest of hollow heroics, that his need, his solitude, his suffered wrong, his exhausted rancour, his foredoomed submission to any shown interest, all hung together too heavy on him to let the weak wings of his pride do more than vaguely tremble. They couldn't, they didn't carry him a single beat further away; according to which he stood rooted, neither retreating nor advancing, but presently correcting his own share of their bleak exchange by looking off at the sea. Deeply conscious of the awkwardness this posture gave him, he yet clung to it as the last shred of his honour, to the clear argument that it was one thing for him to have felt beneath all others, the previous days, that she was to be counted on, but quite a different for her to have felt that *he* was. His checked approach, arriving thus at no term, could in these odd conditions have established that he wasn't only if Kate Cookham had, as either of them might have said, taken it so—if she had given up the game at last by rising, by walking away and adding to the distance between them, and he had then definitely let her vanish into space. It became a fact that when she did finally rise—though after how long our record scarce takes on itself to say—it was not to confirm their separation but to put an end to it; and this by slowly approaching him till she had come within earshot. He had wondered, once aware of it in spite of his averted face, what she would say and on what note, as it were, she would break their week's silence; so that he had to recognise anew, her voice reaching him, that remarkable quality in her which again and again came up for him as her art.

"There are twelve hundred and sixty pounds, to be definite, but I have it all down for you—and you've only to draw."

They lost themselves, these words, rare and exquisite, in the wide bright genial medium and the Sunday stillness, but even while that occurred and he was gaping for it she was herself there, in her battered ladylike truth, to answer for them, to represent them, and, if a further grace than their simple syllabled beauty were conceivable, almost embarrassingly to cause them to materialise. Yes, she let her smart and tight little reticule hang as if it bulged, beneath its clasp, with the whole portentous sum, and he felt himself glare again at this vividest of her attested claims. She might have been ready, on the spot, to open the store to the plunge of his hand, or, with the situation otherwise conceived, to impose on his pauperised state an acceptance of alms on a scale unprecedented in the annals of street charity. Nothing so much counted for him, however, neither grave numeral nor elegant fraction, as the short, rich, rounded word that the breeze had picked up as it dropped and seemed now to blow about between them. "To draw—to draw?" Yes, he gaped it as if it had no sense; the fact being that even while he did so he was reading into her use of the term more romance than any word in the language had ever had for him. He, Herbert Dodd, was to live to "draw," like people, scarce hampered by the conditions of earth, whom he had remotely and circuitously heard about, and in fact when he walked back with her to where she had been sitting it was very much, for his strained nerves, as if the very bench of desolation itself were to be the scene of that exploit and he mightn't really live till he reached it.

When they had sat down together she did press the spring of her reticule, extracting from it, not a handful of gold nor a packet of crisp notes, but an oblong sealed letter, which she had thus waited on him, she remarked, on purpose to deliver, and which would certify, with sundry particulars, to the credit she had opened for him at a London bank. He took it from her without looking at it, and held it, in the same manner, conspicuous and unassimilated, for most of the rest of the immediate time, appearing embarrassed with it, nervously twisting and flapping it, yet thus publicly retaining it even while aware, beneath everything, of the strange, the quite dreadful, wouldn't it be? engagement that such inaction practically stood for. He could accept money to that amount, yes—but not for nothing in return. For what then in return? He kept asking himself for what, while she said other things and made above all, in her high, shrewd, successful way, the point that, no, he needn't pretend that his conviction of her continued personal interest in him wouldn't have tided him over any question besetting him since their separation. She put it to him that the deep instinct of where he should at last find her must confidently have worked for him, since she confessed to her instinct of where she should find *him;* which meant—oh, it came home to him as he fingered his sealed treasure!—neither more nor less than that she had now created between them an equality of experience. He wasn't to have done all the suffering, *she* was to have "been through" things he couldn't even guess at; and, since he was bargaining away his right ever again to allude to the unforgettable, so much there was of it, what her tacit proposition came to was that they were "square" and might start afresh.

He didn't take up her charge, as his so compromised "pride" yet in a manner prompted him, that he had enjoyed all the week all those elements of ease about her; the most he achieved for that was to declare, with an ingenuity contributing to float him no small distance further, that of course he had turned up at their old place of tryst, which had been, through the years, the haunt of his solitude and the goal of his walk any Sunday morning that seemed too beautiful for church; but that he hadn't in the least built on her presence there—since that supposition gave him, she would understand, wouldn't she? the air, disagreeable to him, of having come in search of her. Her quest of himself, once he had been seated there, would have been another matter—but in short, "Of course after all you did come to me, just now, didn't you?" He felt himself, too, lamely and gracelessly grin, as for the final kick of his honour, in confirmation of the record that he had then yielded but to her humility. Her humility became for him at this hour and to this tune, on the bench of desolation, a quantity more prodigious and even more mysterious than that other guaranteed quantity the finger-tips of his left hand could feel the tap of by the action of his right; though what was in especial extraordinary was the manner in which she could keep making him such allowances and yet meet him again, at some turn, as with her residuum for her clever self so great.

"Come to you, Herbert Dodd?" she imperturbably echoed. "I've been coming to you for the last ten years!"

There had been for him just before this sixty supreme seconds of intensest aspiration—a minute of his keeping his certificate poised for a sharp thrust back at her, the thrust of the wild freedom of his saying: "No, no, I *can't* give them up; I can't simply sink them deep down in my soul for ever, with no cross in all my future to mark *that* burial; so that if this is what our arrangement means I must decline to have anything to do with it." The words none the less hadn't come, and when she had herself, a couple of minutes later, spoken those others, the blood rose to his face as if, given his stiffness and her extravagance, he had just indeed saved himself.

Everything in fact stopped, even his fidget with his paper; she imposed a hush, she imposed at any rate the conscious decent form of one, and he couldn't afterward have told how long, at this juncture, he must have sat simply gazing before him. It was so long, at any rate, that Kate herself got up—and quite indeed, presently, as if her own forms were now at an end. He had returned her nothing— so what was she waiting for? She had been on the two other occasions momentarily at a loss, but never so much so, no doubt, as was thus testified to by her leaving the bench and moving over once more to the rail of the terrace. She could carry it off, in a manner, with her resources, that she was waiting with so little to wait for; she could face him again, after looking off at the sea, as if this slightly stiff delay, not wholly exempt from awkwardness, had been but a fine scruple of her courtesy. She had gathered herself in; after giving him time to appeal she could take it that he had decided and that nothing was left for her to do. "Well then," she clearly launched at him across the broad walk—"well then, good-bye."

She had come nearer with it, as if he might rise for some show of express separation; but he only leaned back motionless, his eyes on her now—he kept her a moment before him. "Do you mean that we don't—that we don't——?" But he broke down.

"Do I 'mean'——?" She remained as for questions he might ask, but it was well-nigh as if there played through her dotty veil an irrepressible irony for that particular one. "I've meant, for long years, I think, all I'm capable of meaning. I've meant so much that I can't mean more. So there it is."

"But if you go," he appealed—and with a sense as of final flatness, however he arranged it, for his own attitude—"but if you go shan't I see you again?"

She waited a little and it was strangely for him now as if—though at last so much more gorged with her tribute than she had ever been with his—something still depended on her. "Do you *like* to see me?" she very simply asked.

At this he did get up; that was easier than to say—at least with responsive simplicity; and again for a little he looked hard and in silence at his letter; which, at last, however, raising his eyes to her own for the act, while he masked their conscious ruefulness, to his utmost, in some air of assurance, he slipped into the inner pocket of his coat, letting it settle there securely. "You're too wonderful." But he frowned at her with it as never in his life. "Where does it all come from?"

"The wonder of poor me?" Kate Cookham said. "It comes from *you*."

He shook his head slowly—feeling, with his letter there against his heart, such a new agility, almost such a new range of interest. "I mean so *much* money—so extraordinarily much."

Well, she held him a while blank. "Does it seem to you extraordinarily much— twelve-hundred-and-sixty? Because, you know," she added, "it's all."

"It's enough!" he returned with a slight thoughtful droop of his head to the right and his eyes attached to the far horizon as through a shade of shyness for what he was saying. He felt all her own lingering nearness somehow on his cheek.

"Its enough? Thank you then!" she rather oddly went on.

He shifted a little his posture. "It was more than a hundred a year—for you to get together."

"Yes," she assented, "that was what year by year I tried for."

"But that you could live all the while and have that——!" Yes, he was at liberty, as he hadn't been, quite pleasantly to marvel. All his wonderments in life had been hitherto unanswered—and didn't the change mean that here again was the social relation?

"Ah, I didn't live as you saw me the other day."

"Yes," he answered—and didn't he the next instant feel he must fairly have smiled with it?—"the other day you *were* going it!"

"For once in my life," said Kate Cookham. "I've left the hotel," she after a moment added.

"Ah, you're in—a—lodgings?" he found himself inquiring as for positive sociability.

She had apparently a slight shade of hesitation, but in an instant it was all right; as what he showed he wanted to know she seemed mostly to give him. "Yes—but far of course from here. Up on the hill." To which, after another instant, "At The Mount, Castle Terrace," she subjoined.

"Oh, I *know* The Mount. And Castle Terrace is awfully sunny and nice."

"Awfully sunny and nice," Kate Cookham took from him.

"So that if it isn't," he pursued, "like the Royal, why, you're at least comfortable."

"I shall be comfortable anywhere now," she replied with a certain dryness.

It was astonishing, however, what had become of his own. "Because I've accepted——?"

"Call it that!" she dimly smiled.

"I hope then at any rate," he returned, "you can now thoroughly rest." He spoke as for a cheerful conclusion and moved again also to smile, though as with a poor grimace, no doubt; since what he seemed most clearly to feel was that since he "accepted" he mustn't, for his last note, have accepted in sulkiness or gloom. With that, at the same time, he couldn't but know, in all his fibres, that with such a still-watching face as the dotty veil didn't disguise for him there was no possible concluding, at least on his part. On hers, on hers it was—as he had so often for a week had reflectively to pronounce things—another affair. Ah, somehow, both formidably and helpfully, her face concluded—yet in a sense so strangely enshrouded in things she didn't tell him. What *must* she, what mustn't she, have done? What she had said—she had really told him nothing—was no account of her life; in the midst of which conflict of opposed recognitions, at any rate, it was as if, for all he could do, he himself now considerably floundered. "But I can't think—I can't think——!"

"You can't think I can have made so much money in the time and been honest?"

"Oh, you've been *honest!*" Herbert Dodd distinctly allowed.

It moved her stillness to a gesture—which, however, she had as promptly checked; and she went on the next instant as for further generosity to his failure of thought. "Everything was possible, under my stress, with my hatred."

"Your hatred——?" For she had paused as if it were after all too difficult.

"Of what I should for so long have been doing to you."

With this, for all his failures, a greater light than any yet shone upon him. "It made you think of ways——?"

"It made me think of everything. It made me work," said Kate Cookham. She added, however, the next moment: "But that's my story."

"And I mayn't hear it?"

"No—because I mayn't hear yours."

"Oh, mine——!" he said with the strangest, saddest yet after all most resigned sense of surrender of it; which he tried to make sound as if he couldn't have told it, for its splendour of sacrifice and of misery, even if he would.

It seemed to move in her a little, exactly, that sense of the invidious. "Ah, mine too, I assure you——!"

He rallied at once to the interest. "Oh, we *can* talk then?"

"Never," she most oddly replied. "Never," said Kate Cookham.

They remained so, face to face; the effect of which for him was that he had after a little understood why. That was fundamental. "Well, I see."

Thus confronted they stayed; and then, as he saw with a contentment that came up from deeper still, it was indeed she who, with her worn fine face, would conclude. "But I can take care of you."

"You *have!*" he said as with nothing left of him but a beautiful appreciative candour.

"Oh, but you'll want it now in a way——!" she responsibly answered.

He waited a moment, dropping again on the seat. So, while she still stood, he looked up at her; with the sense somehow that there were too many things and that they were all together, terribly, irresistibly, doubtless blessedly, in her eyes and her whole person; which thus affected him for the moment as more than he could bear. He leaned forward, dropping his elbows to his knees and pressing his head on his hands. So he stayed, saying nothing; only, with the sense of her own sustained, renewed and wonderful action, knowing that an arm had passed round him and that he was held. She was beside him on the bench of desolation.

The Dead

(1914)

James Joyce

Born in Dublin and educated in Jesuit schools, James Joyce (1882–1941) took a degree at University College, Dublin, in 1902 and in 1904 departed for a self-imposed exile in Europe. Between 1904 and 1920 he moved with his common-law wife and family from Trieste to Zurich and finally to Paris, earning a living by teaching and translating. Dublin, however, remained the subject of all his fiction. *Dubliners* (publ. 1914) is a group of fourteen short stories and a novelette, *The Dead*. In 1916 he published his first novel, *A Portrait of the Artist as a Young Man,* and from 1920 to 1922 he published serially his masterpiece, *Ulysses.* As installments appeared (they were at length suppressed), his fame spread, until by the time *Ulysses* was published in book form he was notorious in some quarters, called the father of the modern novel in others, a purveyor of obscenity or the greatest of experimental novelists. The next seventeen years were spent on "Work in Progress," an experiment in language and the subconscious that was eventually published in 1939 as *Finnegan's Wake.* Joyce fled Paris at the time of the Nazi occupation, and still making corrections in *Finnegan's Wake,* died in Zurich.

For further information about Joyce, see Richard Ellman's biography, *James Joyce* (Oxford, 1959); *Letters,* ed. Stuart Gilbert (New York, 1957); *Critical Writings,* eds. Ellsworth Mason and Richard Ellman (New York, 1959). Critical studies on Joyce are legion. For a sampling and a bibliography, see *James Joyce: A Collection of Critical Essays,* ed. Cleanth Brooks (Twentieth-Century Views, Englewood Cliffs, New Jersey, 1964).

The Dead was Joyce's only novelette, written after a trip to Rome in 1907 (for biographical background, see Ellman, *James Joyce,* pp. 252–63). From *Dubliners* by James Joyce. Originally published by B. W. Heubsch, Inc., in 1916. All rights reserved. Reprinted by permission of The Viking Press, Inc.

Lily, the caretaker's daughter, was literally run off her feet. Hardly had she brought one gentleman into the little pantry behind the office on the ground floor and helped him off with his overcoat than the wheezy hall-door bell clanged again and she had to scamper along the bare hallway to let in another guest. It was well for her she had not to attend to the ladies also. But Miss Kate and Miss Julia had thought of that and had converted the bathroom upstairs into a ladies' dressing-room. Miss Kate and Miss Julia were there, gossiping and laughing and fussing, walking after each other to the head of the stairs, peering down over the banisters and calling down to Lily to ask her who had come.

It was always a great affair, the Misses Morkan's annual dance. Everybody who knew them came to it, members of the family, old friends of the family, the members of Julia's choir, any of Kate's pupils that were grown up enough, and even some of Mary Jane's pupils too. Never once had it fallen flat. For years and years it had gone off in splendid style, as long as anyone could remember; ever since Kate and Julia, after the death of their brother Pat, had left the house in Stoney Batter and taken Mary Jane, their only niece, to live with them in the dark, gaunt house on Usher's Island, the upper part of which they had rented from Mr. Fulham, the corn-factor on the ground floor. That was a good thirty years ago if it was a day. Mary Jane, who was then a little girl in short clothes, was now the main prop of the household, for she had the organ in Haddington Road. She had been through the Academy and gave a pupils' concert every year in the upper room of the Antient Concert Rooms. Many of her pupils belonged to the better-class families on the Kingstown and Dalkey line. Old as they were, her aunts also did their share. Julia, though she was quite grey, was still the leading soprano in Adam and Eve's, and Kate, being too feeble to go about much, gave music lessons to beginners on the old square piano in the back room. Lily, the caretaker's daughter, did housemaid's work for them. Though their life was modest, they believed in eating well; the best of everything: diamond-bone sirloins, three-shilling tea and the best bottled stout. But Lily seldom made a mistake in the orders, so that she got on well with her three mistresses. They were fussy, that was all. But the only thing they would not stand was back answers.

Of course, they had good reason to be fussy on such a night. And then it was long after ten o'clock and yet there was no sign of Gabriel and his wife. Besides they were dreadfully afraid that Freddy Malins might turn up screwed. They would not wish for words that any of Mary Jane's pupils should see him under the influence; and when he was like that it was sometimes very hard to manage him. Freddy Malins always came later, but they wondered what could be keeping Gabriel: and that was what brought them every two minutes to the banisters to ask Lily had Gabriel or Freddy come.

"O, Mr. Conroy," said Lily to Gabriel when she opened the door for him, "Miss Kate and Miss Julia thought you were never coming. Goodnight, Mrs. Conroy."

"I'll engage they did," said Gabriel, "but they forget that my wife here takes three mortal hours to dress herself."

He stood on the mat, scraping the snow from his goloshes, while Lily led his wife to the foot of the stairs and called out:

"Miss Kate, here's Mrs. Conroy."

Kate and Julia came toddling down the dark stairs at once. Both of them kissed Gabriel's wife, said she must be perished alive, and asked was Gabriel with her.

"Here I am as right as the mail, Aunt Kate! Go on up. I'll follow," called out Gabriel from the dark.

He continued scraping his feet vigorously while the three women went upstairs, laughing, to the ladies' dressing-room. A light fringe of snow lay like a cape on the shoulders of his overcoat and like toecaps on the toes of his goloshes; and, as the buttons of his overcoat slipped with a squeaking noise through the snow-stiffened freeze, a cold, fragrant air from out-of-doors escaped from crevices and folds.

"Is it snowing again, Mr. Conroy?" asked Lily.

She had preceded him into the pantry to help him off with his overcoat. Gabriel smiled at the three syllables she had given his surname and glanced at her. She was a slim, growing girl, pale in complexion and with hay-coloured hair. The gas in the pantry made her look still paler. Gabriel had known her when she was a child and used to sit on the lowest step nursing a rag doll.

"Yes, Lily," he answered, "and I think we're in for a night of it."

He looked up at the pantry ceiling, which was shaking with the stamping and shuffling of feet on the floor above, listened for a moment to the piano and then glanced at the girl, who was folding his overcoat carefully at the end of a shelf.

"Tell me, Lily," he said in a friendly tone, "do you still go to school?"

"O no, sir," she answered. "I'm done schooling this year and more."

"O, then," said Gabriel gaily, "I suppose we'll be going to your wedding one of these fine days with your young man, eh?"

The girl glanced back at him over her shoulder and said with great bitterness:

"The men that is now is only all palaver and what they can get out of you."

Gabriel coloured, as if he felt he had made a mistake and, without looking at her, kicked off his goloshes and flicked actively with his muffler at his patent-leather shoes.

He was a stout, tallish young man. The high colour of his cheeks pushed upwards even to his forehead, where it scattered itself in a few formless patches of pale red; and on his hairless face there scintillated restlessly the polished lenses and the bright gilt rims of the glasses which screened his delicate and restless eyes. His glossy black hair was parted in the middle and brushed in a long curve behind his ears where it curled slightly beneath the groove left by his hat.

When he had flicked lustre into his shoes he stood up and pulled his waistcoat down more tightly on his plump body. Then he took a coin rapidly from his pocket.

"O Lily," he said, thrusting it into her hands, "it's Christmas-time, isn't it? Just...here's a little...."

He walked rapidly towards the door.

"O no, sir!" cried the girl, following him. "Really, sir, I wouldn't take it."

"Christmas-time! Christmas-time!" said Gabriel, almost trotting to the stairs and waving his hand to her in deprecation.

The girl, seeing that he had gained the stairs, called out after him:

"Well, thank you, sir."

He waited outside the drawing-room door until the waltz should finish, listening to the skirts that swept against it and to the shuffling of feet. He was still discomposed by the girl's bitter and sudden retort. It had cast a gloom over him which he tried to dispel by arranging his cuffs and the bows of his tie. He then took from his waistcoat pocket a little paper and glanced at the headings he had made for his speech. He was undecided about the lines from Robert Browning, for he feared they would be above the heads of his hearers. Some quotation that they would recognise from Shakespeare or from the Melodies would be better. The indelicate clacking of the men's heels and the shuffling of their soles reminded him that their grade of culture differed from his. He would only make himself ridiculous by quoting poetry to them which they could not understand. They would think that he was airing his superior education. He would fail with them just as he had failed with the girl in the pantry. He had taken up a wrong tone. His whole speech was a mistake from first to last, an utter failure.

Just then his aunts and his wife came out of the ladies' dressing-room. His aunts were two small, plainly dressed old women. Aunt Julia was an inch or so the taller. Her hair, drawn low over the tops of her ears, was grey; and grey also, with darker shadows, was her large flaccid face. Though she was stout in build and stood erect, her slow eyes and parted lips gave her the appearance of a woman who did not know where she was or where she was going. Aunt Kate was more vivacious. Her face, healthier than her sister's, was all puckers and creases, like a shrivelled red apple, and her hair, braided in the same old-fashioned way, had not lost its ripe nut colour.

They both kissed Gabriel frankly. He was their favourite nephew, the son of their dead elder sister, Ellen, who had married T. J. Conroy of the Port and Docks.

"Gretta tells me you're not going to take a cab back to Monkstown tonight, Gabriel," said Aunt Kate.

"No," said Gabriel, turning to his wife, "we had quite enough of that last year, hadn't we? Don't you remember, Aunt Kate, what a cold Gretta got out of it? Cab windows rattling all the way, and the east wind blowing in after we passed Merrion. Very jolly it was. Gretta caught a dreadful cold."

Aunt Kate frowned severely and nodded her head at every word.

"Quite right, Gabriel, quite right," she said. "You can't be too careful."

"But as for Gretta there," said Gabriel, "she'd walk home in the snow if she were let."

Mrs. Conroy laughed.

"Don't mind him, Aunt Kate," she said. "He's really an awful bother, what with green shades for Tom's eyes at night and making him do the dumb-bells, and forcing Eva to eat the stirabout. The poor child! And she simply hates the sight of it!...O, but you'll never guess what he makes me wear now!"

She broke out into a peal of laughter and glanced at her husband, whose admiring and happy eyes had been wandering from her dress to her face and hair. The two aunts laughed heartily, too, for Gabriel's solicitude was a standing joke with them.

"Goloshes!" said Mrs. Conroy. "That's the latest. Whenever it's wet underfoot I must put on my goloshes. Tonight even, he wanted me to put them on, but I wouldn't. The next thing he'll buy me will be a diving suit."

Gabriel laughed nervously and patted his tie reassuringly, while Aunt Kate nearly doubled herself, so heartily did she enjoy the joke. The smile soon faded from Aunt Julia's face and her mirthless eyes were directed towards her nephew's face. After a pause she asked:

"And what are goloshes, Gabriel?"

"Goloshes, Julia!" exclaimed her sister. "Goodness me, don't you know what goloshes are? You wear them over your...over your boots, Gretta, isn't it?"

"Yes," said Mrs. Conroy. "Guttapercha things. We both have a pair now. Gabriel says everyone wears them on the Continent."

"O, on the Continent," murmured Aunt Julia, nodding her head slowly.

Gabriel knitted his brows and said, as if he were slightly angered:

"It's nothing very wonderful, but Gretta thinks it very funny because she says the word reminds her of Christy Minstrels."

"But tell me, Gabriel," said Aunt Kate, with brisk tact. "Of course, you've seen about the room. Gretta was saying..."

"O, the room is all right," replied Gabriel. "I've taken one in the Gresham."

"To be sure," said Aunt Kate, "by far the best thing to do. And the children, Gretta, you're not anxious about them?"

"O, for one night," said Mrs. Conroy. "Besides, Bessie will look after them."

"To be sure," said Aunt Kate again. "What a comfort it is to have a girl like that, one you can depend on! There's that Lily, I'm sure I don't know what has come over her lately. She's not the girl she was at all."

Gabriel was about to ask his aunt some questions on this point, but she broke off suddenly to gaze after her sister, who had wandered down the stairs and was craning her neck over the banisters.

"Now, I ask you," she said almost testily, "where is Julia going? Julia! Julia! Where are you going?"

Julia, who had gone half way down one flight, came back and announced blandly: "Here's Freddy."

At the same moment a clapping of hands and a final flourish of the pianist told that the waltz had ended. The drawing-room door was opened from within and some couples came out. Aunt Kate drew Gabriel aside hurriedly and whispered into his ear:

"Slip down, Gabriel, like a good fellow and see if he's all right, and don't let him up if he's screwed. I'm sure he's screwed. I'm sure he is."

Gabriel went to the stairs and listened over the banisters. He could hear two persons talking in the pantry. Then he recognised Freddy Malins' laugh. He went down the stairs noisily.

"It's such a relief," said Aunt Kate to Mrs. Conroy, "that Gabriel is here. I always feel easier in my mind when he's here.... Julia, there's Miss Daly and Miss Power will take some refreshment. Thanks for your beautiful waltz, Miss Daly. It made lovely time."

A tall wizen-faced man, with a stiff grizzled moustache and swarthy skin, who was passing out with his partner, said:

"And may we have some refreshment, too, Miss Morkan?"

"Julia," said Aunt Kate summarily, "and here's Mr. Browne and Miss Furlong. Take them in, Julia, with Miss Daly and Miss Power."

"I'm the man of the ladies," said Mr. Browne, pursing his lips until his moustache bristled and smiling in all his wrinkles. "You know, Miss Morkan, the reason they are so fond of me is——"

He did not finish his sentence, but, seeing that Aunt Kate was out of earshot, at once led the three young ladies into the back room. The middle of the room was occupied by two square tables placed end to end, and on these Aunt Julia and the caretaker were straightening and smoothing a large cloth. On the sideboard were arrayed dishes and plates, and glasses and bundles of knives and forks and spoons. The top of the closed square piano served also as a sideboard for viands and sweets. At a smaller sideboard in one corner two young men were standing, drinking hop-bitters.

Mr. Browne led his charges thither and invited them all, in jest, to some ladies' punch, hot, strong and sweet. As they said they never took anything strong, he opened three bottles of lemonade for them. Then he asked one of the young men to move aside, and, taking hold of the decanter, filled out for himself a goodly measure of whisky. The young men eyed him respectfully while he took a trial sip.

"God help me," he said, smiling, "it's the doctor's orders."

His wizened face broke into a broader smile, and the three young ladies laughed in musical echo to his pleasantry, swaying their bodies to and fro, with nervous jerks of their shoulders. The boldest said:

"O, now, Mr. Browne, I'm sure the doctor never ordered anything of the kind."

Mr. Browne took another sip of his whisky and said, with sidling mimicry:

"Well, you see, I'm like the famous Mrs. Cassidy, who is reported to have said: 'Now, Mary Grimes, if I don't take it, make me take it, for I feel I want it.'"

His hot face had leaned forward a little too confidentially and he had assumed a very low Dublin accent so that the young ladies, with one instinct, received his speech in silence. Miss Furlong, who was one of Mary Jane's pupils, asked Miss Daly what was the name of the pretty waltz she had played; and Mr. Browne, seeing that he was ignored, turned promptly to the two young men who were more appreciative.

A red-faced young woman, dressed in pansy, came into the room, excitedly clapping her hands and crying:

"Quadrilles! Quadrilles!"

Close on her heels came Aunt Kate, crying:

"Two gentlemen and three ladies, Mary Jane!"

"O, here's Mr. Bergin and Mr. Kerrigan," said Mary Jane. "Mr. Kerrigan, will you take Miss Power? Miss Furlong, may I get you a partner, Mr. Bergin. O, that'll just do now."

"Three ladies, Mary Jane," said Aunt Kate.

The two young gentlemen asked the ladies if they might have the pleasure, and Mary Jane turned to Miss Daly.

"O, Miss Daly, you're really awfully good, after playing for the last two dances, but really we're so short of ladies tonight."

"I don't mind the least, Miss Morkan."

"But I've a nice partner for you, Mr. Bartell D'Arcy, the tenor. I'll get him to sing later on. All Dublin is raving about him."

"Lovely voice, lovely voice!" said Aunt Kate.

As the piano had twice begun the prelude to the first figure Mary Jane led her recruits quickly from the room. They had hardly gone when Aunt Julia wandered slowly into the room, looking behind her at something.

"What is the matter, Julia?" asked Aunt Kate anxiously. "Who is it?"

Julia, who was carrying in a column of table-napkins, turned to her sister and said, simply, as if the question had surprised her:

"It's only Freddy, Kate, and Gabriel with him."

In fact right behind her Gabriel could be seen piloting Freddy Malins across the landing. The latter, a young man of about forty, was of Gabriel's size and build, with very round shoulders. His face was fleshy and pallid, touched with colour only at the thick hanging lobes of his ears and at the wide wings of his nose. He had coarse features, a blunt nose, a convex and receding brow, tumid and protruded lips. His heavy-lidded eyes and the disorder of his scanty hair made him look sleepy. He was laughing heartily in a high key at a story which he had been telling Gabriel on the stairs and at the same time rubbing the knuckles of his left fist backwards and forwards into his left eye.

"Good-evening, Freddy," said Aunt Julia.

Freddy Malins bade the Misses Morkan good-evening in what seemed an offhand fashion by reason of the habitual catch in his voice and then, seeing that Mr. Browne was grinning at him from the sideboard, crossed the room on rather shaky legs and began to repeat in an undertone the story he had just told to Gabriel.

"He's not so bad, is he?" said Aunt Kate to Gabriel.

Gabriel's brows were dark but he raised them quickly and answered:

"O, no, hardly noticeable."

"Now, isn't he a terrible fellow!" she said. "And his poor mother made him take the pledge on New Year's Eve. But come on, Gabriel, into the drawing-room."

Before leaving the room with Gabriel she signalled to Mr. Browne by frowning and shaking her forefinger in warning to and fro. Mr. Browne nodded in answer and, when she had gone, said to Freddy Malins:

"Now, then, Teddy, I'm going to fill you out a good glass of lemonade just to buck you up."

Freddy Malins, who was nearing the climax of his story, waved the offer aside impatiently but Mr. Browne, having first called Freddy Malins' attention to a disarray in his dress, filled out and handed him a full glass of lemonade. Freddy Malins' left hand accepted the glass mechanically, his right hand being engaged in the mechanical readjustment of his dress. Mr. Browne, whose face was once more wrinkling with mirth, poured out for himself a glass of whisky while Freddy Malins exploded, before he had well reached the climax of his story, in a kink of high-pitched bronchitic laughter and, setting down his untasted and overflowing glass, began to rub the knuckles of his left fist backwards and forwards into his left eye, repeating words of his last phrase as well as his fit of laughter would allow him.

.   .   .   .   .

Gabriel could not listen while Mary Jane was playing her Academy piece, full of runs and difficult passages, to the hushed drawing-room. He liked music but the piece she was playing had no melody for him and he doubted whether it had any melody for the other listeners, though they had begged Mary Jane to play something. Four young men, who had come from the refreshment-room to stand in the doorway at the sound of the piano, had gone away quietly in couples after a few minutes. The only persons who seemed to follow the music were Mary Jane herself, her hands racing along the key-board or lifted from it at the pauses like those of a priestess in momentary imprecation, and Aunt Kate standing at her elbow to turn the page.

Gabriel's eyes, irritated by the floor, which glittered with beeswax under the heavy chandelier, wandered to the wall above the piano. A picture of the balcony scene in *Romeo and Juliet* hung there and beside it was a picture of the two murdered princes in the Tower which Aunt Julia had worked in red, blue and brown wools when she was a girl. Probably in the school they had gone to as girls that kind of work had been taught for one year. His mother had worked for him as a birthday present a waistcoat of purple tabinet, with little foxes' heads upon it, lined with brown satin and having round mulberry buttons. It was strange that his mother had had no musical talent though Aunt Kate used to call her the brains carrier of the Morkan family. Both she and Julia had always seemed a little proud of their serious and matronly sister. Her photograph stood before the pierglass. She held an open book on her knees and was pointing out something in it to Constantine who, dressed in a man-o'-war suit, lay at her feet. It was she who had chosen the names of her sons for she was very sensible of the dignity of family life. Thanks to her, Constantine was now senior curate in Balbriggan and, thanks to her, Gabriel himself had taken his degree in the Royal University. A shadow passed over his face as he remembered her sullen opposition to his marriage. Some slighting phrases she had used still rankled in his memory; she had once spoken of Gretta as being country cute and that was not true of Gretta at all. It was Gretta who had nursed her during all her last long illness in their house at Monkstown.

He knew that Mary Jane must be near the end of her piece for she was playing again the opening melody with runs of scales after every bar and while he waited for the end the resentment died down in his heart. The piece ended with a trill of octaves in the trebles and a final deep octave in the bass. Great applause greeted Mary Jane as, blushing and rolling up her music nervously, she escaped from the room. The most vigorous clapping came from the four young men in the doorway who had gone away to the refreshment-room at the beginning of the piece but had come back when the piano had stopped.

Lancers were arranged. Gabriel found himself partnered with Miss Ivors. She was a frank-mannered talkative young lady, with a freckled face and prominent brown eyes. She did not wear a low-cut bodice and the large brooch which was fixed in the front of her collar bore on it an Irish device and motto.

When they had taken their places she said abruptly:

"I have a crow to pluck with you."

"With me?" said Gabriel.

She nodded her head gravely.

"What is it?" asked Gabriel, smiling at her solemn manner.

"Who is G. C.?" answered Miss Ivors, turning her eyes upon him.

Gabriel coloured and was about to knit his brows, as if he did not understand, when she said bluntly:

"O, innocent Amy! I have found out that you write for *The Daily Express*. Now, aren't you ashamed of yourself?"

"Why should I be ashamed of myself?" asked Gabriel, blinking his eyes and trying to smile.

"Well, I'm ashamed of you," said Miss Ivors frankly. "To say you'd write for a paper like that. I didn't think you were a West Briton."

A look of perplexity appeared on Gabriel's face. It was true that he wrote a literary column every Wednesday in *The Daily Express,* for which he was paid fifteen shillings. But that did not make him a West Briton surely. The books he received for review were almost more welcome than the paltry cheque. He loved to feel the covers and turn over the pages of newly printed books. Nearly every day when his teaching in the college was ended he used to wander down the quays to the second-hand booksellers, to Hickey's on Bachelor's Walk, to Webb's or Massey's on Aston's Quay, or to O'Clohissey's in the by-street. He did not know how to meet her charge. He wanted to say that literature was above politics. But they were friends of many years' standing and their careers had been parallel, first at the University and then as teachers: he could not risk a grandiose phrase with her. He continued blinking his eyes and trying to smile and murmured lamely that he saw nothing political in writing reviews of books.

When their turn to cross had come he was still perplexed and inattentive. Miss Ivors promptly took his hand in a warm grasp and said in a soft friendly tone:

"Of course, I was only joking. Come, we cross now."

When they were together again she spoke of the University question and Gabriel felt more at ease. A friend of hers had shown her his review of Browning's poems. That was how she had found out the secret: but she liked the review immensely. Then she said suddenly:

"O, Mr. Conroy, will you come for an excursion to the Aran Isles this summer? We're going to stay there a whole month. It will be splendid out in the Atlantic. You ought to come. Mr. Clancy is coming, and Mr. Kilkelly and Kathleen Kearney. It would be splendid for Gretta too if she'd come. She's from Connacht, isn't she?"

"Her people are," said Gabriel shortly.

"But you will come, won't you?" said Miss Ivors, laying her warm hand eagerly on his arm.

"The fact is," said Gabriel, "I have just arranged to go—"

"Go where?" asked Miss Ivors.

"Well, you know, every year I go for a cycling tour with some fellows and so—"

"But where?" asked Miss Ivors.

"Well, we usually go to France or Belgium or perhaps Germany," said Gabriel awkwardly.

"And why do you go to France and Belgium," said Miss Ivors, "instead of visiting your own land?"

"Well," said Gabriel, "it's partly to keep in touch with the languages and partly for a change."

"And haven't you your own language to keep in touch with—Irish?" asked Miss Ivors.

"Well," said Gabriel, "if it comes to that, you know, Irish is not my language."

Their neighbours had turned to listen to the cross-examination. Gabriel glanced right and left nervously and tried to keep his good humour under the ordeal which was making a blush invade his forehead.

"And haven't you your own land to visit," continued Miss Ivors, "that you know nothing of, your own people, and your own country?"

"O, to tell you the truth," retorted Gabriel suddenly, "I'm sick of my own country, sick of it!"

"Why?" asked Miss Ivors.

Gabriel did not answer for his retort had heated him.

"Why?" repeated Miss Ivors.

They had to go visiting together and, as he had not answered her, Miss Ivors said warmly:

"Of course, you've no answer."

Gabriel tried to cover his agitation by taking part in the dance with great energy. He avoided her eyes for he had seen a sour expression on her face. But when they met in the long chain he was surprised to feel his hand firmly pressed. She looked at him from under her brows for a moment quizzically until he smiled. Then, just as the chain was about to start again, she stood on tiptoe and whispered into his ear:

"West Briton!"

When the lancers were over Gabriel went away to a remote corner of the room where Freddy Malins' mother was sitting. She was a stout feeble old woman with white hair. Her voice had a catch in it like her son's and she stuttered slightly. She had been told that Freddy had come and that he was nearly all right. Gabriel asked her whether she had had a good crossing. She lived with her married daughter in Glasgow and came to Dublin on a visit once a year. She answered placidly that she had had a beautiful crossing and that the captain had been most attentive to her. She spoke also of the beautiful house her daughter kept in Glasgow, and of all the friends they had there. While her tongue rambled on Gabriel tried to banish from his mind all memory of the unpleasant incident with Miss Ivors. Of course the girl or woman, or whatever she was, was an enthusiast but there was a time for all things. Perhaps he ought not to have answered her like that. But she had no right to call him a West Briton before people, even in joke. She had tried to make him ridiculous before people, heckling him and staring at him with her rabbit's eyes.

He saw his wife making her way towards him through the waltzing couples. When she reached him she said into his ear:

"Gabriel, Aunt Kate wants to know won't you carve the goose as usual. Miss Daly will carve the ham and I'll do the pudding."

"All right," said Gabriel.

"She's sending in the younger ones first as soon as this waltz is over so that we'll have the table to ourselves."

"Were you dancing?" asked Gabriel.

"Of course I was. Didn't you see me? What row had you with Molly Ivors?"

"No row. Why? Did she say so?"

"Something like that. I'm trying to get that Mr. D'Arcy to sing. He's full of conceit, I think."

"There was no row," said Gabriel moodily, "only she wanted me to go for a trip to the west of Ireland and I said I wouldn't."

His wife clasped her hands excitedly and gave a little jump.

"O, do go, Gabriel," she cried. "I'd love to see Galway again."

"You can go if you like," said Gabriel coldly.

She looked at him for a moment, then turned to Mrs. Malins and said:

"There's a nice husband for you, Mrs. Malins."

While she was threading her way back across the room Mrs. Malins, without adverting to the interruption, went on to tell Gabriel what beautiful places there were in Scotland and beautiful scenery. Her son-in-law brought them every year to the lakes and they used to go fishing. Her son-in-law was a splendid fisher. One day he caught a beautiful big fish and the man in the hotel cooked it for their dinner.

Gabriel hardly heard what she said. Now that supper was coming near he began to think again about his speech and about the quotation. When he saw Freddy Malins coming across the room to visit his mother Gabriel left the chair free for him and retired into the embrasure of the window. The room had already cleared and from the back room came the clatter of plates and knives. Those who still remained in the drawing-room seemed tired of dancing and were conversing quietly in little groups. Gabriel's warm trembling fingers tapped the cold pane of the window. How cool it must be outside! How pleasant it would be to walk out alone, first along by the river and then through the park! The snow would be lying on the branches of the trees and forming a bright cap on the top of the Wellington Monument. How much more pleasant it would be there than at the supper-table!

He ran over the headings of his speech: Irish hospitality, sad memories, the

Three Graces, Paris, the quotation from Browning. He repeated to himself a phrase he had written in his review: "One feels that one is listening to a thought-tormented music." Miss Ivors had praised the review. Was she sincere? Had she really any life of her own behind all her propagandism? There had never been any ill-feeling between them until that night. It unnerved him to think that she would be at the supper-table, looking up at him while he spoke with her critical quizzing eyes. Perhaps she would not be sorry to see him fail in his speech. An idea came into his mind and gave him courage. He would say, alluding to Aunt Kate and Aunt Julia: "Ladies and Gentlemen, the generation which is now on the wane among us may have had its faults but for my part I think it had certain qualities of hospitality, of humour, of humanity, which the new and very serious and hypereducated generation that is growing up around us seems to me to lack." Very good: that was one for Miss Ivors. What did he care that his aunts were only two ignorant old women?

A murmur in the room attracted his attention. Mr. Browne was advancing from the door, gallantly escorting Aunt Julia, who leaned upon his arm, smiling and hanging her head. An irregular musketry of applause escorted her also as far as the piano and then, as Mary Jane seated herself on the stool, and Aunt Julia, no longer smiling, half turned so as to pitch her voice fairly into the room, gradually ceased. Gabriel recognised the prelude. It was that of an old song of Aunt Julia's—*Arrayed for the Bridal*. Her voice, strong and clear in tone, attacked with great spirit the runs which embellish the air and though she sang very rapidly she did not miss even the smallest of the grace notes. To follow the voice, without looking at the singer's face, was to feel and share the excitement of swift and secure flight. Gabriel applauded loudly with all the others at the close of the song and loud applause was borne in from the invisible supper-table. It sounded so genuine that a little colour struggled into Aunt Julia's face as she bent to replace in the music-stand the old leather-bound song-book that had her initials on the cover. Freddy Malins, who had listened with his head perched sideways to hear her better, was still applauding when everyone else had ceased and talking animatedly to his mother who nodded her head gravely and slowly in acquiescence. At last, when he could clap no more, he stood up suddenly and hurried across the room to Aunt Julia whose hand he seized and held in both his hands, shaking it when words failed him or the catch in his voice proved too much for him.

"I was just telling my mother," he said, "I never heard you sing so well, never. No, I never heard your voice so good as it is tonight. Now! Would you believe that now? That's the truth. Upon my word and honour that's the truth. I never heard your voice sound so fresh and so...so clear and fresh, never."

Aunt Julia smiled broadly and murmured something about compliments as she released her hand from his grasp. Mr. Browne extended his open hand towards her and said to those who were near him in the manner of a showman introducing a prodigy to an audience:

"Miss Julia Morkan, my latest discovery!"

He was laughing very heartily at this himself when Freddy Malins turned to him and said:

"Well, Browne, if you're serious you might make a worse discovery. All I can say is I never heard her sing half so well as long as I am coming here. And that's the honest truth."

"Neither did I," said Mr. Browne. "I think her voice has greatly improved."

Aunt Julia shrugged her shoulders and said with meek pride:

"Thirty years ago I hadn't a bad voice as voices go."

"I often told Julia," said Aunt Kate emphatically, "that she was simply thrown away in that choir. But she never would be said by me."

She turned as if to appeal to the good sense of the others against a refractory child while Aunt Julia gazed in front of her, a vague smile of reminiscence playing on her face.

"No," continued Aunt Kate, "she wouldn't be said or led by anyone, slaving there in that choir night and day, night and day. Six o'clock on Christmas morning! And all for what?"

"Well, isn't it for the honour of God, Aunt Kate?" asked Mary Jane, twisting round on the piano-stool and smiling.

Aunt Kate turned fiercely on her niece and said:

"I know all about the honour of God, Mary Jane, but I think it's not at all honourable for the pope to turn out the women out of the choirs that have slaved there all their lives and put little whipper-snappers of boys over their heads. I suppose it is for the good of the Church if the pope does it. But it's not just, Mary Jane, and it's not right."

She had worked herself into a passion and would have continued in defence of her sister for it was a sore subject with her but Mary Jane, seeing that all the dancers had come back, intervened pacifically:

"Now, Aunt Kate, you're giving scandal to Mr. Browne who is of the other persuasion."

Aunt Kate turned to Mr. Browne, who was grinning at this allusion to his religion, and said hastily:

"O, I don't question the pope's being right. I'm only a stupid old woman and I wouldn't presume to do such a thing. But there's such a thing as common everyday politeness and gratitude. And if I were in Julia's place I'd tell that Father Healey straight up to his face..."

"And besides, Aunt Kate," said Mary Jane, "we really are all hungry and when we are hungry we are all very quarrelsome."

"And when we are thirsty we are also quarrelsome," added Mr. Browne.

"So that we had better go to supper," said Mary Jane, "and finish the discussion afterwards."

On the landing outside the drawing-room Gabriel found his wife and Mary Jane trying to persuade Miss Ivors to stay for supper. But Miss Ivors, who had put on her hat and was buttoning her cloak, would not stay. She did not feel in the least hungry and she had already overstayed her time.

"But only for ten minutes, Molly," said Mrs. Conroy. "That won't delay you."

"To take a pick itself," said Mary Jane, "after all your dancing."

"I really couldn't," said Miss Ivors.

"I am afraid you didn't enjoy yourself at all," said Mary Jane hopelessly.

"Ever so much, I assure you," said Miss Ivors, "but you really must let me run off now."

"But how can you get home?" asked Mrs. Conroy.

"O, it's only two steps up the quay."

Gabriel hesitated a moment and said:

"If you will allow me, Miss Ivors, I'll see you home if you are really obliged to go."

But Miss Ivors broke away from them.

"I won't hear of it," she cried. "For goodness' sake go in to your suppers and don't mind me. I'm quite well able to take care of myself."

"Well, you're the comical girl, Molly," said Mrs. Conroy frankly.

"*Beannacht libh*," cried Miss Ivors, with a laugh, as she ran down the staircase.

Mary Jane gazed after her, a moody puzzled expression on her face, while Mrs. Conroy leaned over the banisters to listen for the hall-door. Gabriel asked himself was he the cause of her abrupt departure. But she did not seem to be in ill humor: she had gone away laughing. He stared blankly down the staircase.

At the moment Aunt Kate came toddling out of the supper-room, almost wringing her hands in despair.

"Where is Gabriel?" she cried. "Where on earth is Gabriel? There's everyone waiting in there, stage to let, and nobody to carve the goose!"

"Here I am, Aunt Kate!" cried Gabriel, with sudden animation, "ready to carve a flock of geese, if necessary."

A fat brown goose lay at one end of the table and at the other end, on a bed of creased paper strewn with sprigs of parsley, lay a great ham, stripped of its outer skin and peppered over with crust crumbs, a neat paper frill round its shin and beside this was a round of spiced beef. Between these rival ends ran parallel lines of side-dishes: two little minsters of jelly, red and yellow; a shallow dish full of blocks of blancmange and red jam, a large green leaf-shaped dish with a stalk-shaped handle, on which lay bunches of purple raisins and peeled almonds, a companion dish on which lay a solid rectangle of Smyrna figs, a dish of custard topped with grated nutmeg, a small bowl full of chocolates and sweets wrapped in gold and silver papers and a glass vase in which stood some tall celery stalks. In the centre of the table there stood, as sentries to a fruit-stand which upheld a pyramid of oranges and American apples, two squat old-fashioned decanters of cut glass, one containing port and the other dark sherry. On the closed square piano a pudding in a huge yellow dish lay in waiting and behind it were three squads of bottles of stout and ale and minerals, drawn up according to the colours of their uniforms, the first two black, with brown and red labels, the third and smallest squad white, with transverse green sashes.

Gabriel took his seat boldly at the head of the table and, having looked to the edge of the carver, plunged his fork firmly into the goose. He felt quite at ease now for he was an expert carver and liked nothing better than to find himself at the head of a well-laden table.

"Miss Furlong, what shall I send you?" he asked. "A wing or a slice of the breast?"

"Just a small slice of the breast."

"Miss Higgins, what for you?"

"O, anything at all, Mr. Conroy."

While Gabriel and Miss Daly exchanged plates of goose and plates of ham and spiced beef Lily went from guest to guest with a dish of hot floury potatoes wrapped in a white napkin. This was Mary Jane's idea and she had also suggested apple sauce for the goose but Aunt Kate had said that plain roast goose without any apple sauce had always been good enough for her and she hoped she might never eat worse. Mary Jane waited on her pupils and saw that they got the best slices and Aunt Kate and Aunt Julia opened and carried across from the piano bottles of stout and ale for the gentlemen and bottles of minerals for the ladies. There was a great deal of confusion and laughter and noise, the noise of orders and counter-orders, of knives and forks, of corks and glass-stoppers. Gabriel began to carve second helpings as soon as he had finished the first round without serving himself. Everyone protested loudly so that he compromised by taking a long draught of stout for he had found the carving hot work. Mary Jane settled down quietly to her supper but Aunt Kate and Aunt Julia were still toddling round the table, walking on each other's heels, getting in each other's way and giving each other unheeded orders. Mr. Browne begged of them to sit down and eat their suppers and so did Gabriel but they said there was time enough, so that, at last, Freddy Malins stood up and, capturing Aunt Kate, plumped her down on her chair amid general laughter.

When everyone had been well served Gabriel said, smiling:

"Now, if anyone wants a little more of what vulgar people call stuffing let him or her speak."

A chorus of voices invited him to begin his own supper and Lily came forward with three potatoes which she had reserved for him.

"Very well," said Gabriel amiably, as he took another preparatory draught, "kindly forget my existence, ladies and gentlemen, for a few minutes."

He set to his supper and took no part in the conversation with which the table covered Lily's removal of the plates. The subject of talk was the opera company which was then at the Theatre Royal. Mr. Bartell D'Arcy, the tenor, a dark-complexioned young man with a smart moustache, praised very highly the leading contralto of the company but Miss Furlong thought she had a rather vulgar style of production. Freddy Malins said there was a Negro chieftain singing in the second part of the Gaiety pantomime who had one of the finest tenor voices he had ever heard.

"Have you heard him?" he asked Mr. Bartell D'Arcy across the table.

"No," answered Mr. Bartell D'Arcy carelessly.

"Because," Freddy Malins explained, "now I'd be curious to hear your opinion of him. I think he has a grand voice."

"It takes Teddy to find out the really good things," said Mr. Browne familiarly to the table.

"And why couldn't he have a voice too?" asked Freddy Malins sharply. "Is it because he's only a black?"

Nobody answered this question and Mary Jane led the table back to the legitimate opera. One of her pupils had given her a pass for *Mignon*. Of course it was very fine, she said, but it made her think of poor Georgina Burns. Mr. Browne could go back farther still, to the old Italian companies that used to come to Dublin —Tietjens, Ilma de Murzka, Campanini, the great Trebelli, Giuglini, Ravelli, Aramburo. Those were the days, he said, when there was something like singing to be heard in Dublin. He told too of how the top gallery of the old Royal used to be packed night after night, of how one night an Italian tenor had sung five encores to *Let me like a Soldier fall*, introducing a high C every time, and of how the gallery boys would sometimes in their enthusiasm unyoke the horses from the carriage of some great *prima donna* and pull her themselves through the streets to her hotel. Why did they never play the grand old operas now, he asked, *Dinorah, Lucrezia Borgia?* Because they could not get the voices to sing them: that was why.

"O, well," said Mr. Bartell D'Arcy, "I presume there are as good singers today as there were then."

"Where are they?" asked Mr. Browne defiantly.

"In London, Paris, Milan," said Mr. Bartell D'Arcy warmly. "I suppose Caruso, for example, is quite as good, if not better, than any of the men you have mentioned."

"Maybe so," said Mr. Browne. "But I may tell you I doubt it strongly."

"O, I'd give anything to hear Caruso sing," said Mary Jane.

"For me," said Aunt Kate, who had been picking a bone, "there was only one tenor. To please me, I mean. But I suppose none of you ever heard of him."

"Who was he, Miss Morkan?" asked Mr. Bartell D'Arcy politely.

"His name," said Aunt Kate, "was Parkinson. I heard him when he was in his prime and I think he had then the purest tenor voice that was ever put into a man's throat."

"Strange," said Mr. Bartell D'Arcy. "I never even heard of him."

"Yes, yes, Miss Morkan is right," said Mr. Browne. "I remember hearing of old Parkinson but he's too far back for me."

"A beautiful, pure, sweet, mellow English tenor," said Aunt Kate with enthusiasm.

Gabriel having finished, the huge pudding was transferred to the table. The clatter of forks and spoons began again. Gabriel's wife served out spoonfuls of the pudding and passed the plates down the table. Midway down they were held up by Mary Jane, who replenished them with raspberry or orange jelly or with blancmange and jam. The pudding was of Aunt Julia's making and she received praises for it from all quarters. She herself said that it was not quite brown enough.

"Well, I hope, Miss Morkan," said Mr. Browne, "that I'm brown enough for you because, you know, I'm all brown."

All the gentlemen, except Gabriel, ate some of the pudding out of compliment to Aunt Julia. As Gabriel never ate sweets the celery had been left for him. Freddy Malins also took a stalk of celery and ate it with his pudding. He had been told that celery was a capital thing for the blood and he was just then under doctor's care. Mrs. Malins, who had been silent all through the supper, said that her son was going down to Mount Melleray in a week or so. The table then spoke of Mount Melleray, how bracing the air was down there, how hospitable the monks were and how they never asked for a penny-piece from their guests.

"And do you mean to say," asked Mr. Browne incredulously, "that a chap can go down there and put up there as if it were a hotel and live on the fat of the land and then come away without paying anything?"

"O, most people give some donation to the monastery when they leave," said Mary Jane.

"I wish we had an institution like that in our Church," said Mr. Browne candidly.

He was astonished to hear that the monks never spoke, got up at two in the morning and slept in their coffins. He asked what they did it for.

"That's the rule of the order," said Aunt Kate firmly.

"Yes, but why?" asked Mr. Browne.

Aunt Kate repeated that it was the rule, that was all. Mr. Browne still seemed not to understand. Freddy Malins explained to him, as best he could, that the monks were trying to make up for the sins committed by all the sinners in the outside world. The explanation was not very clear for Mr. Browne grinned and said:

"I like that idea very much but wouldn't a comfortable spring bed do them as well as a coffin?"

"The coffin," said Mary Jane, "is to remind them of their last end."

As the subject had grown lugubrious it was buried in a silence of the table during which Mrs. Malins could be heard saying to her neighbour in an indistinct undertone:

"They are very good men, the monks, very pious men,"

The raisins and almonds and figs and apples and oranges and chocolates and sweets were now passed about the table and Aunt Julia invited all the guests to have either port or sherry. At first Mr. Bartell D'Arcy refused to take either but one of his neighbours nudged him and whispered something to him upon which he allowed his glass to be filled. Gradually as the last glasses were being filled the conversation ceased. A pause followed, broken only by the noise of the wine and by unsettlings of chairs. The Misses Morkan, all three, looked down at the tablecloth. Someone coughed once or twice and then a few gentlemen patted the table gently as a signal for silence. The silence came and Gabriel pushed back his chair and stood up.

The patting at once grew louder in encouragement and then ceased altogether. Gabriel leaned his ten trembling fingers on the tablecloth and smiled nervously at the company. Meeting a row of upturned faces he raised his eyes to the chandelier. The piano was playing a waltz tune and he could hear the skirts sweeping against the drawing-room door. People, perhaps, were standing in the snow on the quay outside, gazing up at the lighted windows and listening to the waltz music. The air was pure there. In the distance lay the park where the trees were weighted with snow. The Wellington Monument wore a gleaming cap of snow that flashed westward over the white field of Fifteen Acres.

He began:

"Ladies and Gentlemen,

"It has fallen to my lot this evening, as in years past, to perform a very pleasing task but a task for which I am afraid my poor powers as a speaker are all too inadequate."

"No, no!" said Mr. Browne.

"But, however that may be, I can only ask you tonight to take the will for the deed and to lend me your attention for a few moments while I endeavor to express to you in words what my feelings are on this occasion.

"Ladies and Gentlemen, it is not the first time that we have gathered together under this hospitable roof, around this hospitable board. It is not the first time that we have been the recipients—or perhaps, I had better say, the victims—of the hospitality of certain good ladies."

He made a circle in the air with his arm and paused. Everyone laughed or smiled at Aunt Kate and Aunt Julia and Mary Jane who all turned crimson with pleasure. Gabriel went on more boldly:

"I feel more strongly with every recurring year that our country has no tradition which does it so much honour and which it should guard so jealously as that of its hospitality. It is a tradition that is unique as far as my experience goes (and I have visited not a few places abroad) among the modern nations. Some would say, perhaps, that with us it is rather a failing than anything to be boasted of. But granted even that, it is, to my mind, a princely failing, and one that I trust will long be cultivated among us. Of one thing, at least, I am sure. As long as this one roof shelters the good ladies aforesaid—and I wish from my heart it may do so for many and many a long year to come—the tradition of genuine warm-hearted courteous Irish hospitality, which our forefathers have handed down to us and which we in turn must hand down to our descendants, is still alive among us."

A hearty murmur of assent ran round the table. It shot through Gabriel's mind that Miss Ivors was not there and that she had gone away discourteously: and he said with confidence in himself:

"Ladies and Gentlemen,

"A new generation is growing up in our midst, a generation actuated by new ideas and new principles. It is serious and enthusiastic for these new ideas and its enthusiasm, even when it is misdirected, is, I believe, in the main sincere. But we are living in a sceptical and, if I may use the phrase, a thought-tormented age: and sometimes I fear that this new generation, educated or hypereducated as it is, will lack those qualities of humanity, of hospitality, of kindly humour which belonged to an older day. Listening tonight to the names of all those great singers of the past it seemed to me, I must confess, that we were living in a less spacious age. Those days might, without exaggeration, be called spacious days: and if they are gone beyond recall let us hope, at least, that in gatherings such as this we shall still speak of them with pride and affection, still cherish in our hearts the memory of those dead and gone great ones whose fame the world will not willingly let die."

"Hear, hear!" said Mr. Browne loudly.

"But yet," continued Gabriel, his voice falling into a softer inflection, "there are always in gatherings such as this sadder thoughts that will recur to our minds: thoughts of the past, of youth, of changes, of absent faces that we miss here tonight. Our path through life is strewn with many such sad memories: and were we to brood upon them always we could not find the heart to go on bravely with our work among the living. We have all of us living duties and living affections which claim, and rightly claim, our strenuous endeavours.

"Therefore, I will not linger on the past. I will not let any gloomy moralising intrude upon us here tonight. Here we are gathered together for a brief moment from the bustle and rush of our everyday routine. We are met here as friends, in the spirit of good-fellowship, as colleagues, also to a certain extent, in the true spirit of *camaraderie,* and as the guests of—what shall I call them?—the Three Graces of the Dublin musical world."

The table burst into applause and laughter at this allusion. Aunt Julia vainly asked each of her neighbours in turn to tell her what Gabriel had said.

"He says we are the Three Graces, Aunt Julia," said Mary Jane.

Aunt Julia did not understand but she looked up, smiling, at Gabriel, who continued in the same vein:

"Ladies and Gentlemen,

"I will not attempt to play tonight the part that Paris played on another occasion. I will not attempt to choose between them. The task would be an invidious one and one beyond my poor powers. For when I view them in turn, whether it be our chief hostess herself, whose good heart, whose too good heart, has become a byword with all who know her, or her sister, who seems to be gifted with perennial youth and whose singing must have been a surprise and a revelation to us all tonight, or, last but not least, when I consider our youngest hostess, talented, cheerful, hard-working and the best of nieces, I confess, Ladies and Gentlemen, that I do not know to which of them I should award the prize."

Gabriel glanced down at his aunts and, seeing the large smile on Aunt Julia's face and the tears which had risen to Aunt Kate's eyes, hastened to his close. He raised his glass of port gallantly, while every member of the company fingered a glass expectantly, and said loudly:

"Let us toast them all three together. Let us drink to their health, wealth, long life, happiness and prosperity and may they long continue to hold the proud and self-won position which they hold in their profession and the position of honour and affection which they hold in our hearts."

All the guests stood up, glass in hand, and turning towards the three seated ladies, sang in unison, with Mr. Browne as leader:

> *For they are jolly gay fellows,*
> *For they are jolly gay fellows,*
> *For they are jolly gay fellows,*
> *Which nobody can deny.*

Aunt Kate was making frank use of her handkerchief and even Aunt Julia seemed moved. Freddy Malins beat time with his pudding-fork and the singers turned towards one another, as if in melodious conference, while they sang with emphasis:

> *Unless he tells a lie,*
> *Unless he tells a lie,*

Then, turning once more towards their hostesses, they sang:

> *For they are jolly gay fellows,*
> *For they are jolly gay fellows,*
> *For they are jolly gay fellows,*
> *Which nobody can deny.*

The acclamation which followed was taken up beyond the door of the supper-room by many of the other guests and renewed time after time, Freddy Malins acting as officer with his fork on high.

. . . . .

The piercing morning air came into the hall where they were standing so that Aunt Kate said:

"Close the door, somebody. Mrs. Malins will get her death of cold."

"Browne is out there, Aunt Kate," said Mary Jane.

"Browne is everywhere," said Aunt Kate, lowering her voice.

Mary Jane laughed at her tone.

"Really," she said archly, "he is very attentive."

"He has been laid on here like the gas," said Aunt Kate in the same tone, "all during the Christmas."

She laughed herself this time good-humouredly and then added quickly:

"But tell him to come in, Mary Jane, and close the door. I hope to goodness he didn't hear me."

At that moment the hall-door was opened and Mr. Browne came in from the doorstep, laughing as if his heart would break. He was dressed in a long green overcoat with mock astrakhan cuffs and collar and wore on his head an oval fur cap. He pointed down the snow-covered quay from where the sound of shrill prolonged whistling was borne in.

"Teddy will have all the cabs in Dublin out," he said.

Gabriel advanced from the little pantry behind the office, struggling into his overcoat and, looking round the hall, said:

"Gretta not down yet?"

"She's getting on her things, Gabriel," said Aunt Kate.

"Who's playing up there?" asked Gabriel.

"Nobody. They're all gone."

"O no, Aunt Kate," said Mary Jane. "Bartell D'Arcy and Miss O'Callaghan aren't gone yet."

"Someone is fooling at the piano anyhow," said Gabriel.

Mary Jane glanced at Gabriel and Mr. Browne and said with a shiver:

"It makes me feel cold to look at you two gentlemen muffled up like that. I wouldn't like to face your journey home at this hour."

"I'd like nothing better this minute," said Mr. Browne stoutly, "than a rattling fine walk in the country or a fast drive with a good spanking goer between the shafts."

"We used to have a very good horse and trap at home," said Aunt Julia sadly.

"The never-to-be-forgotten Johnny," said Mary Jane, laughing.

Aunt Kate and Gabriel laughed too.

"Why, what was wonderful about Johnny?" asked Mr. Browne.

"The late lamented Patrick Morkan, our grandfather, that is," explained Gabriel, "commonly known in his later years as the old gentleman, was a glue-boiler."

"O, now, Gabriel," said Aunt Kate, laughing, "he had a starch mill."

"Well, glue or starch," said Gabriel, "the old gentleman had a horse by the name of Johnny. And Johnny used to work in the old gentleman's mill, walking round and round in order to drive the mill. That was all very well; but now comes the tragic part about Johnny. One fine day the old gentleman thought he'd like to drive out with the quality to a military review in the park."

"The Lord have mercy on his soul," said Aunt Kate compassionately.

"Amen," said Gabriel. "So the old gentleman, as I said, harnessed Johnny and put on his very best tall hat and his very best stock collar and drove out in grand style from his ancestral mansion somewhere near Back Lane, I think."

Everyone laughed, even Mrs. Malins, at Gabriel's manner and Aunt Kate said:

"O, now, Gabriel, he didn't live in Back Lane, really. Only the mill was there."

"Out from the mansion of his forefathers," continued Gabriel, "he drove with Johnny. And everything went on beautifully until Johnny came in sight of King Billy's statue: and whether he fell in love with the horse King Billy sits on or whether he thought he was back again in the mill, anyhow he began to walk round the statue."

Gabriel paced in a circle round the hall in his goloshes amid the laughter of the others.

"Round and round he went," said Gabriel, "and the old gentleman, who was a very pompous old gentleman, was highly indignant. 'Go on, sir! What do you mean, sir? Johnny! Johnny! Most extraordinary conduct! Can't understand the horse!' "

The peal of laughter which followed Gabriel's imitation of the incident was interrupted by a resounding knock at the hall door. Mary Jane ran to open it and let in Freddy Malins. Freddy Malins, with his hat well back on his head and his shoulders humped with cold, was puffing and steaming after his exertions.

"I could only get one cab," he said.

"O, we'll find another along the quay," said Gabriel.

"Yes," said Aunt Kate. "Better not keep Mrs. Malins standing in the draught."

Mrs. Malins was helped down the front steps by her son and Mr. Browne and, after many manœuvres, hoisted into the cab. Freddy Malins clambered in after her and spent a long time settling her on the seat, Mr. Browne helping him with advice. At last she was settled comfortably and Freddy Malins invited Mr. Browne into the cab. There was a good deal of confused talk, and then Mr. Browne got into the cab. The cabman settled his rug over his knees, and bent down for the address. The confusion grew greater and the cabman was directed differently by Freddy Malins and Mr. Browne, each of whom had his head out through a window of the cab. The difficulty was to know where to drop Mr. Browne along the route, and Aunt Kate, Aunt Julia and Mary Jane helped the discussion from the doorstep with cross-directions and contradictions and abundance of laughter. As for Freddy Malins he was speechless with laughter. He popped his head in and out of the window every moment to the great danger of his hat, and told his mother how the discussion was progressing, till at last Mr. Browne shouted to the bewildered cabman above the din of everybody's laughter:

"Do you know Trinity College?"

"Yes, sir," said the cabman.

"Well, drive bang up against Trinity College gates," said Mr. Browne, "and then we'll tell you where to go. You understand now?"

"Yes, sir," said the cabman.

"Make like a bird for Trinity College."

"Right, sir," said the cabman.

The horse was whipped up and the cab rattled off along the quay amid a chorus of laughter and adieus.

Gabriel had not gone to the door with the others. He was in a dark part of the hall gazing up the staircase. A woman was standing near the top of the first flight, in the shadow also. He could not see her face but he could see the terra-cotta and salmon-pink panels of her skirt which the shadow made appear black and white. It was his wife. She was leaning on the banisters, listening to something. Gabriel was surprised at her stillness and strained his ear to listen also. But he could hear little save the noise of laughter and dispute on the front steps, a few chords struck on the piano and a few notes of a man's voice singing.

He stood still in the gloom of the hall, trying to catch the air that the voice was singing and gazing up at his wife. There was grace and mystery in her attitude as if she were a symbol of something. He asked himself what is a woman standing on the stairs in the shadow, listening to distant music, a symbol of. If he were a painter he would paint her in that attitude. Her blue felt hat would show off the bronze of her hair against the darkness and the dark panels of her skirt would show off the light ones. *Distant Music* he would call the picture if he were a painter.

The hall-door was closed; and Aunt Kate, Aunt Julia and Mary Jane came down the hall, still laughing.

"Well, isn't Freddy terrible?" said Mary Jane. "He's really terrible."

Gabriel said nothing but pointed up the stairs towards where his wife was standing. Now that the hall-door was closed the voice and the piano could be heard more clearly. Gabriel held up his hand for them to be silent. The song seemed to be in the old Irish tonality and the singer seemed uncertain both of his words and of his voice. The voice, made plaintive by distance and by the singer's hoarseness, faintly illuminated the cadence of the air with words expressing grief:

> O, the rain falls on my heavy locks
> And the dew wets my skin,
> My babe lies cold...

"Oh," exclaimed Mary Jane. "It's Bartell D'Arcy singing and he wouldn't sing all the night. O' I'll get him to sing a song before he goes."

"O, do, Mary Jane," said Aunt Kate.

Mary Jane brushed past the others and ran to the staircase, but before she reached it the singing stopped and the piano was closed abruptly.

"O, what a pity!" she cried. "Is he coming down, Gretta?"

Gabriel heard his wife answer yes and saw her come down towards them. A few steps behind her were Mr. Bartell D'Arcy and Miss O'Callaghan.

"O, Mr. D'Arcy," cried Mary Jane, "it's downright mean of you to break off like that when we were all in raptures listening to you."

"I have been at him all the evening," said Miss O'Callaghan, "and Mrs. Conroy, too, and he told us he had a dreadful cold and couldn't sing."

"O, Mr. D'Arcy," said Aunt Kate, "now that was a great fib to tell."

"Can't you see that I'm as hoarse as a crow?" said Mr. D'Arcy roughly.

He went into the pantry hastily and put on his overcoat. The others, taken aback by his rude speech, could find nothing to say. Aunt Kate wrinkled her brows and made signs to the others to drop the subject. Mr. D'Arcy stood swathing his neck carefully and frowning.

"It's the weather," said Aunt Julia, after a pause.

"Yes, everybody has colds," said Aunt Kate readily, "everybody."

"They say," said Mary Jane, "we haven't had snow like it for thirty years; and I read this morning in the newspapers that the snow is general all over Ireland."

"I love the look of snow," said Aunt Julia sadly.

"So do I," said Miss O'Callaghan. "I think Christmas is never really Christmas unless we have snow on the ground."

"But poor Mr. D'Arcy doesn't like the snow," said Aunt Kate, smiling.

Mr. D'Arcy came from the pantry, fully swathed and buttoned, and in a repentant tone told them the history of his cold. Everyone gave him advice and said it was a great pity and urged him to be very careful of his throat in the night air. Gabriel watched his wife, who did not join in the conversation. She was standing right under the dusty fanlight and the flame of the gas lit up the rich bronze of her hair, which he had seen her drying at the fire a few days before. She was in the same attitude and seemed unaware of the talk about her. At last she turned towards them and Gabriel saw that there was colour on her cheeks and that her eyes were shining. A sudden tide of joy went leaping out of his heart.

"Mr. D'Arcy," she said, "what is the name of that song you were singing?"

"It's called The Lass of Aughrim," said Mr. D'Arcy, "but I couldn't remember it properly. Why? Do you know it?"

"The Lass of Aughrim," she repeated. "I couldn't think of the name."

"It's a very nice air," said Mary Jane. "I'm sorry you were not in voice tonight."

"Now, Mary Jane," said Aunt Kate, "don't annoy Mr. D'Arcy. I won't have him annoyed."

Seeing that all were ready to start she shepherded them to the door, where good-night was said:

"Well, good-night, Aunt Kate, and thanks for the pleasant evening."

"Good-night, Gabriel. Good-night, Gretta!"

"Good-night, Aunt Kate, and thanks ever so much. Good-night, Aunt Julia."

"O, good-night, Gretta. I didn't see you."

"Good-night, Mr. D'Arcy. Good-night, Miss O'Callaghan."

"Good-night, Miss Morkan."

"Good-night, again."

"Good-night, all. Safe home."

"Good-night. Good night."

The morning was still dark. A dull, yellow light brooded over the houses and the river; and the sky seemed to be descending. It was slushy underfoot; and only streaks and patches of snow lay on the roofs, on the parapets of the quay and on the area railings. The lamps were still burning redly in the murky air and, across the river, the palace of the Four Courts stood out menacingly against the heavy sky.

She was walking on before him with Mr. Bartell D'Arcy, her shoes in a brown parcel tucked under one arm and her hands holding her skirt up from the slush. She had no longer any grace of attitude, but Gabriel's eyes were still bright with happiness. The blood went bounding along his veins; and the thoughts went rioting through his brain, proud, joyful, tender, valorous.

She was walking on before him so lightly and so erect that he longed to run after her noiselessly, catch her by the shoulders and say something foolish and affectionate into her ear. She seemed to him so frail that he longed to defend her against something and then to be alone with her. Moments of their secret life together burst like stars upon his memory. A heliotrope envelope was lying beside his breakfast cup and he was caressing it with his hand. Birds were twittering in the ivy and the sunny web of the curtain was shimmering along the floor: he could not eat for happiness. They were standing on the crowded platform and he was placing a ticket inside the warm palm of her glove. He was standing with her in the cold, looking in through a grated window at a man making bottles in a roaring furnace. It was very cold. Her face, fragrant in the cold air, was quite close to his; and suddenly he called out to the man at the furnace:

"Is the fire hot, sir?"

But the man could not hear with the noise of the furnace. It was just as well. He might have answered rudely.

A wave of yet more tender joy escaped from his heart and went coursing in warm flood along his arteries. Like the tender fire of stars moments of their life together, that no one knew of or would ever know of, broke upon and illumined his memory. He longed to recall to her those moments, to make her forget the years of their dull existence together and remember only their moments of ecstasy.

For the years, he felt, had not quenched his soul or hers. Their children, his writing, her household cares had not quenched all their souls' tender fire. In one letter that he had written to her then he had said: "Why is it that words like these seem to me so dull and cold? Is it because there is no word tender enough to be your name?"

Like distant music these words that he had written years before were borne towards him from the past. He longed to be alone with her. When the others had gone away, when he and she were in the room in the hotel, then they would be alone together. He would call her softly:

"Gretta!"

Perhaps she would not hear at once: she would be undressing. Then something in his voice would strike her. She would turn and look at him. . . .

At the corner of Winetavern Street they met a cab. He was glad of its rattling noise as it saved him from conversation. She was looking out of the window and seemed tired. The others spoke only a few words, pointing out some building or street. The horse galloped along wearily under the murky morning sky, dragging his old rattling box after his heels, and Gabriel was again in a cab with her, galloping to catch the boat, galloping to their honeymoon.

As the cab drove across O'Connell Bridge Miss O'Callaghan said:

"They say you never cross O'Connell Bridge without seeing a white horse."

"I see a white man this time," said Gabriel.

"Where?" asked Mr. Bartell D'Arcy.

Gabriel pointed to the statue, on which lay patches of snow. Then he nodded familiarly to it and waved his hand.

"Good-night, Dan," he said gaily.

When the cab drew up before the hotel, Gabriel jumped out and, in spite of Mr. Bartell D'Arcy's protest, paid the driver. He gave the man a shilling over his fare. The man saluted and said:

"A prosperous New Year to you, sir."

"The same to you," said Gabriel cordially.

She leaned for a moment on his arm in getting out of the cab and while standing at the curbstone, bidding the others good-night. She leaned lightly on his arm, as lightly as when she had danced with him a few hours before. He had felt proud and happy then, happy that she was his, proud of her grace and wifely carriage. But now, after the kindling again of so many memories, the first touch of her body, musical and strange and perfumed, sent through him a keen pang of lust. Under cover of her silence he pressed her arm closely to his side; and, as they stood at the hotel door, he felt that they had escaped from their lives and duties, escaped from home and friends and run away together with wild and radiant hearts to a new adventure.

An old man was dozing in a great hooded chair in the hall. He lit a candle in the office and went before them to the stairs. They followed him in silence, their feet falling in soft thuds on the thickly carpeted stairs. She mounted the stairs behind the porter, her head bowed in the ascent, her frail shoulders curved as with a burden, her skirt girt tightly about her. He could have flung his arms about her hips and held her still, for his arms were trembling with desire to seize her and only the stress of his nails against the palms of his hands held the wild impulse of his body in check. The porter halted on the stairs to settle his guttering candle. They halted, too, on the steps below him. In the silence Gabriel could hear the falling of the molten wax into the tray and the thumping of his own heart against his ribs.

The porter led them along a corridor and opened a door. Then he set his unstable candle down on a toilet-table and asked at what hour they were to be called in the morning.

"Eight," said Gabriel.

The porter pointed to the tap of the electric-light and began a muttered apology, but Gabriel cut him short.

"We don't want any light. We have light enough from the street. And I say," he added, pointing to the candle, "you might remove that handsome article, like a good man."

The porter took up his candle again, but slowly, for he was surprised by such a novel idea. Then he mumbled good-night and went out. Gabriel shot the lock to.

A ghastly light from the street lamp lay in a long shaft from one window to the door. Gabriel threw his overcoat and hat on a couch and crossed the room towards the window. He looked down into the street in order that his emotion might calm a little. Then he turned and leaned against a chest of drawers with his back to the light. She had taken off her hat and cloak and was standing before a large swing-ing mirror, unhooking her waist. Gabriel paused for a few moments, watching her, and then said:

"Gretta!"

She turned away from the mirror slowly and walked along the shaft of light towards him. Her face looked so serious and weary that the words would not pass Gabriel's lips. No, it was not the moment yet.

"You look tired," he said.

"I am a little," she answered.

"You don't feel ill or weak?"

"No, tired: that's all."

She went on to the window and stood there, looking out. Gabriel waited again and then, fearing that diffidence was about to conquer him, he said abruptly:

"By the way, Gretta!"

"What is it?"

"You know that poor fellow Malins?" he said quickly.

"Yes. What about him?"

"Well, poor fellow, he's a decent sort of chap, after all," continued Gabriel in a false voice. "He gave me back that sovereign I lent him, and I didn't expect it, really. It's a pity he wouldn't keep away from that Browne, because he's not a bad fellow, really."

He was trembling now with annoyance. Why did she seem so abstracted? He did not know how he could begin. Was she annoyed, too, about something? If she would only turn to him or come to him of her own accord! To take her as she was would be brutal. No, he must see some ardour in her eyes first. He longed to be master of her strange mood.

"When did you lend him the pound?" she asked, after a pause.

Gabriel strove to restrain himself from breaking out into brutal language about the sottish Malins and his pound. He longed to cry to her from his soul, to crush her body against his, to overmaster her. But he said:

"O, at Christmas, when he opened that little Christmas-card shop in Henry Street."

He was in such a fever of rage and desire that he did not hear her come from the window. She stood before him for an instant, looking at him strangely. Then, suddenly raising herself on tiptoe and resting her hands lightly on his shoulders, she kissed him.

"You are a very generous person Gabriel," she said.

Gabriel, trembling with delight at her sudden kiss and at the quaintness of her phrase, put his hands on her hair and began smoothing it back, scarcely touching it with his fingers. The washing had made it fine and brilliant. His heart was brimming over with happiness. Just when he was wishing for it she had come to him of her own accord. Perhaps her thoughts had been running with his. Perhaps she had felt the impetuous desire that was in him, and then the yielding mood had come upon her. Now that she had fallen to him so easily, he wondered why he had been so diffident.

He stood, holding her head between his hands. Then, slipping one arm swiftly about her body and drawing her towards him, he said softly:

"Gretta, dear, what are you thinking about?"

She did not answer nor yield wholly to his arm. He said again, softly:

"Tell me what it is, Gretta. I think I know what is the matter. Do I know?"

She did not answer at once. Then she said in an outburst of tears:

"O, I am thinking about that song, *The Lass of Aughrim.*"

She broke loose from him and ran to the bed and, throwing her arms across the bed-rail, hid her face. Gabriel stood stock-still for a moment in astonishment and then followed her. As he passed in the way of the cheval-glass he caught sight of himself in full length, his broad, well-filled shirt-front, the face whose expression always puzzled him when he saw it in a mirror, and his glimmering gilt-rimmed eyeglasses. He halted a few paces from her and said:

"What about the song? Why does that make you cry?"

She raised her head from her arms and dried her eyes with the back of her hand like a child. A kinder note than he had intended went into his voice.

"Why, Gretta?" he asked.

"I am thinking about a person long ago who used to sing that song."

"And who was the person long ago?" asked Gabriel, smiling.

"It was a person I used to know in Galway when I was living with my grandmother," she said.

The smile passed away from Gabriel's face. A dull anger began to gather again at the back of his mind and the dull fires of his lust began to glow angrily in his veins.

"Someone you were in love with?" he asked ironically.

"It was a young boy I used to know," she answered, "named Michael Furey. He used to sing that song, *The Lass of Aughrim*. He was very delicate."

Gabriel was silent. He did not wish her to think that he was interested in this delicate boy.

"I can see him so plainly," she said, after a moment. "Such eyes as he had: big, dark eyes! And such an expression in them—an expression!"

"O, then, you are in love with him?" said Gabriel.

"I used to go out walking with him," she said, "when I was in Galway."

A thought flew across Gabriel's mind.

"Perhaps that was why you wanted to go to Galway with that Ivors girl?" he said coldly.

She looked at him and asked in surprise:

"What for?"

Her eyes made Gabriel feel awkward. He shrugged his shoulders and said:

"How do I know? To see him, perhaps."

She looked away from him along the shaft of light towards the window in silence.

"He is dead," she said at length. "He died when he was only seventeen. Isn't it a terrible thing to die so young as that?"

"What was he?" asked Gabriel still ironically.

"He was in the gasworks," she said.

Gabriel felt humiliated by the failure of his irony and by the evocation of this figure from the dead, a boy in the gasworks. While he had been full of memories of their secret life together, full of tenderness and joy and desire, she had been comparing him in her mind with another. A shameful consciousness of his own person assailed him. He saw himself as a ludicrous figure, acting as a pennyboy for his aunts, a nervous, well-meaning sentimentalist, orating to vulgarians and idealising his own clownish lusts, the pitiable fatuous fellow he had caught a glimpse of in the mirror. Instinctively he turned his back more to the light lest she might see the shame that burned upon his forehead.

He tried to keep up his tone of cold interrogation, but his voice when he spoke was humble and indifferent.

"I suppose you were in love with this Michael Furey, Gretta," he said.

"I was great with him at that time," she said.

Her voice was veiled and sad. Gabriel, feeling now how vain it would be to try to lead her whither he had purposed, caressed one of her hands and said, also sadly:

"And what did he die of so young, Gretta? Consumption, was it?"

"I think he died for me," she answered.

A vague terror seized Gabriel at this answer, as if, at that hour when he had hoped to triumph, some impalpable and vindictive being was coming against him, gathering forces against him in its vague world. But he shook himself free of it with an effort of reason and continued to caress her hand. He did not question her again, for he felt that she would tell him of herself. Her hand was warm and moist: it did not respond to his touch, but he continued to caress it just as he had caressed her first letter to him that spring morning.

"It was in the winter," she said, "about the beginning of the winter when I was going to leave my grandmother's and come up here to the convent. And he was ill at the time in his lodgings in Galway and wouldn't be let out, and his people in Oughterard were written to. He was in decline, they said, or something like that. I never knew rightly."

She paused for a moment and sighed.

"Poor fellow," she said. "He was very fond of me and he was such a gentle boy. We used to go out together, walking, you know, Gabriel, like the way they do in the country. He was going to study singing only for his health. He had a very good voice, poor Michael Furey."

"Well; and then?" asked Gabriel.

"And then when it came to the time for me to leave Galway and come up to the convent he was much worse and I wouldn't be let see him so I wrote him a letter saying I was going up to Dublin and would be back in the summer, and hoping he would be better then."

She paused for a moment to get her voice under control, and then went on:

"Then the night before I left, I was in my grandmother's house in Nuns' Island, packing up, and I heard gravel thrown up against the window. The window was so wet I couldn't see, so I ran downstairs as I was and slipped out the back into the garden and there was the poor fellow at the end of the garden, shivering."

"And did you not tell him to go back?" asked Gabriel.

"I implored of him to go home at once and told him he would get his death in the rain. But he said he did not want to live. I can see his eyes as well as well! He was standing at the end of the wall where there was a tree."

"And did he go home?" asked Gabriel.

"Yes, he went home. And when I was only a week in the convent he died and he was buried in Oughterard, where his people come from. O, the day I heard that, that he was dead!"

She stopped, choking with sobs, and, overcome by emotion, flung herself face downward on the bed, sobbing in the quilt. Gabriel held her hand for a moment longer, irresolutely, and then, shy of intruding on her grief, let it fall gently and walked quietly to the window.

She was fast asleep.

Gabriel, leaning on his elbow, looked for a few moments unresentfully on her tangled hair and half-open mouth, listening to her deep-drawn breath. So she had that romance in her life: a man had died for her sake. It hardly pained him now to think how poor a part he, her husband, had played in her life. He watched her while she slept, as though he and she had never lived together as man and wife. His curious eyes rested long upon her face and on her hair: and, as he thought of what she must have been then, in that time of her first girlish beauty, a strange, friendly pity for her entered his soul. He did not like to say even to himself that her face was no longer beautiful, but he knew that it was no longer the face for which Michael Furey had braved death.

Perhaps she had not told him all the story. His eyes moved to the chair over which she had thrown some of her clothes. A petticoat string dangled to the floor. One boot stood upright, its limp upper fallen down: the fellow of it lay upon its side. He wondered at his riot of emotions of an hour before. From what had it proceeded? From his aunt's supper, from his own foolish speech, from the wine and dancing, the merry-making when saying good-night in the hall, the pleasure of the walk along the river in the snow. Poor Aunt Julia! She, too, would soon be a shade with the shade of Patrick Morkan and his horse. He had caught that haggard look upon her face for a moment when she was singing *Arrayed for the Bridal*. Soon, perhaps, he would be sitting in that same drawing-room, dressed in black, his silk hat on his knees. The blinds would be drawn down and Aunt Kate would be sitting beside him crying, and blowing her nose and telling him how Julia had died. He would cast about in his mind for some words that might console her, and would find only lame and useless ones. Yes, yes: that would happen very soon.

The air of the room chilled his shoulders. He stretched himself cautiously along under the sheets and lay down beside his wife. One by one, they were all becoming shades. Better pass boldly into that other world, in the full glory of some passion, than fade and wither dismally with age. He thought of how she who lay beside him had locked in her heart for so many years that image of her lover's eyes when he had told her that he did not wish to live.

Generous tears filled Gabriel's eyes. He had never felt like that himself towards any woman, but he knew that such a feeling must be love. The tears gathered more thickly in his eyes and in the partial darkness he imagined he saw the form of a young man standing under a dripping tree. Other forms were near. His soul had approached that region where dwell the vast hosts of the dead. He was conscious of, but could not apprehend, their wayward and flickering existence. His own identity was fading out into a grey impalpable world: the solid world itself, which these dead had one time reared and lived in, was dissolving and dwindling.

A few light taps upon the pane made him turn to the window. It had begun to snow again. He watched sleepily the flakes, silver and dark, falling obliquely against the lamplight. The time had come for him to set out on his journey westward. Yes, the newspapers were right: snow was general all over Ireland. It was falling on every part of the dark central plain, on the treeless hills, falling softly upon the Bog of Allen and, farther westward, softly falling into the dark mutinous Shannon waves. It was falling, too, upon every part of the lonely churchyard on the hill where Michael Furey lay buried. It lay thickly drifted on the crooked crosses and headstones, on the spears of the little gate, on the barren thorns. His soul swooned slowly as he heard the snow falling faintly through the universe and faintly falling, like the descent of their last end, upon all the living and the dead.

The Burrow

(1924, publ. 1931)

Franz Kafka

Willa and Edwin Muir, translators

Franz Kafka (1883–1924) was born in Prague, the son of a Jewish merchant.
An unsatisfactory father-son relationship overshadowed Kafka's whole life and
influenced his writing. He studied at the Deutsche Universität, Prague (1901–06),
at first reading chemistry and then changing to law. Most of his life was spent
working in an advocate's office and in an accident-insurance office in Prague. In
1912 he met Fräulein "F.B.," and his life was further warped by his inability to
make himself marry the girl he loved. He became engaged to her in 1914, left
his parents to live alone in 1915, and broke off the engagement in 1916; in 1917
he renewed it for a time but then broke it off again. A few of the stories Kafka
wrote during these years were published in his lifetime: "The Judgment" (1913),
The Metamorphosis (1915), "A Country Doctor" (1919), *In the Penal Colony*
(1919), and "A Hunger-Artist" (1924). Most of his writings, however, were not
published until after his early death from tuberculosis. These manuscripts were
brought out by his friend Max Brod: the novels, *The Trial* (1925), *The Castle*
(1926), and *Amerika* (1927); and shorter pieces in *The Great Wall of China*
(1931). For information about Kafka's life, see Max Brod, *Franz Kafka, a
Biography* (New York, 1947); for critical essays and bibliography, see *Kafka:
A Collection of Critical Essays,* ed. Ronald Gray (Twentieth-Century Views,
Englewood Cliffs, New Jersey, 1962).

The Burrow was one of Kafka's last works. As Edwin Muir has noted, it is
"virtually finished, all that remained to be described being the appearance of the
invisible enemy, to whom the hero was to succumb" (Introduction, *Great Wall of
China,* New York, 1946, p. xvii). But one may suspect that the open-ended,
unfinished quality, however arrived at, is an essential part of Kafka's form. A
resolution would have nullified Kafka's effect; and so his inability to finish stories
suggests that his vision of reality precluded the satisfaction of resolution. *The
Burrow* is reprinted by permission of Schocken Books Inc. from *The Great Wall
of China* by Franz Kafka, Copyright 1936, 1937 by Heinr. Mercy Sohn, Prague.
Copyright 1946, 1948 by Schocken Books Inc., New York, translated by Willa and
Edwin Muir.

I have completed the construction of my burrow and it seems to be successful. All that can be seen from outside is a big hole; that, however, really leads nowhere; if you take a few steps you strike against natural firm rock. I can make no boast of having contrived this ruse intentionally; it is simply the remains of one of my many abortive building attempts, but finally it seemed to me advisable to leave this one hole without filling it in. True, some ruses are so subtle that they defeat themselves, I know that better than any one, and it is certainly a risk to draw attention by this hole to the fact that there may be something in the vicinity worth enquiring into. But you do not know me if you think I am afraid, or that I built my burrow simply out of fear. At a distance of some thousand paces from this hole lies, covered by a movable layer of moss, the real entrance to the burrow; it is secured as safely as anything in this world can be secured; yet some one could step on the moss or break through it, and then my burrow would lie open, and anybody who liked—please note, however, that quite uncommon abilities would also be required—could make his way in and destroy everything for good. I know that very well, and even now that I am better off than ever before I can scarcely pass an hour in complete tranquillity; at that one point in the dark moss I am vulnerable, and in my dreams I often see a greedy muzzle sniffing round it persistently. It will be objected that I could quite well have filled in the entrance too, with a thin layer of hard earth on top and with loose soil further down, so that it would not cost me much trouble to dig my way out again whenever I liked. But that plan is impossible; prudence itself demands that I should have a way of leaving at a moment's notice if necessary, prudence itself demands, as alas! so often, the element of risk in life. All this involves very laborious calculation, and the sheer pleasure of the mind in its own keenness is often the sole reason why one keeps it up. I must have a way of leaving at a moment's notice, for, despite all my vigilance, may I not be attacked from some quite unexpected quarter? I live in peace in the inmost chamber of my house, and meanwhile the enemy may be burrowing his way slowly and stealthily straight towards me. I do not say that he has a better scent than I; probably he knows as little about me as I of him. But there are insatiable robbers who burrow blindly through the ground, and to whom the very size of my house gives the hope of hitting by chance on some of its far-flung passages. I certainly have the advantage of being in my own house and knowing all the passages and how they run. A robber may very easily become my victim and a succulent one too. But I am growing old; I am not as strong as many others, and my enemies are countless; it could well happen that in flying from one enemy I might run into the jaws of another. Anything might happen! In any case I must have the confident knowledge that somewhere there is an exit easy to reach and quite free, where I have to do nothing whatever to get out, so that I might never—Heaven shield us!—suddenly feel the teeth of the pursuer in my flank while I am desperately burrowing away, even if it is at loose easy soil. And it is not only by external enemies that I am threatened. There are also enemies in the bowels of the earth. I have never seen them, but legend tells of them and I firmly believe in them. They are creatures of the inner earth; not even legend can describe them. Their very victims can scarcely have seen them; they come, you hear the scratching of their claws just under you in the ground, which is their element, and already you are lost. Here it is of no avail to console yourself with the thought that you are in your own houses; far rather are you in theirs. Not even my exit could save me from them; indeed in all probability it would not save me in any case, but rather betray me; yet it is a hope, and I cannot live without it. Apart from this main exit I am also connected with the outer world by quite narrow, tolerably safe passages which provide me with good fresh air to breathe. They are the work of the field mice. I have made judicious use of them, transforming them into an organic part of my burrow. They also give me the possibility of scenting things from afar, and thus serve as a protection. All sorts of small fry, too, come running through them, and I devour these; so I can have a certain amount of subterranean hunting, sufficient for a modest way of life, without leaving my burrow at all; and that is naturally a great advantage.

But the most beautiful thing about my burrow is the stillness. Of course, that is deceitful. At any moment it may be shattered and then all will be over. For the time being, however, the silence is still with me. For hours I can stroll through my passages and hear nothing except the rustling of some little creature, which I immediately reduce to silence between my jaws, or the pattering of soil, which draws my attention to the need for repair; otherwise all is still. The fragrance of the woods floats in; the place feels both warm and cool. Sometimes I lie down and roll about in the passage with pure joy. When autumn sets in to possess a burrow like mine, and a roof over your head, is great good fortune for any one getting on in years. Every hundred yards I have widened the passages into little round cells; there I can curl myself up in comfort and lie warm. There I sleep the sweet sleep of tranquillity, of satisfied desire, of achieved ambition; for I possess a house. I do not know whether it is a habit that still persists from former days, or whether the perils even of this house of mine are great enough to awaken me; but invariably every now and then I start up out of profound sleep and listen, listen into the stillness which reigns here unchanged day and night, smile contentedly and then sink with loosened limbs into still profounder sleep. Poor homeless wanderers in the roads and woods, creeping for warmth into a heap of leaves or a herd of their comrades, delivered to all the perils of heaven and earth! I lie here in a room secured on every side—there are more than fifty such rooms in my burrow—and pass as much of my time as I choose between dozing and unconscious sleep.

Not quite in the centre of the burrow, carefully chosen to serve as a refuge in case of extreme danger from siege if not from immediate pursuit, lies the chief cell. While all the rest of the burrow is the outcome rather of intense intellectual than of physical labour, this Castle Keep was fashioned by the most arduous labour of my whole body. Several times, in the despair brought on by physical exhaustion, I was on the point of giving up the whole business, flung myself down panting and cursed the burrow, dragged myself outside and left the place lying open to all the world. I could afford to do that, for I had no longer any wish to return to it, until at last, after four hours or days, back I went repentantly, and when I saw that the burrow was unharmed I could almost have raised a hymn of thanksgiving, and in sincere gladness of heart started on the work anew. My labours on the Castle Keep were also made harder, and unnecessarily so (unnecessarily in that the burrow derived no real benefit from those labours) by the fact that just at the place where, according to my calculations, the Castle Keep should be, the soil was very loose and sandy and had literally to be hammered and pounded into a firm state to serve as a wall for the beautifully vaulted chamber. But for such tasks the only tool I possess is my forehead. So I had to run with my forehead thousands and thousands of times, for whole days and nights, against the ground, and I was glad when the blood came, for that was a proof that the walls were beginning to harden; and in that way, as everybody must admit, I richly paid for my Castle Keep.

In the Castle Keep I assemble my stores; everything over and above my daily wants that I capture inside the burrow, and everything I bring back with me from my hunting expeditions outside, I pile up here. The place is so spacious that food for half a year scarcely fills it. Consequently I can divide up my stores, walk about among them, play with them, enjoy their plenty and their various smells, and reckon up exactly how much they represent. That done, I can always arrange accordingly, and make my calculations and hunting plans for the future, taking into account the season of the year. There are times when I am so well provided for that in my indifference to food I never even touch the smaller fry that scuttle about the burrow, which, however, is probably imprudent of me. My constant preoccupation with defensive measures involves a frequent alteration or modification, though within narrow limits, of my views on how the building can best be organized for that end. Then it sometimes seems risky to make the Castle Keep the basis of defence; the ramifications of the burrow present me with manifold possibilities, and it seems more in accordance with prudence to divide up my stores somewhat, and put part of them in certain of the smaller rooms; thereupon I mark off every third room, let us say, as a reserve store-room, or every fourth room as a main and every second as an auxiliary store-room, and so forth. Or I ignore certain passages altogether and store no food in them, so as to throw any enemy off the scent, or I choose quite at random a very few rooms according to their distance from the main exit. Each of these new plans involves of course heavy work; I have to make my calculations and then carry my stores to their new places. True, I can do that at my leisure and without any hurry, and it is not at all unpleasant to carry such good food in your jaws, to lie down and rest whenever you like, and, which is an actual pleasure, to have an occasional nibble. But it is not so pleasant when, as sometimes happens, you suddenly fancy, starting up from your sleep, that the present distribution of your stores is completely and totally wrong, capable of leading to great dangers, and must be set right at once, no matter how tired or sleepy you may be; then I rush, then I fly, then I have no time for calculation; as I am burning to execute my perfectly new, perfectly satisfactory plan, I seize whatever my teeth hit upon and drag it or carry it away, sighing, groaning, stumbling, and nothing will content me but some radical alteration of the present state of things, which seems imminently dangerous. Until little by little full wakefulness sobers me, and I can hardly understand my panic haste, breathe in deeply the tranquillity of my house, which I myself have disturbed, return to my resting-place, fall asleep at once in a new-won exhaustion, and on awakening find hanging from my jaws, say, a rat, as indubitable proof of night labours which already seem almost unreal. Then again there are times when the storing of all my food in one place seems the best plan of all. Of what use to me could my stores in the smaller rooms be, how much could I store there in any case? And whatever I put there would block the passage, and be a greater hindrance than help to me if I were pursued and had to fly. Besides, it is stupid but true that one's self-conceit suffers if one cannot see all one's stores together, and so at one glance know how much one possesses. And in dividing up my food in those various ways might not a great deal get lost? I can't be always scouring through all my passages and cross-passages so as to make sure that everything is in order. The idea of dividing up my stores is of course a good one, but only if one had several rooms similar to my Castle Keep. Several such rooms! Indeed! And who is to build them? In any case they could not be worked into the general plan of my burrow at this late stage. But I will admit that that is a fault in my burrow; it is always a fault to have only one copy of anything. And I confess too that during the whole time I was constructing the burrow a vague divination that I should have more such cells stirred in my mind, vaguely, yet clearly enough if I had only welcomed it; I did not yield to it, I felt too feeble for the enormous labour it would involve, more, I felt too feeble even to admit to myself the necessity for that labour, and comforted myself as best I could with the vague hope that a building which in any other case would clearly be inadequate, would in my own unique, exceptional, favoured case suffice, presumably, because providence was interested in the preservation of my forehead, that unique instrument. So I have only one Castle Keep, but my dark premonitions that one would not suffice have faded. However that may be I must content myself with the one big chamber, the smaller ones are simply no substitute for it, and so, when this conviction has grown on me, I begin once more to haul all my stores back from them to the Castle Keep. For some time afterwards I find a certain comfort in having all the passages and rooms free, in seeing my stores growing in the Castle Keep and emitting their variegated and mingled smells, each of which delights me in its own fashion, and every one of which I can distinguish even at a distance, as far as the very remotest passages. Then I usually enjoy periods of particular tranquillity, in which I change my sleeping-place by stages, always working in towards the centre of the burrow, always steeping myself more profoundly in the mingled smells, until at last I can no longer restrain myself and one night rush into the Castle Keep, mightily fling myself upon my stores, and glut myself with the best that I can seize until I am completely gorged. Happy, but dangerous hours; any one who knew how to exploit them could destroy me with ease and without any risk. Here too the absence of a second or third large store-room works to my detriment; for it is the single huge accumulated mass of food that seduces me. I try to guard myself in various ways against this danger; the distribution of my stores in the smaller rooms is really one of these expedients; but unfortunately, like other such expedients, it leads through renunciation to still greater greed, which, over-ruling my intelligence, makes me arbitrarily alter my plans of defence to suit its ends.

To regain my composure after such lapses I make a practice of reviewing the burrow, and after the necessary improvements have been carried out, frequently leave it, though only for a short spell. At such moments the hardship of renouncing it for a long time seems too punitive, even to myself, yet I recognize clearly the need for my occasional short excursions. It is always with a certain solemnity that I approach the exit again. During my spells of home life I avoid it, steer clear even of the outer windings of the corridor that leads to it; besides, it is no easy job to wander about there, for I have contrived there a whole little maze of passages; it was there that I began my burrow, at a time when I had no hope of ever completing it according to my plans; I began, half in play, at that corner, and so my first joy in labour found riotous satisfaction there in a labyrinthine burrow which at the time seemed to me the crown of all burrows, but which I judge to-day, perhaps with more justice, to be too much of an idle *tour de force,* not really worthy of the rest of the burrow, and though perhaps theoretically brilliant—here is my main entrance, I said in those days, ironically addressing my invisible enemies and seeing them all already caught and stifled in the outer labyrinth—is in reality a flimsy piece of jugglery that would hardly withstand a serious attack or the struggles of an enemy fighting for his life. Should I reconstruct this part of my burrow? I keep on postponing the decision, and the labyrinth will probably remain as it is. Apart from the sheer hard work that I should have to face, the task would also be the most dangerous imaginable. When I began the burrow I could work away at it in comparative peace of mind, the risk wasn't much greater than any other risk; but to attempt that to-day would be to draw the whole world's attention, and gratuitously, to my burrow; to-day the whole thing is impossible. I am almost glad of that, for I still have a certain sentiment about this first achievement of mine. And if a serious attack were attempted, what pattern of entrance at all would be likely to save me? An entrance can deceive, can lead astray, can give the attacker no end of worry, and the present one too can do that at a pinch. But a really serious attack has to be met by an instantaneous mobilisation of all the resources in the burrow and all the forces of my body and soul—that, of course, is self-evident. So this entrance can very well remain where it is. The burrow has so many unavoidable defects imposed by natural causes that it can surely stand this one defect for which I am responsible, and which I recognize as a defect, even if only after the event. In spite of that, however, I do not deny that this fault worries me from time to time, indeed always. If on my customary rounds I avoid this part of the burrow, the fundamental reason is because the sight of it is painful to me, because I don't want to be perpetually reminded of a defect in my house, even if that defect is only too disturbingly present in my mind. Let it continue to exist ineradicably at the entrance; I can at least refuse to look at it as long as that is possible. If I merely walk in the direction of the entrance, even though I may be separated from it by several passages and rooms, I find myself sensing an atmosphere of great danger, actually as if my hair were growing thin and in a moment might fly off and leave me bare and shivering, exposed to the howls of my enemies. Yes, the mere thought of the door itself brings such feelings with it, yet it is the labyrinth leading up to it that torments me most of all. Sometimes I dream that I have reconstructed it, transformed it completely, quickly, in a night, with a giant's strength, nobody having noticed, and now it is impregnable; the nights in which such dreams come to me are the sweetest I know, tears of joy and deliverance still glisten on my beard when I awaken.

So I must thread the tormenting complications of this labyrinth physically as well as mentally whenever I go out, and I am both exasperated and touched when, as sometimes happens, I lose myself for a moment in my own maze, and the work of my hands seems to be still doing its best to prove its sufficiency to me, its maker, whose final judgment has long since been passed on it. But then I find myself beneath the mossy covering, which has been left untouched for so long—for I stay for long spells in my house—that it has grown fast to the soil round it, and now only a little push with my head is needed and I am in the upper world. For a long time I do not dare to make that little movement, and if it were not that I would have to traverse the labyrinth once more, I would certainly leave the matter for the time being and turn back again. Just think. Your house is protected and self-sufficient. You live in peace, warm, well-nourished, master, sole master of all your manifold passages and rooms, and all this you are prepared, it appears, not merely to give up, but actually to abandon; you nurse the confident hope, certainly, that you will regain it; yet is it not a dangerous, a far too dangerous stake that you are playing for? Can there be any reasonable grounds for such a step? No, for such acts as these there can be no reasonable grounds. But all the same I then cautiously raise the trap-door and slip outside, let it solftly fall back again, and fly as fast as I can from the treacherous spot.

Yet I am not really free. True, I am no longer confined by narrow passages, but rush through the open woods, and feel new powers awakening in my body for which there was no room, as it were, in the burrow, not even in the Castle Keep, though it had been ten times as big. The food too is better up here; though hunting is more difficult, success more rare, the results are more valuable from every point of view; I do not deny all this; I appreciate it and take advantage of it as fully as most animals, and probably more fully, for I do not hunt like a vagrant out of mere idleness or desperation, but calmly and methodically. Also I am not permanently doomed to this free life, for I know that my term is measured, that I do not have to hunt here for ever, and that, whenever I am weary of this life and wish to leave it, Someone, whose invitation I shall not be able to withstand, will, so to speak, summon me to him. And so I can pass my time here quite without care and in complete enjoyment, or rather I could, and yet I cannot. My burrow takes up too much of my thoughts. I fled from the entrance fast enough, but soon I am back at it again. I seek out a good hiding-place and keep watch on the entrance of my house—this time from outside—for whole days and nights. Call it foolish if you like; it gives me infinite pleasure and reassures me. At such times it is as if I were not so much looking at my house as at myself sleeping, and had the joy of being in a profound slumber and simultaneously of keeping vigilant guard over myself. I am privileged, as it were, not only to dream about the spectres of the night in all the helplessness and blind trust of sleep, but also at the same time to confront them in actuality with the calm judgment of the fully awake. And strangely enough I discover that my situation is not so bad as I had often thought, and will probably think again when I return to my house. In this connection—it may be in others too, but in this one especially—these excursions of mine are truly indispensable. Carefully as I have chosen an out-of-the-way place for my door, the traffic that passes it is nevertheless, if one takes a week's observation, very great; but so it is, no doubt, in all inhabited regions, and probably it is actually better to hazard the risks of dense traffic, whose very impetus carries it past, than to be delivered in complete solitude to the first persistently searching intruder. Here enemies are numerous and their allies and accomplices still more numerous, but they fight one another, and while thus employed rush past my burrow without noticing it. In all my time I have never seen any one investigating the actual door of my house, which is fortunate both for me and for him, for I would certainly have launched myself at his throat, forgetting everything else in my anxiety for the burrow. True, intruders come in whose neighbourhood I dare not remain, and from whom I have to fly as soon as I scent them in the distance; on their attitude to the burrow I really can't pronounce with certainty, but it is at least a reassurance that when I presently return I never find any of them there, and the entrance is undamaged. There have been happy periods in which I could almost assure myself that the enmity of the world towards me had ceased or been assuaged, or that the strength of the burrow had raised me above the destructive struggle of former times. The burrow has probably protected me in more ways than I thought or dared think while I was inside it. This fancy used to have such a hold over me that sometimes I have been seized by the childish desire never to return to the burrow again, but to settle down somewhere close to the entrance, to pass my life watching the entrance, and gloat perpetually upon the reflection—and in that find my happiness—how steadfast a protection my burrow would be if I were inside it. Well, one is soon roughly awakened from childish dreams. What does this protection which I am looking at here from the outside amount to after all? Dare I estimate the danger which I run inside the burrow from observations which I make when outside? Can my enemies, to begin with, have any proper awareness of me if I am not in my burrow? A certain awareness of me they certainly have, but not full awareness. And is not that full awareness the real definition of a state of danger? So the experiments I attempt here are only half-experiments or even less, calculated merely to reassure my fears and by giving me false reassurance to lay me open to great perils. No, I do not watch over my own sleep, as I imagined; rather it is I who sleep, while the destroyer watches. Perhaps he is one of those who pass the entrance without seeming to notice it, concerned merely to ascertain, just like myself, that the door is still untouched and waits for their attack, and only pass because they know that the master of the house is out, or because they are quite aware that he is guilelessly lying on the watch in the bushes close by. And I leave my post of observation and find I have had enough of this outside life; I feel that there is nothing more that I can learn here, either now or at any time. And I long to say a last goodbye to everything up here, to go down into my burrow never to return again, let things take their course, and not try to retard them with my profitless vigils. But spoilt by seeing for such a long time everything that happened round the entrance, I find great difficulty in summoning the resolution to carry out the actual descent, which might easily draw any one's attention, and without knowing what is happening behind my back and behind the door after it is fastened. I take advantage of stormy nights to get over the necessary preliminaries, and quickly bundle in my spoil; that seems to have come off, but whether it has really come off will only be known when I myself have made the descent; it will be known, but not by me, or by me, but too late. So I give up the attempt and do not make the descent. I dig an experimental burrow, naturally at a good distance from the real entrance, a burrow just as long as myself, and seal it also with a covering of moss. I creep into my hole, close it after me, wait patiently, keep vigil for long or short spells, and at various hours of the day, then fling off the moss, issue from my hole, and summarise my observations. These are extremely heterogeneous, and both good and bad; but I have never been able to discover a universal principle or an infallible method of descent. In consequence of all this I have not yet summoned the resolution to make my actual descent, and am thrown into despair at the necessity of doing it soon. I almost screw myself to the point of deciding to emigrate to distant parts and take up my old comfortless life again, which had no security whatever, but was one indiscriminate succession of perils, yet in consequence prevented one from perceiving and fearing particular perils, as I am constantly reminded by comparing my secure burrow with ordinary life. Certainly such a decision would be an arrant piece of folly, produced simply by living too long in senseless freedom; the burrow is still mine, I have only to take a single step and I am safe. And I tear myself free from all my doubts and by broad daylight rush to the door, quite resolved to raise it now; but I cannot, I rush past it and fling myself into a thorn bush, deliberately, as a punishment, a punishment for some sin I do not know of. Then, at the last moment, I am forced to admit to myself that I was right after all, and that is was really impossible to go down into the burrow without leaving the thing I love best, for a little while at least, at the disposal of all my enemies, on the ground, in the trees, in the air. And the danger is by no means a fanciful one, but very real. It need not be any particular enemy that is provoked to pursue me, it may very well be some chance innocent little creature, some disgusting little beast which follows me out of curiosity, and thus, without knowing it, becomes the leader of all the world against me; nor need it be even that, it may be—and that would be just as bad, indeed in some respects worse—it may be some one of my own kind, a connoisseur and prizer of burrows, a hermit, a lover of peace, but all the same a filthy scoundrel who wishes to be housed where he has not built. If he were actually to arrive now, if in his obscene lust he were to discover the entrance and set about working at it, lifting the moss; if he were actually to succeed, if he were actually to wriggle his way in in my stead, until only his hindquarters still showed; if all this were actually to happen, so that at last, casting all prudence to the winds, I might in my blind rage leap on him, maul him, tear the flesh from his bones, destroy him, drink his blood and fling his corpse among the rest of my spoil, but above all—that is the main thing—were at last back in my burrow once more, I would have it in my heart to greet the labyrinth itself with rapture; but first I would draw the moss covering over me, and I would want to rest, it seems to me, for all the remainder of my life. But nobody comes and I am left to my own resources. Perpetually obsessed by the sheer difficulty of the attempt, I lose much of my timidity, I no longer attempt even to appear to avoid the entrance, but make a hobby of prowling round it; by now it is almost as if I were the enemy spying out a suitable opportunity for successfully breaking in. If I only had some one I could trust to keep watch at my post of observation; then of course I could descend in perfect peace of mind. I would make an agreement with this trusty confederate of mine that he would keep a careful note of the state of things during my descent and for quite a long time afterwards, and if he saw any sign of danger knock on the moss covering, and if he saw nothing do nothing. With that a clean sweep would be made of all my fears, no residue would be left, or at most my confidant. For would he not demand some counter-service from me; would he not at last want to see the burrow? That in itself, to let any one freely into my burrow, would be exquisitely painful to me. I built it for myself, not for visitors, and I think I would refuse to admit him; not even though he alone made it possible for me to get into the burrow would I let him in. But I simply could not admit him, for either I must let him go in first by himself, which is simply unimaginable, or we must both descend at the same time, in which case the advantage I am supposed to derive from him, that of being kept watch over, would be lost. And what trust can I really put in him? Can I trust one whom I have had under my eyes just as fully when I can't see him, and the moss covering separates us? It is comparatively easy to trust any one if you are supervising him or at least can supervise him; perhaps it is possible even to trust some one at a distance; but completely to trust some one outside the burrow when you are inside the burrow, that is, in a different world, that, it seems to me, is impossible. But such considerations are not in the least necessary; the mere reflection is enough that during or after my descent one of the countless accidents of existence might prevent my confidant from fulfilling his duty, and what incalculable results might not the smallest accident of that kind have for me? No, if one takes it by and large, I have no right to complain that I am alone and have nobody that I can trust. I certainly lose nothing by that and probably spare myself trouble. I can only trust myself and my burrow. I should have thought of that before and taken measures to meet the difficulty that worries me so much now. When I began the burrow it would at least have been partly possible. I should have so constructed the first passage that it had two entrances at a moderate distance from each other, so that after descending through the one entrance with that slowness which is unavoidable, I might rush at once through the passage to the second entrance, slightly raise the moss covering, which would be so arranged as to make that easy, and from there keep watch on the position for several days and nights. That would have been the only right way of doing it. True, the two entrances would double the risk, but that consideration need not delay me, for one of the entrances, serving merely as a post of observation, could be quite narrow. And with that I lose myself in a maze of technical speculations, I begin once more to dream my dream of a completely perfect burrow, and that somewhat calms me; with closed eyes I behold with delight perfect or almost perfect structural devices for enabling me to slip out and in unobserved. While I lie there thinking such things I admire these devices very greatly, but only as technical achievements, not as real advantages; for this freedom to slip out and in at will, what does it amount to? It is the mark of a restless nature, of inner uncertainty, disreputable desires, evil propensities that seem still worse when one thinks of the burrow, which is there at one's hand and can flood one with peace if one only remains quite open and receptive to it. For the present, however, I am outside it seeking some possibility of returning, and for that the necessary technical devices would be very desirable. But perhaps not so very desirable after all. Is it not a very grave injustice to the burrow to regard it in moments of nervous panic as a mere hole into which one can creep and be safe? Certainly it is a hole among other things, and a safe one, or should be, and when I picture myself in the midst of danger, then I insist with clenched teeth and all my will that the burrow should be nothing but a hole set apart to save me, and that it should fulfil that clearly defined function with the greatest possible efficiency, and I am ready to absolve it from every other duty. Now the truth of the matter— and one has no eye for that in times of great peril, and only by a great effort even in times when danger is threatening—is that in reality the burrow does provide a considerable degree of security, but by no means enough, for is one ever free from anxieties inside it? These anxieties are different from ordinary ones, prouder, richer in content, often long repressed, but in their destructive effects they are perhaps much the same as the anxieties that existence in the outer world gives rise to. Had I constructed the burrow exclusively to assure my safety I would not have been disappointed, it is true; nevertheless the relation between the enormous labour involved and the actual security it would provide, at least in so far as I could feel it and profit by it, would not have been in my favour. It is extremely painful to have to admit such things to oneself, but one is forced to do it, confronted by that entrance over there which now literally locks and bars itself against me, the builder and possessor. Yet the burrow is not a mere hole for taking refuge in. When I stand in the Castle Keep surrounded by my piled-up stores, surveying the ten passages which begin there, raised and sunken passages, vertical and rounded passages, wide and narrow passages, as the general plan dictates, and all alike still and empty, ready by their various routes to conduct me to all the other rooms, which are also still and empty— then all thought of mere safety is far from my mind, then I know that here is my castle, which I have wrested from the refractory soil with tooth and claw, with pounding and hammering blows, my castle which can never belong to any one else, and is so essentially mine that I can calmly accept in it even my enemy's mortal stroke at the final hour, for my blood will ebb away here in my own soil and not be lost. And what but that is the meaning of the blissful hours which I pass, now peacefully slumbering, now happily keeping watch, in these passages, these passages which suit me so well, where one can stretch oneself out in comfort, roll about in childish delight, lie and dream, or sink into blissful sleep. And the smaller rooms, each familiar to me, so familiar that in spite of their complete similarity I can clearly distinguish one from the other with my eyes shut by the mere feel of the wall: they enclose me more peacefully and warmly than a bird is enclosed in its nest. And all, all still and empty.

But if that is the case, why do I hang back? why do I dread the thought of the intruding enemy more than the possibility of never seeing my burrow again? Well, the latter alternative is fortunately an impossibility; there is no need for me even to take thought to know what the burrow means to me; I and the burrow belong so indissolubly together that in spite of all my fears I could make myself quite comfortable out here, and not even need to overcome my repugnance and open the door; I could be quite content to wait here passively, for nothing can part us for long, and somehow or other I shall quite certainly find myself in my burrow again. But on the other hand how much time may pass before then, and how many things may happen in that time, up here no less than down there? And it lies with me solely to curtail that interval and to do what is necessary at once.

And then, too exhausted to be any longer capable of thought, my head hanging, my legs trembling with fatigue, half-asleep, feeling my way rather than walking, I approach the entrance, slowly raise the moss covering, slowly descend, leaving the door open in my distraction for a needlessly long time, and presently remember my omission, and get out again to make it good—but what need was there to get out for that? All that was needed was to draw to the moss covering; right; so I creep in again and now at last draw to the moss covering. Only in this state, and in this state alone, can I achieve my descent.—So at last I lie down beneath the moss on the top of my bloodstained spoil and can now enjoy my longed-for sleep. Nothing disturbs me, no one has tracked me down, above the moss everything seems to be quiet thus far at least, but even if all were not quiet I question whether I could stop to keep watch now! I have changed my place, I have left the upper world and am in my burrow, and I feel its effect at once. It is a new world, endowing me with new powers, and what I felt as fatigue up there is no longer that here. I have returned from a journey, dog-tired with my wanderings, but the sight of the old house, the thought of all the things that are waiting to be done, the necessity at least to cast a glance at all the rooms, but above all to make my way immediately to the Castle Keep; all this transforms my fatigue into ardent zeal; it is as though at the moment when I set foot in the burrow I had wakened from a long and profound sleep. My first task is a very laborious one and requires all my attention; I mean getting my spoil through the narrow and thin-walled passages of the labyrinth. I shove with all my might, and the work gets done too, but far too slowly for me; to hasten it I drag part of my flesh supply back again and push my way over it and

through it; now I have only a portion of my spoil before me and it is easier to
make progress; but my road is so blocked by all this flesh in these narrow passages,
through which it is not always easy for me to make my way when I am alone,
that I could quite easily smother among my own stores; sometimes I can only
rescue myself from their pressure by eating and drinking a clear space for myself.
But the work of transport is successful, I finish it in quite a reasonable time,
the labyrinth is behind me, I reach an ordinary passage and breathe freely, push
my spoil through a communication passage into a main passage expressly designed
for the purpose, a passage sloping down steeply to the Castle Keep. What is
left to be done is not really work at all; my whole load rolls and flows down the
passage almost of itself. The Castle Keep at last! At last I can dare to rest. Everything is unchanged, no great mishap seems to have occurred, the few little defects
that I note at a first glance can soon be repaired; first, however, I must go my
long round of all the passages, but that is no hardship, that is merely to commune again with friends, as I often did in the old days or—I am not so very
old yet, but my memory of many things is already quite confused—as I often did,
or as I have often imagined I did. I begin with the second passage, but break
off in the middle and turn into the third passage and let it take me back again
to the Castle Keep, and now of course I have to begin at the second passage
once more, and so I play with my task and lengthen it out and smile to myself
and congratulate myself and become quite dazed with all the work in front of
me, but never think of turning aside from it. It is for your sake, ye passages
and rooms, and you, Castle Keep, above all, that I have come back, counting
my own life as nothing in the balance, after stupidly trembling for it for so
long, and postponing my return to you. What do I care for danger now that I
am with you? You belong to me, I to you, we are united; what can harm us?
What if my foes should be assembling even now up above there and their muzzles
be preparing to break through the moss? And with its silence and emptiness the
burrow answers me, confirming my words.—But now a feeling of lassitude over-
comes me and in some favourite room I curl myself up tentatively, I have not
yet surveyed everything by a long way, though still resolved to examine everything
to the very end; I have no intention of sleeping here, I have merely yielded to
the temptation of making myself comfortable and pretending I want to sleep,
I merely wish to find out if this is as good a place for sleeping in as it used to be.
It is, but it is a better place for sleep than for wakening, and I remain lying where
I am in deep slumber.

I must have slept for a long time. I was only wakened when I had reached
the last light sleep which dissolves of itself, and it must have been very light,
for it was an almost inaudible whistling noise that wakened me. I recognised
what it was immediately; the smaller fry, whom I had allowed far too much
latitude, had burrowed a new channel somewhere during my absence, this channel
must have chanced to intersect an older one, the air was caught there, and that
produced the whistling noise. What an indefatigably busy lot these smaller fry
are, and what a nuisance their diligence can be! First I shall have to listen at
the walls of my passages and locate the place of disturbance by experimental

excavations, and only then will I be able to get rid of the noise. However, this new channel may be quite welcome as a further means of ventilation, if it can be fitted into the plan of the burrow. But after this I shall keep a much sharper eye on the small fry than I used to; I shall spare none of them.

As I have a good deal of experience in investigations of this kind the work probably will not take me long and I can start upon it at once; there are other jobs awaiting me, it is true, but this is the most urgent. I must have silence in my passages. This noise, however, is a comparatively innocent one; I did not hear it at all when I first arrived, although it must certainly have been there; I must first feel quite at home before I could hear it; it is, so to speak, audible only to the ear of the householder. And it is not even constant, as such noises usually are; there are long pauses, obviously caused by stoppages of the current of air. I start on my investigations, but I can't find the right place to begin at, and though I cut a few trenches I do it at random; naturally that has no effect, and the hard work of digging and the still harder work of filling the trenches up again and beating the earth firm is so much labour lost. I don't seem to be getting any nearer to the place where the noise is, it goes on always on the same thin note, with regular pauses, now a sort of whistling, but again like a kind of piping. Now I could leave it to itself for the time being; it is very disturbing, certainly, but there can hardly be any doubt that its origin is what I took it to be at first; so it can scarcely become louder, on the contrary such noises may quite well—though until now I have never had to wait so long for that to happen— may quite well vanish of themselves in the course of time through the continued labours of these little burrowers; and apart from that often chance itself puts one on the track of the disturbance, where systematic investigation has failed for a long time. In such ways I comfort myself, and resolve simply to continue my tour of the passages, and visit the rooms, many of which I have not even seen yet since my return, and enjoy myself contemplating the Castle Keep now and then between times; but my anxiety will not let me, and I must go on with my search. These little creatures take up much, far too much, time that could be better employed. In such cases as the present it is usually the technical problem that attracts me; for example, from the noise, which my ear can distinguish in all its finest shades, so that it has a perfectly clear outline to me, I deduce its cause, and now I am on fire to discover whether my conclusion is valid. And with good reason, for as long as that is not established I cannot feel safe, even if it were merely a matter of discovering where a grain of sand that had fallen from one of the walls had rolled to. And even a noise such as this is by no means a trifling matter, regarded from that angle. But whether trifling or important, I can find nothing, no matter how hard I search, or it may be that I find too much. This had to happen just in my favourite room, I think to myself, and I walk a fair good distance away from it, almost half-way along the passage leading to the next room; but I do this merely as a joke, pretending to myself that my favourite room is not alone to blame, but that there are disturbances elsewhere as well, and with a smile on my face I begin to listen; but soon I stop smiling, for, right enough, the same whistling meets me here too. It is really nothing to worry about; sometimes I think that nobody but myself would hear it; it is true, I hear it now more and more distinctly, for my ear has grown keener through practice; though in reality it is exactly the same noise wherever I may hear it, as I have convinced myself by comparing my impressions. Nor is it growing louder; I recognise this when I listen in the middle of the passage instead of pressing my ear against the wall. Then it is only by straining my ears, indeed by lowering my head as well, that I can more guess at than hear the merest trace of a noise now and then. But it is this very uniformity of the noise everywhere that disturbs me most, for it cannot be made to agree with my original assumption. Had I rightly divined the cause of the noise, then it must have issued with greatest force from some given place, which it would be my task to discover, and after that have grown fainter and fainter. But if my hypothesis does not meet the case, what can the explanation be? There still remains the possibility that there are two noises, that up to now I have been listening at a good distance from the two centres, and that while its noise increases, when I draw near to one of them, the total result remains approximately the same for the ear in consequence of the lessening volume of sound from the other centre. Already I have almost fancied sometimes, when I have listened carefully, that I could distinguish, if very indistinctly, differences of tone which support this new assumption. In any case I must extend my sphere of investigation far farther than I have done. Accordingly I descend the passage to the Castle Keep and begin to listen there. Strange, the same noise there too. Now it is a noise produced by the burrowing of some species of small fry who have infamously exploited my absence; in any case they have no intention of doing me harm, they are simply busied with their own work, and so long as no obstacle comes in their way they will keep on in the direction they have taken: I know all this, yet that they should have dared to approach the very Castle Keep itself is incomprehensible to me and fills me with agitation, and confuses the faculties which I need so urgently for the work before me. Here I have no wish to discover whether it is the unusual depth at which the Castle Keep lies, or its great extent and correspondingly powerful air suction, calculated to scare burrowing creatures away, or the mere fact that it is the Castle Keep, that by some channel or other has penetrated to their dull minds. In any case I have never noticed any sign of burrowing in the walls of the Castle Keep until now. Crowds of little beasts have come here, it is true, attracted by the powerful smells; here I have had a constant hunting-ground, but my quarry has always burrowed a way through in the upper passages, and come running down here, somewhat fearfully, but unable to withstand such a temptation. But now, it seems, they are burrowing in all the passages. If I had only carried out the best of the grand plans I thought out in my youth and early manhood, or rather, if I had only had the strength to carry them out, for there would have been no lack of will. One of these favourite plans of mine was to isolate the Castle Keep from its surroundings, that is to say, to restrict the thickness of its walls to about my own height, and leave a free space of about the same width all round the Castle Keep, except for a narrow foundation, which unfortunately would have to be left to bear up the whole. I had always pictured this free space, and not without reason, as the loveliest imaginable haunt. What a joy to lie pressed against the rounded outer wall, pull oneself up, let oneself slide down again, miss one's footing and find oneself on firm earth, and play all those games literally upon the Castle Keep and not inside it; to avoid the Castle Keep, to rest one's eyes from it whenever one wanted, to postpone the joy of seeing it until later and yet not have to do without it, but literally hold it safe between one's claws, a thing that is impossible if you have only an ordinary open entrance to it; but above all to be able to stand guard over it, and in that way to be so completely compensated for renouncing the actual sight of it that, if one had to choose between staying all one's life in the Castle Keep or in the free space outside it, one would choose the latter, content to wander up and down there all one's days and keep guard over the Castle Keep. Then there would be no noises in the walls, no insolent burrowing up to the very Keep itself; then peace would be assured there and I would be its guardian; then I would not have to listen with loathing to the burrowing of the small fry, but with delight to something that I cannot hear now at all: the murmurous silence of the Castle Keep.

But that beautiful dream is past and I must set to work, almost glad that now my work has a direct connection with the Castle Keep, for that wings it. Certainly, as I can see more and more clearly, I need all my energies for this task, which at first seemed quite a trifling one. I listen now at the walls of the Castle Keep, and wherever I listen, high or low, at the roof or the floor, at the entrance or in the corners, everywhere, everywhere, I hear the same noise. And how much time, how much care must be wasted in listening to that noise, with its regular pauses. One can, if one wishes, find a tiny deceitful comfort in the fact that here in the Castle Keep, because of its vastness, one hears nothing at all, as distinguished from the passages, when one stands back from the walls. Simply as a rest and a means to regain my composure I often make this experiment, listen intently and am overjoyed when I hear nothing. But the question still remains, what can have happened? Confronted with this phenomenon my original explanation completely falls to the ground. But I must also reject other explanations which present themselves to me. One could assume, for instance, that the noise I hear is simply that of the small fry themselves at their work. But all my experience contradicts this; I cannot suddenly begin to hear now a thing that I have never heard before though it was always there. My sensitiveness to disturbances in the burrow has perhaps become greater with the years, yet my hearing has by no means grown keener. It is of the very nature of small fry not to be heard. Would I have tolerated them otherwise? Even at the risk of starvation I would have exterminated them. But perhaps—this idea now insinuates itself—I am concerned here with some animal unknown to me. That is possible. True, I have observed the life down here long and carefully enough, but the world is full of diversity and is never wanting in painful surprises. Yet it cannot be a single animal, it must be a whole swarm that has suddenly fallen upon my domain, a huge swarm of little creatures, which as they are audible, must certainly be bigger than the small fry, but yet cannot be very much bigger, for the sound of their labours is itself very faint. It may be, then, a swarm of unknown creatures on their wanderings, who happen to be passing by my way, who disturb me, but will presently cease to do so. So I could really wait for them to pass, and need not put myself to the trouble of work that will be needless in the end. Yet if these creatures are strangers, why is it that I never see any of them? I have already dug a host of trenches, hoping to catch one of them, but I can find not a single one. Then it occurs to me that they may be quite tiny creatures, far tinier than any I am acquainted with, and that it is only the noise they make that is greater. Accordingly I investigate the soil I have dug up, I cast the lumps into the air so that they break into quite small particles, but the noise-makers are not among them. Slowly I come to realize that by digging such small fortuitous trenches I achieve nothing; in doing that I merely disfigure the walls of my burrow, scratching hastily here and there without taking time to fill up the holes again; at many places already there are heaps of earth which block my way and my view. Still, that is only a secondary worry; for now I can neither wander about my house, nor review it, nor rest; often already I have fallen asleep at my work in some hole or other, with one paw clutching the soil above me, from which in a semi-stupor I have been trying to tear a lump. I intend now to alter my methods. I shall dig a wide and carefully constructed trench in the direction of the noise and not cease from digging until, independent of all theories, I find the real cause of the noise. Then I shall eradicate it, if that is within my power, and if it is not, at least I shall know the truth. That truth will bring me either peace or despair, but whether the one or the other, it will be beyond doubt or question. This decision strengthens me. All that I have done till now seems to me far too hasty; in the excitement of my return, while I had not yet shaken myself free from the cares of the upper world, and was not yet completely penetrated by the peace of the burrow, but rather hypersensitive at having had to renounce it for such a long time, I was thrown into complete confusion of mind by an unfamiliar noise. And what was it? A faint whistling, audible only at long intervals, a mere nothing to which I don't say that one could actually get used, for no one could get used to it, but which one could, without actually doing anything about it at once, observe for a while; that is, listen every two hours, let us say, and patiently register the results, instead of, as I had done, keeping one's ear fixed to the wall and at every hint of noise tearing out a lump of earth, not really hoping to find anything, but simply so as to do something to give expression to one's inward agitation. All that will be changed now, I hope. And then, with furious shut eyes, I have to admit to myself that I hope nothing of the kind, for I am still trembling with agitation just as I was hours ago, and if my reason did not restrain me I would probably like nothing better than to start stubbornly and defiantly digging, simply for the sake of digging, at some place or other, whether I heard anything there or not; almost like the small fry, who burrow either without any object at all or simply because they eat the soil. My new and reasonable plan both tempts me and leaves me cold. There is nothing in it to object to, I at least know of no objection; it is bound, so far as I can see, to achieve my aim. And yet at bottom

I do not believe in it; I believe in it so little that I do not even fear the terrors
which its success may well bring, I do not believe even in a dreadful denouément;
indeed it seems to me that I have been thinking ever since the first appearance
of the noise of such a methodical trench, and have not begun upon it until now
simply because I put no trust in it. In spite of that I shall of course start on the
trench; I have no other alternative; but I shall not start at once, but postpone
the task for a little while. If reason is to be reinstated on the throne again, it
must be completely reinstated; I shall not rush blindly into my task. In any
case I shall first repair the damage that I have done to the burrow with my
wild digging; that will take a good long time, but it is necessary; if the new trench
is really to reach its goal it will probably be long, and if it should lead to nothing
at all it will be endless; in any case this task means a longish absence from the
burrow, though an absence by no means so painful as an absence in the upper
world, for I can interrupt my work whenever I like and pay a visit to my house;
and even if I should not do that the air of the Castle Keep will be wafted to
me and surround me while I work; nevertheless it means leaving the burrow
and surrendering myself to an uncertain fate, and consequently I want to leave
the burrow in good order behind me; it shall not be said that I, who am fighting
for its peace, have myself destroyed that peace without reinstating it at once.
So I begin by shovelling the soil back into the holes from which it was taken,
a kind of work I am familiar with, that I have done countless times almost without regarding it as work, and at which, particularly as regards the final pressing
and smoothing down—and this is no empty boast, but the simple truth—I am
unbeatable. But this time everything seems difficult, I am too distracted, every
now and then, in the middle of my work, I press my ear to the wall and listen
and without taking any notice let the soil that I have just lifted trickle back into
the passage again. The final embellishments, which demand a stricter attention,
I can hardly achieve at all. Hideous protuberances, disturbing cracks remain, not
to speak of the fact that the old buoyancy simply cannot be restored again to a
wall patched up in such a way. I try to comfort myself with the reflection that my
present work is only temporary. When I return after peace has been restored I
shall repair everything properly: work will be mere play to me then. Oh yes,
work is mere play in fairy tales, and this comfort of mine belongs to the realm
of fairy tales too. It would be far better to do the work thoroughly now, at
once, far more reasonable than perpetually to interrupt it and wander off through
the passages to discover new sources of noise, which is easy enough, all that is
needed being to stop at any point one likes and listen. And that is not the end
of my useless discoveries. Sometimes I fancy that the noise has stopped, for it
makes long pauses; sometimes such a faint whistling escapes one, one's own
blood is pounding all too loudly in one's ears; then two pauses come one after
another, and for a while one thinks that the whistling has stopped for ever. I
listen no longer, I jump up, all life is transfigured; it is as if the fountains from
which flows the silence of the burrow were unsealed. I refrain from verifying
my discovery at once, I want first to find some one to whom in all good faith
I can confide it, so I rush to the Castle Keep, I remember, for I and everything

in me has awakened to new life, that I have eaten nothing for a long time, I snatch something or other from among my store of food half buried under debris and hurriedly begin to swallow it while I hurry back to the place where I made my incredible discovery, I only want to assure myself about it incidentally, perfunctorily, while I am eating; I listen, but the most perfunctory listening shows at once that I was shamefully deceived: away there in the distance the whistling still remains unshaken. And I spit out my food, and would like to trample it underfoot, and go back to my task, not caring which I take up; any place where it seems to be needed, and there are enough places like that, I mechanically start on something or other, just as if the overseer had appeared and I must make a pretence of working for his benefit. But hardly have I well begun in this fashion when it may happen that I make a new discovery. The noise seems to have become louder, not much louder, of course—here it is always a matter of the subtlest shades—but all the same sufficiently louder for the ear to recognise it clearly. And his growing-louder is like a coming-nearer; still more distinctly than you hear the increasing loudness of the noise, you can literally see the step that brings it closer to you. You leap back from the wall, you try to grasp at once all the possible consequences that this discovery will bring with it. You feel as if you had never really organised the burrow for defense against attack; you had intended to do so, but despite all your experience of life the danger of an attack, and consequently the need to organise the place for defence, seemed remote—or rather not remote (how could it possibly be!)—but infinitely less important than the need to put it in a state where one could live peacefully; and so that consideration was given priority in everything relating to the burrow. Many things in this direction might have been done without affecting the plan of the whole; most incomprehensibly they have been neglected. I have had a great deal of luck all those years, luck has spoilt me; I have had anxieties, but anxiety leads to nothing when you have luck to back you.

The thing to do, really to do now, would be to go carefully over the burrow and consider every possible means of defending it, work out a plan of defence and a corresponding plan of construction, and then start on the work at once with the vigour of youth. That is the work that would really be needed, for which, I need not say, it is now far too late in the day; yet that is what would really be needed, and not the digging of a grand experimental trench, whose only real result would be to deliver me hand and foot to the search for danger, out of the foolish fear that it will not arrive quickly enough of itself. Suddenly I cannot comprehend my former plan. I can find no slightest trace of reason in what had seemed so reasonable; once more I lay aside my work and even my listening; I have no wish to discover any further signs that the noise is growing louder; I have had enough of discoveries; I let everything slide; I would be quite content if I could only still the conflict going on within me. Once more I let my passages lead me where they will, I come to more and more remote ones that I have not yet seen since my return, and that are quite unsullied by my scratching paws, and whose silence rises up to meet me and sinks into me. I do not surrender to it, I hurry on, I do not know what I want, probably simply to put off the hour. I stray so far that I find myself at the labyrinth; the idea of listening beneath the moss covering tempts me; such distant things, distant for the moment, chain my interest. I push my way up and listen. Deep stillness; how lovely it is here, outside there nobody troubles about my burrow, everybody has his own affairs, which have no connection with me; how have I managed to achieve this state of things with all my calculations? Here under the moss covering is perhaps the only place in my burrow now where I can listen for hours and hear nothing. A complete reversal of things in the burrow; what was once the place of danger has become a place of tranquillity, while the Castle Keep has been plunged into the mêlée of the world and all its perils. Still worse, even here there is no peace in reality, here nothing has changed; silent or vociferous, danger lies in ambush as before above the moss, but I have grown insensitive to it, my mind is far too much taken up with the whistling in my walls. Is my mind really taken up with it? It grows louder, it comes nearer, but I wriggle my way through the labyrinth and make a couch for myself up here under the moss; it is almost as though I were already leaving the house to the whistler, content if I can only have a little peace up here. To the whistler? Have I come, then, to a new conclusion concerning the cause of the noise? But surely the noise is caused by the channels bored by the small fry? Is not that my considered opinion? It seems to me that I have not retreated from it thus far. And if the noise is not caused directly by these channels, it is indirectly. And even if it should have no connection with them whatever, one is not at liberty to make *a priori* assumptions, but must wait until one finds the cause, or it reveals itself. One could play with hypotheses, of course, even at this stage; for instance it is possible that there has been a water burst at some distance away, and that what seems a piping or whistling to me is in reality a gurgling. But apart from the fact that I have no experience in that sphere—the ground-water that I found at the start I drained away at once, and in this sandy soil it has never returned—apart from this fact the noise is undeniably a whistling and simply not to be translated into a gurgling. But what avail all exhortations to be calm; my imagination will not rest, and I have actually come to believe—it is useless to deny it to myself—that the whistling is made by some beast, and moreover not by a great many small ones, but by a single great one. Many signs contradict this. The noise can be heard everywhere and always at the same strength, and moreover uniformly, both by day and night. At first, therefore, one cannot but incline to the hypothesis of a great number of little animals; but as I must have found some of them during my digging and I have found nothing, it only remains for me to assume the existence of a great beast, especially as the things that seem to contradict the hypothesis are merely things which make the beast, not so much impossible, as merely dangerous beyond all one's powers of conception. For that reason alone have I stuck out against this hypothesis. I shall cease from this self-deception. For a long time already I have played with the idea that the beast can be heard at such a great distance because it works so furiously; it burrows as fast through the ground as another animal can walk on the open road; the ground still trembles at its burrowing when it has ceased; this reverberation and the noise of the boring itself unite into one sound at such a great distance, and I, as I hear only the last dying ebb of that sound, hear it always at the same uniform strength. It follows from this also that the beast is not making for me, seeing that the noise never changes; more likely it has a plan in view whose purpose I cannot decipher; I merely assume that the beast—and I make no claim whatever that it knows of my existence—is encircling me; it has probably made several circles round my burrow already since I began to observe it. The nature of the noise, the piping or whistling, gives me much food for thought. When I scratch and scrape in the soil in my own fashion the sound is quite different. I can explain the whistling only in this way: that the beast's chief means of burrowing is not its claws, which it probably employs merely as a secondary resource, but its snout or its muzzle, which, of course, apart from its enormous strength, must also be fairly sharp at the point. It probably bores its snout into the earth with one mighty push and tears out a great lump; while it is doing that I hear nothing; that is the pause; but then it draws in the air for a new push. This indrawal of its breath, which must be an earth-shaking noise, not only because of the beast's strength, but of its haste, its furious lust for work as well: this noise I hear then as a faint whistling. But quite incomprehensible remains the beast's capacity to work without stopping; perhaps the short pauses provide also the opportunity of snatching a moment's rest; but apparently the beast has never yet allowed itself a really long rest, day and night it goes on burrowing, always with the same freshness and vigour, always thinking of its object, which must be achieved with the utmost expedition, and which it has the ability to achieve with ease. Now I could not have foreseen such an opponent. But apart altogether from the beast's peculiar characteristics, what is happening now is only something which I should really have feared all the time, something against which I should have been constantly prepared: the fact that some one would come. By what chance can everything have flowed on so quietly and happily for such a long time? Who can have diverted my enemies from their path, and forced them to make a wide detour round my property? Why have I been spared for so long, only to be delivered to such terrors now? Compared with this, what are all the petty dangers in brooding over which I have spent my life! As owner of the burrow I had hoped to be in a stronger position than any enemy who might chance to appear. But simply by virtue of being owner of this great vulnerable edifice I am obviously defenceless against any serious attack. The joy of possessing it has spoilt me, the vulnerability of the burrow has made me vulnerable; any wound to it hurts me as if I myself were hit. It is precisely this that I should have foreseen; instead of thinking only of my own defence—and how perfunctorily and vainly I have done even that— I should have thought of the defence of the burrow. Above all, provision should have been made for cutting off sections of the burrow, and as many as possible of them, from the endangered sections when they are attacked; this should have been done by means of improvised land-slides, calculated to operate at a moment's notice; moreover these should have been so thick, and have provided such an effectual barrier, that the attacker would not even guess that the real burrow only began at the other side. More, these land-slides should have been so devised that they not only concealed the burrow, but also entombed the attacker. Not the slightest attempt have I made to carry out such a plan, nothing at all has been done in this direction, I have been as thoughtless as a child, I have passed my manhood's years in childish games, I have done nothing but play even with the thought of danger, I have shirked really taking thought for actual danger. And there has been no lack of warning.

Nothing, of course, approaching the present situation has happened before; nevertheless there was an incident not unlike it when the burrow was only beginning. The main difference between that time and this is simply that the burrow was only beginning then.... In those days I was literally nothing more than a humble apprentice in his first year, the labyrinth was only sketched out in rough outline, I had already dug a little room, but the proportions and the execution of the walls were sadly bungled; in short everything was so tentative that it could only be regarded as an experiment, as something which, if one lost patience some day, one could leave lying as it was without much regret. Then one day as I lay on a heap of earth resting from my labours—I have rested far too often from my labours all my life—suddenly I heard a noise in the distance. Being young at the time, I was less frightened than curious. I left my work to look after itself and set myself to listen; I listened and listened, and had no wish to fly up to my moss covering and stretch myself out there so that I might not hear. I did listen, at least. I could clearly recognize that the noise came from some kind of burrowing similar to my own; it was somewhat fainter, of course, but how much of that might be put down to the distance one could not tell. I was intensely interested, but otherwise calm and cool. Perhaps I am in somebody else's burrow, I thought to myself, and now the owner is boring his way towards me. If that assumption had proved to be correct I would have gone away, for I have never had any desire for conquest or bloodshed, and begun building somewhere else. But after all I was still young and still without a burrow, so I could remain quite cool. Besides, the further course of the noise brought no real cause for apprehension, except that it was not easy to explain. If whoever was boring there was really making for me, because he had heard me boring, then if he changed his direction, as now actually happened, it could not be told whether he did this because my pause for rest had deprived him of any definite point to make towards, or because—which was more plausible —he had himself changed his plans. But perhaps I had been deceived altogether, and he had never been actually making in my direction; at any rate the noise grew louder for a while as if he were drawing nearer, and being young at that time I probably would not have been displeased to see the burrower suddenly rising from the ground; but nothing of that kind happened, at a certain point the sound of boring began to weaken, it grew fainter and fainter, as if the burrower were gradually diverging from his first route, and suddenly it broke off altogether, as if he had decided now to take the diametrically opposite direction and were making straight away from me into the distance. For a long time I still went on listening for him in the silence, before I returned once more to my work. Now that warning was definite enough, but I soon forgot it, and it scarcely influenced my building plans.

Between that day and this lie my years of maturity, but is it not as if there were no interval at all between them? I still take long rests from my labours and listen at the wall, and the burrower has changed his intention anew, he has turned back, he is returning from his journey, thinking he has given me ample time in the interval to prepare for his reception. But on my side everything is worse prepared for than it was then; the great burrow stands defenceless, and I am no longer a young apprentice, but an old architect and the powers I still have fail me when the decisive hour comes; yet old as I am it seems to me that I would gladly be still older, so old that I should never be able to rise again from my resting-place under the moss. For to be honest I cannot endure the place, I rise up and rush, as if I had filled myself up there with new anxieties instead of peace, down into the house again.—What was the state of things the last time I was here? Had the whistling grown fainter? No, it had grown louder. I listen at ten places chosen at random and definitely note my own disappointment; the whistling is just the same as ever, nothing has altered. Up there under the moss no change touches one, there one is at peace, uplifted above time; but here every instant frets and gnaws at the listener. I go once more the long road to the Castle Keep, all my surroundings seem filled with agitation, seem to be looking at me, and then look away again so as not to annoy me, yet cannot refrain the very next moment from trying to read the saving solution from my expression. I shake my head, I have not yet found any solution. Nor do I go to the Castle Keep in pursuance of any plan. I pass the spot where I had intended to begin the experimental trench, I look it over once more, it would have been an admirable place to begin at, the trench's course would have been in the direction where lay the majority of the tiny ventilation holes, which would have greatly lightened my labours; perhaps I should not have had to dig very far, should not even have had to dig to the source of the noise; perhaps if I had listened at the ventilation holes it would have been enough. But no consideration is potent enough to animate me to this labour of digging. This trench will bring me certainty, you say? I have reached the stage where I no longer wish to have certainty. In the Castle Keep I choose a lovely piece of flayed red flesh and creep with it into one of the heaps of earth; there I shall have silence at least, such silence, at any rate, as still can be said to exist here. I munch and nibble at the flesh, think of the strange beast going its own road in the distance, and then again that I should enjoy my store of food as fully as possible, while I still have the chance. This last is probably the sole plan I have left that I can carry out. For the rest I try to unriddle the beast's plans. Is it on its wanderings, or is it working on its own burrow? If it is on its wanderings then perhaps an understanding with it might be possible. If it should really break through to the burrow I shall give it some of my store and it will go on its way again. It will go its way again, a fine story! Lying on my heap of earth I can naturally dream of all sorts of things, even of an understanding with the beast, though I know well enough that no such thing can happen, and that at the instant when we see each other, more, at the moment when we merely guess at each other's presence, we shall both blindly bare our claws and teeth, neither of us a second before or after the other, both of us filled with a new and different hunger, even if we should already be gorged to bursting. And with entire justice, for who, even if he were merely on his wanderings, would not change his itinerary and his plans for the future on catching sight of the burrow? But perhaps the beast is digging in its own burrow, in which case I cannot even dream of an understanding. Even if it should be such a peculiar beast as to be able to tolerate a neighbour near its burrow, it could not tolerate my burrow, it would not tolerate in any case a neighbour who could be clearly heard. Now actually the beast seems to be a great distance away; if it would only withdraw a little farther the noise too would probably disappear; perhaps in that case everything would be peaceful again as in the old days; all this would then become a painful but salutary lesson, spurring me on to make the most diverse improvements on the burrow; if I have peace, and danger does not immediately threaten me, I am still quite fit for all sorts of hard work; perhaps, considering the enormous possibilities which its powers of work open before it, the beast has given up the idea of extending its burrow in my direction, and is compensating itself for that in some other one. That consummation also cannot, of course, be brought about by negotiation, but only by the beast itself, or by some compulsion exercised from my side. In both cases the decisive factor will be whether the beast knows about me, and if so what it knows. The more I reflect upon it the more improbable does it seem to me that the beast has even heard of me; it is possible, though unimaginable, that it can have received news of me through some other channel, but it has certainly never heard me. So long as I still knew nothing about it, it simply cannot have heard me, for at that time I kept very quiet, nothing could be more quiet than my return to the burrow; afterwards, when I dug the experimental trenches, perhaps it could have heard me, though my style of digging makes very little noise; but if it had heard me I must have noticed some sign of it, the beast must at least have stopped its work every now and then to listen. But all remained unchanged.—

The Virgin and the Gipsy

(1926, publ. 1930)

D. H. Lawrence

Novelist, essayist, and poet, David Herbert Lawrence (1885–1930) was born near Nottingham, England, the son of a coal-miner and his ambitious middle-class wife. Completing his primary education, he taught for three years and then for two years attended Nottingham University on a scholarship. He returned to teaching (in Surrey, near London) and wrote his first novel, *The White Peacock,* which was published in 1911. By the end of the year he was devoting himself entirely to writing. In 1912 he ran off with the wife of a former French professor at Nottingham University, Frieda Werkley-Richtofen, and they were later married. They traveled extensively—in Italy, Switzerland, Germany, France, Ceylon, Australia, Mexico, and New Mexico. Lawrence died of tuberculosis in Vence, on the French Riviera. His works include the following: novels—*Sons and Lovers* (1913), *The Rainbow* (1915), *Women in Love* (1920), *Kangaroo* (1923), *The Plumed Serpent* (1926), and *Lady Chatterley's Lover* (1928); novelettes—*The Fox* (1918–19, revised and expanded in 1921), *The Captain's Doll* (1921), *The Ladybird* (1921–22), *St. Mawr* (1924), and *The Man who Died* (1927); travel books—*Twilight in Italy* (1912), *Sea and Sardinia* (1921), and *Mornings in Mexico* (1927); essays—*Studies in Classic American Literature* (1923) and *Reflections on the Death of a Porcupine* (1925). His collected poems were published in 1928.

For biographies of Lawrence, see Harry T. Moore, *The Life and Works of D. H. Lawrence* (New York, 1951); *The Intelligent Heart: The Story of D. H. Lawrence* (New York, 1954); and Edward Nehls, ed., *D. H. Lawrence: A Composite Biography,* 3 vols. (Madison, Wisc., 1957–59). For critical studies of *The Virgin and the Gipsy,* see F. R. Leavis, *D. H. Lawrence: Novelist* (London, 1955), pp. 288–95; and Kingsley Widmer, *The Art of Perversity: D. H. Lawrence's Shorter Fictions* (Seattle, Wash., 1962), pp. 178–87. See also Mark Spilka, *The Love Ethic of D. H. Lawrence* (Bloomington, Ind., 1955); Eliseo Vivas, *D. H. Lawrence: The Failure and the Triumph of Art* (Evanston, Ill., 1960); and Spilka's anthology, *D. H. Lawrence: A Collection of Critical Essays* (Twentieth-Century Views, Englewood Cliffs, N.J., 1963).

The Virgin and the Gipsy was written in Spotorno, Italy, in 1926, and was published posthumously in 1930. It is reprinted by permission of Laurence Pollinger Limited and the Estate of the Late Mrs. Frieda Lawrence; The Viking Press, Inc.; and Messrs. William Heinemann Limited.

I

When the vicar's wife went off with a young and penniless man the scandal knew no bounds. Her two little girls were only seven and nine years old respectively. And the vicar was such a good husband. True, his hair was grey. But his moustache was dark, he was handsome, and still full of furtive passion for his unrestrained and beautiful wife.

Why did she go? Why did she burst away with such an *éclat* of revulsion, like a touch of madness?

Nobody gave any answer. Only the pious said she was a bad woman. While some of the good women kept silent. They knew.

The two little girls never knew. Wounded, they decided that it was because their mother found them negligible.

The ill wind that blows nobody any good swept away the vicarage family on its blast. Then lo and behold! the vicar, who was somewhat distinguished as an essayist and a controversialist, and whose case had aroused sympathy among the bookish men, received the living of Papplewick. The Lord had tempered the wind of misfortune with a rectorate in the north country.

The rectory was a rather ugly stone house down by the river Papple, before you come into the village. Further on, beyond where the road crosses the stream, were the big old stone cotton-mills, once driven by water. The road curved up-hill, into the bleak stone streets of the village.

The vicarage family received decided modification, upon its transference into the rectory. The vicar, now the rector, fetched up his old mother and his sister, and a brother from the city. The two little girls had a very different *milieu* from the old home.

The rector was now forty-seven years old; he had displayed an intense and not very dignified grief after the flight of his wife. Sympathetic ladies had stayed him from suicide. His hair was almost white, and he had a wild-eyed, tragic look. You had only to look at him, to know how dreadful it all was, and how he had been wronged.

Yet somewhere there was a false note. And some of the ladies, who had sympathized most profoundly with the vicar, secretly rather disliked the rector. There was a certain furtive self-righteousness about him, when all was said and done.

The little girls, of course, in the vague way of children, accepted the family verdict. Granny, who was over seventy and whose sight was failing, became the central figure in the house. Aunt Cissie, who was over forty, pale, pious, and gnawed by an inward worm, kept house. Uncle Fred, a stingy and grey-faced man of forty, who just lived dingily for himself, went into town every day. And the rector, of course, was the most important person, after Granny.

They called her the Mater. She was one of those physically vulgar, clever old bodies who had got her own way all her life by buttering the weaknesses of her menfolk. Very quickly she took her cue. The rector still "loved" his delinquent wife, and would "love her" till he died. Therefore hush! The rector's feeling was sacred. In his heart was enshrined the pure girl he had wedded and worshipped.

Out in the evil world, at the same time, there wandered a disreputable woman who had betrayed the rector and abandoned his little children. She was now yoked to a young and despicable man, who no doubt would bring her the degradation she deserved. Let this be clearly understood, and then hush! For in the pure loftiness of the rector's heart still bloomed the pure white snow-flower of his young bride. This white snow-flower did not wither. That other creature, who had gone off with that despicable young man, was none of his affair.

The Mater, who had been somewhat diminished and insignificant as a widow in a small house, now climbed into the chief arm-chair in the rectory, and planted her old bulk firmly again. She was not going to be dethroned. Astutely she gave a sigh of homage to the rector's fidelity to the pure white snow-flower, while she pretended to disapprove. In sly reverence for her son's great love, she spoke no word against that nettle which flourished in the evil world, and which had once been called Mrs. Arthur Saywell. Now, thank heaven, having married again, she was no more Mrs. Arthur Saywell. No woman bore the rector's name. The pure white snow-flower bloomed *in perpetuum,* without nomenclature. The family even thought of her as She-who-was-Cynthia.

All this was water on the Mater's mill. It secured her against Arthur's ever marrying again. She had him by his feeblest weakness, his skulking self-love. He had married an imperishable white snow-flower. Lucky man! He had been injured. Unhappy man! He had suffered. Ah, what a heart of love! And he had—forgiven! Yes, the white snow-flower was forgiven. He even had made provision in his will for her, when that other scoundrel—but hush! Don't even *think* too near to that horrid nettle in the rank outer world! She-who-was-Cynthia. Let the white snow-flower bloom inaccessible on the heights of the past. The present is another story.

The children were brought up in this atmosphere of cunning self-sanctification and of unmentionability. They too saw the snow-flower on inaccessible heights. They too knew that it was throned in lone splendour aloft their lives, never to be touched.

At the same time, out of the squalid world sometimes would come a rank, evil smell of selfishness and degraded lust, the smell of that awful nettle, She-who-was-Cynthia. This nettle actually contrived at intervals, to get a little note through to the girls, her children. And at this the silver-haired Mater shook inwardly with hate. For if She-who-was-Cynthia ever came back, there wouldn't be much left of the Mater. A secret gust of hate went from the old granny to the girls, children of that foul nettle of lust, that Cynthia who had had such an affectionate contempt for the Mater.

Mingled with all this, was the children's perfectly distinct recollection of their real home, the vicarage in the south, and their glamorous but not very dependable mother, Cynthia. She had made a great glow, a flow of life, like a swift and dangerous sun in the home, forever coming and going. They always associated her presence with brightness, but also with danger; with glamour, but with fearful selfishness.

Now the glamour was gone, and the white snow-flower, like a porcelain wreath, froze on its grave. The danger of instability, the peculiarly *dangerous* sort of selfishness, like lions and tigers, was also gone. There was now a complete stability, in which one could perish safely.

But they were growing up. And as they grew, they became more definitely confused, more actively puzzled. The Mater, as she grew older, grew blinder. Somebody had to lead her about. She did not get up till towards midday. Yet blind or bed-ridden, she held the house.

Besides, she wasn't bed-ridden. Whenever the *men* were present, the Mater was in her throne. She was too cunning to court neglect. Especially as she had rivals.

Her great rival was the younger girl, Yvette. Yvette had some of the vague, careless blitheness of She-who-was-Cynthia. But this one was more docile. Granny perhaps had caught her in time. Perhaps!

The rector adored Yvette, and spoiled her with a doting fondness; as much as to say: am I not a soft-hearted, indulgent old boy! He liked to have this opinion of himself, and the Mater knew his weaknesses to a hair's-breadth. She knew them, and she traded on them by turning them into decorations for him, for his character. He wanted, in his own eyes, to have a fascinating character, as women want to have fascinating dresses. And the Mater cunningly put beauty-spots over his defects and deficiencies. Her mother-love gave her the clue to his weaknesses, and she hid them for him with decorations. Whereas She-who-was-Cynthia—! But don't mention *her,* in this connection. In her eyes, the rector was almost hump-backed and an idiot.

The funny thing was, Granny secretly hated Lucille, the elder girl, more than the pampered Yvette. Lucille, the uneasy and irritable, was more conscious of being under Granny's power, than was the spoilt and vague Yvette.

On the other hand, Aunt Cissie hated Yvette. She hated her very name. Aunt Cissie's life had been sacrificed to the Mater, and Aunt Cissie knew it, and the Mater knew she knew it. Yet as the years went on, it became a convention. The convention of Aunt Cissie's sacrifice was accepted by everybody, including the self-same Cissie. She prayed a good deal about it. Which also showed that she had her own private feelings somewhere, poor thing. She had ceased to be Cissie, she had lost her life and her sex. And now, she was creeping towards fifty, strange green flares of rage would come up in her, and at such times, she was insane.

But Granny held her in her power. And Aunt Cissie's one object in life was to look after the Mater.

Aunt Cissie's green flares of hellish hate would go up against all young things, sometimes. Poor thing, she prayed and tried to obtain forgiveness from heaven. But what had been done to her, *she* could not forgive, and the vitriol would spurt in her veins sometimes.

It was not as if the Mater were a warm, kindly soul. She wasn't. She only seemed it, cunningly. And the fact dawned gradually on the girls. Under her old-fashioned lace cap, under her silver hair, under the black silk of her stout, short, forward-bulging body, this old woman had a cunning heart, seeking forever her own female power. And through the weakness of the unfresh, stagnant men she had bred, she kept her power, as her years rolled on, from seventy to eighty, and from eighty on the new lap, towards ninety.

For in the family there was a whole tradition of "loyalty"; loyalty to one another, and especially to the Mater. The Mater, of course, was the pivot of the family. The family was her own extended ego. Naturally she covered it with her power. And her sons and daughters, being weak and disintegrated, naturally were loyal. Outside the family, what was there for them but danger and insult and ignominy? Had not the rector experienced it, in his marriage? So now, caution! Caution and loyalty, fronting the world! Let there be as much hate and friction *inside* the family, as you like. To the outer world, a stubborn fence of unison.

II

But it was not until the girls finally came home from school that they felt the full weight of Granny's dead old hand on their lives. Lucille was now nearly twenty-one, and Yvette nineteen. They had been to a good girls' school, and had had a finishing year in Lausanne, and were quite the usual thing, tall young creatures with fresh, sensitive faces and bobbed hair and young-manly, deuce-take-it manners.

"What's so awfully *boring* about Papplewick," said Yvette, as they stood on the Channel boat watching the grey, grey cliffs of Dover draw near, "is that there are no *men* about. Why doesn't Daddy have some good old sports for friends? As for Uncle Fred, he's the limit!"

"Oh, you never know what will turn up," said Lucille, more philosophic.

"You jolly well know what to expect," said Yvette. "Choir on Sundays, and I hate mixed choirs. Boys' voices are *lovely*, when there are no women. And Sunday School and Girls' Friendly, and socials, all the dear old souls that inquire after Granny! Not a decent young fellow for miles."

"Oh, I don't know!" said Lucille. "There's always the Framleys. And you know Gerry Somercotes *adores* you."

"Oh, but I *hate* fellows who adore me!" cried Yvette, turning up her sensitive nose. "They *bore* me. They hang on like lead."

"Well, what *do* you want, if you can't stand being adored? *I* think it's perfectly all right to be adored. You know you'll never marry them, so why not let them go on adoring, if it amuses them."

"Oh, but I *want* to get married," cried Yvette.

"Well, in that case, let them go on adoring you till you find one that you can *possibly* marry."

"I never should, that way. Nothing puts me off like an adoring fellow. They *bore* me so! They make me feel beastly."

"Oh, so they do me, if they get pressing. But at a distance, I think they're rather nice."

"I should like to fall *violently* in love."

"Oh, very likely! I shouldn't! I should hate it. Probably so would you, if it actually happened. After all, we've got to settle down a bit, before we know what we want."

"But don't you *hate* going back to Papplewick?" cried Yvette, turning up her young, sensitive nose.

"No, not particularly. I suppose we shall be rather bored. I wish Daddy would get a car. I suppose we shall have to drag the old bikes out. Wouldn't you like to get up to Tansy Moor?"

"Oh, *love* it! Though it's an awful *strain,* shoving an old push-bike up those hills."

The ship was nearing the grey cliffs. It was summer, but a grey day. The two girls wore their coats with fur collars turned up, and little *chic* hats pulled down over their ears. Tall, slender, fresh-faced, naive, yet confident, too confident, in their school-girlish arrogance, they were so terribly English. They seemed so free, and were as a matter of fact so tangled and tied up, inside themselves. They seemed so dashing and unconventional, and were really so conventional, so, as it were, shut up indoors inside themselves. They looked like bold, tall young sloops, just slipping from the harbour into the wide seas of life. And they were, as a matter of fact, two poor young rudderless lives, moving from one chain anchorage to another.

The rectory struck a chill into their hearts as they entered. It seemed ugly, and almost sordid, with the dank air of that middle-class, degenerated comfort which has ceased to be comfortable and has turned stuffy, unclean. The hard, stone house struck the girls as being unclean, they could not have said why. The shabby furniture seemed somehow sordid, nothing was fresh. Even the food at meals had that awful dreary sordidness which is so repulsive to a young thing coming from abroad. Roast beef and wet cabbage, cold mutton and mashed potatoes, sour pickles, inexcusable puddings.

Granny, who "loved a bit of pork," also had special dishes, beef-tea and rusks, or a small savoury custard. The grey-faced Aunt Cissie ate nothing at all. She would sit at table, and take a single lonely and naked boiled potato on to her plate. She never ate meat. So she sat in sordid durance, while the meal went on, and Granny quickly slobbered her portion—lucky if she spilled nothing on her protuberant stomach. The food was not appetizing in itself: how could it be, when Aunt Cissie hated food herself, hated the fact of eating, and never could keep a maid-servant for three months? The girls ate with repulsion, Lucille bravely bearing up, Yvette's tender nose showing her disgust. Only the rector, white-haired, wiped his long grey moustache with his serviette, and cracked jokes. He too was getting heavy and inert, sitting in his study all day, never taking exercise. But he cracked sarcastic little jokes all the time, sitting there under the shelter of the Mater.

The country, with its steep hills and its deep, narrow valleys, was dark and gloomy, yet had a certain powerful strength of its own. Twenty miles away was the black industrialism of the north. Yet the village of Papplewick was comparatively lonely, almost lost, the life in it stony and dour. Everything was stone, with a hardness that was almost poetic, it was so unrelenting.

It was as the girls had known: they went back into the choir, they helped in the parish. But Yvette struck absolutely against Sunday School, the Band of Hope, the Girls' Friendlies—indeed against all those functions that were conducted by determined old maids and obstinate, stupid, elderly men. She avoided church duties as much as possible, and got away from the rectory whenever she could. The Framleys, a big, untidy, jolly family up at the Grange, were an enormous stand-by. And if anybody asked her out to a meal, even if a woman in one of the workmen's houses asked her to stay to tea, she accepted at once. In fact, she was rather thrilled. She liked talking to the working men, they had often such fine, hard heads. But of course they were in another world.

So the months went by. Gerry Somercotes was still an adorer. There were others, too, sons of farmers or mill-owners. Yvette really ought to have had a good time. She was always out to parties and dances, friends came for her in their motor-cars, and off she went to the city, to the afternoon dance in the chief hotel, or in the gorgeous new Palais de Danse, called the Pally.

Yet she always seemed like a creature mesmerized. She was never free to be quite jolly. Deep inside her worked an intolerable irritation, which she thought she *ought* not to feel, and which she hated feeling, thereby making it worse. She never understood at all whence it arose.

At home, she truly was irritable, and outrageously rude to Aunt Cissie. In fact, Yvette's awful temper became one of the family by-words.

Lucille, always more practical, got a job in the city as private secretary to a man who needed somebody with fluent French and shorthand. She went back and forth every day, by the same train as Uncle Fred. But she never travelled with him, and wet or fine, bicycled to the station, while he went on foot.

The two girls were both determined that what they wanted was a really jolly social life. And they resented with fury that the rectory was, for their friends, impossible. There were only four rooms downstairs: the kitchen, where lived the two discontented maid-servants: the dark dining-room: the rector's study: and the big, "homely," dreary living-room or drawing-room. In the dining-room there was a gas fire. Only in the living-room was a good hot fire kept going. Because, of course, here Granny reigned.

In this room the family was assembled. At evening, after dinner, Uncle Fred and the rector invariably played cross-word puzzles with Granny.

"Now, Mater, are you ready! N blank blank blank blank W: a Siamese functionary."

"Eh? Eh? M blank blank blank blank W?"

Granny was hard of hearing.

"No, Mater. Not M! N blank blank blank blank W: a Siamese functionary."

"N blank blank blank blank W: a Chinese functionary."

"SIAMESE."

"Eh?"

"SIAMESE! SIAM!"

"A Siamese functionary! Now what can that be?" said the old lady profoundly, folding her hands on her round stomach. Her two sons proceeded to make suggestions, at which she said Ah! Ah! The rector was amazingly clever at cross-word puzzles. But Fred had a certain technical vocabulary.

"This certainly is a hard nut to crack," said the old lady, when they were all stuck.

Meanwhile Lucille sat in a corner with her hands over her ears, pretending to read, and Yvette irritably made drawings, or hummed loud and exasperating tunes, to add to the family concert. Aunt Cissie continually reached for a chocolate, and her jaws worked ceaselessly. She literally lived on chocolates. Sitting in the distance, she put another into her mouth, then looked again at the parish magazine. Then she lifted her head, and saw it was time to fetch Granny's cup of Horlick's.

While she was gone, in nervous exasperation Yvette would open the window. The room was never fresh, she imagined it smelt: smelt of Granny. And Granny, who was hard of hearing, heard like a weasel when she wasn't wanted to.

"Did you open the window, Yvette? I think you might remember there are older people than yourself in the room," she said.

"It's stifling! It's unbearable! No wonder we've all of us always got colds."

"I'm sure the room is large enough, and a good fire burning." The old lady gave a little shudder. "A draught to give us all our death."

"Not a draught at all," roared Yvette. "A breath of fresh air."

The old lady shuddered again, and said:

"Indeed!"

The rector, in silence, marched to the window and firmly closed it. He did not look at his daughter meanwhile. He hated thwarting her. But she must know what's what!

The cross-word puzzles, invented by Satan himself, continued till Granny had had her Horlick's, and was to go to bed. Then came the ceremony of Good night! Everybody stood up. The girls went to be kissed by the blind old woman, the rector gave his arm, and Aunt Cissie followed with a candle.

But this was already nine o'clock, although Granny was really getting old, and should have been in bed sooner. But when she was in bed, she could not sleep, till Aunt Cissie came.

"You see," said Granny, "I have *never* slept alone. For fifty-four years I never slept a night without the Pater's arm round me. And when he was gone I tried to sleep alone. But as sure as my eyes closed to sleep, my heart nearly jumped out of my body, and I lay in a palpitation. Oh, you may think what you will, but it was a fearful experience, after fifty-four years of perfect married life! I would have prayed to be taken first, but the Pater, well, no I don't think he would have been able to bear up."

So Aunt Cissie slept with Granny. And she hated it. She said *she* could never sleep. And she grew greyer and greyer, and the food in the house got worse, and Aunt Cissie had to have an operation.

But the Mater rose as ever, towards noon, and at the midday meal, she presided from her arm-chair, with her stomach protruding; her reddish, pendulous face, that had a sort of horrible majesty, dropping soft under the wall of her high brow, and her blue eyes peering unseeing. Her white hair was getting scanty, it was altogether a little indecent. But the rector jovially cracked his jokes to her, and she pretended to disapprove. But she was perfectly complacent, sitting in her ancient obesity, and after meals, getting the wind from her stomach, pressing her bosom with her hand as she "rifted" in gross physical complacency.

What the girls minded most was that, when they brought their young friends to the house, Granny always was there, like some awful idol of old flesh, consuming all the attention. There was only the one room for everybody. And there sat the old lady, with Aunt Cissie keeping an acrid guard over her. Everybody must be presented first to Granny: she was ready to be genial, she liked company. She had to know who everybody was, where they came from, every circumstance of their lives. And then, when she was *au fait*, she could get hold of the conversation.

Nothing could be more exasperating to the girls. "Isn't old Mrs. Saywell wonderful! She takes *such* an interest in life, at nearly ninety!"

"She does take an interest in people's affairs, if that's life," said Yvette.

Then she would immediately feel guilty. After all, it *was* wonderful to be nearly ninety, and have such a clear mind! And Granny never *actually* did anybody any harm. It was more that she was in the way. And perhaps it was rather awful to hate somebody because they were old and in the way.

Yvette immediately repented, and was nice. Granny blossomed forth into reminiscences of when she was a girl, in the little town in Buckinghamshire. She talked and talked away, and was *so* entertaining. She really *was* rather wonderful.

Then in the afternoon Lottie and Ella and Bob Framely came, with Leo Wetherell.

"Oh, come in!"—and in they all trooped to the sitting-room, where Granny, in her white cap, sat by the fire.

"Granny, this is Mr. Wetherell."

"Mr. What-did-you-say? You must excuse me, I'm a little deaf!"

Granny gave her hand to the uncomfortable young man, and gazed silently at him, sightlessly.

"You are not from our parish?" she asked him.

"Dinnington!" he shouted.

"We want to go a picnic to-morrow, to Bonsall Head, in Leo's car. We can all squeeze in," said Ella, in a low voice.

"Did you say Bonsall Head?" asked Granny.

"Yes!"

There was a blank silence.

"Did you say you were going in a car?"

"Yes! In Mr. Wetherell's."

"I hope he's a good driver. It's a very dangerous road."

"He's a *very* good driver."

"Not a very good driver?"

"Yes! He *is* a very good driver."

"If you go to Bonsall Head, I think I must send a message to Lady Louth."

Granny always dragged in this miserable Lady Louth, when there was company.

"Oh, we shan't go that way," cried Yvette.

"Which way?" said Granny. "You must go by Heanor."

The whole party sat, as Bob expressed it, like stuffed ducks, fidgeting on their chairs.

Aunt Cissie came in—and then the maid with the tea. There was the eternal and everlasting piece of bought cake. Then appeared a plate of little fresh cakes. Aunt Cissie had actually sent to the baker's.

"Tea, Mater!"

The old lady gripped the arms of her chair. Everybody rose and stood, while she waded slowly across, on Aunt Cissie's arm, to her place at table.

During tea Lucille came in from town, from her job. She was simply worn out, with black marks under her eyes. She gave a cry, seeing all the company.

As soon as the noise had subsided, and the awkwardness was resumed, Granny said:

"You have never mentioned Mr. Wetherell to me, have you, Lucille?"

"I don't remember," said Lucille.

"You can't have done. The name is strange to me."

Yvette absently grabbed another cake, from the now almost empty plate. Aunt Cissie, who was driven almost crazy by Yvette's vague and inconsiderate ways, felt the green rage fuse in her heart. She picked up her own plate, on which was the one cake she allowed herself, and said with vitriolic politeness, offering it to Yvette:

"Won't you have mine?"

"Oh, thanks!" said Yvette, starting in her angry vagueness. And with an appearance of the same insouciance, she helped herself to Aunt Cissie's cake also, adding as an afterthought: "If you're sure you don't want it."

She now had two cakes on her plate. Lucille had gone white as a ghost, bending to her tea. Aunt Cissie sat with a green look of poisonous resignation. The awkwardness was an agony.

But Granny, bulkily enthroned and unaware, only said, in the centre of the cyclone:

"If you are motoring to Bonsall Head to-morrow, Lucille, I wish you would take a message from me to Lady Louth."

"Oh!" said Lucille, giving a queer look across the table at the sightless old woman. Lady Louth was the King Charles' Head of the family, invariably produced by Granny for the benefit of visitors. "Very well!"

"She was so very kind last week. She sent her chauffeur over with a Cross-word Puzzle book for me."

"But you thanked her then," cried Yvette.

"I should like to send her a note."

"We can post it," cried Lucille.

"Oh no! I should like you to take it. When Lady Louth called last time. . . ."

The young ones sat like a shoal of young fishes dumbly mouthing at the surface of the water, while Granny went on about Lady Louth. Aunt Cissie, the two girls knew, was still helpless, almost unconscious in a paroxysm of rage about the cake. Perhaps, poor thing, she was praying.

It was a mercy when the friends departed. But by that time the two girls were both haggard-eyed. And it was then that Yvette, looking round, suddenly saw the stony, implacable will-to-power in the old and motherly-seeming Granny. She sat there bulging backwards in her chair, impassive, her reddish, pendulous old face rather mottled, almost unconscious, but implacable, her face like a mask that hid something stony, relentless. It was the static inertia of her un- savoury power. Yet in a minute she would open her ancient mouth to find out every detail about Leo Wetherell. For the moment she was hibernating in her oldness, her agedness. But in a minute her mouth would open, her mind would flicker awake and with her insatiable greed for life, other people's life, she would start on her quest for every detail. She was like the old toad which Yvette had watched, fascinated, as it sat on the ledge of the beehive, immediately in front of the little entrance by which the bees emerged, and which, with a demonish lightning-like snap of its pursed jaws, caught every bee as it came out to launch into the air, swallowed them one after the other, as if it could consume the whole hive-full, into its aged, bulging, purse-like wrinkledness. It had been swallowing bees as they launched into the air of spring, year after year, year after year, for generations.

But the gardener, called by Yvette, was in a rage, and killed the creature with a stone.

"'Appen tha *art* good for th' snails," he said, as he came down with the stone. "But tha 'rt none goin' ter emp'y th' bee-'ive into thy guts."

III

The next day was dull and low, and the roads were awful, for it had been raining for weeks, yet the young ones set off on their trip, without taking Granny's message either. They just slipped out while she was making her slow trip upstairs after lunch. Not for anything would they have called at Lady Louth's house. That widow of a knighted doctor, a harmless person indeed, had become an obnoxity in their lives.

Six young rebels, they sat very perkily in the car as they swished through the mud. Yet they had a peaked look too. After all, they had nothing really to rebel against, any of them. They were left so very free in their movements. Their parents let them do almost entirely as they liked. There wasn't really a fetter to break, nor a prison-bar to file through, nor a bolt to shatter. The keys of their lives were in their own hands. And there they dangled inert.

It is very much easier to shatter prison bars than to open undiscovered doors to life. As the younger generation finds out somewhat to its chagrin. True, there was Granny. But poor old Granny, you couldn't actually say to her: "Lie down and die, you old woman!" She might be an old nuisance, but she never really *did* anything. It wasn't fair to hate her.

So the young people set off on their jaunt, trying to be very full of beans. They could really do as they liked. And so, of course, there was nothing to do but sit in the car and talk a lot of criticism of other people, and silly flirty gallantry that was really rather a bore. If there had only been a few "strict orders" to be disobeyed! But nothing: beyond the refusal to carry the message to Lady Louth, of which the rector would approve because he didn't encourage King Charles' Head either.

They sang, rather scrappily, the latest would-be comic songs, as they went through the grim villages. In the great park the deer were in groups near the road, roe deer and fallow, nestling in the gloom of the afternoon under the oaks by the road, as if for the stimulus of human company.

Yvette insisted on stopping and getting out to talk to them. The girls, in their Russian boots, tramped through the damp grass, while the deer watched them with big, unfrightened eyes. The hart trotted away mildly, holding back his head, because of the weight of the horns. But the doe, balancing her big ears, did not rise from under the tree, with her half-grown young ones, till the girls were almost in touch. Then she walked light-foot away, lifting her tail from her spotted flanks, while the young ones nimbly trotted.

"Aren't they awfully dainty and nice!" cried Yvette. "You'd wonder they could lie so cosily in this horrid wet grass."

"Well, I suppose they've got to lie down *sometime*," said Lucille. "And it's *fairly* dry under the tree." She looked at the crushed grass, where the deer had lain.

Yvette went and put her hand down, to feel how it felt.

"Yes!" she said doubtfully, "I believe it's a bit warm."

The deer had bunched again a few yards away, and were standing motionless in the gloom of the afternoon. Away below the slopes of grass and trees, beyond the swift river with its balustraded bridge, sat the huge ducal house, one or two chimneys smoking bluely. Behind it rose purplish woods.

The girls, pushing their fur collars up to their cars, dangling one long arm, stood watching in silence, their wide Russian boots protecting them from the wet grass. The great house squatted square and creamy-grey below. The deer, in little groups, were scattered under the old trees close by. It all seemed so still, so unpretentious, and so sad.

"I wonder where the Duke is now," said Ella.

"Not here, wherever he is," said Lucille. "I expect he's abroad where the sun shines."

The motor horn called from the road, and they heard Leo's voice:

"Come on, boys! If we're going to get to the Head and down to Amberdale for tea, we'd better move."

They crowded into the car again, with chilled feet, and set off through the park, past the silent spire of the church, out through the great gates and over the bridge, on into the wide, damp, stony village of Woodlinkin, where the river ran. And thence, for a long time, they stayed in the mud and dark and dampness of the valley, often with sheer rock above them; the water brawling on one hand, the steep rock or dark trees on the other.

Till, through the darkness of overhanging trees, they began to climb, and Leo changed the gear. Slowly the car toiled up through the whitey-grey mud, into the stony village of Bolehill, that hung on the slope, round the old cross, with its steps, that stood where the road branched, on past the cottages whence came a wonderful smell of hot tea-cakes, and beyond, still upwards, under dripping trees and past broken slopes of bracken, always climbing. Until the cleft became shallower, and the trees finished, and the slopes on either side were bare, gloomy grass, with low dry-stone walls. They were emerging on to the Head.

The party had been silent for some time. On either side the road was grass, then a low stone fence, and the swelling curve of the hill-summit, traced with the low, dry stone walls. Above this, the low sky.

The car ran out, under the low, grey sky, on the naked tops.

"Shall we stay a moment?" called Leo.

"Oh yes!" cried the girls.

And they scrambled out once more, to look around. They knew the place quite well. But still, if one came to the Head, one got out to look.

The hills were like the knuckles of a hand, the dales were below, between the fingers, narrow, steep, and dark. In the deeps a train was steaming, slowly pulling north: a small thing of the under-world. The noise of the engine re-echoed curiously upwards. Then came the dull, familiar sound of blasting in a quarry.

Leo, always on the go, moved quickly.

"Shall we be going?" he said. "Do we *want* to get down to Amberdale for tea? Or shall we try somewhere nearer?"

They all voted for Amberdale, for the Marquis of Grantham.

"Well, which way shall we go back? Shall we go by Codnor and over Crosshill, or shall we go by Ashbourne?"

There was the usual dilemma. Then they finally decided on the Codnor top road. Off went the car, gallantly.

They were on the top of the world, now, on the back of the fist. It was naked, too, as the back of your fist, high under heaven, and dull, heavy green. Only it was veined with a network of old stone walls, dividing the fields, and broken here and there with ruins of old lead-mines and works. A sparse stone farm bristled with six naked sharp trees. In the distance was a patch of smoky grey stone, a hamlet. In some fields grey, dark sheep fed silently, sombrely. But there was not a sound nor a movement. It was the roof of England, stony and arid as any roof. Beyond, below, were the shires.

" 'And see the coloured countries,' " said Yvette to herself. Here anyhow they were not coloured. A stream of rooks trailed out from nowhere. They had been walking, pecking, on a naked field that had been manured. The car ran on between the grass and the stone walls of the upland lane, and the young people were silent, looking out over the far network of stone fences, under the sky, looking for the curves downward that indicated a drop to one of the underneath, hidden dales.

Ahead was a light cart, driven by a man, and trudging along at the side was a woman, sturdy and elderly, with a pack on her back. The man in the cart had caught her up, and now was keeping pace.

The road was narrow. Leo sounded the horn sharply. The man on the cart looked round, but the woman on foot only trudged steadily, rapidly forward, without turning her head.

Yvette's heart gave a jump. The man on the cart was a gipsy, one of the black, loose-bodied, handsome sort. He remained seated on his cart, turning round and gazing at the occupants of the motor-car, from under the brim of his cap. And his pose was loose, his gaze insolent in its indifference. He had a thin black moustache under his thin, straight nose, and a big silk handkerchief of red and yellow tied round his neck. He spoke a word to the woman. She stood a second, solid, to turn round and look at the occupants of the car, which had now drawn quite close. Leo honked the horn again, imperiously. The woman, who had a grey-and-white kerchief tied round her head, turned sharply, to keep pace with the cart, whose driver also had settled back, and was lifting the reins, moving his loose, light shoulders. But still he did not pull aside.

Leo made the horn scream, as he put the brakes on and the car slowed up near the back of the cart. The gipsy turned round at the din, laughing in his dark face under his dark-green cap, and said something which they did not hear, showing white teeth under the line of black moustache, and making a gesture with his dark, loose hand.

"Get out o' the way then!" yelled Leo.

For answer, the man delicately pulled the horse to a standstill, as it curved to the side of the road. It was a good roan horse and a good, natty, dark-green cart.

Leo, in a rage, had to jam on the brake and pull up too.

"Don't the pretty young ladies want to hear their fortunes?" said the gipsy on the cart, laughing except for his dark, watchful eyes, which went from face to face, and lingered on Yvette's young, tender face.

She met his dark eyes for a second, their level search, their insolence, their complete indifference to people like Bob and Leo, and something took fire in her breast. She thought: "He is stronger than I am! He doesn't care!"

"Oh yes, let's!" cried Lucille at once.

"Oh yes!" chorused the girls.

"I say! What about the time?" cried Leo.

"Oh, bother the old time! Somebody's always dragging in time by the forelock," cried Lucille.

"Well, if you don't mind *when* we get back, *I* don't," said Leo heroically.

The gipsy man had been sitting loosely on the side of his cart, watching the faces. He now jumped softly down from the shaft, his knees a bit stiff. He was apparently a man something over thirty, and a beau in his way. He wore a sort of shooting-jacket, double-breasted, coming only to the hips, of dark green-and-black frieze; rather tight black trousers, black boots, and a dark-green cap; with the big yellow-and-red bandanna handkerchief round his neck. His appearance was curiously elegant, and quite expensive in its gipsy style. He was handsome, too, pressing in his chin with the old, gipsy conceit, and now apparently not heeding the strangers any more, as he led his good roan horse off the road, preparing to back his cart.

The girls saw for the first time a deep recess in the side of the road, and two caravans smoking. Yvette got quickly down. They had suddenly come upon a disused quarry, cut into the slope of the roadside, and in this sudden lair, almost like a cave, were three caravans, dismantled for the winter. There was also deep at the back, a shelter built of boughs, as a stable for the horse. The grey, crude rock rose high above the caravans, and curved round towards the road. The floor was heaped chips of stone, with grasses growing among. It was a hidden, snug winter camp.

The elderly woman with the pack had gone into one of the caravans, leaving the door open. Two children were peeping out, shewing black heads. The gipsy man gave a little call, as he backed his cart into the quarry, and an elderly man came out to help him untackle.

The gipsy himself went up the steps into the newest caravan, that had its door closed. Underneath, a tied-up dog ranged forth. It was a white hound, spotted liver-coloured. It gave a low growl as Leo and Bob approached.

At the same moment, a dark-faced gipsy-woman with a pink shawl or kerchief round her head and big gold ear-rings in her ears, came down the steps of the newest caravan, swinging her flounced, voluminous green skirt. She was handsome in a bold, dark, long-faced way, just a bit wolfish. She looked like one of the bold, loping Spanish gipsies.

"Good morning, my ladies and gentlemen," she said, eyeing the girls from her bold, predative eyes. She spoke with a certain foreign stiffness.

"Good afternoon!" said the girls.

"Which beautiful little lady like to hear her fortune? Give me her little hand?"

She was a tall woman, with a frightening way of reaching forward her neck like a menace. Her eyes went from face to face, very active, heartlessly searching out what she wanted. Meanwhile the man, apparently her husband, appeared at the top of the caravan steps smoking a pipe, and with a small, black-haired child in his arms. He stood on his limber legs, casually looking down on the group, as if from a distance, his long black lashes lifted from his full, conceited, impudent black eyes. There was something peculiarly transfusing in his stare. Yvette felt it, felt it in her knees. She pretended to be interested in the white-and-liver-coloured hound.

"How much do you want, if we all have our fortunes told?" asked Lottie Framley, as the six fresh-faced young Christians hung back rather reluctantly from this pagan pariah woman.

"All of you? Ladies and gentlemen, all?" said the woman shrewdly.

"I don't want mine told! You go ahead!" cried Leo.

"Neither do I," said Bob. "You four girls."

"The four ladies?" said the gipsy woman, eyeing them shrewdly, after having looked at the boys. And she fixed her price. "Each one give me a sheeling, and a little bit more for luck? A little bit!" She smiled in a way that was more wolfish than cajoling, and the force of her will was felt, heavy as iron beneath the velvet of her words.

"All right," said Leo. "Make it a shilling a head. Don't spin it out too long."

"Oh, *you!*" cried Lucille at him. "We want to hear it *all.*"

The woman took two wooden stools, from under a caravan, and placed them near the wheel. Then she took the tall, dark Lottie Framley by the hand, and bade her sit down.

"You don't care if everybody hear?" she said, looking up curiously into Lottie's face.

Lottie blushed dark with nervousness, as the gipsy woman held her hand, and stroked her palm with hard, cruel-seeming fingers.

"Oh, I don't mind," she said.

The gipsy woman peered into the palm tracing the lines of the hand with a hard, dark forefinger. But she seemed clean.

And slowly she told the fortune, while the others, standing listening, kept on crying out: "Oh, that's Jim Baggaley! Oh, I, I don't believe it! Oh, that's not true! A fair woman who lives beneath a tree! Why, whoever's that?" until Leo stopped them with a manly warning:

"Oh, hold on, girls! You give everything away."

Lottie retired blushing and confused, and it was Ella's turn. She was much more calm and shrewd, trying to read the oracular words. Lucille kept breaking out with: "Oh, I say!" The gipsy man at the top of the steps stood imperturbable, without any expression at all. But his bold eyes kept staring at Yvette, she could feel them on her cheek, on her neck, and she dared not look up. But Framley would sometimes look up at him, and got a level stare back from the handsome face of the male gipsy, from the dark conceited proud eyes. It was a peculiar look, in the eyes that belonged to the tribe of the humble: the pride of the pariah, the half-sneering challenge of the outcast, who sneered at law-abiding men, and went his own way. All the time, the gipsy man stood there, holding his child in his arms, looking on without being concerned.

Lucille was having her hand read—"You have been across the sea, and there you met a man—a brown-haired man—but he was too old——"

"Oh, I *say!*" cried Lucille, looking round at Yvette.

But Yvette was abstracted, agitated, hardly heeding: in one of her mesmerized states.

"You will marry in a few years—not now, but a few years—perhaps four—and you will not be rich, but you will have plenty—enough—and you will go away, a long journey."

"With my husband, or without?" cried Lucille.

"With him——"

When it came to Yvette's turn, and the woman looked up boldly, cruelly, searching for a long time in her face, Yvette said nervously:

"I don't think I want mine told. No, I won't have mine told! No, I won't, really!"

"You are afraid of something?" said the gipsy woman cruelly.

"No, it's not that——" Yvette fidgeted.

"You have some secret? You are afraid I shall say it? Come, would you like to go in the caravan, where nobody hears?"

The woman was curiously insinuating; while Yvette was always wayward, perverse. The look of perversity was on her soft, frail young face now, giving her a queer hardness.

"Yes!" she said suddenly. "Yes! I might do that!"

"Oh, I say!" cried the others. "Be a sport!"

"I don't think you'd *better!*" cried Lucille.

"Yes!" said Yvette, with that hard little way of hers. "I'll do that. I'll go in the caravan."

The gipsy woman called something to the man on the steps. He went into the caravan for a moment or two, then reappeared, and came down the steps, setting the small child on its uncertain feet, and holding it by the hand. A dandy, in his polished black boots, tight black trousers and tight dark-green jersey, he walked slowly across with the toddling child to where the elderly gipsy was giving the roan horse a feed of oats, in the bough shelter between pits of grey rock, with dry bracken upon the stone chip floor. He looked at Yvette as he passed, staring her full in the eyes, with his pariah's bold yet dishonest stare. Something hard inside her met his stare. But the surface of her body seemed to turn to water. Nevertheless, something hard in her registered the peculiar pure lines of his face, of his straight, pure nose, of his cheeks and temples. The curious dark, suave purity of all his body, outlined in the green jersey: a purity like a living sneer.

And as he loped slowly past her, on his flexible hips, it seemed to her still that he was stronger than she was. Of all the men she had ever seen, this one was the only one who was stronger than she was, in her own kind of strength, her own kind of understanding.

So, with curiosity, she followed the woman up the steps of the caravan, the skirts of her well-cut tan coat swinging and almost showing her knees, under the pale-green cloth dress. She had long, long-striding, fine legs, too slim rather than too thick, and she wore curiously-patterned pale-and-fawn stockings of fine wool, suggesting the legs of some delicate animal.

At the top of the steps she paused and turned, debonair, to the others, saying in her naive, lordly way, so off-hand:

"I won't let her be long."

Her grey fur collar was open, showing her soft throat and pale green dress, her little plaited tan-coloured hat came down to her ears, round her soft, fresh face. There was something soft and yet overbearing, unscrupulous, about her. She knew the gipsy man had turned to look at her. She was aware of the pure dark nape of his neck, the black hair groomed away. He watched as she entered his house.

What the gipsy told her, no one ever knew. It was a long time to wait, the others felt. Twilight was deepening on the gloom, and it was turning raw and cold. From the chimney on the second caravan came smoke and a smell of rich food. The horse was fed, a yellow blanket strapped round him, and two gipsy men talked together in the distance, in low tones. There was a peculiar feeling of silence and secrecy in that lonely, hidden quarry.

At last the caravan door opened, and Yvette emerged, bending forward and stepping with long, witch-like slim legs down the steps. There was a stooping, witch-like silence about her as she emerged on the twilight.

"Did it seem long?" she said vaguely, not looking at anybody and keeping her own counsel hard within her soft, vague waywardness. "I hope you weren't bored! Wouldn't tea be nice! Shall we go?"

"You get in!" said Bob. "I'll pay."

The gipsy-woman's full, metallic skirts of jade-green alpaca came swinging down the steps. She rose to her height, a big, triumphant-looking woman with a dark wolf face. The pink cashmere kerchief stamped with red roses, was slipping to one side over her black and crimped hair. She gazed at the young people in the twilight with bold arrogance.

Bob put two half-crowns in her hand.

"A little bit more, for luck, for your young lady's luck," she wheedled, like a wheedling wolf. "Another bit of silver, to bring you luck."

"You've got a shilling for luck, that's enough," said Bob calmly and quietly, as they moved away to the car.

"A little bit of silver! Just a little bit, for your luck in love!"

Yvette, with the sudden long, startling gestures of her long limbs, swung round as she was entering the car, and with long arm out-stretched, strode and put something into the gipsy's hand, then stepped, bending her height, into the car.

"Prosperity to the beautiful young lady, and the gipsy's blessing on her," came the suggestive, half-sneering voice of the woman.

The engine *birred!* then *birred!* again more fiercely, and started. Leo switched on the lights, and immediately the quarry with the gipsies fell back into the blackness of night.

"Good night!" called Yvette's voice, as the car started. But hers was the only voice that piped up, chirpy and impudent in its nonchalance. The headlights glared down the stone lane.

"Yvette, you've got to tell us what she said to you," cried Lucille, in the teeth of Yvette's silent will *not* to be asked.

"Oh, nothing at *all* thrilling," said Yvette, with false warmth. "Just the usual old thing: a dark man who means good luck, and a fair one who means bad: and a death in the family, which if it means Granny, won't be so *very* awful: and I shall marry when I'm twenty-three, and have heaps of money and heaps of love, and two children. All sounds very nice, but it's a bit too much of a good thing, you know."

"Oh, but why did you give her more money?"

"Oh well, I wanted to! You *have* to be a bit lordly with people like that—"

IV

There was a terrific rumpus down at the rectory, on account of Yvette and the Window Fund. After the war, Aunt Cissie had set her heart on a stained glass window in the church, as a memorial for the men of the parish who had fallen. But the bulk of the fallen had been nonconformists, so the memorial took the form of an ugly little monument in front of the Wesleyan chapel.

This did not vanquish Aunt Cissie. She canvassed, she had bazaars, she made the girls get up amateur theatrical shows, for her precious window. Yvette, who quite liked the acting and showing-off part of it, took charge of the farce called *Mary in the Mirror*, and gathered in the proceeds, which were to be paid to the Window Fund when accounts were settled. Each of the girls was supposed to have a money-box for the Fund.

Aunt Cissie, feeling that the united sums must now almost suffice, suddenly called in Yvette's box. It contained fifteen shillings. There was a moment of green horror.

"Where is all the rest?"

"Oh!" said Yvette casually. "I just borrowed it. It wasn't so awfully much."

"What about the three pounds thirteen for *Mary in the Mirror?*" asked Aunt Cissie, as if the jaws of Hell were yawning.

"Oh quite! I just borrowed it. I can pay it back."

Poor Aunt Cissie! The green tumour of hate burst inside her, and there was a ghastly, abnormal scene, which left Yvette shivering with fear and nervous loathing.

Even the rector was rather severe.

"If you needed money, why didn't you tell me?" he said coldly. "Have you ever been refused anything in reason?"

"I—I thought it didn't matter," stammered Yvette.

"And what have you done with the money?"

"I suppose I've spent it," said Yvette, with wide distraught eyes and a peaked face.

"Spent it, on what?"

"I can't remember everything: stockings and things, and I gave some of it away."

Poor Yvette! Her lordly airs and ways were already hitting back at her, on the reflex. The rector was angry: his face had a snarling, doggish look, a sort of sneer. He was afraid his daughter was developing some of the rank, tainted qualities of She-who-was-Cynthia.

"You *would* do the large with somebody else's money, wouldn't you?" he said, with a cold, mongrel sort of sneer, which showed what an utter unbeliever he was, at the heart. The inferiority of a heart which has no core of warm belief in it, no pride in life. He had utterly no belief in her.

Yvette went pale, and very distant. Her pride, that frail, precious flame which everybody tried to quench, recoiled like a flame blown far away, on a cold wind, as if blown out, and her face, white now and still like a snowdrop, the white snow-flower of his conceit, seemed to have no life in it, only this pure, strange abstraction.

"He has no belief in me!" she thought in her soul. "I am really nothing to him. I am nothing, only a shameful thing. Everything is shameful, everything is shameful!"

A flame of passion or rage, while it might have overwhelmed or infuriated her, would not have degraded her as did her father's unbelief, his final attitude of a sneer against her.

He became a little afraid, in the silence of sterile thought. After all, he needed the *appearance* of love and belief and bright life, he would never dare to face the fat worm of his own unbelief that stirred in his heart.

"What have you to say for yourself?" he asked.

She only looked at him from that senseless snowdrop face which haunted him with fear, and gave him a helpless sense of guilt. That other one, She-who-was-Cynthia, she had looked back at him with the same numb, white fear, the fear of his degrading unbelief, the worm which was his heart's core. He *knew* his heart's core was a fat, awful worm. His dread was lest any one else should know. His anguish of hate was against any one who knew, and recoiled.

He saw Yvette recoiling, and immediately his manner changed to the worldly old good-humoured cynic which he affected.

"Ah well!" he said. "You have to pay it back, my girl, that's all. I will advance you the money out of your allowance. But I shall charge you four per cent a month's interest. Even the devil himself must pay a percentage on his debts. Another time, if you can't trust yourself, don't handle money which isn't your own. Dishonesty isn't pretty."

Yvette remained crushed, and deflowered and humiliated. She crept about, trailing the rays of her pride. She had a revulsion even from herself. Oh, why had she ever touched the leprous money! Her whole flesh shrank as if it were defiled. Why was that? Why, why was that?

She admitted herself wrong in having spent the money. "Of course I shouldn't have done it. They are quite right to be angry," she said to herself.

But where did the horrible wincing of her flesh come from? Why did she feel she had caught some physical contagion?

"Where you're so *silly*, Yvette," Lucille lectured her: poor Lucille was in great distress—"is that you give yourself away to them all. You might *know* they'd find out. I could have raised the money for you, and saved all this bother. It's perfectly awful! But you never will think beforehand where your actions are going to land you! Fancy Aunt Cissie saying all those things to you! How *awful!* Whatever would Mamma have said, if she'd heard it?"

When things went very wrong, they thought of their mother, and despised their father and all the low brood of the Saywells. Their mother, of course, had belonged to a higher, if more dangerous and "immoral" world. More selfish, decidedly. But with a showier gesture. More unscrupulous and more easily moved to contempt: but not so humiliating.

Yvette always considered that she got her fine, delicate flesh from her mother. The Saywells were all a bit leathery, and grubby somewhere inside. But then the Saywells never let you down. Whereas the fine She-who-was-Cynthia had let the rector down with a bang, and his little children along with him. Her little children! They could not quite forgive her.

Only dimly, after the row, Yvette began to realize the other sanctity of herself, the sanctity of her sensitive, clean flesh and blood, which the Saywells with their so-called morality succeeded in defiling. They always wanted to defile it. They were the life unbelievers. Whereas, perhaps She-who-was-Cynthia had only been a moral unbeliever.

Yvette went about dazed and peaked and confused. The rector paid in the money to Aunt Cissie, much to that lady's rage. The helpless tumour of her rage was still running. She would have liked to announce her niece's delinquency in the parish magazine. It was anguish to the destroyed woman that she could not publish the news to all the world. The selfishness! The selfishness! The selfishness!

Then the rector handed his daughter a little account with himself: her debt to him, interest thereon, the amount deducted from her small allowance. But to her credit he had placed a guinea, which was the fee he had to pay for complicity.

"As father of the culprit," he said humorously, "I am fined one guinea. And with that I wash the ashes out of my hair."

He was always generous about money. But somehow, he seemed to think that by being free about money he could absolutely call himself a generous man. Whereas he used money, even generosity, as a hold over her.

But he let the affair drop entirely. He was by this time more amused than anything, to judge from appearances. He thought still he was safe.

Aunt Cissie, however, could not get over her convulsion. One night when Yvette had gone rather early, miserably, to bed, when Lucille was away at a party, and she was lying with soft, peaked limbs aching with a sort of numbness and defilement, the door softly opened, and there stood Aunt Cissie, pushing her grey-green face through the opening of the door. Yvette started up in terror.

"Liar! Thief! Selfish little beast!" hissed the maniacal face of Aunt Cissie. "You little hypocrite! You liar! You selfish beast! You greedy little beast!"

There was such extraordinary impersonal hatred in that grey-green mask, and those frantic words, that Yvette opened her mouth to scream with hysterics. But Aunt Cissie shut the door as suddenly as she had opened it, and disappeared. Yvette leaped from her bed and turned the key. Then she crept back, half demented with fear of the squalid abnormal, half numbed with paralysis of damaged pride. And amid it all, up came a bubble of distracted laughter. It *was* so filthily ridiculous!

Aunt Cissie's behaviour did not hurt the girl so very much. It was after all somewhat fantastic. Yet hurt she was: in her limbs, in her body, in her sex, hurt. Hurt, numbed, and half destroyed, with only her nerves vibrating and jangled. And still so young, she could not conceive what was happening.

Only she lay and wished she were a gipsy. To live in a camp, in a caravan, and never set foot in a house, not know the existence of a parish, never look at a church. Her heart was hard with repugnance against the rectory. She loathed these houses with their indoor sanitation and their bathrooms, and their extraordinary repulsiveness. She hated the rectory, and everything it implied. The whole stagnant, sewerage sort of life, where sewerage is never mentioned, but where it seems to smell from the centre to every two-legged inmate, from Granny to the servants, was foul. If gipsies had no bathrooms, at least they had no sewerage. There was fresh air. In the rectory there was *never* fresh air. And in the souls of the people, the air was stale till it stank.

Hate kindled her heart, as she lay with numbed limbs. And she thought of the words of the gipsy woman: "There is a dark man who never lived in a house. He loves you. The other people are treading on your heart. They will tread on your heart till you think it is dead. But the dark man will blow the one spark up into fire again, good fire. You will see what good fire."

Even as the woman was saying it, Yvette felt there was some duplicity somewhere. But she didn't mind. She hated with the cold, acrid hatred of a child the rectory interior, the sort of putridity in the life. She liked that big, swarthy, wolf-like gipsy-woman, with the big gold rings in her ears, the pink scarf over her wavy black hair, the tight bodice of brown velvet, the green, fan-like skirt. She liked her dusky, strong, relentless hands, that had pressed so firm, like wolf's paws, in Yvette's own soft palm. She liked her. She liked the danger and the covert fearlessness of her. She liked her covert, unyielding sex, that was immoral, but with a hard, defiant pride of its own. Nothing would ever get that woman under. She would despise the rectory and the rectory morality, utterly! She would strangle Granny with one hand. And she would have the same contempt for Daddy and for Uncle Fred, as men, as she would have for fat old slobbery Rover, the Newfoundland dog. A great, sardonic female contempt, for such domesticated dogs, calling themselves men.

And the gipsy man himself! Yvette quivered suddenly, as if she had seen his big, bold eyes upon her, with the naked insinuation of desire in them. The absolutely naked insinuation of desire made her lie prone and powerless in the bed, as if a drug had cast her in a new, molten mould.

She never confessed to anybody that two of the ill-starred Window Fund pounds had gone to the gipsy woman. What if Daddy and Aunt Cissie knew *that!* Yvette stirred luxuriously in the bed. The thought of the gipsy had released the life of her limbs, and crystallized in her heart the hate of the rectory: so that now she felt potent, instead of impotent.

When, later, Yvette told Lucille about Aunt Cissie's dramatic interlude in the bedroom doorway, Lucille was indignant.

"Oh, hang it all!" cried she. "She might let it drop now. I should think we've heard enough about it by now! Good heavens, you'd think Aunt Cissie was a perfect bird of paradise! Daddy's dropped it, and after all, it's his business if it's anybody's. Let Aunt Cissie shut up!"

It was the very fact that the rector had dropped it, and that he again treated the vague and inconsiderate Yvette as if she were some specially licensed being, that kept Aunt Cissie's bile flowing. The fact that Yvette really was most of the time unaware of other people's feelings, and being unaware, couldn't care about them, nearly sent Aunt Cissie mad. Why should that young creature, with a delinquent mother, go through life as a privileged being, even unaware of other people's existence, though they were under her nose?

Lucille at this time was very irritable. She seemed as if she simply went a little unbalanced, when she entered the rectory. Poor Lucille, she was so thoughtful and responsible. She did all the extra troubling, thought about doctors, medicines, servants, and all that sort of thing. She slaved conscientiously at her job all day in town, working in a room with artificial light from ten till five. And she came home to have her nerves rubbed almost to frenzy by Granny's horrible and persistent inquisitiveness and parasitic agedness.

The affair of the Window Fund had apparently blown over, but there remained a stuffy tension in the atmosphere. The weather continued bad. Lucille stayed at home on the afternoon of her half holiday, and did herself no good by it. The rector was in his study, she and Yvette were making a dress for the latter young woman, Granny was resting on the couch.

The dress was of blue silk velours, French material, and was going to be very becoming. Lucille made Yvette try it on again: she was nervously uneasy about the hang, under the arms.

"Oh, bother!" cried Yvette, stretching her long, tender, childish arms, that tended to go bluish with the cold. "Don't be so frightfully *fussy*, Lucille! It's quite all right."

"If that's all the thanks I get, slaving my half-day away making dresses for you, I might as well do something for myself!"

"Well, Lucille! You know I never *asked* you! You know you can't bear it unless you *do* supervise," said Yvette, with that irritating blandness of hers, as she raised her naked elbows and peered over her shoulder into the long mirror.

"Oh yes! you never *asked* me!" cried Lucille. "As if I didn't know what you meant, when you started sighing and flouncing about."

"I!" said Yvette, with vague surprise. "Why, when did I start sighing and flouncing about?"

"Of course you know you did."

"Did I? No, I didn't know! When was it?" Yvette could put a peculiar annoyance into her mild, straying questions.

"I shan't do another thing to this frock, if you don't stand still and *stop* it," said Lucille, in her rather sonorous, burning voice.

"You know you are most awfully nagging and irritable, Lucille," said Yvette, standing as if on hot bricks.

"Now, Yvette!" cried Lucille, her eyes suddenly flashing in her sister's face, with wild flashes. "Stop it at once! Why should everybody put up with your abominable and overbearing temper?"

"Well, I don't know about *my* temper," said Yvette, writhing slowly out of the half-made frock, and slipping into her dress again.

Then, with an obstinate little look on her face, she sat down again at the table, in the gloomy afternoon, and began to sew at the blue stuff. The room was littered with blue clippings, the scissors were lying on the floor, the work-basket was spilled in chaos all over the table, and a second mirror was perched perilously on the piano.

Granny, who had been in a semi-coma, called a doze, roused herself on the big, soft couch and put her cap straight.

"I don't get much peace for my nap," she said, slowly feeling her thin white hair, to see that it was in order. She had heard vague noises.

Aunt Cissie came in, fumbling in a bag for a chocolate.

"I never saw such a mess!" she said. "You'd better clear some of that litter away, Yvette."

"All right," said Yvette. "I will in a minute."

"Which means never!" sneered Aunt Cissie, suddenly darting and picking up the scissors.

There was silence for a few moments, and Lucille slowly pushed her hands in her hair, as she read a book.

"You'd better clear away, Yvette," persisted Aunt Cissie.

"I will, before tea," replied Yvette, rising once more and pulling the blue dress over her head, flourishing her long, naked arms through the sleeveless armholes. Then she went between the mirrors, to look at herself once more.

As she did so, she sent the second mirror, that she had perched carelessly on the piano, sliding with a rattle to the floor. Luckily it did not break. But everybody started badly.

"She's smashed the mirror!" cried Aunt Cissie.

"Smashed a mirror! Which mirror! Who's smashed it?" came Granny's sharp voice.

"I haven't smashed anything," came the calm voice of Yvette. "It's quite all right."

"You'd better not perch it up there again," said Lucille.

Yvette, with a little impatient shrug at all the fuss, tried making the mirror stand in another place. She was not successful.

"If one had a fire in one's own room," she said crossly, "one needn't have a lot of people fussing when one wants to sew."

"Which mirror are you moving about?" asked Granny.

"One of our own that came from the vicarage," said Yvette rudely.

"Don't break it in *this* house, wherever it came from," said Granny.

There was a sort of family dislike for the furniture that had belonged to She-who-was-Cynthia. It was most of it shoved into the kitchen, and the servants' bedrooms.

"Oh, *I'm* not superstitious," said Yvette, "about mirrors or any of that sort of thing."

"Perhaps you're not," said Granny. "People who never take the responsibility for their own actions usually don't care what happens."

"After all," said Yvette, "I may say it's my own looking-glass, even if I did break it."

"And I say," said Granny, "that there shall be no mirrors broken in *this* house, if we can help it; no matter who they belong to, or did belong to. Cissie, have I got my cap straight?"

Aunt Cissie went over and straightened the old lady. Yvette loudly and irritatingly trilled a tuneless tune.

"And now, Yvette, will you please clear away?" said Aunt Cissie.

"Oh, bother!" cried Yvette angrily. "It's simply *awful* to live with a lot of people who are always nagging and fussing over trifles."

"What people, may I ask?" said Aunt Cissie ominously.

Another row was imminent. Lucille looked up with a queer cast in her eyes. In the two girls, the blood of She-who-was-Cynthia was roused.

"Of course you may ask! You know quite well I mean the people in this beastly house," said the outrageous Yvette.

"At least," said Granny, "we don't come of half-depraved stock."

There was a second's electric pause. Then Lucille sprang from her low seat, with sparks flying from her.

"You shut up!" she shouted, in a blast full upon the mottled majesty of the old lady.

The old woman's breast began to heave with heaven knows what emotions. The pause this time, as after the thunderbolt, was icy.

Then Aunt Cissie, livid, sprang upon Lucille, pushing her like a fury.

"Go to your room!" she cried hoarsely. "Go to your room!"

And she proceeded to push the white but fiery-eyed Lucille from the room. Lucille let herself be pushed, while Aunt Cissie vociferated:

"Stay in your room till you've apologized for this—till you've apologized to the Mater for this!"

"I shan't apologize!" came the clear voice of Lucille, from the passage, while Aunt Cissie shoved her.

Aunt Cissie drove her more wildly upstairs.

Yvette stood tall and bemused in the sitting-room, with the air of offended dignity, at the same time bemused, which was so odd on her. She still was bare-armed, in the half-made blue dress. And even *she* was half-aghast at Lucille's attack on the majesty of age. But also, she was coldly indignant against Granny's aspersion of the maternal blood in their veins.

"Of course I meant no offence," said Granny.

"Didn't you?" said Yvette coolly.

"Of course not. I only said we're not depraved, just because we happen to be superstitious about breaking mirrors."

Yvette could hardly believe her ears. Had she heard right? Was it possible! Or was Granny, at her age, just telling a barefaced lie?

Yvette knew that the old woman was telling a cool, barefaced lie. But already, so quickly, Granny believed her own statement.

The rector appeared, having left time for a lull.

"What's wrong?" he asked cautiously, genially.

"Oh, nothing!" drawled Yvette. "Lucille told Granny to shut up, when she was saying something. And Aunt Cissie drove her up to her room. *Tant de bruit pour une omelette!* Though Lucille *was* a bit over the mark, that time."

The old lady couldn't quite catch what Yvette said.

"Lucille really will have to learn to control her nerves," said the old woman. "The mirror fell down, and it worried me. I said so to Yvette, and she said something about superstitions and the people in the beastly house. I told her the people in the house were not depraved, if they happened to mind when a mirror was broken. And at that Lucille flew at me and told me to shut up. It really is disgraceful how these children give way to their nerves. I know it's nothing but nerves."

Aunt Cissie had come in during this speech. At first even she was dumb. Then it seemed to her, it was as Granny had said.

"I have forbidden her to come down until she comes to apologize to the Mater," she said.

"I doubt if she'll apologize," said the calm, queenly Yvette, holding her bare arms.

"And I don't want any apology," said the old lady. "It is merely nerves. I don't know what they'll come to, if they have nerves like that, at their age! She must take Vibrofat. I am sure Arthur would like his tea, Cissie."

Yvette swept her sewing together, to go upstairs. And again she trilled her tune, rather shrill and tuneless. She was trembling inwardly.

"More glad rags!" said her father to her, genially.

"More glad rags!" she reiterated sagely, as she sauntered upstairs, with her day dress over one arm. She wanted to console Lucille, and ask her how the blue stuff hung now.

At the first landing she stood as she nearly always did, to gaze through the window that looked to the road and the bridge. Like the Lady of Shalott, she seemed always to imagine that someone would come along singing *Tirra-lirra!* or something equally intelligent, by the river.

V

It was nearly tea-time. The snowdrops were out by the short drive going to the gate from the side of the house, and the gardener was pottering at the round, damp flower-beds, on the wet grass that sloped to the stream. Past the gate went the whitish muddy road, crossing the stone bridge almost immediately, and winding in a curve up to the steep, clustering, stony, smoking northern village, that perched over the grim stone mills which Yvette could see ahead down the narrow valley, their tall chimneys long and erect.

The rectory was on one side the Papple, in the rather steep valley, the village was beyond and above, further down, on the other side the swift stream. At the back of the rectory the hill went up steep, with a grove of dark, bare larches, through which the road disappeared. And immediately across stream from the rectory, facing the house, the river-bank rose steep and bushy, up to the sloping, dreary meadows, that sloped up again to dark hillsides of trees, with grey rock cropping out.

But from the end of the house, Yvette could only see the road curving round past the wall with its laurel hedge, down to the bridge, then up again round the shoulder to that first hard cluster of houses in Papplewick village, beyond the dry-stone walls of the steep fields.

She always expected *something* to come down the slant of the road from Papplewick, and she always lingered at the landing window. Often a cart came, or a motor-car, or a lorry with stone, or a labourer, or one of the servants. But

never anybody who sang *Tirra-lirra!* by the river. The tirra-lirra-ing days seem
to have gone by.

This day, however, round the corner on the white-grey road, between the grass
and the low stone walls, a roan horse came stepping bravely and briskly downhill,
driven by a man in a cap, perched on the front of his light cart. The man swayed
loosely to the swing of the cart, as the horse stepped downhill, in the silent
sombreness of the afternoon. At the back of the cart, long duster-brooms of reed
and feather stuck out, nodding on their stalks of cane.

Yvette stood close to the window, and put the casement-cloth curtains behind
her, clutching her bare upper arms with her hands.

At the foot of the slope the horse started into a brisk trot to the bridge. The
cart rattled on the stone bridge, the brooms bobbed and flustered, the driver sat
as if in a kind of dream, swinging along. It was like something seen in a sleep.

But as he crossed the end of the bridge, and was passing along the rectory
wall, he looked up at the grim stone house that seemed to have backed away
from the gate, under the hill. Yvette moved her hands quickly on her arms.
And as quickly, from under the peak of his cap, he had seen her, his swarthy
predative face was alert.

He pulled up suddenly at the white gate, still gazing upwards at the landing
window; while Yvette, always clasping her cold and mottled arms, still gazed
abstractedly down at him, from the window.

His head gave a little, quick jerk of signal, and he led his horse well aside, on
to the grass. Then, limber and alert, he turned back the tarpaulin of the cart,
fetched out various articles, pulled forth two or three of the long brooms of reed
or turkey-feathers, covered the cart, and turned towards the house, looking up
at Yvette as he opened the white gate.

She nodded to him, and flew to the bathroom to put on her dress, hoping she
had disguised her nod so that he wouldn't be sure she had nodded. Meanwhile she
heard the hoarse deep roaring of that old fool, Rover, punctuated by the yapping
of that young idiot, Trixie.

She and the housemaid arrived at the same moment at the sitting-room door.

"Was it the man selling brooms?" said Yvette to the maid. "All right!" and
she opened the door. "Aunt Cissie, there's a man selling brooms. Shall I go?"

"What sort of a man?" said Aunt Cissie, who was sitting at tea with the
rector and the Mater: the girls having been excluded for once from the meal.

"A man with a cart," said Yvette.

"A gipsy," said the maid.

Of course Aunt Cissie rose at once. She had to look at him.

The gipsy stood at the back door, under the steep dark bank where the larches
grew. The long brooms flourished from one hand, and from the other hung
various objects of shining copper and brass: a saucepan, a candlestick, plates
of beaten copper. The man himself was neat and dapper, almost rakish, in his
dark green cap and double-breasted green check coat. But his manner was subdued, very quiet: and at the same time proud, with a touch of condescension
and aloofness.

"Anything to-day, lady?" he said, looking at Aunt Cissie with dark, shrewd, searching eyes, but putting a very quiet tenderness into his voice.

Aunt Cissie saw how handsome he was, saw the flexible curve of his lips under the line of black moustache, and she was fluttered. The merest hint of roughness or aggression on the man's part would have made her shut the door contemptuously in his face. But he managed to insinuate such a subtle suggestion of submission into his male bearing, that she began to hesitate.

"The candlestick is lovely!" said Yvette. "Did you make it?"

And she looked up at the man with her naive, childlike eyes, that were as capable of double meanings as his own.

"Yes, lady!" He looked back into her eyes for a second, with that naked suggestion of desire which acted on her like a spell, and robbed her of her will. Her tender face seemed to go into a sleep.

"It's awfully nice!" she murmured vaguely.

Aunt Cissie began to bargain for the candlestick: which was a low, thick stem of copper, rising from a double bowl. With patient aloofness the man attended to her, without ever looking at Yvette, who leaned against the doorway and watched in a muse.

"How is your wife?" she asked him suddenly, when Aunt Cissie had gone indoors to show the candlestick to the rector, and ask him if he thought it was worth it.

The man looked fully at Yvette, and a scarcely discernible smile curled his lips. His eyes did not smile: the insinuation in them only hardened to a glare.

"She's all right. When are you coming that way again?" he murmured, in a low, caressive, intimate voice.

"Oh, I don't know," said Yvette vaguely.

"You come Fridays, when I'm there," he said.

Yvette gazed over his shoulder as if she had not heard him. Aunt Cissie returned, with the candlestick and the money to pay for it. Yvette turned nonchalant away, trilling one of her broken tunes, abandoning the whole affair with a certain rudeness.

Nevertheless, hiding this time at the landing window, she stood to watch the man go. What she wanted to know, was whether he really had any power over her. She did not intend him to see her this time.

She saw him go down to the gate, with his brooms and pans, and out to the cart. He carefully stowed away his pans and his brooms, and fixed down the tarpaulin over the cart. Then with a slow, effortless spring of his flexible loins, he was on the cart again, and touching the horse with the reins. The roan horse was away at once, the cart-wheels grinding uphill, and soon the man was gone, without looking round. Gone like a dream which was only a dream, yet which she could not shake off.

"No, he hasn't any power over me!" she said to herself: rather disappointed really, because she wanted somebody, or something, to have power over her.

She went up to reason with the pale and overwrought Lucille, scolding her for getting into a state over nothing.

"What does it *matter*," she expostulated, "if you told Granny to shut up! Why, everybody ought to be told to shut up, when they're being beastly. But she didn't mean it, you know. No, she didn't mean it. And she's quite sorry she said it. There's absolutely no reason to make a fuss. Come on, let's dress ourselves up and sail down to dinner like duchesses. Let's have our own back that way. Come on, Lucille!"

There was something strange and mazy, like having cobwebs over one's face, about Yvette's vague blitheness; her queer, misty side-stepping from an unpleasantness. It was cheering too. But it was like walking in one of those autumn mists, when gossamer strands blow over your face. You don't quite know where you are.

She succeeded, however, in persuading Lucille, and the girls got out their best party frocks: Lucille in green and silver, Yvette in a pale lilac colour with turquoise chenille threading. A little rouge and powder, and their best slippers, and the gardens of paradise began to blossom. Yvette hummed and looked at herself, and put on her most *dégagé* airs of one of the young marchionesses. She had an odd way of slanting her eyebrows and pursing her lips, and to all appearances detaching herself from every earthly consideration, and floating through the cloud of her own pearl-coloured reserves. It was amusing, and not quite convincing.

"Of course I am beautiful, Lucille," she said blandly. "And you're perfectly lovely, now you look a bit reproachful. Of course you're the most aristocratic of the two of us, with your nose! And now your eyes look reproachful, that adds an appealing look, and you're perfect, perfectly lovely. But I'm more *winning*, in a way. Don't you agree?" She turned with arch, complicated simplicity to Lucille.

She was truly simple in what she said. It was just what she thought. But it gave no hint of the very different *feeling* that also preoccupied her: the feeling that she had been looked upon, not from the outside, but from the inside, from her secret female self. She was dressing herself up and looking her most dazzling, just to counteract the effect that the gipsy had had on her, when he had looked at her, and seen none of her pretty face and her pretty ways, but just the dark, tremulous potent secret of her virginity.

The two girls started downstairs in state when the dinner-gong rang: but they waited till they heard the voices of the men. Then they sailed down and into the sitting-room, Yvette preening herself in her vague, debonair way, always a little bit absent; and Lucille shy, ready to burst into tears.

"My goodness gracious!" exclaimed Aunt Cissie, who was still wearing her dark-brown knitted sports coat. "What an apparition! Wherever do you think you're going?"

"We're dining with the family," said Yvette naively, "and we've put on our best gewgaws in honour of the occasion."

The rector laughed aloud, and Uncle Fred said:

"The family feels itself highly honoured."

Both the elderly men were quite gallant, which was what Yvette wanted.

"Come and let me feel your dresses, do!" said Granny. "Are they your best? It *is* a shame I can't see them."

"To-night, Mater," said Uncle Fred, "we shall have to take the young ladies in to dinner, and live up to the honour. Will you go with Cissie?"

"I certainly will," said Granny. "Youth and beauty must come first."

"Well, to-night, Mater!" said the rector, pleased.

And he offered his arm to Lucille, while Uncle Fred escorted Yvette.

But it was a draggled, dull meal, all the same. Lucille tried to be bright and sociable, and Yvette really was most amiable, in her vague, cobwebby way. Dimly, at the back of her mind, she was thinking: Why are we all only like mortal pieces of furniture? Why is nothing *important?*

That was her constant refrain to herself: Why is nothing important? Whether she was in church, or at a party of young people, or dancing in the hotel in the city, the same little bubble of a question rose repeatedly on her consciousness: Why is nothing important?

There were plenty of young men to make love to her: even devotedly. But with impatience she had to shake them off. Why were they so unimportant?— so irritating!

She never even thought of the gipsy. He was a perfectly negligible incident. Yet the approach of Friday loomed strangely significant. "What are we doing on Friday?" she said to Lucille. To which Lucille replied that they were doing nothing. And Yvette was vexed.

Friday came, and in spite of herself she thought all day of the quarry off the road up high Bonsall Head. She wanted to be there. That was all she was conscious of. She wanted to be there. She had not even a dawning idea of going there. Besides, it was raining again. But as she sewed the blue dress, finishing it for the party up at Lambley Close to-morrow, she just felt that her soul was up there, at the quarry, among the caravans, with the gipsies. Like one lost, or whose soul was stolen, she was not present in her body, the shell of her body. Her intrinsic body was away at the quarry, among the caravans.

The next day, at the party, she had no idea that she was being sweet to Leo. She had no idea that she was snatching him away from the tortured Ella Framley. Not until, when she was eating her pistachio ice, he said to her:

"Why don't you and me get engaged, Yvette? I'm absolutely sure it's the right thing for us both."

Leo was a bit common, but good-natured and well-off. Yvette quite liked him. But engaged! How perfectly silly! She felt like offering him a set of her silk underwear, to get engaged to.

"But I thought it was Ella!" she said, in wonder.

"Well! It might ha' been, but for you. It's your doings, you know! Ever since those gipsies told your fortune, I felt it was me or nobody, for you, and you or nobody, for me."

"Really!" said Yvette, simply lost in amazement. "Really!"

"Didn't you feel a bit the same?" he asked.

"Really!" Yvette kept on gasping softly, like a fish.

"You felt a bit the same, didn't you?" he said.

"What? About what?" she asked, coming to.

"About me, as I feel about you."

"Why? What? Getting engaged, you mean? I? No! Why how *could* I? I could never have dreamed of such an impossible thing."

She spoke with her usual heedless candour, utterly unoccupied with his feelings.

"What was to prevent you?" he said, a bit nettled. "I thought you did."

"Did you *really now?*" she breathed in amazement, with that soft, virgin, heedless candour which made her her admirers and her enemies.

She was so completely amazed, there was nothing for him to do but twiddle his thumbs in annoyance.

The music began, and he looked at her.

"No! I won't dance any more," she said, drawing herself up and gazing away rather loftily over the assembly, as if he did not exist. There was a touch of puzzled wonder on her brow, and her soft, dim virgin face did indeed suggest the snowdrop of her father's pathetic imagery.

"But of course *you* will dance," she said, turning to him with young condescension. "Do ask somebody to have this with you."

He rose, angry, and went down the room.

She remained soft and remote in her amazement. Expect Leo to propose to her! She might as well have expected old Rover the Newfoundland dog to propose to her. Get engaged, to any man on earth? No, good heavens, nothing more ridiculous could be imagined!

It was then, in a fleeting side-thought, that she realized that the gipsy existed. Instantly, she was indignant. Him, of all things! Him! Never!

"Now why?" she asked herself, again in hushed amazement. "Why? It's *absolutely* impossible: absolutely! So why is it?"

This was a nut to crack. She looked at the young men dancing, elbows out, hips prominent, waists elegantly in. They gave her no clue to her problem. Yet she did particularly dislike the forced elegance of the waists and the prominent hips, over which the well-tailored coats hung with such effeminate discretion.

"There is something about me which they don't see and never would see," she said angrily to herself. And at the same time, she was relieved that they didn't and couldn't. It made life so very much simpler.

And again, since she was one of the people who are conscious in visual images, she saw the dark-green jersey rolled on the black trousers of the gipsy, his fine, quick hips, alert as eyes. They were elegant. The elegance of these dancers seemed so stuffed, hips merely wadded with flesh. Leo the same, thinking himself such a fine dancer, and a fine figure of a fellow!

Then she saw the gipsy's face; the straight nose, the slender mobile lips, and the level, significant stare of the black eyes, which seemed to shoot her in some vital, undiscovered place, unerring.

She drew herself up angrily. How dared he look at her like that? So she gazed glaringly at the insipid beaux on the dancing floor. And she despised them. Just as the raggle-taggle gipsy women despise men who are not gipsies, despise their dog-like walk down the streets, she found herself despising this crowd. Where among them was the subtle, lonely, insinuating challenge that could reach her?

She did not want to mate with a housedog.

Her sensitive nose turned up, her soft brown hair fell like a soft sheath round her tender, flower-like face, as she sat musing. She seemed so virginal. At the same time, there was a touch of the tall young virgin *witch* about her, that made the housedog men shy off. She might metamorphose into something uncanny before you knew where you were.

This made her lonely, in spite of all the courting. Perhaps the courting only made her lonelier.

Leo, who was a sort of mastiff among the housedogs, returned after his dance, with fresh cheery-o! courage.

"You've had a little think about it, haven't you?" he said, sitting down beside her: a comfortable, well-nourished, determined sort of fellow. She did not know why it irritated her so unreasonably, when he hitched up his trousers at the knee, over his good-sized but not very distinguished legs, and lowered himself assuredly on to a chair.

"Have I?" she said vaguely. "About what?"

"You know what about," he said. "Did you make up your mind?"

"Make up my mind about what?" she asked, innocently.

In her upper consciousness, she truly had forgotten.

"Oh!" said Leo, settling his trousers again. "About me and you getting engaged, you know." He was almost as off-hand as she.

"Oh, that's *absolutely* impossible," she said, with mild amiability, as if it were some stray question among the rest. "Why, I never even thought of it again. Oh, don't talk about that sort of nonsense! That sort of thing is *absolutely* impossible," she reiterated like a child.

"That sort of thing is, is it?" he said, with an odd smile at her calm, distant assertion. "Well, what sort of thing *is* possible, then? You don't want to die an old maid, do you?"

"Oh, I don't mind," she said absently.

"I do," he said.

She turned round and looked at him in wonder.

"Why?" she said. "Why should you mind if I was an old maid?"

"Every reason in the world," he said, looking up at her with a bold, meaningful smile, that wanted to make its meaning blatant, if not patent.

But instead of penetrating into some deep, secret place, and shooting her there, Leo's bold and patent smile only hit her on the outside of the body, like a tennis ball, and caused the same kind of sudden irritated reaction.

"I think this sort of thing is awfully silly," she said, with minx-like spite. "Why, you're practically engaged to—to——" she pulled herself up in time—"probably half a dozen other girls. I'm not flattered by what you've said. I should hate it if anybody knew! Hate it! I shan't breathe a word of it, and I hope you'll have the sense not to. There's Ella!"

And keeping her face averted from him, she sailed away like a tall, soft flower, to join poor Ella Framley.

Leo flapped his white gloves.

"Catty little bitch!" he said to himself. But he was of the mastiff type, he rather liked the kitten to fly in his face. He began definitely to single her out.

VI

The next week it poured again with rain. And this irritated Yvette with strange anger. She had intended it should be fine. Especially she insisted it should be fine towards the week-end. Why, she did not ask herself.

Thursday, the half-holiday, came with a hard frost, and sun. Leo arrived with his car, the usual bunch. Yvette disagreeably and unaccountably refused to go.

"No thanks, I don't feel like it," she said.

She rather enjoyed being Mary-Mary-quite-contrary.

Then she went for a walk by herself, up the frozen hills, to the Black Rocks.

The next day also came sunny and frosty. It was February, but in the north country the ground did not thaw in the sun. Yvette announced that she was going for a ride on her bicycle, and taking her lunch as she might not be back till afternoon.

She set off, not hurrying. In spite of the frost, the sun had a touch of spring. In the park, the deer were standing in the distance, in the sunlight, to be warm. One doe, white-spotted, walked slowly across the motionless landscape.

Cycling, Yvette found it difficult to keep her hands warm, even when bodily she was quite hot. Only when she had to walk up the long hill, to the top, and there was no wind.

The upland was very bare and clear, like another world. She had climbed on to another level. She cycled slowly, a little afraid of taking the wrong lane, in the vast maze of stone fences. As she passed along the lane she thought was the right one, she heard a faint tapping noise, with a slight metallic resonance.

The gipsy man was seated on the ground with his back to the cart-shaft, hammering a copper bowl. He was in the sun, bare-headed, but wearing his green jersey. Three small children were moving quietly round, playing in the horse's shelter: the horse and cart were gone. An old woman, bent, with a kerchief round her head, was cooking over a fire of sticks. The only sound was the rapid, ringing tap-tap-tap! of the small hammer on the dull copper.

The man looked up at once, as Yvette stepped from her bicycle, but he did not move, though he ceased hammering. A delicated barely discernible smile of triumph was on his face. The old woman looked round, keenly, from under her dirty grey hair. The man spoke a half-audible word to her, and she turned again to her fire. He looked up at Yvette.

"How are you all getting on?" she asked politely.

"All right, eh! You sit down a minute?" He turned as he sat, and pulled a stool from under the caravan for Yvette. Then as she wheeled her bicycle to the side of the quarry, he started hammering again, with that bird-like, rapid light stroke.

Yvette went to the fire to warm her hands.

"Is this the dinner cooking?" she asked childishly, of the old gipsy, as she spread her long tender hands, mottled red with the cold, to the embers.

"Dinner, yes!" said the old woman. "For him! And for the children."

She pointed with the long fork at the three black-eyed, staring children, who were staring at her from under their black fringes. But they were clean. Only the old woman was not clean. The quarry itself they had kept perfectly clean.

Yvette crouched in silence, warming her hands. The man rapidly hammered away with intervals of silence. The old hag slowly climbed the steps to the third, oldest caravan. The children began to play again, like little wild animals, quiet and busy.

"Are they your children?" asked Yvette, rising from the fire and turning to the man.

He looked her in the eyes, and nodded.

"But where's your wife?"

"She's gone out with the basket. They've all gone out, cart and all, selling things. I don't go selling things. I make them, but I don't go selling them. Not often. I don't often."

"You make all the copper and brass things?" she said.

He nodded, and again offered her the stool. She sat down.

"You said you'd be here on Fridays," she said. "So I came this way, as it was so fine."

"Very fine day!" said the gipsy, looking at her cheek, that was still a bit blanched by the cold, and the soft hair over her reddened ear, and the long, still mottled hands on her knee.

"You get cold, riding a bicycle?" he asked.

"My hands!" she said, clasping them nervously.

"You didn't wear gloves?"

"I did, but they weren't much good."

"Cold comes through," he said.

"Yes!" she replied.

The old woman came slowly, grotesquely down the steps of the caravan, with some enamel plates.

"The dinner cooked, eh?" he called softly.

The old woman muttered something, as she spread the plates near the fire. Two pots hung from a long iron horizontal bar, over the embers of the fire. A little pan seethed on a small iron tripod. In the sunshine, heat and vapour wavered together.

He put down his tools and the pot, and rose from the ground.

"You eat something along of us?" he asked Yvette, not looking at her.

"Oh, I brought my lunch," said Yvette.

"You eat some stew?" he said. And again he called quietly, secretly to the old woman, who muttered in answer, as she slid the iron pot towards the end of the bar.

Some beans, and some mutton in it," he said.

"Oh thanks awfully!" said Yvette. Then, suddenly taking courage, added: "Well yes, just a very little, if I may."

She went across to untie her lunch from her bicycle, and he went up the steps to his own caravan. After a minute, he emerged, wiping his hands on a towel.

"You want to come up and wash your hands?" he said.

"No, I think not," she said. "They are clean."

He threw away his wash-water, and set off down the road with a high brass jug, to fetch clean water from the spring that trickled into a small pool, taking a cup to dip it with.

When he returned, he set the jug and the cup by the fire, and fetched himself a short log, to sit on. The children sat on the floor by the fire, in a cluster, eating beans and bits of meat with spoon or fingers. The man on the log ate in silence, absorbedly. The woman made coffee in the black pot on the tripod, hobbling upstairs for the cups. There was silence in the camp. Yvette sat on her stool, having taken off her hat and shaken her hair in the sun.

"How many children have you?" Yvette asked suddenly.

"Say five," he replied slowly, as he looked up into her eyes.

And again the bird of her heart sank down and seemed to die. Vaguely, as in a dream, she received from him the cup of coffee. She was aware only of his silent figure, sitting like a shadow there on the log, with an enamel cup in his hand, drinking his coffee in silence. Her will had departed from her limbs, he had power over her: his shadow was on her.

And he, as he blew his hot coffee, was aware of one thing only, the mysterious fruit of her virginity, her perfect tenderness in the body.

At length he put down his coffee-cup by the fire, then looked round at her. Her hair fell across her face, as she tried to sip from the hot cup. On her face was that tender look of sleep, which a nodding flower has when it is full out. Like a mysterious early flower, she was full out, like a snowdrop which spreads its three white wings in a flight into the waking sleep of its brief blossoming. The waking sleep of her full-opened virginity, entranced like a snowdrop in the sunshine, was upon her.

The gipsy, supremely aware of her, waited for her like the substance of shadow, as shadow waits and is there.

At length his voice said, without breaking the spell:

"You want to go in my caravan now, and wash your hands?"

The childlike, sleep-waking eyes of her moment of perfect virginity looked into his, unseeing. She was only aware of the dark strange effluence of him bathing her limbs, washing her at last purely will-less. She was aware of *him*, as a dark, complete power.

"I think I might," she said.

He rose silently, then turned to speak, in a low command, to the old woman. And then again he looked at Yvette, and putting his power over her, so that she had no burden of herself, or of action.

"Come!" he said.

She followed simply, followed the silent, secret, overpowering motion of his body in front of her. It cost her nothing. She was gone in his will.

He was at the top of the steps, and she at the foot, when she become aware of an intruding sound. She stood still, at the foot of the steps. A motor-car was coming. He stood at the top of the steps, looking round strangely. The old woman harshly called something, as with rapidly increasing sound, a car rushed near. It was passing.

Then they heard the cry of a woman's voice, and the brakes on the car. It had pulled up, just beyond the quarry.

The gipsy came down the steps, having closed the door of the caravan.

"You want to put your hat on," he said to her.

Obediently she went to the stool by the fire, and took up her hat. He sat down by the cart-wheel, darkly, and took up his tools. The rapid tap-tap-tap of his hammer, rapid and angry now like the sound of a tiny machine-gun, broke out just as the voice of the woman was heard crying:

"May we warm our hands at the camp fire?"

She advanced, dressed in a sleek but bulky coat of sable fur. A man followed, in a blue great-coat; pulling off his fur gloves and pulling out a pipe.

"It looked so tempting," said the woman in the coat of many dead little animals, smiling a broad, half-condescending, half-hesitant simper, around the company.

No one said a word.

She advanced to the fire, shuddering a little inside her coat, with the cold. They had been driving in an open car.

She was a very small woman, with a rather large nose: probably a Jewess. Tiny almost as a child, in that sable coat she looked much more bulky than she should, and her wide, rather resentful brown eyes of a spoilt Jewess gazed oddly out of her expensive get-up.

She crouched over the low fire, spreading her little hands, on which diamonds and emeralds glittered.

"Ugh!" she shuddered. "Of course we ought not to have come in an open car! But my husband won't even let me say I'm cold!" She looked round at him with her large, childish, reproachful eyes, that had still the canny shrewdness of a bourgeois Jewess: a rich one, probably.

Apparently she was in love, in a Jewess's curious way, with the big, blond man. He looked back at her with his abstracted blue eyes, that seemed to have no lashes, and a small smile creased his smooth, curiously naked cheeks. The smile didn't mean anything at all.

He was a man one connects instantly with winter sports, ski-ing and skating. Athletic, unconnected with life, he slowly filled his pipe, pressing in the tobacco with long, powerful, reddened finger.

The Jewess looked at him to see if she got any response from him. Nothing at all, but that odd, blank smile. She turned again to the fire, tilting her eyebrows and looking at her small, white, spread hands.

He slipped off his heavily-lined coat, and appeared in one of the handsome, sharp-patterned knitted jerseys, in yellow and grey and black, over well-cut trousers, rather wide. Yes, they were both expensive! And he had a magnificent figure, an athletic, prominent chest. Like an experienced camper, he began building the fire together, quietly: like a soldier on campaign.

"D'you think they'd mind if we put some fir-cones on, to make a blaze?" he asked of Yvette, with a silent glance at the hammering gipsy.

"Love it, I should think," said Yvette, in a daze, as the spell of the gipsy slowly left her, feeling stranded and blank.

The man went to the car, and returned with a little sack of cones, from which he drew a handful.

"Mind if we make a blaze?" he called to the gipsy.

"Eh?"

"Mind if we make a blaze with a few cones!"

"You go ahead!" said the gipsy.

The man began placing the cones lightly, carefully on the red embers. And soon, one by one, they caught fire, and burned like roses of flame, with a sweet scent.

"Ah, lovely, lovely!" cried the little Jewess, looking up at her man again. He looked down at her quite kindly, like the sun on ice. "Don't you love fire? Oh, I love it!" the little Jewess cried to Yvette, across the hammering.

The hammering annoyed her. She looked round with a slight frown on her fine little brows, as if she would bid the man stop. Yvette looked round too. The gipsy was bent over his copper bowl, legs apart, head down, lithe arm lifted. Already he seemed so far from her.

The man who accompanied the little Jewess strolled over to the gipsy, and stood in silence looking down on him, holding his pipe to his mouth. Now they were two men, like two strange male dogs, having to sniff one another.

"We're on our honeymoon," said the little Jewess, with an arch, resentful look at Yvette. She spoke in a rather high, defiant voice, like some bird, a jay, or a rook, calling.

"Are you really?" said Yvette.

"Yes! Before we're married! Have you heard of Simon Fawcett?"—she named a wealthy and well-known engineer of the north country. "Well, I'm Mrs. Fawcett, and he's just divorcing me!" She looked at Yvette with curious defiance and wistfulness.

"Are you really!" said Yvette.

She understood now the look of resentment and defiance in the little Jewess's big, childlike brown eyes. She was an honest little thing, but perhaps her honesty was *too* rational. Perhaps it partly explained the notorious unscrupulousness of the well-known Simon Fawcett.

"Yes! As soon as we get the divorce, I'm going to marry Major Eastwood."

Her cards were now all on the table. She was not going to deceive anybody.

Behind her, the two men were talking briefly. She glanced round, and fixed the gipsy with her big brown eyes.

He was looking up, as if shyly, at the big fellow in the sparkling jersey, who was standing pipe in mouth, man to man, looking down.

"With the horses back of Arras," said the gipsy, in a low voice.

They were talking war. The gipsy had served with the artillery teams, in the Major's own regiment.

"*Ein schöner Mensch!*" said the Jewess. "A handsome man, eh?"

For her, too, the gipsy was one of the common men, the Tommies.

"Quite handsome!" said Yvette.

"You are cycling?" asked the Jewess in a tone of surprise.

"Yes! Down to Papplewick. My father is rector of Papplewick: Mr. Saywell!"

"Oh!" said the Jewess. "I know! A clever writer! Very clever! I have read him."

The fir-cones were all consumed already, the fire was a tall pile now of crumbling, shattering fire-roses. The sky was clouding over for afternoon. Perhaps towards evening it would snow.

The Major came back, and slung himself into his coat.

"I thought I remembered his face!" he said. "One of our grooms, A1 man with horses."

"Look!" cried the Jewess to Yvette. "Why don't you let us motor you down to Normanton. We live in Scoresby. We can tie the bicycle on behind."

"I think I will," said Yvette.

"Come!" called the Jewess to the peeping children, as the blond man wheeled away the bicycle. "Come! Come here!" and taking out her little purse, she held out a shilling. "Come!" she cried. "Come and take it!"

The gipsy had laid down his work, and gone into his caravan. The old woman called hoarsely to the children, from her enclosure. The two elder children came stealing forward. The Jewess gave them the two bits of silver, a shilling and a florin, which she had in her purse, and again the hoarse voice of the unseen old woman was heard.

The gipsy descended from his caravan and strolled to the fire. The Jewess searched his face with the peculiar bourgeois boldness of her race.

"You were in the war, in Major Eastwood's regiment?" she said.

"Yes, lady!"

"Imagine you both being here now! It's going to snow." She looked up at the sky.

"Later on," said the man, looking at the sky.

He too had gone inaccessible. His race was very old, in its peculiar battle with established society, and had no conception of winning. Only now and then it could score.

But since the war, even the old sporting chance of scoring now and then, was pretty well quenched. There was no question of yielding. The gipsy's eyes still had their bold look: but it was hardened and directed far away, the touch of insolent intimacy was gone. He had been through the war.

He looked at Yvette.

"You're going back in the motor-car?" he said.

"Yes!" she replied, with a rather mincing mannerism. "The weather is so treacherous!"

"Treacherous weather!" he repeated, looking at the sky.

She could not tell in the least what his feelings were. In truth, she wasn't very much interested. She was rather fascinated, now, by the little Jewess, mother of two children, who was taking her wealth away from the well-known engineer and transferring it to the penniless, sporting young Major Eastwood, who must be five or six years younger than she. Rather intriguing!

The blond man returned.

"A cigarette, Charles!" cried the little Jewess, plaintively.

He took out his case, slowly, with his slow, athletic movement. Something sensitive in him made him slow, cautious, as if he had hurt himself against people. He gave a cigarette to his wife, then one to Yvette, then offered the case, quite simply, to the gipsy. The gipsy took one.

"Thank you, sir!"

And he went quietly to the fire, and stooping, lit it at the red embers. Both women watched him.

"Well, good-bye!" said the Jewess, with her old bourgeois free-masonry. "Thank you for the warm fire."

"Fire is everybody's," said the gipsy.

The young child came toddling to him.

"Good-bye!" said Yvette. "I hope it won't snow for you."

"We don't mind a bit of snow," said the gipsy.

"Don't you?" said Yvette. "I should have thought you would!"

"No!" said the gipsy.

She flung her scarf royally over her shoulder, and followed the fur coat of the Jewess, which seemed to walk on little legs of its own.

VII

Yvette was rather thrilled by the Eastwoods, as she called them. The little Jewess had only to wait three months now, for the final decree. She had boldly rented a small summer cottage, by the moors up at Scoresby, not far from the hills. Now it was dead winter, and she and the Major lived in comparative isolation, without any maid-servant. He had already resigned his commission in the regular army, and called himself Mr. Eastwood. In fact, they were already Mr. and Mrs. Eastwood, to the common world.

The little Jewess was thirty-six, and her two children were both over twelve years of age. The husband had agreed that she should have the custody, as soon as she was married to Eastwood.

So there they were, this queer couple, the tiny, finely formed little Jewess with her big, resentful, reproachful eyes, and her mop of carefully barbered black, curly hair, an elegant little thing in her way; and the big, pale-eyed young man, powerful and wintry, the remnant, surely, of some old uncanny Danish stock:

living together in a small modern house near the moors and the hills, and doing their own housework.

It was a funny household. The cottage was hired furnished, but the little Jewess had brought along her dearest pieces of furniture. She had an odd little taste for the rococo, strange curving cupboards inlaid with mother-of-pearl, tortoise-shell, ebony, heaven knows what; strange tall flamboyant chairs from Italy, with sea-green brocade: astonishing saints with wind-blown, richly coloured carven garments and pink faces: shelves of weird old Saxe and Capo di Monte figurines: and finally, a strange assortment of astonishing pictures painted on the back of glass, done probably in the early years of the nineteenth century, or in the late eighteenth.

In this crowded and extraordinary interior she received Yvette, when the latter made a stolen visit. A whole system of stoves had been installed into the cottage, every corner was warm, almost hot. And there was the tiny rococo figurine of the Jewess herself, in a perfect little frock, and an apron, putting slices of ham on the dish, while the great snow-bird of a major, in a white sweater and grey trousers, cut bread, mixed mustard, prepared coffee, and did all the rest. He had even made the dish of jugged hare which followed the cold meats and caviare.

The silver and the china were really valuable, part of the bride's trousseau. The Major drank beer from a silver mug, the little Jewess and Yvette had champagne in lovely glasses, the Major brought in coffee. They talked away. The little Jewess had a burning indignation against her first husband. She was intensely moral, so moral, that she was a divorcée. The Major too, strange wintry bird, so powerful, handsome, too, in his way, but pale round the eyes as if he had no eyelashes, like a bird, he too had a curious indignation against life, because of the false morality. That powerful, athletic chest hid a strange, snowy sort of anger. And his tenderness for the little Jewess was based on his sense of outraged justice, the abstract morality of the north blowing him, like a strange wind, into isolation.

As the afternoon drew on, they went to the kitchen, the Major pushed back his sleeves, showing his powerful athletic white arms, and carefully, deftly washed the dishes, while the women wiped. It was not for nothing his muscles were trained. Then he went round attending to the stoves of the small house, which only needed a moment or two of care each day. And after this, he brought out a small, closed car and drove Yvette home, in the rain, depositing her at the back gate, a little wicket among the larches, through which the earthen steps sloped downwards to the house.

She was really amazed by this couple.

"Really, Lucille!" she said. "I do meet the most extraordinary people!" And she gave a detailed description.

"I think they sound rather nice!" said Lucille. "I like the Major doing the housework, and looking so frightfully Bond-streety with it all. I should think *when they're married,* it would be rather fun knowing them."

"Yes!" said Yvette vaguely. "Yes! Yes, it would!"

The very strangeness of the connection between the tiny Jewess and that pale-eyed, athletic young officer made her think again of her gipsy, who had been utterly absent from her consciousness, but who now returned with sudden painful force.

"What is it, Lucille," she asked, "that brings people together? People like the Eastwoods, for instance? And Daddy and Mamma, so frightfully unsuitable? And that gipsy woman who told my fortune, like a great horse, and the gipsy man, so fine and delicately cut? What is it?"

"I suppose it's sex, whatever that is," said Lucille.

"Yes, what is it? It's not really anything *common,* like common sensuality, you know, Lucille. It really isn't."

"No, I suppose not," said Lucille. "Anyhow, I suppose it needn't be."

"Because, you see, the *common* fellows, you know, who make a girl feel *low*: nobody cares much about them. Nobody feels any connection with them. Yet they're supposed to be the sexual sort."

"I suppose," said Lucille, "there's the low sort of sex, and there's the other sort, that isn't low. It's frightfully complicated, really! I *loathe* common fellows. And I never feel anything *sexual"*—she laid a rather disgusted stress on the word —"for fellows who aren't common. Perhaps I haven't got any sex."

"That's just it!" said Yvette. "Perhaps neither of us has. Perhaps we haven't really *got* any sex, to connect us with men."

"How horrible it sounds: *connect us with men!"* cried Lucille, with revulsion. "Wouldn't you hate to be connected with men that way? Oh I thing it's an awful pity there has to *be* sex! It would be so much better if we could still be men and women, without that sort of thing."

Yvette pondered. Far in the background was the image of the gipsy as he had looked round at her, when she had said: "The weather is so treacherous." She felt rather like Peter when the cock crew, as she denied him. Or rather, she did not deny the gipsy; she didn't care about his part in the show, anyhow. It was some hidden part of herself which she denied: that part which mysteriously and unconfessedly responded to him. And it was a strange, lustrous black cock which crew in mockery of her.

"Yes!" she said vaguely. "Yes! Sex is an awful bore, you know, Lucille. When you haven't got it, you feel you *ought* to have it, somehow. And when you've got it—or *if* you have it—" she lifted her head and wrinkled her nose disdainfully —"you hate it."

"Oh, I don't know!" cried Lucille. "I think I should *like* to be awfully in love with a man."

"You think so!" said Yvette, again wrinkling her nose. "But if you were you wouldn't."

"How do you know?" asked Lucille.

"Well, I don't really," said Yvette. "But I think so! Yes, I think so!"

"Oh, it's very likely!" said Lucille disgustedly. "And anyhow one would be sure to get out of love again, and it would be merely disgusting."

"Yes," said Yvette. "It's a problem." She hummed a little tune.

"Oh, hang it all, it's not a problem for us two yet. We're neither of us really in love, and we probably never shall be, so the problem is settled that way."

"I'm not so sure!" said Yvette sagely. "I'm not so sure. I believe, one day, I shall fall *awfully* in love."

"Probably you never will," said Lucille brutally. "That's what most old maids are thinking all the time."

Yvette looked at her sister from pensive but apparently insouciant eyes.

"Is it?" she said. "Do you really think so, Lucille? How perfectly awful for them, poor things! Why ever do they *care?*"

"Why do they?" said Lucille. "Perhaps they don't really—Probably it's all because people say: *Poor old girl, she couldn't catch a man.*"

"I suppose it is!" said Yvette. "They get to mind the beastly things people always do say about old maids. What a shame!"

"Anyhow we have a good time, and we do have lots of boys who make a fuss of us," said Lucille.

"Yes!" said Yvette. "Yes! But I couldn't possibly marry any of them."

"Neither could I," said Lucille. "But why should we? Why should we bother about marrying, when we have a perfectly good time with the boys, who are awfully good sorts, and you must say, Yvette, awfully sporting and *decent* to us."

"Oh, they are!" said Yvette absently.

"I think it's time to think of marrying somebody," said Lucille, "when you feel you're *not* having a good time any more. Then marry, and just settle down."

"Quite!" said Yvette.

But now, under all her bland, soft amiability, she was annoyed with Lucille. Suddenly she wanted to turn her back on Lucille.

Besides, look at the shadows under poor Lucille's eyes, and the wistfulness in the beautiful eyes themselves. Oh, if some awfully nice, kind, protective sort of man would but marry her! And if the sporting Lucille would let him!

Yvette did not tell the rector, nor Granny, about the Eastwoods. It would only have started a lot of talk which she detested. The rector wouldn't have minded, for himself, privately. But he too knew the necessity of keeping as clear as possible from that poisonous, many-headed serpent, the tongue of the people.

"But I don't *want* you to come if your father doesn't know," cried the little Jewess.

"I suppose I'll have to tell him," said Yvette. "I'm sure he doesn't mind, really. But if he knew, he'd have to, I suppose."

The young officer looked at her with an odd amusement, bird-like and un-emotional, in his keen eyes. He too was by way of falling in love with Yvette. It was her peculiar virgin tenderness, and her straying, absent-minded detachment from things, which attracted him.

She was aware of what was happening, and she rather preened herself. East-wood piqued her fancy. Such a smart young officer, awfully good class, so calm and amazing with a motor-car, and quite a champion swimmer, it was intriguing to see him quietly, calmly washing dishes, smoking his pipe, doing his job so alert and skilful. Or, with the same interested care with which he made his investigation into the mysterious inside of an automobile, concocting jugged hare in the cottage kitchen. Then going out in the icy weather and cleaning his car till it looked like a live thing, like a cat when she has licked herself. Then coming in to talk so unassumingly and responsively, if briefly, with the little Jewess. And apparently, never bored. Sitting at the window with his pipe in bad weather, silent for hours, abstracted, musing yet with his athletic body alert in its stillness.

Yvette did not flirt with him. But she *did* like him.

"But what about your future?" she asked him.

"What about it?" he said, taking his pipe from his mouth, the unemotional point of a smile in his bird's eyes.

"A career! Doesn't every man have to carve out a career?—like some huge goose with gravy?" She gazed with odd naïveté into his eyes.

"I'm perfectly all right to-day, and I shall be all right to-morrow," he said, with a cold, decided look. "Why shouldn't my future be continuous to-days and to-morrows?"

He looked at her with unmoved searching.

"Quite!" she said. "I hate jobs, and all that side of life." But she was thinking of the Jewess's money.

To which he did not answer. His anger was of the soft, snowy sort, which comfortably muffles the soul.

They had come to the point of talking philosophically together. The little Jewess looked a bit wan. She was curiously naive, and not possessive in her attitude to the man. Nor was she at all catty with Yvette. Only rather wan, and dumb.

Yvette, on a sudden impulse, thought she had better clear herself.

"I think life's *awfully* difficult," she said.

"Life is!" cried the Jewess.

"What's so beastly, is that one is supposed to *fall in love,* and get married!" said Yvette, curling up her nose.

"Don't you *want* to fall in love and get married?" cried the Jewess, with great glaring eyes of astounded reproach.

"No, not particularly!" said Yvette. "Especially as one feels there's nothing else to do. It's an awful chicken-coop one has to run into."

"But you don't know what love is!" cried the Jewess.

"No!" said Yvette. "Do you?"

"I!" bawled the tiny Jewess. "I! My goodness, don't I!" She looked with reflective gloom at Eastwood, who was smoking his pipe, the dimples of his disconnected amusement showing on his smooth, scrupulous face. He had a very fine, smooth skin, which yet did not suffer from the weather, so that his face looked naked as a baby's. But it was not a round face: it was characteristic enough, and took queer ironical dimples, like a mask which is comic but frozen.

"Do you mean to say you don't know what love is?" insisted the Jewess.

"No!" said Yvette, with insouciant candour. "I don't believe I do! Is it awful of me, at my age?"

"Is there never any man that makes you feel quite, quite different?" said the

Jewess, with another big-eyed look at Eastwood. He smoked, utterly unimplicated.

"I don't thing there is," said Yvette. "Unless—yes!—unless it is that gipsy"—she had put her head pensively sideways.

"Which gipsy?" bawled the little Jewess.

"The one who was a Tommy and looked after horses in Major Eastwood's regiment in the war," said Yvette coolly.

The little Jewess gazed at Yvette with great eyes of stupor.

"You're not in love with that *gipsy!*" she said.

"Well!" said Yvette. "I don't know. He's the only one that makes me feel—different! He really is!"

"But how? How? Has he ever *said* anything to you?"

"No! No!"

"Then how? What has he done?"

"Oh, just looked at me!"

"How?"

"Well, you see, I don't know. But different! Yes, different! Different, quite different from the way any man ever looked at me."

"But *how* did he look at you?" insisted the Jewess.

"Why—as if he really, but *really, desired* me," said Yvette, her meditative face looking like the bud of a flower.

"What a vile fellow! What *right* had he to look at you like that?" cried the indignant Jewess.

"A cat may look at a king," calmly interposed the Major, and now his face had the smiles of a cat's face.

"You think he oughtn't to?" asked Yvette, turning to him.

"Certainly not! A gipsy fellow, with half a dozen dirty women trailing after him! Certainly not!" cried the tiny Jewess.

"I wondered!" said Yvette. "Because it *was* rather wonderful, really! And it *was* something quite different in my life."

"I think," said the Major, taking his pipe from his mouth, "that desire is the most wonderful thing in life. Anybody who can really feel it, is a king, and I envy nobody else!" He put back his pipe.

The Jewess looked at him stupefied.

"But, Charles!" she cried. "Every common low man in Halifax feels nothing else!"

He again took his pipe from his mouth.

"That's merely appetite," he said.

And he put back his pipe.

"You think the gipsy is the real thing?" Yvette asked him.

He lifted his shoulders.

"It's not for me to say," he replied. "If I were you, I should know, I shouldn't be asking other people."

"Yes—but——" Yvette trailed out.

"Charles! You're wrong! How *could* it be the real thing! As if she could possibly marry him and go round in a caravan!"

"I didn't say marry him," said Charles.

"Or a love affair! Why, it's monstrous! What would she think of herself! That's not love! That's—that's prostitution!"

Charles smoked for some moments.

"That gipsy was the best man we had, with horses. Nearly died of pneumonia. I thought he *was* dead. He's a resurrected man to me. I'm a resurrected man myself, as far as that goes." He looked at Yvette. "I was buried for twenty hours under snow," he said. "And not much the worse for it, when they dug me out."

There was a frozen pause in the conversation.

"Life's awful!" said Yvette.

"They dug me out by accident," he said.

"Oh!——" Yvette trailed slowly. "It might be destiny, you know."

To which he did not answer.

VIII

The rector heard about Yvette's intimacy with the Eastwoods, and she was somewhat startled by the result. She had thought he wouldn't care. Verbally, in his would-be humorous fashion, he was so entirely unconventional, such a frightfully good sport. As he said himself, he was a conservative anarchist; which meant, he was like a great many more people, a mere unbeliever. The anarchy extended to his humorous talk, and his secret thinking. The conservatism, based on a mongrel fear of the anarchy, controlled every action. His thoughts, secretly, were something to be scared of. Therefore, in his life, he was fanatically afraid of the unconventional.

When his conservatism and his abject sort of fear were uppermost, he always lifted his lip and bared his teeth a little, in a dog-like sneer.

"I hear your latest friends are the half-divorced Mrs. Fawcett and the *maquereau* Eastwood," he said to Yvette.

She didn't know what a *maquereau* was, but she felt the poison in the rector's fangs.

"I just know them," she said. "They're awfully nice, really. And they'll be married in about a month's time."

The rector looked at her insouciant face with hatred. Somewhere inside him, he was cowed, he had been born cowed. And those who are born cowed are natural slaves, and deep instinct makes them fear with poisonous fear those who might suddenly snap the slave's collar round their necks.

It was for this reason the rector had so abjectly curled up, still so abjectly curled up before She-who-was-Cynthia: because of his slave's fear of her contempt, the contempt of a born-free nature for a base-born nature.

Yvette too had a free-born quality. She too, one day, would know him, and clap the slave's collar of her contempt round his neck.

But should she? He would fight to the death, this time, first. The slave in him was cornered this time, like a cornered rat, and with the courage of a cornered rat.

"I suppose they're your sort!" he sneered.

"Well, they are, really," she said, with that blithe vagueness. "I do like them awfully. They seem so solid, you know, so honest."

"You've got a peculiar notion of honesty!" he sneered. "A young sponge going off with a woman older than himself, so that he can live on her money! The woman leaving her home and her children! I don't know where you get your idea of honesty. Not from me, I hope. And you seem to be very well acquainted with them, considering you say you just know them. Where did you meet them?"

"When I was out bicycling. They came along in their car, and we happened to talk. She told me at once who she was, so that I shouldn't make a mistake. She *is* honest."

Poor Yvette was struggling to bear up.

"And how often have you seen them since?"

"Oh, I've just been over twice."

"Over where?"

"To their cottage in Scoresby."

He looked at her in hate, as if he could kill her. And he backed away from her, against the window-curtains of his study, like a rat at bay. Somewhere in his mind he was thinking unspeakable depravities about his daughter, as he had thought them of She-who-was-Cynthia. He was powerless against the lowest insinuations of his own mind. And these depravities which he attributed to the still-uncowed but frightened girl in front of him, made him recoil, showing all his fangs in his handsome face.

"So you just know them, do you?" he said. "Lying is in your blood, I see. I don't believe you get it from me."

Yvette half averted her mute face, and thought of Granny's bare-faced prevarication. She did not answer.

"What takes you creeping round such couples?" he sneered. "Aren't there enough decent people in the world for you to know? Any one would think you were a stray dog, having to run round indecent couples, because the decent ones wouldn't have you. Have you got something worse than lying in your blood?"

"What have I got worse than lying in my blood?" she asked. A cold deadness was coming over her. Was she abnormal, one of the semi-criminal abnormals? It made her feel cold and dead.

In his eyes, she was just brazening out the depravity that underlay her virgin, tender, bird-like face. She-who-was-Cynthia had been like this: a snow-flower. And he had convulsions of sadistic horror, thinking what might be the *actual* depravity of She-who-was-Cynthia. Even his *own* love for her, which had been the lust-love of the born cowed, had been a depravity, in secret, to him. So what must an illegal love be?

"You know best yourself, what you have got," he sneered. "But it is something you had best curb, and quickly, if you don't intend to finish in a criminal-lunacy asylum."

"Why?" she said, pale and muted, numbed with frozen fear. "Why criminal lunacy? What have I done?"

"That is between you and your Maker," he jeered. "I shall never ask. But certain tendencies end in criminal lunacy, unless they are curbed in time."

"Do you mean like knowing the Eastwoods?" asked Yvette, after a pause of numb fear.

"Do I mean like nosing round such people as Mrs. Fawcett, a Jewess, and ex-Major Eastwood, a man who goes off with an older woman for the sake of her money? Why yes, I do!"

"But you *can't* say that," cried Yvette. "He's an awfully simple, straightforward man."

"He is apparently one of your sort."

"Well in a way I thought he was. I thought you'd like him too," she said simply, hardly knowing what she said.

The rector backed into the curtains, as if the girl menaced him with something fearful.

"Don't say any more," he snarled, abject. "Don't say any more. You've said too much, to implicate you. I don't want to learn any more horrors."

"But what horrors?" she persisted.

The very naïveté of her unscrupulous innocence repelled him, cowed him still more.

"Say no more!" he said, in a low, hissing voice. "But I will kill you before you shall go the way of your mother."

She looked at him, as he stood there backed against the velvet curtains of his study, his face yellow, his eyes distraught like a rat's with fear and rage and hate, and a numb, frozen loneliness came over her. For her too, the meaning had gone out of everything.

It was hard to break the frozen, sterile silence that ensued. At last, however, she looked at him. And in spite of herself, beyond her own knowledge, the contempt for him was in her young, clear, baffled eyes. It fell like the slave's collar over his neck, finally.

"Do you mean I mustn't know the Eastwoods?" she said.

"You can know them if you wish," he sneered. "But you must not expect to associate with your Granny and your Aunt Cissie, and Lucille, if you do. I cannot have *them* contaminated. Your Granny was a faithful wife and a faithful mother, if ever one existed. She has already had one shock of shame and abomination to endure. She shall never be exposed to another."

Yvette heard it all dimly, half hearing.

"I can send a note and say you disapprove," she said dimly.

"You follow your own course of action. But remember, you have to choose between clean people, and reverence for your Granny's blameless old age, and people who are unclean in their minds and their bodies."

Again there was a silence. Then she looked at him, and her face was more puzzled than anything. But somewhere at the back of her perplexity was that peculiar calm, virgin contempt of the free-born for the base-born. He, and all the Saywells, were base-born.

"All right," she said. "I'll write and say you disapprove."

He did not answer. He was partly flattered, secretly triumphant, but abjectly.

"I have tried to keep this from your Granny and Aunt Cissie," he said. "It need not be public property, since you choose to make your friendship clandestine."

There was a dreary silence.

"All right," she said. "I'll go and write."

And she crept out of the room.

She addressed her little note to Mrs. Eastwood. "Dear Mrs. Eastwood, Daddy doesn't approve of my coming to see you. So you will understand if we have to break it off. I'm awfully sorry——" That was all.

Yet she felt a dreary blank when she had posted her letter. She was now even afraid of her own thoughts. She wanted, now, to be held against the slender, fine-shaped breast of the gipsy. She wanted him to hold her in his arms, if only for once, for once, and comfort and confirm her. She wanted to be confirmed by him, against her father, who had only a repulsive fear of her.

And at the same time she cringed and winced, so that she could hardly walk, for fear the thought was obscene, a criminal lunacy. It seemed to wound her heels as she walked, the fear. The fear, the great cold fear of the base-born, her father, everything human and swarming. Like a great bog humanity swamped her, and she sank in, weak at the knees, filled with repulsion and fear of every person she met.

She adjusted herself, however, quite rapidly to her new conception of people. She had to live. It is useless to quarrel with one's bread and butter. And to expect a great deal out of life is puerile. So, with the rapid adaptability of the post-war generation, she adjusted herself to the new facts. Her father was what he was. He would always play up to appearances. She would do the same. She too would play up to appearances.

So, underneath the blithe, gossamer-straying insouciance, a certain hardness formed, like rock crystallizing in her heart. She lost her illusions in the collapse of her sympathies. Outwardly, she seemed the same. Inwardly she was hard and detached, and, unknown to herself, revengeful.

Outwardly she remained the same. It was part of her game. While circumstances remained as they were, she must remain, at least in appearance, true to what was expected of her.

But the revengefulness came out in her new vision of people. Under the rector's apparently gallant handsomeness, she saw the weak, feeble nullity. And she despised him. Yet still, in a way, she liked him too. Feelings are so complicated.

It was Granny whom she came to detest with all her soul. That obese old woman, sitting there in her blindness like some great red-blotched fungus, her neck swallowed between her heaped-up shoulders and her rolling, ancient chins, so that she was neckless as a double potato, her Yvette really hated, with that pure, sheer hatred which is almost a joy. Her hate was so clear, that while she was feeing strong, she enjoyed it.

The old woman sat with her big, reddened face pressed a little back, her lace cap perched on her thin white hair, her stub nose still assertive, and her old mouth shut like a trap. This motherly old soul, her mouth gave her away. It always had been one of the compressed sort. But in her great age, it had gone like a toad's, lipless, the jaw pressing up like the lower jaw of a trap. The look Yvette most hated was the look of that lower jaw pressing relentlessly up, with an ancient prognathous thrust, so that the snub nose in turn was forced to press upwards, and the whole face was pressed a little back, beneath the big, wall-like forehead. The will, the ancient, toad-like, obscene *will* in the old woman, was fearful, once you saw it: a toad-like self-will that was godless, and less than human! It belonged to the old, enduring race of toads, or tortoises. And it made one feel that Granny would never die. She would live on like these higher reptiles, in a state of semi-coma, for ever.

Yvette dared not even suggest to her father that Granny was not perfect. He would have threatened his daughter with the lunatic asylum. That was the threat he always seemed to have up his sleeve: the lunatic asylum. Exactly as if a distaste for Granny and for that horrible house of relatives was in itself a proof of lunacy, dangerous lunacy.

Yet in one of her moods of irritable depression, she did once fling out:

"How perfectly beastly this house is! Aunt Lucy comes, and Aunt Nell, and Aunt Alice, and they make a ring like a ring of crows, with Granny and Aunt Cissie, all lifting their skirts up and warming their legs at the fire, and shutting Lucille and me out. We're nothing but outsiders in this beastly house!"

Her father glanced at her curiously. But she managed to put a petulance into her speech, and a mere cross rudeness into her look, so that he could laugh, as at a childish tantrum. Somewhere, though, he knew that she coldly, venomously meant what she said, and he was wary of her.

Her life seemed now nothing but an irritable friction against the unsavoury household of the Saywells, in which she was immersed. She loathed the rectory with a loathing that consumed her life, a loathing so strong that she could not really go away from the place. While it endured, she was spellbound to it, in revulsion.

She forgot the Eastwoods again. After all, what was the revolt of the little Jewess, compared to Granny and the Saywell bunch! A husband was never more than a semi-casual thing! But a family!—an awful, smelly family that would never disperse, stuck half dead round the base of a fungoid old woman! How was one to cope with that?

She did not forget the gipsy entirely. But she had no time for him. She, who was bored almost to agony, and who had nothing at all to do, she had not time to think even, seriously, of anything. Time being, after all, only the current of the soul in its flow.

She saw the gipsy twice. Once he came to the house, with things to sell. And she, watching him from the landing window, refused to go down. He saw her too, as he was putting his things back into his cart. But he too gave no sign. Being a race that exists only to be harrying the outskirts of our society, forever hostile and living only by spoil, he was too much master of himself, and too wary, to expose himself openly to the vast and gruesome clutch of our law. He had been through the war. He had been enslaved against his will, that time.

So now, he showed himself at the rectory, and slowly, quietly busied himself at his cart outside the white gate, with that air of silent and forever-unyielding outsideness which gave him his lonely, predative grace. He knew she saw him. And she should see him unyielding, quietly hawking his copper vessels, on an old, old war-path against such as herself.

Such as herself? Perhaps he was mistaken. Her heart, in its stroke, now rang hard as his hammer upon his copper, beating against circumstances. But he struck stealthily on the outside, and she still more secretly on the inside of the establishment. She liked him. She liked the quiet, noiseless clean-cut presence of him. She liked that mysterious endurance in him, which endures in opposition, without any idea of victory. And she liked that peculiar added relentlessness, the disillusion in hostility, which belongs to after the war. Yes, if she belonged to any side, and to any clan, it was to his. Almost she could have found it in her heart to go with him, and be a pàriah gipsy-woman.

But she was born inside the pale. And she liked comfort, and a certain prestige. Even as a mere rector's daughter, one did have a certain prestige. And she liked that. Also she liked to chip against the pillars of the temple, from the inside. She wanted to be safe under the temple roof. Yet she enjoyed chipping fragments off the supporting pillars. Doubtless many fragments had been whittled away from the pillars of the Philistine, before Samson pulled the temple down.

"I'm not sure one shouldn't have one's fling till one is twenty-six, and then give in, and marry!"

This was Lucille's philosophy, learned from older women. Yvette was twenty-one. It meant she had five more years in which to have this precious fling. And the fling meant, at the moment, the gipsy. The marriage, at the age of twenty-six, meant Leo or Gerry.

So, a woman could eat her cake and have her bread and butter.

Yvette, pitched in gruesome, deadlocked hostility to the Saywell household, was very old and very wise: with the agedness and the wisdom of the young, which always overleaps the agedness and the wisdom of the old, or the elderly.

The second time she met the gipsy by accident. It was March, and sunny weather, after unheard-of rains. Celandines were yellow in the hedges, and primroses among the rocks. But still there came a smell of sulphur from far-away steel-works, out of the steel-blue sky.

And yet it was spring!

Yvette was cycling slowly along by Codnor Gate, past the lime quarries, when she saw the gipsy coming away from the door of a stone cottage. His cart stood there in the road. He was returning with his brooms and copper things, to the cart.

She got down from her bicycle. As she saw him, she loved with curious tenderness the slim lines of his body in the green jersey, the turn of his silent face. She felt she knew him better than she knew anybody on earth, even Lucille, and belonged to him, in some way, for ever.

"Have you made anything new and nice?" she asked innocently, looking at his copper things.

"I don't think," he said, glancing back at her.

The desire was still there, still curious and naked, in his eyes. But it was more remote, the boldness was diminished. There was a tiny glint, as if he might dislike her. But this dissolved again, as he saw her looking among his bits of copper and brass-work. She searched them diligently.

There was a little oval brass plate, with a queer figure like a palm-tree beaten upon it.

"I like that," she said. "How much is it?"

"What you like," he said.

This made her nervous: he seemed off-hand, almost mocking.

"I'd rather you said," she told him, looking up at him.

"You give me what you like," he said.

"No!" she said, suddenly. "If you won't tell me I won't have it."

"All right," he said. "Two shilling."

She found half-a-crown, and he drew from his pocket a handful of silver, from which he gave her her sixpence.

"The old gipsy dreamed something about you," he said, looking at her with curious, searching eyes.

"Did she!" cried Yvette, at once interested. "What was it?"

"She said: 'Be braver in your heart, or you lose your game.' She said it this way: 'Be braver in your body, or your luck will leave you.' And she said as well: 'Listen for the voice of water.' "

Yvette was very much impressed.

"And what does it mean?" she asked.

"I asked her," he said. "She says she don't know."

"Tell me again what it was," said Yvette.

" 'Be braver in your body, or your luck will go.' And: 'Listen for the voice of water.' "

He looked in silence at her soft, pondering face. Something almost like a perfume seemed to flow from her young bosom direct to him, in a grateful connection.

"I'm to be braver in my body, and I'm to listen for the voice of water! All right!" she said. "I don't understand, but perhaps I shall."

She looked at him with clear eyes. Man or woman is made up of many selves. With one self, she loved this gipsy man. With many selves, she ignored him or had a distaste for him.

"You're not coming up to the Head no more?" he asked.

Again she looked at him absently.

"Perhaps I will," she said, "some time. Some time."

"Spring weather!" he said, smiling faintly and glancing round at the sun. "We're going to break camp soon, and go away."

"When?" she said.

"Perhaps next week."

"Where to?"

Again he made a move with his head.

"Perhaps up north," he said.

She looked at him.

"All right!" she said. "Perhaps I *will* come up before you go, and say good-bye to your wife and to the old woman who sent me the message."

IX

Yvette did not keep her promise. The few March days were lovely, and she let them slip. She had a curious reluctance, always, towards taking action, or making any real move of her own. She always wanted someone else to make a move for her, as if she did not want to play her own game of life.

She lived as usual, went out to her friends, to parties, and danced with the undiminished Leo. She wanted to go up and say good-bye to the gipsies. She wanted to. And nothing prevented her.

On the Friday afternoon especially she wanted to go. It was sunny, and the last yellow crocuses down the drive were in full blaze, wide open, the first bees rolling in them. The Papple rushed under the stone bridge, uncannily full, nearly filling the arches. There was the scent of a mezereon tree.

And she felt too lazy, too lazy, too lazy. She strayed in the garden by the river, half dreamy, expecting something. While the gleam of spring sun lasted, she would be out of doors. Indoors Granny, sitting back like some awful old prelate, in her bulk of black silk and her white lace cap, was warming her feet by the fire, and hearing everything that Aunt Nell had to say. Friday was Aunt Nell's day. She usually came for lunch, and left after an early tea. So the mother and the large, rather common daughter, who was a widow at the age of forty, sat gossiping by the fire, while Aunt Cissie prowled in and out. Friday was the rector's day for going to town: it was also the housemaid's half day.

Yvette sat on a wooden seat in the garden, only a few feet above the bank of the swollen river, which rolled a strange, uncanny mass of water. The crocuses were passing in the ornamental beds, the grass was dark green where it was mown, the laurels looked a little brighter. Aunt Cissie appeared at the top of the porch steps, and called to ask if Yvette wanted that early cup of tea. Because of the river just below, Yvette could not hear what Aunt Cissie said, but she guessed, and shook her head. An early cup of tea, indoors, when the sun actually shone? No thanks!

She was conscious of her gipsy, as she sat there musing in the sun. Her soul had the half painful, half easing knack of leaving her, and straying away to some place, to somebody that had caught her imagination. Some days she would be at the Framleys', even though she did not go near them. Some days, she was all the time in spirit with the Eastwoods. And to-day it was the gipsies. She was up at their encampment in the quarry. She saw the man hammering his copper, lifting his head to look at the road; and the children playing in the horse-shelter: and the women, the gipsy's wife and the strong, elderly woman, coming home with their packs, along with the elderly man. For this afternoon, she felt intensely that *that* was home for her: the gipsy camp, the fire, the stool, the man with the hammer, the old crone.

It was part of her nature, to get these fits of yearning for some place she knew; to be in a certain place; with somebody who meant home to her. This afternoon it was the gipsy camp. And the man in the green jersey made it home to her. Just to be where he was, that was to be at home. The caravans, the brats, the other women: everything was natural to her, her home, as if she had been born there. She wondered if the gipsy was aware of her: if he could see her sitting on the stool by the fire; if he would lift his head and see her as she rose, looking at him slowly and significantly, turning towards the steps of his caravan. Did he know? Did he know?

Vaguely she looked up the steep of dark larch trees north of the house, where unseen the road climbed, going towards the Head. There was nothing, and her glance strayed down again. At the foot of the slope the river turned, thrown back harshly, ominously, against the low rocks across stream, then pouring past the garden to the bridge. It was unnaturally full, and whitey-muddy, and ponderous. "Listen for the voice of water," she said to herself. "No need to listen for it, if the voice means the noise!"

And again she looked at the swollen river breaking angrily as it came round the bend. Above it the black-looking kitchen garden hung, and the hard-natured fruit trees. Everything was on the tilt, facing south and south-west, for the sun. Behind, above the house and the kitchen garden hung the steep little wood of withered-seeming larches. The gardener was working in the kitchen garden, high up there, by the edge of the larch-wood.

She heard a call. It was Aunt Cissie and Aunt Nell. They were on the drive, waving Good-bye! Yvette waved back. Then Aunt Cissie, pitching her voice against the waters, called:

"I shan't be long. Don't forget Granny is alone!"

"All right!" screamed Yvette rather ineffectually.

And she sat on her bench and watched the two undignified, long-coated women walk slowly over the bridge and begin the curving climb on the opposite slope, Aunt Nell carrying a sort of suit-case in which she brought a few goods for Granny and took back vegetables or whatever the rectory garden or cupboard was yielding. Slowly the two figures diminished, on the whitish, up-curving road, labouring slowly up towards Papplewick village. Aunt Cissie was going as far as the village for something.

The sun was yellowing to decline. What a pity! Oh, what a pity the sunny day was going, and she would have to turn indoors, to those hateful rooms, and Granny! Aunt Cissie would be back directly: it was past five. And all the others would be arriving from town, rather irritable and tired, soon after six.

As she looked uneasily round, she heard, across the running of water, the sharp noise of a horse and cart rattling on the road hidden in the larch trees. The gardener was looking up too. Yvette turned away again, lingering, strolling by the full river a few paces, unwilling to go in; glancing up the road to see if Aunt Cissie were coming. If she saw her, she would go indoors.

She heard somebody shouting, and looked round. Down the path through the larch trees the gipsy was bounding. The gardener, away beyond, was also running. Simultaneously she became aware of a great roar, which, before she could move, accumulated to a vast deafening snarl. The gipsy was gesticulating. She looked round, behind her.

And to her horror and amazement, round the bend of the river she saw a shaggy, tawny wave-front of water advancing like a wall of lions. The roaring sound wiped out everything. She was powerless, too amazed and wonder-struck, she wanted to see it.

Before she could think twice, it was near, a roaring cliff of water. She almost fainted with horror. She heard the scream of the gipsy, and looked up to see him bounding upon her, his black eyes starting out of his head.

"Run!" he screamed, seizing her arm.

And in the instant the first wave was washing her feet from under her, swirling, in the insane noise, which suddenly for some reason seemed like stillness, with a devouring flood over the garden. The horrible mowing of water!

The gipsy dragged her heavily, lurching, plunging, but still keeping foot-hold both of them, towards the house. She was barely conscious: as if the flood was in her soul.

There was one grass-banked terrace of the garden, near the path round the house. The gipsy clawed his way up this terrace to the dry level of the path, dragging her after him, and sprang with her past the windows to the porch steps. Before they got there, a new great surge of water came mowing, mowing trees down even, and mowed them down too.

Yvette felt herself gone in an agonizing mill-race of icy water, whirled, with only the fearful grip of the gipsy's hand on her wrist. They were both down and gone. She felt a dull but stunning bruise somewhere.

Then he pulled her up. He was up, streaming forth water, clinging to the stem of the great wistaria that grew against the wall, crushed against the wall by the water. Her head was above water, he held her arm till it seemed dislocated: but she could not get her footing. With a ghastly sickness like a dream, she struggled and struggled, and could not get her feet. Only his hand was locked on her wrist.

He dragged her nearer till her one hand caught his leg. He nearly went down again. But the wistaria held him, and he pulled her up to him. She clawed at him, horribly; and got to her feet, he hanging on like a man torn in two, to the wistaria trunk.

The water was above her knees. The man and she looked into each other's ghastly streaming faces.

"Get to the steps!" he screamed.

It was only just round the corner: four strides! She looked at him: she could not go. His eyes glared on her like a tiger's, and he pushed her from him. She clung to the wall, and the water seemed to abate a little. Round the corner she staggered, but staggering, reeled and was pitched up against the cornice of the balustrade of the porch steps, the man after her.

They got on to the steps, when another roar was heard amid the roar, and the wall of the house shook. Up heaved the water round their legs again, but the gipsy had opened the hall door. In they poured with the water, reeling to the stairs. And as they did so, they saw the short but strange bulk of Granny emerge in the hall, away down from the dining-room door. She had her hands lifted and clawing, as the first water swirled round her legs, and her coffin-like mouth was opened in a hoarse scream.

Yvette was blind to everything but the stairs. Blind, unconscious of everything save the steps rising beyond the water, she clambered up like a wet, shuddering cat, in a state of unconsciousness. It was not till she was on the landing, dripping and shuddering till she could not stand erect, clinging to the banisters, while the house shook and the water raved below, that she was aware of the sodden gipsy, in paroxysms of coughing at the head of the stairs, his cap gone, his black hair over his eyes, peering between his washed-down hair at the sickening heave of water below, in the hall. Yvette, fainting, looked too and saw Granny bob up, like a strange float, her face purple, her blind blue eyes bolting, spume hissing from her mouth. One old purple hand clawed at a banister rail, and held for a moment, showing the glint of a wedding ring.

The gipsy, who had coughed himself free and pushed back his hair, said to that awful float-like face below:

"Not good enough! Not good enough!"

With a low thud like thunder, the house was struck again, and shuddered, and a strange cracking, rattling, spitting noise began. Up heaved the water like a sea. The hand was gone, all sign of anything was gone, but upheaving water.

Yvette turned in blind unconscious frenzy, staggering like a wet cat to the upper staircase, and climbing swiftly. It was not till she was at the door of her room that she stopped, paralysed by the sound of a sickening, tearing crash, while the house swayed.

"The house is coming down!" yelled the green-white face of the gipsy, in her face.

He glared into her crazed face.

"Where is the chimney? The back chimney—which room? The chimney will stand——"

He glared with strange ferocity into her face, forcing her to understand. And she nodded with a strange, crazed poise, nodded quite serenely, saying:

"In here! In here! It's all right."

They entered her room, which had a narrow fire-place. It was a back room with two windows, one on each side the great chimney-flue. The gipsy, coughing bitterly and trembling in every limb, went to the window to look out.

Below, between the house and the steep rise of the hill, was a wild mill-race of water rushing with refuse, including Rover's green dog-kennel. The gipsy coughed and coughed, and gazed down blankly. Tree after tree went down, mown by the water, which must have been ten feet deep.

Shudding and pressing his sodden arms on his sodden breast, a look of resignation on his livid face, he turned to Yvette. A fearful tearing noise tore the house, then there was a deep, watery explosion. Something had gone down, some part of the house, the floor heaved and wavered beneath them. For some moments both were suspended, stupefied. Then he roused.

"Not good enough! Not good enough! This will stand. This here still stand. See, that chimney! Like a tower. Yes! All right! All right! You take your clothes off and go to bed. You'll die of the cold."

"It's all right! It's quite all right!" she said to him, sitting on a chair and looking up into his face with her white, insane little face, round which the hair was plastered.

"No!" he cried. "No! Take your things off and I'll rub you with this towel. I rub myself. If the house falls then die warm. If it don't fall, then live, not die of pneumonia."

Coughing, shuddering violently, he pulled up his jersey hem and wrestled with all his shuddering, cold-racked might, to get off his wet, tight jersey.

"Help me!" he cried, his face muffled.

She seized the edge of the jersey, obediently, and pulled with all her might. The garment came over his head, and he stood in his braces.

"Take your things off! Rub with this towel!" he commanded ferociously, the savageness of the war on him. And like a thing obsessed, he pushed himself out of his trousers, and got out of his wet, clinging shirt, emerging slim and livid, shuddering in every fibre with cold and shock.

He seized a towel, and began quickly to rub his body, his teeth chattering like plates rattling together. Yvette dimly saw it was wise. She tried to get out of her dress. He pulled the horrible wet death-gripping thing off her, then, resuming his rubbing, went to the door, tip-toeing on the wet floor.

There he stood, naked, towel in hand, petrified. He looked west, towards where the upper landing window had been, and was looking into the sunset, over an insane sea of waters, bristling with uptorn trees and refuse. The end corner of the house where the porch had been, and the stairs, had gone. The wall had fallen, leaving the floors sticking out. The stairs had gone.

Motionless, he watched the water. A cold wind blew in upon him. He clenched his rattling teeth with a great effort of will, and turned into the room again, closing the door.

Yvette, naked, shuddering so much that she was sick, was trying to wipe herself dry.

"All right!" he cried. "All right! The water don't rise no more! All right!"

With his towel he began to rub her, himself shaking all over, but holding her gripped by the shoulder, and slowly, numbedly rubbing her tender body, even trying to rub up into some dryness the pitiful hair of her small head.

Suddenly he left off.

"Better lie in the bed," he commanded, "I want to rub myself."

His teeth went snap-snap-snap-snap, in great snaps, cutting off his words. Yvette crept shaking and semi-conscious into her bed. He, making strained efforts to hold himself still and rub himself warm, went again to the north window, to look out.

The water had risen a little. The sun had gone down, and there was a reddish glow. He rubbed his hair into a black, wet tangle, then paused for breath, in a sudden access of shuddering, then looked out again, then rubbed again on his breast, and began to cough afresh, because of the water he had swallowed. His towel was red: he had hurt himself somewhere: but he felt nothing.

There was still the strange huge noise of water, and the horrible bump of things bumping against the walls. The wind was rising with sundown, cold and hard. The house shook with explosive thuds, and weird, weird frightening noises came up.

A terror creeping over his soul, he went again to the door. The wind, roaring with the waters, blew in as he opened it. Through the awesome gap in the house he saw the world, the waters, the chaos of horrible waters, the twilight, the perfect new moon high above the sunset, a faint thing, and clouds pushing dark into the sky, on the cold, blustery wind.

Clenching his teeth again, fear mingling with resignation, or fatalism, in his soul, he went into the room and closed the door, picking up her towel to see if it were drier than his own, and less blood-stained, again rubbing his head, and going to the window.

He turned away, unable to control his spasms of shivering. Yvette had disappeared right under the bedclothes, and nothing of her was visible but a shivering mound under the white quilt. He laid his hand on this shivering mound, as if for company. It did not stop shivering.

"All right!" he said. "All right! Water's going down!"

She suddenly uncovered her head and peered out at him from a white face. She peered into his greenish, curiously calm face, semi-conscious. His teeth were chattering unheeded, as he gazed down at her, his black eyes still full of the fire of life and a certain vagabond calm of fatalistic resignation.

"Warm me!" she moaned, with chattering teeth. "Warm me! I shall die of shivering."

A terrible convulsion went through her curled-up white body, enough indeed to rupture her and cause her to die.

The gipsy nodded, and took her in his arms, and held her in a clasp like a vice, to still his own shuddering. He himself was shuddering fearfully, and only semi-conscious. It was the shock.

The vice-like grip of his arms round her seemed to her the only stable point in her consciousness. It was a fearful relief to her heart, which was strained to bursting. And though his body, wrapped round her strange and lithe and powerful, like tentacles, rippled with shuddering as an electric current, still the rigid tension of the muscles that held her clenched steadied them both, and gradually the sickening violence of the shuddering, caused by shock, abated, in his body first, then in hers, and the warmth revived between them. And as it roused, their tortured, semi-conscious minds became unconscious, they passed away into sleep.

X

The sun was shining in heaven before men were able to get across the Papple with ladders. The bridge was gone. But the flood had abated, and the house, that leaned forwards as if it were making a stiff bow to the stream, stood now in mud and wreckage, with a great heap of fallen masonry and debris at the south-west corner. Awful were the gaping mouths of rooms!

Inside, there was no sign of life. But across-stream the gardener had come to reconnoitre, and the cook appeared, thrilled with curiosity. She had escaped from the back door and up through the larches to the high-road, when she saw the gipsy bound past the house: thinking he was coming to murder somebody. At the little top gate she had found his cart standing. The gardener had led the horse away to the Red Lion up at Darley, when night had fallen.

This the men from Papplewick learned when at last they got across the stream with ladders, and to the back of the house. They were nervous, fearing a collapse of the building, whose front was all undermined and whose back was choked up. They gazed with horror at the silent shelves of the rector's rows of books, in his torn-open study; at the big brass bedstead of Granny's room, the bed so deep and comfortably made, but one brass leg of the bedstead perching tentatively over the torn void; at the wreckage of the maid's room upstairs. The housemaid and the cook wept. Then a man climbed in cautiously through a smashed kitchen window, into the jungle and morass of the ground floor. He found the body of the old woman: or at least he saw her foot, in its flat black slipper, muddily protruding from a mud-heap of debris. And he fled.

The gardener said he was sure that Miss Yvette was not in the house. He had seen her and the gipsy swept away. But the policeman insisted on a search, and the Framely boys rushing up at last, the ladders were roped together. Then the whole party set up a loud yell. But without result. No answer from within.

A ladder was up, Bob Framley climbed, smashed a window, and clambered into Aunt Cissie's room. The perfect homely familiarity of everything terrified him like ghosts. The house might go down any minute.

They had just got the ladder up to the top floor, when men came running from Darley, saying the old gipsy had been to the Red Lion for the horse and cart, leaving word that his son had seen Yvette at the top of the house. But by that time the policeman was smashing the window of Yvette's room.

Yvette, fast asleep, started from under the bedclothes with a scream, as the glass flew. She clutched the sheets round her nakedness. The policeman uttered a startled yell, which he converted into a cry of: "Miss Yvette! Miss Yvette!"

He turned round on the ladder and shouted to the faces below:

"Miss Yvette's in bed!—in bed!"

And he perched there on the ladder, an unmarried man, clutching the window in peril, not knowing what to do.

Yvette sat up in bed, her hair in a matted tangle, and started with wild eyes, clutching up the sheets at her naked breast. She had been so very fast asleep, that she was still not there.

The policeman, terrified at the flabby ladder, climbed into the room saying:

"Don't be frightened, Miss! Don't you worry any more about it. You're safe now."

And Yvette, so dazed, thought he meant the gipsy. Where was the gipsy?

This was the first thing in her mind. Where was her gipsy? This was the first thing in her mind. Where was her gipsy of this world's-end night?

He was gone! He was gone! And a policeman was in the room! A policeman! She rubbed her hand over her dazed brow.

"If you'll get dressed, Miss, we can get you down to safe ground. The house is likely to fall. I suppose there's nobody in the other rooms?"

He stepped gingerly into the passage and gazed in terror through the torn-out end of the house, and far off saw the rector coming down in a motor-car, on the sunlit hill.

Yvette, her face gone numb and disappointed, got up quickly, closing the bedclothes, and looked at herself a moment, then opened her drawers for clothing. She dressed herself, then looked in a mirror, and saw her matted hair with horror. Yet she did not care. The gipsy was gone, anyhow.

Her own clothes lay in a sodden heap. There was a great sodden place on the carpet where his had been, and two blood-stained filthy towels. Otherwise there was no sign of him.

She was tugging at her hair when the policeman tapped at her door. She called him to come in. Her saw with relief that she was dressed and in her right senses.

"We'd better get out of the house as soon as possible, Miss," he reiterated. "It might fall any minute."

"Really!" said Yvette calmly. "Is it as bad as that?"

There were great shouts. She had to go to the window. There, below, was the rector, his arms wide open, tears streaming down his face.

"I'm perfectly all right, Daddy!" she said, with the calmness of her contradictory feelings. She would keep the gipsy a secret from him. At the same time, tears ran down her face.

"Don't you cry, Miss, don't you cry! The rector's lost his mother, but he's thanking his stars to have his daughter. We all thought you were gone as well, we did that!"

"Is Granny drowned?" said Yvette.

"I'm afraid she is, poor lady!" said the policeman, with a grave face.

Yvette wept away into her hanky, which she had had to fetch from a drawer.

"Dare you go down that ladder, Miss?" said the policeman.

Yvette looked at the sagging depth of it, and said promptly to herself: "No! Not for anything!" But then she remembered the gipsy's saying: "Be braver in the body."

"Have you been in all the other rooms?" she said, in her weeping, turning to the policeman.

"Yes, Miss! But you was the only person in the house, you know, save the old lady. Cook got away in time, and Lizzie was up at her mother's. It was only you and the poor old lady we was fretting about. Do you think you dare go down that ladder?"

"Oh, yes!" said Yvette, with indifference. The gipsy was gone anyway.

And now the rector in torment watched his tall, slender daughter slowly stepping backwards down the sagging ladder, the policeman, peering heroically from the smashed window, holding the ladder's top end.

At the foot of the ladder Yvette appropriately fainted in her father's arms, and was borne away with him, in the car, by Bob, to the Framley home. There the poor Lucille, a ghost of ghosts, wept with relief till she had hysterics, and even Aunt Cissie cried out among her tears: "Let the old be taken and the young spared! Oh I *can't* cry for the Mater, now Yvette is spared!"

And she wept gallons.

The flood was caused by the sudden bursting of the great reservoir, up in Papple Highdale, five miles from the rectory. It was found out later that an ancient, perhaps even a Roman mine tunnel, unsuspected, undreamed of, beneath the reservoir dam, had collapsed, undermining the whole dam. That was why the Papple had been, for that last day, so uncannily full. And then the dam had burst.

The rector and the two girls stayed on at the Framleys', till a new home could be found. Yvette did not attend Granny's funeral. She stayed in bed.

Telling her tale, she only told how the gipsy had got her inside the porch, and she had crawled to the stairs out of the water. It was known that he had escaped: the old gipsy had said so, when he fetched the horse and cart from the Red Lion.

Yvette could tell little. She was vague, confused, she seemed hardly to remember anything. But that was just like her.

It was Bob Framley who said:

"You know, I think that gipsy deserves a medal."

The whole family suddenly was struck.

"Oh, we *ought* to thank him!" cried Lucille.

The rector himself went with Bob in the car. But the quarry was deserted. The gipsies had lifted camp and gone, no one knew whither.

And Yvette, lying in bed, moaned in her heart: "Oh, I love him! I love him! I love him!" The grief over him kept her prostrate. Yet practically, she too was acquiescent in the fact of his disappearance. Her young soul knew the wisdom of it.

But after Granny's funeral, she received a little letter, dated from some unknown place.

"Dear Miss, I see in the paper you are all right after your ducking, as is the same with me. I hope I see you again one day, maybe at Tideswell cattle-fair, or maybe we come that way again. I come that day to say good-bye! and I never said it, well, the water give no time, but I live in hopes. Your obdt. servant Joe Boswell."

And only then she realized that he had a name.

Old Mortality

(1939)

Katherine Ann Porter

Short-story writer, essayist, and novelist, Katherine Anne Porter (1890–   )
was born in Indian Creek, Texas, a country to which she has returned in much
of her fiction. She made her reputation as a short-story writer and master of the
novelette form in *Flowering Judas* (1930) and *Hacienda* (1934), combined in
Flowering Judas and Other Stories (1935). These were followed by *Noon Wine*
(1937), *Pale Horse, Pale Rider* (1939), and *The Leaning Tower* (1944). In 1952
she published a book of essays, *The Days Before,* and in 1962 her novel, *Ship of
Fools.* She has traveled widely, living in Mexico, Paris, and Berlin, which have
served as locales for her stories; she now lives in Washington, D.C. For some
comments of her own on her fiction, see the *Paris Review* interview in *Writers at
Work, Second Series* (New York, 1963), pp. 137–63.

Part I: 1885-1902

She was a spirited-looking young woman, with dark curly hair cropped and
parted on the side, a short oval face with straight eyebrows, and a large curved
mouth. A round white collar rose from the neck of her tightly buttoned black
basque, and round white cuffs set off lazy hands with dimples in them, lying at
ease in the folds of her flounced skirt which gathered around to a bustle. She sat
thus, forever in the pose of being photographed, a motionless image in her dark
walnut frame with silver oak leaves in the corners, her smiling gray eyes following
one about the room. It was a reckless indifferent smile, rather disturbing to her
nieces Maria and Miranda. Quite often they wondered why every older person
who looked at the picture said, "How lovely"; and why everyone who had known
her thought her so beautiful and charming.

There was a kind of faded merriment in the background, with its vase of flowers and draped velvet curtains, the kind of vase and the kind of curtains no one would have any more. The clothes were not even romantic looking, but merely most terribly out of fashion, and the whole affair was associated, in the minds of the little girls, with dead things: the smell of Grandmother's medicated cigarettes and her furniture that smelled of beeswax, and her old-fashioned perfume, Orange Flower. The woman in the picture had been Aunt Amy, but she was only a ghost in a frame, and a sad, pretty story from old times. She had been beautiful, much loved, unhappy, and she had died young.

Maria and Miranda, aged twelve and eight years, knew they were young, though they felt they had lived a long time. They had lived not only their own years; but their memories, it seemed to them, began years before they were born, in the lives of the grown-ups around them, old people above forty, most of them, who had a way of insisting that they too had been young once. It was hard to believe.

Their father was Aunt Amy's brother Harry. She had been his favorite sister. He sometimes glanced at the photograph and said, "It's not very good. Her hair and her smile were her chief beauties, and they aren't shown at all. She was much slimmer than that, too. There were never any fat women in the family, thank God."

When they heard their father say things like that, Maria and Miranda simply wondered, without criticism, what he meant. Their grandmother was thin as a match; the pictures of their mother, long since dead, proved her to have been a candle-wick, almost. Dashing young ladies, who turned out to be, to Miranda's astonishment, merely more of Grandmother's grandchildren, like herself, came visiting from school for the holidays, boasting of their eighteen-inch waists. But how did their father account for great-aunt Eliza, who quite squeezed herself through doors, and who, when seated, was one solid pyramidal monument from floor to neck? What about great-aunt Keziah, in Kentucky? Her husband, great-uncle John Jacob, had refused to allow her to ride his good horses after she had achieved two hundred and twenty pounds. "No," said great-uncle John Jacob, "my sentiments of chivalry are not dead in my bosom; but neither is my common sense, to say nothing of charity to our faithful dumb friends. And the greatest of these is charity." It was suggested to great-uncle John Jacob that charity should forbid him to wound great-aunt Keziah's female vanity by such a comment on her figure. "Female vanity will recover," said great-uncle John Jacob, callously, "but what about my horses' backs? And if she had the proper female vanity in the first place, she would never have got into such shape." Well, great-aunt Keziah was famous for her heft, and wasn't she in the family? But something seemed to happen to their father's memory when he thought of the girls he had known in the family of his youth, and he declared steadfastly they had all been, in every generation without exception, as slim as reeds and graceful as sylphs.

This loyalty of their father's in the face of evidence contrary to his ideal had its springs in family feeling, and a love of legend that he shared with the others. They loved to tell stories, romantic and poetic, or comic with a romantic humor; they did not gild the outward circumstance, it was the feeling that mattered.

Their hearts and imaginations were captivated by their past, a past in which worldly considerations had played a very minor role. Their stories were almost always love stories against a bright blank heavenly blue sky.

Photographs, portraits by inept painters who meant earnestly to flatter, and the festival garments folded away in dried herbs and camphor were disappointing when the little girls tried to fit them to the living beings created in their minds by the breathing words of their elders. Grandmother, twice a year compelled in her blood by the change of seasons, would sit nearly all of one day beside old trunks and boxes in the lumber room, unfolding layers of garments and small keepsakes; she spread them out on sheets on the floor around her, crying over certain things, nearly always the same things, looking again at pictures in velvet cases, unwrapping locks of hair and dried flowers, crying gently and easily as if tears were the only pleasure she had left.

If Maria and Miranda were very quiet, and touched nothing until it was offered, they might sit by her at these times, or come and go. There was a tacit understanding that her grief was strictly her own, and must not be noticed or mentioned. The little girls examined the objects, one by one, and did not find them, in themselves, impressive. Such dowdy little wreaths and necklaces, some of them made of pearly shells; such moth-eaten bunches of pink ostrich feathers for the hair; such clumsy big breast pins and bracelets of gold and colored enamel; such silly-looking combs, standing up on tall teeth capped with seed pearls and French paste. Miranda, without knowing why, felt melancholy. It seemed such a pity that these faded things, these yellowed long gloves and misshapen satin slippers, these broad ribbons cracking where they were folded, should have been all those vanished girls had to decorate themselves with. And where were they now, those girls, and the boys in the odd-looking collars? The young men seemed even more unreal than the girls, with their high-buttoned coats, their puffy neckties, their waxed mustaches, their waving thick hair combed carefully over their foreheads. Who could have taken them seriously, looking like that?

No, Maria and Miranda found it impossible to sympathize with those young persons, sitting rather stiffly before the camera, hopelessly out of fashion; but they were drawn and held by the mysterious love of the living, who remembered and cherished these dead. The visible remains were nothing; they were dust, perishable as the flesh; the features stamped on paper and metal were nothing, but their living memory enchanted the little girls. They listened, all ears and eager minds, picking here and there among the floating ends of narrative, patching together as well as they could fragments of tales that were like bits of poetry or music, indeed were associated with the poetry they had heard or read, with music, with the theater.

"Tell me again how Aunt Amy went away when she was married." "She ran into the gray cold and stepped into the carriage and turned and smiled with her face as pale as death, and called out 'Good-by, good-by,' and refused her cloak, and said, 'Give me a glass of wine.' And none of us saw her alive again." "Why wouldn't she wear her cloak, Cousin Cora?" "Because she was not in love, my dear." Ruin hath taught me thus to ruminate, that time will come and take my love away. "Was she really beautiful, Uncle Bill?" "As an angel, my child." There were golden-haired angels with long blue pleated skirts dancing around the throne of the Blessed Virgin. None of them resembled Aunt Amy in the least, nor the type of beauty they had been brought up to admire. There were points of beauty by which one was judged severely. First, a beauty must be tall; whatever color the eyes, the hair must be dark, the darker the better; the skin must be pale and smooth. Lightness and swiftness of movement were important points. A beauty must be a good dancer, superb on horseback, with a serene manner, an amiable gaiety tempered with dignity at all hours. Beautiful teeth and hands, of course, and over and above all this, some mysterious crown of enchantment that attracted and held the heart. It was all very exciting and discouraging.

Miranda persisted through her childhood in believing, in spite of her smallness, thinness, her little snubby nose saddled with freckles, her speckled gray eyes and habitual tantrums, that by some miracle she would grow into a tall, cream-colored brunette, like cousin Isabel; she decided always to wear a trailing white satin gown. Maria, born sensible, had no such illusions. "We are going to take after Mamma's family," she said. "It's no use, we are. We'll never be beautiful, we'll always have freckles. And *you*," she told Miranda, "haven't even a good disposition."

Miranda admitted both truth and justice in this unkindness, but still secretly believed that she would one day suddenly receive beauty, as by inheritance, riches laid suddenly in her hands through no deserts of her own. She believed for quite a while that she would one day be like Aunt Amy, not as she appeared in the photograph, but as she was remembered by those who had seen her.

When Cousin Isabel came out in her tight black riding habit, surrounded by young men, and mounted gracefully, drawing her horse up and around so that he pranced learnedly on one spot while the other riders sprang to their saddles in the same sedate flurry, Miranda's heart would close with such a keen dart of admiration, envy, vicarious pride it was almost painful; but there would always be an elder present to lay a cooling hand upon her emotions. "She rides almost as well as Amy, doesn't she? But Amy had the pure Spanish style, she could bring out paces in a horse no one else knew he had." Young namesake Amy, on her way to a dance, would swish through the hall in ruffled white taffeta, glimmering like a moth in the lamplight, carrying her elbows pointed backward stiffly as wings, sliding along as if she were on rollers, in the fashionable walk of her day. She was considered the best dancer at any party, and Maria, sniffing the wave of perfume that followed Amy, would clasp her hands and say, "Oh, I can't *wait* to be grown up." But the elders would agree that the first Amy had been lighter, more smooth and delicate in her waltzing; young Amy would never equal her. Cousin Molly Parrington, far past her youth, indeed she belonged to the generation before Aunt Amy, was a noted charmer. Men who had known her all her life still gathered about her; now that she was happily widowed for the second time there was no doubt that she would yet marry again. But Amy, said the elders, had the same high spirits and wit without boldness, and you really could not say that Molly had ever been discreet. She dyed her hair, and made jokes about it. She had a way of collecting the men around her in a corner, where she told them stories. She was an unnatural mother to her ugly daughter Eva, an old maid past forty while her mother was still the belle of the ball. "Born when I was fifteen, you remember," Molly would say shamelessly, looking an old beau straight in the eye, both of them remembering that he had been best man at her first wedding when she was past twenty-one. "Everyone said I was like a little girl with her doll."

Eva, shy and chinless, straining her upper lip over two enormous teeth, would sit in corners watching her mother. She looked hungry, her eyes were strained and tired. She wore her mother's old clothes, made over, and taught Latin in a Female Seminary. She believed in votes for women, and had traveled about, making speeches. When her mother was not present, Eva bloomed out a little, danced prettily, smiled, showing all her teeth, and was like a dry little plant set out in a gentle rain. Molly was merry about her ugly duckling. "It's lucky for me my daughter is an old maid. She's not so apt," said Molly naughtily, "to make a grandmother of me." Eva would blush as if she had been slapped.

Eva was a blot, no doubt about it, but the little girls felt she belonged to their everyday world of dull lessons to be learned, stiff shoes to be limbered up, scratchy flannels to be endured in cold weather, measles and disappointed expectations. Their Aunt Amy belonged to the world of poetry. The romance of Uncle Gabriel's long, unrewarded love for her, her early death, was such a story as one found in old books: unworldly books, but true, such as the Vita Nuova, the Sonnets of Shakespeare and the Wedding Song of Spenser; and poems by Edgar Allan Poe. "Her tantalized spirit now blandly reposes, Forgetting or never regretting its roses. . . ." Their father read that to them, and said, "He was our greatest poet," and they knew that "our" meant he was Southern. Aunt Amy was real as the pictures in the old Holbein and Durer books were real. The little girls lay flat on their stomachs and peered into a world of wonder, turning the shabby leaves that fell apart easily, not surprised at the sight of the Mother of God sitting on a hollow log nursing her child; not doubting either Death or the Devil riding at the stirrups of the grim night; not questioning the propriety of the stiffly dressed ladies of Sir Thomas More's household, seated in dignity on the floor, or seeming to be. They missed all the dog and pony shows, and lantern-slide entertainments, but their father took them to see "Hamlet," and "The Taming of the Shrew," and "Richard the Third," and a long sad play with Mary, Queen of Scots, in it. Miranda thought the magnificent lady in black velvet was truly the Queen of Scots, and was pained to learn that the real Queen had died long ago, and not at all on the night she, Miranda, had been present.

The little girls loved the theater, that world of personages taller than human beings, who swept upon the scene and invested it with their presences, their more than human voices, their gestures of gods and goddesses ruling a universe. But there was always a voice recalling other and greater occasions. Grandmother in her youth had heard Jenny Lind, and thought that Nellie Melba was much overrated. Father had seen Bernhardt, and Madame Modjeska was no sort of rival. When Paderewski played for the first time in their city, cousins came from all over the state and went from the grandmother's house to hear him. The little girls were left out of this great occasion. They shared the excitement of the going away, and shared the beautiful moment of return, when cousins stood about in groups, with coffee cups and glasses in their hands, talking in low voices, awed and happy. The little girls, struck with the sense of a great event, hung about in their nightgowns and listened, until someone noticed and hustled them away from the sweet nimbus of all that glory. One old gentleman, however, had heard Rubinstein frequently. He could not but feel that Rubinstein had reached the final height of musical interpretation, and for him, Paderewski had been something of an anticlimax. The little girls heard him muttering on, holding up one hand, patting the air as if he were calling for silence. The others looked at him, and listened, without any disturbance of their grave tender mood. They had never heard Rubinstein; they had, one hour since, heard Paderewski, and why should anyone need to recall the past? Miranda, dragged away, half understanding the old gentleman, hated him. She felt that she too had heard Paderewski.

There was then a life beyond a life in this world, as well as in the next; such episodes confirmed for the little girls the nobility of human feeling, the divinity of man's vision of the unseen, the importance of life and death, the depths of the human heart, the romantic value of tragedy. Cousin Eva, on a certain visit, trying to interest them in the study of Latin, told them the story of John Wilkes Booth, who, handsomely garbed in a long black cloak, had leaped to the stage after assassinating President Lincoln. "Sic semper tyrannis," he had shouted superbly, in spite of his broken leg. The little girls never doubted that it had happened in just that way, and the moral seemed to be that one should always have Latin, or at least a good classical poetry quotation, to depend upon in great or desperate moments. Cousin Eva reminded them that no one, not even a good Southerner, could possibly approve of John Wilkes Booth's deed. It was murder, after all. They were to remember that. But Miranda, used to tragedy in books and in family legends—two great-uncles had committed suicide and a remote ancestress had gone mad for love—decided that, without the murder, there would have been no point to dressing up and leaping to the stage shouting in Latin. So how could she disapprove of the deed? It was a fine story. She knew a distantly related old gentleman who had been devoted to the art of Booth, had seen him in a great many plays, but not, alas, at his greatest moment. Miranda regretted this; it would have been so pleasant to have the assassination of Lincoln in the family.

Uncle Gabriel, who had loved Aunt Amy so desperately, still lived somewhere, though Miranda and Maria had never seen him. He had gone away, far away, after her death. He still owned racehorses, and ran them at famous tracks all over the country, and Miranda believed there could not possibly be a more brilliant career. He had married again, quite soon, and had written to Grandmother, asking her to accept his new wife as a daughter in place of Amy. Grandmother had written coldly, accepting, inviting them for a visit, but Uncle Gabriel had somehow never brought his bride home. Harry had visited them in New Orleans, and reported that the second wife was a very good-looking well-bred blonde girl who would undoubtedly be a good wife for Gabriel. Still, Uncle Gabriel's heart was broken. Faithfully once a year he wrote a letter to someone of the family, sending money for a wreath for Amy's grave. He had written a poem for her gravestone, and had come home, leaving his second wife in Atlanta, to see that it was carved properly. He could never account for having written this poem; he had certainly never tried to write a single rhyme since leaving school. Yet one day when he had been thinking about Amy, the verse occurred to him, out of the air. Maria and Miranda had seen it, printed in gold on a mourning card. Uncle Gabriel had sent a great number of them to be handed around among the family.

> "She lives again who suffered life,
>   Then suffered death, and now set free
>   A singing angel, she forgets
>   The griefs of old mortality."

"Did she really sing?" Maria asked her father.

"Now what has that to do with it?" he asked. "It's a poem."

"I think it's very pretty," said Miranda, impressed. Uncle Gabriel was second cousin to her father and Aunt Amy. It brought poetry very near.

"Not so bad for tombstone poetry," said their father, "but it should be better."

Uncle Gabriel had waited five years to marry Aunt Amy. She had been ill, her chest was weak; she was engaged twice to other young men and broke her engagements for no reason; and she laughed at the advice of older and kinder-hearted persons who thought it very capricious of her not to return the devotion of such a handsome and romantic young man as Gabriel, her second cousin, too; it was not as if she would be marrying a stranger. Her coldness was said to have driven Gabriel to a wild life and even to drinking. His grandfather was wealthy and Gabriel was his favorite; they had quarreled over the racehorses, and Gabriel had shouted, "By God, I must have *something*." As if he had not everything already: youth, health, good looks, the prospect of riches, and a devoted family circle. His grandfather pointed out to him that he was little better than an ingrate, and showed signs of being a wastrel as well. Gabriel said, "You had racehorses, and made a good thing of them." "I never depended upon them for a livelihood, sir," said his grandfather.

Gabriel wrote letters about this and many other things to Amy from Saratoga and from Kentucky and from New Orleans, sending her presents, and flowers packed in ice, and telegrams. The presents were amusing, such as a huge cage full of small green lovebirds; or, as an ornament for her hair, a full-petaled enameled rose with paste dewdrops, with an enameled butterfly in brilliant colors suspended quivering on a gold wire about it; but the telegrams always frightened her mother, and the flowers, after a journey by train and then by stage into the country, were much the worse for wear. He would send roses when the rose garden at home was in full bloom. Amy could not help smiling over it, though her mother insisted it was touching and sweet of Gabriel. It must prove to Amy that she was always in his thoughts.

"That's no place for me," said Amy, but she had a way of speaking, a tone of voice, which made it impossible to discover what she meant by what she said. It was possible always that she might be serious. And she would not answer questions.

"Amy's wedding dress," said the grandmother, unfurling an immense cloak of dove-colored cut velvet, spreading beside it a silvery-gray watered-silk frock, and a small gray velvet toque with a dark red breast of feathers. Cousin Isabel, the beauty, sat with her. They talked to each other, and Miranda could listen if she chose.

"She would not wear white, nor a veil," said Grandmother. "I couldn't oppose her, for I had said my daughters should each have exactly the wedding dress they wanted. But Amy surprised me. 'Now what would I look like in white satin?' she asked. It's true she was pale, but she would have been angelic in it, and all of us told her so. 'I shall wear mourning if I like,' she said, 'it is *my* funeral, you know.' I reminded her that Lou and your mother had worn white with veils and it would please me to have my daughters all alike in that. Amy said, 'Lou and Isabel are not like me,' but I could not persuade her to explain what she meant. One day when she was ill she said, 'Mammy, I'm not long for this world,' but not as if she meant it. I told her, 'You might live as long as anyone, if only you will be sensible.' 'That's the whole trouble,' said Amy. 'I feel sorry for Gabriel,' she told me. 'He doesn't know what he's asking for.' "

"I tried to tell her once more," said the grandmother, "that marriage and children would cure her of everything. 'All women of our family are delicate when they are young,' I said. 'Why, when I was your age no one expected me to live a year. It was called greensickness, and everybody knew there was only one cure.' 'If I live for a hundred years and turn green as grass,' said Amy, 'I still shan't want to marry Gabriel.' So I told her very seriously that if she truly felt that way she must never do it, and Gabriel must be told once for all, and sent away. He would get over it. 'I have told him, and I have sent him away,' said Amy. 'He just doesn't listen.' We both laughed at that, and I told her young girls found a hundred ways to deny they wished to be married, and a thousand more to test their power over men, but that she had more than enough of that, and now it was time for her to be entirely sincere and make her decision. As for me," said the grandmother, "I wished with all my heart to marry your grandfather, and if he had not asked me, I should have asked him most certainly. Amy insisted that she could not imagine wanting to marry anybody. She would be, she said, a nice old maid like Eva Parrington. For even then it was pretty plain that Eva was an old maid, born. Harry said, 'Oh, Eva—Eva has no chin, that's her trouble. If you had no chin, Amy, you'd be in the same fix as Eva, no doubt.' Your Uncle Bill would say, 'When women haven't anything else, they'll take a vote for con-solation. A pretty thin bed-fellow,' said your Uncle Bill. 'What I really need is a good dancing partner to guide me through life,' said Amy, 'that's the match I'm looking for.' It was no good trying to talk to her."

Her brothers remembered her tenderly as a sensible girl. After listening to their comments on her character and ways, Maria decided that they considered her sensible because she asked their advice about her appearance when she was going out to dance. If they found fault in any way, she would change her dress or her hair until they were pleased, and say, "You are an angel not to let your poor sister go out looking like a freak." But she would not listen to her father, nor to Gabriel. If Gabriel praised the frock she was wearing, she was apt to disappear and come back in another. He loved her long black hair, and once, lifting it up from her pillow when she was ill, said, "I love your hair, Amy, the most beautiful hair in the world." When he returned on his next visit, he found her with her hair cropped and curled close to her head. He was horrified, as if she had willfully mutilated herself. She would not let it grow again, not even to please her brothers. The photograph hanging on the wall was one she had made at that time to send to Gabriel, who sent it back without a word. This pleased her, and she framed the photograph. There was a thin inky scrawl low in one corner, "To dear brother Harry, who likes my hair cut."

This was a mischievous reference to a very grave scandal. The little girls used to look at their father, and wonder what would have happened if he had really hit the young man he shot at. The young man was believed to have kissed Aunt Amy, when she was not in the least engaged to him. Uncle Gabriel was supposed to have had a duel with the young man, but Father had got there first. He was a pleasant, everyday sort of father, who held his daughters on his knee if they were prettily dressed and well behaved, and pushed them away if they had not freshly combed hair and nicely scrubbed fingernails. "Go away, you're disgusting," he would say, in a matter-of-fact voice. He noticed if their stocking seams were crooked. He caused them to brush their teeth with a revolting mixture of prepared chalk, powdered charcoal and salt. When they behaved stupidly he could not endure the sight of them. They understood dimly that all this was for their own future good; and when they were snivelly with colds, he prescribed delicious hot toddy for them, and saw that it was given them. He was always hoping they might not grow up to be so silly as they seemed to him at any given moment, and he had a disconcerting way of inquiring, "How do you *know?*" when they forgot and made dogmatic statements in his presence. It always came out embarrassingly that they did not know at all, but were repeating something they had heard. This made conversation with him difficult, for he laid traps and they fell into them, but it became important to them that their father should not believe them to be fools. Well, this very father had gone to Mexico once and stayed there for nearly a year, because he had shot at a man with whom Aunt Amy had flirted at a dance. It had been very wrong of him, because he should have challenged the man to a duel, as Uncle Gabriel had done. Instead, he just took a shot at him, and this was the lowest sort of manners. It had caused great disturbance in the whole community and had almost broken up the affair between Aunt Amy and Uncle Gabriel for good. Uncle Gabriel insisted that the young man had kissed Aunt Amy, and Aunt Amy insisted that the young man had merely paid her a compliment on her hair.

During the Mardi Gras holidays there was to be a big gay fancy-dress ball. Harry was going as a bull-fighter because his sweetheart, Mariana, had a new black lace mantilla and high comb from Mexico. Maria and Miranda had seen a photograph of their mother in this dress, her lovely face without a trace of coquetry looking gravely out from under a tremendous fall of lace from the peak of the comb, a rose tucked firmly over her ear. Amy copied her costume from a small Dresden-china shepherdess which stood on the mantelpiece in the parlor;

a careful copy with ribboned hat, gilded crook, very low-laced bodice, short basket skirts, green slippers and all. She wore it with a black half-mask, but it was no disguise. "You would have known it was Amy at any distance," said Father. Gabriel, six feet three in height as he was, had got himself up to match, and a spectacle he provided in pale blue satin knee breeches and a blond curled wig with a hair ribbon. "He felt a fool, and he looked like one," said Uncle Bill, "and he behaved like one before the evening was over."

Everything went beautifully until the party gathered downstairs to leave for the ball. Amy's father—he must have been born a grandfather, thought Miranda —gave one glance at his daughter, her white ankles shining, bosom deeply exposed, two round spots of paint on her cheeks ,and fell into a frenzy of outraged propriety. "It's disgraceful," he pronounced, loudly. "No daughter of mine is going to show herself in such a rig-out. It's bawdy," he thundered. "Bawdy!"

Amy had taken off her mask to smile at him. "Why, Papa," she said very sweetly, "what's wrong with it? Look on the mantelpiece. She's been there all along, and you were never shocked before."

"There's all the difference in the world," said her father, "all the difference, young lady, and you know it. You go upstairs this minute and pin up that waist in front and let down those skirts to a decent length before you leave this house. *And wash your face!*"

"I see nothing wrong with it," said Amy's mother, firmly, "and you shouldn't use such language before innocent young girls." She and Amy sat down with several females of the household to help, and they made short work of the business. In ten minutes Amy returned, face clean, bodice filled in with lace, shepherdess skirt modestly sweeping the carpet behind her.

When Amy appeared from the dressing room for her first dance with Gabriel, the lace was gone from her bodice, her skirts were tucked up more daringly than before, and the spots on her cheeks were like pomegranates. "Now Gabriel, tell me truly, wouldn't it have been a pity to spoil my costume?" Gabriel, delighted that she had asked his opinion, declared it was perfect. They agreed with kindly tolerance that old people were often tiresome, but one need not upset them by open disobedience: their youth was gone, what had they to live for?

Harry, dancing with Mariana who swung a heavy train around her expertly at every turn of the waltz, began to be uneasy about his sister Amy. She was entirely too popular. He saw young men make beelines across the floor, eyes fixed on those white silk ankles. Some of the young men he did not know at all, others he knew too well and could not approve of for his sister Amy. Gabriel, unhappy in his lyric satin and wig, stood about holding his ribboned crook as though it had sprouted thorns. He hardly danced at all with Amy, he did not enjoy dancing with anyone else, and he was having a thoroughly wretched time of it.

There appeared late, alone, got up as Jean Lafitte, a young Creole gentleman who had, two years before, been for a time engaged to Amy. He came straight to her, with the manner of a happy lover, and said, clearly enough for everyone near by to hear him, "I only came because I knew you were to be here. I only want to dance with you and I shall go again." Amy, with a face of delight, cried out, "Raymond!" as if to a lover. She had danced with him four times, and had then disappeared from the floor on his arm.

Harry and Mariana, in conventional disguise of romance, irreproachably betrothed, safe in their happiness, were waltzing slowly to their favorite song, the melancholy farewell of the Moorish King on leaving Granada. They sang in whispers to each other, in their uncertain Spanish, a song of love and parting and that sword's point of grief that makes the heart tender towards all other lost and disinherited creatures: Oh, mansion of love, my earthly paradise...that I shall see no more...whither flies the poor swallow, weary and homeless, seeking for shelter where no shelter is? I too am far from home without the power to fly.... Come to my heart, sweet bird, beloved pilgrim, build your nest near my bed, let me listen to your song, and weep for my lost land of joy....

Into this bliss broke Gabriel. He had thrown away his shepherd's crook and he was carrying his wig. He wanted to speak to Harry at once, and before Mariana knew what was happening she was sitting beside her mother and the two excited young men were gone. Waiting, disturbed and displeased, she smiled at Amy who waltzed past with a young man in Devil costume, including ill-fitting scarlet cloven hoofs. Almost at once, Harry and Gabriel came back, with serious faces, and Harry darted on the dance floor, returning with Amy. The girls and the chaperones were asked to come at once, they must be taken home. It was all mysterious and sudden, and Harry said to Mariana, "I will tell you what is happening, but not now—"

The grandmother remembered of this disgraceful affair only that Gabriel brought Amy home alone and that Harry came in somewhat later. The other members of the party straggled in at various hours, and the story came out piecemeal. Amy was silent and, her mother discovered later, burning with fever. "I saw at once that something was very wrong. 'What happened, Amy?' 'Oh, Harry goes about shooting at people at a party,' she said, sitting down as if she were exhausted. 'It was on your account, Amy,' said Gabriel. 'Oh, no, it was not,' said Amy. 'Don't believe him, Mammy.' So I said, 'Now enough of this. Tell me what happened, Amy.' And Amy said, 'Mammy, this is it. Raymond came in, and you know I like Raymond, and he is a good dancer. So we danced together, too much, maybe. We went on the gallery for a breath of air, and stood there. He said, "How well your hair looks. I like this new shingled style." ' She glanced at Gabriel. 'And then another young man came out and said, "I've been looking everywhere. This is our dance, isn't it?" And I went in to dance. And now it seems that Gabriel went out at once and challenged Raymond to a duel about something or other, but Harry doesn't wait for that. Raymond had already gone out to have his horse brought, I suppose one doesn't duel in fancy dress,' she said, looking at Gabriel, who fairly shriveled in his blue satin shepherd's costume, 'and Harry simply went out and shot at him. I don't think that was fair,' said Amy."

Her mother agreed that indeed it was not fair; it was not even decent, and she could not imagine what her son Harry thought he was doing. "It isn't much of a way to defend your sister's honor," she said to him afterward. "I didn't want Gabriel to go fighting duels," said Harry. "That wouldn't have helped much, either."

Gabriel had stood before Amy, leaning over, asking once more the question he had apparently been asking her all the way home. "Did he kiss you, Amy?"

Amy took off her shepherdess hat and pushed her hair back. "Maybe he did," she answered, "and maybe I wished him to."

"Amy, you must not say such things," said her mother. "Answer Gabriel's question."

"He hasn't the right to ask it," said Amy, but without anger.

"Do you love him, Amy?" asked Gabriel, the sweat standing out on his forehead.

"It doesn't matter," answered Amy, leaning back in her chair.

"Oh, it does matter; it matters terribly," said Gabriel. "You must answer me now." He took both of her hands and tried to hold them. She drew her hands away firmly and steadily so that he had to let go.

"Let her alone, Gabriel," said Amy's mother. "You'd better go now. We are all tired. Let's talk about it tomorrow."

She helped Amy to undress, noticing the changed bodice and the shortened skirt. "You shouldn't have done that, Amy. That was not wise of you. It was better the other way."

Amy said, "Mammy, I'm sick of this world. I don't like anything in it. It's so *dull*," she said, and for a moment she looked as if she might weep. She had never been tearful, even as a child, and her mother was alarmed. It was then she discovered that Amy had fever.

"Gabriel is dull, Mother—he sulks," she said. "I could see him sulking every time I passed. It spoils things," she said. "Oh, I want to go to sleep."

Her mother sat looking at her and wondering how it had happened she had brought such a beautiful child into the world. "Her face," said her mother, "was angelic in sleep."

Some time during that fevered night, the projected duel between Gabriel and Raymond was halted by the offices of friends on both sides. There remained the open question of Harry's impulsive shot, which was not so easily settled. Raymond seemed vindictive about that, it was possible he might choose to make trouble. Harry, taking the advice of Gabriel, his brothers and friends decided that the best way to avoid further scandal was for him to disappear for a while. This being decided upon, the young men returned about daybreak, saddled Harry's best horse and helped him pack a few things; accompanied by Gabriel and Bill, Harry set out for the border, feeling rather gay and adventurous.

Amy, being wakened by the stirring in the house, found out the plan. Five minutes after they were gone, she came down in her riding dress, had her own horse saddled, and struck out after them. She rode almost every morning; before her parents had time to be uneasy over her prolonged absence, they found her note.

What had threatened to be a tragedy became a rowdy lark. Amy rode to the border, kissed her brother Harry good-by, and rode back again with Bill and Gabriel. It was a three days' journey, and when they arrived Amy had to be lifted from the saddle. She was really ill by now, but in the gayest of humors. Her mother and father had been prepared to be severe with her, but, at sight of her, their feelings changed. They turned on Bill and Gabriel. "Why did you let her do this?" they asked.

"You know we could not stop her," said Gabriel helplessly, "and she did enjoy herself so much!"

Amy laughed. "Mammy, it was splendid, the most delightful trip I ever had. And if I am to be the heroine of this novel, why shouldn't I make the most of it?"

The scandal, Maria and Miranda gathered, had been pretty terrible. Amy simply took to bed and stayed there, and Harry had skipped out blithely to wait until the little affair blew over. The rest of the family had to receive visitors, write letters, go to church, return calls, and bear the whole brunt, as they expressed it. They sat in the twilight of scandal in their little world, holding themselves very rigidly, in a shared tension as if all their nerves began at a common center. This center had received a blow, and family nerves shuddered, even into the farthest reaches of Kentucky. From whence in due time great-great-aunt Sally Rhea addressed a letter to *Mifs Amy Rhea*. In deep brown ink like dried blood, in a spidery hand adept at archaic symbols and abbreviations great-great-aunt Sally informed Amy that she was fairly convinced that this calamity was only the forerunner of a series shortly to be visited by the Almighty God upon a race already condemned through its own wickedness, a warning that man's time was short, and that they must all prepare for the end of the world. For herself, she had long expected it, she was entirely resigned to the prospect of meeting her Maker; and Amy, no less than her wicked brother Harry, must likewise place herself in God's hands and prepare for the worst. *"Oh, my dear unfortunate young relative,"* twittered great-great-aunt Sally, *"we must in our Extremity join hands and appr before ye Dread Throne of Jdgment a United Fmly if One is Mssg from ye Flock, what will Jesus say?"*

Great-great-aunt Sally's religious career had become comic legend. She had forsaken her Catholic rearing for a young man whose family were Cumberland Presbyterians. Unable to accept their opinions, however, she was converted to the Hard-Shell Baptists, a sect as loathsome to her husband's family as the Catholic could possibly be. She had spent a life of vicious self-indulgent martyrdom to her faith; as Harry commented: "Religion put claws on Aunt Sally and gave her a post to whet them on." She had out-argued, out-fought, and out-lived her entire generation, but she did not miss them. She bedeviled the second generation without ceasing, and was beginning hungrily on the third.

Amy, reading this letter, broke into her gay full laugh that always caused everyone around her to laugh too, even before they knew why, and her small green lovebirds in their cage turned and eyed her solemnly. "Imagine drawing a pew in heaven beside Aunt Sally," she said. "What a prospect."

"Don't laugh too soon," said her father. "Heaven was made to order for Aunt Sally. She'll be on her own territory there."

"For my sins," said Amy, "I must go to heaven with Aunt Sally."

During the uncomfortable time of Harry's absence, Amy went on refusing to marry Gabriel. Her mother could hear their voices going on in their endless colloquy, during many long days. One afternoon, Gabriel came out, looking very sober and discouraged. He stood looking down at Amy's mother as she sat sewing, and said, "I think it is all over, I believe now that Amy will never have me." The grandmother always said afterward, "Never have I pitied anyone as I did poor Gabriel at that moment. But I told him, very firmly, 'Let her alone, then, she is ill.' " So Gabriel left, and Amy had no word from him for more than a month.

The day after Gabriel was gone, Amy rose looking extremely well, went hunting with her brothers Bill and Stephen, bought a velvet wrap, had her hair shingled and curled again, and wrote long letters to Harry, who was having a most enjoyable exile in Mexico City.

After dancing all night three times in one week, she woke one morning in a hemorrhage. She seemed frightened and asked for the doctor, promising to do whatever he advised. She was quiet for a few days, reading. She asked for Gabriel. No one knew where he was. "You should write him a letter; his mother will send it on." "Oh, no," she said. "I miss him coming in with his sour face. Letters are no good."

Gabriel did come in, only a few days later, with a very sour face and unpleasant news. His grandfather had died, after a day's illness. On his death bed, in the name of God, being of a sound and disposing mind, he had cut off his favorite grandchild Gabriel with one dollar. "In the name of God, Amy," said Gabriel, "the old devil has ruined me in one sentence."

It was the conduct of his immediate family in the matter that had embittered him, he said. They could hardly conceal their satisfaction. They had known and envied Gabriel's quite just, well-founded expectations. Not one of them offered to make any private settlement. No one even thought of repairing this last-minute act of senile vengeance. Privately they blessed their luck. "I have been cut off with a dollar," said Gabriel, "and they are all glad of it. I think they feel somehow that this justifies every criticism they ever made against me. They were right about me all along. I am a worthless poor relation," said Gabriel. "My God, I wish you could see them."

Amy said, "I wonder how you will ever support a wife, now."

Gabriel said, "Oh, it isn't so bad as that. If you would, Amy—"

Amy said, "Gabriel, if we get married now there'll be just time to be in New Orleans for Mardi Gras. If we wait until after Lent, it may be too late."

"Why, Amy," said Gabriel, "how could it ever be too late?"

"You might change your mind," said Amy. "You know how fickle you are."

There were two letters in the grandmother's many packets of letters that Maria and Miranda read after they were grown. One of them was from Amy. It was dated ten days after her marriage.

"Dear Mammy, New Orleans han't changed as much as I have since we saw each other last. I am now a staid old married woman, and Gabriel is very devoted and kind. Footlights won a race for us yesterday, she was the favorite, and it was wonderful. I go to the races every day, and our horses are doing splendidly; I had my choice of Erin Go Bragh or Miss Lucy, and I chose Miss Lucy. She is mine now, she runs like a streak. Gabriel says I made a mistake, Erin Go Bragh will stay better. I think Miss Lucy will stay my time.

"We are having a lovely visit. I'm going to put on a domino and take to the streets with Gabriel some time during Mardi Gras. I'm tired of watching the show from a balcony. Gabriel says it isn't safe. He says he'll take me if I insist, but I doubt it. Mammy, he's very nice. Don't worry about me. I have a beautiful black-and-rose-colored velvet gown for the Proteus Ball. Madame, my new mother-in-law, wanted to know if it wasn't a little dashing. I told her I hoped so or I had been cheated. It is fitted perfectly smooth in the bodice, very low in the shoulders—Papa would not approve—and the skirt is looped with wide silver ribbons between the waist and knees in front, and then it surges around and is looped enormously in the back, with a train just one yard long. I now have an eighteen-inch waist, thanks to Madame Duré. I expect to be so dashing that my mother-in-law will have an attack. She has them quite often. Gabriel sends love. Please take good care of Graylie and Fiddler. I want to ride them again when I come home. We're going to Saratoga, I don't know just when. Give everybody my dear dear love. It rains all the time here, of course. . . .

"P.S. Mammy, as soon as I get a minute to myself I'm going to be terribly homesick. Good-by, my darling Mammy."

The other was from Amy's nurse, dated six weeks after Amy's marriage.

"I cut off the lock of hair because I was sure you would like to have it. And I do not want you to think I was careless, leaving her medicine where she could get it, the doctor has written and explained. It would not have done her any harm except that her heart was weak. She did not know how much she was taking, often she said to me, one more of those little capsules wouldn't do any harm, and so I told her to be careful and not take anything except what I gave her. She begged me for them sometimes but I would not give her more than the doctor said. I slept during the night because she did not seem to be so sick as all that and the doctor did not order me to sit up with her. Please accept my regrets for your great loss and please do not think that anybody was careless with your dear daughter. She suffered a great deal and now she is at rest. She could not get well but she might have lived longer. Yours respectfully. . . ."

The letters and all the strange keepsakes were packed away and forgotten for a great many years. They seemed to have no place in the world.

Part II: 1904

During vacation on their grandmother's farm, Maria and Miranda, who read as naturally and constantly as ponies crop grass, and with much the same kind of pleasure, had by some happy chance laid hold of some forbidden reading matter, brought in and left there with missionary intent, no doubt, by some Protestant cousin. It fell into the right hands if enjoyment had been its end. The reading matter was printed in poor type on spongy paper, and was orna- mented with smudgy illustrations all the more exciting to the little girls because they could not make head or tail of them. The stories were about beautiful but unlucky maidens, who for mysterious reasons had been trapped by nuns and priests in dire collusion; they were then "immured" in convents, where they were forced to take the veil—an appalling rite during which the victims shrieked dreadfully—

and condemned forever after to most uncomfortable and disorderly existences. They seemed to divide their time between lying chained in dark cells and assisting other nuns to bury throttled infants under stones in moldering rat-infested dungeons.

Immured! It was the word Maria and Miranda had been needing all along to describe their condition at the Convent of the Child Jesus, in New Orleans, where they spent the long winters trying to avoid an education. There were no dungeons at the Child Jesus, and this was only one of numerous marked differences between convent life as Maria and Miranda knew it and the thrilling paper-backed version. It was no good at all trying to fit the stories to life, and they did not even try. They had long since learned to draw the lines between life, which was real and earnest, and the grave was not its goal; poetry, which was true but not real; and stories, or forbidden reading matter, in which things happened as nowhere else, with the most sublime irrelevance and unlikelihood, and one need not turn a hair, because there was not a word of truth in them.

It was true the little girls were hedged and confined, but in a large garden with trees and a grotto; they were locked at night into a long cold dormitory, with all the windows open, and a sister sleeping at either end. Their beds were curtained with muslin, and small night-lamps were so arranged that the sisters could see through the curtains, but the children could not see the sisters. Miranda wondered if they ever slept, or did they sit there all night quietly watching the sleepers through the muslin? She tried to work up a little sinister thrill about this, but she found it impossible to care much what either of the sisters did. They were very dull good-natured women who managed to make the whole dormitory seem dull. All days and all things in the Convent of the Child Jesus were dull, in fact, and Maria and Miranda lived for Saturdays.

No one had even hinted that they should become nuns. On the contrary Miranda felt that the discouraging attitude of Sister Claude and Sister Austin and Sister Ursula towards her expressed ambition to be a nun barely veiled a deeply critical knowledge of her spiritual deficiencies. Still Maria and Miranda had got a fine new word out of their summer reading, and they referred to themselves as "immured." It gave a romantic glint to what was otherwise a very dull life for them, except for blessed Saturday afternoons during the racing season.

If the nuns were able to assure the family that the deportment and scholastic achievements of Maria and Miranda were at least passable, some cousin or other always showed up smiling, in holiday mood, to take them to the races, where they were given a dollar each to bet on any horse they chose. There were black Saturdays now and then, when Maria and Miranda sat ready, hats in hand, curly hair plastered down and slicked behind their ears, their stiffly pleated navy-blue skirts spread out around them, waiting with their hearts going down slowly into their high-topped laced-up black shoes. They never put on their hats until the last minute, for somehow it would have been too horrible to have their hats on, when, after all, Cousin Henry and Cousin Isabel, or Uncle George and Aunt Polly, were not coming to take them to the races. When no one appeared, and Saturday came and went a sickening waste, they were then given to understand that it was a punishment for bad marks during the week. They never knew until it was too late to avoid the disappointment. It was very wearing.

One Saturday they were sent down to wait in the visitors' parlor, and there was their father. He had come all the way from Texas to see them. They leaped at sight of him, and then stopped short, suspiciously. Was he going to take them to the races? If so, they were happy to see him.

"Hello," said father, kissing their cheeks. "Have you been good girls? Your Uncle Gabriel is running a mare at the Crescent City today, so we'll all go and bet on her. Would you like that?"

Maria put on her hat without a word, but Miranda stood and addressed her father sternly. She had suffered many doubts about this day. *"Why* didn't· you send word yesterday? I could have been looking forward all this time."

"We didn't know," said father, in his easiest paternal manner, "that you were going to deserve it. Remember Saturday before last?"

Miranda hung her head and put on her hat, with the round elastic under the chin. She remembered too well. She had, in midweek, given way to despair over her arithmetic and had fallen flat on her face on the classroom floor, refusing to rise until she was carried out. The rest of the week had been a series of novel deprivations, and Saturday a day of mourning; secret mourning, for if one mourned too noisily, it simply meant another bad mark against deportment.

"Never mind," said father, as if it were the smallest possible matter, "today you're going. Come along now. We've barely time."

These expeditions were all joy, every time, from the moment they stepped into a closed one-horse cab, a treat in itself with its dark, thick upholstery, soaked with strange perfumes and tobacco smoke, until the thrilling moment when they walked into a restaurant under big lights and were given dinner with things to eat they never had at home, much less at the convent. They felt worldly and grown up, each with her glass of water colored pink with claret.

The great crowd was always exciting as if they had never seen it before, with the beautiful, incredibly dressed ladies, all plumes and flowers and paint, and the elegant gentlemen with yellow gloves. The bands played in turn with thundering drums and brasses, and now and then a wild beautiful horse would career around the track with a tiny, monkey-shaped boy on his back, limbering up for his race.

Miranda had a secret personal interest in all this which she knew better than to confide to anyone, even Maria. Least of all to Maria. In ten minutes the whole family would have known. She had lately decided to be a jockey when she grew up. Her father had said one day that she was going to be a little thing all her life, she would never be tall; and this meant, of course, that she would never be a beauty like Aunt Amy, or Cousin Isabel. Her hope of being a beauty died hard, until the notion of being a jockey came suddenly and filled all her thoughts. Quietly, blissfully, at night before she slept, and too often in the daytime when she should have been studying, she planned her career as jockey. It was dim in detail, but brilliant at the right distance. It seemed too silly to be worried about arithmetic at all, when what she needed for her future was to ride better—much better. "You ought to be ashamed of yourself," said father, after watching her gallop full tilt down the lane at the farm, on Trixie, the mustang mare. "I can see the sun, moon and stars between you and the saddle every jump." Spanish style meant that one sat close to the saddle, and did all kinds of things with the knees and reins. Jockeys bounced lightly, their knees almost level with the horse's back, rising and falling like a rubber ball. Miranda felt she could do that easily. Yes, she would be a jockey, like Tod Sloan, winning every other race at least. Meantime, while she was training, she would keep it a secret, and one day she would ride out, bouncing lightly, with the other jockeys, and win a great race, and surprise everybody, her family most of all.

On that particular Saturday, her idol, the great Tod Sloan, was riding, and he won two races. Miranda longed to bet her dollar on Tod Sloan, but father said, "Not now, honey. Today you must bet on Uncle Gabriel's horse. Save your dollar for the fourth race, and put it on Miss Lucy. You've got a hundred to one shot. Think if she wins."

Miranda knew well enough that a hundred to one shot was no bet at all. She sulked, the crumbled dollar in her hand grew damp and warm. She could have won three dollars already on Tod Sloan. Maria said virtuously, "It wouldn't be nice not to bet on Uncle Gabriel. That way, we keep the money in the family." Miranda put out her upper lip at her sister. Maria was too prissy for words. She wrinkled her nose back at Miranda.

They had just turned their dollar over to the bookmaker for the fourth race when a vast bulging man with a red face and immense tan ragged mustaches fading into gray hailed them from a lower level of the grandstand, over the heads of the crowd, "Hey, there, Harry?" Father said, "Bless my soul, there's Gabriel." He motioned to the man, who came pushing his way heavily up the shallow steps. Maria and Miranda stared, first at him, then at each other. "Can that be our Uncle Gabriel?" their eyes asked. "Is that Aunt Amy's handsome romantic beau? Is that the man who wrote the poem about our Aunt Amy?" Oh, what did grown-up people *mean* when they talked, anyway?

He was a shabby fat man with bloodshot blue eyes, sad beaten eyes, and a big melancholy laugh, like a groan. He towered over them shouting to their father, "Well, for God's sake, Harry, it's been a coon's age. You ought to come out and look 'em over. You look just like yourself, Harry, how are you?"

The band struck up "Over the River" and Uncle Gabriel shouted louder. "Come on, let's get out of this. What are you doing up here with the pikers?"

"Can't," shouted father. "Brought my little girls. Here they are."

Uncle Gabriel's bleared eyes beamed blindly upon them. "Fine looking set, Harry," he bellowed, "pretty as pictures, how old are they?"

"Ten and fourteen now," said father; "awkward ages. Nest of vipers," he boasted, "perfect batch of serpent's teeth. Can't do a thing with 'em." He fluffed up Miranda's hair, pretending to tousle it.

"Pretty as pictures," bawled Uncle Gabriel, "but rolled into one they don't come up to Amy, do they?"

"'No, they don't," admitted their father at the top of his voice, "but they're only half-baked." *Over the river, over the river,* moaned the band, *my sweetheart's waiting for me.*

"I've got to get back now," yelled Uncle Gabriel. The little girls felt quite deaf and confused. "Got the God-damnedest jockey in the world, Harry, just my luck.

Ought to tie him on. Fell off Fiddler yesterday, just plain fell off on his tail—
Remember Amy's mare, Miss Lucy? Well, this is her namesake, Miss Lucy IV.
None of 'em ever came up to the first one, though. Stay right where you are,
I'll be back."

Maria spoke up boldly. "Uncle Gabriel, tell Miss Lucy we're betting on her."
Uncle Gabriel bent down and it looked as if there were tears in his swollen eyes.
"God bless your sweet heart," he bellowed, "I'll tell her." He plunged down
through the crowd again, his fat back bowed slightly in his loose clothes, his thick
neck rolling over his collar.

Miranda and Maria, disheartened by the odds, by their first sight of their
romantic Uncle Gabriel, whose language was so coarse, sat listlessly without
watching, their chances missed, their dollars gone, their hearts sore. They didn't
even move until their father leaned over and hauled them up. "Watch your
horse," he said, in a quick warning voice, "watch Miss Lucy come home."

They stood up, scrambled to their feet on the bench, every vein in them
suddenly beating so violently they could hardly focus their eyes, and saw a thin
little mahogany-colored streak flash by the judges' stand, only a neck ahead, but
their Miss Lucy, oh, their darling, their lovely—oh, Miss Lucy, their Uncle
Gabriel's Miss Lucy, had won, had won. They leaped up and down screaming
and clapping their hands, their hats falling back on their shoulders, their hair
flying wild. *Whoa, you heifer,* squalled the band with snorting brasses, and the
crowd broke into a long roar like the falling of the walls of Jericho.

The little girls sat down, feeling quite dizzy, while their father tried to pull
their hats straight, and taking out his handkerchief held it to Miranda's face,
saying very gently, "Here, blow your nose," and he dried her eyes while he was
about it. He stood up then and shook them out of their daze. He was smiling with
deep laughing wrinkles around his eyes, and spoke to them as if they were grown
young ladies he was squiring around.

"Let's go out and pay our respects to Miss Lucy," he said. "She's the star of
the day."

The horses were coming in, looking as if their hides had been drenched and
rubbed with soap, their ribs heaving, their nostrils flaring and closing. The jockeys
sat bowed and relaxed, their faces calm, moving a little at the waist with the
movement of their horses. Miranda noted this for future use; that was the way
you came in from a race, easy and quiet, whether you had won or lost. Miss Lucy
came last, and a little handful of winners applauded her and cheered the jockey.
He smiled and lifted his whip, his eyes and shriveled brown face perfectly serene.
Miss Lucy was bleeding at the nose, two thick red rivulets were stiffening her
tender mouth and chin, the round velvet chin that Miranda thought the nicest
kind of chin in the world. Her eyes were wild and her knees were trembling, and
she snored when she drew her breath.

Miranda stood staring. That was winning, too. Her heart clinched tight; that
was winning, for Miss Lucy. So instantly and completely did her heart reject that
victory, she did not know when it happened, but she hated it, and was ashamed
that she had screamed and shed tears of joy when Miss Lucy, with her bloodied

nose and bursting heart, had gone past the judges' stand a neck ahead. She felt empty and sick and held to her father's hand so hard that he shook her off a little impatiently and said, "What is the matter with you? Don't be so fidgety."

Uncle Gabriel was standing there waiting, and he was completely drunk. He watched the mare go in, then leaned against the fence with its white-washed posts and sobbed openly. "She's got the nosebleed, Harry," he said. "Had it since yesterday. We thought we had her all fixed up. But she did it, all right. She's got a heart like a lion. I'm going to breed her, Harry. Her heart's worth a million dollars, by itself, God bless her." Tears ran over his brick-colored face and into his straggling mustaches. "If anything happens to her now I'll blow my brains out. She's my last hope. She saved my life. I've had a run," he said, groaning into a large handkerchief and mopping his face all over, "I've had a run of luck that would break a brass billy goat. God, Harry, let's go somewhere and have a drink."

"I must get the children back to school first, Gabriel," said their father, taking each by a hand.

"No, no, don't go yet," said Uncle Gabriel desperately. "Wait here a minute, I want to see the vet and take a look at Miss Lucy, and I'll be right back. Don't go, Harry, for God's sake. I want to talk to you a few minutes."

Maria and Miranda, watching Uncle Gabriel's lumbering, unsteady back, were thinking that this was the first time they had ever seen a man that they knew to be drunk. They had seen pictures and read descriptions, and had heard descriptions, so they recognized the symptoms at once. Miranda felt it was an important moment in a great many ways.

"Uncle Gabriel's a drunkard, isn't he?" she asked her father, rather proudly.

"Hush, don't say such things," said father, with a heavy frown, "or I'll never bring you here again." He looked worried and unhappy, and, above all, undecided. The little girls stood stiff with resentment against such obvious injustice. They loosed their hands from his and moved away coldly, standing together in silence. Their father did not notice, watching the place where Uncle Gabriel had disappeared. In a few minutes he came back, still wiping his face, as if there were cobwebs on it, carrying his big black hat. He waved at them from a short distance, calling out in a cheerful way, "She's going to be all right, Harry. It's stopped now. Lord, this will be good news for Miss Honey. Come on, Harry, let's all go home and tell Miss Honey. She deserves some good news."

Father said, "I'd better take the children back to school first, then we'll go."

"No, no," said Uncle Gabriel, fondly, "I want her to see the girls. She'll be tickled pink to see them, Harry. Bring 'em along."

"Is it another race horse we're going to see?" whispered Miranda in her sister's ear.

"Don't be silly," said Maria. "It's Uncle Gabriel's second wife."

"Let's find a cab, Harry," said Uncle Gabriel, "and take your little girls out to cheer up Miss Honey. Both of 'em rolled into one look a lot like Amy, I swear they do. I want Miss Honey to see them. She's always liked our family, Harry, though of course she's not what you'd call an expansive kind of woman."

Maria and Miranda sat facing the driver, and Uncle Gabriel squeezed himself in facing them beside their father. The air became at once bitter and sour with his breathing. He looked sad and poor. His necktie was on crooked and his shirt was rumpled. Father said, "You're going to see Uncle Gabriel's second wife, children," exactly as if they had not heard everything; and to Gabriel, "How *is* your wife nowadays? It must be twenty years since I saw her last."

"She's pretty gloomy, and that's a fact," said Uncle Gabriel. "She's been pretty gloomy for years now, and nothing seems to shake her out of it. She never did care for horses, Harry, if you remember; she hasn't been near the track three times since we were married. When I think how Amy wouldn't have missed a race for anything...She's very different from Amy, Harry, a very different kind of woman. As fine a woman as ever lived in her own way, but she hates change and moving around, and she just lives in the boy."

"Where is Gabe now?" asked father.

"Finishing college," said Uncle Gabriel; "a smart boy, but awfully like his mother. Awfully like," he said, in a melancholy way. "She hates being away from him. Just wants to sit down in the same town and wait for him to get through with his education. Well, I'm sorry it can't be done if that's what she wants, but God Almighty—And this last run of luck has about got her down. I hope you'll be able to cheer her up a little, Harry, she needs it."

The little girls sat watching the streets grow duller and dingier and narrower, and at last the shabbier and shabbier white people gave way to dressed-up Negroes, and then to shabby Negroes, and after a long way the cab stopped before a desolate-looking little hotel in Elysian Fields. Their father helped Maria and Miranda out, told the cabman to wait, and they followed Uncle Gabriel through a dirty damp-smelling patio, down a long gas-lighted hall full of a terrible smell, Miranda couldn't decide what it was made of but it had a bitter taste even, and up a long staircase with a ragged carpet. Uncle Gabriel pushed open a door without warning, saying, "Come in, here we are."

A tall pale-faced woman with faded straw-colored hair and pink-rimmed eyelids rose suddenly from a squeaking rocking chair. She wore a stiff blue-and-white-striped shirtwaist and a stiff black skirt of some hard shiny material. Her large knuckled hands rose to her round, neat pompadour at sight of her visitors.

"Honey," said Uncle Gabriel, with large false heartiness, "you'll never guess who's come to see you." He gave her a clumsy hug. Her face did not change and her eyes rested steadily on the three strangers. "Amy's brother Harry, Honey, you remember, don't you?"

"Of course," said Miss Honey, putting out her hand straight as a paddle, "of course I remember you, Harry." She did not smile.

"And Amy's two little nieces," went on Uncle Gabriel, bringing them forward. They put out their hands limply, and Miss Honey gave each one a slight flip and dropped it. "And we've got good news for you," went on Uncle Gabriel, trying to bolster up the painful situation. "Miss Lucy stepped out and showed 'em today, Honey. We're rich again, old girl, cheer up."

Miss Honey turned her long, despairing face towards her visitors. "Sit down," she said with a heavy sigh, seating herself and motioning towards various rickety chairs. There was a big lumpy bed, with a grayish-white counterpane on it, a marble-topped washstand, grayish coarse lace curtains on strings at the two small windows, a small closed fireplace with a hole in it for a stovepipe, and two trunks, standing at odds as if somebody were just moving in, or just moving out. Everything was dingy and soiled and neat and bare; not a pin out of place.

"We'll move to the St. Charles tomorrow," said Uncle Gabriel, as much to Harry as to his wife. "Get your best dresses together, Honey, the long dry spell is over."

Miss Honey's nostrils pinched together and she rocked slightly, with her arms folded. "I've lived in the St. Charles before, and I've lived here before," she said, in a tight deliberate voice, "and this time I'll just stay where I am, thank you. I prefer it to moving back here in three months. I'm settled now, I feel at home here," she told him, glancing at Harry, her pale eyes kindling with blue fire, a stiff white line around her mouth.

The little girls sat trying not to stare, miserably ill at ease. Their grandmother had pronounced Harry's children to be the most unteachable she had ever seen in her long experience with the young; but they had learned by indirection one thing well—nice people did not carry on quarrels before outsiders. Family quarrels were sacred, to be waged privately in fierce hissing whispers, low choked mutters and growls. If they did yell and stamp, it must be behind closed doors and windows. Uncle Gabriel's second wife was hopping mad and she looked ready to fly out at Uncle Gabriel any second, with him sitting there like a hound when someone shakes a whip at him.

"She loathes and despises everybody in this room," thought Miranda, coolly, "and she's afraid we won't know it. She needn't worry, we knew it when we came in." With all her heart she wanted to go, but her father, though his face was a study, made no move. He seemed to be trying to think of something pleasant to say. Maria, feeling guilty, though she couldn't think why, was calculating rapidly, "Why, she's only Uncle Gabriel's second wife, and Uncle Gabriel was only married before to Aunt Amy, why, she's no kin at all, and I'm glad of it." Sitting back easily, she let her hands fall open in her lap; they would be going in a few minutes, undoubtedly, and they need never come back.

Then father said, "We mustn't be keeping you, we just dropped in for a few minutes. We wanted to see how you are."

Miss Honey said nothing, but she made a little gesture with her hands, from the wrist, as if to say, "Well, you see how I am, and now what next?"

"I must take these young ones back to school," said Father, and Uncle Gabriel said stupidly, "Look, Honey, don't you think they resemble Amy a little? Especially around the eyes, especially Maria, don't you think, Harry?"

Their father glanced at them in turn. "I really couldn't say," he decided, and the little girls saw he was more monstrously embarrassed than ever. He turned to Miss Honey, "I hadn't seen Gabriel for so many years," he said, "we thought of getting out for a talk about old times together. You know how it is."

"Yes, I know," said Miss Honey, rocking a little, and all that she knew gleamed forth in a pallid, unquenchable hatred and bitterness that seemed enough to bring her long body straight up out of the chair in a fury, "I know," and she sat staring at the floor. Her mouth shook and straightened. There was a terrible silence, which was broken when the little girls saw their father rise. They got up, too, and it was all they could do to keep from making a dash for the door.

"I must get the young ones back," said their father. "They've had enough excitement for one day. They each won a hundred dollars on Miss Lucy. It was a good race," he said, in complete wretchedness, as if he simply could not extricate himself from the situation. "Wasn't it, Gabriel?"

"It was a grand race," said Gabriel, brokenly, "a grand race."

Miss Honey stood up and moved a step towards the door. "Do you take them to the races, actually?" she asked, and her lids flickered towards them as if they were loathsome insects, Maria felt.

"If I feel they deserve a little treat, yes," said their father, in an easy tone but with wrinkled brow.

"I had rather, much rather," said Miss Honey clearly, "see my son dead at my feet than hanging around a race track."

The next few moments were rather a blank, but at last they were out of it, going down the stairs, across the patio, with Uncle Gabriel seeing them back into the cab. His face was sagging, the features had fallen as if the flesh had slipped from the bones, and his eyelids were puffed and blue. "Good-by, Harry," he said soberly. "How long you expect to be here?"

"Starting back tomorrow," said Harry. "just dropped in on a little business and to see how the girls were getting along."

"Well," said Uncle Gabriel, "I may be dropping into your part of the country one of these days. Good-by, children," he said, taking their hands one after the other in his big warm paws. "They're nice children, Harry. I'm glad you won on Miss Lucy," he said to the little girls, tenderly. "Don't spend your money foolishly, now. Well, so long, Harry." As the cab jolted away he stood there fat and sagging, holding up his arm and wagging his hand at them.

"Goodness," said Maria, in her most grown-up manner, taking her hat off and hanging it over her knee, "I'm glad that's over."

"What I want to know is," said Miranda, "*is* Uncle Gabriel a real drunkard?"

"Oh, hush," said their father, sharply, "I've got the heartburn."

There was a respectful pause, as before a public monument. When their father had the heartburn it was time to lay low. The cab rumbled on, back to clean gay streets, with the lights coming on in the early February darkness, past shimmering shop windows, smooth pavements, on and on, past beautiful old houses set in deep gardens, on, on back to the dark walls with the heavy-topped trees hanging over them. Miranda sat thinking so hard she forgot and spoke out in her thoughtless way: "I've decided I'm not going to be a jockey, after all." She could as usual have bitten her tongue, but as usual it was too late.

Father cheered up and twinkled at her knowingly, as if that didn't surprise him in the least. "Well, well," said he, "so you aren't going to be a jockey! That's very sensible of you. I think she ought to be a lion-tamer, don't you, Maria? That's a nice, womanly profession."

Miranda, seeing Maria from the height of her fourteen years suddenly joining with their father to laugh at her, made an instant decision and laughed with them at herself. That was better. Everybody laughed and it was such a relief.

"Where's my hundred dollars?" asked Maria, anxiously.

"It's going in the bank," said their father, "and yours too," he told Miranda. "That is your nest-egg."

"Just so they don't buy my stockings with it," said Miranda, who had long resented the use of her Christmas money by their grandmother. "I've got enough stockings to last me a year."

"I'd like to buy a racehorse," said Maria, "but I know it's not enough." The limitations of wealth oppressed her. *"What* could you buy with a hundred dollars?" she asked fretfully.

"Nothing, nothing at all," said their father, "a hundred dollars is just something you put in the bank."

Maria and Miranda lost interest. They had won a hundred dollars on a horse race once. It was already in the far past. They began to chatter about something else.

The lay sister opened the door on a long cord, from behind the grille; Maria and Miranda walked in silently to their familiar world of shining bare floors and insipid wholesome food and cold-water washing and regular prayers; their world of poverty, chastity and obedience, of early to bed and early to rise, of sharp little rules and tittle-tattle. Resignation was in their childish faces as they held them up to be kissed.

Be good girls," said their father, in the strange serious, rather helpless way he always had when he told them good-by. "Write to your daddy, now, nice long letters," he said, holding their arms firmly for a moment before letting go for good. Then he disappeared, and the sister swung the door closed after him.

Maria and Miranda went upstairs to the dormitory to wash their faces and hands and slick down their hair again before supper.

Miranda was hungry. "We didn't have a thing to eat, after all," she grumbled. "Not even a chocolate nut bar. I think that's mean. We didn't even get a quarter to spend," she said.

"Not a living bite," said Maria. "Not a nickel." She poured out cold water into the bowl and rolled up her sleeves.

Another girl about her own age came in and went to a washbowl near another bed. "Where have you been?" she asked. "Did you have a good time?"

"We went to the races, with our father," said Maria, soaping her hands.

"Our uncle's horse won," said Miranda.

"My goodness," said the other girl, vaguely, "that must have been grand."

Maria looked at Miranda, who was rolling up her own sleeves. She tried to feel martyred, but it wouldn't go. "Immured for another week," she said, her eyes sparkling over the edge of her towel.

Part III: 1912

Miranda followed the porter down the stuffy aisle of the sleeping-car, where the berths were nearly all made down and the dusty green curtains buttoned to a seat at the further end. "Now yo' berth's ready any time, Miss," said the porter.

"But I want to sit up a while," said Miranda. A very thin old lady raised choleric black eyes and fixed upon her a regard of unmixed disapproval. She had two immense front teeth and a receding chin, but she did not lack character. She had piled her luggage around her like a barricade, and she glared at the porter when he picked some of it up to make room for his new passenger. Miranda sat, saying mechanically, "May I?"

"You may, indeed," said the old lady, for she seemed old in spite of a certain brisk, rustling energy. Her taffeta petticoats creaked like hinges every time she stirred. With ferocious sarcasm, after a half second's pause, she added, "You may be so good as to get off my hat!"

Miranda rose instantly in horror, and handed to the old lady a wilted contrivance of black horsehair braid and shattered white poppies. "I'm dreadfully sorry," she stammered, for she had been brought up to treat ferocious old ladies respectfully, and this one seemed capable of spanking her, then and there. "I didn't dream it was your hat."

"And whose hat did you dream it might be?" inquired the old lady, baring her teeth and twirling the hat on a forefinger to restore it.

"I didn't think it was a hat at all," said Miranda with a touch of hysteria.

"Oh, you didn't think it was a hat? Where on earth are your eyes, child?" and she proved the nature and function of the object by placing it on her head at a somewhat tipsy angle, though still it did not much resemble a hat. "Now can you see what it is?"

"Yes, oh, yes," said Miranda, with a meekness she hoped was disarming. She ventured to sit again after a careful inspection of the narrow space she was to occupy.

"Well, well," said the old lady, "let's have the porter remove some of these encumbrances," and she stabbed the bell with a lean sharp forefinger. There followed a flurry of rearrangements, during which they both stood in the aisle, the old lady giving a series of impossible directions to the Negro which he bore philosophically while he disposed of the luggage exactly as he had meant to do. Seated again, the old lady asked in a kindly, authoritative tone, "And what might your name be, child?"

At Miranda's answer, she blinked somewhat, unfolded her spectacles, straddled them across her high nose competently, and took a good long look at the face beside her.

"If I'd had my spectacles on," she said, in an astonishingly changed voice, "I might have known. I'm Cousin Eva Parrington," she said, "Cousin Molly Parrington's daughter, remember? I knew you when you were a little girl. You were a lively little girl," she added as if to console her, "and very opinionated. The last thing I heard about you, you were planning to be a tight-rope walker. You were going to play the violin and walk the tight-rope at the same time."

"I must have seen it at the vaudeville show," said Miranda. "I couldn't have invented it. Now I'd like to be an air pilot!"

"I used to go to dances with your father," said Cousin Eva, busy with her own thoughts, "and to big holiday parties at your grandmother's house, long before you were born. Oh, indeed, yes, a long time before."

Miranda remembered several things at once. Aunt Amy had threatened to be an old maid like Eva. Oh, Eva, the trouble with her is she has no chin. Eva has given up, and is teaching Latin in a Female Seminary. Eva's gone out for votes for women, God help her. The nice thing about an ugly daughter is, she's not apt to make me a grandmother.... "They didn't do you much good, those parties, dear Cousin Eva," thought Miranda.

"They didn't do me much good, those parties," said Cousin Eva aloud as if she were a mind-reader, and Miranda's head swam for a moment with fear that she had herself spoken aloud. "Oh at least, they didn't serve their purpose, for I never got married; but I enjoyed them, just the same. I had a good time at those parties, even if I wasn't a belle. And so you are Harry's child, and here I was quarreling with you. You do remember me, don't you?"

"Yes," said Miranda, and thinking that even if Cousin Eva had been really an old maid ten years before, still she couldn't be much past fifty now, and she looked so withered and tired, so famished and sunken in the cheeks, so *old*, somehow. Across the abyss separating Cousin Eva from her own youth, Miranda looked with painful premonition. "Oh, must I ever be like that?" She said aloud, "Yes, you used to read Latin to me, and tell me not to bother about the sense, to get the sound in my mind, and it would come easier later."

"Ah, so I did," said Cousin Eva, delighted. "So I did. You don't happen to remember that I once had a beautiful sapphire velvet dress with a train on it?"

"No, I don't remember that dress," said Miranda.

"It was an old dress of my mother's made over and cut down to fit," said Eva, "and it wasn't in the least becoming to me, but it was the only really good dress I ever had, and I remember it as if it were yesterday. Blue was never my color." She sighed with a humorous bitterness. The humor seemed momentary, but the bitterness was a constant state of mind.

Miranda, trying to offer the sympathy of fellow suffering, said, "I know. I've had Maria's dresses made over for me, and they were never right. It was dreadful."

"Well," said Cousin Eva, in the tone of one who did not wish to share her unique disappointments. "How is your father? I always liked him. He was one of the finest-looking young men I ever saw. Vain, too, like all his family. He wouldn't ride any but the best horses he could buy, and I used to say he made them prance and then watched his own shadow. I used to tell this on him at dinner parties, and he hated me for it. I feel pretty certain he hated me." An overtone of complacency in Cousin Eva's voice explained better than words that she had her own method of commanding attention and arousing emotion. "How *is* your father, I asked you, my dear?"

"I haven't seen him for nearly a year," answered Miranda, quickly, before Cousin Eva could get ahead again. "I'm going home now to Uncle Gabriel's funeral; you know, Uncle Gabriel died in Lexington and they have brought him back to be buried beside Aunt Amy."

"So that's how we meet," said Cousin Eva. "Yes, Gabriel drank himself to death at last. I'm going to the funeral, too. I haven't been home since I went to Mother's funeral, it must be, let's see, yes, it will be nine years next July. I'm going to Gabriel's funeral, though. I wouldn't miss that. Poor fellow, what a life he had. Pretty soon, they'll all be gone."

Miranda said, "We're left, Cousin Eva," meaning those of her own generation, the young, and Cousin Eva said, "Pshaw, you'll live forever, and you won't bother to come to our funerals." She didn't seem to think this was a misfortune, but flung the remark from her like a woman accustomed to saying what she thought.

Miranda sat thinking, "Still, I suppose it would be pleasant if I could say something to make her believe that she and all of them would be lamented, but— but—" With a smile which she hoped would be her denial of Cousin Eva's cynicism about the younger generation, she said, "You were right about the Latin, Cousin Eva, your reading did help when I began with it. I still study," she said. "Latin, too."

"And why shouldn't you?" asked Cousin Eva, sharply, adding at once mildly, "I'm glad you are going to use your mind a little, child. Don't let yourself rust away. Your mind outwears all sorts of things you may set your heart upon; you can enjoy it when all other things are taken away." Miranda was chilled by her melancholy. Cousin Eva went on: "In our part of the country, in my time, we were so provincial—a woman didn't dare to think or act for herself. The whole world was a little that way," she said, "but we were the worst, I believe. I suppose you must know how I fought for votes for women when it almost made a pariah of me—I was turned out of my chair at the Seminary, but I'm glad I did it and I would do it again. You young things don't realize. You'll live in a better world because we worked for it."

Miranda knew something of Cousin Eva's career. She said sincerely, "I think it was brave of you, and I'm glad you did it, too. I loved your courage."

"It wasn't just showing off, mind you," said Cousin Eva, rejecting praise, fretfully. "Any fool can be brave. We were working for something we knew was right, and it turned out that we needed a lot of courage for it. That was all. I didn't expect to go to jail, but I went three times, and I'd go three times three more if it were necessary. We aren't voting yet," she said, "but we will be."

Miranda did not venture any answer, but she felt convinced that indeed women would be voting soon if nothing fatal happened to Cousin Eva. There was something in her manner which said such things could be left safely to her. Miranda was dimly fired for the cause herself; it seemed heroic and worth suffering for, but discouraging, too, to those who came after: Cousin Eva so plainly had swept the field clear of opportunity.

They were silent for a few minutes, while Cousin Eva rummaged in her handbag, bringing up odds and ends: peppermint drops, eye drops, a packet of needles, three handkerchiefs, a little bottle of violet perfume, a book of addresses, two buttons, one black, one white, and, finally, a packet of headache powders.

"Bring me a glass of water, will you, my dear?" she asked Miranda. She poured the headache powder on her tongue, swallowed the water, and put two peppermints in her mouth.

"So now they're going to bury Gabriel near Amy," she said after a while, as if her eased headache had started her on a new train of thought. "Miss Honey would like that, poor dear, if she could know. After listening to stories about Amy for twenty-five years, she must lie alone in her grave in Lexington while Gabriel sneaks off to Texas to make his bed with Amy again. It was a kind of life-long infidelity, Miranda, and now an eternal infidelity on top of that. He ought to be ashamed of himself."

"It was Aunt Amy he loved," said Miranda, wondering what Miss Honey could have been like before her long troubles with Uncle Gabriel. "First, anyway."

"Oh, that Amy," said Cousin Eva, her eyes glittering. "Your Aunt Amy was a devil and a mischief-maker, but I loved her dearly. I used to stand up for Amy when her reputation wasn't worth that." Her fingers snapped like castanets. "She used to say to me, in that gay soft way she had, 'Now, Eva, don't go talking votes for women when the lads ask you to dance. Don't recite Latin poems to 'em,' she would say, 'they got sick of that in school. Dance and say nothing, Eva,' she would say, her eyes perfectly devilish, 'and hold your chin up, Eva.' My chin was my weak point, you see. 'You'll never catch a husband if you don't look out,' she would say. Then she would laugh and fly away, and where did she fly to?" demanded Cousin Eva, her sharp eyes pinning Miranda down to the bitter facts of the case, "To scandal and to death, nowhere else."

"She was joking, Cousin Eva," said Miranda, innocently, "and everybody loved her."

"Not everybody, by a long shot," said Cousin Eva in triumph. "She had enemies. If she knew, she pretended she didn't. If she cared, she never said. You couldn't make her quarrel. She was sweet as a honeycomb to everybody. *Everybody*," she added, "that was the trouble. She went through life like a spoiled darling, doing as she pleased and letting other people suffer for it, and pick up the pieces after her. I never believed for one moment," said Cousin Eva, putting her mouth close to Miranda's ear and breathing peppermint hotly into it, "that Amy was an impure woman. Never! But let me tell you, there were plenty who did believe it. There were plenty to pity poor Gabriel for being so completely blinded by her. A great many persons were not surprised when they heard that Gabriel was perfectly miserable all the time, on their honeymoon, in New Orleans. Jealousy. And why not? But I used to say to such persons that, no matter what the appearances were, I had faith in Amy's virtue. Wild, I said, indiscreet, I said, heartless, I said, but *virtuous* I feel certain. But you could hardly blame anyone for being mystified. The way she rose up suddenly from death's door to marry Gabriel Breaux, after refusing him and treating him like a dog for years, looked odd, to say the least. To say the very least," she added, after a moment, "odd is a mild word for it. And there was something very mysterious about her death, only six weeks after marriage."

Miranda roused herself. She felt she knew this part of the story and could set Cousin Eva right about one thing. "She died of a hemorrhage from the lungs," said Miranda. "She had been ill for five years, don't you remember?"

Cousin Eva was ready for that. "Ha, that was the story, indeed. The official account, you might say. Oh, yes, I heard that often enough. But did you ever hear about that fellow Raymond somebody-or-other from Calcasieu Parish, almost a stranger, who persuaded Amy to elope with him from a dance one night, and she just ran out into the darkness without even stopping for her cloak, and your poor dear nice father Harry—you weren't even thought of then—had to run him down to earth and shoot him?"

Miranda leaned back from the advancing flood of speech. "Cousin Eva, my father shot *at* him, don't you remember? He didn't hit him. . . ."

"Well, that's a pity."

". . .and they had only gone out for a breath of air between dances. It was Uncle Gabriel's jealousy. And my father shot at the man because he thought that was better than letting Uncle Gabriel fight a duel about Aunt Amy. There was *nothing* in the whole affair except Uncle Gabriel's jealousy."

"You poor baby," said Cousin Eva, and pity gave a light like daggers to her eyes, "you dear innocent, you—do you believe that? How old are you, anyway?"

"Just past eighteen," said Miranda.

"If you don't understand what I tell you," said Cousin Eva portentously, "you will later. Knowledge can't hurt you. You mustn't live in a romantic haze about life. You'll understand when you're married, at any rate."

"I'm married now, Cousin Eva," said Miranda, feeling for almost the first time that it might be an advantage, "nearly a year. I eloped from school." It seemed very unreal even as she said it, and seemed to have nothing at all to do with the future; still, it was important, it must be declared, it was a situation in life which people seemed to be most exacting about, and the only feeling she could rouse in herself about it was an immense weariness as if it were an illness that she might one day hope to recover from.

"Shameful, shameful," cried Cousin Eva, genuinely repelled. "If you had been my child I should have brought you home and spanked you."

Miranda laughed out. Cousin Eva seemed to believe things could be arranged like that. She was so solemn and fierce, so comic and baffled.

"And you must know I should have just gone straight out again, through the nearest window," she taunted her. "If I went the first time, why not the second?"

"Yes, I suppose so," said Cousin Eva. "I hope you married rich."

"Not so very," said Miranda. "Enough." As if anyone could have stopped to think of such a thing!

Cousin Eva adjusted her spectacles and sized up Miranda's dress, her luggage, examined her engagement ring and wedding ring, with her nostrils fairly quivering as if she might smell out wealth on her.

"Well, that's better than nothing," said Cousin Eva. "I thank God every day of my life that I have a small income. It's a Rock of Ages. What would have become of me if I hadn't a cent of my own? Well, you'll be able now to do something for your family."

Miranda remembered what she had always heard about the Parringtons. They were money-hungry, they loved money and nothing else, and when they had got some they kept it. Blood was thinner than water between the Parringtons where money was concerned.

"We're pretty poor," said Miranda, stubbornly allying herself with her father's family instead of her husband's, "but a rich marriage is no way out," she said, with the snobbishness of poverty. She was thinking, "You don't know my branch of the family, dear Cousin Eva, if you think it is."

"Your branch of the family," said Cousin Eva, with that terrifying habit she had of lifting phrases out of one's mind, "has no more practical sense than so many children. Everything for love," she said, with a face of positive nausea, "that was it. Gabriel would have been rich if his grandfather had not disinherited him, but would Amy be sensible and marry him and make him settle down so the old man would have been pleased with him? No. And what could Gabriel do without money? I wish you could have seen the life he led Miss Honey, one day buying her Paris gowns and the next day pawning her earrings. It just depended on how the horses ran, and they ran worse and worse, and Gabriel drank more and more."

Miranda did not say, "I saw a little of it." She was trying to imagine Miss Honey in a Paris gown. She said, "But Uncle Gabriel was so mad about Aunt Amy, there was no question of her not marrying him at last, money or no money."

Cousin Eva strained her lips tightly over her teeth, let them fly again and leaned over, gripping Miranda's arm. "What I ask myself, what I ask myself over and over again," she whispered, "is, what connection did this man Raymond from Calcasieu have with Amy's sudden marriage to Gabriel, and *what* did Amy do to make away with herself so soon afterward? For mark my words, child, Amy wasn't so ill as all that. She'd been flying around for years after the doctors said her lungs were weak. Amy did away with herself to escape some disgrace, some exposure that she faced."

The beady black eyes glinted; Cousin Eva's face was quite frightening, so near and so intent. Miranda wanted to say, "Stop. Let her rest. What harm did she ever do you?" but she was timid and unnerved, and deep in her was a horrid fascination with the terrors and the darkness Cousin Eva had conjured up. What was the end of this story?

"She was a bad, wild girl, but I was fond of her to the last," said Cousin Eva. "She got into trouble somehow, and she couldn't get out again, and I have every reason to believe she killed herself with the drug they gave her to keep her quiet after a hemorrhage. If she didn't, what happened, what happened?"

"I don't know," said Miranda. "How should I know? She was very beautiful," she said, as if this explained everything. "Everybody said she was very beautiful."

"Not everybody," said Cousin Eva, firmly, shaking her head. "I for one never thought so. They made entirely too much fuss over her. She was good-looking enough, but why did they think she was beautiful? I cannot understand it. She was too thin when she was young, and later I always thought she was too fat, and again in her last year she was altogether too thin. She always got herself up to be looked at, and so people looked, of course. She rode too hard, and she danced too freely, and she talked too much, and you'd have to be blind, deaf and dumb not to notice her. I don't mean she was loud or vulgar, she wasn't, but she was *too free*," said Cousin Eva. She stopped for breath and put a peppermint in her mouth. Miranda could see Cousin Eva on the platform, making her speeches, stopping to take a peppermint. But why did she hate Aunt Amy so, when Aunt Amy was dead and she alive? Wasn't being alive enough?

"And her illness wasn't romantic either," said Cousin Eva, "though to hear them tell it she faded like a lily. Well, she coughed blood, if that's romantic. If they had made her take proper care of herself, if she had been nursed sensibly, she might have been alive today. But no, nothing of the kind. She lay wrapped in beautiful shawls on a sofa with flowers around her, eating as she liked or not eating, getting up after a hemorrhage and going out to ride or dance, sleeping with the windows closed; with crowds coming in and out laughing and talking at all hours, and Amy sitting up so her hair wouldn't get out of curl. And why wouldn't that sort of thing kill a well person in time? I have almost died twice in my life," said Cousin Eva, "and both times I was sent to a hospital where I belonged and left there until I came out. And I came out," she said, her voice deepening to a bugle note, "and I went to work again."

"Beauty goes, character stays," said the small voice of axiomatic morality in Miranda's ear. It was a dreary prospect; why was a strong character so deforming? Miranda felt she truly wanted to be strong, but how could she face it, seeing what it did to one?

"She had a lovely complexion," said Cousin Eva, "perfectly transparent with a flush on each cheekbone. But it was tuberculosis, and is disease beautiful? And she brought it on herself by drinking lemon and salt to stop her periods when she wanted to go to dances. There was a superstition among young girls about that. They fancied that young men could tell what ailed them by touching their hands, or even by looking at them. As if it mattered? But they were terribly self-conscious and they had immense respect for man's worldly wisdom in those days. My own notion is that a man couldn't—but anyway, the whole thing was stupid."

"I should have thought they'd have stayed at home if they couldn't manage better than that," said Miranda, feeling very knowledgeable and modern.

"They didn't dare. Those parties and dances were their market, a girl couldn't afford to miss out, there were always rivals waiting to cut the ground from under her. The rivalry—" said Cousin Eva, and her head lifted, she arched like a cavalry horse getting a whiff of the battlefield—"you can't imagine what the rivalry was like. The way those girls treated each other—nothing was too mean, nothing too false—"

Cousin Eva wrung her hands. "It was just sex," she said in despair; "their minds dwelt on nothing else. They didn't call it that, it was all smothered under pretty names, but that's all it was, sex." She looked out of the window into the darkness, her sunken cheek near Miranda flushed deeply. She turned back. "I took to the soap box and the platform when I was called upon," she said proudly, "and I went to jail when it was necessary, and my condition didn't make any difference. I was booed and jeered and shoved around just as if I had been in perfect health. But it was part of our philosophy not to let our physical handicaps make any difference to our work. You know what I mean," she said, as if until now it was all mystery. "Well, Amy carried herself with more spirit than the others, and she didn't seem to be making any sort of fight, but she was simply sex-ridden, like the rest. She behaved as if she hadn't a rival on earth, and she pretended not to know what marriage was about, but I know better. None of them had, and they didn't want to have, anything else to think about, and they didn't really know anything about that, so they simply festered inside—they festered—"

Miranda found herself deliberately watching a long procession of living corpses, festering women stepping gaily towards the charnel house, their corruption concealed under laces and flowers, their dead faces lifted smiling, and thought quite coldly, "Of course it was not like that. This is no more true than what I was told before, it's every bit as romantic," and she realized that she was tired of her intense Cousin Eva, she wanted to go to sleep, she wanted to be at home, she wished it were tomorrow and she could see her father and her sister, who were so alive and solid; who would mention her freckles and ask her if she wanted something to eat.

"My mother was not like that," she said, childishly. "My mother was a perfectly natural woman who liked to cook. I have seen some of her sewing," she said. "I have read her diary."

"Your mother was a saint," said Cousin Eva, automatically.

Miranda sat silent, outraged. "My mother was nothing of the sort," she wanted to fling in Cousin Eva's big front teeth. But Cousin Eva had been gathering bitterness until more speech came of it.

" 'Hold your chin up, Eva,' Amy used to tell me," she began, doubling up both her fists and shaking them a little. "All my life the whole family bedeviled me about my chin. My entire girlhood was spoiled by it. Can you imagine," she asked, with a ferocity that seemed much too deep for this one cause, "people who call themselves civilized spoiling life for a young girl because she had one unlucky feature? Of course, you understand perfectly it was all in the very best humor, everybody was very amusing about it, no harm meant—oh, no, no harm at all. That is the hellish thing about it. It is that I can't forgive," she cried out, and she twisted her hands together as if they were rags. "Ah, the family," she said, releasing her breath and sitting back quietly, "the whole hideous institution should be wiped from the face of the earth. It is the root of all human wrongs," she ended, and relaxed, and her face became calm. She was trembling. Miranda reached out and took Cousin Eva's hand and held it. The hand fluttered and lay still, and Cousin Eva said, "You've not the faintest idea what some of us went through, but I wanted you to hear the other side of the story. And I'm keeping you up when you need your beauty sleep," she said grimly, stirring herself with an immense rustle of petticoats.

Miranda pulled herself together, feeling limp, and stood up. Cousin Eva put out her hand again, and drew Miranda down to her. "Good night, you dear child," she said, "to think you're grown up." Miranda hesitated, then quite suddenly kissed her Cousin Eva on the cheek. The black eyes shone brightly through water for an instant, and Cousin Eva said with a warm note in her sharp clear orator's voice, "Tomorrow we'll be home again. I'm looking forward to it, aren't you? Good night."

Miranda fell asleep while she was getting off her clothes. Instantly it was morning again. She was still trying to close her suitcase when the train pulled into the small station, and there on the platform she saw her father, looking tired and anxious, his hat pulled over his eyes. She rapped on the window to catch his attention, then ran out and threw herself upon him. He said, "Well, here's my big girl," as if she were still seven, but his hands on her arms held her off, the tone was forced. There was no welcome for her, and there had not been since she had run away. She could not persuade herself to remember how it would be; between one home-coming and the next her mind refused to accept its own knowledge. Her father looked over her head and said, without surprise, "Why, hello, Eva, I'm glad somebody sent you a telegram." Miranda, rebuffed again, let her arms fall away again, with the same painful dull jerk of the heart.

"No one in my family," said Eva, her face framed in the thin black veil she reserved, evidently, for family funerals, "ever sent me a telegram in my life. I had the news from young Keziah who had it from young Gabriel. I suppose Gabe is here?"

"Everybody seems to be here," said Father. "The house is getting full."

"I'll go to the hotel if you like," said Cousin Eva.

"Damnation, no," said Father. "I didn't mean that. You'll come with us where you belong."

Skid, the handy man, grabbed the suitcases and started down the rocky village street. "We've got the car," said Father. He took Miranda by the hand, then dropped it again, and reached for Cousin Eva's elbow.

"I'm perfectly able, thank you," said Cousin Eva, shying away.

"If you're so independent now," said Father, "God help us when you get that vote."

Cousin Eva pushed back her veil. She was smiling merrily. She liked Harry, she always had liked him, he could tease as much as he liked. She slipped her arm through his. "So it's all over with poor Gabriel, isn't it?"

"Oh, yes," said Father, "it's all over, all right. They're pegging out pretty regularly now. It will be our turn next, Eva?"

"I don't know, and I don't care," said Eva, recklessly. "It's good to be back now and then, Harry, even if it is only for funerals. I feel sinfully cheerful."

"Oh, Gabriel wouldn't mind, he'd like seeing you cheerful. Gabriel was the cheerfullest cuss I ever saw, when we were young. Life for Gabriel," said Father, "was just one perpetual picnic."

"Poor fellow," said Cousin Eva.

"Poor old Gabriel," said Father, heavily.

Miranda walked along beside her father, feeling homeless, but not sorry for it. He had not forgiven her, she knew that. When would he? She could not guess, but she felt it would come of itself, without words and without acknowledgment on either side, for by the time it arrived neither of them would need to remember what had caused their division, nor why it had seemed so important. Surely old people cannot hold their grudges forever because the young want to live, too, she thought, in her arrogance, her pride. I will make my own mistakes, not yours; I cannot depend upon you beyond a certain point, why depend at all? There was something more beyond, but this was a first step to take, and she took it, walking in silence beside her elders who were no longer Cousin Eva and Father, since they had forgotten her presence, but had become Eva and Harry, who knew each other well, who were comfortable with each other, being contemporaries on equal terms, who occupied by right their place in this world, at the time of life to which they had arrived by paths familiar to them both. They need not play their roles of daughter, of son, to aged persons who did not understand them; nor of father and elderly female cousin to young persons whom they did not understand. They were precisely themselves; their eyes cleared, their voices relaxed into perfect naturalness, they need not weigh their words or calculate the effect of their manner. "It is I who have no place," thought Miranda. "Where are my own people and my own time?" She resented, slowly and deeply and in profound silence, the presence of these aliens who lectured and admonished her, who loved her with bitterness and denied her the right to look at the world with her own eyes, who demanded that she accept their version of life and yet could not tell her the truth, not in the smallest thing. "I hate them both," her most inner and secret mind said plainly, *"I will be free of them, I shall not even remember them."*

She sat in the front seat with Skid, the Negro boy. "Come back with us, Miranda," said Cousin Eva, with the sharp little note of elderly command, "there is plenty of room."

"No, thank you," said Miranda, in a firm cold voice. "I'm quite comfortable. Don't disturb yourself."

Neither of them noticed her voice or her manner. They sat back and went on talking steadily in their friendly family voices, talking about their dead, their living, their affairs, their prospects, their common memories, interrupting each other, catching each other up on small points of dispute, laughing with a gaiety and freshness Miranda had not known they were capable of, going over old stories and finding new points of interest in them.

Miranda could not hear the stories above the noisy motor, but she felt she knew them well, or stories like them. She knew too many stories like them, she wanted something new of her own. The language was familiar to them, but not to her, not any more. The house, her father had said, was full. It would be full of cousins, many of them strangers. Would there be any young cousins there, to whom she could talk about things they both knew? She felt a vague distaste for seeing cousins. There were too many of them and her blood rebelled against the ties of blood. She was sick to death of cousins. She did not want any more ties with this house, she was going to leave it, and she was not going back to her husband's family either. She would have no more bonds that smothered her in love and hatred. She knew now why she had run away to marriage, and she knew that she was going to run away from marriage, and she was not going to stay in any place, with anyone, that threatened to forbid her making her own discoveries, that said "No" to her. She hoped no one had taken her old room, she would like to sleep there once more, she would say good-by there where she had loved sleeping once, sleeping and waking and waiting to be grown, to begin to live. Oh, what is life, she asked herself in desperate seriousness, in those childish unanswerable words, and what shall I do with it? It is something of my own, she thought in a fury of jealous possessiveness, what shall I make of it? She did not know that she asked herself this because all her earliest training had argued that life was a substance, a material to be used, it took shape and direction and meaning only as the possessor guided and worked it; living was a progress of continuous and varied acts of the will directed towards a definite end. She had been assured that there were good and evil ones, one must make a choice. But what was good, and what was evil? I hate love, she thought, as if this were the answer, I hate loving and being loved, I hate it. And her disturbed and seething mind received a shock of comfort from this sudden collapse of an old painful structure of distorted images and misconceptions. "You don't know anything about it," said Miranda to herself, with extraordinary clearness as if she were an elder admonishing some young misguided creature. "You have to find out about it." But nothing in her prompted her to decide, "I will now do this, I will be that, I will go yonder, I will take a certain road to a certain end." There are questions to be asked first, she thought, but who will answer them? No one, or there will be too many answers, none of them right. What is the truth, she asked herself as intently as if the question had never been asked, the truth, even about the smallest, the least important of all the things I must find out? and where shall I begin to look for it? Her mind closed stubbornly against remembering, not the past but the legend of the past, other people's memory of the past, at which she had spent her life peering in wonder like a child at a magic-lantern show. Ah, but there is my own life to come yet, she thought, my own life now and beyond. I don't want any promises, I won't have false hopes, I won't be romantic about myself. I can't live in their world any longer, she told herself, listening to the voices back of her. Let them tell their stories to each other. Let them go on explaining how things happened. I don't care. At least I can know the truth about what happens to me, she assured herself silently, making a promise to herself, in her hopefulness, her ignorance.

Julie de Carneilhan

(1941)

Colette

Patrick Leigh Fermor, translator

The French novelist Sidonie Gabrielle Colette (1873–1954) was born at Saint-Sauveur-en-Puisaye in the department of the Yonne. Two periods in her life served as sources for her major fictional themes: her childhood and adolescence, spent in a French provincial town and dominated by her mother, from which stem her concerns with the unit of the family and with nature; and her first marriage (1893–1906), to Henri Gauthier-Villars ("Willy"), which took her to Paris and introduced her to the Bohemian life. Willy, himself a hack novelist and pornographer, also started her career as a novelist by locking her in a room to write novels published under his name (the *Claudine* novels, 1900–1903). After her divorce from Willy, Colette carried on a music hall career as a mime (1906–1912); her second marriage was to Henri de Jouvenel, the wealthy editor of *Matin* (1912–1924). Her third marriage in 1935 was to Maurice Goudeket, twenty years her junior, who had been her lover since 1925.

Her literary work continued through these years, and through the 1940's in spite of crippling attacks of arthritis. She produced novels, short stories, *nouvelles,* plays, personal remembrances, meditations, chronicles; but her most successful writings mingle fiction, reminiscence, and meditation. Among her novels and *nouvelles* are *La Vagabonde* (1911), *Chéri* (1920), *La fin de Chéri* (1926), *La Naissance du Jour* (1928), *La Seconde* (1929), *La Chatte* (1933), and *Gigi et autres nouvelles* (1944).

For further information, see Maurice Goudeket, *Près de Colette,* trans. Edin McLeod (New York, 1957); Pierre Trahard, *L'Art de Colette* (Paris, 1941); and Elaine Marks, *Colette* (New Brunswick, N. J., 1960).

Julie de Carneilhan (1941) was included in *Gigi et autres nouvelles,* which was translated into English in 1944. From *Gigi, Julie de Carneilhan & Chance Acquaintances* by Colette, translated by Patrick Leigh Fermor, by permission of Farrar, Straus & Company, Inc., and Martin Secker & Warburg Limited. Copyright 1952 by Farrar, Straus and Young, Inc., and Martin Secker & Warburg Limited.

Mme. de Carneilhan turned off the gas, leaving the earthen-ware saucepan on the stove. Beside the stove she laid out the Empire teacup, the Swedish spoon and the rye-bread folded in a rough silk Turkish napkin. The smell of hot chocolate made her yawn with hunger, for she had not eaten much for luncheon—a cold pork cutlet, a slice of bread and butter, half a pound of red currants and a cup of excellent coffee. During the meal she had worked away at a triangular cushion, cut out of an old pair of faded grey corduroy riding breeches. A fine-linked steel chain, which had once belonged, so Julie de Carneilhan said, to a monkey (though according to her brother the monkey had belonged to the chain) was to be sewn on one side of the cushion in the shape of a C, or possibly a J. "C would be easier to sew, but J is more decorative: it'll look terrific," she said to herself.

She put the lid on the steaming saucepan, mopped the kitchen slab with a cloth, and then filled the milk-can with water and shut the dust-bin. Feeling that she had lived up to her principles as the perfect housewife, she went into the studio. In front of a looking-glass in the hall, she put on a certain expression, a sort of contraction of the nostrils, to which she was specially attached. It accentuated, she maintained, the 'wild animal' side of her character.

Thinking that she heard voices on the stairs, Julie hurriedly put on her hat and a light overcoat the color of her ash-blonde hair, which she wore cut short and curled *à la Caracalla*. She threw down a pair of not quite clean gloves, and picked them up again—'Good enough to go to the pictures in'—then switched off two of the four lights, and sat down to wait in the best armchair. 'This is the last time,' she thought as she glanced round the studio, 'that I'll ever do up a room in red and blue. The color positively eats up the light, and costs the earth in electricity!'

One of the walls was red, one grey, and the other two were blue. The furniture was an odd mixture of style, the effect slightly too colonial, perhaps, but not unpleasing. The room was encumbered with a twelve-sided bronze tray-table from Indo-China, an armchair of South African oxhide, bits of tooled leather from Fez, and basket work which had originally been plaited round English tobacco tins by the natives of the Gold Coast. The rest of the furniture was good eighteenth-century work, but it remained on its legs only because Mme. de Carneilhan's strong, deft hands were clever with glue-pot and pegs, and could even, when necessary, slide thin metal rods inside old bamboo and the broken chair-legs.

She waited ten minutes. Her patience came from fundamental humility. Her training and a superficial pride made her sit upright in her chair.

The studio gained depth from a long, unframed looking-glass. She looked with pleasure at the reflection of her well-set neck, at her bust which stubbornly retained its shape and firmness. A sheaf of dog whips and riding switches, valued as collector's pieces because they came from the Caucasus or Siberia, hung down in coils over the looking-glass.

Julie de Carneilhan resumed work on the cushion, boldly marking out the lines of the letter. And then suddenly she lost heart. 'It's no good,' she thought; 'it would be hideous.'

After ten minutes of waiting, Julie's proud and charming nose and her small well-defined mouth began to twitch nervously, and two large tears sparkled in the corners of her blue eyes. Her spirits revived at the sound of the bell, and she ran to the door.

"This is a fine time to come! It's no good trying to get round me, I loathe people who..."

She drew back and her voice changed.

"Oh, it's you."

"Yes, it's me. May I come in?"

"Have I ever kept you out?"

"Oh, once or twice—perhaps three times. Are you going out?"

"Yes. I'm waiting for some friends, that is, and they're disgustingly late."

"It's wretched weather, you know."

Léon de Carneilhan pulled off his gloves and rubbed his hands together. They were tanned by his open air life and polished by everyday contact with bridles. As he passed the looking-glass he contracted his nostrils like his sister, and, with his fair greying hair and blue eyes, this underlined the resemblance between them.

"What are you up to with those old breeches of mine?"

"Making a cushion. Do you mind?"

"It's too late to mind, seeing you've already cut them up."

His presence exuded an atmosphere of absent-minded distrust, and Julie scrutinised him with a similar look of suspicion. They lighted their cigarettes with the same match.

"Do you mind if I leave you?" Julie said. "I'm going to the pictures."

"I'm afraid I've come at an awkward time," Carneilhan said. Her only answer was a vague shrug. He then turned on his sister. Judging horseflesh had given his eyes a keen look, and her eyes, though softened by her make-up, wore an identical expression.

"Your husband is very ill."

"You don't say so!" said Julie in tones of mock horror. "Poor old Becker!"

"No, not Becker. Your second, Espivant."

For a moment she remained motionless, her mouth half open.

"How do you mean, Espivant?" she asked in a hesitant voice. "He was out and about yesterday, talking of a question he intended to ask in the *Chambre*. I heard that from one of the barmen at Maxim's who used to be my butler. What's wrong with him?"

"He suddenly collapsed, flat on his face, and had to be carried home."

"What about his wife? What's she got to say about it?"

"Nobody knows. It only happened at three this afternoon."

"She's probably letting down her long tresses and beseeching a last kiss while counting her rows of pearls with the other hand." They both gave a short laugh and continued smoking in silence. Julie blew the smoke out through her narrow and faultless nostrils.

"Do you think he'll die?"

Léon struck his bony knees with his hand. "How should I know? You might as well ask me to whom he'll leave the money that Marianne brought him in the marriage settlement."

"I bet it was the only way of getting him to make up his mind," said Julie with a grin.

"You may laugh, my dear. But think of Marianne's money and her looks! Herbert might well be tempted by less than that."

"Might be? He was," Julie said.

"You're too modest."

She lifted her smooth arrogant nose. "I'm not talking about me! I mean Galatée des Conches, and that idiot Béatrix."

Léon wagged his head with an experienced air. He was a fair haired, fierce and aging man, who had had great success with women.

"Béatrix is not bad, not bad at all."

"Do you know, I'm rather bored by the whole business," said Julie shortly.

She put on her gloves, and, straightening her little hat of plaited felt, made it quite clear that she wished to see the last of her visitor.

"Tell me, Julie," Léon went on reflectively, "has Herbert been feeling friendly to you these last months?"

"Friendly? Yes. As with all the women he drops. He's always one move behind in his friendliness."

"Much more so with you than with the others. Didn't he pay your debts when he remarried?"

"What nonsense. I only had about twenty-two thousand francs' worth. One can't run up debts any more. Everything's cash nowadays."

"Supposing he leaves you a token of his friendship, a really solid one, when he dies!"

Julie's blue eyes assumed an expression of childish credulity.

"No? Do you really think he might die?"

"Of course I don't! I only said supposing when he died, he left you..."

Julie had stopped listening. She was running through her furniture in her mind, banishing her Colonial freaks and her Louis XIV relics, planning a change of house, a bathroom in yellow and black. She was not really grasping; only improvident and rather careless.

"Listen, my dear, I'm going out, as my young friends haven't put in an appearance. I'm going to the pictures."

"Do you really think you should? The news of Herbert's illness is already in the later edition of the evening papers. *'The physicians have so far issued no statement as to the gravity of the sudden illness which at five o'clock overcame the Comte d'Espivant, right-wing Deputy....'* "

"What about it? Am I expected to put on mourning in advance for a man who was unfaithful to me for eight years and has been married again for another three?"

"It makes no difference. You were the wife people talked about. You can bet that everyone to-night has forgotten Marianne and is asking how Julie de Carneilhan is taking it."

"Do you really think so? You may be right."

Flattered by the thought, she smiled and brushed back a pretty little lock of hair that half covered her ear. But at the sound of a footfall on the stairs and loud laughter she at once became nervous and flustered.

"Do you hear that? They were supposed to pick me up at a quarter past eight. It's turned nine, and there they are kicking up a row on the stairs. Aren't people awful nowadays? What a crew!"

"Who are they?"

Julie shrugged her shoulders.

"Nobody. Some young friends of mine."

"Our sort of age?"

She gave him a long, challenging look.

"My dear, would you expect them to be!"

"Well for Heaven's sake, drop them for this evening."

She blushed, and tears came to her eyes.

"No, no, I won't! Why should I remain all alone when everybody else is having fun? There is a very good film at the Marboeuf and the program changes tomorrow."

She protested as though she were struggling against some violent danger, and flogged the arm of her chair with her gloves. Her brother contemplated her with a kind of bad-tempered patience. He was used to dealing with mares that were far more intractable.

"Listen to me. Don't behave like an idiot. It's only for this evening, and who knows if Herbert..."

"But I don't *care* about Herbert. I don't see why I should in any way concern myself each time he catches a chill! I forbid you to mention it in front of my friends."

"What do you bet they don't already know? There goes the bell. Shall I let them in?"

"No, no. I'll go."

She ran to the door like a little girl. Léon de Carneilhan, pricking his ears, could hear only his sister's voice.

"Ah! So there you are, only an hour late! Come on in; we can't stand talking here."

Two women and a young man came in without a word.

"My brother, the Comte de Carneilhan, Madame Encelade, Mademoiselle Lucie Albert, Monsieur Vatard, my brother, the Comte de Carneilhan. No, don't sit down. What have you got to say for yourselves?"

M. Vatard and Mme. Encelade tacitly delegated the spokesmanship to Mlle. Lucie Albert, who seemed the shyest of the three, her eyes were so enormous.

"We weren't going to come. I said we ought to telephone.... We read in the papers that...that the Count was ill...."

Julie, unwillingly admitting defeat, shot a glance at her brother, and the three newcomers did the same. In answer to these deferential glances, Léon de Carneilhan put on the expression that his sister called "the mask of a fox that has betrayed its king by hunting with humans." But Julie gave up the struggle.

"My dears, it can't be helped," she declared. "Herbert and I got ourselves talked about far too much for his illness not to draw a certain amount of attention to me. So..."

"I understand," said Coco Vatard.

"You're not the only one who understands," said Mme. Encelade tartly. "Lucie and I understand too."

"I'll give you a ring to-morrow."

"Is there anything I can do to help?" asked Lucie Albert.

"Nothing, darling. You're an angel. Let's all meet again soon, dears. I'll see you out."

From the studio Carneilhan could hear the four of them laughing and talking in low voices. One of the three women called Coco Vatard a crackpot, and then the door closed.

Her brother displayed no surprise when Julie returned. He knew of old the sudden weaknesses of this beautiful creature: she flouted public opinion, emerged cool and serene from conjugal disasters and put up with the make-shift existence of a woman living without money or help, but was unable to miss a treat, to which she'd been looking forward, without crying a little and bowing her shoulders and suddenly looking her age.

"My poor Julie, won't you ever change?"

She sat upright. Her eyes were wet but furious.

"I'm not 'your poor Julie' for a start! You stick to selling old hacks and young pigs and leave me alone?"

"Shall I take you out to dinner somewhere?"

"No!"

"Have you got anything in the flat?"

"I've got some chocolate. . . ."

"To eat?"

"What a horrid thought! No; to drink. I was going to have it when I came home. You know, young people are quite capable of dropping you at your door after the pictures without so much as giving you a drink. They're like that. There are some plums, and three eggs...yes, and some tinned tunny and a lettuce."

"Any whisky?"

"Of course. That's one thing I've always got."

"It's started raining. Would you like me to go?"

She caught at her brother with a gesture of alarm.

"No; please don't!"

"Well, let's try and soften the shock we've had! I'll lend you a hand. How do you want the eggs?"

"Don't care."

"I'll do you a tunny omelette. Put the chocolate on the stove for afterwards."

Gaily, as though armed against the worst by a frivolity that closely resembled courage (and which frequently promoted it), they forgot everything except getting their meal ready. They set about it with the skill and competitiveness of overgrown Boy Scouts. Léon de Carneilhan discovered the remains of some crème d'Isigny, and poured it into the salad. He tied a red-striped towel round his waist under his coat, and Julie took off her dress and put on a dressing-gown.

They escaped all trace of absurdity by the deftness of their movements, their long and unself-conscious practice in handling humble everyday objects. While Lêon was beating the eggs for the omelette, Julie laid the card table with two blue and two red plates, a handsome decanter and a rather ugly jug, and, then, putting a small pot of bright blue lobelias between the places, cried, "That looks grand!"

The gusto with which they ate had its roots in their indestructible appetites and digestions. In their friendship they were like two of a litter that can never play together without leaving traces of tooth and claw, wounding each other in the most sensitive places. Neither of them complained about their frugal supper; they rose nourished, but without having eaten their fill. The plates were replaced by ash trays and cards. Relaxed at last, Julie answered all her brother's questions with a good grace. A rainy draught from the window stirred her ringlets; and from her brother's 'traitor-fox' look, she perceived that the arrogant carriage of her head, her blue eyes, so prompt to sparkle with tears, and the radiance of her downy complexion and her hair, made her still the beautiful Julie de Carneilhan. Julie de Carneilhan, as people, in spite of a couple of marriages and divorces, still called her.

Lêon had taken off his coat. He never wore a waist-coat and he felt stifled the moment he was confined in a room. The body under the shirt was lean and hard—all table corners, Julie called it—a body almost numb to feeling and pitilessly ill-treated by its owner.

"How are the ducks going, Lêon?"

"Badly. If only I hadn't got those wretched little pigs on my hands! I've sent one of the brood-mares back to Père Carneilhan. Henrietta, the bay."

"Sent it back? By train?"

"No fear. By road. Gayant rode her."

"Lucky chap! I'd have loved to have ridden her there for you."

"You're too busy," said Carneilhan, not without irony. "It took him twelve days. He and the mare slept in the fields, a blanket apiece. She stuffed herself with all the oats she came across on the way! They'd have been in the soup if anybody'd caught them. Gayant's fodder was bread and cheese and garlic. She was so fat when they arrived that Père Carneilhan thought she was in foal, and Gayant had to disillusion him."

"When was all this?"

"In June."

Without more words, they both fell into a day-dream of roads in June running through the green oat-fields. Thinking of the lulling gait of the mare, the cool freshness between four and eight o'clock in the morning, the little rhythmical creak of the saddle and the first red streak of sunlight over the squat towers of Carneilhan, Julie felt her eyes growing moist once again. She flung a quick malevolent glance at her brother.

"It's very odd, when you're in shirt-sleeves, you look like a cavalry lieutenant who's taken to the bottle."

"Thanks."

"Don't mention it, dear."

"I mean thanks for 'lieutenant.' Who on earth's that chap you call Coco Vatard?"

"Nothing. Just somebody with a motor-car."

"A flame?"

"No."

"What about the girl, the one you called an angel? Is she your fancy?"

"Heavens no," sighed Julie. "I'm absolutely heart-whole. I think my life's heading for a big change. She's a very interesting little thing; a pianist and cashier in a night club, and to-day's her night off."

"It's none of my business, Julie, but what exactly would you do if you had any money?"

"Oh, thousands of idiotic things," said Julie haughtily. "Why?"

"Well, this Herbert affair. I can't help thinking about it, that's all."

She put her hand on her brother's arm, and he looked at it as though taken unawares by the fraternal gesture.

"It's not worth worrying about. That flighty line of his took us all in. If he dies, he dies. No one will see the color of any money that he has."

"You're talking like a fortune teller."

Julie's eyes lit up.

"Oh, my dear, I know one! It's priceless. She tells your fortune in melted candlewax! She told me, all in one sitting, that another war would break out, that I should have a sensational meeting and that Marianne would die of cancer."

"Marianne? How did you know she was talking about Marianne?"

The blood flowed into Julie's cheeks. She was splendid in attack, but inclined to lose her head when she was on the defensive.

"Why, I understood perfectly well from her description. It's the kind of thing you feel."

"How did you know she was talking about Marianne?" repeated Léon. "Tell me, or I'll tickle you up and down your spine!"

"Pax! I'll tell you, I promise!" Julie cried in haste. "Well, it was Toni. . . ."

"Toni? Marianne's son?"

"Yes. I asked him, my dear—we're on the best of terms—I asked him to pinch one of his mother's silk stockings, when she took them off before going to bed. You see, the candle woman has to have something worn by the person concerned."

"And did he bring it?"

Junie nodded.

"What a queer family," said Carneilhan. "It's all rather comic," he went on lightly. "It's getting late, and I must be on my way, old girl. It's an hour past midnight."

"How small. . . ." said Julie.

"How do you mean, small?"

"Only that people always talk about 'the small hours.' Ha! ha ha!"

She burst out laughing, and he realised that she was slightly tipsy. But she managed to walk steadily as far as the window.

"There's still a taxi on the rank. Shall I whistle for it?"

"Don't bother. I'll walk back. It's not raining."

She did not insist. Her brother often walked back to Saint Cloud, crossing the Bois de Boulogne with a tireless stride. One night, at the approach of an ugly-looking customer, he had jumped straight into a thicket with a leap of such length and swiftness that the stranger, frightened out of his wits, had taken to his heels. He loved the hours of the night as day began to break, always got home before six, and his horses started to whinny expectantly while he was still a long way off.

He shook Julie's hand in a vague manner and made off towards the thing he cared for most in the world; the shrill whinny of his faithful mares, and the friendly language of their great affectionate lips close to their master's expert ear.

"It must be Friday," thought Mme. de Carneilhan, still half asleep. "I can smell fish."

There was a large general grocer's shop at the corner of the street. When Julie had taken the lease of the "studio with every modern comfort" she had sacrificed smartness to convenience, a bargain she never ceased regretting, especially on fish days, cabbage days and melon days.

The presence of the daily cleaning woman washing up in the kitchen-bathroom indicated that it was only about half-past nine, so Julie went to sleep again; but not without twinges of guilt dating from her earliest childhood, when she had been used to sharp little cuts with a riding-crop from her father's stern but equitable hand. In those days Julie and Léon, barefoot and in silence, used to fight in front of the door (which opened ineluctably at seven in winter and six in summer) to avoid being beaten the first. Well warmed up and still tingling, they put on their sole-worn shoes without an atom of rancor, and threw themselves upon the backs of their ponies and galloped to catch up with the Comte de Carneilhan. Their father would be mounted on a Breton nag with a back like a basket, or on a bag of bones as high as a church, or even on a saddled cow. She was a light-colored animal, as fair as himself, oat-fed and fiery-eyed, and she cocked up her tail when she took the jumps with her teats swinging to and fro like bell-clappers. He used to ride her just to demonstrate what he could get out of anything with hooves and flat teeth, and to draw attention to himself at the horse-fairs and important market days in Périgord.

On such days he lent Julie and Léon the pick of his stable. Having set out from Carneilhan on horseback, the children often had to trudge home with their saddles on their shoulders or get a lift in a peasant's cart, their smart appearance and good seats having helped to sell the ponies on the spot. For a time they would remain obdurate and embittered, shedding secret tears for the little horse they had loved. But, as they grew up, they developed a taste for these frequent changes of mount. And when, at the age of seventeen, Julie de Carneilhan married a rich man from Holland called Julius Becker, she was not particularly worried. "I'll change him," she thought vaguely to herself, "next market day."

As other people dream longingly of university degrees or legal briefs, Julie would often dream that she was on horseback. Mme. Encelade, who was given to interpreting dreams, declared: "That means that you ought to go to bed with somebody."

"No it doesn't," Julie insisted. "It simply means that I want to be on horseback."

And she would plan to borrow her brother's mare, Hirondelle. But the next morning she would wake up late, and fall into a brown study. Léon, what's more, refused to lend her Hirondelle, and suggested Tullia—a quiet, uninteresting, sure-footed animal, compact of all the virtues of a nursery governess. Julie was on her dignity at once.

"My dear boy, you don't expect me to appear in the Bois on a dappled mare?"

The water, as it gurgled into the bath in the kitchen next to the studio, set the narrow partition shaking musically. "Ten o'clock!" Julie got out of bed and pulled her pyjama belt tight. Feeling well and sprightly, with a clean taste on her tongue and throat, she remembered that she had been drinking the night before. Spirits treated her mercifully, as they did Père Carneilhan. They cleared her complexion and her brain. She could boast without lying that never a drop of syrupy liqueur had been allowed to pass the barrier of her mouth. Her teeth were healthy and unevenly set, the two middle incisors being on the large side and the two others smaller and slanting slightly backwards.

"I'm going to dip my teeth in a glass of water," she would say in the morning, and then go and drink a tumblerful at the kitchen tap. This family catch-phrase, she was in the habit of telling her friends, had cost her the affections of a good-looking lieutenant she had hardly got to work on; failing to catch the joke, he had assumed that she wore a set of false teeth.

She stopped in front of the looking-glass and screwed up her nose. Sleep had put all her ringlets out of curl: they stood out stiffly all over her head like bits of straw.

"I look as though I'd been sleeping in the stables," she observed to herself. She stopped again to telephone, and listened motionlessly to the prolonged ringing tone at the other end. "Hello? Hello?...Really, what a bore this is! What? M. Vatard has gone out? Already? Good, thank you." Grimacing scornfully, she pulled a stray slipper towards her with her big toe. "Oh dear, oh dear, that boy and his beastly factory..." and made for the part of the kitchen curtained off by a waterproof hanging fitted to a rod, and known as the bathroom.

An electric stove with two rings was fitted to the top of a cupboard beside the bath. When the cleaning woman was out, Mme. de Carneilhan could have her bath and keep an eye on her breakfast at the same time. She had retained, from a childhood steeped in assured if penurious family pride, a profound lack of bashfulness and a total disregard for the presence of servants. "Stir up the water for me, Peyre," she used to shout to the kitchen gardener at Carneilhan when she was thirteen, fourteen, fifteen years old. The man would then beat the surface of the fish pond by the spring, for Julie could not bear the sinuous, invisible creatures that haunted its depths. Then she would shout: "Turn round and look the other way!" and throwing off her dress, slip into the water—it was warm on top, but ice-cold lower down—swim round a bit and then get out, as oblivious of the man who beat the water for her as she was of her own beauty.

"Good morning to you, Madame du Sabrier," she called to her daily woman in tones of mock ceremony as she pulled off her crumpled pyjamas.

Before getting into the bath, she did some deep breathing exercises and a few knee-bends like a dancer. Disapproving of naked beauty, Mme. Sabrier turned the other way.

"Are you having lunch in, Madame? What would you like to eat?"

"I'd like—let me see—cream cheese and skate in black butter. The black and white together would look particularly smart."

She laughed under a helmet of lather. When she was in her bath, Julie soaped herself all over, including her head, like a man.

Mme. Sabrier heaved a deep sigh.

"It's not fair. There's no justice in the world," she said. "You were up drinking last night, weren't you? I saw the glasses. And there you are, spry as a goldfish. And I've never drunk a drop, and here am I all doubled up. And you are forty-four, too.... It's not fair...."

"I don't want to seem inquisitive, but I'd like to know the name of the pig who told you how old I was?"

Mme. Sabrier smiled at last.

"Well now! I've got my little ways and means, Madame. It was the chauffeur who brought a letter for you one day. A chauffeur who brought a letter for you one day. A chauffeur from the left bank of the river."

"So that's how they behave on the left bank? They'll catch it when I get at them. Give me my dressing-gown."

"Now don't you go making wet footmarks all over my clean floor, please. He told me he got it from your first husband."

'It's Herbert's chauffeur,' thought Julie as she went out. She stopped at the doorway—she made 'good exits' through force of habit—and said "My second, Madame Sabrier. My second husband. And not the last either!"

"It's not fair," sighed Mme. Sabrier. "Here are your newspapers."

'Dead? Or not? If he's dead, it'll be on the front page.' Clutching the papers in her wet hand, she went and sat on her bed. 'Nobody on the front page. He must be just ill on page two: What did I say? *We are happy to announce that the sudden illness of the Comte d' Espivant appears to offer no cause for alarm.*'

"There," Julie cried out loud, "I was sure of it! I could have gone to the pictures after all! The dirty dog! And Professors Hattoutant and Giscard at his bedside, if you please! Marianne must be getting worried about her source of..."

She threw the paper aside and opened the only cupboard in the studio, which she had lined with looking-glass as a make-up cabinet and fitted with electric light. She was clever with her fingers and impulsively attacked any job in hand; but she soon grew bored and her unfinished handiwork would remain as a series of little monuments to her skill and her inconstancy.

'A chauffeur from the left bank,' she thought. 'That must have been my old Beaupied bringing a letter from Toni. It's Toni's fault.... What a nuisance boys of that age are! He decided he wanted to see me, and who does he send with the letter. His stepfather's chauffeur! Herbert has a mania for keeping on his chauffeurs till they fall to bits. He thinks that what was "aristocratic" where coachmen were concerned now applies to mechanics.'

She brushed her wet hair back till it lay flat against her scalp. Taken unawares like this, with nothing on her face and plunged in disgruntled thoughts, Julie resembled her brother in certain characteristics—a wild look, with narrowing temples and the chin and jawbone fining down into a muzzle. But everything was redeemed by her nose and a rosy coloring that could stand up to anything. She dabbed a patch of face-cream on her delicious nose, and spread it on with her forefinger. She made herself up with skill, plucked a couple of hairs from her upper lip, curled her hair with lively twists of the hand. 'I'll walk in the Bois for a bit,' she said to herself. 'I won't put on my lizard-skin shoes, or they won't last out the year.'

She ran to answer the telephone, cursing jubilantly to herself. She did this whenever her restless indolence and over-encumbered solitude were forced into action.

"Hello? Is that you, Coco? Does that mean that it's past twelve and you've got away from the office? Oh! What rotten luck.... I wanted to go for a tremendous walk. What? No, I wanted to go to-day. To-morrow's not the same thing at all. What? Herbert? He's better, of course. All he cares about is being a nuisance to other people. All right, to-night then, but I loathe having to wait for anything I enjoy. What? My dear boy, who on earth do you think you're talking to? See you this evening." She put the receiver back and broke into a little urchin-like smile that put years on her all at once. She quickly resumed her serious expression and became once more a tempestuous and masterful blonde. In five minutes' time she was dressed in a white tailored shirt, a skirt with a pattern of black and white birds' feet and a black jacket that flouted every current fashion. Her slightly overdone trimness betrayed the fact that Julie de Carneilhan was approaching the age when women decide to sacrifice their faces to their figures.

'I ought to have a purple carnation. Ten francs...no joke at the moment.' She rummaged among her handkerchiefs and found a small one of mauve crepe which she twisted into the shape of a flower. She snipped at it deftly with her scissors and then frilled it out in her buttonhole. 'Marvellous!' Then her face clouded over with the same alacrity. 'What an idiot I am! The handkerchief cost a whole *louis*.' She always reckoned in louis out of smartness and what she called 'good form.' A cloud drifted across the sky and chased away all desire to go for a walk. 'Shall I ring up Lucie? Or find out when the sales begin at Hermés? Or...'

She trembled at the sound of the telephone, which started to ring just as she was stretching out her hand for the receiver. Like many creatures leading an unprotected life, she regarded the telephone as her only source of help.

"Hello! Yes, speaking. What? I can't hear. Would you say it again? Who did you say was speaking?" The tone of her voice altered and her shoulders fell into a slight stoop.

"Is...is that you, Herbert? Yes, of course, I read it in the papers like everybody else. So it wasn't anything serious?" She saw herself across the room in the looking-glass and sat up straight. "Frightening us all like that! What? Well, *us* means the whole of Paris, my dear, half of France, and a good hunk of abroad."

She laughed, listened for a moment and then stopped laughing.

"Where are you telephoning from? What? Come there, to your house? Oh, nothing. I was going to have luncheon alone. No, nobody. No, of course I'm not saying no, but...what about Marianne? All right. Yes. But it's nothing. Don't be absurd. Yes; I'll keep an eye out of the window."

Julie replaced the receiver slowly. She put on a black straw hat that reminded her of her early childhood, and opened the door into the kitchen.

"Madame Sabrier," she said, in an uncertain voice. Then she was suddenly on the alert with her nostrils wide.

"What's that awful stink of fish?"

"Why, it's the skate, Madame. Madame told me. White cheese and black butter."

"But it's frightful. You didn't really think..."

The corners of her mouth sank, and she said, in piteous tones: "I only thought I was saying something funny. You can eat your wretched skate. But leave me the cream cheese. I'll buy...well, we'll see...."

She sank back into uncertainty, fiddling idly with some oddments on the chimney-piece, and then she went to lean on the window-sill, with one foot resting on top of the other. When a long black motor drew up among the delivery-tricycles outside the grocers', Julie pulled herself together and ran downstairs like a girl, feeling all the exhilaration of her firm, slim legs, her light breasts and her freedom from a single ounce of extra flesh.

"Why, of course, it's Beaupied. How are you, Beaupied? You never change a bit."

"Madame la Comtesse flatters me."

"No, Beaupied, really. You're always the same, specially since I can't turn my back on you for five minutes without your telling my charwomen that I'm forty-four!"

"Me? Oh! I can promise your Ladyship..."

"Anyway, I'm not forty-four, Beaupied. I'm forty-five. Drive home, would you."

"Er—home," repeated the grey-haired chauffeur. "Which..."

"Yours," said Mme. de Carneilhan kindly. "Ours, I mean the same one, in the Rue Saint-Sabas."

Once the door was shut, she brought the stern and critical eye of the im-pecunious to bear on the car. 'A real bounder's turn-out! They bought it at a motor show. It must have been left over by a Maharajah. Herbert always did have a tendency to buy motor-hearses. And all upholstered in pearl-grey! Why not mauve satin? And a chauffeur rigged up in summer livery. I suppose one can't have everything—millions and taste as well....' Her critical sense was equally hard upon the cutout flower in her buttonhole. She took it off and threw it out of the window as they drove into the flower-planted courtyard.

Julie had not foreseen the evocative power of the surroundings which she herself had once chosen and loved. Her pulse was thumping in her eardrums, and before shaking her head to the chauffeur when he asked if her ladyship would like to be driven back later, she raised her eyes to the first floor. Her second husband, drawn to the window by the sound of the motor-car, was leaning out and shouting "Two o'clock sharp!" to Beaupied.

'Two o'clock sharp,' she repeated to herself, 'and the car used to hang about till four! Unless, of course, Herbert slunk off in a taxi to see some wretched girl-friend.' She ascended the little flight of steps and went through the door of the hall almost without being aware of it, guided unerringly by the memory of her foot on the stone stairs, her hand on the door knob. The moment she crossed the threshold, a heavy atmosphere of feminine scent pulled her together. 'Marianne's scent...too much of it, too much money, too many diamonds, too much hair....' An unexpected irritation sharpened her faculties. On the first floor she thought she caught, through a half-open door, the thread of a brilliant glance, an intake of breath; and the door closed. Her room! A footman paced along in front of her. She expected him to open the door of the study next to Espivant's room, but he asked her to wait in a little room that she could not remember. She could hear Espivant's voice somewhere behind the thin walls, and for a moment she lost all sense of time. The present became meaningless, as if lost in the heart of a dream, yet she was aware that she was dreaming. The footman came back and she followed him.

'Where on earth does Herbert sleep?' she wondered, counting the closed doors. 'My room...the lined cupboard...his room...the room we used to call the nursery...' She stopped dead all at once with a gesture of despair. 'I forgot to change my old shoes!' She almost turned right about and took to her heels. Her calm was restored by a second's consideration. 'After all, what does it matter? Well I never, he's gone and settled in the nursery. How very odd!' Her guide vanished and Julie made a fine entrance with her charming nose in the air, her eyes feigning short sight, her small mouth half open in an agreeable but un-affectionate smile, and her gaze focused straight ahead at the level of her eyes. But Herbert's voice rose from a little bed much lower down.

"So I'm reduced to sending for you? It never occurred to you to come and ask how I was?"

His voice was young and cheerful and pitched in a key that Julie was still unable to hear without anger and pain. She lowered her eyes and saw Herbert in bed. She took him in at a glance. 'Oh!' she said to herself. 'He's done for.' The smell of ether, well-known to Julie from many a disreputable haunt, suddenly assumed a terrible significance. It gave her the cue for her words and behaviour.

"Herbert," she said, a little too fulsomely. "What's this new stunt of yours, and all this publicity in the papers? And are those pale grey silk pyjamas for my benefit? What sort of opinion do you expect me to carry away of a man who interviews me in pale grey silk?"

The hand that Herbert stretched out to her seemed to have thickened. It waved her into a little armchair close to the bed.

"Would you like to smoke?" he said. "You can."

"What about you?"

"Not this morning, my dear. I don't even want to."

She was unable to single out any definite sign of deterioration in Espivant's face. He was 'switching on the charm' for her, as he did for everybody, from pure force of habit. But a mysterious process seemed imperceptibly to have puffed up all that had been hollow the day before, and conversely, to have scooped out the convexities of the slim brown Gascon mask. Julie had long realised that his handsome face was merely, under its masculine brow, a collection of slightly effeminate features. But the fire in the light brown eyes, the mouth retaining all its youthful delicacy and the deliberately unfashionable moustache, there they all were before her eyes again, and once again she bit the edge of her tongue to punish herself for still being hurt by them.

"Have you had luncheon yet, Youlka? Do have something with me! Just to please me!"

' "Just to please me"...D, E flat, E natural, A flat. Same phrase on the same notes,' thought Julie.

"But..." she began, turning towards the door.

"I'm having my tiny luncheon all alone. Marianne, who was up all night— there was not the slightest need for it—is having a rest."

"Just anything, then. Some fruit.... It's my day for fruit."

"Lovely. Darling, I'm going to ring. Nobody will disturb us once they've brought the food. I'll tell you all about my tiresome attack, if you'd like to hear it. But perhaps it would be a bore. Youlka, does being here mean anything to you?"

Julie understood, from the caressing tone of his voice, that he still enjoyed hurting her.

"No," she said coldly.

In came a male nurse, in white, followed by a secretary with a handful of telegrams. Espivant began speaking before the latter could get a word out.

"No, no, Cousteix. Nothing for the moment. You just see to them all, there's a good chap. After all, I *am* ill!" he said with a laugh. "I'll have a look at my letters this evening. Perhaps...!"

He propped himself on his fists to hoist himself into a sitting position. The effort lasted only a moment, but his mouth gaped strangely open, and Julie perceived genuine anxiety rather than mere officiousness in the haste with which the nurse ran to help him.

"What a ridiculously narrow bed," Julie reproached him. "It's only about eighty centimetres wide like a house-maid's!"

The nurse glanced at her approvingly as he left the room. "Sh!" whispered Espivant. "It's all part of my plan! It's my self-defence bed!"

They were still laughing with spiteful complicity when two tables laden with fruit were wheeled in. Julie found it all faultless: late cherries, rose-colored peaches, thin-skinned Marseilles figs, cloudy hot-house grapes that had been care-fully protected from the wasps. Iced water and champagne trembled in thick cut-glass jugs, chiselled with a pattern of nail-heads. Julie's nostrils opened wide to the fumes of the coffee and the smell of the yellow rose standing next to a pot of fresh cream. She carefully concealed the pleasure she derived from all this luxury.

"Who asked for this ham, Herbert? Nobody wants it."

Espivant made a careless gesture.

"No, thanks. So Marianne knew that I . . . ?"

"Marianne, I expect. Anything else you want?"

"What are you worrying about? Please don't tire me!"

A ray of sunshine fell across the gleaming silver. Herbert chose the best of the peaches, still adorned with its living green leaf, and let it rest in the palm of his hand.

"How lovely it is. . ." he sighed. "Take this one. Do you still drink your coffee while you're eating fruit?"

This reminder of their old life together caught Julie unawares. She flushed, and steadied herself by drinking a glass of champagne.

"How pretty the table looks," she said. "Cherries too! Let me play with all this for a bit; don't you worry about me. Is there some medicine or other you ought to take?"

Espivant, who had cut one of the peaches, left it on his plate. He took a handful of cherries and held them up to the full light.

"Look, they're so clear you can almost see the stones inside! What have I ever had of my own after all? All I'll have to say goodbye to amounts to just about this."

He dropped the cherries and waved towards the little sunlit table. His gesture did not exclude the tall fair-haired woman sitting slant-wise in her chair, facing the light, and feeling as happy as a wasp in the sun. She wiped her lips, wrinkling her brows as she did so.

"Goodbye? How do you mean?"

Espivant leaned towards her. As he emerged from the shadow, the strange almost vegetable color of his face became at once apparent, the greenish white of his forehead and temples and of the skin around his mouth. Round his brown eyes were dark circles; so many women, too many women, had painted them there and loved them.

"It's all up with me, Youlka," he said with affected lightness. "No, do let me talk about it! Pour out the coffee. Yes, yes, I'm allowed coffee. Aren't you surprised to see so few doctors 'at my bedside,' as they say? No? What a brute you are; you never notice anything! You don't even notice what a man looks like unless you've got him face to face. And, when I use the expression 'face to face,' it's only because I respect the precincts of a dwelling that matrimony has doubly sanctified."

He laughed, and made Julie laugh too. This she did with constraint at first; then she gave way to a helpless fit of laughing as easily as she might have burst into tears.

"Suppose she heard us. . ." she said.

"Who? Marianne? She's bound to, a bit."

"You behave like a cad to her, Herbert."

"No, I lie to her. I...I was a cad to you because I used to tell you the truth."

Her nostrils stiffened as she tore open a fig with her teeth.

"You've got to admit I paid you back in the same coin."

"Only because I wrung your neck until you owned up."

He threw her one of those deep and slanting glances that he had employed when he was still her unfaithful and jealous husband. He even stuck his fist on his hip. Some divine intervention had stripped him forever of the most effectual elements of his attractiveness, and all the violence aroused in Julie by these accents of a bygone day melted in pity. 'Poor man...' And since, through lack of vocation or from habit, she was prone to confuse pity with boredom, she felt herself practically a prisoner between the bedridden Herbert, the elaborate silver and the various knick-knacks that were calling her. She longed for her street full of shops and for Coco Vatard and Lucie Albert with all their youth and naïve intentness on their work and amusements. She looked about her and began to criticise the furniture.

"Herbert, are you really attached to that chintz? Has nobody ever told you that the pink-and-black chintz suited you about as well as a rope of pearls would a bulldog? Haven't you got any real friends?"

"Very few."

"And what on earth are you doing, all tucked up here in the nursery? Is it an attempt to make yourself seem younger? That's *too* much."

Espivant, leaning on the pillow, was drinking his coffee.

"Shove the table to one side, would you?" he asked her without answering her question. "Put your coffee on top of mine, and bring the cigarettes over. I want to talk to you."

Julie obeyed quickly lest he should catch sight of her old shoes and went on pulling the furniture to pieces in order to distract his attention.

"Lovely lemon-wood. But surely a bit chichi for a man's room?"

The secretary came back holding a telephone with a long trailing wire. "It's the President of the Republic asking for news."

"How well all those spirals of telephone wire suit you, Cousteix! You look like a vine. This is my friend Cousteix, who is kind enough to be my secretary: the Comtesse de Carneilhan. Thank the President, Cousteix. Say I'm ill. Not very ill. Just fairly ill—anything you like. Oh, and while you're there, Cousteix——Julie, will you excuse me a moment?"

'It's very odd,' Julie was thinking, 'Herbert has never been able to talk naturally to a secretary or an inferior. The authority of the Espivants is just about as recent as their title. Saint-Simon saw them moving in, and Viel-Castel made fun of them. And now, there's Herbert bitching about in the hopes of putting his secretary into an ecstasy.'

She cried "Oh!" and leapt forward. For, the moment the door was closed behind Cousteix, Espivant fell back with his eyes shut. Julie found a bottle, opened it, damped a napkin with sal volatile, and fanned Herbert's nostrils so vigorously that his fainting fit lasted less than sixty seconds.

"Don't call anyone; it's nothing," Herbert said in a clear voice. "I'm getting used to it. Any coffee left? Do give me some. You were so quick. I didn't have time to lose consciousness. Thank you."

He sat up without any help and breathed deeply. The whole of his greenish face was smiling.

"It's queer, you know, the feeling of well-being, of optimism, that accompanies each of these, what shall I call them—little deaths. Would you like some brandy, Youlka? I've got some here that dates from—oh, from Pepin the Short."

He was slightly out of breath and overcome by a sudden gloom. She could not take her eyes off his pale face and deep eye-sockets.

"Thanks, I won't. I drank too much last night."

"Ah? Who with? Where? Was it fun? Go on, tell!"

He leant forward and the blood returned to his cheeks. Julie recognised his mode of speech, his veiled eyes, the wild hope of widening the range of his senses, and began to hate him again.

"No, it was nothing. I sat up drinking whiskey with Léon, that's all. Pure hygiene! Do you want to talk to me, or shall I let you rest? I can always come back."

"Yes, but perhaps I shan't always be able to. Do stay! Even if it bores you. You're so easily bored."

He smiled at her without a trace of goodwill, but went on holding her hand. 'We know each other too well,' thought Julie. 'We're still quite capable of playing dirty tricks on each other, but we can no longer deceive each other.' She shook her head in token of denial, sat down opposite Espivant and poured cream into a second cup of coffee. A young male voice shouted a few words in the courtyard below.

"It's Toni," Espivant explained.

Julie lowered her eyes to conceal a smile. 'If you really think I need you,' she thought, 'to tell me that it's Toni...'

"My darling pet," Herbert began, "we were saying that I was going to die. You can't always be there to intervene.... Oh, I remember one day, when you'd got a saucepan of milk on the stove, the telephone began ringing, the milk was rising and you dealt with the telephone and the milk at the same time, turning off the gas with your elbow without letting go of the saucepan or the receiver. You were superb. We were poor then."

'I still am,' she thought to herself and hid her feet under the chair. But, as Espivant grew less pale and vague and more animated, she felt strangely happy and proud that he owed his present well-being to her.

"How's Becker, by the way?"

"All right. He's in Amsterdam."

"Does he still give you an allowance? How much?"

Julie blushed, and did not answer. She was hesitating between the truth and a lie, and finally voted for the truth.

"Four thousand a month."

"Not what you'd call royal."

"Why should it be royal? He's only a baron, and then only if you don't look too close."

"Including rent?"

"Yes."

"He hasn't cancelled the insurance in his own favor?"

"No."

Espivant gazed at her with what she always called his 'small look'; pointed, expert, and pressed tight between his eyelids. She knew that his attention had alighted at last on her slightly faded black jacket and her white shirt, spotless, but so often laundered. His eyes came to rest on her feet. 'That's done it. He's seen them.' She heaved a breath of deliverance, ate the last of the cherries, and slowly powdered her nose. Her bag was almost new.

"You never told me," Espivant coldly reproached her.

"It's against all my principles," she answered in the same tone. He made his voice still harder.

"Of course, your way of life has got nothing to do with me."

"No, nothing at all."

She lowered her forehead, arming herself against whatever blows were coming; but Espivant remained calm. 'He's sparing himself, not me,' thought Julie.

"Idiot," he said gently, "let's talk. I've announced my impending dissolution to you three times, and all you do is talk about furniture and interior decoration because you don't like this sexless room. Give me a cigarette. You haven't grasped the fact that I 'happen' to sleep here at least three times a week; 'No, no, don't change a thing in this ugly room, my darling, you know I only want your—our—room. But I've got to work late this evening, and I'm feeling tired and ugly.' "

He imitated himself talking to his second wife, and Julie could not help admiring so much langour and amorous authoritativeness. 'He's a past master in treachery,' she thought.

"Do you call her *vous* like that?"

"Not always. She likes contrasts. So you see, that's how I'm able to wriggle out of it."

"Wriggle out of it?" Julie repeated thoughtfully.

"Well," Herbert said crossly, "you don't need a translation, do you?"

"Oh, no...only I say it in a different way. Go on, though. I'd never have thought that Marianne was so—— It's true she's only thirty-five: the age when a woman doesn't know that, once out of twice, she ought to say 'No' to a man of ...our age. A respectable spouse will finish off a man of fifty twice as quickly as a clever tart who knows better than to wear out her own property."

"Here, I'm not fifty!"

"I know. Not for another six months. I was talking in general terms."

She gazed at Espivant with a look that derived nearly all of its kindness from the blue make-up round her eyes. 'Perhaps,' she thought, 'he will never be fifty.'

"Well," she resumed, "you've got a wife who stands no nonsense. Go on."

He absent-mindedly crushed out his half-smoked cigarette.

"Go on? There's nothing more to say. You've just told my entire story...and my wife's."

"Rich wives are expensive."

"So are beautiful ones. Oh, I realize now what an idiot I was! I've tried all sorts of things, gadgets, pills."

"Like the Duc de Morny?"

"Like the Duc de Morny. We'll not come to much good copying the Napoleonic nobility."

'We? How does he mean "we"?'—malicious gaiety suddenly overcame her·at the thought—'Once "we" no longer means Herbert and Julie. He's surely not lumping together the Carneilhans and the Espivants?' She was careful to conceal the pride that bound her to the name of her family, to its ragged antiquity and to the remains of the massive-walled castle, half manor and half farmhouse, which, for the last nine hundred years, had never been called anything but Carneilhan.

"Don't be rude to the Second Empire," she said. "I'm having my boudoir all quilted and buttoned like the Comtesse de Teba's. But, seriously, Herbert, why don't you just go away? Surely you've had enough of this house and its dismal little box-hedges? Go away. Take your pale grey pyjamas...and your dowry."

"Ah! My dowry!"

He gazed dreamily at the chintz-covered ceiling and seemed on the point of a decision.

"How they talked about the 'dowry' that fixed my election! Five millions? Four millions? How much, Julie?"

"Some people said five. Some two."

She wanted to please and insult him at the same time. She stroked his lip and his small musketeer's moustache.

"Five or two, you were cheap at the price."

He caught her hand, the hand so skilful at every task it touched, and kissed it vaguely as she withdrew it.

"Did you hear that? There have been at least four rings at the door since you arrived. I bet Marianne's been entertaining in my place and that she's already promised since this morning to build a bridge, a school, a wash-house and an orphanage."

"And will she really do it?"

"They'll bring her the estimates, and she'll have them looked into. All that takes time."

He sat up and undid the button of the pale grey pyjamas at his thick neck.

"She pays for things; she doesn't give. Do you get the idea, Youlka?"

"American style?"

"I don't know. I haven't married any American so far. My dowry! She's put 'all her worldly goods' at my disposal. You see the difference?"

"Of course I do. You've been had."

They went on smoking in silence. Espivant, from tiredness and perhaps from chronic flirtatiousness, lowered his dark eyelids. Julie listened to light feminine footsteps in the corridor. 'Perhaps that's her. I've been here over an hour,' she thought. 'Is that all he wanted to tell me?'

"Actually, why *did* you marry her?"

Herbert opened his eyes again and looked at her like a reproachful schoolmaster.

"My dear child, what a question! Four months to run an election campaign, a widowed beauty paying me her *devoirs*, a...an extremely embarrassed financial situation. That was my position."

"Nobody quite knows what's going on, even in a very dicky financial situation. But a marriage like yours makes everything as clear as daylight."

"Yes, but supposing I'd only been Marianne's lover, just think of the massed howling going up from my old friends and political enemies. *'Where does the money come from?'* "

"Nobody asks where the money comes from once the candidate's elected."

Espivant sat up laughing.

"You seem to know a lot all at once! Who told you all this?"

"You did. I'm just dishing up what you told me about Puylamere's candidature."

Herbert gave her an attentive look from between his lashes, and she met it without embarrassment.

"It seems you're always destined to fill me with admiration, Youlka."

"Yes; like a racehorse that starts winning the moment it's been sold. You're simply a child with a moustache. You thought you'd be rich because Marianne was; that's your excuse. You were desperately in need of a lot of useless odds and ends, you wanted motor-cars like the Argyropoulos; you wanted to throw Venetian parties like the Fauchier-Magnans; you even wanted a more beautiful wife than anyone else."

She was talking airily, knitting round her eyes the network of wrinkles blurred by her grey-blue make-up. Herbert let her run on, greedy for flattery and insult. He made a gesture of protest, and the sunlight on his bloated white hand for an instant robbed Julie of speech.

"I wanted," Herbert went on plaintively, "I wanted a sheaf of Corneille's unpublished manuscripts enough to fill a great book...and then I wanted a chateau. Oh! how I wanted a chateau!"

He jerked himself into a sitting position with the agility of a healthy young man.

"Just imagine it, Julie. It was called Maucombe. The whole castle lies reflected in a magnificent lake. It looks as if it doesn't take itself quite seriously, as if it felt almost too fifteenth-century with all those corner-towers and pinnacles and gateways and gothic arches! And the looking-glass it is built in the middle of! I wanted things I'd been dreaming of for so long!"

He looked at Julie and went on. "...That we'd been dreaming of for so long!"

She smiled at him generously.

"Oh, I'm quicker than you at forgetting what I want. I do think Marianne might have..."

The swollen white hand reappeared in the sunbeam and made a gesture of indecision. 'I'd have given it him, in the old days, if I'd been Marianne,' she went on thinking. 'He's never more irresistible than when he wants something for entirely selfish reasons!'

"So you didn't get your fairy-tale Robida castle in the end? Why not?"

"Oh, it's most involved. It meant draining a swamp that had formed because they'd allowed the dykes to go to pot. Too dear; not a healthy enough region. Too isolated. People like that have got two passwords that crop up the whole time —'too much,' and 'not enough.' "

"Who have?"

Espivant looked for a moment like a man who is being spied on. "I really don't know, to tell you the truth. You don't tumble bang into the *middle* of a fortune like Marianne's; you fall *alongside* it, somewhere in the neighborhood. You arrive there. . . . I'm not boring you, Julie?"

"Don't be silly."

"Well, you arrive there like a chap who has been forced by a motor accident to spend half a day with a strange family that live by the roadside, and whose new hosts will keep on repeating, 'This is Uncle Reveillaud, and that lady is my sister-in-law, Charlotte's aunt, and that tall boy, over there is George, who is going to Saint-Cyr next term.' As if the poor wretch could remember any of it after five minutes!"

He was interrupted by a fit of coughing.

"Herbert, you're tiring yourself. Shall I give you something to drink?"

He made a gesture of refusal.

"I'm not coughing from my throat, but from my heart. Never mind. Marianne's fortune is a. . .a huge foreign body, something fearful, enormous and secretive, talking every known language and always having something wrong with it, just as I might feel sick or you'd have a pain in the back."

"I *beg* your pardon, I never have a pain in the back," said Julie proudly.

"Yes, yes, we all know it's made of solid steel!" Espivant said, raising his shoulders. "Unlike the mineral resources of Marianne. Whenever you want. . .well, I don't know."

"The moon?" Julie suggested.

"Let's say the moon—you suddenly discover that copper has got chlorosis that year, weevils have got at the diamonds, and the swallows have gobbled up all the ground-nuts from the trees."

Julie burst into one of her real laughs, with tears in her eyes and her mouth wide open. She thought she heard a rustle outside the door, and laughed a bit louder, while Espivant dropped his voice.

"Reams and reams of paper, portfolios, calculating machines, arctically cold offices in impossible parts of the town, hideous malformed little brats carting piles of documents about, and lawyers better dressed than I am, who say: 'The Comte d'Espivant is no concern of ours. Our business is direct with the lady, called Anfredi Marianne-Hélène, widow of Hortiz Ludovic-Ramon. . . .' That's Marianne's fortune for you, that and lots of other things; but it's not what you would call 'money.' It's a board of directors. It's a labyrinth. At last, at the end of a corridor, you bump up against a tiny old man called Saillard, who is racked with asthma, and whose name is always just mentioned like that. Just Saillard. Marianne's always going to see Saillard, or coming back from seeing Saillard. She *often* comes back with a face as long as your arm, saying, 'It's no good. Saillard was against it!' "

"Against what?"

"Against immobilising four millions for the purchase of a country estate, against advancing eighteen hundred thousand francs to buy a ravishing little Fragonard, an extraordinary bargain. Saillard would like to point out to Madame la Comtesse d'Espivant that her diamonds were reset in the modern fashion at the time of her marriage, and besides there is that new set of emeralds which was recently acquired. That, as guardian of her son, who is still a minor, Hortiz Antoine-René, she is obliged to...Oh! I'm fed up with it all!" cried Espivant, stretching his arms. "It's a funny thing, when I open my arms wide, there's a place here where..."

He pricked his ears towards the garden. "Oh, I know who that is. Professor Giscard. Oh dear, I can't just put him off like an office-boy. Julie, you must come again. We've only had time to talk nonsense. Tell me, would you like to? Would it amuse you in the slightest to come again?"

"Of course, I'm quite ready to."

"Quite ready to! You'd catch it, you condescending bitch, if only I were better!"

Julie thought he was making a sort of heavy joke, but she was astounded to see that he was heading for one of those sharp, unpredictable outbursts that used to rock their conjugal household, and reach a resounding climax that died away only in the dust and ashes of broken plates. 'Oh really,' she thought, 'he's too tiresome....' But she hastened to laugh as though she were still afraid of him, and promised to come again.

"You know, a bus brings me straight to your door. I'd prefer it to Beaupied. The back of his neck wobbles and it looks beastly if you're sitting behind him. Your servants' hall always looks like an almshouse for old age pensioners. And that motor! Do you think I like bowling about in an archbishop's car all done up in pearl-grey? And you might tell the Countess—I mean the second of the name—that in Paris, in a motor-car like that, one doesn't dress up one's chauffeur in white linen."

"If you don't go, you'll have to tell her yourself," Espivant interrupted, "because she'll be coming upstairs with Giscard. Off you go, my darling. I'll give you a ring. God, what a lovely figure you've got! Indestructible monster!"

He looked at her enviously and then turned away to fix his eyes on the door through which could come help and condemnation.

On the landing Julie realised that she had lost some of the self-assurance which, two hours earlier, had lightened her step and predisposed her for adventure. All the closed doors along the gallery, which she had slyly scrutinised on the way up, now seemed suspicious. Downstairs she manhandled the old iron latch that had been swinging on the glass-panelled door since Louis XV's day, and almost sprained her ankle on the gravel. 'Ah,' she sighed when she was on the pavement at last, 'that's better. I'm sure Marianne watched me leaving. She was watching me from all those doorways. She hoped I'd break my leg in the garden. And, with all that fuss, what did I have for lunch? I don't feel an ounce heavier! A peach, some cherries, a few figs. And, I must say, wonderful coffee.'

Cheered by having turned her back on what she most abhorred, a sick-bed, she breathed in the brief Parisian summer. The yellow rose-bud pinned to her lapel was beginning to droop. 'One of Marianne's roses.' Far from wishing to throw it away, she pressed it tight in her hand like plundered treasure. Two or three times her thoughts returned, almost gluttonously, to the two hours she had just spent in the forbidden zone. But she wisely postponed analysing them. She would pull everything to pieces when she got home. The men who passed her ran their eyes from the ash-blonde nape of her neck down to her shabby shoes, and she stopped a moment in front of all the shoe-shops. 'It'll be time to start thinking about gloves next,' she sighed. And she sought sanctuary from temptation inside a bus.

She felt a spasm of affection, as though she were just returning after a long absence, at the sight of the quavering little lift and the ramshackle staircase with its peeling plaster. On a sudden impulse she changed the position of several bits of furniture in the studio. Then, plugging in the electric iron, she spread a cloth over the kitchen table, and set to work. A black marocain crepe dress, that had been overworked for both evening and afternoon wear, was attacked with the iron and diluted ammonia. Water mixed with glycerine was dabbed on to elbows and hips that were threatening to turn shiny. A navy-blue tailor-made, whose four little pockets were covered with dull blue and red sequins, received the same careful treatment, and Julie was busy soaping a blouse, two pairs of camiknickers and some silk stockings when she was disturbed by three rings on the bell. She kept her overall on while she answered the door and brought her visitor back into the kitchen.

"What's the time, Coco? I wasn't expecting you yet!"

"Five o'clock."

"Already!"

"You might say 'at last.' "

"I was busy, as you see. The day seems to have flown."

"Lucky you!"

"Me?"

She surveyed the young man with cheerful derision. How odd that anyone should call her 'lucky.'

"You can wait in the studio, if you like."

"May I stay here?"

"You won't be in my way. Sit down on Madame Sabrier's stool. I'll only be another ten minutes."

She went on with her work, rolled her washing up in a damp towel, ironed the pleats of a skirt, changed her shoes and stitched up a hem. Coco Vatard followed her every movement since his arrival. Julie had devoted a slightly insulting attention to her various tasks, spreading cream on the heels of her shoes and plying the velvet polishing-rag with rapid strokes of her forearm.

"Is it fun watching?" she asked him.

His light-colored eyes remained fixed upon her. "Yes," he said in an earnest voice. "Nobody works like you. If only my dyers at the factory worked like that! You've such a deft and easy knack of doing things. I could watch you forever."

"Wouldn't you care to help me? Or for me to have a rest?"

Sitting on the edge of the bath-tub, she unfastened her overall and whisked it off with an aggressive gesture. She splashed cold water on her downy arms, on her shoulders and throat, barely distinguishable in color from her hair. Her one concession to modesty was to tie a little Tyrolean scarf round her neck. Only under her chin could she detect the least sign of flabbiness.

"No," Coco said after a moment's reflection. "I haven't got your knack of doing things so well. And why should you want to rest? You're always bored when you're not busy."

"That's not true!" she exclaimed.

Anger could bring tears to her eyes as promptly as laughter. But Coco showed no feeling other than admiration. He lifted the edge of his jacket and punctiliously pulled up the knees of his trousers. He was so near to being impeccably dressed that Julie hoped that she might actually make him so by putting a finishing touch to the knot of his tie. But she gave up the attempt almost at once, and drew back as he was about to take her into his arms.

"How good you smell," he said, with a sincerity which never deserted him. "You smell of under the arms and polish. Won't you be kind to me to-day?"

She gave him a distant look, her head tilted to one side. 'He really is rather nice,' she thought, 'in spite of his Sunday-best look on every day of the week. A decent young industrialist with big childish eyes and a turned-up nose. But as for...'

She sighed, and said, "I'm hungry."

"Hungry? Why on earth?"

She dilated her nostrils and raised her chin.

"Because, my dear boy, I had no time for luncheon. The Comte d'Espivant sent his car for me, and I sat by his bed for three or four hours, perhaps longer."

"Is he better?" asked Coco carelessly.

"No. Worse."

As she wanted to dine out and go to the cinema afterwards, she added, in a business-like way, "Professor Giscard is pessimistic, that's to say, but there is no immediate danger."

"And what does his wife think of your going to see your—her husband?"

"Nothing. She wasn't present at our meeting."

"Ah," said Coco reflectively, before he finally made up his mind. "It's disgusting!"

"What's disgusting?"

"Calling on each other like that. It's disgusting of him to have sent for you, disgusting of you to have gone, and disgusting of the other woman to have stood for it."

Julie did not react, and went on soaping her hands under the kitchen tap, looking at Coco's reflection in the small looking-glass over the sink. 'A lot he knows about it,' she thought. 'A first-rate executive in the cleaning and dyeing industry, no doubt, and treats himself to a mild binge at regular intervals. I bet he's got a faded photograph of his father in his wallet, dressed as a private. He's a nice boy.'

"You poor wretch," she said out loud. "What do you suppose you and I have got in common?"

"What?"

"I suppose that we both want to go out. Where are we going to dine? Are you meeting Lucie Albert? But not old Encelade, I presume?"

"No," Coco said. "Neither. You gave me no marching orders. Will it bore you if there's just the two of us?"

She smoothed out the three little vertical lines that the slightest vexation incised between her eyebrows.

"Of course not. But make me swallow something before dinner, or I'll eat one of your cheeks off."

Julie gently touched with her painted lips the clean-shaven cheek he proffered.

She was still in bed at ten o'clock next morning. She listened through her sleep to the familiar sounds of activity in the kitchen. When Mme. Sabrier half opened the studio door, Julie allowed her no time for her usual grievances.

"A glass of cold water, and some cocoa made with water, not milk. No breakfast or luncheon. No electric cleaner. See to my shoes and my tailor-made suit, and then off you go. I'm asleep. No letters? See you to-morrow, Madame Sabrier. Don't brush the sequins on the little pockets; they might come off."

She rolled over like a gun-dog and lay with her forehead against the wall. But she was unable to slip back into the pleasant, slumbrous condition that usually followed her brief and tumultuous nights of imbibing mixed drinks. 'It's the fault of the champagne,' she thought. 'Anyway, to be good at all, champagne must be marvelous. Nowadays, night clubs are all supplied with a standard champagne that tastes metallic. Give me brandy every time, with or without water, or a decent whisky that leaves you with a clean tongue.' The smell of cold tobacco smoke still lingered in her hair. 'My mouth and nose feel positively poisonous this morning. What on earth's the matter with me?'

A glass of cold water swept away the morning fog.

"Of course!" she cried aloud, "I had a row with Coco Vatard!"

She got back into bed and carefully pulled up the single sheet; it was worn, but made of linen and large enough to double over and tuck into her narrow divan bed. Gazing at the ceiling, she went back over the course of her evening. Shadow Number One had been the tête-à-tête dinner in the outskirts of Paris. When they left, in spite of Coco's misgivings, she had sat at the steering-wheel. "Do be careful," he begged her. "It's Papa's car; mine's being re-lined. If Papa saw you taking corners like that!"

"We ought to have brought Papa along too," she had said at length. "You'd have been happier then."

Her harmless little remark transformed Coco. He became mute and pompous and unready to accept any joke against his family. In other circumstances, the restaurant and the dinner would have met with Julie's approval. The dusk was darkening into night, the lights were reflected in the diminutive lake, the soft damp air carried the smell of geraniums and there was music which set her humming. But all this was too much for Coco.

"Why is it all so sad, Julie?"

She surveyed him with what remained of her benevolence, still humming softly to avoid having to say: 'It's so sad, because you're the wrong person to be here with me. And nothing here is really meant for you. You're not made for drinking or for dining with a woman who doesn't love you, somebody who comes from far away and remains there even when you hold her to your heart. You're really cut out for family dinners at home, for having a night out on Saturdays, for pretending to have outstripped your father when you are barely able to follow in his tracks or even to respect him as he deserves. It makes me sad to be here, too. But then I've been here often enough with other men, so it's not so serious in my case. I share out the sadness between Becker and Espivant and Puylamare, and others you've never heard of. Or perhaps you have, and it makes no difference. Once, for instance, I had dinner at that table down there with my first husband. I was called Baroness Becker then. At another table sat a lieutenant in uniform, with a civilian. I couldn't take my eyes off the lieutenant. It's a funny thing, nowadays one no longer sees those really fair-haired lieutenants. This one got up all of a sudden, came straight over to our table, apologised, and then stated his name, adding, "Your humble cousin, Madame!" Then up he climbed into a genealogical tree, reeling off strings of names and marriages and kinships. Becker kept nodding his head and saying, "Of course...yes, yes, I see.... Quite right. It's true there is quite a family likeness between my wife and you." And there wasn't a shred of truth in it, except the lieutenant's spun-gold hair and certain other qualities, very authentic ones, that he revealed later. But I can't tell that sort of story to someone like you. You're only sitting beside me because we went home together after supper—two? three months ago?—I've forgotten. I must say, we both had a wonderful time. But why should we begin all over again? You're like one of those old-fashioned French girls, who say "Mama, I'm engaged to be married, a gentleman kissed me in the garden!" Yes, that's the way, order some more champagne. Two hundred and sixty francs are my entire fortune at the moment, and there are still several days till Becker's cheque turns up. After all, I can't soak you for anything, my-poor-boy-who-is-not-yet-rich! I've never liked taking money from men. Treat the Comtesse de Carneilhan to food and drink. She's not really a countess, anyway, but only, this evening, disgustingly Carneilhan, and a bad lot like all of them!'

But she knew that with her flat dark blue felt hat tilted over one eye, and her yellow rose-petal skin toning with her hair, both the time of night and the lighting were becoming to her.

Others dining there had recognised her, and Coco found her ravishing. It was just about then that her young companion had tried to snatch her hand and kiss it under the table, and she had slapped his face. As bad luck would have it, this gesture, applied to Coco's flat compact cheek, was as clear and resounding as a stage-smack, and everyone who did not see it heard it.

They laughed, and Coco had the sense to do the same. So Julie wrinkling up her nose 'like a wild animal' was the only one to be cross, and she had trouble in recovering her temper.

'Going on to the Bal Tabarin was my idea. The drive back. Oh yes! He didn't want me to drive Papa's car. He wanted us to pull up by the side of the road in the Bois des Fausses-Reposes and make love. A regular picnic! A charming idea, really, and I can't think why I put a stop to it. Just my luck, I'm hungry again?'

Getting out of bed, she hunted through the food locker, which did its best to look like a frigidaire, and found a triangle of white cheese left over from the day before. Sprinkling a slice of bread with salt and pepper, most of her optimism returned to her as she munched away. But she always dreaded, during these difficult last days of the month, her punctual and ineluctable yearnings for food. Spurned and postponed by endless cigarettes on an empty stomach, these yearnings came back again to torment her digestion. Julie had broken herself in to every kind of diet and could cope with anything except hunger. 'Too early for oysters, but there are all sorts of little things I could swallow piping hot. I could do myself proud on ten francs, on the terrace of the little café. With a glass of muscadot to wash it down!' As she ate her bread and cheese, she sniffed the warm, damp noon-day. 'If only we could have two more months of this weather, two months without having to think about a warm coat!'

Without looking at the time, she went and smoked her first cigarette on her bed. All the details of the night before came back to her, from the gloomy dinner to the floor-show at the Tabarin, and the encounter with Beatrix de la Roche-Tannoy. She was an ex-society woman turned cabaret singer. 'Third star on the posters of the Ba-Ta-Clan! Poor Beatrix imagines a scandal in high life remains exciting for ever! We all went to see her when she first appeared on the stage at the Casino. But it didn't take long to see that the big la Roche-Tannoy nose, under all those paste tiaras and ostrich feathers, was even more tiresome than in ordinary life. So we all forgot about it.'

Julie was still bored, despite the castles of naked flesh piled up on the stage and dance floor of the Tabarin, so she made room for her friend. She was on the plump side and dressed in a little conical mediaeval headdress covered with sequins. Julie introduced Coco Vatard.

"Coco, order some more champagne for Madame de la Roche-Tannoy."

"Here we go," said Coco with a sort of polite familiarity.

"Are you alone, Beatrix?"

"Yes. I came on business. I've got to see Sandrini after the show. He wants to sign me up for the winter Revue."

"Are you...happy about it?"

"Delighted. Goodness, if only I'd known, I'd have dropped that gang of stuck-up idiots ten years sooner!"

"You didn't lose much time as it was," said Julie with a certain ferocity.

"And what about you? How is your father keeping?"

"My dear, he's amazing. He's still training a few colts at Carneilhan."

"No, really?" said Coco. "I say, I never knew you had a father."

Julie looked at him without saying a word, and then exchanged smiles with Beatrix.

"You never told me you had a father. Why didn't you tell me?"

"Haven't had time," Julie said.

With a pointed laugh, she made clear to Beatrix the recent date and the unimportance of her relationship with Coco Vatard. Beatrix, amused, buried her big nose in her big glass.

"And how's your mother?" Julie asked her.

"Married again, my dear, just to spite me. At seventy-one!"

"Well, I must say!" said Coco Vatard. "That's going it."

"Coco," Julie said, "pour out some champagne for Madame de la Roche-Tannoy. But what did Volodia say about her marrying again?"

"Volodia? He wanted to commit suicide. Just imagine, he'd been officially engaged to my mother for thirty years!"

"Good God!" said Coco Vatard. "Do you mean to say he wanted to commit suicide because of the old ha—— I mean, because of a person of seventy-one? I must be dreaming!"

Neither of the two women appeared to have heard. Julie pushed the plate of little sandwiches to one side and put her elbows on the table so that she could lean closer to Beatrix, who followed her lead.

"Do you still see your sister Castelbeluze?" Julie asked.

Beatrix sat up straight and opened her fur coat, revealing breasts pressed tightly together by her low-cut dress.

"Her? most certainly I don't! She took sides the moment I changed my way of living, and stirred up my whole family against me." The huge, historical nose was lowered confidentially. "But, I must say, my brother-in-law behaved very well. He didn't chime in with the rest of the pack. He gets nicer the more you know him," Beatrix whispered. "And talking of that, do tell me how things are between you and Espivant?"

"Much the same! We dote on each other as long as we're not married. I spent at least three hours with him to-day! So you see."

"At his house?"

"At his house, of course. He's still laid up."

"But, Julie! What about his wife all this time?"

"Marianne? Nothing to do with me, darling. She was minding her own business, I expect."

Beatrix's close-set eyes and long nose registered such utter if belated astonishment that Julie, relishing its full flavor, blushed and then laughed exultantly. 'She'll repeat that to the whole of Christendom!' she thought.

"It it true that Espivant is going to die?"

"Of course it isn't! His pulse is violently irregular; that's all due to the strain of parliamentary life, and so on. . . ."

"You told me," interrupted Coco, "that the Comte d'Espivant was in a really bad way."

"Your lighter, Coco. Thanks."

"I asked you," Madame de la Roche-Tannoy went on, "because Espivant, after all, has got no relations."

"Don't I know it, my dear! None at all."

A prolonged glance, fanned into flame by the champagne, passed between them. No alcoholic languor, however, loosened the fibre of these two steady drinkers or made their intimacy less cautious.

"Of course, you know the rumor that has been going round for the last few days? About Espivant's divorce?"

"I know something even more interesting," Julie answered smoothly. "Not an immediate divorce, perhaps, but a separation. It seems that Marianne is suffering from some very serious illness."

Beatrix whinnied with laughter.

"A serious illness is a promise people very seldom keep."

"Pure gossip," Julie said.

"If you aren't certain," said Coco, "why do you talk about it? What business is it of yours?"

Julie pushed the young man's glass and ash-tray to one side, and leaning forward, covered half of the little table with her bust. Her sleeves were once again beside Beatrix's bare arms and bracelets. They both gave way to the need, which they would have denied hotly if they had had nothing to drink, of stealing back, like burglars, into the world they had abandoned with such pointless ostentation. Their conversation became an exchange of scandals and mendacious confidences, of slanders and boasts which they only half believed. Dates were quoted and, above all, names usually qualified by outrageous epithets. A *rinforzando* of the orchestra wrenched them back from this passionate preoccupation.

"My dear," cried Beatrix, "it's the end. The Apotheosis of Woman! Where's your young friend got to?"

"Powdering his nose, I suppose."

"Will you excuse me if I leave you now? I don't want to miss Sandrini. Do let's meet soon."

"Darling, do let's."

Julie, left alone, watched the lights going out one by one while the crowd thronged towards the exit, stirring up, as they went, a nimbus of hanging dust. She made a sign to the barman, and he came up to her table.

"The gentleman apologised for not being able to wait. Everything is paid for."

"Splendid," said Julie.

She went down as far as the church of Saint-Augustin on foot. The cool night air played about her coatless shoulders, her face, whose warm colors were lost in the gloaming. She felt acutely aware of her solitude all of a sudden, and at once lost the sense of well-being she had felt after hours in the open air, the good dinner and the abundance of wine. 'Ah, why isn't that young idiot here?' As it was long past midnight, she climbed into a *fiacre* to save money, bewailing, in

a confused fashion, the lot of the old broken-down cab-horse, Espivant's incon-
sequent greed and the taciturn mood of the cabby who refused, as they drove
from the eighth to the sixteenth *arrondissement,* to tell his life story to Julie de
Carneilhan.

Once she was out of her bath and had made up her face, she planned to lie
down for an hour on her newly made bed; but she was summoned by the ring
of the telephone. She ran into the studio stark naked, with muttered objurations
and an assumed bad temper that changed tone as soon as she heard the voice
of Lucie Albert.

"Is that you, my pet? Did you have a nice evening? Oh, of course, it was
Saturday. It's no use, I'll never get used to Saturday."

In the looking-glass opposite, a tall, naked woman was watching her. From
her feet to her small head with its golden-beige hair she was the color of a yellow
tea-rose, with the rather spare, flat belly of a barren woman, a pretty navel placed
high at her middle and breasts that had lost none of their fineness, except in her
own severely critical eyes. 'Just a shade more like jelly-fish than apples cut in
half these days,' was her verdict. Reiterated squeaks of "Hello! Hello!" were
calling her, and she realised that she was not listening.

"Yes, my pet, we were cut off. What? Oh! A procession of Beauty Queens!
Yes, yes, it would be great fun, the prize-winners are always so wonderfully
inadequate, aren't they? What, tea thrown in? What a Saturnalia! I said, 'What
a Saturnalia!' No, 'Saturnalia'. . . . It doesn't matter, darling. All right, I'll meet
you here about four."

She remained standing there naked, with her hand on the telephone, overcome
with gloom at the thought of the emptiness of the day ahead, though it was no
different from most of her days. 'It's Beatrix's fault. That great nose of hers
brings me bad luck. To be quite fair, it's also because it's the eighth of the month.
From the eighth to the fifteenth, my morale varies with the state of my finances.'
She struck a few becoming attitudes with her feet together and her arms above
her head, and then stopped because the need for food was gnawing the pit of
her stomach. 'How I loathe eating alone, but I suppose I'd better resign myself
to doing so till the Becker check turns up!'

The telephone sounded once more and for a moment she stood in nervous
immobility, thinking that Espivant might be calling her. But it was only Coco
Vatard, for whose benefit she quite pointlessly raised her eyebrows, dilated her
nostrils, and rested a hand on her hip. She spoke to him in the second person
plural.

"What? You're phenomenally ignorant of how to behave, my dear boy. Angry?
Me? But you're merely grotesque! What did you say? You needn't bother about
me. Besides, Beatrix had her car and very kindly drove me home."

Far away, in an echoing atmosphere where Julie could hear a typewriter at
work and the slower rhythm of some kind of motor, Coco was obstinately and
sincerely attempting to explain. "You don't understand. Do let me speak, Julie.
No, I didn't mean to play you a dirty trick, but I had Papa's car, and I saw

that it was past one o'clock, and the cleaners turn up at home at five and always tackle the cars first. I get up at six-thirty on Sundays and weekdays alike, and I said to myself, 'Those two with their interminable mutterings have dropped me flat as if I wasn't there, and then supposing I strike lucky and Julie is kind to me, I know I'll be out till half-past five in the morning. I'll cut my losses and go home, at least I'll have a full working day and no rows with Papa. Julie, no, do listen. Julie, I'll come and collect you. We'll have lunch in the Bois. Listen, Julie. I was only doing everything for the best."

All of a sudden Mme. de Carneilhan renounced her dignity and the pompous *vous*, and burst out laughing as she sized herself up in the looking-glass.

"Come here now, you idiot! Didn't I take you in beautifully? See you in a moment."

She looked fiercely at the telephone, believing she hated the person to whom, without appearing to, she had just surrendered. From Becker to Coco Vatard how many men had she given in to on a tone of command?

She had to answer the telephone yet a third time, and listen to a grating, constricted voice that she did not recognize at first.

"Oh!" she said. "It's you, Toni? Have you got a sore throat? Good morning. I didn't recognise your voice. Is everybody well?"

"You went to the Rue Saint-Sabas."

"Yes. I even heard you talking in the garden."

"You went to the Rue Saint-Sabas," the voice grated. "You went and saw your—my stepfather. I don't want you to go and see that man. I forbid you to see him. Yes, that's it. I forbid you. No, it's *not* because of my mother. I don't want you to see him again, nor him to see you. Yes, I forbid you."

Julie put the receiver gently back on its hook without listening further. She heard another ring, and a second explosion of the broken voice punctuated by tears. 'As for that one,' she thought, 'he's the most difficult of the lot.'

She dressed with automatic deftness, putting on her black-and-white dress. 'Don't talk to me about boys in their "teens," ' she thought. 'What business is it of his? Young boys are a real pest. It's lucky I don't like them. A kiss on the forehead and a couple of dabs of my scent behind his ears, and he thinks he's my lover, if you please! All the same, I've a feeling he may turn out to be most tiresome. I might get rid of him by seeing Espivant only very rarely.' She knew, as she looked at her reflection, that she would do nothing so reasonable.

A moment later, she was completely taken up with Coco's arrival, and with the only too well known pleasure she derived from the presence of a man. 'A tree in the desert,' she thought, looking at Coco. However, she listened to Coco's version of the night before with an expression of supreme mockery.

"You see, Julie..." As he spoke he bumped into the twelve-sided table and almost upset the pot of lobelias. "...I've got my dignity as well, Julie."

To punish him for the word she tweaked the ends of his bow tie, rucked up his hair and pulled him about in all directions, like a sharp-toothed bitch that pretends to play so that she can bite. He only just managed to laugh, and tried to protect himself. "Julie, it's my new suit! I hate anyone touching my tie!"

She kissed him absent-mindedly, and at the touch of her strong, cold, painted lips, he stopped speaking in devout expectancy. But Julie rewarded him no further and led the way downstairs.

They both took trouble to be pleasant while they ate their luncheon. In front of some worried-looking businessmen and a few young women destined for a cinema career and a Deputy who greeted her a shade too familiarly, Julie posed as a woman indifferent to her reputation, calling Coco *tu* in a loud voice. Coco automatically slipped into the part of an adored young man. He plunged his honest grey eyes into Julie's, where they struck shallow bottom on a spangled, cold and unconfiding blue sand.

"Who was the chap you said 'Hello' to, Julie, over there in the corner?"

"A Deputy called Puylamare."

"Do you know him well?"

"Enough not to want to know him better."

"So you don't mind him seeing us together?"

"My dear infant, please get it into your head that I don't care a damn. Not only Puylamare, I mean, but everybody."

"How nice you are!"

But, even as he spoke he did not seem sure that she was so nice after all. Near the muddy little lake a swarm of starlings, about a hundred strong, settled among the branches where the leaves were already turning to gold. They were plump and heavy, and their whistling sounded like a winter wind.

"What are you doing to-day, Julie?"

"It all depends. What is to-day?"

"Don't you ever know what day it is, Julie?"

"Yes, whenever the fifteenth turns out to be a Saturday or Sunday."

"Why?"

"Because then I can't get my...my allowance till Monday."

"Julie," he said kindly, "it's the ninth to-day. You wouldn't be needing any money, would you?"

Julie turned to him in surprise.

'It's usually women,' she thought, 'who make these offers so diffidently.' She said "No" with her head, preferring not to speak. 'I should only say something silly,' she pondered, 'or rather I couldn't help saying "Yes," that I've got to pay Madame Sabrier for the week, that I've only got two hundred and forty francs left, that...yes, that I do need some money.'

Leaning on the table, she kept brushing Coco's hand with a rose she had been given by the *maître d'hôtel*. She felt a faint wave of friendship towards the hand with its thumb deformed by an accident with some piece of machinery: the manicurist did not always succeed in removing a line of vivid green round the edge of the nail, the acid stain of some color test.

"Once," she said, "I tried to dye a blouse by myself. Oh, my dear, for a month I could never take my gloves off, except at home."

"Of course you couldn't manage it; you're only a beginner," said Coco. "Julie, please be kind and tell me—wouldn't you like a little money?"

She shook her head once more. 'If I start talking about it I'll let myself go, and admit I'm gnawed all of a sudden by a longing for all kinds of things I need; I'd say I'd like some stockings, gloves, a fur coat, two new tailor-mades, scent by the litre and cakes of soap by the dozen. I haven't been like this for ages. What's got into me? If I don't hold myself back, if this blessed innocent gives me some of his salary and then thinks I'm in his debt, life will again be a hell.'

She shook herself, smiled, and began powering her nose.

"You're an angel. Send me a little bottle of *Fairyland*. And take me home. I've got to change my suit. I've got a date with Lucie. We're going to have a great time at the procession of Beauty Queens in the banqueting hall of *Le Journal*."

"What about me?" Coco begged.

Julie put on her fareway look, and glanced at Coco between her darkened lashes.

"If you'd like to...if you're free."

"Free as air. But only till half-past seven. We've got a dinner to-night for the anniversary of my parents' wedding."

"Really? You haven't talked about them for ages. Come on, then; it's three o'clock! It's absurd, sitting on at a table as though we were at a wedding breakfast. Just look at Puylamare on the job! He arrived long before us, and there he is still, drinking *Franciscaine*. He's not fifty yet, and he looks old enough to be my grandfather!"

As they crossed the room, she vaguely acknowledged an inquisitive and familiar greeting from the Deputy, who looked Coco up and down.

They drove back to Paris the long way round, and Coco's grey eyes made it clear to Julie how much he longed for her to be 'kind' to him. With a glance and a dilation of the nostrils, she promised she would, and he began driving the car like a taxi-man at the outset of his career.

Feeling relaxed and faintly perturbed and at the mercy of a melancholy she forbade herself to explore, Julie laughed at the speed of his driving and the rash way he took the corners. 'He's not a clumsy lover by any means,' she thought. 'He's full of instinct and warmth. I am too. We've got lots of time before Lucie comes to pick me up. I won't take the cover off the divan. I've only got one sheet on the bed, and it's a turned one with a seam down the middle. We'll carry on just as if we were on the grass.'

In the hall Julie saw that Coco Vatard's face had turned into the very picture of carnal desire—foolish-featured, and lilac-colored, as if bruised, under the eyes. She had to push him aside and say, "Wait, wait a minute," in a low voice, feeling an access of indulgence for this healthy and uncomplicated young male in all the confusion of his impatience.

But, before the elevator began to move, the *concierge* ran up and pushed an envelope through the bars.

"A chauffeur brought this for you."

"When?" shouted Julie, sailing up into the air.

"Just a moment ago!" squeaked the concierge. "No message!"

In spite of the half-darkness, Julie recognised Espivant's writing—sharp, incisive writing which often cut into the paper. Coco Vatard's hand pressed hers softly.

"Do leave me alone, you!" she said crossly.

He recoiled as far as the narrow elevator would allow.

"Why 'me'?" he asked in an offended voice.

"Really, Coco, you might at least behave in the elevator."

When they were in her flat, she left him standing while she read the letter. He walked up and down the studio, and, of course, banged into the twelve-sided table, to which he said "Sorry." When he saw Julie folding the letter up, he risked a question.

"Nothing nasty?"

"No, no," said Julie quickly. Then she added, more slowly, "Only it's rather a bore. I shan't be able to go with Lucie to the Beauty Queens at five. . . . Quick. Go and open the door. That's Lucie ringing. She's early for once."

Coco Vatard came back, followed by Lucie.

"Julie can't come with us to the Beauty Queens at five," he repeated in a gloomy voice.

"Why?" asked Lucie Albert.

At the slightest provocation she would open her anxious eyes wide: eyes which a year before had taken the first prize as 'the largest in Paris.' But everybody had forgotten that by now, although she would still unveil those vast orbs— beyond the bounds of decency or tact—till they seemed the size of a mare's; swamped by dark irises and equally devoid of intelligence.

"You might at least say good afternoon, Julie!"

"Good afternoon, my angel. You look very pretty today," Julie added without thinking.

"But why can't you come? Why did you tell me you could come, then? What shall I do if you don't come?"

'She's awful,' thought Julie. 'When she opens her eyes like that, it makes my head ache. And that little purple hat!' She turned to Coco, as though in search of help.

"Coco can tell you that a letter I've just received has upset all my plans for the afternoon, can't you, Coco?"

"Yes," said Coco impassively. "Julie's not coming with us because she wants to go and see Monsieur d'Espivant."

"How do you mean? Nobody said anything about Monsieur d'Espivant that I know."

"That's got nothing to do with it. I say you want to go and see him. And that this is rotten for us. And also that you're wrong to go. If you want my advice, you oughtn't to."

'What on earth is he talking about? Advising me not to go... He offers me his good advice. It's grotesque, it's...' She had grown so red in the face that the down on her cheeks and close to her ears veiled her skin like silver gauze.

"That's quite right," said Lucie Albert. "You oughtn't to go. Anyway, what did the Count say in his letter? Probably lies. Just think, after the way he treated you!"

"Oh, she knows all right," said Coco Vatard.

"And we'd have a lovely time at *Le Journal*. Maurice de Waleffe told me he'd put us in the very best places and that he'd keep some chocolate for us, whatever happens. Because you know how people carry on when the refreshments are free, the chocolate's always the first to go."

Coco frowned.

"No need to bother about free refreshments if I'm coming with you."

Julie emerged painfully from her silence, lifted her nose in the air and adopted her thin head-voice.

"When you've quite finished, may I say something? I'm not compelled to account for my actions to either of you. But I admit it is a question of Monsieur d'Espivant's health, which is in a bad enough condition..."

"To have you on toast," said Coco.

"What exactly does that mean?"

He became very young and contrite: "Oh! Nothing, Julie. You know, you hurt my feelings, and then I get spiteful. Julie, anybody else in my place...."

She calmed down, smiled at his grey eyes and turned-up nose, and thought, vaguely, 'I'd have done much better to let him have a few moments of fun and, incidentally, enjoyed myself too into the bargain. It's too late now. Also, they're bound to be right, he and that little idiot. Probably all lies.' Four strokes chimed from the clock of the neighboring school. Julie picked Coco's gloves up from the table and Lucie's bag and tossed them over to their owners.

"Off you go. Quick."

"Oh!" Lucie was outraged.

"And supposing I don't come back?" ventured Coco in a challenging tone.

Julie gazed at him from a long way off.

"You're a good boy," she said.

She went up to him and diplomatically stroked his clear cheek.

"And very good-looking...very. Lucie, my love, do excuse me."

She pushed them both out and shot the bolt in order to feel more definitely separated from them, free to remain standing with her arms hanging at her sides and listen to their footsteps dying away down the staircase. She dressed herself with her usual speed and efficiency, and, when she was ready, wondered why she was going. 'Probably lies,' as Lucie says, 'nothing but lies.'

She had lived a great deal among lies, before plumping for a small life of her own, a sincere and restricted life from which all pretence, even in matters sensual, was banished. How many crazy decisions and allegiances to successive aspects of the truth! Had she not, one day when her costume for a fancy dress had demanded short hair, cut off the great chestnut mane that fell below her waist when she let it down? 'I could have hired a wig,' she thought. 'I might also, at a pinch, have passed the rest of my life with Becker, or with Espivant. If it comes to that, I could also have gone on stirring puddings in an old saucepan at Carneilhan. The things "one might have done" are, in fact, the things one could not do. Lies? After all, why not?' She had not always taken sides against the fascination of destroying truth and confidence. 'The man who wrote this knew what he was about!'

When she had found a seat in the bus, she unfolded the letter, thinking she might have read it too hastily. But she remembered the most important words: "Please come," that is to say, and "darling Youlka."

Julie was not particularly surprised to find Herbert d'Espivant up and dressed and in his study. 'But why, oh why,' she thought, 'that maroon-colored velvet jacket?' No trace remained of the exhilarated mood in which she had stepped on to the bus, with the letter crackling in her bag like a new bank-note. She felt absent-minded, aware of her surroundings, sharply critical and rather coarse-grained, and she had the bad taste to go and lean, for a moment, on the open window-sill.

"Did I introduce my friend Cousteix?"

"Of course," she said, and she stretched out her hand with the gracious gesture of a hostess, to a young man slightly aged by a beard. 'Model secretary for a pretentious politican. Young tutor for an adolescent prince. Herbert always knew how to choose his secretaries.' Cousteix vanished like a shadow and Herbert took Julie by the elbow and led her into the sunlight by the window.

"What if they see us from the garden?" she said. "You're not interesting any more, now you're well on the road to recovery."

"I thought," Herbert said, "you were only interested in men in full possession of their powers. No, I'm not well yet. But I almost look it, don't I?"

He confronted the daylight, and she observed his clean-shaven cheek, his short hair, the moustache skilfully clipped and trimmed. 'It's a disaster,' thought Julie and her eyes grew moist, not with pity, but with regret for the past, for this faithless musketeer of hers, with his delicate beauty and his faintly martial pose. Espivant's smile died away. He became hard, businesslike and preoccupied once more.

"Sit down. Get it into your head that I'm lonely here. Lonely as I suppose everybody is. Are you? You wouldn't tell me. I'm absolutely alone, living beside a woman who's in love with me, and ill now that I'm faced with a political life I started too late. Anyway, there's going to be a war."

"A war?" said Julie.

"Does that surprise you? You read the papers, don't you?"

"The illustrated ones, now and then. But I only looked surprised because a fortune-teller told me we were going to have a war."

"Is that all you care?"

"Yes," Julie said. "All I know about wars is how to be glad if we win, and how to die if I have to."

Espivant looked at her with envy.

"But don't you realise what a terrible war it would be? Worse than the last one?"

She made a gesture of indifference.

"I don't bother my head about it. After all, it's nothing to do with women." She reflected a moment and then went on: "But you're fifty. And you're not—not at the moment—outstandingly fit. . . ."

"My dear, I know I'm not up to much," said Espivant bitterly, "and I don't need reassuring."

"It's not you I'm reassuring," said Julie, "but me."

Espivant fixed his whole attention on her. He seemed to believe her. He kissed her hand and then put an arm around her shoulders. She disengaged herself, cleverly pivoting away from him.

"Palace furniture, Herbert?"

"Yes. Kept, as one might say, in Boulle."

"Are you the culprit?"

"I had accomplices. But don't start on interior decorating again. I haven't the time."

"Nor have I."

Julie stared him in the face with studied insolence, for she was feeling inferior to her normal self—dry-skinned, less rose-complexioned than usual, small-eyed— and she hated it. Espivant shrugged his shoulders.

"It's no day for rows, Youlka. I've only been up a couple of hours."

"But you haven't had any more of those attacks since my visit, have you?"

"Only one. Let's forget about it. My house gets on my nerves. Oh, don't keep listening towards the gallery; nobody's there. Do you know where Marianne is?"

"No."

"She's gone in search of her son."

"In search...? What did you say?"

"Of her son. I wish you'd listen, Youlka! Toni didn't come home last night. My opinion is, he's with some woman. But his mother's off her head with anxiety. After all, seventeen is young to stay out all night, especially without warning. And then, he's too good-looking, much too good-looking. Are you listening? What are you thinking about?"

"What you're saying. Didn't he leave any clue?"

"Yes, an idiotic note for his mother: 'I'll never set foot in this house again,' or something of the kind. Marianne swears nothing had gone wrong between them, but I simply can't believe it."

"Did he take any money with him?"

"Very little. Marianne doesn't give him much. Only in driblets."

"Why?"

"She says that that's the right thing. I slip him five louis now and then."

"Are you on good terms with your stepson?"

"Very good terms. He's not specially communicative, but he's very sweet-tempered, rather difficult to size up—the least troublesome child in the world. He's got a little flat, two and a half rooms on the second floor, and I haven't seen him for...let me see, for forty-eight hours. Do you know him?"

"I've caught glimpses of him. You're on good terms with him, but you don't like him. Is that right? No, you don't like him. Of course you don't like him. You've got your hands full with one Marianne; a pair of them would be too much. She and the boy look so much alike that you can hardly stand it. Is that it? Go on, do tell. Surely you can tell *me?*"

She advanced, pushing Espivant with her forefinger, and putting her face close to his, which was exactly on a level with her own; and attacking the hazel of his eyes with the blue of hers, hardening their expression and harassing him as she used to in the old days when she wanted to make him own up to an infidelity in thought or deed. Caught by surprise, he gave way, and took refuge in cynicism.

"Well, as far as that goes, I don't really care a damn one way or the other. If he had been my own son... But I've neither the years nor the temperament for an adoptive father. But I'm worried about this business, for Marianne's sake. Anything that interferes with her normal course of life makes her...how shall I put it? When something tiresome happens to either of us, you or me, we just call it tiresome."

"Or even worse."

"While Marianne calls it an unheard-of event, an unimaginable catastrophe."

"She's the sensitive sort."

"No; but she's fundamentally gloomy. And actually, nothing but the most fortunate things ever happen to her."

"Herbert, you're forgetting yourself!"

They both burst out laughing, when the bell of the private telephone interrupted them.

"What is it, Cousteix? They've found the boy? No? But that's too much of a good thing! No; don't go there now. Stay here, and take all incoming calls, but only tell me when there's something urgent. I want to be left in peace. Hang on to Mademoiselle Billecoq and get her to take down anything important from the foreign wireless stations. Thank you. Oh, and Cousteix—give me Billecoq—I want to dictate. There are one or two odds and ends."

While he was dictating, Julie made a tour of the room. 'Herbert and I never managed to furnish this study. I'd worked out a rather Balzacian decoration, the furnishings all imaginary, the name of the nonexistent picture written up on the walls. And now it's much too full. That huge Panini! And those Guardis, thirteen to the dozen. And that array of telephones! It's a funny thing, all those symbols of activity; I can never quite believe that Herbert really needs them.'

She was striving to distract her mind from an awkward fact. 'Toni refuses to set foot here again. Toni has disappeared. It's no business of mine. Really none.' Then she remembered the telephone conversation, the tearful and discordant voice, the childish threats. 'Toni didn't sleep at home. And he wrote that he *refused* to come back.'

Julie wandered about the room, peered at a little picture entirely filled with Venice, stroked with disgusted hands the brass and tortoiseshell of the Boulle while she listened to Espivant's voice dictating into the mouthpiece "...*the points, my dear colleague, that you have kindly brought to my notice by no means imply that I must consider....* Are you following, Mademoiselle Billecoq? For Heaven's sake try and keep up."

'Toni stayed out all night. He doesn't want to set foot in his stepfather's house.' She frowned, ferociously calling to mind the fair adolescent face so like Marianne's. 'If only he were dead,' she exclaimed to herself, 'we should be well rid of him!' It escaped her notice that her thoughts had been expressed as 'we should' instead of 'I should.'

"That's all. Take me off the office line, Billecoq. Tell Monsieur Cousteix to put me on only if Madame d'Espivant telephones. Come, Youlka. I'm so sorry."

He pulled up a great, unfriendly crimson armchair for Julie. 'Venetian Louis XIV,' she thought; 'the nastiest style in the world. The whole room stinks of Venice. I loathe rooms furnished according to a single idea. If I know anything of Herbert, he's probably very proud of it.' She made her wild-animal grimace and sat down gingerly. Espivant cast a slow glance over her crossed legs and her shoes. His look put her in a good mood at once.

"I've got my pretty shoes on to-day," she said with a laugh.

"And your pretty legs every day," Herbert answered. "How do you find me, Youlka?"

"Dangerous."

He leant back in his chair, beaming. "That's the right sort of talk, but it would not be the right sort of behavior."

"Would you like to tie my hands, for safety?"

"You've got so many other weapons."

He contemplated her thoughtfully and without desire.

"Youlka, I want to go to the country."

"I give you my full permission."

"I need some money."

"I've got two hundred and forty francs."

"What did you do with that receipt I gave you, for fun—and also because I was furious—when you sold your diamond necklace during your divorce suit? Before we were married. You remember.... *I hereby testify that I have received from Madame Julius Becker, Baroness of the early pink Dutch variety, the exorbitant sum of...*"

"What a memory."

"...the exorbitant sum of a million, Youlka!"

"That's it. A million that didn't last long, to give it its due."

"What's a million?"

"It was tiny, done up in two rubber bands...."

"Had no staying-power, eh?"

They laughed, rubbing shoulders and cold-heartedly provoking each other.

"Did you throw the paper away? Because, my dear child, that comic document is an absolutely genuine receipt. Do you remember I mentioned—idiotically!—that the sum was 'in the nature of a loan.' And I can still see the beautiful sheet of paper, all stamped and engraved, that I consecrated to that masterpiece of prose."

He was consulting his extraordinary memory, which never played him false. 'He's like a starling. Léon's right,' thought Julie. 'When Herbert makes an effort to remember anything he squints a bit.'

"You put the paper away in..."

"In that lovely box inlaid with mother-of-pearl, a chocolate box, with your other letters and your love-letters. I've still got the box, even if I haven't got the stamped paper."

On the alert, she lied in exactly the level and sociable tones she had used in former contests: fencing-matches that used to end in sudden sharp squalls. But to-day, talking as he was only of money, Julie was frightened, not of his violence, but of his diplomacy.

"Have a good hunt for it," he said in a cajoling voice. "I owe you a million, Julie, do you realise?"

"No," Julie said in all sincerity.

"But I do, really. I'd like to pay it back to you. Why don't you claim it? Because I wouldn't give it back? Wrong for once! Marianne can't bear debts, especially mine. Do you get me?"

Julie blushed so much that there was no need to answer.

"Well, don't let's say any more about it. I was only saying..."

She bowed her head.

"I quite realise why you said it. But I shouldn't think Marianne's the sort of woman to believe, on the strength of a mere affirmation..."

Herbert interrupted her as though he had his answer pat.

"Marianne's the sort of woman who believes what she sees," he said.

He lowered his glance from her eyes the instant he felt that she was about to bridle, and began stroking her shoulders. "You're the only person I enjoy playing dangerous games with, Youlka. I forgot to tell you that the two medical big-wigs, Hattoutant and Giscard, have given me an ultimatum. I've got to quit Paris and political life. The country—and do you see me in the country?"

"I've seen you there. But you don't like it."

He gave her a melancholy smile that had all the appearance of being genuine.

"When we used to go riding at Carneilhan, you used to have your great mane of hair knotted up tight like the tail of a cart-horse. It was in a terrible mess sometimes when you got home...."

She thrust the glowing evocation from her with a wave of the hand.

"No, please. Can't you go to the country alone?"

He lowered his head.

"Politics aren't the only thing I've been warned off. You know, in Paris, some-how, the intimacy of married life seems to be a very small part of the twenty-four hours."

"You don't say so!"

"And Deauville wouldn't be too bad either. Everybody goes to bed late. But the country..."

Listening reflectively, Julie repressed an awkward temptation to burst out laughing.

"Did they tell your wife there would be...certain restrictions?"

"Heavens, no. I put a stop to that. That's the sort of commission I undertake myself."

"What will she say?"

"Oh, nothing. She'll settle in a different room, quite straightforwardly. On nights when there is a full moon or a smell of new-mown hay, she'll get as far away as possible, but not quickly enough for me not to see what her feelings are. Stop laughing, you beast, or I'll chuck the Regent's ink-pot at your head. It's a fake, anyhow," he went on coldly.

"And...what about divorce?"

"Too soon. I've got absolutely nothing of my own."

He grew angry again and shouted, "Good heavens! After all, I'm not demanding anything extraordinary. That million francs was Becker's money, the proceeds of Becker's presents. You gave it to me, and a fine shindy there would have been if I'd refused it!"

"I agree. But it was my money as well. I had a right to give that. But how can I give Marianne's?"

"Oh, we'd share it," he said naively. "I mean...I'd give you some."

Julie smiled in spite of herself.

Espivant, certain now that she would consent, pressed his point home.

"Marianne's money is—ought to be—everybody's. It's gloomy, mysterious money with a sombre, Mexican face, and it makes a sound like metal held prisoner underground. A million is only a tiny spangle of all those remote minerals."

She listened, trembling and overswept by a breath from former times. Her practised ear could single out the spurious anger, the incurable gaiety, the knack of seduction in the very avowal of unworthiness, the gusts of marital hatred and, above all, the positive refusal to be poor again. 'I've never hesitated,' she thought, 'almost flinging myself headlong into poverty, if it was a question of escape. What's he saying? He's still going on about Marianne?'

She saw him break off and press the region of his heart with both hands.

"I swear to you, when I first found myself with that rose-colored body—it was the color of pink wax—in my arms, and that endless mass of hair, so long and thick I was almost frightened when it was all spread out in my bed, I thought I'd overturned the statue barring the entrance—you know, Youlka, it comes in the *Arabian Nights*—the entrance of the underworld with a cave full of emeralds, a cave full of rubies, a cave full of sapphires. And as the statue was fond of me into the bargain—fond, much too fond really—the whole thing seemed easy, agreeable, intoxicating, lasting, and I thought myself an astonishing fellow."

He sat on the arm of Youlka's chair and leaned up against her.

"My poor beautiful darling, my poor, poor beautiful darling. These are things that I ought never to tell you! My poor beautiful darling, if you only knew how cheated of everything I feel. And then I go and send for *you.*"

Leaning against Julie, he tipped up her little black straw boater. She believed not a word he was saying; but spurred by an overmastering curiosity, she laid her cheek against his velvet jacket. Herbert froze into immobility and Julie knew that he was expecting and fearing one of those gentle but imperious advances— so friendly and so amorous—which he used to call 'the Youlka manner.' 'Always on the look-out for sensuality,' she thought, 'pleasure-blackmail, pleasure-panacea, pleasure-death-blow. Is that all he knows about or understands?'

Through the cloth of his suit she felt the irregular beating of Herbert's damaged heart, and thenceforward it dominated every other sound. She was scared all of a sudden by the broken rhythm, scared lest the unequal beats should stop, and she sat up straight. A voice that was studiedly, miraculously deep and precise, floated down to her.

"Didn't you like it there, Youlka darling?"

She shook her head to avoid answering and took Herbert by the arm. "Don't sit perched like that on the arm of the chair!"

"Like a bird on a branch!" he said. "By the way, Youlka, has Becker's remittance turned up?"

"No. It comes on the fifteenth. Three notches in the girth, as Léon would say."

"What's Léon's rank in the Army?"

"Captain. The dried-up remains of one, that's to say. Why?"

"Because of the war."

"Oh, really . . ." Julie said with a sigh of boredom.

"Yes, really, just as you say; what does Léon think about it?"

"Well, if war breaks out he's going to sell his pigs. Kill his mare Hirondelle, and join up again."

"How do you mean, kill his mare? Poor wretch! What a brute Léon is. Why?"

Julie looked at him disdainfully.

"If you don't understand, it's no use explaining."

"You Carneilhans are very lucky. You never see further than your noses."

He glanced furtively at his reflection in the brass and tortoiseshell looking-glass. Julie realised that he was thinking about his illness and the uncertainty of his life.

"Here, Youlka. I wish you'd have this."

He unclasped from his wrist a watch attached to a platinum curb-chain, and handed it to her.

"Is it eatable, Herbert?"

"Yes; when one's got teeth like yours. It's too heavy for me. Everything seems to tire me now. The bracelet presses just where a vein is beating, or an artery. Sell it or pawn it. . . . I'd like it to be a sort of link between us, a sort of something . . ."

"Something on account," said Julie.

He slid the warm chain into her hand.

"Oh, my poor old darling, don't pretend to be tougher than you really are! It doesn't fool me. Let's each of us do what we can for the other. It would be our only virtue! If only I had some money! It's pretty odd, you'll admit, that I never do have any. Would you like to carry off one of the Guardis for breakfast to-morrow? Or would you prefer a Panini three metres by five?"

"Oh, a little slice of the Panini would be ample, thanks! Do they all belong to you?"

"Nothing here belongs to me. It was a decision I made at the time of my marriage. I stuck to it afterwards out of good manners, and now I have to go on, because I've no option. But . . ."

He leaned over Julie, making his brown eyes shine with a more brilliant lustre and bringing his sinuous moustached mouth close to her ear. "But I can steal," he said archly.

Julie shook her head.

"You're flattering yourself," she said. "That's what one thinks. But after all, what *can* one carry away from a luxurious marital establishment? I know something about it! It boils down to three trunks full of clothes, some books you don't really care about, a few knick-knacks, a necklace, a couple of clips and three rings. And a pair of hideous cuff-links left lying about in a bowl, that you take on principle. Pictures, yes. But rich people haven't owned pictures for very long"—she raised her eyes to the Panini—"and what pictures!"

She opened her hand and looked at the warm chain.

"It certainly looks a very good watch," she said.

"But you must certainly keep the watch!" Espivant cried. "There are two little platinum prongs that fit on to a link of the chain; you press them and the watch comes off. Let's have it a moment. It's beautifully made."

They both sat down, leaning over the watch. A sunbeam turned the nape of Julie's neck into a solid pillar of silver. Herbert's over-silky hair, surrounding a small and carefully hidden tonsure, curled like a woman's. Both of them, quite oblivious of their age, were as fascinated as children with a mechanical toy.

"Marvellous!" said Julie. "What are they called, these sort of fat links, more or less square? They're like a convict's chains."

"I'll give another in exchange," said Espivant.

"Who to?"

"To Marianne, of course when she's found her lost chick. Hello, that's her. Idiot," he said, laughing. "That's her, calling I mean—that little wooden buzzer ringing under the desk. Hello, Cousteix? Put her through, quick. Hello? Darling, at last! Where are you? Where? But that's miles away! I can't hear at all well."

Julie had withdrawn to the end of the room, and watched him going through the motions of love and concern; questioning with raised eyebrows, pursing his lips into a heart-shape and sticking his chin out to underline 'very badly' with a note of plaintiveness. 'Anyone else would come to bits under the ludicrousness of it all,' she thought! 'Yet he gets away with it. It's a star turn.'

"Found him? Alive? Ah! But why is your voice so tragic, then, my Black Rose?"

He threw Julie a gay little kiss across the telephone with the tips of his fingers. 'A star turn with all its execrable taste and all its bounderishness. If he thinks I like it...' The mask of the caressing musketeer froze under her eyes and the seductive voice stumbled over the words: "With...with what? Veronal? But...but is he out of danger? Oh, the idiot child! Neuilly Hospital? Of *course* I understand it's not your fault in any way. But try and talk more clearly, for God's sake. I beg your pardon, darling, but you can imagine that your emotion and mine don't make things easier."

He fell silent and listened for a long time without interrupting. Holding a pencil in his free hand, he began to draw little rabbits, traced in a single outline, on the blotting paper. Julie's piercing eyes counted them automatically. But she gave up counting after the word "veronal' and lay in wait for some unknown and vaguely threatening event. She breathed in deeply and felt ready for what was to come. 'It will be the moment when he stops drawing those little rabbits.' He stopped drawing, threw down his pencil and raised his eyes to Julie.

"All right," he said. "The rest isn't particularly important; you'll tell me when you get here," he said into the telephone. "To-morrow, the whole business will seem no more than a bad dream for both of us. Of course you must leave him there. It's the wisest thing to do. Don't... don't hurry, darling; the urgent thing was for me to know where you were. Me too, darling, me too."

He hung up the receiver without lowering his eyes from Julie and lit a cigarette.

"Well, Youlka," he said at last, "so you've developed a taste for young boys."

As she did not answer, he went on:

"To clear up anything that remains obscure, I'd like to inform you that Toni was discovered unconscious at the Hotel Continental. A photograph of you was found beside his bed. Also, a letter saying that he was taking his life voluntarily, and a note from you putting off a rendezvous. That's all. What have you got to say to all that?"

"Nothing," Julie said.

He stood up with violence.

"What do you mean, nothing?"

"Ah yes, of course! I'd like to know if you'd have preferred the note from me to have been an acceptance of the rendezvous, instead of a refusal. I *didn't put it off*. I *refused* it."

She felt at the top of her form, a condition of which her moral solitude had for a long time robbed her. Once again she was deep in the atmosphere where women, the permanent objects of men's rivalry, bear all their suspicions light-heartedly, listen to their insults, yield under varied assaults and hold their own against masculine presumption and derive from it all a simple and lively pleasure. Her horse-woman's muscles twitched in her thighs and she felt in her breast the rhythm of her full and regular heart-beats. 'He's got no idea what to say or do,' she thought. 'In point of fact, men scarcely ever have. But what's this particular one looking so cross about?'

She was disturbed by her feeling of jubilation. Besides, the presence of several former Julies was blinding her to the implications of the moment. One of her vanished selves was in full flight from good old Becker and flinging herself at the head of a poor but very handsome young officer who was almost demolished by so splendid a catastrophe. Another Julie, naked and golden this time, shivered with cold and impatience between two men who were on the point of coming to blows, but they finally thought better of it. A credulous Julie followed, blindly absorbed by her passion for Espivant, then betrayed, desperate, and, in the end, consoled. They were Julies ready for any drama, provided they were dramas of love. Julies who were only capable of triumph, subtlety, kindness, ferocity or stoicism if these were the byproducts of love. These and the easy chastity and the physical passion that it engendered were the fruits of Julie's faithful and unflagging appetite for love.

"And when, if I'm not being indiscreet, did this story begin?"

She fixed on Espivant a tenacious blue gaze that over-flowed with the spirit of hazard and defiance. 'So he's made up his mind,' she thought, 'Men are not very quick thinkers.'

"Your question would be extremely indiscreet if there *were* any story. But there isn't."

"As if I"d believe that!"

"Young Mr. Hortiz wanted to behave like his step-papa. Yes, you don't like that name, do you? I think it's rather fun. It was perfectly natural for him to fall in love with me, at his age and mine. And that's the whole story, as you call it. I've just learnt the rest from you. A bit more and it would have been the end."

"I shouldn't advise you to laugh about it!"

"Thanks, I've never needed your advice or permission to laugh. After all, nobody's been killed by the business. And who on earth doesn't commit suicide, more or less, between fifteen and twenty?" She walked up to the desk and took a cigarette from a vase as she would have drawn an arrow from a quiver.

"A light, please, Espivant."

He held out his lighter without a word. The blood was in her cheeks, and she carried herself like a figure-head. Her lips trembled slightly. She surrounded herself with smoke and went on.

"A little fellow less than eighteen years old! A sort of delicate little Borgia! I agree, he's very beautiful. But pff! you ought to know, unless you've quite forgotten what I think of the Italian statuette kind of beauty. I bet he's got two lilac-colored buttons on his chest and a dismal little——"

"That's enough!" Espivant said.

"Enough of what?" Julie innocently asked.

"Enough of all that...of all that filth."

"But what filth, Herbert? Here am I cudgelling my brains to tell the truth: I clear myself of the slur of corrupting children—whom I hold, anyway, in holy abomination. I can't bear veal, lamb or kid, and I can't bear adolescents. If there's anybody who knows my amorous proclivities, surely that person is not very far from here, at this very moment?"

She was longing to overstep the mark, to hear insulting words and slamming doors, to twist her wrists free from somebody's hands again—either a lover's or a stranger's—to measure her strength against that of another, voluptuously, or in a struggle. But Espivant, she saw, was holding himself back and breathing with difficulty. A generous impulse overcame her. "Here we are with only this scrap of nonsense between us," she went on, "and he's not worth all this fuss! You're not really cross, are you?"

"Yes," said Herbert.

"Cross-*cross*, or just cross?"

He answered with a gesture and avoided looking at her.

"Seriously? But really, Herbert, why?"

Herbert remained standing, his eyes lowered. Julie saw that he was rumpling with one hand under his jacket the place where his heart lay. She shoved a chair from behind into the hollow of his knees, briskly enough to jerk him into the seat by surprise.

"Herbert, will you please tell me how I'm to blame in all this business? Because I really don't see..."

"Leave me alone," he cried in a low voice. "I don't see either! But I'm not going to stand your—that in front of me, talking to me—I'm not going to have you discussing any male creature as if you were deciding to use it or not to use it! You're free and I'm married. I quite realise all that. But your liberty doesn't extend to coming here and then, under my very nose, appraising the Hortiz boy's physique."

As Julie merely shrugged her shoulders, he struck the desk with his fist.

"The Hortiz boy or anyone else! You are the field that I've mown and trampled! But I swear that if others have done the same after me, you're not going to come here and shove the marks they've left on you under my nose!"

He looked her up and down, trying to master his irregular breathing, and Julie admired him with a growing anxiety. She felt a danger swelling inside her that she would be unwilling to escape. But Espivant made a gesture of affliction, and only said: "Go away."

"What do you mean, go away?"

"What I say. Go away!"

She pivoted round on her heel, went out and slammed the door behind her. Strangers gazed at her as she crossed the garden, but she did not even see them.

She plunged into the warm street as into a bath. Then, mastering her passion, she called Espivant a cad and a fool. But, deep down in herself, she went over and over the insulting words, weighting up all they contained of promise or of threat. Towards the south, a storm hung heavy over the city. Paris waited for it supinely with all her *concierges* out of doors on the watered and steaming pavements. 'This kind of weather,' grinned Julie, 'must make Marianne curse herself for being a redhead!' For she knew that the strange purplish hair of Mme. d'Espivant owed nothing to dye.

Now and then she accorded a thought, a 'poor kid' to Toni Hortiz, coldly summoning up the loosened, prostrate body, the inanimate beauty of the child who had wished to sleep for ever. 'It was his right. But it was idiotic. At that age, luckily, one's as clumsy at dying as at living. It's hot. A cold river to swim in, that's what I want.' She noticed that her bag seemed heavier on her arm. 'Of course, the chain. I've got it. I'll sell it tomorrow morning.'

She took a cab to *Le Journal*. Under irregular rain-drops, each the size of a flower petal, the curiosity aroused by the Beauty Queens had filled the streets. Lucie Albert, in her joy at seeing Julie, made her signs as though she had been shipwrecked, to which Julie gave cold response. But she was determined to enjoy herself to the full. They sat side by side in the hottest part of the room. Bereft of all pity for the exhausted Beauties, Julie sized them up with a whip-like glance, which lashed them from head to heel: she commented on hair falling out of curl, on the delicacy or coarseness of wrist or ankle, the stoop of a shoulder-blade, the little constellations of freckles at the top of young arms, the dress from a foreign capital. This cannibal feast only ended when she saw that Lucie Albert was on the point of fainting or being sick.

The storm, lightened by the shower, had drifted by without a downpour and now it was sailing up and away, opening its lips of fire across a pale yellow sunset.

"Come on, my angel. I'll take you out to dinner," Julie said.

The girl looked at her with her enormous eyes—vast globes unaccustomed to the light of day—and said, "Oh no, Julie. I'm feeling sick...and it's too expensive."

"Come on. I'm rich. We'll dance afterwards to cool ourselves down!"

"And what about Coco Vatard?" suggested Lucie Albert. "You've no idea what the poor fellow said to me when we were going downstairs."

"No," said Julie. "No Coco to-day, thanks. That'll do."

She made the usual grimace with her nostrils. Her cheeks were hot under their silver down and her blue eyes sombre and aggressive. She rubbed the make-up even over her eyelids in a shop-window looking glass.

She fed her little slave in the Place du Tertre. She filled her up with Asti-Spumante, but only drank iced water and coffee herself.

"But you're eating nothing, Julie. What's the matter? Julie, you haven't told me anything about this afternoon. Did you have words with that gentleman?"

"No, my love. He was very nice. But when I'm not hungry I don't eat, that's all."

She went on listening in a vague way to the childish chatter of the simple little creature. Gay and downcast by turns, Lucie would willingly have joined her solitude in all docility to Julie's, had she been given the chance. But this Julie refused to give. She had always scorned the help that one woman gives to another.

"The other night," Lucie was saying, "one of the clients paid his bill with a thousand-franc note, and Gaston brought it to me at the cash desk. It was about three in the morning. It was a new note, but it didn't seem quite smooth enough between the fingers. I didn't want to make a fuss, but..."

Julie breathed in the air of the Parisian night, a pleasure costing little, and reserved for people who refuse to stay indoors. A shooting star streaked briefly across the upper sky and soon lost itself in the vaporous zone hanging over Paris.

"Are you sure it's not later than ten, Julie? You know, I've got to be in the night club at ten forty-five."

They danced for a few minutes to the accordion, but Julie, still dreaming of violence and free fights, grew tired of leading all the time a partner who was too fragile and submissive.

"You look as though you're on the warpath to-night, Julie! Who have you got your knife into?"

"I'm wondering," Julie said. "Come on. I'll drop you at your night club by taxi."

Julie went home, although it was hardly eleven. A little family café next door supplied her with half a bottle of water, which she swallowed at a draught on the deserted terrace, under the reddened leaves of a chestnut tree. The late passers-by turned round to look at this fair-haired woman, as she sat smoking all by herself. Her legs were crossed, her face was lost in shadow and a silver reflection played over the nape of her neck and her silk stockings. She allowed herself to be gazed at without displeasure. Her evening, already half over, no longer held any terrors for her.

She undressed slowly, and created a breath of air between the studio and the kitchen before going straight to a little mother-of-pearl fitted box, without a lock, which was hidden in the hanging-cupboard. She undid a bundle of letters picked out a sheet of paper bearing a sixty-centime stamp, and re-read it. *"I hereby testify that I have received, in the nature of a loan, from Madame Julius Becker..."* She folded it up at once, and put back everything in good order.

She scattered her remaining hundred and forty francs and the platinum chain over her bedside table. Then she put on her damp bath-robe and sat down to make out a list. 'Two tailor-made suits. Four blouses. Two v. pretty pullovers. A long overcoat. An afternoon dress. Stockings, gloves, shoes, hats (two only). Underclothes. A very smart mackintosh.' She took the chain solemnly into the kitchen to weigh it on the scales; but she could not find the weights. She lay listening to the wind sweeping across the sheet-zinc of the roof, and then turned the lamp on again and picked up the list. Opposite 'underclothes' she wrote 'For whose benefit? and then crossed it out and went back to bed.

The days following were measured out to Julie in equal doses of disappointment and intoxication. She went to a Dressmaking House where she unearthed an elderly and rebellious saleswoman, who wore a bang of carrot-colored tow on her forehead, told horrifying tales about the days of vitriol-throwing, and smoked in the w.c. But she made the clumsy mistake of saying to Julie, "Ah, in our day, Countess...," and Julie squandered eight out of her ten thousand francs at another dressmaker's.

"But what are you doing?" Lucie Albert complained into the telephone. "Nobody seems to see you any more."

"I'm working," Julie answer importantly. "Come round if you like and I'll teach you how to knit washable sportsgloves."

Her experimental bent and her skill with her hands had returned to her. She gilded a pair of mules, and tried painting a solution of *vernis-Martin* over an old biscuit box, which turned out like an enormous caramel. Finally, she knitted some gloves and a scarf out of very thick pink string, over which Lucie Albert was lost in admiration. The huge, nocturnal eyes of the little pianist-cashier blinked sleepily as she tried to follow the needles, for she could only manage to relax when sitting at a table in a bar or outside of a café.

"I've seen some lovely washable gloves in the Rue Fontaine," she said. "They've even got some sky-blue ones."

"Knitted by machinery," said Lucie.

"Yes. And what if they are? They're just as good."

Brand-new, dashing, self-centered, dressed up in grey and black, smartly gloved and wearing a pink scarf, Julie went out one morning at eleven o'clock. There was a yellow, end-of-August sun, and she stopped in front of the glass between two shop windows. 'A woman like that,' she thought, 'can still look a knock-out if she's properly dressed. That little felt hat with the wood-pigeon's feather is a pure marvel. All the outfit needs is a dark grey man. But that's an expensive accessory.'

She was surprised to discover that her new wardrobe filled her with melancholy and a thirst for further luxuries. She found herself standing absent-mindedly on the kerb and waiting, not for *a* motor-car, but *the* motor-car, *her* motor-car. Only half awake, she would reach out for the cool contact of another body asleep outside the discarded sheets. She fingered the old place of the wedding ring on her fourth finger. Then she remembered that, in her impetuosity and unreason, she had lost the sleeper with the cold knees, the motor-car, the tiresome but charming house, the ring and the trace of the ring. All that she had frittered away became almost tangible, and she opened her lovely nostrils to the memory of the tonic smell exhaled, when they grew warm to each other's contact, by the copper-red mare she used to ride and her Russia-leather saddle. 'A Russia-leather saddle! Heavens, how flush I must have been! A saddle that must have cost—God knows how much! The mare, too. After the mare, I had a little car. Then I had the old Encelade woman instead of my Carneilhan Rocquencourt cousins and my Espivant sister-in-law, and Coco Vatard instead of Puylamare. And anybody who came and told me I had lost on the deal would have caught it hot!' But so far there had been only Julie de Carneilhan to reproach her with the social status of Mme. Encelade (expert in massage and removing tattoo marks and threading pearl necklaces), with the opinionated youth of Coco Vatard and the transparent emptiness of Lucie Albert.

A little later, she thought she had fallen ill. But, inexperienced as she was in illnesses, she thought it might be something to do with the change of life. 'Already?' she thought, 'And for a sou I should have said I was going strong.' But when she questioned her bodily state, she was rewarded with neither instruction nor blame. She thought about Espivant every day, and about Marianne and young Toni, and in all sincerity said to herself. "It's odd how little I think of those people!'

Coco Vatard was the beneficiary of this sudden access of superficial democracy. Recalled and amnestied, he duly admired the hats and the dresses, the bronze-colored stockings stretched tight on legs with small, well-placed muscles. In token of her new gentle disposition, Julie was 'kind' to him, at last, one silent afternoon in the half-darkness of the studio. But he had no chance of putting into words the overwhelming gratitude he felt for the long, fair and faintly luminous reef lying beside him. At the first word, the tip of a cigarette reddened in the shadows and Julie's muffled voice reached his ears.

"No. I hate talking about it afterwards."

Julie could not help noticing that, apart from his effusiveness, Coco was becoming gloomy in the extreme. One day she tried to make him laugh by telling him how, in order to fit herself out with new clothes, she had sold a wrist-watch. But he failed to laugh.

"Oh! I was sure you must have done something silly. You never consult me about anything. That wrist-watch—which, by the way, I never saw you wearing—

you may need it some day. You ought to have sold it only in the event of war. God knows what will happen to you when I'm gone."

"You think a lot about the war, Coco."

"I'm twenty-eight, Julie."

They were just finishing luncheon in the Bois. Julie powdered her nose and strengthened the red on a mouth which was the same pink color inside as her scarf and her cord gloves. The melancholy that she discerned in Coco's wide-open eyes did not disturb her, for she knew that love seldom finds expression in gaiety.

"I'll be recalled to the infantry. But I'll wangle to get into a motorised unit."

As he was talking only about himself and a hypothetical war, she interrupted him without hesitation.

"By the way, Coco. I've fallen out with Monsieur d'Espivant."

"Oh," Coco said. "I don't like that."

She laughed in his face and opened her jacket, showing her grey and pink-edged blouse drawn tight across her bosom.

"Well, I don't want to argue. But may one know why you're so keen, all of a sudden, that my relationship with Monsieur d'Espivant should be marked by cordiality?"

"That's easy. Your falling out, as you say, with that gentleman means that something pretty—well, pretty tough—must have occurred between you."

"We'll admit that. And then?"

"Well, something pretty tough could only be the result of something intimate, so I wonder. . . But you'll jump down my throat again."

"What do you think?"

Coco did not turn his eyes away, although Julie was searching them with a blue, unloving gaze.

"I wonder what you can both have been up to that was so intimate, in your past or your present, for the conversation to turn nasty. Quarrelling with a man so 'gravely ill,' as you call it. . .weren't you afraid that it might have done for him?"

She avoided answering him. Her one desire was to be elsewhere, far away from him. Sooner begin the last three years all over again! Three years that had destroyed her bit by bit, with every hour worsening the last hour's work and each month evoking a more facile surrender than the month before, leading to a life that she was too frivolous and too proud to consider vain, a life to which her physical health, like the optimism of strong children, alone gave any value. Haphazard months, needy periods of waiting. Does all this, then, happen in a woman's life because of certain definite infractions and disobediences, through individual omissions, the breach of a companionship with one man, the choice of another, and then the fact of being chosen by yet a third? The long sequence of household cares, of toil with the needle, of turned skirts—"My dear, I swear it's better than right-side out!"—of ingenuities which one pretends are so many little triumphs, are not, then, the result of pure hazard, but of a hostile, of an almost fatalistic power? She thought without gratitude of good old Becker's gratuitous alms-giving. She called to mind those little festivities of the flesh, swiftly conducted and swiftly forgotten, exasperated moments from which a broken masculine voice seemed to rise to Julie's ears. 'It's not their real voice,' thought Julie, 'but the voice of an instant.' Three, four years of improvised meals on a card-table—"Delicious, these radishes with mustard. Julie's really *full* of ideas!"—and restaurants where one went with one's lips properly made up and a dazzling complexion and a smile that pretended to be short-sighted, but revealed the authentic lady; champagne and caviar, or, perhaps, oysters, and *paté de foie de porc*. Forty—forty-two—forty-five years old. "Who is that? Why it's the beautiful Madame de Carneilhan. Do you mean to say that name means nothing to you?"

The wind, blowing up the corners of the tablecloth, announced the fact that rain was gathering in the sky, and that the bottom of the shallow lower lake was only mud.

"Julie, you're not feeling ill, are you?"

She shook her head and smiled patiently. 'No,' she answered within herself. 'I'm just waiting for the moment when you are no longer there. Because you're something I've never come across, and something I shan't be able to put up with much longer: a really clear-sighted man. You read through me into another man, and you treat him as an enemy. One would really think that Herbert has no secrets for you. You have him and understand him. When I think of Espivant you ask me if I'm feeling ill. What good advice you could give me from the height of your twenty-eight years! An honest little counsellor, one of those little plebeian marvels that chance sometimes placed at the elbows of queens. But the bitches of queens go to bed with the marvel and turn him into a trumpery duke, an embittered lover and a misunderstood statesman. With you as my adviser I'd never do "anything silly," as you so nicely put it.'

She emptied her glass of brandy at a gulp, though it was a very old brandy and worth serious attention, a smooth and civilised brandy.

"Alley-oop!" said Julie, putting her glass down.

"Bravo!" said Coco Vatard.

'If he only knew what he was applauding! Nothing silly any more—that's tantamount to saying I'll never be any use to anyone again—not even to myself. He'd keep me from ruining myself, or from being taken in. People can always ruin themselves again, even when they've got nothing. The clever ones pick them out a mile off. And he is full of scruples. Coco would never try to turn a receipt written as a joke into ready money, for instance. Chance has fortunately placed a good seventeen years between us; to mention only *that* particular distance.'

"The brandy makes your eyes shine, Julie. They're so blue—a frightening blue," Coco said in a low voice. "But you don't say a word to me. Won't you talk to me at least with your eyes?"

By half closing her eyelids, she softened the blue that he found so terrible.

'The clear-sighted little wretch!' she thought. 'It makes his company intolerable.'

"It's the Carneilhan blue," she said. "My father used to scare us with that blue when we were children. And then my brother and I discovered that we'd inherited it. Léon maintains that that particular blue tames horses."

"Really?" said Coco sarcastically. "And what color does he break in his pigs with?"

Julie did not flicker an eyelid, for Coco's fate was sealed.

'He's impossible,' her thoughts continued. 'He suspects everything with any likeness to me. I hope he'll soon detest me too.'

"You'd much prefer me to have no family, wouldn't you, Coco?"

"I don't wish anybody's death," Coco said.

She looked at him prudently, well aware of the profound distrust that a man feels after a recent act of possession.

"Take me home, my dear, will you? I'm in a bit of a hurry to-day."

Her companion had the unwisdom to look surprised, a fact that she attributed to his clandestine espionage. The tired summer all round their luncheon table was cruel to her skin, thirsting as it was for the touch of salt water and deprived of the wind which, in the country round Carneilhan, would be ruffling the aspens and scattering the chaff in the threshing-yard. The smell of the yawning melon on a neighbor's dessert plate suddenly ruined the smell of her coffee.

'He spies on me. He keeps a check on how I spend my hours and days. He knows I've got nothing to do, apart from all that soaping and darning he finds so reassuring, and knows that Espivant is forbidden fruit for me at the moment. Had I realised that myself?'

She became playful, as if she had some crime to conceal, throwing crumbs to the sparrows, exclaiming in front of a great barrier of red geraniums. On the way back to the car she picked up a tomtit's feather with a silver tip and stuck it into Coco's buttonhole.

"You should never give feathers away, or birds. It brings bad luck to friendships."

"Throw it away, then."

He laid his hand flat on the little feather as though to protect it.

"No," he said. "What's given is given."

But she put an arm round his shoulders, and, letting her fingers fall, sought and plucked out the tit's feather and abandoned it to the stormy wind. She turned her head away from his grateful glance. '*I* know, I know, you're humbly thankful. But you won't be humble for long. That was the very last thing I shall do for you,' she thought. She hummed a tune. She went on humming inside the car so that he shouldn't dare to speak.

"Drop me there, Coco, in front of the chemist's. I've got to pick something up."

She jumped out nimbly before the car had stopped. Taken unawares, Coco bumped against the pavement with the near-side front wheel.

"Your driving's become hopeless these days, my child."

"I know," Coco admitted.

He got out, and touched a scratch on the rim with his finger.

"I'll wait, Julie. Be quick."

"No, no!" she cried. "I'm almost at home."

But at that moment the downpour turned the pavement blue, and Julie ran and bought the first tube of tooth-paste she saw, went back to the car, and let herself be driven home. She seemed to hear, resounding through her whole body, the warning drone of a terrible intolerance. Already she was unable to bear Coco approaching her refuge and drawing up outside her door.

"Till this evening..." Coco began.

"This evening," Julie said, "I've got my brother coming."

Coco raised his eyebrows and opened his eyes wide.

"Your brother?"

"My brother. Don't ask which. I've only got one. We're dining together."

She thrust the lower part of her face forward, in imitation of Léon, sucking in her cheeks and pulling down over her eyes brows as yellow, under the brown pencil strokes, as the flowers of a willow, and clamped on her features a disfiguring and specifically Carneilhan mask, as if she were loosing dogs on a trespasser.

"All right," Coco said. "You needn't make faces at me like that. We'll telephone each other, then. Wait a moment, Julie! You'll spoil your lovely suit."

But she opened the door and ran across the pavement under the warm lash of the rain. She hid behind the second door in the hall, and only went up in the lift after she had seen the car drive off. Tears and rain-drops were running down her cheeks, relaxing the almost convulsive tension of her intolerance.

She allowed the last slanting arrows of the downpour to come into the studio. A pure blue, harbinger of clear skies, was rising in the west. She looked after her wet clothes before telephoning Léon de Carneilhan. As she waited beside the instrument, well-known sounds penetrated the wide and murmurous enclosure at the other end—a sharp whinny, and then the grave bell-note of a wooden bucket striking the flagstones. She recalled the stables opening on to the yard, the terrible little office on ground-floor level and the room on the first floor. This was the habitat of the bachelor Léon de Carneilhan; and that was all Julie knew about it. She suspected that her brother had a leading toward adventures in deserted lanes and open-air village laundries; a tendency that sprang from a certain grossness of appetite and the pride of a man bereft of fortune. Their particular brand of fraternal relationship shied away from any exchange of confidences. "We're too much relations to be friends," Julie would say. But because she was the younger in age and strength, something deeprooted in Julie compelled her to respect Léon de Carneilhan and his capacity for living alone.

With her first glance that evening, she noticed his drawn muzzle, his tanned and hollow cheeks, and said nothing. But she asked him about his mare Hirondelle. Carneilhan lowered his eyes.

"I've changed all my ideas," he said: "I don't think we'll be able to avoid war much longer, but I've decided to take Hirondelle to Carneilhan. After all, she's entitled to live out her life in peace. She's nineteen, and still a beauty."

Julie stopped beating the vinaigrette sauce.

"You're taking her? Taking her yourself?"

"Yes, Gayant will ride La Grosse and lead Tullia. They're all I've got left. I've sold out. I couldn't carry on."

"Well done!" Julie said at a venture.

She looked him furtively up and down for any sign of prosperity. But he was not even wearing a new tie. Nothing he wore ever seemed quite able to rise above a certain level of threadbare cleanliness.

"But," Julie asked, "will Hirondelle be able to do the journey?"

He smiled gently, as though the mare were looking at him.

"She'll do it slowly, at her ease. I'm quitting the high road after Le Mans, it's too hard on her feet. She'll be wild with delight. What are you giving us to eat?"

"Beef the way—you know—they used to do it in Périgord. Then salad, cheese and fruit. Go down and get the rolls, would you? I clean forgot."

She followed him out with her eye. 'There's white pack thread showing in his moustache and his nose is getting bigger. That's how the end starts, even with Carneilhans.'

After a few short and regulation questions, they began their meal, without talking.

"Has selling out made things any easier?" Julie asked.

"It's given me breathing space," Léon answered. He went and put the beef back in the oven and returned the compliment with another question.

"And Espivant, still at death's door?"

"He's not so bad," Julie said. "Remind me to tell you about him after dinner."

Carneilhan, with Julie's permission, dined in his shirt-sleeves, drinking away serenely at a nondescript red wine that showed black in the lamplight.

"But," Julie said all of a sudden, "if you're taking the whole lot to Carneilhan —does that mean you're going to stay there?"

"Not that I know."

The ambiguous answer was not enough for Julie. The deep mauvish night closing over Paris warned her of summer's end and made her dread the disappearance of this long-faced, fair-haired man out of the same mold as herself; sitting with grim eyes on his plate, eating with peasant's hands and the movements of a gentleman.

"These are real greengages," he said "They're excellent."

"Tell me, Léon, when do you think you'll start?"

"Why do you want to know? A week to-day."

"As soon as that?"

He surveyed his sister through the smoke of a mediocre cigar that lit unevenly.

"It's not as soon as all that. The nights are getting longer. But it'll be cooler in the daytime."

"Yes. Do you remember when we went to Cabourg with my lovely chestnut mare?"

"Yes. And Espivant too, don't forget! He soon packed up."

"Yes. So your mind's made up?"

"Unless it comes down in buckets that day, of course."

"Yes. Have you any news from Carneilhan? What's the weather like down there?"

"Magnificent."

Julie was afraid of insisting. Nevertheless, there were twenty questions on the tip of her tongue about the downstairs room, the 'blue room,' three poultry-yard pheasants, the brood-mares and even old Father Carneilhan. She felt a strange weakness in her that sighed for somewhere cut in the rick's side, to lie down in the hay, for the afternoon torpor of that pale and shingly soil. She got up suddenly.

"Stay where you are. I'll go and make the coffee. Will you clear the table?"

When she came back with the brown coffee-pot, the cloth had been straightened on the card-table, the whisky and brandy, glasses and cigarettes and the cups laid out. Julie gave a whistle of approval. Before sitting down she took the stamped sheet of paper out of the box of love-letters and laid it down in front of her brother.

"What do you think of that?"

He read it slowly, and, before putting it down, verified the watermark by holding it up to the light.

"I understand your keeping it. It's your affair. But apart from that, I don't think it's specially interesting. Why did you show it to me?"

"But it was you who...who told me that you felt there might be a lot of money that Espivant..."

Carneilhan interrupted her.

"I meant if he died, and not what advantage might be got out of him during his lifetime. This paper dates from before that ridiculous marriage of yours. Who would dream of stirring up that ugly old story and spattering everyone with mud?"

"Oh, all right," said Julie disconcertedly. "Let's pretend I never mentioned it."

"Once and for all, nothing that puts you in touch with Espivant can do you any good."

"Why, pray?"

"Because you're so weak."

He kept his eyes fixed on his sister. She merely lowered hers, started shelling almonds and burnt her lips with the boiling coffee, while keeping well out of range of his blue irises and their pinhead black pupils.

"But who can have been putting that into your head?"

"Only me, really."

"Or one of your little pals who thought he might get something out of it."

Julie straightened up with a jerk and assumed a lofty tone of voice.

"Really, my dear boy, I may have all sorts of nonsense with 'my little pals,' but not to the extent of telling them my family affairs!"

"Espivant's not part of your family," Carneilhan observed.

"No. But don't let's split hairs. Let's drop the whole thing. My idea was no good. Yours wasn't any better, as Herbert's well again now. Do you know, by the way, that he never saw a penny of that famous dowry? He told me so himself."

"I can quite believe it," grunted Carneilhan. "He's such a fool."

"I agree that he's not a genius, but a fool?..."

"Yes. Don't you see that he's done nothing but idiotic things all his life— always in a bright and intelligent manner? That stroke of genius, his last marriage, let's take a look at that! If I married a rich woman, I'd have her cleaning my boots."

"It's always so nice to be at your feet."

"You can always get out of anything," Carneilhan went on. "Anyway, I'd never marry a rich woman." He thought for a moment, and then jerked up his lean head. "If he failed to get hold of 'his' dowry, how can you have thought of asking for all or part of the million back?"

Julie went purple, and feigned stupidity.

"Oh, as for me, you know there's not a single blunder I don't make! But you must give me credit for consulting you first."

"Delighted to do so."

She felt uneasy at his suspicions and tried to put him off the scent by dragging him away from Espivant. She managed to do so by telling him, with exaggerated abandon, the tale of Toni's attempted suicide, and Carneilhan emitted a hard laugh when he learnt that Espivant had flown off the handle.

"You know how he is," Julie elaborated, "when he hears that a man is after a woman he has known! He feels ever so slightly a cuckold."

When Léon swept the crumbs off the table with the edge of his hand—a gesture that seemed to say, 'None of this is of any use to anyone'—Julie breathed again and poured herself out a middling drink. Her stiffness fell away, she beamed in the lamplight and felt the warmth of the alcohol rise to her temples. She felt that her efforts had been crowned with success when she heard Carneilhan, in good spirits at last, say, "I don't know how you manage it, but you don't look a day over thirty to-night." She longed to become even more deserving of this praise and its undertow of silent, fraternal jealousy; so, like a bird trailing a supposedly broken wing, she had to direct attention away from the truth. She burst out with her ringing laugh, shed two tears, and told Carneilhan that she wanted to "ditch Coco Vatard," who was getting on her nerves.

Then she seemed to lose her head, and, with it, all discrimination between what she should and should not confide to a Carneilhan very much on the alert. She pulled to shreds poor harmless little Coco, brandished his scalp, plunged it into dye-steeped vats. "Can you see me, my dear, waking up beside a chap with a violet stomach and a green nose!" Carneilhan did not allow himself to be blinded all at once. While Julie, her lips shining with brandy and her straw-colored hair all uncurled by the rain, deliberately stripped her cast-off playmate down to the skin and beyond, Carneilhan risked, in a level tone of voice, a harmless question: "Didn't Herbert impress you as being rather a sham? And don't you find it slightly odd that Herbert seems to need you so much all of a sudden?" He tired of it in the end, and Julie no longer noticed the name that he kept dropping between her snippets of chatter in the hope of tripping her up. The conversation became a confused noise in her ears, and Julie was suddenly struck down by the need for sleep. She rolled herself up in the blanket of her divan-bed and stopped talking. Léon de Carneilhan pushed the leaves of the french window to, switched off all the lights except the one beside the bed and turned out the gas in the kitchen. When he left, Julie was asleep under the dark red cover, and the short locks of her hair shone with the same pallor as her skin. She did not so much as tremble at the slam of the hall door.

Next morning she determined to take action, and laid her plans. By 'plans' she always meant a series of decisions which seemed quite incoherent to other people, often earning censure from her friends and ridicule from her acquaintances, for she acted in defiance of what either would have advised. On this occasion, she took one precaution—which was to consult the candlewoman. With a new candle tucked into her breast next to the skin, she went and woke up Lucie Albert, to drag her off, pale from fatigue, with gaping eyes and a body in the throes of a kind of walking hypnosis. But that little creature of the night did not forget to take a candle from the piano for herself, one of two pink and faded spirals, which she slipped inside her blouse.

"What, Julie, another taxi?"

"Another taxi. And that's not all. Jump in, and go to sleep until we get to the Avenue Junot."

When the open taxi drove past a looking-glass, Julie passed stern judgment on the slender, rocking silhouette, the pallor and the drowsiness of her companion, which made her all the more satisfied with her own upright reflection, her old black-and-white tailor-made (which had just been cleaned yet again), and the pink-and-yellow color of the nosegay formed by her face and her short froth of curly hair. Her secret state of mind and body was patent in her determined expression, her nostrils particularly open to the wind, and her mouth at its largest, painted a challenging red.

At the candlewoman's, an unchanging temperature not unlike the chill of the inside of a church prevailed in the little parlor. Cane-bottomed chairs stood against the wall, and the only decoration was a kind of diploma framed in black.

"*I certify,*" Julie read out loud, "*that Madame Elena did everything in her power to prevent my late lamented daughter Génevlève from leaving on the yacht, having told her that she would be going to her death.* I say, this is a scream."

"Oh, Julie! There's nothing to laugh at! Think of that poor young woman being drowned! It's not funny at all!"

Julie gazed at her little friend.

"How on earth could you know, my poor darling, what's funny or not?"

Mme. Elena came in yawning, wagging her head over the arduous duties of her profession and complaining that she did not get enough sleep: apparently she did not qualify as sleep the sort of permanently torpid state that smeared her eyes with a vague blue haze. The rest of her, from the check apron to the loaf-like bun of hair, might have belonged to a self-respecting charwoman. She started on the lighted candle with a knife as though she were scraping a carrot, and mumbled darkly to excite her two consultants. She spelt out, in the pools of hardened wax, that Julie would become involved with a rather unreliable man, that she would go on a journey and, finally, that she would climb a spiral staircase. With Lucie she became even more sibylline, and pronounced, as she pressed the old twisted candle on a sham Rouen plate, vague sentences about a hidden child. But what did the untrustworthy man and the clandestine child matter to Julie and Lucie Albert? All they wanted was to give themselves up to the enjoyment of a mystery that would never be elucidated. Lucie kept on saying, "Yes, yes," nodding her head as though she were memorising an order. Julie took refuge behind an expression of mute Carneilhan aloofness. She left Mme. Elena's as though she had just been to a masseuse, and settled down outside a café. Lucie Albert managed to wake up at last when faced with a coffee and cream.

"I feel as hungry as I used to be after High Mass at Carneilhan," cried Julie.

"I'm feeling ever so peckish, too!" cried Lucie Albert. "Julie, just think! A hidden baby! It's amazing!"

"But have you got one?"

"Oh no, Julie! But everybody I meet now will make me think of hidden babies; it's fascinating. And do you see yourself in what she told you?"

Julie smiled as she buttered her *croissant.*

"Not at all! So you see how much easier I feel about things! I mean about what I'm going to do."

"But what things?"

Julie buried her teeth in the *croissant,* and swept the Place Clichy with an optimistic glance. Now, in the August heat, it was as dusty and deserted as a cross-roads in the provinces.

"Anything, any nonsense. But, you know, *sensible* nonsense for once."

"Julie, you're not going to marry Coco?"

"What did you say?"

Lucie Albert retreated scared to the back of her chair.

"It wasn't *my* idea, Julie. Coco's the one who's always saying, 'I'm very much afraid that woman is the woman of my life.' Don't curl your lip up like that; it looks awful. But do you believe what she foretells, Julie?"

"For five minutes. Then I hardly think about it."

She thought it wiser to lie no further. She was gauging the length of the next few days, swept clean of any observant intruder. Even Toni Hortiz, packed off by Marianne to the top of some wretched Alp, was recovering from his first suicide, and Mme. Elena had only read into her destiny those jumbled images of staircases and journeys. Far away from indiscreet surveillance, she was breathing in deeply a new atmosphere of freedom, through which, when the moment came, she could advance alone, and select her blunder, and cherish her last fling of folly. 'But why should it be the last?' her pride whispered. Whenever she was in the throes of activity or impatience, she tensed the muscles in her thighs as though she were on horse-back.

"You go and sleep," she told Lucie Albert. "When can you sleep till?"

"Four, five o'clock. Specially after having eaten. I only have to dress and make up."

Julie's over-sensitive nostrils suspected the little thing of not washing much; her hair had gone lack-lustre from long hours, night after night, in a fog of cigar and cigarette smoke. Her skin, she thought, looked as pale and damp as chicory.

"Poor kid," she said. "I'll drop you."

The enormous eyes, which betrayed only the signs of accumulated sleepless nights grew larger still.

"Oh, Julie, Julie! You'll end up by sleeping on straw!"

"On straw? But you've no idea of the price of straw. It's terrible!" Julie laughed. "Goodbye. I might drop in for a glass of something this evening."

"O *do! Do* Julie! I'll play that pretty little tune out of *Les Biches* for you in the *entr'acte!* Do you promise?"

Between eleven and one in the morning, Julie made her way down to the night club. Alone, dressed in a new black tailor-made, she sat down in front of a gin-fizz at a table smaller than a tea-tray, attracting attention by her fine stature, the sulphur-colored carnation echoing the shade of her hair, and her blue eyes as unabashed as those of the blind. She exchanged smiles now and then with her little friend, who left the cash desk to sit at the piano and play, very prettily, a fragment from *Les Biches*. After midnight, she accompanied the songs of the star who owned the place.

The narrow room differed little from other narrow rooms devoted to songs and alcohol. A layer of smoke clung to the low ceiling, and the size of the room and of the stage left no scope for attempts at eccentric decoration. Lucie waited for a sign from Julie before coming over to sit sideways near her friend and accepting a gin-fizz.

"Oh, Julie, you are beautiful, you know!"

"Have to be," said Julie pensively.

She forced herself to keep up a semblance of conversation. But she was conscious of no reality beyond the thin, dry taste of the gin. All the rest was merely a background to her last actions of the afternoon: removing the stamped paper from the mother-of-pearl box, folding it in a new shape, adding the few words "Do what you like," signing it "Youlka," and sending the whole thing to Herbert d'Espivant. The brevity and the ease of it all left her slightly astonished. She was not regretting her decision; nor did she regret it later during a night of calm insomnia. She only doubted, on the brink of sleep, whether she had really done it, and this doubt woke her up again. She was surprised, in the fine weather of the following morning, to find herself singing, and the morning slipped quickly by. 'How easy waiting is, when one's really waiting for something or someone!' She touched the wood under the table-top three times with her middle finger. After that she had to answer Coco's telephone call. Serene and out of all danger, she dismissed him in affectionate tones.

"No, my dear child, I can't. I really can't. Oh, but it's not a mystery at all, don't be absurd. My brother...Yes, him again, as you say. My brother has sold his— what's it called?—his establishment, thanks. Apart from the ducks and the pigs, there's the furniture, which will go for at least a hundred and fifty louis, but poor old Léon hasn't any idea of how to set about it, so I have to. No, really not, not to-morrow. To-morrow I'll be at Ville d'Avray all day. Telephone me there? My dear, just imagine, it's been cut off for the last three months. He hadn't paid the bill. Ah, my brother's an odd card! Fortunately, I've only got one. What? Come here straight away? Oh no, my dear. No, no...I really wouldn't."

An urgent voice at the other end kept saying, "Why? But why?" Julie pondered for a moment and answered in a friendly voice: "Because I'd chuck you downstairs. Yes; that's the gospel truth. Yes. True as I'm standing here."

She put the receiver gently back on its stand and smiled at the world of uncertainty that was opening in front of her. She put on the little felt hat with the wood-pigeon's feather and went down to the street to buy eggs and shell-fish and fruit. The day drifted by with such a soft and imperturbable flow, and Julie's waiting mood populated every moment so densely that the silence surrounding her was like a continual murmuring. 'My letter reached him by the morning post, about nine o'clock. He must have recognised my writing.' In imagination she moved across to the Rue Saint-Sabas and installed herself there. 'At nine o'clock, the mail was put on the little table outside his room as usual. He may be unfaithful, but in everything else he's a slave to habit. Bath. Hairdresser and manicure at the same time. Marianne? It's true, Marianne's there. Smothered in her purple hair, shaped into fringes and coils and shells. Marianne at that time would be. . . . Anyway, who cares? Marianne can do what she likes.' Julie waved Marianne away with her hand and came back to Espivant. 'At ten o'clock he must have looked at his nails before dressing and said, "It's an odd thing, but no manicurist has ever understood the first thing about nails." Then he opened my letter. Then he called Marianne. . .unless he screwed his eyes up and said, "Let's see. . . . Better wait a bit!" '

She lowered her head and clasped her hands between her knees because, saying "Better wait," she realised what a stern gymnastic exploit it can be just to wait. At eight she gave up and went and had buckwheat pancakes washed down with cider at a little Breton establishment, and finished her evening at the local cinema.

She was scrubbing herself in the bath next morning when the telephone rang. "Run, Madame Sabrier, run for heaven's sake!"

She heard the charwoman answering "Yes, sir," "No, sir," and leapt out of the water. When she saw her naked and dripping, and flowering with crimped yellow sea-weed, Mme. Sabrier let out a shocked squawk and fled.

"Hello," said Julie in a high slow voice. "Hello? Who's speaking? Ah! Monsieur Cousteix, of course. How is Monsieur d'Espivant? To-day between four and seven? No; I wasn't thinking of going out. Actually I had planned to stay at home. I won't be going out. Goodbye, Monsieur Cousteix."

Drops of water, while she talked, ran down off her hair in parallel lines, hung for a moment on the tip of her breasts, and fell to the floor. Julie trembled with imaginary cold. She caught sight of her hair and her lashes all stuck together. 'I'm going to look awful to-day.'

She dressed and put on white canvas shoes and walked up and down in the Bois for an hour and a half. Then she came home and cooked herself a well-chosen beef-steak on the ring. 'As thick,' she thought, 'as a dictionary.'

But she left the washing up, and painted her nails red. The hours of the afternoon were faithfully, tritely similar to the swift, exciting hours that precede the arrival of a man one is waiting for. She got ready a tray with two cups and wrapped a bunch of green mint up in a damp cloth to scent the tea made in the Moroccan way. 'Moroccan tea doesn't tire the heart.' Then she lay down in the ox-hide armchair. Now and then she turned towards her reflection and congratulated it with a vague smile on having its hair done neatly, on being dressed in a grey tailor-made and rejuvenated by the lowered shutters. Made for meeting a man and being desired by him, for loving him often and too much, she played with the thought of the man who would soon come in. 'I wish he'd come. I can't go on looking ahead like this. Afterwards...afterwards is a long way off.'

She gave no free rein, in her mind, to the thought of physical pleasure. The best part of her vigil was a deep passivity and entire ignorance, for never once in her life had she picked up the threads of a broken liaison, regained the taste for a savour she had forgotten. A faint red flush rose to her cheeks and neck at the thought that perhaps at this moment Espivant might be fearing or desiring the amorous conflict of their two bodies. 'No, no. Of course there is no question of it. To-day's the day when I do my best to get him out of the hole he's in. To-day he'll find out that I'm his real ally in spite of all we've said and done and hurled at each other's heads.'

The sum of money he coveted, the impudent misuse of a few written lines, no longer tormented her. A 'practical joke' either comes off or falls flat. If it's a flop, so much the worse. Nothing had accustomed Julie to thinking of Marianne as a moral creature capable of judging the acts of others. She remained a Marianne whom she had never seen at close quarters, Marianne the millionaire, a precious object calculated to discourage all rivals, a sort of Eastern conquest thrown open to competition once more by widowhood. A slightly sordid mystery did in point of fact surround Marianne. Julie was almost astonished that she knew how to read and write, spoke French, was not a deaf-mute! A woman loaded with so much beauty, with so heavy a fortune. Irritated, Julie gave way to a false little laugh. 'It's almost as if she were a cripple or a woman with six toes,' she thought.

The school clock chimed four and she leapt from her seat to open the shutter and gaze questioningly at the street and the weather, to make sure that the magnificent day and the light warmth had not changed; to chew a leaf of mint and powder her face. At the timid and uncertain ring of the bell, she laughed. 'What punctuality!'—and she gave a finishing touch, before answering the door, to a bunch of cornflowers, and shook loose a sheaf of red poppies that spread round them, along with their dark blue pollen, a smell of dust and opium.

Upright, with her feet together and her mouth slightly open to reveal her white front teeth, she opened the door, 'No, it's not him yet...'

"Madame? Yes; it's here."

Automatically her features maintained the half-smile over the white front teeth, the look of impertinent false myopia. 'But—but it's Marianne...Marianne,' she said to herself. 'No; it can't be Marianne? It mustn't be Marianne!'

"I am Madame d'Espivant," said the stranger.

Julie dropped her free arm, accepted the reality at last, and stepped backwards. "Come in, Madame."

She slipped into her duties as a properly trained woman of the world, and Madame d'Espivant gave all the necessary answers. "Do sit down!" "Thank you." "This chair's rather low." "No. I'm perfectly all right, really...." And then they both lapsed into silence. Carneilhan frivolity was already at grips with anxiety. 'It's Marianne. What a story! Lucie will be knocked sideways. And what about Léon? Here, right in front of my eyes, is the famous Marianne.'

"Madame, my presence here must seem. . .strange to you."

"But of course not, Madame."

'We're going to waste a lot of time,' thought Julie. 'She's got a charming tone of voice. Lovely pitch. And downstairs in his driver's seat, Beaupied must be wondering what's going on!'

"But I only came because my husband asked me to."

"Oh? It was he who. . ."

"Yes. He's ill to-day. Really ill," she repeated as though Julie were about to protest. "I waited till it was time for his injection before leaving his side."

"I do hope it's not serious," Julie said.

'A very pretty pitch her voice has, soft, with a something acid in the higher registers. But if we go on like this,' she thought, 'I'll have to ask her to dinner. Fancy going out at four o'clock in a black afternoon dress! And that hat, with its little floating veil! I must say, I don't find the lovely Marianne so staggering after all!'

Then Julie shook off her feminine reactions and began to isolate Marianne from her general renown and from her own private criticism. She searched avidly for "the statue of rose-colored wax" described by Espivant, did not at once discover it, and thought her complexion of untransparent carnation, a complexion with the grain and opacity of marble, had about it a touch of slightly Jewish pallor. 'Yes. In broad daylight it must be pink.'

"Unfortunately, it is rather serious. I believe my husband himself—so he told me—has informed you that the doctors diagnosed his illness as heart trouble."

"Yes, indeed, Madame, indeed. But the future of an organic ailment depends so much on general conditions, and Espivant is supposed—was supposed—to have plenty of natural resistance."

'And so on and so forth, and what lovely weather we are having,' Julie went on to herself. She was regaining her self-control. 'Oh! I hadn't seen the plaits! Oh, what hair!'

Mme. d'Espivant had just thrown back her veil, laying bare part of the red-brown mass of her hair, the brilliant swellings and bosses of a diadem of plaits that crossed and re-crossed and invaded her ears and tightly clasped her temples and her brow. 'It's amazing!' Julie said to herself. 'She's a woman, like certain statuettes, made up entirely of precious materials—jade, green-spangled quartz, ivory, amethyst. Can she really be alive? Yes; she is. And here she is in my flat. Here she is, and not trembling at all, and less impressed at having me in front of her than I am to see her here. Let us get to the point, Madame d'Espivant, to the point!'

"I wish I could share your optimism, Madame," said Marianne, "but I feel I must tell you that your recent demand has greatly alarmed my husband."

She turned slightly in her chair and raised her very dark eyes to Julie. They were wide open, like ancient Greek eyes, and armed with lashes on either lid, and the whites were tinted with blue. 'Lovely, lovely eyes,' thought Julie in admiration. 'And how little she uses them! And she's simple. She must be simple to come and see me, even if he's sent her. What was she just saying? My recent demand? I should think it was recent, my letter only having been posted the day before yesterday.'

"Were you able to judge in such a short time whether my...demand had an adverse effect on Espivant?"

The dark eyes fixed themselves on Julie.

"My husband, Madame, even before his illness, suffered greatly from his nerves." 'Thanks for the inside information!' Julie said to herself. The passivity of Marianne, and her gravity, put her out of reach of all irony. "...and worry can cause definite ravages on a nervous patient in the space of a fortnight...."

Julie flinched at the word "fortnight." 'Look out! Things are beginning to slip and slide, and I don't quite see. A fortnight? Oh, the dirty dog, what's he been telling her?'

She repeated pensively: "A fortnight?"

"Perhaps a little more," said Madame d'Espivant. "It was a fortnight ago, I remember, when I came in and found my husband so terribly upset."

'She's got a rim round her mouth like some pretty Indian woman and a little hollow at the corner of her lips. She's a magnificent creature, without the faintest idea of what she ought to wear.'

"Upset, Madame? I don't see my share of blame in this...this upset?"

Julie opened her jacket as she was feeling hot, and also, especially, so that Marianne might see her slender throat and the long noble lines of her figure under the grey-and-pink shirt. 'There! She must have seen at once that I'm not a complete hunchback myself!' As she was longing to smoke, she offered her case to Marianne, who refused.

"I hope my smoking doesn't bother you. I was forgetting, Herbert smokes, of course. You said that you held me responsible for his getting worse. It's Monsieur d'Espivant's heart that is causing the trouble? His heart. Of course, his habit of hiding his feelings must have over-taxed his heart...."

'I can wear myself out being ironical; she doesn't even appear to understand. Perhaps that's the most touching thing about her, that vague sadness, that widowed look, that warm-blooded womanish apathy. One thing seems obvious— she's sad, so Herbert must be really ill, as she says.'

"Madame, please believe me when I say that I came here without pleasure and that I speak with deep regret," Mme. d'Espivant said. "You cannot have forgotten that your demand—the legitimacy of which my husband does not question—was accompanied by certain terms."

'She looks a bit matronly when she bridles,' thought Julie. 'It's not a question of flesh, because she's still slim. It's lack of breeding. A miraculously beautiful woman, with something unspeakably common about her. She blushed when I called Espivant by his first name. But, my good lady, you must get used to the idea that there used to be "something," as they say, between Herbert and me. Second Madame d'Espivant, don't lose your head!'

"...was accompanied by certain terms that could be interpreted in a disturbing way, that made one foresee a...a disagreeable publicity round my husband's name, his personality, his honor, even. Am I mistaken?"

'How! What? Publicity! His honor? I can't ask her to repeat it, she'd think I was either deaf or an idiot. If I were at all reasonable, I'd get up and lead her politely to the door, and the farce of the two Comtesses d'Espivant would be at an end.'

"You know, I should quite understand," Marianne insisted, "if necessity or some feeling drove you to use arguments, such as one employs only as a last resort. It's essential that I should not misrepresent what my husband told me, isn't it?"

Julie gazed in stupefaction at this beautiful woman in black who, even in accusing her, displayed such nervousness. 'He did that! He's done this to me. He's put the whole thing on me. Everything, he's put everything on my shoulders. He's made her believe that his idea of a kind of blackmail was really mine. Oh! It's not to be borne. I can't have Marianne thinking I'm capable of..." But she was already in the grips of a still more prevailing blindness. She shook her head and cleared her throat.

"Espivant told you the truth, Madame."

She turned away, crushed out her cigarette, saw her hand shaking as she heard her voice shake, and felt an extraordinary joy because of it. 'It's done now. I've said it! I've said what he wanted me to. I'm drowned, lost, done for, everything has happened as he wanted it to. But she must go now. I must tell her to go.'

"So don't think about it any more. Don't let's think about it, Madame," cried Marianne. "A woman cannot always be equal to circumstance," she added with a touch of plebeian *naïveté*. "You mustn't think about it any more."

Julie grew gloomy again as a result of all this encouragement. 'Don't think about it, indeed! Everybody under the sun seems to take it into their heads to give me advice—Coco Vatard, the beautiful Marianne! Don't think about it! As if I'd be able not to think that Herbert's put the whole dirty business on to me, has rolled me in filth. There's still time for me to say the word and put Marianne wise. She's not sure of him yet. She feels that Herbert's cunning white hand is somehow mixed up in all this, and I can change everything with a word if I want to. That, at least, he can't steal.'

A line, written in a jagged, stabbing handwriting, floated in front of her eyes, and she read it through again: *"Youlka, please come."* She could not help herself, the saliva of sudden tears filled her mouth and she burst out into sobs.

"Madame...Madame..." Marianne's voice was murmuring close beside her. Julie struggled in vain, mopping her eyes with the help of a little handkerchief. She heard her own hiccoughs, but was unable to master them. 'Nothing, absolutely nothing worse could have happened to me. In front of her! Crying in front of her! If only she'd go. No, there she is, rooted to the floor. She's watching the damage.' All in a muddle, she thought of her swollen eyes, of the tear-spots all over her blouse, and Espivant's treachery. 'Doing that to me! How sure of me he must be! Surer of me than of his own wife.'

She got herself in hand at last, blew her nose and felt no embarrassment in powdering her nose and smoothing out her eyelashes with a damp forefinger.

"I'm making an exhibition of myself," said Julie, "and a very unpleasant exhibition, too. I'm so sorry."

Mme. d'Espivant made a movement with her hand that simultaneously excused itself, put to rights a tulle collar that nothing had disturbed and felt at her throat for a non-existent string of pearls. 'She took it off to come and see me,' thought Julie, always prompt to change her mood.

"Madame," Marianne said. "I was deeply moved by your tears. Yes, yes, deeply moved. You seem so spontaneous, so...so impulsive. Seeing you, I can hardly believe my ears and what my husband was forced to tell me."

They were both standing up, with the folding table between them. Marianne's heavy scent assailed her. She recognised scented air that had its source in the vestibule in the Rue Saint-Sabas, sailed up to the 'children's room' where Herbert lay in his pearl-grey pyjamas, and then dispersed under the icy fan of the ether. She wrinkled her brows which, dabbed now with her handkerchief, had become completely fair. 'I can clear myself in a few words,' she thought. 'It would be over in a moment. She's waiting for it. She practically invited me to. I'll speak. I'll speak!'

She spoke, without asking Marianne to sit down again. "Madame, the action I took needed no publicity; but I thought, for several reasons, that you couldn't be ignorant of it. I resigned myself to doing it under conditions that were...painful and offensive to me."

"Why offensive? The decision was entirely yours, if I understood properly."

'Careful,' thought Julie. 'This middle-class creature knows better than I do myself what I'm talking about, and wants to get me in a muddle. I'd give absolutely anything for a glass of really cold water. Ah, now she's really listening! She'd like to know what sort of man she's married to! Her little ears and her huge eyes are wide open for the truth. But she won't hear it from me. She'll only get a rotten, made-up story out of me, and she'll have to swallow it.'

"Monsieur d'Espivant's extreme frankness doesn't put me on a bed of roses, Madame. The demand that your husband thinks is legitimate..."

Marianne interrupted her. "He only said that he did not contest its legitimacy."

"I'm delighted for his sake," Julie said. "As Espivant has told you everything, you also know how long this *démarche* was delayed. Putting it off was not always easy for me."

"Oh! I quite understand," said Marianne.

Julie leant towards Marianne, smaller than herself, and managed to smile.

"But there's nothing sure about it, or I do not make myself properly understood. Living from hand to mouth, and on very little, is a sort of game for certain kinds of character, a bet that one simply has to win once every twenty-four hours. It's very exciting. I'm a bit of a gambler.... And so it went on, until the day when I'd lost everything. And what I did then, you know."

As Marianne did not move, and seemed to be waiting for her to go on speaking, Julie said in a low voice: "I think you know as much about it now as I do."

The intonation obliged Mme. d'Espivant to pick up her bag and her gloves and pull her veil down again, while Julie hastened to guide her to the door. On the landing, they both took refuge once more in automatic good manners and the exchange of commonplaces.

"But really, please don't bother. . ."

"The landing's so tiny that one's in danger of falling when one comes out of my door. I'll get the lift."

"No, no, really. I'd rather walk."

'No, I couldn't have managed five minutes more of it! Oh! And "I hope you don't mind the smoke, Madame," and "I quite understand, Madame," and "the demands I made, Madame." Like school girls playing at visiting.' Julie slaked her thirst with long gulps. Then, driven by some odd impulse, she went and sprawled in the only chair in the dark and claustrophobic little hall. Her mood grew calmer, and she felt grateful to Marianne for having left, for being so far away and already on the other bank of the Seine. 'That woman's superb—or beautiful, actually, rather than superb. She hasn't got that nasty side to her that spoils so many of the Mme. Thingummies one meets. In evening dress, or at home—I'll bet anything she wears tea-gowns—smothered with her hair and her eyes and with silks and satins and harem-jewels, she must be tremendous. . .tremendous.'

She leaned her head against the rough pink plaster. 'Oh dear, I'm no good at that sort of diplomacy. Marianne soon saw that. Nor at any other sort, for the matter of that. I just about got him out of the business by the skin of my teeth, my poor traitor. I'm not quite sure yet whether I did get him out of it.'

She suddenly leapt to her feet. 'And what about the money, the money he wanted? We're no better off if she doesn't give him the money he wants, if she hasn't given it him yet. Poor Herbert! It hurts him here if he stretches his arms out. Poor Herbert needs the wretched little sum, the chance to be a bachelor, his gamekeeper's pension.'

She went and washed her reddened eyes at the tap, telling herself to keep calm. 'He'll ring me up. Or I'll call up Cousteix. What was the good woman saying, all honeyed up with plaits and veils and crèpe-de-chine? That Herbert was *really* ill to-day? After all, perhaps it's true. I'd better wait. If only he'd tell me, or let me know. If it hasn't come off, I'll begin all over again. I'll fix it, whatever happens. Oh Herbert, my greatest love of all, happiest part of my life, and my greatest sorrow!'

She pressed a pad soaked in salt and water on her eyes. Under her eyelids, mixed up with luminous globules and zigzags, little mirages flickered past—a memory, a hope as simple as herself: the small, luxurious table, the fruit, the aromatic fumes of the coffee, a bright sunbeam falling on the burnished silver, and in front of her, pale from his heart attack, the man she was fanning with a napkin soaked in cold ether coming back to life in the hollow of her arm. A rough thirst for rescue work, and unquestioning feminine longing to prove her devotion, assailed her. She made her shoulders and her finger-joints crack to test her strength, promising Espivant all her help meanwhile in threatening tones. 'You'll have your beastly little million. I'll shove it at you on the table beside the cherries, slap in the middle of the bowl of figs, or in your great foot-bath of a coffee-cup. If that Marianne of yours doesn't cough up, I'll have a thing or two to tell her! And if we pull it off, I won't think twice about whatever share of the swag you toss me! I'll snap it up in mid-air like a dog! And, who cares, I'll go and telephone.'

She ran into the studio where, from the doorway, her eyes fell on an envelope that looked blindingly white and frighteningly thick. 'Marianne must have put that there! When did she do it? Oh, of course, when I went in front of her to open the door. Nobody could say Madame d'Espivant is the sort of a woman to lose her head.'

She felt the packet, weighing it in her hand. 'How light it is! Much lighter, I should have said, than that odd million of ours. The address is in Herbert's handwriting.'

The top envelope enclosed another in which, wrapped in several thicknesses of tissue paper, was a bundle of blue and pinkish notes that finally emerged, pinned together in trusses of ten, brand new, and smelling faintly of tallow. 'Is that all? Why, there are only a hundred thousand francs, and not a word. Not even an impertinent little "Thank you,"—not even the sort of joke a cheerful swindler might scribble, to make me laugh?' She looked questioningly at the door through which Marianne had just left, as though she could call her back. 'He split the bundle up into our two stakes with his own hands—those swollen and masterful hands...and that's all there is to it. It's the last straw of cruelty. It's...'

"It's ten per cent; what a middle-man or a house agent would get," she said out loud, on what she hoped was a cynical and bantering note. But the sound jarred on her.

She rolled up the notes and slipped an elastic band round them, and then, at a loss what to do with them, she went and put them into the mother-of-pearl box. She came back and leant idly over the balcony, vaguely marvelling at the fact that the approach of evening had already assembled the sparrows in the ivy of a dusty neighboring courtyard.

'Not even a line,' she sighed. 'Not a single word to break this silence. The last words I heard him say were "Go away." An hour before, less than an hour, he'd said "Didn't you like it there, Youlka?"'

She was inflicting bruises on herself purposely, trying out the two tones of voice, the harsh and the tender, and she proudly decided that the harsh, the insulting tone, was the one she preferred. It had at least a faint smack of the truth about it, of active jealousy, of flattering iniquity. 'I'd have liked just one word, a word that would have turned us into accomplices, soft on the ear, and comforting to look at on the white paper. He really might have taken the trouble.'

She leant there, motionless under the approach of the violet hour, until her arms grew numb. Then she pulled down the blind and switched on the top light. Making up her mind to go out, she opened her make-up box. 'Oh! No, I daren't show myself this evening.' She felt sorry for her poor face. She made do with another of her scratch meals, with soup and meat replaced by sardines and cheese. She sprinkled sugar on yesterday's fruit which was beginning to shrivel, but she felt defeated by the thought of making coffee. She kept turning, as she ate, towards the telephone, as though demanding an explanation for its silence.

She washed up with deft gestures, and carefully avoided plunging her hands into the dish-water. Everything she did seemed easy and even pleasant, but not entirely satisfying. 'Haven't I forgotten something?' she wondered. When the plates were in the rack and the bed turned down, she gave herself a clean answer to all this uncertainty: 'No; there's nothing I've forgotten. There's no hurry. There's nothing left I can do for him. Or for anybody else.'

As the hours passed, she thought out plan after plan—to telephone to Espivant to thank him, to insult him, but most of all, to summon him to her, to beseech him. 'But beseech him for what? What I really want from Herbert can't be put into words.'

She opened a book. But she had never, in her whole life, succeeded in giving the greatest of books precedence over the most insignificant of worries about love. 'Well,' she sighed, 'I suppose I'd better go to bed. The only thing is, I'm not tired.' She lay motionless in bed and listened to the hours striking. As the clock of the neighboring school tolled the succeeding hours she wondered, 'How could I have stood that clock chiming the hours and the halves and quarters all this time? I'll never be able to get used to it again. I'll have to move.' She fell asleep nevertheless, but woke up with a feeling that something or someone was living in the flat besides herself. At about four o'clock, she got out of bed, slipped into the bath-robe that never quite had time to get dry, and opened the step ladder so that she could climb to the top shelves of the hanging cupboard. There she began reaching and rummaging for things that seldom saw the light of day. After hanging on the back of a chair a beige gabardine coat and a pair of brown whipcord riding-breeches, Julie de Carneilhan sat down under the naked bulb of the kitchen lamp and fell to polishing her riding-boots.

The alarm-clock and the bell in the hall both rang at the same moment. A clear whinnying sound, shrill as a cavalry-trumpet, echoed from the street. Julie, booted, dressed in riding-breeches and a flannel shirt, was tying a white scarf round her neck.

"Is that you already, Léon?" she shouted through the door. "It may interest you to know I'm all ready to be off."

"No, Madame la Comtesse, it's Gayant. I've come for the bags and things."

She opened the door, and shook the dry and horny hand that was held out to her by a little man on the threshold.

"Do you think it is going to rain to-day? I'm taking a mackintosh, just in case."

"No rain, Madame la Comtesse. Mist and dew, and then we'll have the wind and the sun between the stroke of a quarter to seven and seven."

"Is that Hirondelle kicking up such a fuss down there?"

"That's it, Madame. She always knows when the least preparations are in the wind. There's been no holding her since yesterday. She's seen the nosebags and straps and everything."

"Give me my jacket, Gayant. Thanks. Gayant, do you think I'm still up to this sort of trip?"

"I think so," said Gayant. "Madame la Comtesse is a horse-woman. How much does your ladyship weigh?"

"Fifty-five kilos."

"That's all right. Last year your ladyship weighted fifty-six and a half. Fifty-five's all to the good."

The little man with the over-long arms sized Julie up, from her boots to her soft felt hat.

"Do you think so?"

"Yes. Better for Tullia."

"Oh, you only bother about the mares, of course. It doesn't matter if I do myself in! Here, take this and this, and this. Take care, that's our breakfast! Go downstairs and tell my brother to come up. His coffee's ready."

She buttoned up her jacket and saw to it that the fork of her riding breeches fitted properly, with that shocking and masculine gesture with which classical dancers adjust their tights. She felt at ease in these clothes. Her boots and gloves fitted her on the large side, and she was securely hatted against the wind. She slapped herself over the thighs and cursed. 'All this cash is making my pockets bulge. I'll hand half of it over to Léon.'

She gazed at her reflection in the looking-glass, festooned with crops and switches: a tall pale figure, with long, clean-cut legs. Her short and sleepless night, devoted by turns to agreeable preparations and sad thoughts, had just come to an end. She was all ready to go, but she still felt uncertain of her departure. Gayant's discreet "Whoa back there!" rose from the silent street, and the sound of Carneilhan lovingly scolding his mare. Julie could hear the horses moving across the road in the direction of departure. She sat down and wrote a few lines to the *concierge* and the charwoman, leaving a tip for each of them. The sight of the envelopes placed so prominently on the card-table reminded her of the faked-up parcel padded with white paper. She felt weak and agitated. 'I'm not going. No; I won't go! To begin with, I'm no longer up-and-coming enough for this sort of jaunt. And then, nothing decisive has been said yet. Herbert has often played a mouse longer than this, and perhaps to-day's the day he'll send for me, or even come here. I don't want to leave. I'm not going to leave!'

She leant over the balcony, and could just descry the sombre group formed by the two saddled mares, the little harnessed luggage-trap and the two men busy with the three horses. She breathed in the dampness that prevails before daybreak, the smell of ivy, and the impalpable watery powder that hung in the air. She was moved. 'How cool,' she thought, 'this spindrift of fresh water.' Her wounded and versatile spirits veered round to the impending journey and sang in double time the songs that are improvised to and maintained by the gait of a horse; drew rein by a stream under the high timbers of a forest. Quenching their thirst, the mares would tread their hoofs and play their muzzles in the running water. 'La Grosse and Tullia can be re-shod anywhere by the roadside, while Léon will have taken at least four pairs of dancing shoes for Hirondelle. I didn't ask Gayant whether he'd taken the curry-comb and the hoof-picker. But Gayant never forgets anything!'

Julie sat down on her unmade bed. It would never be open again for Coco

Vatard. 'What did that sententious young man say? Ah, yes! That he feared I was the woman of his life. Well, it wasn't so wide of the mark, that shop-girl cliché of his. He didn't say I was his Great Love; he'd get it quite clear; he said I was the Woman of his Life. Coco Vatard will have plenty of mistresses and at least one wife. Each of them will open up a wound, an anxiety of which none of them will be the real cause. I'll recover from Herbert once again, I think. And perhaps another man, not Herbert, will hurt me once again. But it will always be from him, that damned "Man of my Life" that I shall draw all my consolation and my desolation.'

She thought she had been dreaming a long while, but, when her brother climbed the stairs, the brow of dawn had not yet risen above the neighboring school buildings, nor painted green the ivy leaves in the walled garden.

Instead of ringing, Léon de Carneilhan knocked three times, fairly hard, on the door: a sound which shook away Julie's dreams and set her once more a-jangle. 'I don't want to go! I won't go! I'll explain to Léon that I've got serious reasons for staying behind. After all, I'm a free agent!'

When Léon came in, she wrinkled her brows, and apostrophised him in the vigorous terms that had become a sort of ritual between them.

"What on earth were you up to down there, taking such a time, I'd like to know?"

"And who do you think's going to tighten the girths? And stow everything that rattles in the bottom of the trap? Including your bags and suitcases? And one of the bins of oats that was leaking through the bottom? Gayant never forgets anything, but he has no idea of how to stow things. If I didn't keep my eyes open, the trap would make as much row as a motor-car, once we got going."

Like Julie, Carneilhan had lowered his reddish eyebrows. He relaxed as he contemplated his sister.

"You know, that kit still suits you, though Lord knows I've never been keen on women riding astride."

Julie could have returned a similar compliment to her brother, who was dressed in some indestructible material. Russet-colored like their owner, his riding clothes had faded over the shoulders, his coarse and thickly planted hair was going white on the crown, and his forehead, owing to the strange cut of his features, was more deeply tanned than his narrow temples. A meagre Adam's apple shifted up and down his throat as he swallowed his bowl of hot coffee.

"Shall we go down?"

Julie's blue eyes wavered.

"Listen, Léon, I'd rather...I'd rather not go. I'm not feeling well-today..."

He interrupted her, moving a step towards her.

"Is that true or not true?"

She pulled herself together, and admitted courageously: "It's not true. I wanted to...to stay on a few days, to...to please somebody."

Carneilhan's glance slid across to the open bed and came back to Julie.

"Do you mean Espivant?"

She quivered, flinging herself against the suspicion.

"No, no! What on earth are you dreaming of?"

Then she laughed and cried tauntingly, "Really, my dear! You've no imagination. Or else too much."

She lowered her eyes in a comic imitation of bashfulness.

"Poor little Coco. He's very nice, you know."

She seemed to change her mind all of a sudden, and started rummaging in her pockets.

"Here, take this off my hands. Put it in your breast-pocket."

She tossed him half of the roll of new bank-notes.

"What's this?"

"Fifty thousand. Look after them for me while we're on the road. Good old Becker, believe it or not! He sent me that to celebrate his sixtieth birthday."

Carneilhan slowly arranged the notes, fumbling them incredulously.

"Good old Becker. Poor little Coco. It sounds as if you only knock around with saints and martyrs. Espivant will be an archangel soon."

Julie gave a little sigh of exasperation.

"Oh, you can keep that one. He's tougher than a seven-year-old hen. Are we going, Léon, or are we not? We're wasting so much time."

Swift and rose-colored light was already mounting in the sky. Julie's face materialised in the looking-glass, her pallor, the rings under her eyes, her faded air.

"Oh!" she said with a start.

"What's wrong now?"

She pointed to her washed-out reflection.

"I don't think I'm up to it, Léon. I'd be under my horse within a mile from here. I didn't sleep last night, I'm not in training, I . . ."

She turned away, dabbings at her eyelashes. Her brother caught hold of her elbow, and made her swing round towards him. "What a great goose you are! You know what an old armchair Tullia is. Your nice, awful old Tullia, dappled like a circus horse; the beautiful remains of my Hirondelle, La Grosse pulling the old trap with half the paint off, Gayant dressed like nothing on earth. Do you want not to come because you're ashamed of joining such a wretched band of gipsies?"

She put her arms on his shoulders, laughing and crying.

"No, no, no! Of course not, I'm not ashamed! Look at my breeches, they've got two moth-holes in them! Have you still got *the* trap?"

"You don't suppose I went and bought a new one for Gayant? Of course it's *the* trap. There's not an inch of paint left on it. It's peeling all over like a plane tree losing its bark. But it's still got a smart little umbrella-basket, and luckily the rubber on the wheels is still intact. When you're tired, you can get into the trap, and let Gayant ride Tullia."

Julie gazed at the russet-colored muzzle and the piercing blue eyes that were losing their stern and threatening look.

"So I *shall* get tired?" she said sadly. "You see, even you say, already, that I'll get tired!"

"I wouldn't swear to it," said Léon, shaking his head. "But I advise you to. *Be* tired. Come on; let's be off. We're not trying to impress anyone any more. I've got everything I possess on me. I see you're taking your whole fortune. Don't leave anything behind. The road to Carneilhan will be a one-way journey for me. Do you think you can say the same?"

He tightened his leather belt in order to avoid seeming to wait for a reply. But Julie said nothing.

"Off we go, Julie."

"Yes. Where shall we stop?"

"Wherever you like."

She smiled at such an unexpected statement.

"How long do you think it'll take us to get to Carneilhan?"

For the first time Julie saw her brother make a gesture of uncertainty. He raised his arms and let them drop.

"Three weeks...three months...all our lives."

He listened in the direction of the mares, who were growing restive. They heard the clink of the horse-shoes on the cobblestones below.

"Isn't it an astounding feeling, Julie, having some money and no home, instead of having a home and no money?"

These few words, the lofty voice, the large, quivering nose, the movement of the jaw muscles under the reddened and clean-shaven cheek were accepted by Julie as precious symbols of brotherly affection.

"I want to breathe, Julie. It gets me in the ribs, having no money for oats, no money for straw, for the harness-maker's bill and the blacksmith's."

Julie put her hand on her brother's arm to interrupt a litany that she knew by heart. The arm responded. She felt the muscles move, and rejoiced in so much strength. It seemed a token of hope and support.

"The sun's up," said Carneilhan. "We're going the long way round, Julie. The long way will tire the mares least, and also the horsewoman. We'll be far better off in the by-ways, with grass on either side. Gayant knows some tracks and pathways that are almost Red Indian, they're so remote."

Julie opened her nostrils and her whole body leaned forward in a movement of consent.

"You didn't warn old Père Carneilhan that I was coming too?"

"He'll know soon enough," Léon said, wryly. "If we'd told him, he might have taken to writing again just to stop you starting. Your presence will bother him a lot, at first. He'll have to clear all his stuff out of your blue room, his salt-stores and millet-cobs, his provisions of dried bread, everything that the damp and the rats can get at."

As he spoke, Julie's recollections passed through a porch, sniffed the cold hall and fumblingly hung a straw hat on a stag's antler. 'Shall I still like my home,' she wondered. 'Shall I still love my two Carneilhans enough, with their silence, their pride and their frugality?' She reached a blue room discolored by sunlight under a beamed ceiling. 'I'll re-paint it pink.' The white underside of the aspen leaves cast their light over her memory like the reflections of a river, and she leaned out of the window of the blue room. 'Unless I re-paint it pale yellow!' From her oval room at the top of the tower, Julie de Carneilhan, aged fifteen, with the frontiers of her stubborn forehead marked out by her blonde plaits, peered down at the rounded tops of two lime trees casting their shade upon the terrace, at the brood-mares resting their heads on the railings of the meadow, at Père Carneilhan in his flat cap with his little hazel switch thrust into his coat pocket. So the network or roads, the staircase 'turning like a corkscrew' promised by the candlewoman simply led, as though predestined, to the room she had lived in as a girl?

Careless of the sleep which still enfolded the house, they went downstairs with an indiscreet clatter of boots and talk.

"Do you think I should take the spirit-stove?"

"I kept out the first-aid set; it's rolled up in a blanket."

When they appeared, the horses pawed the ground affectionately, and Julie greeted each of them with a lump of sugar to make amends and revive their friendship. The saddles and bridles and the stirrup-leathers stretched by long use were shining with age and endless polishing. In order to make much of her dappled mare, such an ugly and meritorious beast, Julie threw her useless quirt into the trap.

Julie, who had been deprived so long of outdoor life and travel, found herself slightly astray among the seasons and the regions; she expected, almost, to gather plums and lilies-of-the-valley on the way, wild strawberries and dog-roses. She longed for the towing-paths and the resilient turf of the heathland. But, above all, she summoned up remembrance of certain sandy pathways, soft under the horses' feet and hemmed in with prickly burdocks and bitter blackberries, with gorse bushes that plucked at manes and tails, and hollowed out pathways that used to force Julie and another horseman, both happy to ride side by side, close up against each other. 'Herbert! And my long hair that used to come down over my shoulders when he tilted back my head.' She pressed her forehead for an instant against Tullia's neck, hiding a last fleeting weakness. Then she turned resolutely towards her brother, at the very moment when the tall mare Hirondelle, immaculately gaitered in white, was coming to search out and caress the hand of Carneilhan with her wide, fanatic nostrils.

'Ah,' thought Julie, 'he, at least, is taking with him what he loves best in the world.'